Clare

Clare

a Novel

Susan Lynn Peterson

Alcuin House Publishing
Tucson, Arizona

Alcuin House Publishing, Tucson, Arizona
A division of Alcuin Communications, LLC

© 2006, 2011 by Susan Lynn Peterson
All rights reserved. First edition 2006
Second edition 2011
Printed in the United States of America

ISBN: 978-0-9830652-2-7
LCCN: 2011913880

In memory of
Clara Elizabeth Keane Magnuson, my grandmother,
who with her mother, Hannah, and brother, Thomas,
boarded the S.S. Laconia in 1912
to emigrate from Cork, Ireland, to St. Paul, Minnesota

Prologue

All these years later, I sit in my study beneath my nursing school diploma, beneath photos of children and grandchildren and of Colum, my husband, gone now these three years. I write and I feel. For the first time in many years I slow down long enough to feel. What I feel is a lifetime's worth of feelings; and for the life of me, I can't seem to get enough of it. I feel pride, to be sure, pride in that frightened fourteen-year-old girl I was. I feel sadness as page-by-page the losses roll from the point of my pen, one after another like a slow-moving freight train carrying my life off into the horizon.

All these years later, if I close my eyes on a cold Minnesota night, if I'm quiet enough, I can still listen in on the fear and anxiety of Ellis Island, back when the great liners disengorged great loads of "huddled masses" into its front door. I can make my way back over the endless water. I can taste the salt air of Queenstown harbor in the back of my throat. If I breathe deeply through my nose, smelling past the smell of cars and the lake beneath my window, I can smell all the way back to the lanes of Cork—the potatoes boiling, the horse manure, the musk from the Beamish brewery clinging to the damp bricks of the tenement where I grew up. All these years later, I can feel once again the curious mix of excitement and emptiness that comes from leaving the bones of one's ancestors in the soil of a continent one may never see again.

I look up from my writing, and on the wall of my study is a painting my oldest girl did. In it a beautiful woman sits at the keyboard of a magnificent grand piano. A vase of purple lilacs sits atop, its image reflected in the polished surface of the instrument. Hannah, my mother's namesake, was nineteen when she painted that painting. She painted it left handed, just to see if she could, so it leans to the left, the woman threatening to fall backward off the piano bench, and the piano itself threatening to come down on top of her, lilacs and all. Hannah is thirty-seven now, not much younger than Mama was when she died. Hannah married a good man, a businessman and a teetotaler, saints be praised. Sally, my younger girl, married an engineer with dark brown hair like my brother Tom. When the girls moved out, we turned their bedroom into a study—lined it with books and moved in a big walnut desk where I now sit. There I ponder things that happened when I was young, young like Hannah's and Sally's children are now young, not that I was ever young in that way. I ponder a world without walnut desks and studies, without grand pianos tipsy or not, without the luxury of looking back on a long life well-lived.

My mother always had a weak chest. That's what it all comes down to, all my memories, all the flood of feelings. The shawlies who lived on our lane, blamed the weakness on the Lee, the river that ran from hills to harbor through

1

the center of Cork. Da, before he died, himself a young man, blamed it on years of breathing other people's house dust. I know now what modern medicine would have to say on the subject. Modern medicine would say it was the *Streptococcus pneumoniae* bacteria that killed her; it was pneumonia that put her in her grave and us on a path that would take us across the ocean to a life utterly unimaginable to the young Irish girl I was those many years ago. But I'm not so sure that Da and the shawlies weren't right.

Outside the window, the snowplow throws aside a plume of new snow. Inside the air is warm and dry, warm enough that I should perhaps feel a little guilty. But I am done with such guilt, or at least would like to be. The ink still flows freely from the nib of my pen, and I have much more important memories to feel.

One

The day hung wet about my ears. Outside the door of the scullery, dew weighed down every leaf, every blade of grass. Clouds grayed the sky. Puddles sat heavily on the drive. And the petticoats Mama was hanging on the line to dry were, if anything, getting wetter in the thick air. It was the kind of spring day we had often in Cork, Ireland. The kind of day when God reminds you that green and living things require a good soaking every now and again if they are to grow.

"Beat those shirts good now, Clareen," Mama called from the back yard where she was hanging the boys' vests beside the damp petticoats.

"That'll do, Mama," I called through the doorway of the tradesmen's entrance.

"Mr. Quillan has a big meeting tomorrow, and we can't be sending him in a dingy shirt." Mama's voice was hoarse, choked almost.

"We can't at that, Mama." I emptied the rest of the pot of boiling water into the washing vat and leaned heavy into the washing board. A sweaty strand of hair made its way loose and into my eye. I brushed it back with the back of my wrist. It didn't stay.

From the back yard I could hear Mama coughing, then clearing her throat again. I glanced out the window. Mama looked as sweaty and disheveled as I did. No surprise, that. It was Monday, wash day, after all. But she also looked pale—a grey, flat, frightening color of pale.

"Mama," I called through the door, "do you want me to finish the laundry and you do the silver?"

"And how will you be doing all this laundry yourself?" she called back. She laughed and coughed again. "You didn't hire yourself a maid, now, did you?"

"No, Mama," I said. "'Tis only me and the wash board in here."

"I'll do, Clare," she said, making her way to the top of the steps. She leaned on the doorframe while she assessed my work.

"'Tis only a touch of the croup, sounds worse than it is. The hot water and steam will probably do me good, clear my chest." She coughed again. It didn't sound as though the steam was doing her much good at all, but I didn't say so. "Finish those, and I'll hang them while you start on the stockings," she said, then coughed again as she descended the steps to the yard.

* * *

The spring of 1906. Cork, Ireland, it was. Fifty-eight years and a half a world away from where I sit today. The tangy smell of the washing soda, the barely warm, muggy breeze blowing through the open door. It was a turning point in my life, though I didn't know it at the time. After that day, nothing would be the same.

I was barely fourteen. More than a girl, but less than a woman. For the last three years, I had lived in a small closet under the stairs at the Quillan house. I was the Quillan's maid. Mama was their cook and housekeeper.

It wasn't a bad life. I would rise at the crack of dawn, wet the tea, then start the water boiling for eggs. Across town, Mama would rise, get the boys ready for school, then make her way through the streets of Cork, out of the lanes and alleys and into the respectable neighborhood were the Quillans lived. Once there she would come up behind me, hug me, and place a kiss on the back of my head as I cleaned the kitchen after breakfast. Then together we spent the day scrubbing floors, preparing meals, making beds, and washing clothes. Every evening, Mama would cook supper for the Quillans, and while I was serving, she would eat her meal quickly in the kitchen before leaving for home to feed my two brothers. I would wash up the plates and dishes and tidy the kitchen. If all my work was done, I could sit for a while in the kitchen before raking the fire and laying the coals for the morning.

Friday was payday. Saturday was a half-day and confession. Sunday morning was Mass. Sunday afternoon I spent with Mama and the boys. Monday was washday.

I stopped the steady rhythm I had set up on one of Mr. Quillan's white shirts. From outside came a sound, a terrible, murderous rasping sound. I didn't recognize it, not at first. Then I did.

"Mama," I called, running out the door. "Mama, are you all right?"

She knelt bent at the waist, leaning against a tree, her apron pressed tightly to her mouth. The kinks of coughing shook her shoulders in great spasms.

"Mama, what can I do?" I asked, kneeling beside her. She was coughing too hard to answer, so I just stroked her back and prayed. Gradually, the fearful spasms stopped. Mama looked up at me, her face pale. The apron she held in her clenched hand was soaked with blood.

"The springtime's no good at all for my chest," she said, her voice thin.

"Blood," I said, my eyes still fixed on her apron. "Mama, you were coughing up blood."

"Ah, well, it wouldn't be the first time," she answered. "And probably not the last. 'Tis only a spot. I can spare it, I think." She untied her apron and smiled thinly at me. The ashen color of her lips frightened me.

"Mama," I said. "I'll finish the laundry. You need to rest."

"A good girl, yourself," she replied.

* * *

That night, we climbed the four stone steps that led from the main street to Walsh Lane, the lane where Mama and the boys lived. I would need to leave early tomorrow to be back at the Quillan's at first light, but I didn't want Mama to walk home alone. The night was moonless, and the mucky cobblestones of the lane were lit by no more than a single gas street lamp. On either side of us, deteriorating brick walls rose like a steep canyon. The canyon led to the yard, a stone-covered open area surrounded by three-storey tenements. In America, such a yard would be called a "dead end." I can't say that I'd argue with that description. Any number of people were born in those tenements, lived in the tenements, died in the tenements, some managing the entire process in a matter of mere months.

Along one wall, at the tap, giggling children splashed water on their faces, their hands, each other. The evening breeze dipped tentatively into the yard, washing the smell of the toilet and the rubbish heap over us. Our tenement shared two toilets, each in their own cubby, each with a battered metal roof, through which the toilet's only light came during the day, and into which poured a steady stream of muddy water when it rained. The women of the tenement took turns scrubbing down the inside with boiling water, once each day. But that did nothing for the smell from the pit, which in the summers hung in the air like a thick syrup. The air that night was cool and the breeze gentle. But still I held my breath, then breathed through my mouth trying not to take the stink into my nose.

"A good evening to you," a man called from across the yard, where he was hauling two full buckets of water into the house. He was dressed in his working clothes, a coal-darkened jacket and trousers that blended into the night.

"A very good evening to you, John Sullivan," Mother called back. "Don't you have boys to do that for you?"

"I do seem to remember feeding them this evening, but when there's work to be done, it seems Sarah and I are always childless."

Mama threw back her head and laughed. I smiled.

"I see you have your Clare home with you this evening," he said. "No problems, I trust."

Mama coughed. The laughing seemed to have loosened something in her chest again. She braced herself, a hand on the wall, the other grasping her shawl tightly about her throat. Mr. Sullivan waited respectfully at a distance, then set the buckets down and came by as the coughing eased.

"'Tis nothing a little honey and vinegar won't cure, or maybe one of Mr. Carey's linseed tonics come payday," Mama wiped her lips with her handkerchief.

"Will I send my Sarah over later to take a look at you?" he asked. "She's nursed the children through more ailments than I can count. I'm sure she'd be pleased to stop by."

"Thank you, John, but I think what I need most is a good night's sleep," Mama said. "I'll send Clare if I need Sarah."

"You do that," Mr. Sullivan said. "A good rest, then."

"And to you," Mama said.

"Thank you, Mr. Sullivan," I added. He nodded and tipped his cap.

We entered the tenement door, unlocked as always—I doubted it had ever had a lock. The light in the stairway was out as usual, and we made out way carefully, avoiding the places where tenants had pulled up parts of the steps for firewood last winter. Mama laid a hand lightly on my back.

"Take care," she said. The railing is missing up a bit. "When they've the drink taken, it seems some of the neighbors can't tell wall from wood." Her voice was ragged, choked. It pained me to listen to it.

"Don't talk this minute, Mama," I said. But the cough was finding its way up her throat again. She, paused, leaned against the wall, coughed lightly, then more deeply. Her chest heaved, trying to wrench out another kink. I held her elbow, and the spasm passed. We climbed the remaining two flights in the dark and in silence.

* * *

Mick and Tom were waiting for us when we opened the door. Tom was sitting on the old horsehair chair beneath the window, squinting at his school books in the fading light. Beneath his weight the frame of the chair listed slightly, and its stuffing strained against the patches Mama and I had darned in its cushions.

Mick sat on an old coal box covered with a thin strip of red cloth near the fireplace. In his lap was a small wooden dog Papa had carved for him some five or more years ago. He had a kitchen knife and a small hunk of wood and was trying without much success to replicate the dog. Even when the fire was out, Mick would drift toward the fireplace. He was twelve, small-boned but tall, straight and finely made like Papa had been. Before Papa died, the two would huddle together by the fire on cold winter days. Yet still the chill would seep into the both of them, and as the embers died back for the night, they would shake with it and climb quickly into bed.

Tom, on the other hand, was like a small stove. At ten he was shorter than most boys his age, much shorter than Mick. Mama said he was built like her father, with a full chest and strong arms and legs. On the nights I was home, we would curl up together in the big, iron bed all four of us shared, Mama and I at the head, Tom and Mick at the foot. On a cold night, Tom would be like a big warm stone radiating heat beneath the threadbare blankets and Papa's old warm coat on top of us. The neighbors said that Tom would make a fine laborer some day. Perhaps he would hold a steady job on the docks or in the brewery. But Mama would look at him with his nose in a book and would whisper a prayer for her son to become a priest.

"I'll start a fire," I said. "You rest, Mama."

Mama nodded and sank into a creaky chair by the table. She loosened her shawl, then stopped, as though taking it off all together would be too much effort.

"Mam," Tom said, rising to stand beside her, propped against the table, "you don't look well at all. Will I go with you to the infirmary tomorrow?"

"Tom, you have school. What will the Brothers think if you miss classes?"

"I will tell them that I was taking care of my mother," Tom replied. "Surely not a man in the entire Irish Christian Brothers would tell me I was wrong."

Tom may have looked like a boy of ten, but he talked like an adult and had for several years. Da used to tell him he had the gift of gab, a very Irish gift if ever there was one. Mama used to say that Tom must have sneaked out to kiss the blarney stone one day when we weren't looking. I think Tom just spent so much time inside his books that eventually he began to sound like a book himself.

"Well, you may be able to may be able to charm the brothers into giving you the day off," Mama said, "but I have a whole house full of floors at the Quillan's that aren't going to scrub themselves if I'm standing in line at the infirmary."

"Mama," I said, touching a match to the small piece of paper I wedged beneath the turf in the fireplace, "I'll take care of the floors. You should see the doctor." I looked down at the bag where she had stuffed the bloodied apron.

"They're right, Mam," Mick said. "You look terribly pale."

"I'm fine," she said, leaning hard on the table and lifting herself to her feet. "I only need some rest." She walked to the bed in the corner of the room, lay down in her shawl, and immediately fell asleep.

Tom, Mick, and I looked at each other. We knew that we had to get Mama to the infirmary tomorrow whether she wanted to go or not.

* * *

I lay in bed, still in my clothes from the night before, dozing on and off, not really sleeping. A feeling hung in the air, the feeling that I needed to be prepared, ready for anything. Mick was sleeping on one side of my legs. Tom was at the other, his toasty warm feet against my back. The terrible noise of that afternoon was back. I opened my eyes, only a little bit, so Mama wouldn't know her coughing woke me. She was sitting in a chair beside the bed still in her dress, still in her shawl. In her hand she held a bloody rag. I watched her as the kink passed and she sank against the wall, tears in her eyes. She reached out a hand and stroked Mick's hair.

"Too young," she whispered. "Sweet Mary, they're too young." I saw the last light of the fire flicker on her face. "Give me only a little more time," she said. "Sweet Jesus, give me only a little . . . " Another cough split the air. I closed my eyes and began to pray.

* * *

"Clare," Mama's voice came to me from across the room. I opened my eyes. The first light of morning was beginning to show through the window. I must have slept, though I can't imagine how. "Clare." I climbed over Mick and out of bed.

"Yes, Mama," I said. Mama was sitting slumped on the floor in the corner. I knelt beside her. "Mama, why are you on the floor? It's cold here. Let me help you into bed. We still have an hour or so before we have to get up." I took her elbow, and she looked up at me. In the faint morning light I saw the dark stain that soaked the front of her dress.

"Mama!"

"Clare, be a good girl and make me a cup of tea, won't you. And wake Mick. Let him go down to the chapel and fetch the priest."

"Mama, you need a doctor," I said trying to hide the fear in my voice. "Mick can go fetch a doctor."

"No, Clare. Tell him to fetch the priest. "'Tis the priest I need."

I stumbled to my feet, went to shake Mick awake. But when I got to the bed, I could see his eyes were open. Tears were welling in the corners of them. His shoulders quivered.

"Mick," I said pulling back the blankets. "Mick, you need to go to St. Finbarr's and fetch the priest. Tell him Mama needs him right away." I looked at Mama in the corner clutching her shawl tightly around her trying to hide the bloodstain that seemed to be growing ever larger with the morning light. "Take Tom with you."

I reached out a hand and gently shook Tom's shoulder. He rolled over and pulled the blanket more tightly around his chin. The boy could sleep through anything.

"Tom," I said. "Tom, come on, now; rouse up. You need to help Mick with an important job." Tom opened his eyes.

"What job?" he mumbled.

"Mick will tell you on the way there."

Tom sat up in bed and rubbed his eyes. "Why are you on the floor, Mam?" he asked.

"Tom," I said, "Mama's going to go back to bed now. But you have to get up and go with Mick. No questions this minute. Do you understand?"

He nodded. Mick had dressed and pulled on his jacket. He handed Tom his trousers and gansey, and fished his boots from under the bed. The thump of their feet on the stairs rattled the thin walls as they trotted down to the yard below.

I pushed aside the ashes from last night and lit a block of turf. Thankfully, the battered old kettle still held water from last night. I wouldn't have to go down to the tap. I hung it on the hob over the slowly catching fire and turned to Mama.

"Can you stand?" I asked.

"Help me," she said. I moved a chair next to her and took her elbow. Between Mama, the chair, and I, it was all we could do to get her to her feet. She shuffled toward the bed, leaning heavily on me. Her hands were burning hot and her body was stiff. She sank onto the bed and lay back. I wadded up the old blanket and put it under her head.

"Mama," I said. "What will we do about your dress?"

The cough took her again before she could reply. She rolled onto her side and doubled over with it. Her mouth was red and frothy. Droplets of the stuff spattered the sheet with each bark. I pulled her shawl up around her and stroked her forehead. It was grey and slippery beneath my touch. I wished I were Mick, running right now through the streets of Cork. But all I could do was sit and wait—wait for the coughing to stop, wait for the kettle to heat up, wait for Mick to return with the priest.

"Hail Mary full of grace," I began to whisper the words of the prayer I had prayed every day for as long as I could remember. "The Lord is with Thee." Help my mother, I thought, help her. "Blessed aren't thou amongst women . . . "

I was two or three decades into my beads when the tea kettle began to rattle and steam. I rose from the chair, stroking Mam's hair as I turned to the hearth. "Hail Mary full of grace." I started again, but my mind was not on my prayer. Neither was it on the tea. Rather it filled with images, terrible images surrounded by the haze of a deep grey dread. The tea leaves, tea pot, and cups were in a sideboard in the corner. I assembled them on the table. "Holy Mary, Mother of God, pray for us sinners." I bundled some of my skirt around my hand and took the kettle from the fire. Not bothering to warm the pot first, I put a pinch of leaves into the pot, and poured the water over them. "Now and at the hour of our death."

I looked over at my mother, the kinks had stopped for the moment. She lay motionless, like a pile of bloody rags bundled in the black of her shawl. "Now and at the hour of our death," I whispered again, blinking back the fear. "Please, holy Mary, pray for us. Not now. Not now."

When the tea was ready, I poured it into a cup. "Mama," I said. "Mama, the tea is ready." Her eyes were open, but she didn't respond.

"Mama!" I set the cup down on the chair. I bent over, my ear to her face. Her ragged breath was still finding its raspy way in and out. I touched her forehead, and she smiled slightly. "Do you want tea?" I asked.

"Later," Mama whispered. Her eyes closed and she slept.

I sat down on the floor, my cheek resting on the edge of the mattress. I squeezed my eyes shut against the tears, and focused on the sound of Mama's breath, raspy and strained. In and out. I willed it to continue. In and out.

* * *

In what seemed like hours, I could hear the sounds of the steps on the stairway. Two men, with heavy slow steps. Two children, running then stopping, running then stopping. Tom burst through the door, then froze in the middle of the room, his eyes falling hard on Mama lying grey beneath the old blanket. Behind him was Mr. Connor from downstairs and a priest I didn't recognize.

"Come on, son," Mr. Connor said, laying a hand on Tom's shoulder. "Sit you down here while we tend to your mother." He led Tom to a chair at the table. Mick sank heavily onto the old coal box by the fire.

"God bless you, Father," I said and curtsied as the bulky man in black stepped through the door, his cassock swishing about his ankles. The Father didn't pause, even to acknowledge my presence, but made a line straight for Mama's bed.

"Mrs. Keane," he said gently. "Hannah, can you hear me, now?" Mama opened her eyes.

"Father," she said in a whisper. "'Tis too soon. I can't die and leave my children. Please tell me God knows 'tis too soon."

"Mama, you're not going to . . . ," I paused, the word stuck behind a lump in my throat. I swallowed. "You're not going to leave, Mama," I said. "We'll go to the infirmary. Or Mick and I will fetch the doctor. That would be better. They'll give you medicine. And I'll take care of Tom and Mick and do your work until you get better. Maybe I can get the Vincent men to give me another blanket and some coal. And, and you'll be better before you know it." All the anxiety I had been holding inside me suddenly spilled out in a torrent of words.

"Mr. Connor," the priest said, looking first at Connor and then at me. "Would you take the children downstairs for a bit? I need a word with Mrs. Keane."

Mr. Connor nodded, his eyes solemn. I was old enough to know that the more solemn the grownups looked, the less they were likely to tell children. I stood. Mama lay almost motionless in the bed. I laid a hand on her forehead, smoothed a damp strand of hair back from her face.

"You go with Mr. Connor, now," the Father said.

I bent to kiss her, the corner of her eye that always crinkled when she smiled. I didn't want to leave.

"Clare," she whispered to me. I leaned in close. "Keep the boys together. You are all they have. Keep them with you. Promise me."

"I promise, Mama," I said.

"Do you promise?" Mama said.

"I do," I said.

"Go on with you, now," the Father said. "The angels and I will take good care of your mother."

Mr. Connor reached out a hand to me. I took it for a second, then pulled away.

"Come on, Tommeen," I said, taking his hand as he slid out of the chair. "We need to leave the Father alone with Mama for a while." I looked at Mick as he rose heavily off the coal box. He looked at me. Behind his tears was the same numbness I felt through every bone in my body.

* * *

Mr. Connor's apartment was tucked under the stairs on the ground floor. As we entered the door, we were assailed by a barrage of smells, each more insistent than the next. A chamber pot sat full just outside the door, waiting to be emptied in the privy. A plate with yesterday's cabbage lay on the table. The smell of old pipe smoke, old sweat, old cooking fires long dead clung to the walls thicker than both the fleas and the peeling paint put together. A pile of tattered coats lay on the bed. A single chair held together with twine was the only place to sit. Mr. Connor pulled it out for me, then turned to the mantle to light the paraffin lamp.

"I need to see about . . . , um . . . , cleaning, um . . . , fixing something. Abroad. In the yard," he said, reaching for a sack of tools under the bed, not meeting my eyes. "You three wait here."

"I'm going to go up to Mam," Tom said.

"And keep your brothers here," Mr. Connor said, making quick eye contact with me before heading quickly to the door. He paused, turned to look first at Tom, then me. His eyes were full of something I couldn't quite understand. "You need to stay here until the priest or I come for you. Do you understand?"

"I do, Mr. Connor," I said. I understood what he said. What I didn't understand was why he was saying it. Why should we stay here when Mama needed us? I knew it would do little good to ask.

"That's a good lass," he said. Turning to leave, he paused. For a flicker, it looked as though he wanted to say something more. Instead he laid a hand lightly on Mick's shoulder, turned his eyes to the door, and left.

I sat at the in the chair, smelling the stale cabbage on the plate beside me. My stomach growled with hunger, but I couldn't imagine eating.

"Do you think he would mind if we ate his cabbage?" Tom asked.

"I don't know," I said.

"I don't think he'd mind," Tom said. "It's pretty old. It looks like he only left it."

Mick stood beside the hearth, gazing into the low flame of the lamp, his back to me. His hands were stuffed hard into the pockets of his jacket. I could see his shoulders shake.

"I wouldn't mind if it were my cabbage. It looks like he only left it." Tom said. His words came out in a nervous rush.

"Go on, then," I said to Tom, who snatched a limp leaf off the plate with his fingers and began munching.

Mick dragged a sleeve across his eyes and turned to me.

"Is Mama going to die?" he asked quietly, turning to look into my eyes.

"I think so," I said. He nodded, walked over the doorway and stared absently out it.

"Who will take care of us?" he said finally.

Tom snatched another cabbage leaf from the plate, listening solemnly to the conversation.

"I suppose I will," I said.

"I don't want to go to an orphanage," Mick said, his voice shaking. "A boy at school went to one of those industrial school orphanages for a year after his father went away to England. He said they beat him, sometimes in the middle of the night. He said the monks don't sleep like regular people and sometimes they come in the middle of the night and make boys get up for a flaking."

"I can't imagine they would do such a thing," I said. "Why would they wake up boys to cane them?"

"I don't know," Mick said. "I only know I don't want to go there. He said all the monks were good for was praying and caning the knackers out of him."

"And did he deserve it?" I asked.

"One boy died," Mick said. "He had a weak chest, and the monks said he was shamming. And when he wouldn't work they beat him until he died. Murdered him where he stood. Only cause he was alone in the world, that and had a weak chest. I don't want to go there."

"I can't imagine," I said. But then I couldn't have imagined the conversation we were having either. The whole world seemed surreal. "Can we talk about this later? We should be praying."

"Can we get some bread?" Tom asked. The cabbage was gone. His fingers mopped up the last of the juices on the plate. When he first started school, he had sucked his two center fingers when he was upset or nervous. The boys teased him mercilessly, called him Fingers. Gradually he had broken the habit, but had replaced it by a fierce desire to eat when he was anxious. "I could go out and watch for the bread cart," he offered.

"Not this minute," I said. "We should be praying."

"I don't want to go to an orphanage," Mick said. "I won't go to an orphanage."

I sat between the two boys, Tom licking the cabbage juice from his fingers, Mick leaning on the door jam, staring at the lid of the slops. I brushed the crumbs on the table into a small pile. I couldn't seem to pray either, not beyond the gasping cries for help of a drowning victim. More than anything I wanted to charge out the front door and up the stairs to Mama's bedside.

"Go rinse that plate at the tap outside," I said to Tom. Mr. Connor's been kind enough to let us wait here. The least we can do is help him clean the place up a bit."

Tom picked up the chipped plate, and gnawing at his thumbnail, made his way outside to the tap.

"Mama might be fine," he said, brushing past Mick on his way out. "We might not have to go to the orphanage."

"We won't have to go to the orphanage," I said, feeling the strength of the promise in my chest. "I'll see to that."

* * *

It didn't take us long to clean Mr. Connor's room. He had just the table, chair, and bed, and there wasn't much to be done about the bed since it had no sheets and just a pile of old coats instead of blankets. Mick carried out the slops, holding it at arms' length, his head turned away. I wiped the table with an old rag I found on the mantle and rinsed the jelly jar Mr. O'Connor used as a glass. He didn't appear to have a broom, so there was little I could do about the floor.

I suppose it didn't matter much. Everyone knew that since his wife died a year or so ago of the typhoid, Mr. Connor was rarely home. He spent his days tending to the houses of the respectable people, greasing a hinge here, fixing a step there. When he was well, that is. Now that he was alone, Mr. Connor seemed to be drying up like a piece of old shoe leather. His color was flat and grey, and sometimes he had a rattle in his chest that scared the little kidgers no less than if he had risen from the grave himself. He did odd jobs for the landlord, cleaning the yard, collecting the rent. For that, he earned a room that he seemed to avoid like the devil in all his terror lived there. Looking around at the windowless hole with its slanting ceiling and mossy walls, I could understand that Mr. Connor's primary allegiance was to the pub, and that his room was no more than a place to sleep and get out of the weather after his real home closed.

I took a last swipe with the rag over the mantle, then backed up to see if there was anything more I could do. Shy of boiling a great vat of water and scrubbing the tiny apartment from top to bottom, I couldn't do much more than I had. I returned the rag to the mantle.

That's when I saw it. A single large clock, a cockroach it was, climbing its way out of the fireplace. It was a sign of death and no mistaking, a sign that someone nearby was passing on.

I stumbled out the door, shocked to my very core by the omen. Tom and Mick were leaning against the front door of the tenement in the long early morning light. Tom was picking at a button on his jacket. Mick simply stood motionless, leaning heavily against the jam, his eyes fixed and far away. Mom used to say that men were great leaners—they leaned on walls, on shovels, on the bar rail at the pub. Women, she said, never had time to lean. They were either too busy working, or, if they finished their work, were too tired to do anything but sit.

Mama used to say that, I thought. It wasn't right that the Father should keep us from Mama. It wasn't right.

"I want to back upstairs," Mick said.

"Me, too," said Tom.

"We shouldn't," I said without conviction. "Mr. Connor and the Father said to wait here."

But I needed to see her. It suddenly didn't matter if we got in trouble. I needed to be with my mama.

* * *

Outside our door on the landing, Mrs. Sullivan from across the yard and her sister from down the lane stood, heads bowed and hands folded. Never missing a beat in the saying of their beads, they raised their eyes and motioned for us to come up the last flight of stairs. Marking her place on the rosary with her thumb, Mrs. Sullivan reached out a hand and gently stroked my face, a quick, quavering stroke before returning to the beads.

Inside the priest bent over the bed. His narrow purple stole was thin and wrinkled from having been folded. It lay lightly against the black cassock. I stared at it, noticing the little flakes of dandruff that littered his shoulders. How strange that I should notice the dandruff. Mama lay silent on the bed, and I notice dandruff, wrinkles. I forced my eyes from the priest's shoulders. He held a bottle of amber liquid—oil I guessed—in one hand and was dabbing some of it on Mama's hands with the other. He said something in Latin, then moved to the foot of the bed and dabbed more of the oil on her feet.

I knew what was happening. These were the last rites. Mama was dying, or maybe dead. "Mama is dead." The words rattled in my mind, not finding a place to settle. "Mama is dead. Da is dead. Grandmama is dead. Granddad was dead long before I was born myself. Nana and Papa were not only dead, they were dead in America." I reached out for Tom's hand. It was cold.

The priest removed the stole from around his neck.

"Children," he said, "come to me." He put an arm around Mick's shoulders. "Do you have someone you could stay with? An aunt or an uncle, maybe?" He looked at us each in turn.

"Is our mother dead?" I asked.

"She is," he said. "She was a good woman, made a good confession, and died in the arms of the church. You will see her again in heaven."

Tom walked to the foot of the bed. His face was blank as he looked at Mama, as though he were waiting, merely waiting.

"Do you have family?" the priest asked again.

"Yes," Mick said. I looked at him surprised. Our only family was Uncle Ronan, and he was all the way across the sea in America. We had never even met him, had only read the short letters he had written Da before he died. "We have family, but we will have to write them to send for us. So we would be grateful for help with . . . " He looked over at Mama and began to cry.

"We will need someone to prepare Mama for the wake," I said. The words felt like they were coming from some far away place, certainly not from my mouth. As if on cue, Mrs. Sullivan pushed the door open and walked into the apartment her hands clasping the rosary in front of her. She approached us reverently, as though approaching the altar at the Mass.

"I'll give Mr. Connor a few pence for your food today," the priest said. He walked over to where Mama lay, took a rosary from her still fingers. "You best keep this." He handed the rosary to me.

"Thank you," I said, clutching it, trying to feel in the beads the last warmth of Mama's fingers. The tears began to rise, from a bottomless place, a place so full of tears I believed it would never empty.

"I must go say morning Mass," he said. "We will pray for you children and for your mother's soul."

* * *

Mrs. Sullivan and the three other women who had appeared mysteriously just after the Father left were now scattered to fetch water, soap, combs, and a pair of copper pennies.

"You need some time to yourself," she had said, again stroking my face as she left. "Make your goodbyes. We'll be back presently." That was an hour ago. Maybe an hour ago. Maybe not. I wasn't certain. I looked out the window trying to gauge the height of the sun by the shadow of our tenement on the building across the yard. Time seemed to be shrinking and stretching inside me. Each moment was an eternity, but those eternities passed smoothly, quickly, in a deep grey haze that made everything look not quite real.

I was kneeling by the side of the bed. The tears had stopped. I almost wished for more of them because where they had been was now a frightened, empty place inside me. Tom napped at the foot of the bed, his face blotchy from the tears. Mick was at the table, pencil in hand, bent over a piece of paper.

I stood and went to him, laid a hand on his shoulder, stroked his hair.

"I'm writing Uncle Ronan at the Lakeside Inn," he said.

"We're not sure he still works there," I said.

"He does," Mick replied, still writing. Unlike Tom, he had never been comfortable with words and books. He wielded the pencil like a blunt object.

"Mick," I said. "Why did you tell the priest we have family?"

"We have Uncle Ronan," he said.

"Uncle Ronan is in America," I said. "He can't take care of us."

"I don't want to go to the orphanage," Mick said. "Maybe he can send us some money."

"I don't think we should depend on it," I said.

"Maybe he can bring us to live with him in America."

"I doubt he has that kind of money."

"Maybe we can go live with him. We could catch fish in the lake to eat, and I could get a job as a delivery boy, and you could clean houses for the rich people. America has lots of rich people. We could pay him back."

"I suppose it doesn't hurt to write him. He needs to know about Mama, anyway."

"He does," Mick said.

I wondered when the women would arrive.

Two

I don't remember much of the wake or the funeral. They seemed like a dream even while they were happening. Once they were over, the memory faded quickly, leaving only a few dull images resting heavily in my mind. I do remember Mama lying stretched out on the bed in a new nightdress, a blue and white one even though Mama had always worn yellow. The sheet was pulled up nearly to her chin, but her arms were on top of it, a flower in one hand and her grandmother's rosary in the other. Beneath her head was a strange, white pillow the handywomen had brought in. And what with the strange pillow and the new nightdress, and the, well, the *look* of her face, she seemed like she wasn't really herself, which she wasn't, I suppose. Still, as I stood looking down at her, it seemed as though not only she, but also the apartment, the candles atop the table, the sounds of the women praying the rosary, the smell of the strong soap they washed her in — all those were not quite real either.

The neighbors came by for the wake, of course. I remember the noise, the sandwiches everyone chipped in to buy, the tobacco smoke and the laughter as Paddy Doohan told a story about his boss tripping over his own feet. I remember the keening that would break out every now and again, the high, mournful, barely human wailing, some of it from my very throat. Our apartment was packed to the rafters with neighbors. The smell of porter, damp wool, and living, breathing bodies filled up the only available air, so eventually I made my way down the crowded stairs and out the front door. The rain was falling lightly. That's what I remember. The rain, the sounds of a crowd from the open window above.

* * *

The rain was still falling as we stood in the graveyard the next day. Mick shivered beside me. Beside him, Tom stood rigid, his jaw clamped so tight I could see the muscles in his neck.

It wasn't much of a grave. After Da's death, Mama got behind on the dead money. The burial insurance policy never got paid up. The neighbors helped, chipped in a few pence each. But because we couldn't afford any better, because most of the money went to the wake and the hearse, they buried Mama in a shroud instead of a casket, and on top of Papa. At least it isn't a pauper's grave Mrs. Sullivan tried to reassure me. At least she'll have a place near her husband.

They tied her up in a canvas sheet, a shroud the women called it, and three men lowered her down into a big hole in the ground. The mud from the freshly dug hole sucked at the men's boots. It seeped into the canvas when they laid her down with a hollow sound atop what must have been Da's casket, Da's casket deep in the soggy hole. Standing up top, I could still feel the mud, feel it in my very flesh, cold and sticky, almost as though it were my shroud it was seeping into.

The priest, a different one this time, murmured to himself in Latin as he sprinkled yet more water into the grave. The hem of his cassock was sticky with the mud. The rain ran in small rivers down the creases of his old face.

Mr. Connor stood, hat in hands, a fair distance from the grave. Mrs. Sullivan and the other women who had washed and bound Mama's body stood two steps behind the Father, their hands folded prayerfully. Other neighbors, huddled in blue serge suits and black shawls, bowed their heads against the rain and the occasion.

On the very edge of the grave, though, were just the three of us, the three of standing in a tight knot, our hair pasted to our heads by the rain, our clothes dark with the damp of it. The men from the graveyard drew their ropes from the hole and grabbed at shovels stuck into a nearby mound. The dirt fell in light clumps and landed with hollow thuds on the gritty canvas below.

* * *

"Do you have family?" the priest asked us when he finished his words in Latin. "Do you need someone to take care of you?"

I looked at Mick. He looked back at me.

"If you don't have family, you need to tell me so I can send one of the brothers to come for you."

"We have family." I said. "We wrote our Uncle Ronan yesterday."

"And where would your Uncle Ronan be, then?" the priest asked.

I hesitated. Surely it was a sin to lie to a priest.

"Uncle Ronan lives west of here," Mick said. "Abroad in the country."

"Ah, well, I'm glad of it," the priest said. "It will do you no harm to get out of this city, and you being left in God's hands and no others."

"Thank you, Father," I said. "Bless you."

"Bless you, Father," echoed Tom and Mick.

He left. After they had stooped to hug us, so did the neighbors. Some of them headed back to work, others felt there was no excuse like a funeral to spend the afternoon in the pub.

Mr. Connor stepped forward gingerly, almost as through he were afraid the grave would reach out and capture him. He shot nervous glances at the men with shovels.

"Well then," Mr. Connor said, "We should be getting you home. When will your uncle be sending for you?"

"We just wrote him," said Mick.

"I'm hungry," Tom said.

"Surely you are," Mr. Connor said. "When did you last eat? The wake?"

I couldn't seem to remember. Somehow it didn't seem important.

"Why don't I buy you some nice fish and chips?" he said. "You really should eat something after all you went through."

"We should," I thought. We would need to eat something. I would have to feed us from now on.

* * *

We sat together around the table, greasy newspapers spread out in front of us. The deep-fried fish and potatoes that had been in them were gone. Tom ran his finger over the last of the grease and put it in his mouth. Mr. Connor had left. Someone had complained that the tap was working poorly again, and he had gone to see about it.

"I think we should send a telegram to Uncle Ronan," Mick said.

"Can you send a telegram all the way to America?" I asked.

"Of course," Mick answered. "A boy at school said his brother in America sends them money all the time by telegraph."

"How much would it cost?" I asked.

Mick shrugged. "How much money do we have?"

I looked over at Da's coat, hanging on a hook by the door. Mick looked, too.

"Go on," he said. "'Tis ours now"

I stood, walked to the coat, and lifted it gently from the hook. It was one of our only relics of Da, a relic of decency, from a time long gone when we could afford a coat, a brand-new one if we wanted. It was warmth on cold nights huddled together in bed. And it was our bank, the place we sewed the few pence we'd managed to save.

I bundled the coat over my arm, clutched it tightly to me. A light scent rose from it, the smell of Mama's hair freshly washed. For a moment, she was there beside me, there in the smell of her. Then just as suddenly she was down at the bottom of the hole, bound like a bundle of rags, wet from the rain and the mud. I buried my face in the worn brown fabric, clutching furiously at the faint aroma. Mama. The tears came again, the deep sobs. What am I going to do, Mama? What am I going to do?

When the tears subsided, I picked myself up from the floor and put the coat back on the hook. I looked up. The boys were sitting bent over the table, their faces buried in their sleeves, crying into soggy newspaper.

"Let's go to bed," I said. "You have school tomorrow, and I have to work."

* * *

I was awake with the sun. For a moment I didn't remember. Then I did. I crawled over Mick out of bed and peed in the chamber pot. I threw my shawl around my shoulders and lifted Da's coat from the hook. Taking a knife from the shelf, I sat with the coat at the table. In the shadowy light of the new day, I carefully picked the stitching in the left pocket. From a secret pouch, Mama had sewn there, I pulled a handful of pennies, a couple of shillings, a half a crown, and another. Eight and four in all. Just under a week's wages for Mama and me.

We would eat today, would eat for the rest of the week. But the rent for next Monday wasn't there. That two and six would have to come out of my Friday pay. Three and six minus two and six—that left a shilling for us to eat off for the rest of the week. I couldn't feed us on that, not even if we ate no better than stirabout and bread. I picked up the water bucket and stepped out the door onto the landing. The weathered wood of the stairs felt soggy, slippery under my bare feet. Through the open door at the foot of the stairs came a breeze, the air was cool and damp, but the rain had stopped. I waited my turn, then filled the bucket and scrubbed my face and hands at the tap in the end of the yard.

Back in our room, I filled the teapot and set it to boil before waking the boys. Mick, got up, put on his jacket, and sat down at the table, where the money lay.

"Eight and four," he said. "We can send the telegram this morning on the way to school."

I nodded.

"Do we have breakfast?" he asked.

"Only tea," I said filling the pot. "I'll buy us some bread on way to the telegraph office. What shall we say in the telegram?"

"Well," said Mick, "I suppose we should know before we go to the office." He snatched a piece of newspaper left over from the fish and chips last night and found a piece of margin that wasn't too greasy. From his jacket pocket he pulled his school pencil.

"What do you think?" he said.

"Dear Uncle Ronan," I began. "We are sorry to tell you that our mother, your sister-in-law, is gone to join Father in heaven."

"You can't say that," Mick broke into my thoughts.

"Why not," I said. "I thought it sounded fine."

"It sounded fine, but a telegram has to be short. Every word costs money."

"It does?" I said.

"Of course it does," he said. "How do you think they pay the man who sits and clicks out the messages?"

"Then we'll write a shorter one," I said simply. "We're not made of money."

As I said it, I heard Mama's voice in my mind. "We're not made of money," she used to say. No we're not, I thought.

"How about this?" Tom said, reading what he wrote. "Dear Uncle Ronan, Mama died last Friday. The three of us children are alone. Will you bring us to America? Your nephew, Michael Finbarr Joseph Keane."

"You best say 'mother,' not 'mama'," I said.

"Just so," said Mick making the change.

"And I think it should be from all of us, not only you."

"But it will cost more money if we put all three names on it," Mick said.

"Then only put mine," I said.

"Why only yours?" Mick asked. "I wrote it."

"But I'm paying for it."

"'Tis Mama's money," Mick said.

"But I'm the only one with a job," I replied. "And I'm the oldest. We'll put my name on the telegram."

"Fine," Mick said. He crossed out the last sentence and wrote, "Your niece, Clare Elizabeth Keane."

I poured him a glass of tea from the pot.

"We need to leave soon," I said. "Be sure you scrub your face and hands before we go."

* * *

The man at the telegraph office squinted at the greasy piece of newspaper. He pulled out a small, clean sheet of paper.

"Are you really alone?" he said.

"We are, sir," I answered.

"A terrible thing," he said. "How old is the lad?" He gestured toward Tom.

"Ten, sir" I said.

"And yourself?" he said.

"Fourteen, sir. Just."

Mick spoke up. "I'm twelve, sir."

"So you are," said the man, shaking his head. "So you are. So young." He began writing on the small sheet of paper. "A terrible thing," he said to himself.

"This will save you a few farthings," he said. "By the looks of you, I would say you need it." He pushed the paper sideways across the paper so I could see it and read, "Mama died. We three children alone. Will you bring us America? Your niece, Clare Keane."

It sounded so hard, so cold, when put like that.

"'Tis powerful short," I said.

"Thank you," he replied with a nod. "Then we'll send it, we will?"

I looked at Mick. He nodded.

"We will, sir," I said, reaching in my pocket for the money.

"Ah, don't you be bothering with that," he said. He reached into his own pocket and pulled out a few coins. "My mother is still alive, and me a grown man. 'Tis the least I can do."

"We thank you, sir," Mick said.

"God increase you," I added.

"And you," he said. In his eyes were the same look of sadness we seemed to see all around us.

* * *

The sun was up for some time, a couple of hours maybe, when I entered the Quillan's house through the tradesmen's entrance. I made my way through the back hallway to my room, where I dropped my shawl on the cot and picked up a clean apron from the stack under the wash stand. Mrs. Quillan was adamant about clean aprons, making me put on a fresh apron first thing in the morning, then again before serving dinner. I tied it neatly behind me and returned to the kitchen.

Straightening my skirt, and smoothing back my hair, I looked through the kitchen door into the dining room. The Quillans were seated at table eating breakfast. They had tea in matching cups, bread and jam on matching plates. They even had eggs, one each in little cups made only for eggs. Mrs. Quillan must have cooked. She hated cooking breakfast, and I was sure to hear about it.

Around the table, the three boys were decked out in their school jackets, crisply pressed navy jackets with the school crest stitched to the pocket. One was wiping at an egg stain on his tie with his sleeve.

"Stop that, Andrew," Mrs. Quillan snapped at him. She was in a sour humor, to be sure. "Just take the tie off and put on a clean one."

Andrew stood, the legs of his chair making a scraping sound against the floor.

"First ask to be excused," Mrs. Quillan directed.

I retreated into the kitchen and began wiping the counters of the crumbs Mrs. Quillan had left there. I would tell her when she finished breakfast. As soon as she finished breakfast. I tried the words out in my head.

"Mrs. Quillan," I thought to myself. "I'm afraid my mother is gone to be with the angels. She always did have a weak chest you know. But now that I am fourteen, I can do an adult's work for an adult's pay." No wait, that wasn't right. "But now that I am fourteen, I'm sure I could do her work as well as mine, and if you could see your way clear to giving me a rise." That wasn't right either. "Mrs. Quillan, I'm sorry to tell you that my mother passed on."

"Why are you mumbling to yourself, child?" Mrs. Quillan stood right behind, her hands full of dishes and her eyes shooting out little jets of ire. I jumped at her voice. "Where have you been the last two days? And where is your mother? I need to talk to her about Saturday's menu, and the wood needs to be done and the brass on the front door needs to be polished. I should dismiss both of you on the spot for leaving me like this."

"My mother is dead," I said. The tears welled up in the corner of my eyes. I blinked them back. I had promised myself I wouldn't cry. "Yesterday was her funeral. And I'm alone now with my two brothers. And I have to make more money, because we have to go to America. And . . . ," I looked up into her eyes. "My mother is dead," I said simply.

"I'm sorry for your loss," she said quietly. That's all: I'm sorry for your loss. But then she was a Protestant, and perhaps they weren't taught the proper things to say at such a time. I wasn't sure what to say when someone said, "I'm sorry for your loss," so I simply nodded and concentrated on fighting back the tears.

Mrs. Quillan set the dishes she was carrying in the sink. "Come," she said simply, leading me into the small table in the kitchen where Mama and I used to eat our meals. "Sit," she said motioning to a chair.

"Was it her chest?" she asked.

I nodded, then remembered my manners. "It was, ma'am," I said.

"A terrible thing," she said. "Can you work today and tomorrow, until I can find someone to replace her?"

"Certainly, I can," I said, surprised at the question. "Ma'am," I said. "I can replace her. I can keep working for you, do my mother's job and my own."

"No, Clare," Mrs. Quillan said. "I need an adult for the job, someone who can do the heavy lifting, someone I can trust to buy food, and cook for parties, and no, Clare. You are a good girl, a hard worker, but you are a child."

"I'm fourteen," I said. "Almost an adult. I could find a woman to do Mother's work, and I could keep doing my work, and . . . "

"Please don't make things worse for yourself," Mrs. Quillan said abruptly. "I didn't get where I am today by allowing children to choose my servants for me. Lord knows your mother was a fine cook, and you were a good servant. The two of you will be hard to replace."

I sat, stunned. I was out of work. These three years I scrubbed the Quillan's floors, cleaned their grates, emptied their slops, made their beds. Now I was out of work. The tears welled up in my eyes.

"You can stay through the end of the week," she said quietly. "I'll give you a good character, and I'll put a little extra in your pay on Friday."

"Thank you, Mrs. Quillan," I said.

"I'm sorry for your loss, dear," she said reaching over gently to touch my knee. "But I have a house to run. I have to think of my husband and children first."

"I understand, Mrs. Quillan," I said.

"I'm glad," she said. "Now I need you to polish the brass on the front door especially well. A very important business associate of Mr. Quillan's is coming this weekend, and it just won't do to make a poor first impression. I'll be at Mrs. Daly's house until late this afternoon. Can you manage on your own?"

"Yes, ma'am," I said, rising to tend to the breakfast dishes.

* * *

The lamps were trimmed. The feather beds were shaken and turned. The house was dusted. The brass was polished up to the nines. The good silver and china were clean, shined, and laid out on clean white towels. I had just finished scrubbing the entryway floor when Mrs. Quillan came home.

"Very nice," she said, stepping gingerly across the wet floor. "The door latch looks very nice. But I think you missed a spot atop the knocker."

"I'll see to it, Mrs. Quillan," I said, standing and wiping my hands on my apron.

"That's what I was talking about, Clare," Mrs. Quillan said, removing her gloves and dropping them on the table in the hallway. "You're too small, too young for your mother's job.

I wanted more than anything to tell her she was wrong. She was wrong. But I held my tongue. Mama always used to tell me that it just didn't pay to talk back to the rich folks. Even if you were clearly right and they were clearly wrong, you would still lose. It was best to simply agree and get on with your work.

"A shame," she said handing me her coat to hang up. "A terrible pity." She strolled into the living room and sank into the sofa. "Clare," she said, "Would you be a dear and make me a cup of tea?"

* * *

"I got sacked," I said sinking into the chair without even taking off my shawl.

Tom, as usual, was seated near the window, squinting at a book. Mick, who was outside leaning with his friends, came through the door just after me. The sun was nearly down. They had been home from school for hours.

"You got sacked?" Mick said. "What did you do?" It sounded like he was accusing me of something.

"I was fourteen years old," I snapped back at him. "Mrs. Quillan wants someone older. She doesn't think I can do the job without Mama."

"I'll get a job," Mick said.

"You need to go to school," I replied.

"I need to get a job," he said, rummaging through the sideboard for whatever stray crumbs he could find. There were none. And somehow I'd forgotten to stop by the market on the way home.

"What if the truancy officers catch you?" I said. "If you mitch from school five or six times, they'll be sending you off to an industrial school. Or they'll come looking for Mam and Da and find out we're alone and send us all off to an industrial school." I was beginning to think that maybe that wasn't a bad thing. I was unemployed. The money was disappearing fast, and our only relative was thousands of miles away. Despite Mick's objections, an industrial school was beginning to look mighty good.

"We'll be in America before the truancy officers can catch up to me. Besides, you were younger than I was when you quit school to work."

"I had to," I said.

"Now I have to." He stood before me, his arms crossed over his chest and his jaw set. "I'm the man of the family. 'Tis my responsibility." I looked at him, him with his fine bones and his hairless jaw and marveled to think that he was right.

Tom rose from the horsehair chair and sat down at the table across from me. "Maybe we should all find work. If we do, we can save faster and get to America sooner."

"No," I said simply. "You need to be in school. Mama would want you to be in school. I'll find a job. I can go to the registry office tomorrow."

"Clare!" Tom exclaimed, his face registering shock. "You can't go to one of those places. They're filled with, with, "He paused, tracing his forefinger along the spine of the book in his hands. "They're filled with women of the unfortunate class," he said finally.

"'Women of the unfortunate class'?" Mick guffawed. He gave Tom a shove. Tom's chair let of a terrible squawk as it shifted beneath his weight. "Women of the unfortunate class? Don't you mean 'whores'? And what would you know about whores, boyo?"

Tom's ears colored. "I know enough to know that Clare doesn't want to be around them."

"And why is that?" Mick leaned back on the table and locked eyes with his younger brother, a practiced leer on his face.

"Mick, stop," I said. "This is no joke. We're talking about how we can keep you in school."

"We were until Tom brought up *whores*." His eyes remained locked on Tom's ever reddening face. I reached across the table and slapped Mick on the side of the head. He glared at me.

"Stop acting like such a child," I said. "Is this what you and your corner boy friends do, bait each other with dirty prattle?"

"Do you want me to be a man?" he replied. "All right, I'll be one. Listen to me," he said, leaning across the table. "When we get to Uncle Ronan's, I'll go back to school. But now we need the money more than we need me to know British history. I'll find a job."

"Mick," I said. "We have another choice."

"Not that I can see," he said.

"We do, and you know it."

"No," he said.

"We could go to the industrial school," I said firmly.

"No."

"Mick."

"No."

"Listen to me, Mick," I said. "I saw some industrial school boys themselves. They wore clean clothes, no holes." I looked up at him. His shirt was more mending than shirt, and his trousers looked as though they were being held together by dirt. I ached with the knowledge that Mama and I hadn't been able to do better for him. "Mick, those boys sleep in a clean bed every night. They eat good food without having to worry where their next meal is coming from. They learn a good trade so they don't have to spend their life as dray horses and dogsbodies, hauling whatever the rich people put on their shoulders."

"No," Mick said.

"'Tis a better life than we have now," I said. "And 'tis a better life than I'm likely to ever give us."

Mick collapsed into the horsehair chair. "Are you going to try to make us go there?" he said. "I won't go, you know. I'll run away if you try to make me." The "man of the family" was sitting, arms crossed tightly on his chest, a definite pout twisting up his face.

I sighed. "Do you want to tell me just what you think is so bad about the industrial schools that you'd turn down three meals a day and a clean bed?"

Mick twisted around and stared out the window silently. I waited. Finally he spoke, his eyes still looking far out the window.

"I don't know really," he said. "Andy Jewitt was in an industrial school. That time his father went to England looking for work. Andy told me about it. He said it was terrible. He said they dress you all alike, cut your hair all alike. They parade you everywhere in long lines, your feet marching in time with everyone else's feet. You eat when they say eat. You sleep when they say sleep. You would laugh and joke when they say, but they never say. You work all day long, from sunup to sunset, and when you're not working you're praying. If you step out of line, they thrash you. Sometimes they come in the middle of the night and thrash you. The monks walk around the dormitory in the middle of the night wearing these soft padded slippers so you can't hear them, and if you aren't sleeping the way they want you to sleep, they take you out and beat the knackers out of you. It's no better than a prison. I won't go," he said.

"Mick," I said, "they feed you. They clothe you. They teach you a trade. And I have a hard time believing they come around and beat you in the middle of the night, no matter what Andy Jewitt says."

"I won't go," Mick said.

"Would you go, too, Clare," Tom asked, "if we do have to go?" He'd been sitting quietly listening to Mick's description.

"I wouldn't turn away a clean bed all to myself," I said.

"They'd separate us," Mick said. "They wouldn't let us stay together."

"Clare would have to go to the girl's school," Tom agreed.

"And you'd be with the junior boys, and I'd be with the older boys, and we'd never see each other again," Mick said.

The room went silent. Mick's words hung in the air. "We'd never see each other again." I wasn't sure he was right. But the thought of it was enough to set my mind working again. It began turning it over again—the long litany of losses, the long catalog of things that had been snatched from my grasp before I was ready to let them go. First Da, then the house, then all our possessions abandoned at the pawns one by one, then my schooling, my place in the bed beside Mama and the boys, finally Mama, my job, and the last clear glimpse I had of tomorrow. I looked up at the boys. Both wore the same far away look. Could we trade each other in for a hot meal, and a charity meal at that?

"I don't want to go either," Tom said quietly.

"I think we should go to America," Mick added. "I think we have a better chance there. At the very least we can stay together."

"I don't know if we can afford to go to America," I said. "I don't know how much it costs. I don't know if I can make a living there."

"A boy at school said it costs twenty-five pounds per person to travel on one of those big ocean liners," Tom supplied. "That's seventy-five pounds for three. If we all find jobs, we can start saving now."

I have to say I was shocked. I had no notion it would cost so much. "Do you know how long it would take to earn seventy-five pounds?" I said. America suddenly looked impossible. At five shillings a week, I made a pound a month. That was twelve pounds a year, barely enough to live off. It would take me six or seven years to earn enough to get us to America, and that's assuming the boys could make enough to keep us pulling the devil by the tail while I did.

"We don't have to earn our whole fare," Mick said. "We only have to earn enough for new traveling clothes. Uncle Ronan will send the fare."

"We don't know that," I replied.

"He will," Mick said.

"What about money for the train ticket?" Tom asked.

I looked at him. "The train ticket," I said. "To where? We can walk to Queenstown."

"Not to Queenstown, to St. Paul," he said. "You can't get to St. Paul by boat." He reached over to the chair and snatched up one of the books in the stack he was reading. "I got this at the library," he said. "It has everything you'd ever want to know about America." He flipped through its pages to a map.

"Here's Ireland," he said pointing to a tiny shape roughly in the center of the map. "Here's the Atlantic Ocean. And here's New York." He pointed at a dot with New York printed beside it. "I think New York is the capital of the United States. At least it's where most of the boats from Ireland go."

Mick leaned over the table to look at the book with us, looking interested despite himself.

"Where's St. Paul?" I asked.

Tom flipped to another page in the book. "Here," Tom said. He pointed to another dot.

"We wouldn't have to live in St. Paul," Mick said.

"That's where Uncle Ronan is, or close to there, anyway," Tom replied.

"But if we can save money for the boat fare, we can live in New York until we can save money for the train," Mick said.

I was still looking at the map, trying to make sense of it. Maps weren't my strength even when I was in school, and that seemed an eternity ago. "What's this?" I pointed to something that looked a little like a leaf or a bunch of leaves.

"Those are the Great Lakes," Tom said. "This one is Lake Superior. It's in the state of Minnesota, like St. Paul is. You could fit all of Ireland into Lake Superior and still have lots of room to do some fishing."

"Go on with you!" Mick said.

"No, it's true," Tom said. "It would take months to walk from New York to St. Paul because you have to walk over mountains and around the Great Lakes. But you don't have to walk because you can get anywhere you want in America only by riding a train. So we have to have enough money for boat fare, train tickets, clothes, and food."

"Uncle Ronan will send us the fare for the ship," Mick amended. "And we'll have to earn the rest."

"Maybe," I said. "We still don't know if Uncle Ronan will send for us."

"He will," Mick said. "He has to."

That was true enough. If he didn't, there would be no way for us to get to America. I wondered if the boys understood that. If they didn't now, I imagined they would soon enough.

"Here's what we'll do, then," I said. "I'll look for work. Mick will look for work, work after school if he can find it, otherwise work during the day. Tom, you'll stay in school for now. Learn as much as you can about America. We'll save what we can and wait to hear from Uncle Ronan. But if we run out of money, or if the truancy officers come for Mick, or if Uncle Ronan can't send for us, we go present ourselves to the industrial school."

I looked at Tom. He nodded in agreement. I looked at Mick. Reluctantly, he nodded too.

Three

When Americans find out I grew up in the tenements, the question they invariably ask me is "how did you end up there?" Americans, it seems, find comfort in reasons and explanations. They honestly believe that if they can find the reason for someone else's misfortune, they can avoid that misfortune themselves. If they could find out how I ended up in the tenements, they could assure themselves that it could never have happened to them.

The truth is that many of my neighbors lived where they did because that was where their mother and father lived, and their parents before them. Each generation left school early to earn a wee bit of money for the family. They then spent the rest of their lives earning just that, a wee bit of money. It was the way of things. The poor, my people when I was growing up, were smiled upon when they knew their place and slapped down and booted out if they tried to ease so much as a toe into a better class. You see, we all believed that the children of servants and laborers were born to be the next generation of servants and laborers. It was their reason for being. We all believed it. Except those of us who didn't, and they either emigrated or learned to keep quiet. That or lived in the constant power of trouble their attitude cost them. It's the way it was back then.

In my case, the truth is that we ended up in the tenements when my father died. Before he died, Da was a butcher and Mama did day work, cleaning offices for some solicitors. We weren't rich, probably not even middle class. But we had a small clean house with a bedroom and a tap in the kitchen, and we had meat and vegetables, and could afford Sunday clothes to go to Mass in. Mama and the boys ended up in the tenement, and I quit school to go do for the Quillans when Da died. If anyone could have found another way, we would have been glad to take it.

Of course, some of our neighbors lived where they did because of the drink. Some call it the curse of the Irish. I say living in drunken poverty is a curse no matter if you're Irish or not. Still, if a man makes twenty shillings a week—a good wage for a laborer—and then drinks three or four pints a day at nine pence a pint, he's left with no better than three or four shillings a week to bring home to his wife and family. Three or four shillings is murderous little to live off of no matter how you slice it. But then if a man slaves like a beast all day long, then goes home to a squalid apartment in a run-down building with a wife who complains to him that there is never enough money, well then doesn't that man deserve a pint or two now and again? You live poor because you drink, then you drink because you live poor—it's a little like a starving dog eating itself from the tail up. Yet more than a few of my neighbors did just that.

The Purcells who lived across the landing were living eight to a room mostly because of drink, not that Ned Purcell had much in the way of either ambition or cunning even when he was sober. Every payday Ned would stumble home when the pubs closed, coughing and barking from the pipe tobacco he could only afford when he'd had work that day. If his family was lucky, he'd have enough left in his pocket to pay for both the week's rent and food. If they weren't lucky, Mrs. Purcell would try to extract the lack from Ned's hide. That, too, was the way of things.

* * *

It was the dead of night. I had been sleeping deeply enough to dream, a strange and tumbling dream of coming home only to find everyone missing—not only Mama and the boys but all the neighbors, the local guard, everybody. I ran from place to place, down the stairs of the tenement, through the yard, to the church, to the Quillan's house, but everywhere I went, I found nobody but strangers. I returned home to decide what to do. I was lying alone in bed, my knees tucked up to my chest, when suddenly I heard a pounding at the door. I went to answer. Nobody was there, but still the pounding continued.

At the foot of the bed, Mick rolled over. He kneed Tom's legs, and Tom responded by kicking a foot into my chest. I propped myself up on an elbow, suddenly awake, feeling weak in the gut from the dream. The pounding from my dream found its way into the air of my real world.

"Maura, pet, let us in, won't you?" a man called in a slurred voice. I recognized it as Ned Purcell's voice. "Be a dear and let us in."

"Go away, you bowsie bastard," Maura called. Our door was open a crack to keep the air from getting too thick. Between that and the paper-thin walls, the drama outside could as well be held in our bedroom itself. "If you think I'll be letting you in before you sober up," Maura said, "you're not only on the drink, you're entirely dead in the head."

"Go away, Da. She's got the carving knife." A boy's voice chimed it. It was probably Charlie, their oldest.

"Go away, Ned or I'll give you a powerful clout in the head, better yet in the arse, give you permanent brain damage, I will."

The pounding stopped for a bit. Then the sound of coughing and retching split the air. Silence. Then the pounding resumed and with it a sharp, sour smell that crept steadily into our apartment.

"You let me in, right now, woman. I shouldn't have to beg to be let me into my own house," Ned answered. "I'm your husband, and this is my house. I pay the rent and I should be able to come and go as I please."

"Go on then, Ned," Maura answered. "Show us the rent. Slide it under the door so we can see it, you great souse of a man. I know where the rent money is. 'Tis lying in a puddle on my clean landing." I had no doubt about the truth of what she said. The smell was working its way past my nose into my throat.

"Let me in, Maura." Ned stopped banging the door with his fists and started kicking it. The hollow thud's of his boots echoed in the hallway.

I sat up, wide-awake now. Mick rolled over, I could see the dim outline of his face in the full moonlight that streamed in the window.

"He'll leave soon," he said. "We'll find him sobering up on the front stoop in the morning." Ned switched back to pounding with his fists. Between bouts, I could hear Tom snoring quietly at the foot of the bed.

"How can he sleep through this?" I said.

"He almost always does," Mick said.

"This happens often?"

"As often as fingers and toes." Mick answered. "Whenever Mrs. Purcell doesn't catch Ned between the docks and the pub, he comes home rolling. Charlie says giving money to his Da is like tossing it into the Lee. He says that most days his Mam or he goes out to the pubs trying to find Mr. Purcell before he drinks the rent entirely. He's worse tonight, though. The stevedore likely picked him for a good job."

I lowered myself back down onto the bed, and pulled the old coat up to my chin. The pounding next door slowed, then stopped. The sound of uneven footsteps on the stairs was followed by Mrs. Purcell's voice. She had opened the door and was on the landing just outside the door.

"What kind of a man steals bread from his children's mouths to buy drink?" she shouted at the top of her lungs. "If you never come back, Ned Purcell, it will be too soon for me, by goats."

The door across the hall slammed. Then the front door of the tenement slammed. Then it was quiet again. I heard stirring across the landing, then more stirring in the apartment beneath us, the sound of a man peeing into a chamber pot downstairs.

It was an unspoken rule that though everyone knew if a husband and wife were fighting, nobody interfered unless the blood was running freely. When you live as closely as we all did, you learn to hide your neighbors' secrets for them.

I was wide-awake, with a full bladder and a choking feeling in the back of my nose from the stink. So I got out of bed, thought about opening the window, but decided against it. The last thing any of us needed was to take a chill. I closed the door and squatted over the pot. The smell from the landing still seeped in.

"Finished?" Mick said quietly.

"Almost," I replied. "Do you think she'll clean that tonight?"

"Mrs. Purcell's no martyr to the mop," Mick replied. "She might get to it by afternoon."

"I can't sleep with the smell," I said. "Slops I don't mind. I don't like the smell, but I don't mind. But that smell, I can't abide that smell. It makes me want to puke myself."

"I'll draw the water if you clean," Mick said.

"We ought to get Tom to clean it. The smell doesn't seem to bother him." Tom was still spread out on his back, his arm outstretched and his hand dangling over the side of the bed. He was snoring lightly, completely oblivious to our conversation, to all that had happened.

"I think the cleaning might be easier than waking him," Mick said dryly. "That boyo can sleep with the best of them."

"Get the water," I said. "I'll start the fire."

Tom dug under the bed for his trousers and tiptoed out the door and around the ever-spreading puddle.

I lit a bit of scraw, piled a brick of turf against it, then sat myself atop the coal box to watch the flame draw up. My tiny room under the stairs at the Quillans hadn't been much. In fact 'twasn't much more than a cot, a wash stand, and some pegs for clothes. But it was more than I had now. I thought about it with a fondness that surprised me. The floor was left over linoleum. The walls were painted a soft white. And nobody in all the three and a half years I had lived there had ever thrown up a half dozen pints of porter outside my door.

The flame began to catch in earnest, and in its light I could see the crumbling masonry of the hearth. I ran a hand over the rough mortar, and some of it crumbled a bit under my fingers. The room was dismally grey in the light of the fire and the moon. But then in the clear light of day it was nearly as grey — grey, bare board floors, sooty grey walls, grey rocks around the hearth and grey ashes within it. I took a bit of kindling, lit it off the fire, and touched it to the wick of the paraffin oil lamp. It sputtered and smoked. I had planned to trim the wick in the morning, so now it burned dirty, sending sinews of grey smoke into the air. I watch them rise and disappear into the dark of the room.

The sound of footsteps on the stairs brought me out of my thoughts. Mick's and somebody else's. My first thought was that it was Mr. Purcell, but the footsteps were even and steady. Mick opened the door. Standing outside, his eyes averted, was a great shambles of a man.

"Clare," Mick said. "This is Benny. He sleeps on the landing sometimes, when the guard doesn't roust him out."

Benny tipped his threadbare cap, eyes still averted. I reached for my shawl hanging on the back of a chair and wrapped it around me.

"Lass, if you'll be so good as to heat the water and show me a bit of soap, I'll clean this mess here for you. After all, it was my bedroom he dropped it in." Benny chuckled.

"I would be grateful to you," I said.

"And if you'd want to do a quick wash up," Mick said, "the shadows on the landing are deep enough, I'd say. 'Twould be a pity to waste clean water, on a mucky floor."

"'Twould indeed," Benny said, tipping his cap again.

I poured the water into the kettle and set it to boil. Mick directed Benny to the chair. He tipped his cap again and sat, his smells mingling with the smell of the dirty lamp flame and the puddle on the landing. We sat there, the three of us, silently watching the kettle and the musky turf fire. When the water finally got hot enough, I poured it into the vat. I gathered together a bit of old newspaper, a scrub brush, some soap, and a bit of bread wrapped in a washrag, and I handed it all over to Benny.

I fell asleep that night to the sound of the scrub brush. When I woke the next morning, the vat was rinsed clean and the brush and rag lay inside. The floor was as pure as butter. Benny was nowhere to be seen.

* * *

The next morning I went to the registry office to see if they had a new job for me. They were kindly people, and I saw none of Tom's "unfortunate women." But they wanted two and six to put my name on the books and more when I was hired. I thanked them and left. Two and six would more than keep us fed for a week.

Not knowing where else to turn, I walked to the church to talk to the Father. He said he hadn't heard of free situations here in town, but he knew of three people in less than a month who had been hired by the rich folks out on Front Douglas Road. I asked him how far he thought that would be. He said he didn't know exactly but that he supposed it would be two miles if it were a foot. So

I made my way south, stopping to knock at the tradesmen's entrance of every respectable house I passed.

* * *

I was three days walking and knocking my way down Front Douglas Road when I arrived at the back door of a large brick house set deep in a great expanse of spring-green lawn and lilac bushes. The housekeeper answered.

"My name is Clare Keane," I said. "I am an orphan looking for work to support my two brothers and myself. I can do any kind of housework. I'm strong, and I work hard." I was halfway into my prepared speech, when the housekeeper interrupted.

"Clare Keane," she said, "You wouldn't be Hannah's girl, would you?"

"I am, ma'am," I said.

"Sure if you don't have her hair and face," she said. "I'm Mary Kellogg O'Rourke. I know your Mama, don't you know. When your mother worked for Mrs. Quillan, she would come with messages for Mrs. Good. That's the lady of the house, you know. I'm her cook and lady's maid. Your mother, she would sometimes sit for a while and rest her feet before going back. But you say you're an orphan. You don't mean . . ."

"She passed on last week," I said.

"Sweet Jesus, Mary and St. Joseph. The blessing of grace with her soul," she said quickly crossing herself. "She's gone, you say?"

"She is," I said.

"How?" she asked.

"'Twas her chest," I said.

"'Tis always the chest," she said and sighed. "The Lee, you know. The damp of it seeps into your lungs. And once the Lee is in your chest, you can't cough it out. Well don't only stand here. Come in, lassie, you poor lassie, come in."

I made my way past a large pile of old linoleum in the foyer of the tradesmen's entrance. The entrance was a mess of scraps and bits of dried up glue. But the kitchen was spotless and sunny, with the smell of fresh bread and spring air already banishing the last of the glue smell. The curtains were finely made, and the floors were shiny with fresh linoleum. A brand-new gas range and oven radiated a homey warmth.

"Do you think I can find work here?" I asked, amazed that the Goods would spend such money on the kitchen.

"Well, I can't say for certain, now," she said. "The work we have, surely, what with young master Michael getting married and Mr. Good bringing more and more people from his milling business home to be entertained. The work we have. 'Tis the pay that's the problem. Mrs. Good can squeeze a shilling 'til the king turns blue." She winked at me. "But I think I can come round her to turn loose his majesty this once." She pulled a bottle of lemonade from the icebox and a beautiful silver tray from the shelf. She lifted a towel from a loaf of bread, which she sliced and buttered. On the butter she sprinkled a little sugar.

"Herself is a wee bit sweetmouthed, don't you know," she said. "You follow me. But stay back. Don't let her see you just yet."

* * *

Mrs. Good was a noble woman, clad in a silk dressing gown. Her chestnut brown hair was swept back from her face and held by a fine jeweled comb. The sweep of her hair showed off high cheek bones and a delicate nose. Papa would have said she had a face so thin she could kiss a goat between the horns. But to me she looked elegant and finely made. She sat before the window of her bedroom at a small writing table with the bearing of a queen expecting to receive guests at any time. Mrs. O'Rourke slipped quietly into the room, with the practiced stealth of those who make their living being noticed only when it suits their purposes. She set the tray on the table and began to make the bed.

"Mary," Mrs. Good said, looking up from the cards she was lettering with great concentration, "have you beaten the rugs in the dining room?"

"I did, ma'am," Mrs. O'Rourke replied, fluffing a pillow and setting in down in place.

"And the floors, they're swept?"

"As clean as a new pin. But the windows still need to be washed. I'll have Kennedy see to them this afternoon. If he has time. Otherwise, I'll do them. The last of the silver needs to be polished. And the linen needs to be pressed on the table. I'll do them this afternoon, too." Mrs. O'Rourke sighed dramatically.

"Bridget should be helping you, shouldn't she?" Mrs. Good asked, turning away from her writing.

"Bridget is at the market as we speak. It will take her until midafternoon to get everything we need. I'll find my way around it all, ma'am. I'll just do the silver now and then press the linens while things are cooking. That leaves the wood in the drawing room, though." Her voice trailed off slightly. Then she sighed again.

"What about the wood?" Mrs. Good demanded.

"'Tis only that it's gotten a bit dingy, don't you know? Could use a little wax. I doubt anyone will notice." Mrs. O'Rourke smoothed the wrinkles from the bedspread. "They'll all be looking at your son and daughter-in-law-to-be, now won't they? They'll hardly notice that your wood needs a bit of elbow grease."

"Mary," Mrs. Good said sharply. "You know how much this party means to me. It's my first chance to entertain the Gardiners since my Michael was engaged to their Anna. Everything has to be perfect."

"Well, now, I suppose," Mrs. O'Rourke said, her brow furrowed in thought, "I suppose I could get young Clare in to help for the afternoon. He's the daughter of an old friend of mine—a good girl herself, clean and steady. She could do the wood and the linens, so I could spend a little extra time in the kitchen."

"Do what you have to," Mrs. Good said. "Tonight has to be perfect."

"That'll do, Ma'am," Mrs. O'Rourke said. "You just leave everything to me."

* * *

Mrs. O'Rourke winked at me as she left the bedroom. "If Mrs. Good isn't a bit proud about her wood," she whispered. "I suppose we ought to make it gleam for her." The smile on Mrs. O'Rourke's face lit up the hallway. In the light of it, for the first time since Mama had died, I relaxed. I had work, at least for now. And I had Mrs. O'Rourke.

She led me to the front parlour, which she made a great point of calling the "drawing room." I said the words over inside my head a few times, "drawing room, drawing room." It would not do to be calling it a parlour at the wrong time.

The drawing room, which contained no evidence that people might actually draw within its confines, was a large, sumptuous room weighted down with deep mahogany wood and real Persian carpets in maroons and gold. The light that filtered in through in through lace curtains, seemed thick and velvety itself.

"The sideboard and china cabinet are needing the most elbow grease," Mrs. O'Rourke said. "Don't empty them. Bridget did them only a fortnight ago. It will be enough if you run the rubber over the doors a bit. When you finish them, do the piano, then the sofa and chairs. If you have time, we'll put you to work on the table. It won't be needing as much attention with all the bric-a-brac herself keeps on it. It won't be as though any of the guests will be able to see the top of it." She threw back her head and laughed heartily at her own joke. I liked her laugh, and laughed myself as much for the joy of hearing it as for the joke itself.

I looked at the table, stretching out beneath the window. Its shining surface glowed. Apart from a few fingerprints it didn't seem to need polishing at all. A narrow silk runner edged with lace and embroidered with flowers ran down the center. Atop the runner sat two vases empty and waiting for the gardener to bring flowers from the yard. Clustered around the vases were photographs in frames, a couple of small statues, including one of a girl reading a book beneath a tree, and at least a dozen small, silver boxes.

"You best get to work," Mrs. O'Rourke said. "I want everything to be just so for young master Michael and his new lady." With that she swept out of the room.

* * *

I finished the wood in the drawing room quickly. It was obviously well cared for, a point of pride for Mrs. Good. I found Mrs. O'Rourke in the dining room. Beside her was a pile of linens waiting to be spread over the table. She was going over the serving spoons with a cloth.

"Would you like me to wash the windows, now?" I asked.

"The windows?" she looked up. She dragged her mind out of her reverie, and that with great difficulty. "The windows. No, the windows are fine. 'Tis like to rain anyway—my knee is aching like the devil. No, I need you to take a rag and make sure Bridget didn't miss a bit of the dusting. She's a fair kitchen maid, but can she keep her mind on the cleaning? What we need around here is a housemaid who knows her way around a dusting rag and wash tub." She held up the spoon up, inspected it, laid it carefully on a clean cloth, and picked up another one. "Start here in the dining room, Clareen. God knows I could use the company."

I took the rag she handed me and began to go over the window sills. They were spotless. Mrs. O'Rourke kept a tidy house; there was no doubt about it.

"Tell me about your dear mother," she said. "I can't keep myself from thinking about her. She didn't look to be a day over thirty-five. And now this." She tisked quietly to herself.

"She was thirty-eight," I said. "No more than a grey hair or two in amongst the copper." I thought of Mama's hair, taken down in the evening before bed. When I was home on Sunday nights, I would brush it for her, and she would hum contentedly. Mrs. O'Rourke's reverie was contagious it seemed. We both sank into it as we worked.

"Do you have brothers and sisters?" she asked eventually.

"Two brothers," I said. "Younger." I was losing the picture of Mama in my mind. It had been replaced by a picture of Tom and Mick. I achingly let the mood slip through my fingers.

"And they'll be living with a grandmother or an aunt," she said, dipping her cloth into more silver polish.

"Not this minute," I answered.

"And what would you mean by 'not this minute'?" she asked.

"They live with me," I said. "Mama always said that family should stay together no matter what. You see when Da died, Mama's friends said she should send at least one of the boys off to the industrial school, at least until she got back on her feet. We don't have family in Cork, don't you know—only an uncle in America is all. But Mama said, no, family should stay together no matter what. So she got a job for the two of us with the Quillans and a smaller, cheaper apartment for her and the boys. I lived with the Quillans, and Mama arranged to go home after supper. I'm hoping Mrs. Good might allow me the same thing."

"You can't mean that you and the boys are living by yourself," she said, setting the spoon down and looking hard in my direction.

I was hoping she wouldn't ask. "Our uncle in America," I said, "he'll be sending for us soon."

"And you're living with your brothers all alone then?" she asked again.

"I am," I said quietly.

"And how old would you be?"

"Fourteen, but . . . " I felt I should add something, something that said that I was quite able to take care of myself and my brothers, something that said that fourteen wasn't as young as she thought. But I knew deep inside me that fourteen *was* just as young as she thought, maybe younger.

"You'll not have anyone, then," she said, "no one to watch out for you?"

"Uncle Ronan will be sending for us presently," I said. "We thought it wouldn't be any good for us to go into an orphanage for only a month or two." I finished the windowsills and looked around the room for something else to dust. Mrs. O'Rourke seemed to have fallen back into her reverie. I picked up my polishing cloth and began attacking the fingerprints on the sideboard.

"Your mother and I were not that different in age," she said. "I never married, myself. I'm nearly thirty years working here for the Goods. They were newly married and I no more than a day out of school when my Da brought me here as a general servant. I wept for a month. And behind the door of her bedroom, I could hear herself weeping as well. We were quite the holy show bumping through the house with our eyes red and puffy, trying to figure out how to put the meals on the table on time. But together we made do. A good life it's been, all in all." She bundled the polished spoons into the cloth. "'Tis a puzzlement, it is—why the good Lord takes one and not another."

"'Tis," I said.

"I'm glad you came by this morning, Clareen," she said, touching my shoulder lightly on her way into the kitchen.

* * *

The dinner was magnificent: Fragrant onion soup. Sliced goose and spring lamb with gravy and mint. Fresh asparagus and sweet, green peas from Spain.

Long, pure-white elephant potatoes served in a thick creamy sauce that Bridget had fussed over until it was smooth as white velvet. Bottles of wine with exotic pictures on the labels. And dates and figs from far off in Asia. I stood in the kitchen, my arms up to my elbows in soapy water and watched Bridget carry plate after plate of the wonderful stuff into the dining room. My belly growled and my mouth watered. And I hoped the Goods and their guests were not very hungry because whatever was left over we could sample along with our own dinner.

Through the doors I heard the sound of Mrs. Good's laughter high and clear over the low hum of voices. She seemed a wee bit high strung, but Mrs. O'Rourke insisted that I wouldn't find a better employer. I leaned into the roasting pan, scrubbing hard at the grease and little bits of lamb that stuck to the sides. Outside the rain beat against the windowpanes. In the fading light I could see the branches of an old willow tree whipping madly in the wind. It would be a cold walk home. I hoped I would arrive with the news of a new job.

"Clare." Mrs. O'Rourke had been poking her head out through the kitchen door to check on Bridget and the progress of the dinner. "Let's get the afters out of the oven. It can go on the table to cool a bit."

"That'll do," I said, drying my hands and taking a dry cloth from the counter to fetch the rhubarb and strawberry tart. It too smelled like heaven, and my belly growled loud enough to be heard over the drum of the rain on the window. It had been a good while since I had seen a strawberry, longer since I had tasted one. The Goods had bought these imported all the way from the Mediterranean in an attempt to impress the new in-laws. I couldn't say much about the Gardiners, but I was impressed enough that it was all I could do to keep my fingers out of the heavenly stuff. I set the tart on the table right next to the window, where the chill leaking in around the glass would cool it to pleasantly warm by serving time.

The rain outside spattered the glass as though great buckets full were being hurled against it. And the willow, well, its branches were swinging with such force that I imagined it might be the one throwing those buckets. If the rain didn't die down, I would have to stay the night. A person could catch their death going out in a rain like that. I hoped Mick and Tom had the sense to stay home and close to the fire.

"Will I fill this wee jug, then" I said. "We'll be serving the cobbler with cream?"

"You're a quick one, Clare," Mrs. O'Rourke said. "I can imagine I'd need to tell Bridget at least twice, bless her heart."

I pulled the bottles of milk from the icebox, and ever so gently tipped them so I could get at the thick layer of cream with a spoon.

"Take a fork to it, only a couple of strokes," Mrs. O'Rourke said, accepting the breadbasket Bridget handed in through the door to the kitchen. "Enough to thicken it a bit. Then add a touch of that sugar there." She pointed to a bowl in the corner of the counter, and began refilling the basket with bread.

"The tart smells wonderful," I said.

"'Twas my Aunt Bernice's recipe," she said. "The secret is a touch of nutmeg, not in the fruit but in the crust. When you're sifting the flour . . . "

The terrible sound drowned out the rest of Mrs. O'Rourke's recipe. It was a great groan followed by a crack, followed by a crash. Suddenly rain, wind, and broken glass flew through the kitchen. Instinctively I turned my back. The debris pelted my shoulders and soaked my back right to the skin in a matter of seconds.

"Are you hurt?" Mrs. O'Rourke asked, quickly, checking herself for damage. The wind continued to whip through the now-open kitchen.

"I, I'm not," I said, looking up timidly.

"Good," Mrs. O'Rourke said. "Good." She cracked the dining room door open. Mrs. Good was on her feet and on the other side. Mrs. O'Rourke slid through, not wanting Mrs. Good to see the mess surrounding me.

"It was only the old willow," she said in whispered tone on the other side of the door. "Nothing to worry about this minute, though I imagine Kennedy is going to have his hands full tomorrow taking the last of it down."

"I loved that old willow," Mrs. Good said with a sigh. "Is it bad? Did it hit the house? The noise was so loud, I'd swear it hit the house."

"You go back to your guests," Mrs. O'Rourke said. "Clare and I have it all in hand."

I was surveying the damage when she slipped back into the kitchen. The tart lay strewn across the table amidst branches and jagged bits of broken glass. The rain streamed in and soaked the whole mess in icy, muddy puddles.

"We have to get that window covered," Mrs. O'Rourke said. "I wonder if Kennedy has something that would do."

"Maybe the linoleum in the tradesmen's entrance?" I said. "Did Kennedy take it to the cellar yet?"

"My tart," Mrs. O'Rourke moaned, suddenly identifying the deep red smear across the table and down onto the floor. She bent down for a closer look, not that she would have needed it.

I stepped around her to the door. The linoleum was still there. I pulled a good-sized piece of it from the pile, and wrestled it to the window. It was big enough to cover and then some. I pressed it into place, and immediately the kitchen felt like a room again instead of a part of the yard.

"Well done, Clare," Mrs. O'Rourke said. "Well done, indeed. Now if we could only find a way to keep it there." Just then, as if on cue, an older man slipped in through the tradesman's entrance, bundled in a thick wool coat against the cold and the rain.

"Would you help Clare then, Kennedy?" Mrs. O'Rourke said.

"You'll be Clare," the man said. "Pleased to make your acquaintance." He edged in beside me, knocking the cobbler plate to the floor in the process. Sizing up the situation quickly, he began bending the linoleum to fit more snugly into the window. "Hold it here." He pointed to the side closest to me. He fished through his pocket for a nail.

"You're standing on my cobbler," Mrs. O'Rourke said to him with mock severity. "How am I supposed to serve that to guests with your footprints all over it?"

"I think your cobbler is beyond the point where you need to be worrying about it," Kennedy said dryly and he kicked a hammer out of the loop on his belt and began nailing the linoleum to the window frame. "Didn't it already pass over, shuffle off this mortal coil, go to meet its Maker? More's the pity if it was your Aunt Bernice's recipe."

"Pfft," Mrs. O'Rourke said. "'Gone to meet its Maker,' indeed. I was its maker."

"We'll be needing that bread now," Bridget said, sticking her head in the door from the dining room. She gasped. "Sweet Saint Jude," she exclaimed. "What happened?"

"Willow tree came down," Mrs. O'Rourke replied, handing her the breadbasket.

"What about the afters?" Bridget said, seeing the tart, tracked as it was all over the floor beneath the window.

"That's not your worry," Mrs. O'Rourke said nudging her out the door and closing it.

"Do we have any more berries?" I asked, calling back over my shoulder.

"Not enough for six," Mrs. O'Rourke replied.

"Rhubarb?" I asked.

"A few stalks only."

"Apples?" I said.

"Last year's," she said, "nothing I'd feed to guests let alone young Michael's bride."

"Wine glasses?" I said. "Something thin and a little shorter than a spoon."

"Clare, what are you thinking?"

"I can make something if you have some nice crystal to serve it in," I replied, hoping what I had in mind would work.

"Herself has some nice champagne flutes," Mrs. O'Rourke said, "Shall I get them?"

"Do," I said. Mrs. O'Rourke looked like she was going to say something, then turned and snuck into the dining room to the china cabinet.

Kennedy finished nailing his side of the window and took over my side. I stepped away and hurried to the icebox. I rinsed berries and rhubarb, then transferred the cream into a large bowl and began whipping it with a fork. Mrs. Sullivan returned with a beautiful silver tray and six crystal glasses. I handed her the cream. "Until it's stiff," I said.

"Mr. Kennedy," I said. He was tacking down the last corner or the linoleum. He looked over his shoulder at me. "Would you be so good as to bring up three or four apples when you're finished there?" He looked over at Mrs. O'Rourke and she nodded, a big grin on her face.

I emptied the last of the berries into a bowl, hulled and sliced them, chopped the rhubarb paper thin, then rummaged through the pantry for some sugar. "Skillet?" I said. Mrs. O'Rourke pointed. She had settled herself on a chair with the cream and was watching me with an amused look in her eyes. I set the skillet on the new gas range, then froze.

"Get yourself a lit taper from the lamp, then turn the knob over there on the far right," Mrs. O'Rourke said. I touched the taper to the burner and it whooshed to life. While the skillet was warming, I set about grating a bit of cinnamon.

"And what would this be that you're making?" Mrs. O'Rourke asked.

"Well," I said, "I'm not sure it has a name. My mother sometimes used to stir a bit of apple in some butter for me as a special treat. I don't know that she had a name for it."

"Clare," Mrs. O'Rourke said. I looked up. "Do you know what you're doing? I need to know."

"I do," I said. I hoped it was more boast than lie.

Mr. Kellogg came up from the root cellar holding two hands full of shriveled old apples. I had hoped for better, but once I set about peeling and chopping them I saw that they were reasonably unblemished if not firm. I smeared a chunk of butter in the bottom of the skillet, then added the apples, the rhubarb, the berries, the cinnamon, a splash of flat lemonade from the icebox, and a couple of big handfuls of sugar. Shaking and stirring I watched the mix slowly soften as the berries and rhubarb released their juices and the apples absorbed them and the melted butter. The smell filled the kitchen.

"Let's put just a dab of that cream in bottom of each glass," I said. "Just a teaspoon or so."

Mrs. Sullivan leaned over the skillet. "Pretty," she said. She dipped her little finger into the corner of the juices and brought it to her mouth. Her shoulders relaxed a bit. "Bridget is going to be green with envy," she said, patting my shoulder. "You didn't tell me you could cook."

"Mrs. Quillan didn't think I could," I replied. "That's why she sacked me."

"Mrs. Quillan's loss," Mrs. O'Rourke said spooning the cream into the glasses. "Our gain."

For each of the glasses, I followed the cold cream with a layer of warm fruit, and another of cream, and another of fruit, and then a dab of cream and a mint leaf left over from the lamb atop only for show. When Bridget called through the door for afters, I handed the glasses out on the silver tray.

Ear to the door, I waited. Hearing the exclamations that greeted the arrival of afters, I knew we were all right. A sudden wave of relief flooded over me. I walked across the kitchen and collapsed in a damp chair by the window. Kennedy had cleaned up most of the broken glass, but a bit of it crunched beneath my foot as I stretched my legs out in front of me. Mrs. O'Rourke smiled down at me, then cast a quick glance at the rest of the dirty pots in the sink. Remembering myself, I scrambled to my feet.

"No, no. Sit yourself down Clare," Mrs. O'Rourke said. "Bridget can finish the pots when she's done serving." She removed a cloth from the last of the lamb and began slicing it onto what was obviously the servants' plates. "Would you have much of a hunger on you?" she asked casually.

I began to giggle. The laugh rose from the same place the feeling of relief was coming from. It spread out from there until finally Mrs. O'Rourke caught it, too. Together we muffled out giggles with our aprons, sitting over elegantly roasted lamb and debris-laden puddles.

"The lamb looks good," I said. "But what do we have for afters?"

* * *

I've heard it said that servants in an English household are judged by their ability to create and maintain an orderly environment. The ideal English butler is so stern, the ideal English housekeeper so staid that disorder would never consider setting so much as a foot onto the property. English servants are paid to keep inconvenience at bay. Perhaps that's why so many of the English who settled our shores never fully adapted to having Irish servants.

Irish servants, you see, judge themselves not by their ability to maintain order but by their ability to function with flexibility and alacrity in the midst of total chaos. It's not that we neglect our employer's comfort. Quite the contrary. But we Irish, you know, do love a bit of drama. And the servant who can keep her head as that drama plays itself out, well, she is not only the model employee, she's the model character in the drama of life, a drama we cherish from the bottom of our storytelling hearts.

That was all to the good, I suppose when Mrs. Good flung open the door of the kitchen, thinking to show off her the new linoleum and range to Mrs. Gardiner. What they found instead was an unholy mess—puddles of water, rhubarb footprints, and the linoleum not only on the floor but nailed to the window frame as well. Well, Mrs. Good didn't have to say much more than "what in heaven's name happened here?" before Mrs. O'Rourke was off to the races with the whole story of it.

I listened with absolute rapture as Mrs. O'Rourke recounted the story, my story, to the Goods. In it, I was St. George fighting the dragon; I was the little Dutch boy holding back the great waters of chaos. Having both lived it and heard it told as tale, I much preferred the tale myself. Mrs. Good, who after nearly thirty years of living cheek by jowl with the very-Irish Mrs. O'Rourke, appreciated a good story with the best of them and hired me on the spot. It didn't hurt, I suppose, that the afters I whipped up drew rave reviews from the critics seated in the dining room. But what more than likely turned the key was that I had kept not only my head but my sense of humor in the midst of a crisis.

When the Gardiners had left, bundled home in a carriage with extra blankets, Mrs. Good called me into the drawing room to work out the details. I would come in every morning before breakfast, work as a maid all day and leave after I had finished washing the pots and pans from dinner. I'd work full days Monday through Friday and only half days on Saturday and Sunday, when such a schedule was convenient for Mrs. Good, of course. I would eat breakfast and lunch at their house, dinner at home with the boys. And, she said, casting a critical eye at my dress, I would be expected to provide suitable attire for myself within two weeks' time. I agreed. It was not until I was halfway home, snug in the fine carriage Mr. Good had hired for the night to impress the Gardiners, that I remembered to ask how much I would be paid. But that oversight aside, I fairly floated with relief. I had work again.

Four

If I worked in the old horsehair chair, I found, I could get enough light from the front window to do a bit of mending. The sun was barely down, but there was no sense lighting the lamp just yet. Paraffin was fairly cheap, but even cheap is dear when you're living on nothing, or just shy of nothing.

The two old shirts in my lap didn't look like much in the fading light. They'd belonged to Michael, the Good's oldest boy. But since he was about to marry, his wardrobe was undergoing a major renovation, and Mrs. Good was tossing everything not fitting for an up-and-coming young mill owner. When I heard she was planning to turn a couple of tattered, but still quite serviceable, shirts into cleaning rags, I summoned up my courage and asked if she would mind if I took them instead.

I hated to do it. I hated to ask, that is, to approach Mrs. Good like some pauper who couldn't care for her own family. That's not to mention that I'd been at the Good's house for no more than three weeks. Asking for castoffs that soon seemed a bit nervy. But the truth of the matter was that Mick had completely worn through his second shirt, and Tom, who was always waiting for Mick's hand-me-downs, hadn't had a second shirt in as long as I could remember. That meant that the boys had nothing to wear when while wash was being done, so wash was rarely if ever getting done. Moreover, Easter was coming, and fast. We might not be able to afford new clothes, but neither could we afford the inevitable bad luck that would come from wearing rags and jags to Easter Mass.

I held up the shirts one at a time for inspection. They were pale blue dress shirts, meant to be worn with a stiff detachable collar and cuffs. Michael and some of his chums had taken up throwing a medicine ball about in the Good's back yard. The fronts of the shirts were worn and stained with dirt and grass stains from being hammered by the large heavy ball. But a good scrubbing and some darning cotton would take care of the worst of it. They were still much better shirts than most of what I saw in lanes. I measured a sleeve against my arm. They would be far too big for either Mick or Tom. In fact, they would probably hang to their knees or beyond. But that suited me fine as the trousers they wore were their only pair as well. I'd darn a few holes, then on Saturday could put the boys into their new shirts while I washed both shirts and trousers.

* * *

Supper was over. The sun was down and then some. Tom was squinting at a book by the light of the paraffin lamp, and I was back to mending the shirts when Mick finally came through the door, cap in hand, a long slat of wood tucked under one arm.

"We ate without you," I said.

"Mmhmm, fine," he said noncommittally. He was obviously in a bad humor, angry at something and a wee bit jumpy.

"Were you looking for work?" I thought maybe that would account for his mood. Looking for work had certainly done my mood no good at all.

"No," he said shortly.

He dropped his cap onto the peg by the door, propped the stick in the corner, and sat down heavily at the table. His hair was matted and damp. Gingerly he touched the top of his head. That's when I noticed. His fingers were covered with dried blood.

I set down the mending and walked over. Standing above him, I could see the gash clearly through his sandy-colored hair. It was about two inches long and a good two or three hours old. Not bothering to ask permission, I teased the hair away from the wound for a better look. Dried blood caked the edges, but the wound still oozed and bled a bit when I pulled the hair back.

"Be careful, would you," he said, jerking away.

"How?" I asked.

"Hurling," he said simply.

I sighed. "When?"

"Before sunset," he said. A couple of hours, then. "But I think I opened it up again taking my cap off."

"If it didn't stop bleeding yet, it will probably need to be stitched," Tom commented, rising from the table and leaning in for a better look.

"And there goes more of the money from the tin," I said. It gnawed at me—the thought that here I was saving on paraffin, saving on clothing, saving a farthing her and a farthing there everywhere I could, and now we'd have to pay it all out to a doctor. "I thought you were going to be looking for work after school. What were you doing hurling? With the cost of the infirmary these days, I have half a mind to let you bleed," I said.

"Fine," Mick said. "Let me bleed, then. I didn't ask for your help, did I?"

"You could do it," Tom said appraising the wound like someone who knew what he was looking at.

"No, Tom," I said, "as much as I'd like to, I can't let him bleed."

"No, I mean you could stitch it up. Mrs. Sullivan stitched up Wally that time one of the north-side boys laid him open with a chair leg."

"And what do I know about stitching up heads?" I said.

"It will be just like stitching up clothes, I would imagine," Tom said. "Any old woman can do that. How hard can it be?"

"And what would you know about stitching up clothes?" I replied sharply. He'd hit a nerve, I'm afraid. "There's more to keeping you ruffians in clothes than you'll ever know, I can tell you that much. You'll keep coming home with holes in your trousers, holes in your shirts, holes in yourself, and who has to patch you up?"

Tom, taken aback, dropped himself onto the horsehair chair, his arms crossed tightly across this chest. I didn't mean to shout, not at Tom at least, but now that I had, it was too late to back down.

"Don't be sitting there pouting," I said. "Make yourself useful. Pour some water from the kettle onto that plate. I want to clean this mess up." I slapped Mick's hand away from his head and teased back most of the hair from the wound. The half-dried blood functioned quite handily as a hair tonic to lay it into place. My stomach rolled at the sight of it and at the sticky feel beneath my fingers.

"You'll be luck if you don't get lock jaw," I said. "It looks like you have half the dirt on the south-side stuck to your head."

"I fell," he said.

"You blacked out? The blow knocked you out?" I said. The worry rose again inside me, but I beat it down to a manageable spot just over my stomach.

"Only for a second or two," he said. "Got right up, shook it off, and kept playing." There was a note of pride in his voice. Tom, rising to fetch the kettle, gave him a congratulatory clip on the shoulder on his way past.

"So you got clubbed over the head with a hurley, blacked out for a bit, and bled all over your hair and shirt. Then once you woke up, you went right back to playing without checking the damage?" I commented. Mick nodded. "Your brain fell out through the hole in your head, then?" I said. "Or didn't you have one to begin with?"

"You don't know what you're talking about," Mick muttered.

I took a rag from the shelf, dipped a corner in the water, and started dabbing at the wound. Mick squirmed. "Ouch," he said. "Be careful."

"Sit still," I said. "If you're eejit enough to get your head split open, you can just sit while I patch it." Mick grabbed a wad of his trouser and gritted his teeth. I cleaned away the worst of the grit.

"Are you going to stitch him?" Tom asked. He seemed eager to think that

I might try it.

"I suppose I have to," I answered. "I'm not about to turn over every penny we have to some doctor."

I went over to pick up the mending I was doing, bit loose the needle and cotton from the shirt I'd just finished. If I stopped to think about it too much, I probably wouldn't be able to do it. So I bit off the cotton, and made a beeline for Mick's head. The wound was ugly, long, and still a bit crusty. But it was a clean cut, with straight sides.

I put a thumb on one side of the gash, a finger on the other and pushed the sides together. The wound immediately responded with a fresh flow of blood. I set down the needle and dabbed at oozing mess with the cloth.

"Ow," Mick said jerking away.

"I didn't start yet," I replied.

"Then don't," Mick said, pulling out of my reach. "I'll go to the infirmary tomorrow morning."

"You won't spend the whole night dripping blood on the bed, not if I have anything to say about it," I replied. "Let me finish."

Mick sat down heavily. I dabbed again with the rag, pulled the wound closed, then came in with the needle. I wasn't sure how much skin to take. It would have to be enough so the cotton didn't rip through when I tightened it. I decided on about a half inch, and gingerly inserted the needle. It went in cleanly, came out the other side of the wound. I grasped the point and tugged gently. The cotton slipped through an inch or so, then tangled. The blood stuck to the cotton, stuck to the hair, and as I pulled, I pulled the whole mass into the entrance hole. Mick whinged loudly, swatted at my hand, and scooted away, the needle still dangling from his scalp.

"Let Mrs. Sullivan do it," he said, his back to the wall. "You don't know what you're doing." I looked over at Tom.

"I'll see if she can come," he said, pulling his cap from the peg and stepping out the door.

"Fine," I said. "Fine." I meant it. I was relieved at not having to stab him again. My hands shook. I crossed my arms, tucking my hand into my armpits. "Do you want to tell me how it happened?"

"Hurling," he said. "I told you that."

"So you said. You were fighting, were you?"

"I said I was hurling." Mick reached up and found the needle dangling from his head.

"You wouldn't be the first boyo who was able to do both at the same time."

"I wasn't fighting," he said. "Can't you cut this free?"

I nodded and pointed to the chair. Mick sat. I clipped the cotton close to the wound and teased the end loose. It was deep red. I threw it into the fire. Mick sat tight-lipped. I looked at him and sighed.

"You sounded like Mam just then," he said, his voice suddenly softer.

"When," I asked.

"Just now. Mam used to sigh like that."

"I suppose she did," I said. I suppose she did, indeed.

* * *

Mrs. Sullivan entered the room like an army advancing with banners unfurled. Behind her were Tom and Wally, who snatched their caps from their heads immediately upon crossing the threshold. Though she was always gentle with me, Mrs. Sullivan could call forth fear even in grown men when she wanted to. In boys like Tom and Wally, she could be a source of stark terror.

"Good evening, Mrs. Sullivan," I said. "I'm grateful for your help."

"'Tis no great trouble," she said, unwrapping the shawl from her shoulders and handing it to me. "We'll have the boyo patched in no time at all, at all." The look in Mick's eyes said he wasn't so sure.

"Now then," she said, "you have scissors?" I handed her the pair on the chair. She stepped behind Mick, and without missing a beat, began cutting the hair from around the wound. Mick's eyes went wide, but he said nothing.

"We have to get the gash ready, clean away the hair and dirt," she said snipping hunks of hair in random patterns from Mick's crown.

"How did you do it, lad?" she asked.

"Hurling," Mick said again.

"Now that doesn't tell me much, does it?" The scissors continued to click. "How did you do it?"

Mick didn't pause to think, he simply opened his mouth and a story spilled out.

"We were talking, my mates and I. We were talking about how last season, the hurling cup went over across to the other side."

"They cheated," Mrs. Sullivan said simply.

"They did," Mick replied. "But when the team was carrying the cup over the bridge, and singing and shouting, some boys from the north, some rich, public school boys in purple blazers and striped ties, came across and started saying how the scum always builds up on the south bank of the river. And we said the cheaters always build up on the north bank. And they said any of the old shawlies from the north-side could beat the best of our players, no need for cheating. And we said we would beat them next year. Our team would beat theirs for the cup, and me and my mates would beat them and their mates, too . . . at hurling," he added nervously. "We were practicing. That's all."

"You took a hurley to your skull?" Mrs. Sullivan stopped snipping.

"I did," Mick replied quietly. Mrs. Sullivan fixed a glare on him. "Actually, it was John Kennedy's grandfather's cane," he amended. We only have a couple of hurleys for the team."

"A hard skull is a blessing," she said, brushing the hair from his shoulders. "Go down, now and stick your head under the tap. Run some water over the wound and get it as clean as you can."

Mick stood, and he and the two other boys made haste out the door.

"Thank you," I said quietly, after they'd left. "I wasn't sure how to do it."

"'Tis no great matter," she said with a wave of the hand. "Stitching up men's skulls is a valuable skill for any woman, more so for one with a brother like Mick there." She pawed through my sewing box and pulled out a skein. I handed her the needle.

"I hear you are working down on Front Douglas Road," she said concentrating on threading the needle.

"I am," I said.

"'Tis a fair walk," she said, stabbing the cotton unsuccessfully at the eye of the needle. She licked the cotton and tried again. "And a fair walk home after a long day."

"'Tis," I said quietly.

"You must not be home much."

"Weekends," I said.

"'Tis honest work, though." The cotton finally slipped into the eye. She paused. "Clare," she said finally, in a tone that brought my eyes to hers surer than had they been on a leash. "Clare, Mick's wound wasn't made by any hurley."

"How do you know?" I asked.

"After raising three boys, one all the way to manhood, how could I not know?" she said. "Besides," she added, "the wound is a cut, not a bash. It was made by a knife or some such thing."

I stared at her in shock. "A knife?" I said. Outside the door the sound of slow, steady footsteps rose from the stairway. Visions of the animal gangs rose before my eyes, of boys and young men clad in black, flasks in their breast pockets and blades tucked into the brims of their caps. I shivered.

"Clare," she said, "You do know that there are folks around here, folks on the lane who wouldn't mind giving you a little help every now and then? With the boys, I mean. Or anything else you need."

"I'd be grateful," I said.

"You only have to ask," she said as the boys pushed the door open and entered.

* * *

Mick's hair dripped onto the shoulders of his jacket. It stood up in spikes and patches around the bald spot at the crown. He stepped into the room like a condemned man, and sat compliantly on the coal box Mrs. Sullivan had placed next to the lantern on the table.

"Wally," she said, "come hold this shoulder. Tom, you hold the shoulder on your side." Mrs. Sullivan encircled Mick's head with her arm, holding it snugly into her belly. "Clare, you stand next to me and watch. You need to learn to do this."

We surrounded Mick, all eyes on his scalp. It was as though he were not there in his entirety, but only his hair and the wound laid bare and dripping. Mrs. Sullivan wasted no time. As soon as everyone was in place, she dipped the needle in quickly and steadily.

"Take about this much in one bit," she said. Mick whimpered beneath her arm. "Loop it through like this. Then move up and do the whole thing all over again." Her single hand worked quickly, surely, stitching tight even stitches. The way she did it was not too much different from mending a shirt.

I looked over at Tom. He was still holding Mick's shoulder, but was staring at reflection in the window, his face pale. Wally gazed down at his feet as though they were the most fascinating things he ever did see. I, for my part, was riveted by Mrs. Sullivan's hands, how she dipped surely, confidently into the skin, how each stitch securely knit the edges of the wound together. Bit by bit, the gash closed.

"You'll need to wake him two or three times during the night," Mrs.

Sullivan said to me as she turned loose of Mick's head. "It looks like he has a nice sized goose egg here," she poked a finger at a second spot, one I hadn't even seen. Mick jumped. "Don't move yet," she said to him. I handed her the scissors and she clipped the cotton. "You need to wake him during the night to make sure he doesn't sleep too deep and slip into a stupor. And make sure he's still clear-headed in the morning." She handed the scissors back to me. "If he's dazed or confused at all, you need to bring him to see the doctor."

"And you." She addressed herself to Mick, who squirmed under her intense gaze. "You need to stay away from the kind of people who club other people with hurleys or cut them with knives. Those kind of people aren't good for yourself at all, at all."

Mick's eyes grew wide. He bowed his head beneath the rebuff. "I will," he muttered meekly.

"See that you do," Mrs. Sullivan said. "Because if you don't, it'll myself you'll have to answer to." Mick nodded gravely.

"Thank you," I said. "Will you take some tea with us?"

"'Tis late," she said. "Thank you just the same. Wally has school tomorrow." As if on cue, Wally reached for his cap on the peg. "You did well, Clare," Mrs. Sullivan said quietly.

"I didn't do anything," I said.

"But you kept your head," Mrs. Sullivan said. "Your mother would be proud." Almost as an afterthought she added, "You did fine, too, Mick." Her face softened somewhat. "But you remember what I said." With that she strode out the door, Wally following behind her.

Mick stood leaning against the table, fingering the stitches.

"Don't fiddle with those," I said. "Do you want a spud? I kept yours warm beside the fire. 'Twill be a bit dry, but I'd say you're in no place to complain."

Mick nodded gently and sat at the table again. I set the roasted potato on a plate and placed it in front of him.

"Do we have butter?" he asked casting an eye at the water bucket.

"No," I said simply. He picked at the warm skin and began to eat.

"Mick," I said, "no more 'hurling' until we get to America. Next time you might not be so lucky and we might have a doctor to pay."

"I promised the boys I would play," Mick said softly. "I mean I did say I'd *play*, you know?"

"Mick," I said. "No more. No more hurling. No more fighting. This is no time to take a hurley or anything else to the head. We can't afford the trouble."

"But I promised the boys . . . "

"Then tell the boys you promised me that you won't. When we get to America, and you have Uncle Ronan to patch you up all the time, then you can play at hurling."

"And if there's no hurling in America?" Tom spoke up for the first time since Mrs. Sullivan walked through the door. His voice startled me for an instant. Tom had a way of making himself invisible when he wanted to.

"If there are Irish men in America there will be hurling," I said, wiping the needle and returning to my mending. "It would be a shame to waste those thick Irish skulls on any less of a game."

* * *

"Did I ever tell you about Uncle Andy, my mother's sister's husband who worked for old Mr. Logan?" Mrs. O'Rourke bit off the cotton she was using and reached into the basket for a new spool. The afternoon's work was finished, and she had invited me up the back stairs to her room where she kept her sewing basket. We sat together beneath the window that looked out over the side yard, me on the edge of her bed, her in an old rocking chair. The old kitchen linoleum covered the floor.

"Uncle Andy Fitzgerald?" she said. I shook my head. "No? Well, he was a stable hand, looked after the master's horses and hunting dogs. He didn't like the dogs much, but he sure did love those horses."

"How's this?" I said, holding up the half-finished seam for inspection. It was the side seam for a new dress Mrs. O'Rourke had agreed to help me make. At the Quillan's I'd been able to wear a single dark blue, general-purpose dress, the same dress I wore during my off hours, the same dress I wore to Mass. Mr. Quillan was no more than a shopkeeper, so his servants needed to be no more than work around the house. But Mr. Good was a mill owner, a fine important man. His servants needed to be not only labor, but decoration, symbols of ever-growing wealth and prestige. For the last week or so, until I could save enough for the fabric, I'd been borrowing a dress from Bridget. Now finally I was to have a dress of my own, a proper maid's dress, and a brand-new one at that.

The fabric we chose was just like the dress Mrs. O'Rourke wore but in yellow, not blue. It was a good, serviceable cotton, printed with tiny flowers and twining vines. We were making it ankle length. Technically, of course, only women servants wore ankle length dresses. Girls wore mid-calf length. It was stretching a point for me to wear the longer length, but the dress had to last me. And besides, as Mrs. O'Rourke pointed out, I'd done a fair bit of growing up in the past month or so, even if I wasn't precisely a woman yet.

She reached for the skirt piece I was stitching, and holding it at near arms' length, squinted to examine my work. "Well, now," Mrs. O'Rourke said, "That's a good bit better. The stitches are getting much more even. Now rip out the last few inches and do it again. Your seam is getting too small. It'll give you a bulge right here on the hip." She patted herself high on the outside thigh. She licked a piece of cotton and holding it far out in front of her, threaded it tidily through the needle. She had reading glasses, which she would remove carefully from their pouch and settle on her nose when she and Mrs. Good went over the menus for the week. I wondered why she didn't wear them for sewing.

"Anyway, my Uncle Andy used to say that training dogs was a simple matter of horse flesh," she said. I wasn't quite sure what dogs, and horse flesh, and Uncle Andy had to do with what we had been talking about, namely Mick and the fact that I wasn't sure how to handle him and his fighting. But still, Mrs. O'Rourke told a good story, so tongue in the corner of my mouth, I settled in to sew and listen.

"Horse flesh?" I said, slipping the scissors into the last few stitches.

"Horse flesh," she said. "That's what they feed the dogs, you know, old horses that have to be put down from some injury or some such thing. Well, Uncle Andy would keep a wee sack full of it when it was time to train the dogs. When a dog behaved, he got some of it. When a dog was contrary, he got to watch his mates eat while he himself got none. Uncle Andy swore by the method. What he didn't know was that Aunt Bernice was using the very same method on him. When he came home on time, when he brought his pay home straight away without spending it all at the pub or when he was kind and gentle with her, his favorite foods would seem to magically appear from the pantry. When he came home on the drink or when he was foul to her and the children, he would find himself eating gristle. 'Tis all a matter of horse flesh." She nodded with finality.

"She fed him horse flesh when he was contrary?" I asked.

"You're not listening, girl," Mrs. O'Rourke said. She reached over, and I handed her the seam I was working on. "Good," she said. "Make sure you keep it running straight like that. What do you say to a bit of gathers about the neck?" I nodded.

"Boys," she said, "men, too, are not all that different from dogs. You can train them to be good husbands and fathers if you're willing to put a bit of work into them. You let them know that if they mind their manners, you'll keep them well fed. If they act like thugs and ruffians, you'll feed them naught but gristle and bones. They think with their stomachs, they do. If you're a good cook, they fall in line."

"Does it really work?" I asked.

"It did for my Aunt Bernice," she said.

"But you never tried it yourself?" Mrs. O'Rourke fixed me with that look grownups give children who speak out of turn. I instantly regretted the question.

"Who do you think has the final word over the biscuit tin?" she said. "I hate to brag, but why do you think young Michael turned into the gentleman he is, so well mannered, so well dressed?"

I had never really thought of Michael as a gentleman. A fop, perhaps. Maybe a dandy in the straw boater and striped blazer he seemed to wear everywhere these days. But he was a gentleman in the sense that he would never have to get dirt under his nails if he chose not to. His father's money would see to that.

"Mmm," I said, not really committing myself to a comment.

"When he played nicely in the yard, kept his clothes clean, didn't fight with the other boys, I would give him a biscuit," Mrs. O'Rourke said. "When he would come in with grass stains on his knees or dirt on his hands, I would tell him we had no biscuits left. Then I would make him go wash and change clothes. All these years of biscuit/no biscuit, just look at him—the finest young gentleman you would ever want to meet."

"I don't think we could really afford biscuits this minute," I commented tentatively. "For Mick, I mean."

"No matter," Mrs. O'Rourke said. "'Tis all the same whether you're talking biscuits or potatoes, horse flesh or gravy. Boys think with their stomach. Control the stomach and you control the boy." She nodded her head with finality.

* * *

Most days on my way home I would stop by the market to pick up a few things—a handful of potatoes perhaps, maybe a loaf of bread from the baker. This evening, though, I decided to give Mrs. O'Rourke's advice a go. It was Friday, and my pay jingled in my pocket. Five shilling, six pence a week was good pay for a girl my age, but it spread powerfully thin when divided between the landlord, the baker, the grocer, and dozens of other folks who always seemed to have their hands open beneath my nose.

During the walk home, I had formulated a plan, a never-miss plan if Mrs. Rourke was to be believed. God knows it would be hard on the pocketbook. But then trips to the infirmary, even funeral costs, God forbid, weren't cheap either. I had to get Mick under control before he went out and did something that would ruin his life, or mine.

The quay was crowded to be sure, but tables in the market were a bit sparse that early in the spring. Vegetables from the farms were not yet ready, and vegetables brought in by ship from various ports along the Mediterranean were so dear that most of the folks who shopped on the quay couldn't afford them. I stopped in front of a table littered with a few remaining vegetables—spuds, hanks of onions, a couple of bunches of carrots and two small cabbages. A couple of cooked potatoes sat front-and-center on an enameled plate. My stomach growled.

"Good day," I greeted the woman who presided over the goods.

"And a good day to you," she answered, standing and brushing down her bright red apron. "Balls of temptation aren't they?" She nodded at the potatoes. I nodded. "Tuppence for three pounds."

"I only need a pound," I said. "Ha'penny?"

"A penny," she said. "I'll throw in an extra."

I nodded. "And the cabbage?"

She gave me a queer look. A laner buying cabbage on a weekday was not unheard of, but I guess it must have looked unlikely in my case. I pretended not to notice. "Two heads, nine pence," she said.

"And one head?" I asked. Two was out of the question.

"Five pence," she said.

"I'll give you four and a half," I said.

"Will you then?" the woman replied. "But then it is Friday. And a girl your age shouldn't be having any vices worse than cabbage to spend her week's pay on. Four and a half it is," she said, picking the larger of the two heads off the table. "Hold up your bib there, and I'll throw them in."

With one hand I clutched the vegetables in my apron and dug with the other in my pocket. I delighted in the feel of a cabbage as I made my way to the butcher tables. It had been a long while since I had so much as paused before the butcher's table. It was rare for me to do the shopping for the house I worked for, and Mick, Tom and I hadn't had meat at home since Mama died.

I followed the sound of the butcher's voice along the quay and into an alley. "Buy away, buy away, new shop open." He called. His table stood amidst a pile of sawdust. Flies and bluebottles buzzed about, landing ever so briefly before being fanned away. The butcher in his blue and white overalls greeted me politely.

"Come on over to me, Miss," he said. "I have some beef cuttings fresh. Good for beef tea, or a nice stew. Or maybe a sheep's head. Four pence. I crack it for you here."

"I was looking for a wee bit of bacon," I said.

"For the cabbage," he said, gesturing at the head in my apron.

"For the cabbage," I said.

"You'd be shopping for Sunday already?" he said, stabbing a slab of bacon with his knife. "Or is it an occasion?"

"Of sorts," I replied, not really wanting to reveal my plan.

"Well," he said, "my bacon is worthy of an occasion if I do say so myself. How much d'you fancy?"

I made a sliver-sized gesture with my thumb and forefinger. The butcher laughed. "Not much of an occasion then," he said, slicing carefully. He balanced the piece on a scale. "Three pence," he announced.

I paid him. Further down the quay I paid out tuppence for a pint of milk, another tuppence for bread, and a ha'penny for some sweets. Bundled in my shawl I had nearly a day and a half's pay, and I hadn't even thought about paying rent yet. That would be another two and six. I sincerely hoped Mrs. O'Rourke was right.

* * *

It didn't take long before the smell of frying bacon brought Tom up from the yard. In fact the smell, a smell like heaven on earth if I dared say so, brought not only Tom but a small clutch of boys who perched just outside the door on the landing inhaling with gusto.

"And what's the occasion?" Tom said.

"No occasion," I replied.

"You got a rise?" Tom asked. "Mrs. O'Rourke decided to pay you more than five and six?"

"No, five and six is all," I replied, dumping the cabbage I'd just chopped into the pot with the bacon to cook.

"The bacon was a gift, then?" he asked.

"It wasn't," I said. "And if you want any of it, you'll sit quietly and stop harrying me with all your questions." Tom immediately dropped himself into a chair, interlaced his fingers, and set them in front of him on the table. I recognized the posture immediately. It was the one the nuns at my old school believed most conducive to children's salvation and general blessedness. Apparently Tom's teachers were of the same opinion. Perhaps Mrs. O'Rourke was right.

"How was school?" I asked.

"Good," he replied. "I was the only one who could figure out a fraction problem."

"You always were good at figures," I said, stirring the cabbage gently. "Did you walk home with Mick?"

"He, um . . . " Tom paused. "He, um, went with some other boys."

I turned to look. Tom was fiddling with the skin around one of his fingers, picking at it, then biting it off. He was lying. I knew it immediately.

I should say here that Tom was the kind of boy who was destined to honest work from the very beginning. Not only was he an upright Christian soul, he was also totally unsuited to lying. Tom could no more hide a lie than he could flap his arms and fly. It just wasn't in his nature. I fixed him with my best I-can-tell look. He blushed deeply.

"Tell me," I said.

"Mick went home with, um, some boys from school."

"Tell me the truth," I said.

"He didn't go," his shoulders slumped, as though unloading the lie was like unloading a great burden from his back. "Mick didn't go to school today."

"Where was he?" I asked. "Was he looking for work?"

"I don't know," Tom replied. "I don't think so. He's been spending time with the Connor boys, Mr. Connor's youngest brother's boys. They live two lanes down."

I sighed. The Connor boys did not have the best reputations on the lane.

"Well if that's how Mick is going to spend his time," I said. "You and I will eat by ourselves." I scooped the cabbage out of the pot and put two huge helpings on plates for the two of us.

"We'll not save any for Mick?" Tom asked.

"No," I said. "If he wants to eat with us, he'll have to mend his ways."

Tom shrugged and dug into his cabbage as though nothing else in the world mattered. I had lost most of my appetite, but I ate. I was bound that Mick would have none of it.

* * *

He came in well after dark. Tom was in bed. I would have been had I not been fairly humming with anger and quite incapable of sleeping. He came through the door, dropped his cap on the peg and kicked off his boots right were he stood. I rose from the horsehair chair where I had been sitting in the dim silvery light of the moon, and stood before him.

"Where were you?" I said.

"Out," he said, stripping off his jacket.

"Out with the Connor boys," I said.

"Do I smell bacon?" he asked.

"Out with the Connor boys mitching school, and getting into God only knows what kind of trouble."

"Yes I was out with Micky and Ryan Connor," he said. "No, we were not getting into trouble. Not that it's any of your business. That is bacon, isn't it? Bacon and cabbage."

"We ate it," I said. "If you'd been home instead of out with your corner boys, you'd have some for yourself. But as it is, well, 'tis gone." I crossed my arms across my chest and waited for the effect.

"Do we have bread?" he asked.

"No," I said.

"Spuds?"

"No."

"Well, only a cup of tea, then," he said. "We had fish and chips for lunch."

"And where would you be finding the money for fish and chips?" I asked. "You didn't take anything from the tin?" I spun on my heel and grabbed at the tin, stubbing my toe on the table leg in the process. I limped back to the table and emptied the tin on it. The moonlight was too dim to count, but the number of coins seemed about right.

"Do we have anything to eat?" Mick asked, then almost as though it were an afterthought added, "I didn't touch your precious tin."

"Get in bed, Mick," I said. "Get in bed before I do you harm. If you were home, you could have had bacon and cabbage with us, bacon and cabbage that cost me dearly I might say. But you were out on the streets, so you can just go to bed without anything to eat. Go to bed, Mick. Just go to bed."

"Clare," he said in a tone so calm it made my blood boil. "I'm after a hard day. I've a terrible hunger on me. I could eat a horse this very minute. Now do we have food, or do I have to go down to the pub and find something for myself. He reached into his pocket and snatched something out. He tossed it into the air and caught it again. It was silver. I could tell by the way the moonlight hit it. It was silver.

"Where did you get that?" I fairly screamed.

"We don't have food, then," he replied.

"Where did you get that?" I said again, bolting out of the chair and reaching for his hand. He stuffed it into his pocket.

"Earned it," he said. "And now since we don't seem to have any food in the house, I'm going to go spend it." He stuffed his feet into his boots, snatched up his hat and jacket, and was gone with a slam of the door.

I dropped myself into the chair. The tears started to flow. No not "flow," gush, pour forth. Nothing makes me cry like anger, unless it's frustration, or helplessness, and just then I was filled to my jowls with them all. I stood again and kicked over the chair. I tried to kick over the table too but only managed to hurt my stubbed toe again.

"Damn you, Mick," I whispered. I regretted it immediately. But the truth of the matter was that he could be damning himself, and there wasn't a thing I could do about it. I righted the chair and again sat.

"The bacon was good, Clare." Tom's voice came quietly from the bed across the room. He sat up with a creak of springs. "I liked it."

"Go back to bed, Tom," I replied, and mercifully he did.

* * *

The next morning I woke, and opened my eyes to one of Mick's feet. He must have come in some time in the middle of the night. I'd cried myself into exhaustion before finally falling asleep. I probably wouldn't have heard him had he come in trailing the entire Barrack Street Band. I crawled out from under the coat, and as an afterthought, picked it up and draped it over Mick's shoulders. The anger from the night before had dissolved in the night, and seeing him laying there asleep I saw not the cocky corner boy of last night but simply my brother.

I tucked the coat up around his neck, and he woke.

"Sorry," I said, not meaning to wake him.

"I'm sorry, too," he said. "I shouldn't speak to you that way."

"Ah, well then," I said. I hadn't meant to apologize for last night, but since it seemed that I already had, I wasn't about to take it back.

Mick rose, lifting his feet quietly over Tom, who was still stretched out, head at the foot of the bed.

"Hungry?" I said, checking the water bucket beside the hearth. "I can make us tea. And we have bread from last night."

"Last night, I thought you said . . . "

I interrupted. "I think 'tis best if we both forget what was said last night," I replied.

Mick nodded. "Micky Connor says the telegraph office is looking for a delivery boy," he said, pulling his trousers from under the bed. "I thought I'd apply today."

"Are you sure?" I asked.

"We need the money," Mick replied. "And being a delivery boy is *respectable* work." He made sure I caught the word "respectable."

"It is," I said. "And we do need the money." I paused. "Mick," I said finally, pulling the loaf of bread from the sideboard, "where did you get that sixpence last night?"

"It was a shilling," he said. "And I earned it doing some errands for, um, a lady, um, down by the docks."

"Are you lying to me, Mick Keane?" I said, the anger from the night before beginning to rise again.

"Clare," he said. "Please. I'm telling you the truth. I earned it running errands. Please don't ask me any more."

I sighed. I knew he was lying. "Mick," I said. "I think you should take that delivery boy job."

"I'll need a bath, then," he said.

"You'll need a clean shirt, too," I said. I reached for Michael's old shirt, lying draped over the sewing basket. I tossed it to him. He looked it over.

"A good shirt," he said.

"A bit big," I said, but 'tis clean, and there are no holes.

Mick pulled off his old shirt and slipped into the new one. The sleeves hung to his fingertips. He rolled them up and tucked the ample tails into his trousers.

It looks good on you," I said. He was stroking the fabric, a much finer fabric than he had probably ever felt.

"Well," he said, "Please God the man at the telegraph office thinks the same."

I placed the bread before him, and pulled the tea off the shelf. He did look good in that color. But still I wanted to take him by the front of his fine new shirt and shake him. I wanted to slap him until he told me what kind of trouble he had been getting into. I wanted to lock him in the house and bar the door against the ruffians and thugs I imagined him with. And as for the "lady" he had been running errands for, well, I wasn't sure what I wanted to do with her, whoever she was. But the fact is that I hadn't the stomach for another fight, and that quite literally. My belly felt like I had strained something down there with all the crying last night. I couldn't do it again. Not this minute.

"The man at the telegraph office will think you the best prospect he's seen in ages," I said, reaching for the washing vat. "Now fill this at the tap, and I'll heat some water for your bath."

Five

"M ary," Mrs. Good's voice broke the silence in the kitchen. "Mary, have you seen my keys?" From the dining room, we could hear sounds of drawers being opened.

"St. Jude, help us," Mrs. O'Rourke murmured under her breath. "If that woman isn't hopeless sometimes." She set aside the bowl of peas she was shucking.

I looked up from potatoes I was peeling. I was supposed to be straightening bedrooms at this time of day, but for some reason or another, Bridget had disappeared right around the time the milkman came. Mrs. O'Rourke had grumbled for a few minutes about girls who weren't really serious about service, and then had put me to work doing Bridget's job.

"Mary," Mrs. Good's voice came in from the dining room. "Did you hear me?"

"I did, ma'am," Mrs. O'Rourke responded. "Don't only sit there," she said to me. "Put those in some water. And cover these peas with a damp cloth. The great key hunt is about to begin."

"The great key hunt?" I asked, but Mrs. O'Rourke was already halfway across the kitchen.

"Where did you last see them, ma'am?" she called, wiping her hands on her apron and striding purposefully through the door into the dining room. I poured some water from the bucket over the potatoes I'd peeled, then washed my hands.

I was covering the bowl of peas when Brigid came in the tradesmen's entrance, her hands full of flowers for the various vases scattered through the house. "What's happened?" she asked, spotting the covered peas and potatoes.

"Mrs. Good lost her keys," I said.

Brigid sighed dramatically. "And are we surprised at all?" She sighed again. "Every week, sometimes twice, Mrs. Good loses her keys. Every week we turn the house inside out looking for them. Every week she goes on and on about someone stealing them. Usually she's dropped them in a linen drawer or one of those fancy silver boxes she keeps. But until we find them, the whole household can't get a lick of work done. We're all about searching for her poor, lost keys." She sighed again and laid the flowers on the kitchen counter.

"She needs a hook for them," I commented.

Bridget looked at me curiously, like I had sprouted a third eye or some such thing. She shook her head. "She's the lady of the house. She doesn't want a hook. She doesn't need a hook; she has us. I don't know what she needs those keys for anyway. Nothing around here is ever locked."

Mrs. O'Rourke poked her head around the corner. "Bridget, Clare, come here, now. And don't you let herself hear you chin wagging so. 'Tis disrespectful."

Once in the dining room, Mrs. Good lined us up and addressed us like a general preparing troops for battle. "Mary," she said. "I want you to search my bedroom. Don't let anyone else go through my things, do you hear?"

"That will do, ma'am," Mrs. O'Rourke said.

"Bridget, you look in the drawing room and the dining room." Bridget nodded slightly.

"And Clare, I want you to go out to the potting shed and fetch Kennedy and the new man. They can look in the yard."

"Yes, ma'am," I said.

"I don't want that new man searching the house," she said. "You can never tell about someone until they've worked for you a bit. For all I know he was the one who took the keys in the first place." She fixed her eyes on me, giving me a meaningful look.

"Yes, ma'am," I said. What else could I say?

"Go, go," Mrs. Good said. "I need those keys."

* * *

Kennedy was out behind the house, tending the kitchen garden. He was seated on the grass beside some new sprouts, plucking the occasional weed in the late afternoon sun. He looked comfortable, in his element, and I hated to bother him.

"'Tis a fine day, isn't it young Clare?" he said by way of greeting.

"'Tis indeed, Mr. Kennedy," I said, "But Mrs. Good will be needing you in the house, just the same. It seems her keys went missing again."

Kennedy smiled, showing several deep-grey teeth. He shook his head and grinned at me. Then he raised his fist to his mouth, placed the thumb near his lips and made the sound of fox horn. "To the hunt, me boys," he said, raising himself to his feet and motioning with a great sweep of his arm for me to follow. "Round up the dogs, saddle the horses, and we'll scour the countryside. The keys will not escape."

I smiled back at him. "She called for the new man, as well."

"Murphy?" Kennedy brushed the dirt and bits of grass from his trousers and smoothed the lapels of his jacket. "He supposed to be out front grubbing up the weeds in herself's new flower bed. Whether or not he's actually there or actually working is anybody's guess." He snorted a blast of air through his nose. "Laziest man I ever met, and I served my time in the army." He laughed again. "Just between the two of us, I hear Mrs. Good hired him as a favor to the Gardiners. Though why the Gardiners would care about such a shiftless lout of a man is beyond my ken."

"Will I fetch him, then?" I asked.

"I suppose you had better if herself asked for him." Kennedy straightened his cap. He cast an eye at the house, then sounded the "fox horn" again, winked at me, and began making his way up the hill to the back door.

* * *

Murphy was, as predicted out front by the drive. He was also, as predicted, leaning on his spade, staring into space. He was in his mid-twenties probably, maybe younger. As I approached, he turned and looked me up and down. The smile he smiled caused a great shiver to roll through by shoulders. He laughed.

"I do seem to have that effect on women," he said, still smiling.

"Mrs. Good wants you in the house," I said and turned to leave as quickly as possible. There was something about him that made my flesh crawl.

"Wait, wait," he said, tossing his shovel casually on the ground. "Why does she want me?" His accent was strange, the slick, iffy tones of a northern man. "Does she need me to bring tools?"

"She needs you to help find her keys," I said over my shoulder. "She needs both of us," I added.

"Oh, well then, why don't you let me walk you to the house?" he said, trotting up beside me. He removed his cap and ran a hand through his jet-black hair. It was slightly wavy, shiny, and smelled of hair oil or some such thing. He grinned at me.

"Name's Murphy," he said.

"Clare," I said simply.

"Clare," he said. "'Tis an old Irish name meaning pale of skin and straight of limb. I see it's appropriate for your skin? Is the other part true as well?"

I could feel his gaze heavy on me. I kept my eyes on the house, picked up the pace. "We have a task to do, Mr. Murphy. And I find your question rather inappropriate. Besides 'Clare' means bright and clear."

"Begging your pardon, I'm sure," he replied, again tipping his hat. "Simply making conversation."

We continued to walk. I picked up the pace, but Murphy matched it easily.

"I'm working here for a week only," he said. "Does gardening for the Good household typically involve searching for keys?"

"I'm sure I wouldn't know," I said. "I'm new myself."

"Well, now," he said. "If that isn't a fine coincidence." He sidled up to me until we were walking nearly shoulder to shoulder. I could almost feel the heat of him on my upper arm. Eyes still riveted on the house, I found myself nearly trotting, angling off away from Murphy's slippery presence. But he matched me step for step all the way to the tradesmen's entrance.

"Maybe we could find our way around the place together." He laid a hand on my arm and motioned toward the steps. I nearly leapt onto the first of them. My toe caught in the hem of my new dress and I stumbled, going down on one knee before I caught my balance. Murphy chuckled and slipped a hand under my elbow.

"I like a girl with enthusiasm," he said. I shook my arm free and dashed up the steps.

* * *

In the drawing room, Bridget was systematically searching one silver box after another. Watching over her housemaid's shoulder, Mrs. Good was verbally retracing all her movements of the day.

"I came into the drawing room to play the piano at about two," she said. "I know I had the keys then. After that I went to the kitchen to check the dinner menu with Mary."

I watched from the doorway, not sure where I should search first. Murphy, cap in hand, stood beside me, a bit too close for my taste.

"Then I went out back to see if Mr. Kennedy was planning to plant a new bed out by the road." She paused and looked up. "Clare, Murphy, why are you just standing there?"

"Where would you like us to look?" I asked.

"Anywhere, anywhere," Mrs. Good said impatiently. "I need those keys before tonight."

"That will do, ma'am," I said.

"Yes, ma'am," Murphy echoed.

"You look in the yard," I said, as Murphy followed me through the dining room into the kitchen. "You heard Mrs. Good, she needs those keys before tonight."

"Yes, ma'am, of course, ma'am," Murphy said tugging at his forelock and bowing. He looked up and grinned. I found the man unsettling, but he did have a nice smile. Now that we were in my territory, he didn't seem so threatening. I smiled back.

"That's more like it," he said and headed toward the tradesmen's entrance. I began scanning the kitchen.

"If you find them, let me know and we'll split the reward." Murphy reached under the damp cloth and grabbed a handful of peas in his grubby paw.

"I don't think there is a reward," I said, lifting a towel that lay on counter. "And stay out of Mrs. O'Rourke's peas." Beneath the towel lay the keys. I picked them up and with them hanging from my forefinger showed them to Murphy.

"Very nicely done, young Clare." He reached out and snatched them from me.

"*I* found them," I said, reaching to take them back.

"So you did," Murphy said, elbowing his way past me into the dining room. "I'll make sure herself knows as much."

I followed him as he strode into drawing room, the keys held out in from of him like a standard.

"You found them!" Mrs. Good exclaimed as he made his grand entrance into the drawing room. "Where did you find them?"

"In the kitchen," Murphy said. "Under a wee towel." He paused a second, looked at me, and added. "Clare helped, of course."

"Well, I thank you," Mrs. Good said, clutching the keys tightly. "And thank you too, Clare. I have no idea how they might have found their way into the kitchen." It sounded a little like an accusation, so I kept my eyes lowered. I figured it never hurt to look meek, even when you weren't to blame.

"Then I'll be getting back to my digging," Murphy said, inclining his head slightly and smiling. Mrs. Good nodded back. Murphy took a step toward the door, then paused.

"Before I do, though," he said. "Could I be asking you a bit of a favor, ma'am?"

"And what would that be?" Mrs. Good replied, dropping the newly found keys into the pocket of her skirt.

"Well, 'tis only that—I really hate to ask—but I could use nine pence from this Friday's pay a few days early." He wadded up the crown of his cap in his clenched fists.

"You know we're not in the habit of paying servants on any day but Friday," Mrs. Good replied.

"Oh, and I know that," Murphy said apologetically. "And I wouldn't ask normally, if it were only for myself. It's only that when I saw how troubled you were about losing your keys, I said a bit of a prayer to St. Antony, don't you know. I prayed, 'St. Antony, if you help me find Mrs. Good's keys, I'll stop by the church on my way home, light a candle and drop a shilling in the box.' I really thought I had the shilling, but now that I look, I see I don't have anything more than threepence." He reached in his pocket and drew out a threepenny bit and displayed it in the heel of his fist. "So if you could see it in your heart to show me nine pence from my Friday's pay, I would be most grateful. And so would St. Antony, I'm sure." He smiled his most unassuming smile at Mrs. Good, and dropped the three penny bit back into his pocket.

"You know I don't go in for all that saints nonsense," Mrs. Good replied.

"Oh, yes, I know ma'am," Murphy said. "I've always worked for Protestants, and I won't tell you a word of a lie—I prefer it. Good folks, all of them."

"I might not hold with all that saints nonsense, but I do admire a man who makes good on his word." She pulled a small change purse from her pocket and picked a shilling from it. "They were my keys. Let me pay the debt to your saint."

"You're more than generous," he said.

"Just this once," Mrs. Good said, holding the shilling over his outstretched palm.

"Of course, ma'am," Murphy replied.

"And this doesn't mean I approve of such prayers," she said. Murphy nodded. "But I won't have a man break his word on my account." He nodded again. She dropped the shilling.

"I thank you for understanding," Murphy said, closing his hand and touching his forelock lightly.

"Now, don't you have a flower bed to dig?" Mrs. Good returned the purse to her pocket.

"Of course, ma'am. Thank you again, ma'am." Murphy turned on his heels, still clutching the shilling in front of him.

"You too, Clare," she said to me. "Get back to work." I followed Murphy to the kitchen.

"A bob to the good for my trouble," he said quietly, tossing the shilling in the air and catching it.

"I think you might be misremembering," I said. "Wasn't it my 'trouble'? And isn't it St. Antony himself who's a bob to the good?"

"Well, right you are for certain, Sister Clare," he said, smoothing his hair back with his hand and settling his cap on his head. "And if either you or the good saint would like to join me at Becky Butler's tonight, 'tis myself who will be buying."

* * *

Father Matthew stood above me, his great metal hand outstretched. The statue stood at the foot of Patrick Street, surrounded by the bustle of Cork's finest shopping district. We used to walk along Pana—that's what Patrick Street was known as in those days—Mama, Da, Mick, and Tom when he was so young he was only a bundle inside Mama's shawl. Every time we passed the statue, Da used to say Father Matthew was reaching for another pint. Mama said that was no way to talk about the man who brought temperance to Ireland, and him nearly a saint at that. Da said any man who would stand between a workingman and his Beamish was no saint.

Despite the long walk from Douglas, despite the fact that it was more than a few steps out of my way, I had swung up Anglesea Street and along the north channel for a bit before heading home. Mama and I used to walk that way on Sunday afternoons on our way home from the Quillans. We'd amble across the Brian Boru Bridge, and along the north channel, watching the water and the folks in their Sunday best out for a stroll. We'd stroll ourselves for a bit past the shops that lined St. Patrick Street. I wasn't sure why I had made the detour that night. But for whatever reason, I found myself sitting, watching the water in the fading light of twilight.

I looked up. From my perspective it looked as though the good father was reaching down to pat me on the head. It had been a good long time since anyone had done that. I wasn't in the mood to quibble though the man's hands were probably as cold as stone.

Mama had been dead and buried these seven weeks. The sound of the sentence in my mind was still foreign, alien. Mama was dead. A couple of months ago I would have said that I knew death. God knows I had seen enough of it growing up in the lanes and the tenements. I'd been to the wakes, stood before the bodies of men, women, children. I'd buried friends, children I'd grown up with. But this was different, so different it seemed like something utterly alien.

Mama was dead. The hard reality of it nestled in beside me, almost like a physical presence, a specter that hung with me, sometimes close, sometimes across the room, but always there. In the last weeks, I'd resigned myself to being in charge of the family. It wasn't that different really. I'd been working since Da died, contributing a bit less than half of the family's income for the last few years. Now I simply had to find a way to support us entirely. It was either that or the industrial school. The knowledge was hard, but I could live with it. Being orphans in that sense was simply a matter of pounds and shillings and the things one had to do to secure them.

But the specter that hung over me since Mama died, the specter that sat next to me that evening beneath the cold hand of Father Matthews, that specter was not about money or food or any of the other things I now had to think about. In fact, the specter was not even a matter of losing Mama herself. It was that, of course. It was the empty spot in the bed at night. It was the empty place at the table, the shawl with no one to wear it.

But more than that, it was the loss of all the small moments, the small habits. It was the loss of Mama's company on the road on the way home from work on Sundays. She and I would talk about the day, gossip about Mrs. Quillan and the family, discuss Mick and Tom and the way they were growing. Now as I walked home I would look up from the walk and find myself alone, and the sound of my footfalls on the stones and the sounds of horses and carts and people milling about seemed hollow, less real somehow than the hard reality of that space where Mama used to be.

Death was the loss of Mama's cooking and the smell of it filling the house. Death was the loss of her hands on my hair, combing, smoothing, braiding. Death was the loss of her laughter as she laughed generously at Mick's jokes, or tried to tell one herself, always forgetting large parts, the parts that would make it funny. Death was the loss of her look, the one she would fix on Mick and Tom to bring them immediately to heel. Death was the loss of her hand on my shoulder while I did the Quillans' laundry, her quiet *"Go m-beannuighe Dia air bhur n-obair"* blessing my work. Mama was gone and with her all the little actions that blessed my existence.

I looked up a Father Matthew his hand stretched out above me. "Bless me, Father," I whispered. "And my brothers, too." The air was turning cool; the light was beginning to fade. In the shadows of a doorway across the way a pair of young lovers clung to each other. His hand nestled in the small of her back and pressed her tightly to himself. She tilted her head back at an impossible angle as they kissed. The man's arms seemed to envelope her, enclose her. A breeze blew off the water and caught her hair, whipping it into a golden cloud around them.

The night air had a chill to it. I wrapped my shawl more tightly around me and rubbed my upper arms, trying to work some warmth into them. They ached from the polishing. Mrs. Good's wood had never looked better. If I could only keep this job, we might be able to manage. Maybe.

* * *

As I opened the door to the flat, an unfamiliar smell rose up to meet me. Mick and Tom were bent over the fire. The smell from the kettle before them tickled the back of my nose and made my belly growl with hunger.

"Did you get the delivery job?" I said. Mick had mitched school again that afternoon to check on a job delivering messages for a local solicitor.

"This is the job," Mick answered. He ladled a big spoon of something from the pot to a waiting rag on the table, dripping grease the whole way. From a sack, he drew a large pinch of salt.

"What are those?" I asked.

"Peanuts," he said. "I bought them raw from a man on the quay. They came all the way from America."

"So you didn't get the delivery job?" I said.

"No," Mick said, "they didn't need me. They hired some boyo in a tie, like someone who could afford a tie needed the work anyway."

Tom reached out a hand and gingerly picked one of the hot peanuts from the pile and popped it into his mouth. "They're good," he said. "Are they supposed to be this crunchy?"

"They can be if I want," Mick replied. "These are Keane's Peanuts. My own special recipe."

"Mick," I said. "If you didn't get the delivery boy job, where did you get the peanuts and the oil?" I looked down into the pot where a handful of peanuts continued to sizzle and smoke. I'd seen peanuts before, of course, but they weren't nearly as common back in Cork as they are in America. In Cork people were much more likely to by chestnuts or chips. The man on the quay must have recognized an easy mark when he saw one.

"I told you," Tom said, "I got them from a man on the quay. He got them from a boat that just arrived from America." He fished in the pot to scoop out the remaining nuts.

"Cheeky little kidger," I wedged myself between him and the rag on the table, fully intending to stand there until I got some answers. "You know very well that's not what I meant. Where did you get the money?"

He looked up at me, then down at the peanuts dripping grease at his feet.

He thrust the spoon at me. To get away from the dripping grease, I took a step back and Mick slipped past me to the table.

"I pawned Papa's coat," he said quietly.

I looked up at the hook by the door. It was empty. I looked at Mick. He was focused intently, too intently, on the peanuts piled before him.

"I took the last of the money from the secret pocket first," he said checking one of the peanuts from the second batch. "'Tis in the biscuit tin with the household money, most of it."

"Mama kept that coat for a reason," I said simply. I untied the shawl and sat down opposite him at the table. I couldn't believe he had actually pawned the coat.

"I know," he said. "But it takes money to make money. I forgot who said that, but he was rich, I know that much."

"You know what she used to say about that coat. She used to say that that coat was her relic of decency, her reminder of the good times. You may not remember that life, but I do."

Suddenly it was not the coat I was upset about. It was not the money. It was everything—the grayness of the room, the boys' tattered clothing, the way our teeth ached all the time, the way we coughed our way through the nights. It was the bedbugs, the roaches, the fleas and lice, and it was the stinky pink stuff the landlord sprayed every now and then to try to kill them all off. I was suddenly tired, tired of it all. I wondered if Mick could begin to understand that.

"When Papa was alive," I said quietly, "we could afford the odd nice thing. We didn't live like this." I gestured at the bare walls around us. "Papa could afford the coat, and Mama's ring." Mama's ring had been long ago pawned, just like the coat was now. The memory stabbed through me like a knife. I looked around, scanning the room for something, anything that had been theirs. The best I could do was Mama's old sewing kit, Mama's patch on the horsehair chair, and Mama's shawl, now my own. I clutched it more tightly to me.

"When Papa was alive, he'd sometimes bring home a joint of beef," I said, my memory wandering. "And he and Mama would take all day Sunday off from work, and we'd go down to the Lough to watch the swans. And sometimes we would go up to the quay and buy apples or an orange just come in from Spain. You don't remember that, do you?"

"I do," Mick said defensively.

"If you remembered, you wouldn't be pawning the coat," I countered.

"It was the only way," Mick said. "I can sell these peanuts at the hurling match. We'll take the money and get the coat out of hock before we go to America. It was the only way."

"It wasn't," I said simply. "You could be finding yourself a real job." I took the shawl from my shoulders, thought to lay it over the chair, but instead took it with me to the bed. I lay back onto the threadbare sheets made of old flour sacks. And draped an arm over my eyes as if to block of the images that floated across my memory. Papa in the coat feeding the ducks at the Lough. Mama lying in bed her face pale from the coughing, the coat draped over her for warmth. Mick and Tom and I huddling beneath its weight on a cold Monday morning while Mama teased the fire back to life.

"How much did you get for it?" I asked, not moving.

"Ten and six," Mick said.

"A good amount," I said.

"The man said it was for Mama's sake."

"Ah, well, then." I sat up. "He always was good to us."

The smell of the peanuts made my stomach growl. They smelled good, tempting. Tom apparently thought so too as he picked another morsel from the pile. What was done was done. The boys would have to sell the peanuts if were going to get the coat back. It was a simple as that.

"Take Tom with you to the match," I said. He can help sell. And don't either of you being eating them all before you get our money back? We're going to get that coat out of hock next week, do you hear?"

* * *

The peanuts were wrapped by the handfuls in bits of newspaper and lined up in ranks of six on the table. It was Saturday morning. The boys were ready to try their hand selling Keane's Peanuts at the weekly hurling match. I was on my way out the door to work. It was a sunny day, and there would be a good crowd at the match. Yet I knew we'd be lucky to make back the money Mick spent on those infernal things. Da's coat was probably long gone.

I sat at the table to pull on my boots. From the foot of the stairs I heard a voice calling up.

"Clare Keane," it said. It was the voice of a boy about Mick's age. "Clare Keane. Telegram."

"Up here," I called, and I heard footsteps as the boy began the three-storey climb. I waited at the door.

"Clare Keane?" he said climbing the last few steps.

I nodded and extended my hand, feeling a bit numb with the surprise. He handed over the bit of paper.

"Wait, please," I said, returning to the room for his tip.

Tom snatched the telegram from my hand, opened it with a rustle, and began to read: "'Will wire boat fare to Cunard S.S.Co. office Minneapolis three weeks. You pay other expenses. Ronan.'"

"We're going to America," he shouted, loud enough that I'm sure half the people in the tenement heard him. "Can you imagine?"

I said fishing a couple farthings from the biscuit tin and bringing them to the boy. "Can you imagine?" Tom asked the boy. The boy doffed his cap, smiled, and trotted down the stairs to his bicycle.

"I told you," Mick said. "I told you Uncle Ronan would send for us."

"You did," I replied. I had been hoping, but truth be told, I never truly thought it possible.

"America," Tom said. "Can you imagine?"

Mick snatched the telegram from my hand to read it for himself.

"I wonder how much the other expenses will be," Tom said. "Do we need to bring food for the journey?"

"I don't know," I said. "We'll need new clothes. I'm certainly not going to enter America dressed as a maid."

"And I'll need new boots," Mick said, laying the telegram on the table. "I can barely get my feet in these."

"I'll need boots too," Tom added.

"You can have these," Mick said.

"They have holes in them," Tom replied.

"That doesn't matter," Mick said. "The soles are still good."

"It matters to me," Tom said. "I always get your old boots, and they always have your holes in them. Only for once I'd like to make my own holes in my own boots."

"We'll get you new boots if we can, Tom," I said. "I'm not sure we'll be able to afford it."

"We'll be able to afford a new dress for you, though. Is that it?" Tom snatched up the telegram and dropped himself onto the horsehair chair, which sighed and listed under his weight.

"We're not made of money," Mick chimed in.

"How much do you expect to make today?" I asked. "If you can sell all these?" I motioned to the little packets on the table.

"I don't know," he said. "Not right off hand," he amended. "How much can we make today, Tom?"

"This telegram is from someplace called Wyoming, Minnesota," Tom replied, ignoring Mick's question. Mick reached over and snatched the paper from Tom's hands.

"What do you mean?" I asked examining it over Mick's shoulder. "I thought we sent our telegram to Lindstrom."

"We did," Tom replied. But that telegram is from someplace called Wyoming. Wyoming is a state." He climbed out of the chair and held out is hand for Mick to return the telegram. Mick turned his back, examining the paper.

"'Wyoming, Minn.' it says." He pronounced it 'min.' Tom walked around Mick, who again turned his back.

"Mick," Tom said in exasperation. "Give."

"Do you think he's moved?" Mick asked, handing me the telegram. I looked at it briefly then handed it to Tom.

"Not 'min'. Minnesota. Wyoming, Minnesota," Tom said. "Wyoming is a state. Minnesota is a state. How can it be from both?"

"Maybe Wyoming's also a city," Mick said. "Cork is a city and a county both."

"But that would mean Wyoming is a city in Wyoming," Tom replied.

"Let me see that," Mick replied, reaching for the paper. Tom turned his back and hunched over the telegram.

"The important thing," I said, snatching the telegram out of Tom's hands and stuffing it into the biscuit tin, "is that the telegraph company and Uncle Ronan know where Wyoming, Minnesota is. We'll take the train to St. Paul. Then we'll wire Uncle Ronan. He'll come to get us, and he'll take us to his house wherever it is."

"But where should we wire him, Wyoming or Lindstrom?" Tom said, standing on the coal box to fish the telegram out of the tin.

"The telegram we sent to him in Lindstrom got to him," Mick said. "Just like I said it would," he added.

"But he was in Wyoming when he sent this," Tom said, spreading it out on the table, smoothing out the wrinkles.

"He'll let us know where he is," I said, snatching up the telegram again and putting it back in the biscuit tin. "And don't you go mauling that telegram, Tom. Leave it in the tin where we can find it if we need it." Tom returned to the chair, dropping himself into it, his arms crossed.

"In the meantime," I said, "we have money to make. How much do you expect to make today, Tom?"

Tom fished a scrap of paper from one of his pockets and handed it to me. "I figure about half a bar," he said. "Minus about four pence for expenses."

"And we still have most of the raw peanuts and oil left," Mick said.

"We can buy food with that, and save what Mrs. Good pays me for the trip," I said trying to appear casual as I admired Tom's fine figures. The boy had not only a head for such things but a fair hand as well. It would be a pity for him to leave school early and take some job as a beast of burden. Maybe in America he could avoid such a thing. It would be unlikely that he could here.

"How much is Mrs. Good paying you?" Mick asked as he began to bundle the tiny packets into a big piece of newspaper.

"Five and six," I said. Six pence less than what Tom estimated they could make in a single afternoon if they sold all the peanuts.

"That's a good wage," Mick replied, "for a girl."

"Well, 'tis money that not resting on some dead-head plan that may or may not work, I can tell you that. My work is good steady work."

"But it will never see us rich," Mick replied.

"And peanuts will?"

"They might," Mick said.

"You'll pardon me if I wait before I buy our new horse and cart," I said.

"She laughs now," Mick addressed himself to Tom. "But once we fill her mouth with sweets and fine meat and puddings of all sorts, well then she'll stop laughing, won't she?"

"She will," Tom replied, but without much conviction.

"When that day comes, Mick Keane, I'll be the first to allow I was wrong." I checked to make sure the fire in the hearth was out, then sat to button my boots. On that day I will shout it from the rooftops that I was wrong and glad of it. But in the meantime I need to get on the road. Mrs. O'Rourke isn't paying me to sit here and gab with you two. I wrapped my shawl around my shoulders. "Luck to you," I added motioning at the peanuts.

* * *

Now I should say something about Uncle Ronan and why we believed that he was our last and only hope. In those days everyone had family, and that family took it upon itself to see you through your childhood and old age, should you live long enough to have an old age, that is. The fact is that far fewer people lived to see past their forties in those days. Illness, dangerous work, poor food and poorer living conditions all conspired to weed out the weak. So children were often raised not by their parents but their uncles, aunts, grandparents, even older brothers or sisters.

Large tight-knit families were the norm. Most of the families on our lane had five children or more. The family down below us had eighteen, some of them theirs, some of them her late sister's. Mama used to say that if she was going to be neighbors with a family with eighteen children, eleven of them boys, she'd rather be living above them than below them. Still, just the sound of feet on the old wooden boards of the tenement was like a great herd of cattle thundering through the place. That thunder of family was the sound of the tenements.

It's true that everyone had family, often large a family. But not everyone had family that was still living. Mama's father died before I was born aboard a merchant ship were he was cook. Mama had four sisters—five girls there were in that family. All of them died of the consumption. The doctor said Mama was lucky. She was the oldest, had already gone as a maid, and was living in her employer's house in Limerick. The doctor said that was what saved her from getting the consumption when all of her sisters did. Mama's mother died mere months later—of either grief, consumption or the sack factory, depending on who you asked.

On the other side, Da had only one brother and a sister. The brother, Ronan, who was older by five years, up and emigrated before he was twenty. Da's sister died as a baby during a spell when granddad was out of work. Then Granddad, Da's da, who worked on the docks when he could, was killed when a great pallet of butter fell on him. Grandmama never remarried, said one man per lifetime was more than enough. She lived alone, only her and Da. She wasn't well herself, but she resolved to see Da up and married before she died. Grandmama danced at Da's wedding, then took a fit and died the very next week.

So that left Uncle Ronan and us, the only members of the Keane family not felled by disease or accident, or work or the lack of it. We didn't know Uncle Ronan, had never met him. He was one of the many poor Irish tenement dwellers who had begged, borrowed or stole for a ticket out. But he was family. More importantly, he was all we had.

Six

Maybe it was the fact that we saw so little of it. Maybe it was watching the rich folks we worked for spending it like water. Maybe it was the scars that earning it left on our bodies. Whatever it was, the folk of our tenement were obsessed with it.

With money, that is, more particularly with schemes that would make them the greatest piles of that money with the least amount of sweat off their foreheads. The easy shilling occupied not a little bit of the talk on the stoop and street corners. Toss schools—clusters of men gathered on the sidewalks pitching pennies—saw penny-starved workers make and lose money faster than they could blink. From the depths of our being, we knew that there had to be an easier way to make a living than the one we engaged in day in and day out. Finding that easier way was like a slow burning fever in some of us.

On the first floor of our tenement lived three bachelor brothers, the Doohan brothers. The three of them had the fever as badly as anyone I knew. Nobody was sure just how old they were, but Con, the oldest of the three had hands like ancient oak branches. Cracked and gnarled they were, so crippled up he no longer worked. Thomsy, his younger brother, sold song birds down at the Coal Quay for a living, or at least that's what he did as far as the guard was concerned. Paddy, the youngest of the three, brought in the highest wages, such as they were. He worked as a tugger for a shopkeeper over in Barrack Street.

Truth be told, though, the three of them probably took in the most money betting on Thomsy's birds. Thomsy may have sold songbirds, but his heart belonged to his fighting cockerels. Big, nasty beasts they were, with eyes like a damned soul and combs as red as blood. He kept most of them on a friend's farm just outside town. But the cocks that were in training, those he kept in his room. He said the lanes hardened a bird like a cushy farm life never could. He set them to wander in the yard, saying the paving stones toughened the birds' talons. There they terrorized the kidgers, one minute strolling nonchalantly, the next flying into a furious flurry of feathers and claws. And God help the boy who decided to get his own back on the bird by throwing a stone or poking it with a stick. Thomsy, who kept a keen eye on his birds from the window, would storm out the door, huffing and wheezing, his fat fists balled at his side. He would pick up pebbles and bounce them off the pate of the offender yelling, "How do you like that? How does that feel?"

Those cocks were his life. "Birds," he would say, "are a comfort. A man would do better to keep a canary, or a cock, or even a pigeon than keep a wife. A wife is a boil on a man's backside for the rest of his natural life. A bird is comfort." His brothers apparently agreed with him. The three of them never so much nodded at a woman, but they lived with Thomsy's cocks in that tiny room, and they would no more eat chicken stew than they would boil their own grandmother.

Now and then a particularly mean cockerel would return Thomsy's affection by making him great piles of fast money in the ring. Thomsy would buy drinks all around at the pub, and the fever would ignite itself again and spread its hot fingers up and down the lane.

That was Mick's heritage, and he was as true to it as any boy I've met. The quick shilling was as much a part of him as the very air he breathed.

* * *

On Saturdays I worked a half day at the Goods', from breakfast until lunch. That meant that as soon as the dishes from the noon meal were clean, I could go. I could work my six or seven hours, then come home to take care of my own house.

On that particular Saturday I worked like a fiend from the moment my toe touched my doorstep. The thought of the telegram stuffed into the biscuit tin buoyed my spirits, gave me energy. By the time the sun sank below the roof of the tenement across the way, the floors of both the room and the landing were clean. The window was washed, the table scrubbed down with boiling water. Mick and Tom each had a clean shirt for the next week, and my work dress was ready for a new week. The sun set on a room as clean as hot water, black soap, and elbow grease could make it.

For a while I sat by the hearth waiting for the boys, wishing for a bit of mending, something to occupy my hands and mind. The potatoes in the pot were disintegrating from overcooking, and the little dabs of mustard I'd put on the three plates for want of anything better to do were beginning to harden into something that vaguely resembled the floor of the old cattle market down by the quays. I was beginning to wonder if I should be asking Mrs. Sullivan for help finding the boys when I heard a thunder of steps on the stairs.

"You should see the Keane boys sell," Mick announced as he and Tom barged through the door. "A wonder, it was. A great wonder indeed." He set an empty tray on the table, and turned out his pockets. A great pile of coins tumbled out. "I think Tom sold three times what I did. After I showed him how the selling works." Mick practically glowed with pride.

"Did you make enough to buy back Da's coat?" I asked Mick, not looking up from the mushy remains of the cooked potatoes that I scooped onto the plates. They had cooked to baby rags and were turning a dingy grey as the air hit them.

"What is that mess?" he said looking with distaste at his plate.

"How much did you make, Tommeen?" I ignored him and addressed my question to Tom.

"Six and six," Tom replied, "after expenses." He fished in his pocket and brought out the scrap of paper I'd seen that morning. "Ten and six minus four for the peanuts, oil, and extra turf. Six and six. That's six pence more than we thought."

"Six and six you say." I set the last of the plates on the table. Their contents didn't resemble food as much as I would have liked, but I had the hunger of the world on me and didn't mind one little bit.

"Not too bad for a 'dead-head' scheme," Mick said. "Don't you think?"

"I *know* I'll be making five and six next week," I replied. "How about you?"

"You just can't admit that my scheme worked," Mick said.

"I admit that your scheme worked today," I said. "I'll need to see more before I admit more."

Mick harrumphed, pulled the coal box to the table and sat, eying the dried up mustard on his plate suspiciously. He pushed the coins into a tighter pile in the center of the table and then picked up the tray he had come in with and set it aside on the horsehair chair.

"Where did you get the tray?" I asked.

"Got the lend of it from a friend," he said. It seemed like the kind of tray that one might use in an eating house or pub.

"Which friend," I asked.

"A friend," he said, then quickly crossed himself and bowed his head. Tom and I did the same to bless ourselves as we always did before eating. Tom's head barely hit bottom before it bobbed up again.

"Don't you want to know how we did it?" Tom asked. He fingered the coins in the center of the table. I looked over at Mick, and nodded. "Tell me," I said, offering an olive branch.

"It was Tom," Mick said. "It was his scheme that sold most of them. A regular Andrew Carnegie with the selling, that boy is." He grinned over at Tom.

"So what's your secret, 'Andrew'?" I looked over at Tom who was beaming with obvious pride. I had to admit it was nice to see them both happy. Tom had been so quiet, and Mick so contrary lately that I wasn't sure what to do with them. It was nice to see smiles for a change.

"Well," Tom began, leaning in over his potatoes, his elbows on the table. "The boys were down by two. And those Blackrock blackguards were egging us on, saying maybe we ought to have our grandmothers come out and play for us, that maybe they would do a better job of it than our team, and we said our grandmothers truly could beat their players hollow. And presently one of the blackguards gave one of our boys a clout on the jaw, and . . . "

"Tom," I interrupted. "Could we have a little less about 'blackguards' and a little more about the peanuts?"

"He's getting to it," Mick said.

"I am," Tom agreed. "Well our boys were breaking their hearts with the trying and our people were mad with shouting to encourage them to fight on. So I called out 'Barr's peanuts.' and 'Cheer on the St. Finbarr boys by buying Barr's peanuts.' They laughed at me, but they bought the peanuts. And just then Billey Moloney managed to get loose and pick up a stray ball, and he lifted the sliotar and swung, and another 'Barr man caught it on the drop and hit it with a terrible force. And away up and through the goal it went."

"Mr. O'Connor says that Tom has great hansel, that luck follows him about like a shadow," Mick said. "The more people bought his peanuts, the better the team did."

"We beat them by 1-9 to 1-5," Tom stated simply.

"Only so you know 'tis not because of your peanuts," I said, trying to loosen up the clot of mustard on my plate with a tine of my fork before deciding to eat the potatoes dry.

"Maybe 'tis; maybe 'tisn't," Tom said smashing his potatoes and mustard together into a nasty looking mess.

"God gave those boys their skills, and it was those skills and the boys' heart that carried the game," I said. "Peanuts and your 'hansel' have nothing to do with it."

"Maybe so," Mick said. "But peanuts have a good bit to do with pennies, and pennies have a good bit to do with the expense money we need to go to America. So if people want to think the peanuts made the 'Barrs win the match, I'll not tell them different."

"Hmmph," I said. "Are you going to tell that to the priest this evening at confession?" The situation bothered me, though I wasn't sure why. That much money in one afternoon sounded like some kind of temptation. I couldn't place my finger on just what kind of sin it might be leading to, but I could feel in my bones that it was some kind of trouble. Six and six. Many a grown man, even some tradesmen, would not be sorry for that kind of pay for a day's work. Two boys making it, and for work that barely broke a sweat—it didn't feel right.

"You sold all your peanuts?" I finally asked.

"All of them," Tom said. "We sold about half, maybe less at the match. Then after the match a few of the men went in to Becky Butler's, to celebrate don't you know. They asked us to join them, and wouldn't you know we sold the rest there."

I heard a shuffle under the table. "Ow," Tom shouted and recoiled. Mick was staring him down across the table.

"I wasn't supposed to notice that, was I, Mick?" I said. Mick shifted in his chair to get a better angle on a second kick, but Tom pulled away in time.

"Is Becky Butler's a pub?" I asked. The name seemed somewhat familiar, but I couldn't place it.

"'Tis no great thing," Mick said. "We didn't go to drink. We only went to sell the rest of the peanuts."

"I don't want you selling at a pub," I replied. "You can sell your peanuts at the hurling match."

"We can sell more of them at the pub," Mick said. "Becky says we can sell them there any time we want. I can sell them after school, so I wouldn't have to miss any more. And we don't have to wait until there's a hurling match. Don't you see? That means we can sell more peanuts and faster. It won't take us as long to save for America."

"No," I said. "I don't want you spending your evenings in a pub."

"We could drop them off with the doorman, and Becky could sell them," Tom offered. "We wouldn't have to go inside the pub itself. 'Tis good money," he added.

Six and six every day was amazingly good money. And it would go a long way toward getting us new clothes, maybe even a suitcase. Maybe that was the temptation. I wasn't sure.

"Let me think about it," I said. "For now, I don't want you going back to the pub. I want to see what kind of a place it is, first."

"Fine," Mick said. "If you don't want us spending all night in the pub, we won't. You don't have to go checking up on us all the time." Mick slouched over his potatoes.

"You'll stay out of the pub, then?" I asked.

"Isn't that what I said?" Mick replied.

"Could we only drop off the peanuts and leave?" Tom asked.

I thought about it for a moment. I couldn't see that it made a difference where people ate their peanuts. "I suppose that wouldn't hurt," I said. "But you have to promise me you won't go in."

Mick scowled at me.

"Mick?"

"Yes, yes," Mick said testily. "We'll drop off the peanuts and leave. Are you content?" The smiles were gone, and it seemed we were back to squabbling. Squabbling and silence. Mick picked at his potatoes. Tom mopped up the last of his mustard with a piece of bread.

"How do you like working for Mrs. Good?" Tom finally asked, breaking the silence.

"It brings us regular money. I like that just fine," I said dropping the subject.

My mood was bad enough, with the boys being late, and the news of the pub. I couldn't see that it would be improved by talking about work. Truth be told, the job at the Goods wasn't nearly as good a job than I had had at the Quillans. At the Quillans, Mama cooked, but beyond that we split the duties down the middle. At the Goods, Mrs. O'Rourke got the pick of the jobs, Bridget then took the few remaining good tasks, and I spent my time emptying slops, doing laundry, scrubbing floors, and slogging through all the other jobs nobody wanted.

Still I could think of worse jobs—factory work came to mind. Throughout the tenements one could hear the coughs of factory workers bringing up the day's dust and grime from their lungs. Or at least some of the day's dust, the rest sat like a wet blanket clogging the chest something terrible. Even slops and privy cleaning were better than that. For the first time that day, I slowed down, relaxed, and instead of working thought of all the work I'd done that day. That's when I discovered it—I was weary right to my very bones.

Mick finished his potatoes and rose to lift the old biscuit tin from the mantle. He dumped the contents in a pile with their earnings from the day and began to count.

"I need to rest," I said, suddenly too tired to move. "Tommeen would you be a dear and rinse the plates down at the tap?" Tom didn't seem to mind. He quietly gathered the plates and carried them out.

"Don't you go turning him into a Colleen," Mick said when Tom had left.

"Washing a few dishes won't hurt him," I replied.

"'Tis women's work," Mick responded.

"'Tis you who should be careful with him, Michael Finbarr Joseph Keane," I said, "taking him into a crowd of gambling, swearing, spitting men. He's your brother."

"They don't spit that much," Mick replied.

"You know what I mean," I said. Mick bent over the coins on the table. I watched him for a bit as he piled them carefully by denomination.

"Mick," I said finally. "I don't want Tom thinking that 'tis right to lie about the peanuts. And I don't want him getting a taste for spending his time in pubs. Not at his age. You're his older brother. You need to watch him. You need to keep him away from those places."

"I do," Mick said. "But he has a knack for the selling. He may soon be making better than you or I do."

"And the devil makes better than all three of us." I wasn't sure I was getting through to him. "'Tisn't the money. 'Tis Tom I worry about. Will you watch him? Will you make sure he knows what's right and what's wrong?"

Tom returned with the dishes, dripping a line of water drops into the room.

"Will you?" I said to Mick.

Mick shot a look at Tom and nodded.

Seven

Twas a cruel wet evening. The rain came down in a steady drizzle, not enough to soak me right away, but enough that I could feel it slowly seeping, first through my shawl, then through the light fabric of my dress. The drizzle was steady, relentless, and I firmly believed that it was only a matter of time before it seeped through my skin itself and into my very bones.

The walk, which had seemed so far the first week, had now become second nature, not easy certainly, but at least second nature. I needed simply to point my feet toward home, and habit would do part of the work. The houses were coming closer together now, and I would soon be in amongst the lanes that smeared themselves across the southernmost edges of the city. I hunched over and pulled the shawl tighter around my face. The cold damp of it clung to the back of my neck. But that was better than the cold pins and needles I felt as the drizzle struck my face. As the last bit of light dipped beneath the horizon, with it went the last bit of warmth in my arms and shoulders. My God, it was a cruel evening.

Behind me I heard hoof beats and I moved over to the far edge of the road. A covered car bounced past me on the rutted road. One of many, it was, and I took no more notice of it than I needed to stay out of its way. But when I looked up after it had passed, I saw a man's face in the back window that looked familiar, though I couldn't quite make out the features. The cart slowed and then stopped a good hundred yards ahead. The man jumped out and began walking toward me. He had the collar of his coat turned up and the peak of his cap pulled down over his face. He hunched against the rain as I had. I could not see his face.

As casually as I could, I crossed to the other side of the road. The man crossed over as well. I looked up and down the street. It was empty of pedestrians, and no surprise that. It was no kind of night to be out walking. The next house lie on the other side of the cart. I had no lane between me and the stranger. I slowed my pace, considered turning around. But if he wanted to outrun me, he could surely do that. Well, then, I thought, it looks as though I must simply face the situation. I pulled my shoulders back, lifted my chin, and strode forward.

"Clare," the man said. "What are you doing on a night like this? The wetting'll do you no good at all." He raised his chin, and I saw the face of Murphy. I relaxed a little, but not much. Murphy was the kind of man who always seemed to be trying to put a body at ease. It was for that very reason I didn't trust him. That and the fact that after the incident with the keys I knew him to be a petty liar, if there were such a thing.

"'Tis not a fit day for walking," he said. "Not a fit day at all."

"That's God's own truth, Mr. Murphy," I said. "But I'll be blessed if my driver isn't home in bed with the croup and his fine team of horses with him. What is a lady to do?" I kept walking.

Murphy laughed, perhaps a bit too hard. "Join me," he said. "'Tis a welcome day for a covered car."

"Well, thank you just the same, Mr. Murphy," I said. "'Tisn't much of a walk. I couldn't impose."

"Ah, but I insist, Sister Clare," he said. "I had a bit of luck betting on the hurling match yesterday and 'twould be a shame to keep such good fortune all to myself, so it would. I thought what better way to spend the lads' money that to look out at them from a warm cozy covered car on a cold rainy day."

"You're very kind," I said thinking about the cozy little cart and the chance to get out of the rain. "But I'm afraid my mother would not approve."

"The summer stars never shone on a better woman than your mother, God rest her. Murphy crossed himself hastily. I looked up at him in surprise. "I used to haul coal to the Quillan's," he said. "Your mother would let me in the back gate. She always had a smile and a kind word. I was so sorry to hear of her passing."

"Thank you," I said simply.

"I don't think she would mind if I repaid her kindness by offering to share the comfort of my car."

"Perhaps not," I said. Cold and damp is bad enough when you know you have no choice. But cold and damp when a warm car stands waiting and available, well now that is more than a body can take. "I would be most grateful, Mr. Murphy," I said.

"Well, that is grand." He gestured toward the car and offered his arm. I took it gingerly. He led me back to where the driver waited, perched on a seat atop the car, a thick, damp blanket wrapped around his shoulders. Murphy took my elbow as I climbed in. The car rocked slightly on its single pair of wheels then settled. It smelled vaguely of porter and sour men, but it was dry and out of the wind. I took a seat in the front of the car and rearranged my shawl around my shoulders. Murphy climbed in and sat across from me. He smiled pleasantly and tapped the front wall of the car for the driver to proceed.

"Miss," the driver called down through the front window. "I'll be needing your to move a little more behind, if you don't mind. "We're too heavy on the poor horse's back."

"Oh, certainly," I said. Murphy shifted his knees to the side, and I squeezed in across from him. "Walk on," the driver called from his damp box seat. The cart lurched and began to roll.

Now I should say that covered cars were none too big. Certainly they were nothing like the carriages the rich folks rode in. In fact they weren't much more than a way to get off your feet and out of the rain. So when I moved to the back of the car, I found myself shoulder to shoulder with Murphy himself. My knee rested lightly against his. I was suddenly acutely aware of how his leg brushed mine as we rocked and bounced over the muddied road. I smoothed my skirt down, shifted my legs, and tired to make myself small.

"Do you like working for the Goods?" he asked.

"One floor is much like the next when you're on your hands and knees," I answered.

"So it is," he laughed again, turning himself slightly in the seat. Again his knee rested against mine. I brought up as pleasant a smile as I could muster. Now that I had warmed up a bit, I was beginning to feel clammy. I shifted the shawl further down on my shoulders. My eyes were in my lap, but out of the corner of my eye I could see Murphy watching me. I turned my head and set my eyes on the front of the car.

"I think I'll like being a gardener better than hauling coal. I could never get the coal dust off of me. No matter how hard I scrubbed, I was covered with it from head to toe. Even that skin that rarely sees the light of day was black and thick with it."

I wasn't sure how to respond to that, so I just smiled.

"I'd like to be the head gardener of a big estate some day. My own cottage, and the extra fruit if there is any. A man like that could marry, raise some children."

I wondered if we were close to town yet. I couldn't see much through the front window, and to see out the back, I would have to twist in my seat and maneuver my knees around Murphy's somehow. I decided to try. Shifting a bit, I turned my head all the way, and squinted through the dirty window.

"Are you tired of my company so soon, Clare?" I felt a hand on my knee. I froze, then turned slowly to the front, trying not to meet Murphy's eye.

"Did anyone ever tell you what beautiful hair you have?" He leaned to touch a strand that had flown free of the pins.

I knocked on the roof of the car. "Driver," I called. "I'd like to get out now."

The car slowed. Murphy leaned forward and spoke through the front window. "Don't you pay my niece any mind," he said. "She's only having a bit of a screech. Drive on."

The cab picked up speed again. "I'm not his niece," I shouted. "I'm not his niece."

Murphy laid his hand on my thigh, gently sinking his fingers into the flesh.

"No need to fuss," he said. "I don't mean any harm by it."

"Remove your hand," I said.

"Give us a kiss then," he said.

"Driver," I called, "stop the car."

"Give us a kiss." He reached for my face. I pulled away, backed all the way to the side wall, but not far enough. Murphy leaned in.

"Driver!" I called. The cart continued to roll. I slipped along seat and moving forward as much as I could. Murphy leaned forward too, and the balance of the cart shifted. I moved over to the other side.

"Beggin' your pardon," the driver called down through the window, "but the horse is feeling the bounce."

"Good," I said and began bouncing up and down, forward and back as hard as I could. "If you don't like it, you can let me out." I threw myself hard against the side wall. Murphy's eyes went wide as the cart tilted dangerously to the side.

"Halt," the driver called to the horses, and the cart came to a halt. I bolted for the door. Murphy caught my arm.

"I didn't mean anything by it," he said. "No harm in a bit of fun now is there?" I ignored him and stumbled out the door into the mud. The driver shot me a nasty look as I gathered my shawl about me.

"Go," I said to him, closing the door in Murphy's face. "Go, go!"

The covered car drove off. I huddled down inside my shawl and continued the trudge toward home.

* * *

"I'll murder the bounder," Mick stated matter of factly. His voice was loud enough that it carried to the next pew of penitents waiting for confessional. They turned and stared. I elbowed him hard in the ribs.

It was Saturday night. I'd kept silent all last night, all morning as I worked my half-day at the Goods. Finally, not being able to hold it inside anymore, I'd burst out with the story on the way into confession. It was a relief to let someone know, but now I was wishing I hadn't. Mick knelt beside me, his every muscle tense. "I'll cave his worthless skull," he whispered.

"I'll help," Tom added from his place on my other side.

"Nobody's killing anyone," I whispered. "A fine thing it is to be talking about murdering in a church. You be sure to add that to your list of sins when you confess."

"At the very least I'll bloody his nose for him," Mick said. The woman in the pew in front of us turned and fixed a glare on us that could melt glass. I grabbed Tom by the wrist and Mick by the jacket and hauled them out the front door and around the side wall.

"With what? How are you going to bloody his nose?" I asked when we were out of earshot of the parishioners milling about the front door. "Murphy is twice your age and twice your size. You listen to me, Mick Keane. There's nothing you can do here. A good run is better than a bad stand any day of the week. A wise man knows when to fight and when to walk away."

"A coward knows when to walk away," Mick said. "A wise man knows how to fight and win."

"Did they tell you that down at Becky Butler's? Them with their drunken fist fights." Every night that week, when I came home Mick had peeled himself off a dark huddle of boys a lane or two up Barrack Street. Each night he had met me as I walked up the lane, wordlessly followed me inside, and sulked while I cooked supper. And though he made a point of being home in the evening, the sack of peanuts in the corner continued to diminish. Sales had slowed considerably since that first incredible day, but the money in the biscuit tin continued to increase. He was supposed to be in school. But he was still selling the peanuts, and I had a fair notion where and when.

"Becky Butler's is business," Mick said, shaking his arm loose from my grasp.

"Phhff. Becky Butler's is a bad influence on you all together. I want you to quit selling your peanuts there. You can sell them at the hurling matches or on the quay."

"We're not talking about Becky Butler's or peanuts," Mick said. "We're talking about Murphy. How could you get into the car with him in the first place?"

"Is that what you're angry at?"

"It was foolish," Mick said. "Anyone with an eye in his head could see he was a bounder."

"'Tis *my* fault then, is it?" I asked.

"Is it?" I asked myself. "Is it?"

Mick stood, his jaw set, his hands balled into fists at his side. He was staring at a piece of moss growing up the side of the old church.

"I won't make the mistake again," I said quietly. Tom had drifted off. I watched him wander around the corner and probably back into the church. Mick slouched against the building.

"Don't go looking for Murphy," I said. "It won't do you a bit of good to be picking fights."

"I have to protect you," he said quietly. "I'm the only man left in the family." I looked at him in his short trousers, his wrists hanging down a good inch and a half below the sleeves of his jacket, his beardless chin buried in the front of his shirt. I resisted the urge to smile. He was right. God help us; he was the only man in my family.

"Mick," I said, "You're right. 'Tis a fact I shouldn't be forgetting. I do need you to be the man in the family. I depend on it more than you know." He looked up at me, disbelief in his eyes. "But what that means in this case is doing what's best for the family. If you hurt Murphy, and the guard lays hands on you, it will mean we can't go to America. The magistrate will want to put you in the reformatory. And the Americans won't let in a man with a criminal past. That means we'll all be staying here, you tugging like a mule for some factory, me scrubbing rich people's floors, Tom getting into God knows what kind of trouble without a Mama and Da around."

Mick kicked at the ground with the toe of his boot.

"What would Da do when he was still with us?" I asked, then thought better of it. Da had never been one to back away from a fight.

Mick thought for a moment. "Da likely would find Murphy and flatten his snot," he said, a smile creeping across his face.

"You're probably right," I replied, smiling. "But Da didn't have the opportunity we have. Don't go after, Murphy."

"You're right," Mick said. "It would be a foolish thing to do."

"So you won't go looking for a fight?"

"If that's what you want."

"Swear?"

"As much as I'd like to do him no end of harm," Mick said, "I swear I won't try to kill him."

* * *

Now I must say that Mick was usually true to his word. But he had a quick mind, no mistake. And if I'd thought better of it, I would have asked him to swear not to try to hurt Murphy, *not to hurt him*, in just those words. But I didn't and that was my undoing as well as his.

It was Monday. Mick had been on a slow burn all day Sunday. He seemed quieter Monday as I sent him off to school. So by the time I had finished washing the Good's breakfast dishes, my mind was on something else entirely.

I was putting the plates back in the china cabinet. Mrs. O'Rourke was seated at the dining room table discussing the week's meals with Mrs. Good. That's when the set-to broke out. We heard it all the way through the kitchen into the dining room. A terrible racket it was—shrieks and oaths and all manner of blue bloody murder. Mrs. Good ignored it at first—she was never one to look trouble in the eye if she could avoid it. But finally, when the racket refused to stop, she rose and made her way to the kitchen to look out the window. I followed, thinking only to catch a quick peek before getting back to my work.

There on the lawn just outside the tradesmen's entrance, stood Murphy, Mick, and Tom, with Kennedy holding a bloody slat between his thumb and forefinger well away from his body. Murphy had his handkerchief pressed to the crown of his head. Mick was cradling his right wrist in his other arm, his face a mixture of pain and fury.

I wanted to run out into the yard, slap Mick silly and then demand to know what he was doing here. Instead I followed a pace or two behind Mrs. Good, who, nose wrinkled and face screwed into a sour fist, was striding to the group as though it were a pile of fetid garbage.

"Would you care to tell me what this is all about Kennedy?" She shot quick looks at Mick and Tom, then returned her gaze to Kennedy.

"Well, Mrs. Good, we were planting the bluebells, just as you asked out by the front drive. I sent Murphy back for a spade—some of the bed wasn't dug quite deep enough you see." He gave Murphy a meaningful look. Murphy's lip curled as he looked away. "It wasn't more than a minute or two before I hear this terrible racket, kidgers screaming and Murphy here swearing terrible oaths. I made my way to the potting shed, and Murphy had this boyo"—he motioned to Mick—"on the ground all trussed up like a goose, his arm wrenched behind his back and his legs all tied up in his own. And the other one was standing over them with this slat. And Murphy was bleeding from his pate and shouting about how these two clubbed him over the head, and him just going about his own business. And the boys were screaming threats and bloody murder. So I pulled them apart and the rest you can see for yourself. That's about all there is to tell."

"Who would you be, then?" Mrs. Good addressed herself to Mick.

"I'm Michael Keane, ma'am," Mick snatched his cap quickly from his head, then went back to clutching his wrist. Tom, taking his lead, snatched off his cap as well. "This is my brother Thomas."

"And why have you come on my property and assaulted my gardener?"

"I'm here for my sister's honor," Michael said, straightening his shoulders as much as he could without letting go his wrist. He looked over at me, a look of utter rectitude on his face. "This filthy scut tried to take advantage of her. Last week, in a covered car he tried to take advantage of Clare."

"This boy is your brother?" Mrs. Good turned to question me.

"He is, ma'am. They both are, though I can't say I'm proud to own them this minute."

"And is what they say true? Did Mr. Murphy try to take advantage of you?"

I wasn't sure how to answer the question. My thoughts went back to the covered car. I searched my memory, searched the events. Did he indeed try to take advantage of me? He tried to make me do something I didn't want to do. He lied to the driver to keep me in the car against my will. He made me more uncomfortable than I had ever been around another person.

"He did, ma'am," I said.

"And did you lead him on in any way?

"No, ma'am, not a bit of it!"

"But you were alone in a covered car with him?"

"Yes, ma'am, but it was raining, and the walk was long, and I wasn't feeling well, and Murphy stopped and offered, and he said he knew my mother. I didn't see the harm."

"Murphy?"

"What is a man to do, ma'am?" Murphy's look was one of complete innocence. "She asked to share my car, then when we were alone, she kissed me. Of course, I was concerned about her good name, but with the way she kissed, I wasn't of a mind to resist."

"Liar!" Mick threw himself at Murphy, shoving him hard with his good hand. "Take that back, or so help me I'll give you the devil to eat."

"Get a hold of yourself, boy," Kennedy wrapped an arm around Mick and pulled him away.

"Take it back," Mick said through clenched teeth. Murphy simply smiled back and shrugged. "Take it back." Tears were welling in the corners of Mick's eyes.

"Now's not the time," Kennedy whispered quietly in the general direction of Mick's ear, so quietly I had to think a moment to figure out what he said. Then louder, as much for Mrs. Good as for Mick he added. "A man has to defend his family's honor, 'tis true. But for now you must get a hold."

Mick stopped struggling, going so limp so suddenly that Kennedy had to catch his balance. Kennedy slowly unwrapped his arm, and Mick stepped free, pale, shaky, clutching his right wrist again.

"I'll see you two in the drawing room directly," Mrs. Good said, casting a look at first me and then Murphy. She was visibly shaken by the experience. I too could feel the backs of my arms quiver and my stomach hollow out. Murphy's face still held the same implacable look as always. Only his skull seemed the worse for the wear.

* * *

"I can't have my servants behaving this way," Mrs. Good said. She had obviously pulled herself together between the yard and the drawing room. She fixed on me a hard glare, one that made me want to crawl beneath the table and never come out. "I will not have you disrupting the tranquility of this house," she continued. I bowed my head humbly. Beside me I could see Murphy doing the same.

"I trusted you Clare," she said. "I took you in before checking your character, without knowing anything but the barest scraps about your abilities. I did it for Mary, and I did it for your mother. And this is how you repay my kindness?"

Mrs. Good, sat down on the sofa, then turned her head to look unseeing out the window. "Clare, Murphy I'm afraid your services are no longer required. You may pick up your wages on Friday, but you are dismissed effective immediately."

I looked up in shock. "Mrs. Good, ma'am . . . "

"I will not discuss the matter further," she said. I stood frozen in my tracks. "That will be all, Clare."

"Yes, ma'am," I said, and turned to leave, then remembered my manners, "Thank you, ma'am," I said over my shoulder and headed for the kitchen.

"A brief word, ma'am," Murphy said. I paused just inside the kitchen door to listen.

"No, Murphy," Mrs. Good interrupted, "no more words, brief or not. I knew you were trouble from the moment I hired you. I could feel it in my bones, I could. If it weren't for the Gardiner's good word, I would never have allowed you to set so much as a toe in my house. But, I thought, sometimes a black hen lays white eggs. Mrs. Gardiner said you were a good worker. For her sake I gave you a chance. But for the sake of my own house, I'll not give you another. You are dismissed, Mr. Murphy."

Murphy found me in the kitchen before I had the chance to make my way into the yard. He grabbed my shoulder, spun me around to face him. I reached up and slapped him. He smiled, an unsettling smile, the kind of smile one might expect a dog to smile just before it tucks into a freshly killed rabbit. He grabbed me around back of my neck and pulled me into a kiss. I pushed at him, clawed at him. He let me go, that same sickening smile on his lips. I wadded up a fist and punched him, landing the fist square in the middle of the smile.

"Clare," Mrs. Good's voice came from the door. "Clare, leave this instant. I never want to see you near my house again."

I turned, grabbed my shawl from the hook near the back door, and dashed down the back steps. I ran past Tom and Mick, past Mr. Kennedy calling for me to wait. I ran to the end of the drive and out into the road, pumping my legs, trying to outrun the feeling inside me. But try as I may, the anger, the fear, the feelings of violation pulsed within me, harder even than my pounding heart.

I was well past the neighbor's drive when Tom and Mick caught up to me. I slowed to a walk, and they did too.

"Clare," Mick said.

"Shut your gob, Mick," I said.

"I didn't try to kill him," he said. "I didn't break my promise."

I was silent, choked by the fury that rose in my throat. I wanted to lash out, to knock Mick down and pound him senseless. My knuckles throbbed with both the blow I'd already thrown and the one I ached with my every fiber to throw.

"Clare, I think he broke my wrist," Mick said.

"Shut your gob, or I'll break the other one."

"Is that the thanks I get?" Mick whined. "I did this for you."

"You did this *to* me, you cocky little snot. You eejit. You ass. I lost my job because of your 'help'." I picked up my pace. Mick and Tom did, too.

"'Twould be better if I killed him," Mick mumbled.

"You're lucky you didn't end up in the dead house yourself. What you were thinking I can't begin to imagine."

"I was thinking about you," Mick said.

"Next time use your head when you do."

* * *

All that afternoon, I roamed the streets of Cork, supposedly looking for work, actually looking for some kind of resolution within myself. That evening Mick didn't show up for supper. Tom and I ate our potatoes and bread in silence. When Mick did come home, he threw off his boots at the door and his trousers at the bed. He then fairly threw himself onto the mattress, curled up his back to the room, and made like he was going to sleep. He didn't fool anyone. Tom joined him shortly. I waited, but soon the anger was edged out by total exhaustion.

I should say here that very few modern child psychologists would approve of our sleeping arrangements back in the tenements. Boys and girls, mothers and fathers all in the same bed. The parents, of course, found other times and places for their adult relations. And the children were never allowed to look when their brothers or sisters were in a state of less than full dress. Thanks to the church and the strict mores of their society they learned to keep their flesh under a tight leash, perhaps too tight for their later emotional health. But all that aside, I'd say the benefits of families sleeping together on the same mattress more than made up for the various emotional adjustments the practice required.

That angry evening, I hung my dress on the peg by the door, and slipped into bed, the only bed we had. Tom was lying on his back, his head at the foot, his arm outstretched and dangling off the edge of the mattress. Mick still lay next to him, curled into a tight ball, his back to me. I pulled the old coat over me, and shoved at the boys trying to make room for myself. Tom shifted in his sleep. Mick barely budged. I eased in, but still my hip hung over the edge of the mattress in the cool air. I could either put up with the draft, or I could close the gap between Mick and myself.

Suddenly I was aware of it, the space between the two us—not just the real space, but the distance that had formed between Mick and me since Mama's death. I wasn't sure how it had formed, but the gap was there and it was growing. Truth be told, I barely knew this boy who had grown so much during my three years at the Quillans. I remembered him as the little lad on Da's knee. Now he was nearly as tall as I was.

I edged deeper into the mattress. Tom pulled into a ball, and my hip came to rest lightly against Mick's calf. I could feel him tighten. He was awake. The contact had been made.

"How's your wrist?" I said.

"I don't think it's broken," he said quietly from the foot of the bed. "I'll do."

He relaxed. Not much but enough that I could sense it through our tenuous connection.

"I'm sorry," I said finally.

"For what?" he asked.

"I don't know. Everything."

"Me, too," he replied.

"Thank you," I said. "You made a real mess of things, but thank you."

Mick rolled over onto his back and lifted his head to look my way. "Do you mean it?" he said.

"I do," I replied. "You really did make a mess, and I really do thank you."

We lay quietly, shoulder to foot, hip to hip. "I wanted to think that Murphy would just go away if I ignored him. I think now that he probably wouldn't. I'm glad . . . " I paused, not sure what I wanted to say. Murphy's face passed in front of my closed eyes. The feel of his hands on me, his rough lips on mine, it all came back in a flood. Then I felt Mick's hand at my side, searching for my own. "I'm glad I didn't have to face him alone," I finally said.

"What are brothers for?" Mick replied.

"I'm blessed if I know," I said.

Eight

The rain was a steady roar on the roof. From the warm place under Papa's coat, my feet snug against the steady heat of Tom's back, I listened to the tattoo of dripping. The roof of the tenement, which merely seeped during most rains, had fully saturated this time, and was giving up not only damp patches but full-fledged leaks. Sometime in the middle of the night I'd risen to put the cooking pot under the largest drip, the water bucket under another and the slop bucket and washing vat under smaller drips by the door. But the steady seep in the corner by the window was creating its own puddle, and a half dozen smaller leaks rolled along the ceiling before dropping to the floor any place they chose.

Between the drum beat of water on water, I listened to the sounds of the tenement coming to life—quiet voices, growls and groans, footsteps on the stairs. It was time to get up. The job search awaited. I dreaded the day.

Finding day work was beginning to seem impossible. Nobody wanted to hire a maid without a "character," and Mrs. Good had refused me that utterly indispensable scrap of paper. Without the blessing of my prior employer, without her positive assessment of my abilities, attitude, and overall moral fiber, my chances of finding a new employer were severely limited. For a week and a half I had traipsed the city, suffering excessively polite and excessively impolite rejections both. I was beginning to come to terms with my prospects: thanks to Murphy, my days as a general servant were likely over.

Yet I needed a job, and I needed it now. Despite the continued slow but steady sale of Mick's peanuts, despite our tightening our belts still further, the money in the biscuit tin was oozing out. On Monday we had to dip into Mick and Tom's earnings to pay rent. Then on Tuesday, Tom lost his cap and needed a new one. Food was a steady drain. Not only were we not saving for America, we were actually losing ground. We'd be out of money in another week, week and a half at the most.

That steady leak in the money tin left me with only one sure alternative. I would have to find work at a factory. It would be bad, to be sure. But factory work itself had its advantages. Unlike service, at a factory I could work my ten hours and come home. I would work five, maybe five and a half days a week, not the six and a half I used to work in service. I could be there with Mick and Tom in the morning when they left for school. We could eat together before the sun went down.

"I hope you aren't disappointed with me, Mama," I whispered as I rolled out of bed and reached for my shawl. "I know what you say about such places, but if I get the boys to America, we can start a new life. I have to do this."

I lit the lamp and checked the cooking pot in the center of the room. The water was dripping into it a double jig pace. I assessed the slop bucket and the water bucket. The slop bucket was filling faster, so I took the water bucket for the cooking pot leak. Opening the window, I shouted, "Beware of the water," and tossed the contents of the pot into the street. It wouldn't make much difference for anyone below. In this weather they would have been soaked to the skin anyway and might not have noticed had someone tossed a pot of water on their head. But courtesy is courtesy all the same.

On the mantle, the lamp sputtered. A leak was dripping onto the globe. I found a relatively dry place on the table for it. Beneath my feet, the floorboards were slippery. A smell rose from them, a decades-old smell now reconstituted by the standing water—mildew, the grease from old cooking fires, and the stink of well-worn human flesh. With the back of my throat, I could taste it as much as smell it.

I needed something in my stomach to face this day. Just tea would not suffice, not if I was to walk into a factory for the first time. The sideboard contained little better than a sack of oatmeal. Oatmeal stirabout was considered famine food, and rightly so. It was cheaper than potatoes, cheaper even than bread. We hadn't had much more for the last few days. Still the thought of a warm bowl of oatmeal warming the inside of me against the rain outside was an appealing notion. I made ready to light the fire. That's when I remembered that the water bucket was full not of fresh water but of the brownish sludge that had come in from the roof. I looked out at the rain, knowing I would have to trudge through it to tap outside. I couldn't face it just yet. Not just yet.

"Mick," I said walking over to the bed. "Mick, 'tis time to get up. You need to go out and fetch water for stirabout and tea."

"Can't you do it?" he said, his jacket still pulled like a blanket up about his ears and his back still to me.

"While you lay abed all morning? What kind of a lazy lout are you?" Mick's lack of movement answered my question. I yanked the jacket off him. "Rouse up," I said. "There's work to be done." Tom curled reflexively into a tight ball.

Mick rolled over and glared at me. "You get water every morning. Why is it suddenly my job now 'tis raining?"

"Because today I'm going over to Cornmarket Street to see if one of the sack factories will give me work. I have to make myself presentable, and I need your help." I was improvising, and he knew it. There was no fear that I would be presentable by the time I reached the factory, what with the rain and all.

Mick looked at me, then rose silently, pulled on his trousers and jacket, snatched up the bucket and stepped out into soggy hallway. Tom, too, rose.

"Mam said she would never work at a factory," he said pulling on his trousers. "Not even if she had to scrub clothes and empty privy pots all her life. She said 'twas the dust and disease of a factory that sent Grandma to an early grave." He looked up; a drip of water had landed squarely on his head. I made a mental note to ask Mick to move the bed to a drier part of the room when he came in.

"The consumption sent Grandma to an early grave," I replied, digging a match from the box on the mantle. The matchbox was damp. Even the embers of the fire seemed soggy as I stirred them and lit piece of turf. "And factory is steady work. We'll never be able to save enough for America if I have to spend any more time looking for day work."

"Can't you look a little longer?" Tom said. "I don't want you getting sick in one of those places."

In answer I pulled the biscuit tin from the mantle. I pulled loose the top and dumped the contents on the table. A handful of coins rolled around a bit before settling. Most of them were copper.

Tom looked at them briefly, then scooped them up and handed them back to me. "Do you want me to walk you to the factory?" he asked quietly.

"I want you to empty those." I gestured at the two containers still sitting on the floor. "Dirty water in the house is unlucky, and I can use all the luck I can get today."

"If dirty water in the house is unlucky. This place must be the unluckiest house in all of Cork," he muttered, ducking around one of the drips to fetch the slop bucket.

* * *

The deluge had stopped with the dawn. But a steady drizzle continued to fall, a light drip it was, almost a mist. We Irish, you see, have an eye for rain and are able to distinguish all manner of different degrees of precipitation. The rain that morning was enough to make a body huddle, but not enough to make her rush. It was, as such, an ignorable rain, and in that sense not really rain at all. But as I stood under the tiny overhang before the front office of the factory, that rain that was no real rain was making me decidedly damp, and that did nothing for my general sense of anxiety. I shook as much of it as I could off my shawl and shivered.

People were beginning to arrive, women, mostly, huddled deep in their shawls, and a few men in dungarees and tattered jackets, picking their way between puddles, finding their way around the side of the building. Finally a small man in a long black coat and a bowler stepped around the corner and strode quickly up the front walk. He was a short stump of a man with a terrible nose on him. His face was all pulled in on itself like it was trying to avoid the world all together. The nasty little man hunched down inside his coat and pushed past me up the stairs as though I didn't exist at all. He unlocked the door, shook off his umbrella onto my feet, and entered. After weighing the misery of the weather against the sourness of the man I followed him inside.

The front office was no more than a handful of desks, each piled with papers and official-looking leather bound books. The sour man removed his coat and hat and lowered himself heavily into one of the desk chairs.

"Beg your pardon, sir," I said. "My name is Clare Keane, and I'm here about the work . . . "

"We're not open for business yet" he said, pulling open one of his desk drawers. "We don't open until 7:30." He looked up from the drawer and poked a finger toward a large, industrial-looking clock hanging on the wall by the door. The clock read 7:26. "Wait there," he said pointing at a bench beneath the front window.

"I will, sir, thank you," I said. I rearranged my soggy shawl about my shoulders and sat. The sour looking man had pulled a flask from the drawer and was attempting to clean something from a small glass with his index finger. He looked up, saw me watching him and glared. I lowered my eyes.

He was an unpleasant man to be sure, but if he was the man in charge, he didn't really need to be pleasant. I, on the other hand, needed the job, so I tried as hard as I could to make myself as inoffensive as possible, eyes lowered, raising them only to glance at the clock every now and then. At precisely 7:30, another man and two boys about my age strode through the door. Each wore a dark overcoat over a dark suit. The man wore a fine, deep-grey hat with a crease in the crown; the boys wore caps. They hung their coats, cast a dismissive glance at me, and took their places at the desks. The boys immediately went to work with pen and ink bent over the large leather books and stacks of loose papers speared on shiny metal spikes in the corner of their desks.

I glanced at the clock again. It read 7:31, so I walked over to the sour man's desk to draw down about the job.

"Beg your pardon, sir," I said. My name is Clare Keane, and I'm here looking for work."

"Talk to Houlihan about that," he said. He jabbed a finger in the direction of the other man in the office. Houlihan looked up and smiled.

"You're looking for work?" he said.

"I am, sir," I said, walking over to stand before him, returning his smile, but keeping my eyes lowered in respect.

"How old are you?" he asked.

"Fifteen," I said, then added "almost" silently to myself.

"Do you know how to operate a sewing machine?" he asked.

"I don't, sir," I said. "But I learn quickly."

"No matter," he said. "Most of the girls didn't know how to work the machines when they first got here. We teach you."

"Yes, sir," I said.

"Are you willing to show up on time every day and work hard?" he asked. The question seemed perfunctory, a mere formality. He and I both knew that if I didn't, I would simply be dismissed. People like me were highly replaceable.

"I will, sir," I said.

"And can you start today?"

"I can, sir," I replied.

"Good," he said. "Follow me." He snatched his hat off the rack, and threw his coat about his shoulders. Hunched against the rain, which was falling heavier again, he led me outside to a large exterior door on the side of an attached dark brick building. Women huddled in limp black shawls were beginning to arrive, dozens of them hurrying into the building by way of the double door. The sign over the door said "T.D. Roche and Company" in large block letters. "Meet me inside," he said and trotted back the way we had come.

I stepped through the door, which a girl about my age held for me.

"Thank you," I said, slowing as I entered the building to take it all in.

The room was one large floor with metal poles running floor to ceiling at regular intervals. On the one side of the room, beneath tall, rain-streaked windows, were the machines, three rows of dusty, black sewing machines. On the other side of the room were great piles of sacks. A young man was already bringing them in on carts and dumping them on the well-worn wooden floor.

I stood in the middle of it, scanning the crowd for Houlihan. A small crowd of women and girls trickled through the doors on either side of me. Their chatter filled the air like the dust that seemed to be everywhere. Finally Houlihan entered via a small door at the front of the building. He had taken off his hat and coat and was adjusting the button at the neck of his shirt. The eyes of a dozen or more women making ready at the machines lifted when he entered, then just as quickly fell back to the machines. One of the women stood and walked toward him. I did the same.

"Good morrow," Houlihan said.

"Good morrow kindly," replied the woman, a plain woman in her thirties maybe, though something about her looked much older.

"I have a new girl for you, Betty," Houlihan said.

"Bluebell will be glad to hear that," Betty replied.

"Right," said Houlihan, turning already to leave. "And Betty, we need that shipment for Murphy's by closing," he said over his shoulder. "See to it."

"I will, Mr. Houlihan," Betty said. "And don't I always," she added under her breath when she was sure Mr. Houlihan was out of earshot.

She turned to me and looked me up and down. "I'm Betty Houlihan," she said. "Mrs. Houlihan. No relation, obviously." She laughed as though she had made a grand joke. She didn't look nearly as old when she was smiling. "I'm the senior worker here. You'll take instructions from the supervisors, of course, but if you have any problems, you come to me."

"I will, ma'am," I said.

"What's your name?" she asked.

"Clare Keane," I said.

"Ina," Mrs. Houlihan called to one of the girls taking a light blue smock from one of dozens of pegs set into the wall by the door. The girl removed her shawl and hung it on the peg, which was labeled *Ina*. "Where's Bluebell?"

"I didn't her his morning," Ina replied trotting over to Mrs. Houlihan. "But then she almost always steps through the door the very second the bell rings."

"All right, then," Mrs. Houlihan said, turning to me, "you follow me." I followed her to the end of the row of pegs. The last label said "Bluebell."

Mrs. Houlihan pulled a smock from a shelf containing several of them stacked in neat piles. She held the smock up to me, and satisfied it would fit, shook the dust from it and handed over. She took a pen and a small piece of paper from the shelf. She dipped the pen in a small portable inkwell and handed pen and paper to me as well.

"Write your name on the paper," she said. "It will mark your peg."

I took the pen, and began to write my name. My tongue protruded of its own accord. It had been some time since I had a pen in my hand.

"Not much of a scholar?" Mrs. Houlihan commented.

"Only in my leisure time," I said, smiling.

Mrs. Houlihan laughed. "Every now and again I like to write a sonnet or two meself," she said. "When my family and I summer at our cottage on the coast." I chuckled.

"You can wait here 'til Bluebell comes," she said. "She'll teach you the job."

* * *

Bluebell, as predicted, dashed through the door just as the bell sounded at 8:00. She whipped her shawl from her shoulders as she trotted toward me. She paused only for the briefest of seconds before her peg. Then smock in hand, she dashed toward the growing pile of sacks along the far wall. I dashed after her.

"My name is Clare," I said when we finally stopped in front of the sacks.

"My name is Rebecca," the girl said. "But you can call me Bluebell. Everyone does."

"I'm the new girl," I explained.

"Do you have a nickname?" she asked.

"No," I said, "not really." It was not the first question I expected to be asked.

"Why not?" Bluebell asked. "Everyone has a nickname."

"I guess I never got one," I replied.

"Well, then," Bluebell said, "We'll only have to think of one for you."

"Mrs. Houlihan said you could teach me the job," I offered, feeling a bit self-conscious merely standing there while everyone else had begun work.

"You're the new girl?" Bluebell asked.

"I am," I said. "I'm going to be working here," I added. "Mrs. Houlihan said . . . "

"Yes, I know, Mrs. Houlihan said I could show you the job. You said that already." Bluebell was turning one of the sacks inside out in a single smooth motion. Then without warning she grasped it by the corners and gave it a few quick shakes over a trough in the floor. The dust from the sack rose into the air and landed on me, in my eyes, all over my face. I reflexively pawed at my eyes.

"It helps if you keep your eyes all squinted up like this when you shake the sacks." She screwed her face into a tight squint. She snatched a stiff brush from a collection hanging on the wall, and attacked a small clump of mildew on the sack. She then turned the sack this way and that, inspecting it before tossing it onto the floor.

"Not much to it," she said. "Turn the sack inside out. Shake out the dirt and barley dust. Then get any clumps or stains with a brush. If the sack is sound, put it in that pile." She pointed at the single sack lying by itself on the floor. "If it needs mending, toss it on that pile." She pointed at the open floor. "The ones that need mending will go over to the machines."

"You don't sew yourself?" I asked.

"No," said Bluebell, a smirk on her face. "I don't sew. And neither will you until we get enough new girls in to replace you. Do you see Anne there? She carries, folds and stacks. She taught me this job. And Daisy," she pointed to another girl about our age over by the machines, "she cuts the fabric for new sacks and winds the cotton onto the bobbins." A young man, about sixteen or seventeen I would guess, brought another load of sacks on a pushcart through the great double doors and dumped them in front of us.

"You two need to gab less and work more," he said, kicking a stray sack into the pile.

"We can do both, Doolan," Bluebell said, snatching up another sack. "I don't see you breaking your back this minute."

The young man grunted. "Unlike some people, I earn my pay around here." He spun his cart around and headed out the door.

"Doolan," Bluebell said. "The supervisor's son. He doesn't do anything but tug loads of sacks, but his Daddy's the supervisor, so he thinks he's in charge. He's a cad, he is, and pure trouble."

I picked up a sack from the stack, turned it inside out, though not with Bluebell's ease of motion. Turning aside, I shook it over the trough. The dust, however, landed as much on me as in the trough.

"What do you mean 'he's trouble'?" I asked.

Bluebell shrugged. "If I'm Bluebell, and Daisy's Daisy, maybe you should be Pansy. Or Buttercup. Buttercup's better. That's you now, Buttercup."

I didn't think of myself as a Buttercup. It seemed a rather arbitrary nickname. I pulled a brush from the wall and went to work on a resistant lump of grain. Already the clack, clack of machines and the quiet hum of conversations filled the air.

"I don't think I ever did see such a power of sacks," I said trying to make conversation.

"What a strange thing to say," Bluebell replied.

"I only meant," I paused, not sure what I meant. "I only wondered where they all come from."

"Breweries, mostly," Bluebell said, poking her finger through a hole in one of the sacks. "Murphy's, Beamish. And distilleries. A few bakeries, but not many." She tossed the defective sack on the empty floor, starting the new pile.

"Does everyone over there mend sacks?" I asked.

"Of course not," Bluebell answered. "Some *make* sacks. Some in the far corner make covers for railway wagons. But you'll not be making covers for many years. First you shake sacks. Then you stack sacks. Then you cut sacks and wind bobbins. Then you repair sacks. Then you make sacks. Then you make covers. And before you can move up, someone has to come in and someone has to leave. That's the way of things." She paused to blow a bit of straw from her mouth. "I'll hold that you'll be breathing barley dust for, oh, two or three years before you move up to new sacks."

Two or three years. I didn't hope to be here that long. As I stood in the growing cloud of dust rising around me, I wished with all my might to out of that factory before the buttercups bloomed that summer.

* * *

By the end of the day, I had developed a perpetual tickle in the back of my throat. I coughed at it, tried to shake it loose, but it clung to my throat like a burr. The dust in the air grew steadily thicker as the day wore on. Bluebell didn't seem to notice it. Neither did the women hunched over their machines on the other side of the room. But if I stopped to listen, I noticed that a steady bark of coughs rang through the air almost continually. I scratched my nose, and snatched up another sack.

After issuing basic instructions about the sacks, Bluebell hadn't much more to say about the job itself. There wasn't much more to say, I suppose—turn the sack, shake the sack, scrub the sack, sort the sack. I wondered if I'd done a thousand yet. The movement had already become second nature.

Bluebell's chief value was not as a job tutor but as a source of information about my coworkers. I now knew that Mrs. Houlihan's husband was a part of the socialist movement and so had a hard time keeping a job. Daisy was in love with a baker, but his family didn't approve of her family, so they saw each other mostly on the sly. Anne, who was sixteen or seventeen, Bluebell couldn't remember, had supported her mother and younger sister since her father abandoned them for a painted woman from Dublin. "The Irish divorce," she said with a wink. "He ran out on them." I got the life stories of everyone in the factory, and I do have to admit, the litany did help make the day pass.

Toward the end of the day, a barrel-chested bear of a man strode through the double doors. His nearly white hair had a reddish tinge, turning it a pinkish color that seemed utterly incompatible with his otherwise bear-like stature. Across the room a dozen faces looked up from their machines, then quickly went back to work. Bluebell's pace picked up slightly. I knew immediately that this was Mr. Doolan, young Doolan's father, the supervisor.

Doolan strode the factory floor like a man who owned everything he surveyed. The women nodded briefly as he passed, and he acknowledged them only when the whim took him. He made a cursory inspection of the machines, then headed toward Bluebell and me. Mere feet from where I stood, he stopped. I looked up from the sack I was scrubbing only long enough to see if I could catch a look in his eyes. He was clearly not interested in me but rather in how clean the sacks were getting. I leaned into the stain I was scrubbing. He must have been satisfied because he left without saying a word.

"What did he want?" I asked Bluebell quietly when he'd moved on. She shrugged. "What do supervisors ever want?" she replied. She paused briefly to run the back of her wrist over her forehead. The unheated room had warmed considerably since that morning, owing to the presence of dozens of hard-working bodies. Though the air was still cool, it was muggy enough that every bit of dust that floated past stuck to our skin. Bluebell's forehead now bore a wide streak of brown dust. I imagined mine did too.

"Do you want to hear what I know about Mr. Doolan?" she asked conspiratorially after himself had left through the double doors that led to the loading dock. I nodded.

"He spends all his money at a kiphouse," she whispered.

"He does?" I replied.

"He does," she confirmed. She looked as though he had just conveyed the most scandalous information anyone could ever imagine. It suppose it was possible that she had, though you'd never know asking me.

"Bluebell," I whispered. She leaned in. "What's a kiphouse?"

She jumped back in amazement, then leaned in again to whisper. "You don't know what a kiphouse is?" I shook my head. "The Lord preserve your innocence. A kiphouse is a house of fallen women," she said, "where women, you know, sell, um, themselves."

"A house of women of the unfortunate class," I said, remembering Tom's description.

"Mmhmm," she said.

"And Mr. Doolan goes there to, um, buy?" I asked.

"That's what they say," she replied. "They say that he spends all his money at a place called Becky Butler's. Daisy says she saw him going in the door once."

"Becky Butler's is, what did you call it?"

"A kiphouse," Bluebell confirmed. "You didn't ever hear of it? It is positively infamous. A terrible place all together."

"I did hear a few things," I said. "I thought it was a pub."

"Oh it is that," Bluebell said. "But only downstairs. Upstairs is where the women are."

"So a man could only go in for a drink," I said. "And not, um, anything else."

"I suppose," Bluebell answered. "But they say that Mr. Doolan's not content with only a drink."

"A kiphouse," I said, coming up with all kinds of pictures of Tom and Mick in such a place.

"I can't believe you didn't know what a kiphouse was," Bluebell laughed at what I suppose she considered my naivety. I wasn't about to tell her otherwise.

Nine

Where's Tom?" I asked, hanging my dusty shawl on the nail behind the door.

"You're home early," Mick said.

"The factory lets out at six," I answered. I came right home. I checked the water bucket. It was half full, so I dipped a cup and drank, trying to clean the dust from the back of my throat.

"Six, you say," Mick replied. He was used to having me home between eight and ten.

"Where's Tom?" I repeated the question.

"He's, um, out with his friends," Mick answered. He was fishing more peanuts from a vat of hot oil on the fire. His eyes were glued on the vat far more than the task warranted.

Mick, you see, had an ailment common to Irish men. He couldn't seem to lie convincingly to the women in his life. It's surprising in some ways given how often he tried. He had the Irish male gift for blarney. He told a good story. But he could never lie to me or to Mama. The best he could hope for was misdirection, finagling the truth, and he was mighty good at that. But as for outright, bald-faced lying, well that was something he couldn't manage, at least not with us. We could always tell by the blush of him. After that it was merely a matter of locking eyes with him, and it would eventually all come spilling out.

"Mick," I said. "Where is Tom? Really."

"I think we're out of turf," he said. "Did you bring some, or should I get it tomorrow?"

"Mick."

"Tom is fine."

"I'm sure he is, but *where* is he fine?"

"He's at Becky's. We were selling peanuts, and Becky had a job for him in the back room, and he said he'd be home before you got here, but you were early. . . ."

"You left him?" I shouted. "You left your brother in that, that place? I told you I didn't want you in that place."

"You said to drop the peanuts off at the door," Mick said. "We do that."

"And then you follow them in?" I fairly shouted. "Do you know what kind of a place Becky Butler's is, Mick?"

Mick fished another spoonful of peanuts from the oil. His lips were pressed so tightly together they were practically blue.

"Do you know what goes on in a place like that?" I was hoping he didn't.

"Do you?" Mick replied. "Did you ever set foot in the place? I know what 'tis like. Do you?"

"I know enough," I said. "I know I don't want you and Tom to ever set foot in that place again. 'Tis no place for a good Christian, and no place for boys. I can't imagine what you were thinking, leaving Tom in a place like that."

"'Tisn't like you think," Mick protested. "The bottom floor is only a pub, nothing more."

"And that's better? Leaving your brother in a pub?"

"Becky watches out for him. She likes Tom."

"I'm sure she *likes* the girls who work for her, too. Am I the only one in the family with any sense? Take me there. I'll fetch him myself."

"He'll be home soon," Mick said. "I told him he had to be home before you were. 'Tis only that you got home early."

"Beg your pardon," I replied. "I didn't mean to interrupt your carefully planned schedule. Take me there. Now."

Mick fished the last of the peanuts out of the oil, set them out on paper to cool, and still never meeting my eyes, reached for his jacket.

* * *

We walked briskly along the quays, watching the debris drift slowly down the river beneath us. Not surprisingly, the house was down by the docks, no more than a short spit from where ships from all over the world moored. In front of the innocuous brick facade, a few men sat at the curb, playing cards for match sticks, waiting for a friend to some by and stand them a pint. Along the quay, a couple of sailors lounged against a bollard, speaking a language I didn't understand. As we crossed the street, the card players suddenly erupted.

"Jesus Christ," one of them said, throwing down his cards. "Damn my bloody rotten luck tonight. I couldn't draw a respectable hand if my feckin' life depended on it."

I placed a hand on Mick's back and hurried him along, hugging the wall as far from the card players as I could manage. I'd never been to a kiphouse, but this was exactly how I imagined people in them would talk. I wondered if I would have to confess the whole incident tomorrow evening. Mick pointed out the front door.

"Do you want me to go in and get him?" he asked. Before I could answer, a voice interrupted.

"Hellooo. Hello on the street." the woman said. "Mick, honey is that you?" The lilting voice seemed to float down on the night air from above. I looked up in time to see a tin tied to a string drop out of the sky atop my head.

"So sorry," the voice came from the dark of one of the windows a storey above. I took a couple of steps out to get a better look, then wished I didn't. The threadbare sheet the young woman was clutching to her chest was barely covering her obviously naked torso. The light from the gas lamp behind her cast a hard outline of her body on the sheet. I looked quickly over at Mick, who was fishing a shilling from the tin. In two long steps I closed the distance and I put a hand on his chest, holding him in close to the wall.

"Mick would you be a dear and run into the pub and fetch me a quick gargle?" the voice from above said. "And if Miss Butler has some Woodbines would you see if she'll part with one or two?" The young woman's words were laced with sugar. They had a visible effect on Mick.

"It would be my pleasure, Polly." Mick tossed the coin into the air and caught it before dropping it in his pocket. He grinned up into the night with that buttery smile Irish men use when they're trying to impress a woman.

"It will *not* be your pleasure," I said, still holding close in to the building. "We're here to collect Tom. That's all. Give her the shilling back."

"I said I'd do it," Mick said.

"Give it back."

"She'll let me keep the change."

"Give it back."

Mick looked as though he was going to protest, but decided better of it. He grasped the tin on its string with one hand and reached into his pocket with the other. Sullenly, he stuffed his fist into the tin, then released it for its upward trip. He took a couple of steps back and winked an exaggerated wink to the woman reeling in the string above. I slapped him hard against the side of the head.

"Ow," he said. "What was that for?"

I slapped him again. "That one was for not knowing what the first one was for," I said.

* * *

We walked to the front door. Standing in front of it, arms crossed across his chest, was a great big whacker of a man in a dark wool jacket and bowler hat. As he watched us approach, the stern look on his face melted into a friendly smile.

"If it isn't Mick the Stick," he said heartily by way of greeting. "I thought you'd gone home for the night."

"Franky," Mick said, extending his hand.

"Is this your sister, then, Micky?" the man asked. He swallowed Mick's hand in his own huge mitt.

"'Tis, Franky," Mick said. "My sister Clare. A fine night, isn't it?" I glared at him. I didn't like the idea of my brother being on a first name basis with a brothel doorman. I didn't like it a bit.

"'Tis that," Franky replied.

"We're only here to collect Tom." I interrupted their assessment of the weather rather rudely, I'm afraid. But I wanted nothing more at the moment than to snatch up Tom and get us home. "He's inside?"

Franky nodded and held the door for us. The knuckles of his hand had obviously been split and healed several times over.

"We need to talk," I said as we passed through the ornate doors into an equally ornate pub. "When we get home, we surely do need to talk."

"We will," Mick whispered. "But not this minute." His eyes were glowing.

I looked up to see what he beaming at. Toward us came a large woman, a beautiful woman, a stunningly gorgeous woman. She was six foot three if she was an inch, and her fiery red hair piled high atop her head added another four inches to the measure. She was dressed in a deep kelly green, a silky flowing skirt and a bodice of velvet or some such thing that fit snug against her ample bosom. She passed through the sea of men's eyes like a tall ship with sails unfurled. In the shadow she cast, I believe I would have disappeared altogether had she not held her hands out to me in welcome.

"And who is this beautiful young woman?" she said. "Is this the sister you told me so much about, Micky?"

"'Tis," Mick said. "My sister, Clare. Clare, this is Becky Butler. She owns this place."

I wasn't sure what to say. "Delighted to meet you" seemed rather inappropriate. So I just nodded.

"You didn't tell me she was such a beauty," Becky said, looking me up and down. I was suddenly acutely aware of my hands, that there seemed no good place for them at the moment. I clasped them behind my back. That was no good. I dropped them at my side. Too stiff. I finally settled on folding them lightly in front of me. Becky's hands, however, were a symphony of subtle graceful movement. She reached out and stroked Mick's chin ever so slightly. "Your mother certainly has handsome children," she said to him. Mick blushed deeply in response.

"We're here for my brother," I said. "For Tom."

"Of course," she said. "'Tis a school night. It was remiss of me to keep him so long. He's in the back counting bottles for me. The boy has a head for figures. He's the only one who will give me an accurate inventory of my goods without nipping a bit on the sly."

"I'll get him," Mick said, and before I could say anything more, he had disappeared into the smoke and chatter of the pub.

"You have two wonderful brothers," Becky commented, gesturing for me to sit with her at a free table. I nodded. "The peanuts Micky brings in are selling very well. I have to say I'm a bit surprised at that, but they do sell well. And the two of them help me sweep up and collect glasses. They are good workers, the both of them, a godsend."

"I'm sorry," I said, "but our mother wouldn't approve of them being here if she were still with us."

"Yes, of course," Becky said. "Your mother. The blessing of grace with her soul." She crossed herself quickly. "'Tis a terrible thing when a boy loses his mother at such a young age. It's been hard on poor Tom, especially. He feels things so deeply." I looked into her eyes. She did seem to care. But how would she know so much about Tom? How much had they been here?

"I don't think Mama would approve of the boys being here."

"And they won't be, not for long," she said. "I only want to help you earn your money for America. That's what I do. Boys and girls both come to me when they're down on their luck or in trouble. And I give them a leg up. It's a way of taking money from those that have it and putting it in the pockets of unfortunates."

I thought of the young woman in the window, the outline of her shape on the sheet. No pockets there. None at all.

"I thank you, Miss Butler," I said. "But I am able to care for my own people."

"In that wretched sack factory," she said. "Tom told me you took that terrible job yourself. What do they pay you there? Seven, eight shillings a week? Small money for such hard work. I tell you there are worse ways to make a living than what my girls do."

"No ma'am," I said quietly. "I don't mean to be cheeky, but I don't think there are worse ways." I stood. Mick was making his way through the crowd with Tom in tow and a half pint of stout in his hand.

"For Polly," he said before I had a chance to say anything. I glared at him, but his eyes were already on Becky. So were Tom's.

"Home," I said between my teeth. "Now."

* * *

"I don't want you going there anymore," I said closing the door to the room. The Purcells seemed to feel no shame at airing their family problems for the whole building to hear, but I'd rather my neighbors not learn where the boys had been working lately. "I don't want you to set foot in that place. I don't want you taking any more money from the girls. I don't even want you handing peanuts in through the door."

"We need the money. You said so yourself," Mick replied. "Besides, I make more money selling peanuts at Becky's than you do at your precious sack factory."

"My sack factory?" I said, my voice rising with my temper. "My sack factory? I'm breaking my back every day at that, that, *place* for you, for us. My sack factory?! I work there for you, you clot!"

"I didn't ask you to," Mick shouted. "I can make my own money."

"Not at Becky Butler's," I said. "Not at that sinful place, you don't. I don't want you spending time with girls like that. Who was that girl in the window? I don't want you spending any more time with girls like that."

"They're not all sinful," Tom said quietly.

"And where will we get the money for America?" Mick shouted. "Your pay barely covers rent. We'll never get to America unless I keep selling my peanuts."

"We'll find a way," I said. "I don't want you there. Do you understand? That's the end of it."

"You're not my mother," Mick shouted. "You can't tell me what to do. You're not my mother." Suddenly tears sprang to his eyes. He bolted for the door, tipping over a chair on his way, and slamming the door so hard the walls shook with it.

"Go after him," I said to Tom. "We aren't finished."

"He'll be back," Tom said.

"I don't want the two of you spending any more time at that place, with those girls," I said, not ready to let go of the matter yet. "Go after him!"

"He'll be back." He righted the tipped chair.

"What do I have to do to make the two of you listen?" I shouted. "Go after him!"

"The girl Mick got the drink for was Polly," he said quietly, almost in a whisper. "Her name was Polly." The hush in his voice brought me up short. It took me a moment to get my bearings. "She's from a farm near Macroom," Tom added.

"You know her?" I asked. The shouting inside me had died down, but I was still bruising for a fight. "You talked to her? Tom, how could you talk to someone like that?" I looked him in the eye. What I saw there, the heart scald I saw there, made me forget Mick if just for a moment.

"I talked to her," Tom admitted. He sat down on the coal box and began tracing the lines in the table with his finger. "I asked her how she came to such a place. She said a man forced himself on her one day when she went into town to sell the eggs."

"Do you know what that means?" I asked. "That a man forced himself on her."

"Not exactly," Tom said. I wasn't exactly sure either.

"But she was in trouble. That's what she said — 'in trouble.' And one day her father tied her hand and foot and dumped her into the back of a rented wagon. And he took her to the sisters here in Cork."

My anger was beginning to drain away. I sat down in the chair across from Tom, whose eyes were fixed on the table, not that he could have seen much of it in the fading evening light.

"The sisters made her do laundry every day, sheets for the hospital, and she scrubbed floors, and herself getting bigger every day with the child. They kept her for a year. She had the baby, and they took it, and she just kept washing sheets and scrubbing floors until after a year they gave her the boot. And she was in the street with just the rags on her back and no way to go home to her family, not that they would want her."

I rose, went to the window to see if Mick was out in the yard. He wasn't. "Her name was Polly," I thought. The woman in the window at the kiphouse. The girl at the window. Her name was Polly. Tom had risen too and was pawing through the boxes on the sideboard looking for food. We had dry oatmeal, not much more than that.

"What happened to her," I asked. How did she find Becky, Miss Butler?"

"Becky found her," Tom said, coming to stand beside me at the window. "Becky has a way of finding girls who are down on their luck. She's a good woman, a good Christian."

"I wouldn't be so sure about that," I said.

"Becky found Polly," Tom said. "And she bought her new clothes, beautiful dresses, and shoes. And she fed her, and gave her a chance to earn a living."

"Tom," I said, "do you understand that 'tis wrong to earn a living like that? 'Tis sinful. It means those girls are going to hell."

"And what choice did Polly have?" he said. "That's what she says, 'what choice did I have?'"

"Tommeen," I said. "You have to trust me. You need to stay away from that place. Polly hadn't a choice. You have. We'll find another way to make the money to go to America. Will you promise me you'll not go back?"

"I think I should go find Mick," he said, making his way to the door.

"Tommeen," I said. "Promise me."

He slipped out the door and down the steps.

"Mama," I thought. "Help me. I don't know what to do."

Ten

The way I see it," Tom said after we'd walked together in silence for a block or two, "The way I see it, Mama isn't really dead." For the last couple of days, since our talk about Polly and his not returning to Becky's, Tom had taken to meeting me after work and walking home with me. I suspected he needed some time to talk, some time without Mick's steady stream of comments and challenges.

"I was thinking," he said, "If Mama's in heaven, she's alive. The priest did say she was in heaven." He looked up at me for affirmation. The topic caught me a bit off my guard.

"He did," I said. Actually what he had said was that we would see her there. I knew enough about purgatory to doubt that she had arrived at heaven's gate quite so soon. And as for what she was going through in purgatory, well, that was something I'd rather not think about.

"So that means she's alive."

"Tom," I said. "Mama's dead."

"Well, yes," he replied. "She died. But then she went to heaven. And if she's living in heaven, she can't be dead anymore. You can't live somewhere when you're dead."

I sighed. I couldn't have put words to it then, but I think I suspected then what I know for a fact now, all these many losses later. What I know for a fact now—now that I've lived over and over again through one death after another and out the other side again—what I know is that heaven is a comfort that belongs exclusively to the future. We *will* go to heaven. We *will* see our loved ones again. And I have no doubt that we'll be glad of it when we do. But as for the present, heaven does us very little good. We still live in the "veil of tears" as the Fathers say. Heaven does us little good as we stand ankle-deep in the dust of this world. It does us little good when we're trying to scratch out a living alone, without parents and family. They call it the "hope of heaven," and that's exactly right, for it hangs there just out of reach, close enough to be tempting, but far enough away that it's not sullied by the muck and grief of earthly life. For those of us here on earth, there is little difference between "in heaven" and simply "dead." But I'm not sure I could have put words to that reality back then. And even if I could have, I doubt I could have made Tom understand them.

"The way I see it," Tom said. "It's more like she's on a long trip. Like a trip to America only she can't write us or come back on a boat."

We passed over the bridge and into Barrack Street. The air was saturated with a cool drizzle, and I was going to be glad to be out of it. I wondered if it rained so much in America. I knew Minnesota was cold, but I hoped it would be drier than Cork. No cold went right through you as easily as damp cold.

"It doesn't rain in heaven, you know," Tom said as though he could see into my mind. "That's what the brothers said. They said that in heaven God provides all our needs, so we don't need rain for crops and to keep the rivers flowing."

"I'm glad of it," I said. We walked together in silence for a while. "Tom," I finally said, "Can you picture Mama's face? Can you see it if you close your eyes?"

"Sometimes I can't," he said. "But sometimes I'll think of something we did together, like the time she fell asleep on the front stoop one Sunday afternoon. And Mick and I came home and there she was sleeping propped up against the door jam, with the sweetest smile on her face. And we just stood there and looked. It was like looking into the face of an angel. And then she felt us looking and she woke up all flustered. When I close my eyes, I can still see that. I think that's the way she looks now in heaven. Like she did that day when she was asleep."

I looked over at him. He looked back. The expression on his face was that of a boy who had caught a glimpse through the gates of heaven. I remember thinking that years from now, should we ever part, I could think back to this day and see his face like that burned into the very walls of my mind.

* * *

The boys stood leaning against the wall at the entrance to our lane. There was quite a clutch of them, ten at least, maybe twelve. The oldest members of the gang looked to be around seventeen. They wore black shirts and trousers and black caps pulled to a tight peak. The youngest were little older than Tom. They wore the ever-present uniform of the lanes, short trousers with dirty bare legs and tattered jackets the one color with the dirty cobblestones.

"Don't look at them," I whispered to Tom.

"Is The Stick home?" one of them said as we walked by. He was a couple years older than me and was wearing a nearly new black gansey buttoned all the way from chest to neck. My eyes were on the cobblestones, and I didn't realize at first that he was talking to me. He broke rank and trotted out in front of me, blocking my path.

"Is The Stick home?" he repeated, one hand on the side of the gate, the other crammed into the pocket of his trousers.

"I'm sure I wouldn't know anyone named The Stick," I replied.

"Micky. Mick the Stick," the boy said. "Your brother. Is he home?"

"No," I said, remembering that that was what the doorman at the kiphouse had called Mick as well. Mick the Stick. That was another thing he and I would have to talk about.

"Oh, well, thank you then," the boy said, removing his hand from the gate and tipping his hat ever so slightly. He didn't move, though. Rather he just replaced the hand and stood there, a menacing grin on his face.

"I'd like to pass," I said.

"Where are my manners?" the boy replied. He stepped the slightest fraction of an inch to the side. Tom's fist balled up, and he took as step forward. The boy's shoulders tightened visibly.

"Come on, Tom," I said, taking him by the hand and elbowing my way into the tight space between the boy and the wall. He gave way and laughed. I hustled Tom and myself down the lane to a chorus of forced laughter coming from just beyond the gate.

* * *

"The Stick?" I said as we made our way into the yard. Tom shrugged. "Do you know those boys?" I asked.

"I've seen them," Tom said. "Don't know them. Do we have food?"

"Potatoes," I said. "Bread. Does Mick know them?"

"They know Mick," Tom said. "Obviously."

"Wait upstairs," I said. "I'll put the potatoes on in a minute or two." Tom trotted up the stairs, lured by the promise of bread. I crossed the yard for the Sullivan's house. The upper half of the door was open and I called in: "God bless all here."

"Clare," Mrs. Sullivan said. "Come in. Come in. Would you care to take some tea?" She had been cutting carrots and dried her hands on her apron.

"I can't stay long," I said. "If I do, Tom will be eating our whole supper single-handedly." She laughed.

"Then I assume this isn't a social call," she said, motioning at one of the chairs pushed under the table. I pulled it out and sat.

"Do you know the boys at the end of the lane?" I asked.

"What boys would those be?" she said.

"A power of boys, about ten of them I'd guess, dressed in black." I let her draw her own conclusion. It was the same as mine.

"Street gang," she said.

I nodded. "I think so."

"At the end of the lane, you say?"

I nodded. She sighed. "John will be home soon. And our Roddy. I'll go across the way and talk to Nora. She can send her Tom over when he's finished work, and maybe Mary's Sean, too. I think we can persuade them to leave."

"They asked for Mick," I said quietly.

"The animal gang?" she said.

I nodded. "'Mick the Stick', they said."

She sighed again. "I worry about Wally," she said. "But he knows his father would thrash him raw if he so much as talked to a gang. But Mick." She paused. "He's always been headstrong. Your mother used to tell me stories." She shook her head. "Do you want Mr. Sullivan to talk to Mick?"

"I would be grateful," I said, rising to leave.

"Clare," she said to me, "do you have supper?"

"Oh, yes," I said. "Bread *and* potatoes. If Tom didn't eat them all raw already." She laughed.

"Boys are a blessing, aren't they?" she said, a tired look in her eye.

"And I'm twice blessed," I said. "God help me."

* * *

"Look what I have," Tom said as soon as I came through the door. "It's written by a man named Father Byrne." He showed me the spine of the book he was reading at the table amidst an ample scattering of breadcrumbs. "*Irish*

Emigration to the United States."

"Where did you get it?" I hung my shawl on the coat peg by the door, straightened my hair, and brushed down the front of my skirt. It was Mama's routine. Every time she came home, she did the same thing—shawl, hair, skirt. Some time in the last week or so, I had picked up the habit quite without thinking about it. It was a good habit. I liked it. I'd keep it.

Tom flipped over to one of the first pages of the book. "Look here," he said. "'Approbatio Ordinis. Imprimatur.' That means the Church approves of it. It should be a good guide."

"Did you find it at the library then?" I piled together a small pile of light turf and lit it. Since agreeing to stay away from Becky Butler's, Tom had been spending his afternoons after school in the new Carnegie free library just down the street. He'd come home each day with a fact about America to share. I'd stopped worrying quite so much about him, not that I had much worry left after I finished spending it all on Mick.

"I bought it down on Paddy's Market," Tom said, closing the book and gathering it to his chest. "But before you say anything, hear me out."

"How much did you spend?" I reached for the biscuit tin and popped the lid. A couple of coppers rested at the bottom. "How could you?" I snapped.

"Hear me out."

"How much?"

"Three pence," Tom said. "Three pence each."

"How many did you buy?" I grabbed for the book, but Tom continued to hug in close.

"Only the two, well, three if you count the atlas. We need them, Clare. We haven't the least notion what America is going to be like. These books will tell us."

"We don't have to know what America is like. Uncle Ronan knows what it's like. We'll live with him once we get to Minnesota."

"Look," Tom said, stepping to the far side of the table. "Maps. We need a map to find our way to Minnesota."

"Get a good look at your precious map now, for you'll be selling it tomorrow on the quay." I dove across the table and snatched the book. I caught a bit of the cover, but Tom grabbed it away.

"Be reasonable," Tom said.

"Reasonable?" I said. "Here's reasonable. I spent ten hours today standing in a great room amidst so much dust I nearly had to chew my air before I could breathe it. My feet ache. My legs ache. And my shoulders feel like I'm carrying fifty stone of iron beneath my skin. I shook out dozens, hundreds, of the devil's own sacks today, carrying that ache with me for every one of them. And for that they give me nine and six a week. It's no great shakes, but it gets us one step closer to America. I carry the ache gladly for I know we'll have a better life for it."

Tom stood, rooted in place, his eyes on the book in his hands resting on the table.

"Is that book worth three, nearly four hours of work? Is it worth what that work takes out of me? Is it worth the chance that we may never be able to leave because we haven't the money?"

"It's not that bad," Tom said, looking up not quite in my eyes, but roughly at my throat. "You're making it sound worse than it is."

"You stand on a bare board floor breathing naught but barley dust for days on end and then tell me how bad it is."

Tom sat down heavily on the coal box.

I added a block of turf to the fire and set about peeling a few potatoes. My hands were shaking.

"Where's Mick," I asked. "Do you know? Did he say where he was going?"

"He said he'd be with his mates up the lane. He'll be back presently."

"With his mates," I said. "Hmmph. I'd hold he's off at Becky's again. Becky's or worse. Are you sure you don't know anything more about those boys at the gate?" Tom shook his head.

I dipped water from the bucket into the cooking pot, added the potatoes, and hung it over the fire. Tom still sat atop the coal box hugging the book. I pulled the chair over by the fire and sat heavily. By contrast to the boys at the end of the lane, Tom with his stack of books seemed positively angelic. By contrast to Mick, he was no trouble at all. I supposed there were worse vices than second-hand books.

"Nine pence," I said shaking my head. "And you didn't ask me first. Can you take them back?" He shook his head. I sighed. "I suppose the damage is done. Since you spent our money on them already, tell me about those books. Do they say how much a train ticket to St. Paul will cost us?"

"It doesn't say anything about St. Paul," he said. "But it does say one to Chicago is ten dollars."

"How much is that?"

"I'm not quite sure," he said.

"And how far is Chicago from St. Paul?"

"About four hundred miles." I looked up at him in disbelief. "Too far to walk," he added.

"I should say," I said.

"We'll probably need forty or fifty dollars at least, then," I said. "Maybe more if we have to hire a cart from Chicago. Are you sure it doesn't say how much a dollar is."

"It does, I'm sure," Tom replied. "I just didn't read it though yet."

"Well then do so," I said. "Tell me what you learn. We need to know how much to save. I'll be blessed if I'm to spend one day more than I have to in that factory."

"You'll not sell the books, then?"

"Not just yet. We'll sell them just before we leave if we need the money."

"That's reasonable," Tom said.

"I'm glad you approve," I replied.

* * *

Mick came home that evening with a split knuckle. It wasn't much, a scratch only, but surrounded by puffy red skin fast turning purple. He wouldn't tell me what happened. He wouldn't tell me who he was with when it happened. He simply sat bent over his supper, silently ignoring my every question. I was torn between worry and bubbling rage. If I thought I could, I'd have beaten Mick silly for the trouble he was causing me. But I had the feeling that if I tried, he might walk out the door never to return. I was losing him.

That evening, I walked across the yard to the Sullivan's house and returned with Mr. Sullivan. It was admitting defeat to do so, but I knew right down to my bones that I could make no more of an impression on Mick. I'd done as much as I could. What he needed was a man, someone a good deal larger than he was, to show him right from wrong.

"It sounds as though you need a good talking to, Mick Keane," Mr. Sullivan said as I led him through the door to our room that evening. "Those black-shirted ruffians out at the gate said they were waiting for you. We don't want those kind in our neighborhood."

"I didn't . . . ," Mick interjected, but Mr. Sullivan cut him off.

"I didn't ask for you to speak now, did I?" Mick shook his head. "We chased them off like a no-good pack of dogs, and that's what they are. But you, you're better than that."

Mick stood, his hands forced in his pockets and his jaw tight. His eyes were fixed out the window, not that there was anything out there to see. He was stonewalling Mr. Sullivan just as he had me.

"You've been causing your sister no end of grief. That's no way for a man to act. A man should respect his sisters, protect them, cherish them." Mick continued to stare out the window.

"Do you understand me?" Mr. Sullivan asked, moving to stand between Mick and whatever he was looking at. Mick shifted his gaze to the door.

"Clare," Mr. Sullivan said with a sigh. "Why don't you and Tom go down to our house? Mrs. Sullivan bought some cocoa this afternoon, and I do believe she had a wee bit extra. It looks like Mick and I need to talk man-to-man."

By the time I'd thanked Mr. Sullivan, Tom was already halfway out the door. It had been quite some time since we'd been able to afford cocoa. He bounded down the stairs. I moved more slowly, straining to hear what was taking place in our room. One floor down, I no longer had to strain. Mick's cries of pain bounced off the walls.

When I got back home he was already in bed, asleep, backside up.

* * *

I have noticed in my years on this earth that sometimes, on rare occasions, life will sneak up on you from behind, clubbing you into senselessness before you know what happened. But most of the time it comes at you straight on, slowly enough that you can plainly see that it's your name on the business end of the club it's brandishing.

One evening, a couple of days after Mr. Sullivan's "talk" with Mick, I was hauling my aching shoulders home from the factory. I rounded the corner and made my way up the lane, and there it was: life, club in hand, waiting for me on the doorstep. It took the form of two guards and a stone-faced man in a black suit. Tom walked before one of the guards. The other had Mick by the back of the collar. They were all marching through the yard and up the steps of our tenement.

Without thinking, I turned on my heel and made my way back down the lane. I didn't care what trouble Mick had made for himself, he could bloody well get his own self out of it. Of course, after not many steps I thought better of it. Rather than find my way home directly, I headed across the yard to Mrs.

Sullivan's door. As usual, her door was on the push, left slightly ajar in welcome to visiting neighbors. I gave the top half a tug and called in. The smell of fresh-made stew rolled over me. My stomach growled and gripped down on itself.

"Clareen," Mrs. Sullivan said. "What brings you by?" I explained the situation, the two guards and the gentry man, and Mick and Tom looking like they'd rather be at the bottom of the sea rather than in the heavy hands of the three of them. Mrs. Sullivan's face hardened itself. She patted her hair, brushed down her apron, and strode across the yard with a purposefulness that might make life itself think twice before shaking a fist.

"Are you these boys' mother?" the stone face addressed Mrs. Sullivan as we caught up to them at the top of the stairs. The light was poor, the handrail gone, and several of the steps loose enough to give a body pause. They had apparently been picking their way up slowly.

"Before you go throwing your questions about, shouldn't you be telling me who you are?"

"My name is Desmond. I'm a School Attendance Officer. I report to the magistrate on the state of delinquent minors. Are you these boys' mother?"

"My name is Sarah Sullivan. Delighted to make your acquaintance. Would you tell what it is these boys did that you're mistaking them for delinquent minors?"

"Are you their mother?"

"No, sir, I am not," Mrs. Sullivan replied. "Their mother and their father both are no longer living, God rest them."

"Are you their guardian, then?"

"Well, I suppose that fits as well as anything. Their mother and I were close, and my husband and I watch out for them now that they have no one else."

"Well, you apparently don't watch them very closely. We found them over at Becky Butler's speaking with a known prostitute."

"Mick!" I said.

"We were selling her peanuts," Mick protested. "Is selling peanuts illegal?"

"I told you to stay away from that place," I said. It came out not angrily but like a sigh, like the last whimper of a small wounded animal. It was over. We'd just used our last chance.

"And who would you be?" Desmond asked.

"Clare Keane, sir. I'm their sister."

"And what age are you?"

"Fourteen, sir." He looked me over, a disbelieving look on his face. "Since January," I added.

"So the three of you are orphans, all under age. And you live how? By begging?"

"We do not, sir!" I protested. "I work at the sack factory. I support us. We do not beg."

"Umhmm," Desmond made a note on the pad of paper he carried. "And the boys, what school do they attend?"

"The Christian Brothers' school, sir," Mick offered. "At Sullivan's Quay. Tom and I both are students at the Brothers'."

"And if I check with the headmaster at that school, would I find that you both are students in good standing?"

"I am," Tom replied. I had no doubt that he was. Mick on the other hand was silent. Finally he spoke up, "I am too, sir." He said it quite without conviction. I wondered how much he'd been bunking off lately.

"We'll see," Desmond replied. "I believe I've heard enough. You three will come with me. You'll stay at the station house tonight. I'll make my recommendation to the magistrate in the morning."

"You'll not send us to gaol, will you?" Tom said.

"An industrial school, actually," Desmond replied.

"I don't want to go," Mick said.

"And do you think you have any say in the matter?" Desmond asked. "The law is clear. You may not live alone. You may not beg in the streets or in public buildings. You may not associate with known prostitutes. You must attend school."

Mick collapsed into a chair, hanging his head. "We don't beg," he muttered.

"On your feet, Mick," I said. "Have you no manners?"

"'Tis not so bad, Mick," Tom offered. "They'll feed us, give us a roof over our head." The corners of his eyes were filling with tears.

"The industrial school will educate you," Desmond added, "teach you a trade. We've come a long way from the old orphanages and reform schools."

"Mr. Desmond," Mrs. Sullivan finally spoke. "I understand you have your duty. And I think 'tis a generous, Christian thing you taking in children who have nobody, and feeding them, and clothing them, and teaching them a trade. But these children have family in America. Their uncle will be sending for them directly."

Taking her lead, I walked across the room to the biscuit tin and pulled from it Uncle Ronan's telegram. I smoothed it open and handed it to Mr. Desmond. He tipped it to the light from the front window and read it quickly.

"This telegram is six weeks old," he said. "He didn't wire the money yet?"

"He didn't," I said. "Not yet. But we expect to hear from him any day."

"You can wait to hear from him in the industrial school, then," Desmond made another note in his pad, handed me the telegram, closed his pad and placed it in his inside jacket pocket. It was evident he considered the matter finished.

"Mr. Desmond," Mrs. Sullivan said, shifting ever so slightly to block the door. "Perhaps we could discuss another option?"

Desmond crossed his arms over his chest. "Minor children cannot be allowed to live alone," he said.

"Did I say alone?" Mrs. Sullivan asked. "They can live with me until they hear from their uncle. It would save you some paperwork, now wouldn't it? There's no sense to their entering an industrial school when they may well hear from their uncle tomorrow."

"You live nearby?" Desmond said.

"Just across the yard," Mrs. Sullivan nodded in the general direction.

"Show me," Desmond said.

"Since you'll be asking so politely, how could I refuse?" Mrs. Sullivan replied. "Stay here," she said to the boys and me, and strode out the door, Desmond and the guards in tow.

* * *

"Maybe Mrs. Sullivan can talk them into letting us stay here," Tom said.

"You aren't going to school," I said, fixing my sights on Mick. "Do you want to tell me why?"

"We should sneak out," Mick said, "while they're not looking. We can find someplace else to live, and by the time the catch up to us, we'll be in America." He rose and looked out the door.

"Sit yourself," I said. Mick walked back into the room and slumped back into the chair again.

"But if Mrs. Sullivan can't persuade them, we'll be in that industrial school in the shake of a lamb's tail."

"Just sit," I said. Suddenly I felt tired, tired of the factory, tired of trying to raise Mick, tired of being an adult, tired of being tired. I almost hoped Mr. Desmond would pick us up and drag us against our will to the industrial school, where someone would feed us, and watch over us, and where someone else could lock horns with Mick for a change. I laid my head on the table, and aching to be somewhere else, I drifted off thinking about being a girl again.

* * *

"Come on now," Mrs. Sullivan was shaking my shoulder gently. "Rouse up now. He's gone."

I blinked my eyes open. "We're not going to the industrial school?"

"No, not just yet," Mrs. Sullivan said taking me gently under the elbow. "You'll have to go before the magistrate, and he'll decide if they're going to write you a detention order or not. But that won't be for another few weeks."

"We can stay here until then?" I asked.

"No," Mrs. Sullivan said. "You're coming with me,"

"Where?" I asked.

"My house, of course." She held the door open. "Bring the mattress, boys. We're not exactly the Ritz, but I think we can find a corner to put it in.

The Sullivan's house was, of course, not much larger than ours. None of the houses on the lane were much more than a way to keep the rain off one's head. The Sullivan house, was, however, unique on the lane. In old days, the house we lived in had been a manor house. After it had fallen apart too much for respectable people to live in anymore, the landlord had come in, put in walls, torn out walls, and made it into a hive of single rooms, each occupied by a family. The Sullivan house, back in respectable times, had been the stable for that manor house. It was a small, square, freestanding building. When the Sullivan's moved in, it had been cold and drafty, with a dirt floor, and windows that leaked chill like all the other windows in the tenement. Mrs. Sullivan continually hounded the landlord to fix things—the windows, the roof, the floor. He didn't of course. If a repair would take more than a single nail, you could always count on our landlord to ignore it. But Mrs. Sullivan's complaining did have an effect. The landlord finally offered to sell her their house.

That was an offer too good to pass up. Mrs. Sullivan dug first into the didley, then the dead money, then the stash she kept hidden from her husband behind a chimney brick. She pawned nearly everything they owned—the sideboard, the table, the bed frame itself. Then she came round her sisters to do the same. Together they scraped together nearly all they needed for the house. So Mrs.

Sullivan went to the local Jewmen—that's what the moneylenders were called in that day whether they were Jewish or not—and they lent her the rest at five shilling to the pound. The family had to live mighty closely for the next few years to pay that back. But in the end the Sullivans became the first on the lane to own their own house.

When Roddy started working, Mr. Sullivan put in a wood floor. When Angela started doing for some rich people in the evenings after school, Mrs. Sullivan made lace curtains. They added a flower box to the window and painted the walls. The windows still leaked, and keeping the roof patched was still like holding back the waves of the sea. But the tiny one-room house was theirs. That was the main difference between the Sullivan house and ours. The other crucial difference was that while our single room was crowded with three people, theirs was crowded with seven, soon to be ten.

"A thousand welcomes," Mrs. Sullivan said, leading us through the door. "Stand that mattress against the wall there beside the trunk," Mick and Tom wrestled it around the edge of the table and half propped, half piled it into the place where Mrs. Sullivan pointed. Two girls, both a few years older than I, sat near the fire. They watched us with eyes narrowed. I matched them glare for glare, and soon they turned back to fire, poking spuds with the poker and stirring whatever was in the pot.

"Angela, make yourself useful, now. Go on and find Kevin and Wally. Your father and Roddy will be home presently, and they'll not take kindly to waiting for their supper." The younger of the two girls rose reluctantly and headed out the door.

"Clare, you can put out the plates and glasses. Mick, you and Tom will need to go fetch your chairs. We'll be needing them this evening. The rest of your things we have until Saturday to tend to."

I went to the shelves. Nine plates and nine glasses. I spread them out over the table. Nine forks, nine spoons and four knives. I spread them around as well. We were one short of everything. The boys could share.

The door opened. I turned, expecting to see Mick and Tom come in with the chairs. Instead, two tall men, covered head to toe with coal dust stood shoulder to shoulder in the entryway.

"Give us a kiss, then, Sarah," the older of the two said. I recognized Mr. Sullivan from his grin, the only thing that wasn't covered with soot.

"Go on with ya," Mrs. Sullivan said, obvious affection in her eyes. "And why would I want to kiss such a ghastly mess?" Her apron wrapped around her hand, she grasped one of the pots hanging over the fire, poured hot water into a metal washing vat, and handed it and a cake of black soap out the door. Mr. Sullivan and Roddy handed in their jackets, which Mrs. Sullivan hung on nails pounded into the wall. The two appeared a few minutes later, their faces and hands scrubbed to a pale grey.

Mr. Sullivan sat at the head of the table, snapping open an obviously thumbed-through edition of the *Evening Echo*. Mrs. Sullivan bent over him to give him a quick kiss. Just then Tom and Mick came through the door with our two chairs followed by Angela, Kevin and Wally.

"Guests?" Mr. Sullivan said.

"I've been hoping to talk with you about that," Mrs. Sullivan replied. "Just put those there," she said to Mick, motioning to the nearest corner of the table. Kevin and Wally grasped the two ends of the trunk by the wall and hauled it with a loud creak to the table.

"Wash up," Mrs. Sullivan said, and Kevin and Wally quickly trotted out the door. "You, too," she said looking at the boys and me. We followed the Sullivan boys out the door.

"Hey, Fingers," Wally said to Tom. "I saw the guard at your house. So they've finally brightened themselves and are going to haul your scrawny arse off to gaol."

"I'll give my regards to your sister while I'm there," Tom replied.

Wally shoulder barged Kevin, and the younger boy tripped into Tom's path.

"Hey," said Kevin. "What did I do?"

Mick reached down a hand, and Kevin pulled himself up. "Let me explain about your big brother," Mick said. "He doesn't think before he pushes people about. A small blame to him. Thinking hurts that wee bit of a brain of his too much. They don't call him Brick Wally for nothing, you know."

"They call me that because I could find old bricks to sell better than anyone else in the city," Wally boasted.

"Thick as a brick," Mick said to Kevin. "Thick as a brick and he doesn't know it himself."

"Fine talk from a lad who slept through most of the last year of school."

"Fine talk about my own brother," echoed Kevin. He tried to jostle Mick but kept merely bouncing off.

"If the bluebottles aren't all over me this summer," Mick said, flicking at Kevin like he would an insect buzzing around him.

I trotted out ahead of the pack toward the pump. I always amazed me how boys could talk for hours, doing little more than stringing insults together one after another like beads on a string. By the time the boys shoved and wrestled their way to the pump, Kevin had a scraped knee, and I was already on my way back.

* * *

The soup was watered, no doubt about that. But it was good soup, filled with potatoes and carrots, scraps of this and that, and juicy cuts of pigs cheek. Mrs. Sullivan served Mr. Sullivan and Roddy first, then me. "Working folk first," she said finally ladling the rest of the soup into the remaining bowls.

Mr. Sullivan crossed himself, and we all followed suit, bowed our head for the blessing. At the "Amen," Roddy dived on his food like a wolf on a fresh kill. Mr. Sullivan reached a long grey arm in front of me and snatched up the mustard.

"Nothing like a day's work to make any meal a feast," he said, putting a large glob on the edge of his plate.

"And is this just 'any meal' you're eating then?" Mrs. Sullivan replied. "Why tomorrow I'll save myself the trouble. You can eat dry bread and see how you like it."

"But Sarah," Mr. Sullivan said, a twinkle in his eye, "didn't I just call this fine fare a feast?"

"Hmpphh," Mrs. Sullivan, smiling a quiet, familiar smile at him. "As fast as you eat, a feast could be in one end out you and out the other before you'd had the chance to wish it a good evening."

Mr. Sullivan laughed. He put a finger delicately into the mustard and smeared a little bit of it behind his ear.

"Tooth still bothering you, then?" Mrs. Sullivan asked.

"Good evening," Mr. Sullivan said, addressing himself to his soup. "Good evening." He addressed his bread before taking a bit. "And a good evening to you, too, my fine wife."

"Good evening, yourself, John Sullivan. You heard me. Is your tooth still bothering you?"

"And why shouldn't it? 'Tis rotten to the root."

"You should have old Mr. Carey pull that for you." Mrs. Sullivan sliced a cut of soda bread and handed to me. I was savoring a piece of carrot and only noticed the bread when Mrs. Sullivan wagged it a bit under my nose.

"Half a crown he wants to pull it," Mr. Sullivan said. "And what does he do? He puts a knee in your chest and a huge forceps in your mouth and nearly pulls your head right off your shoulders. No, thank you, ma'am. I'll wait until it falls out."

"I heard," Roddy said, his mouth half full of potato, "I heard that John Murphy's brother Jimmy went to Mr. Carey to have a tooth pulled." He swallowed and washed the potato down with a huge swig of tea. "Mr. Carey grabs onto the rotten tooth, and he tugs for all he's worth, and the tooth just breaks off right in Jimmy's head. And Mr. Carey has to go digging around for the bottom of it, and he gets most of it, but some of it is still there in Jimmy's jaw. And Jimmy goes back to work the next day, but by the end of the shift he's feeling poorly. By the next morning his whole head is green, and he couldn't get up to go to work if it meant his life. And his wife goes to the chemist's and gets Mr. Carey to give her something for Jimmy and his pain. But by the time she gets back, poor Jimmy is stretched out on the bed, dead as can be, his mouth full of green pus, and him no more than twenty-five years old. That's what I heard," he said, stuffing another piece of potato into his mouth.

"Thank you, Roddy," Mrs. Sullivan said dryly. "There's nothing like a good story with one's stew." Roddy grinned broadly, showing little pieces of carrot and bread in his teeth. Mrs. Sullivan shook her head.

"I say if it's paining you, you should go have it pulled," she said.

"Or I could spend the half crown down at the pub, get into a set-to, and maybe someone will knock it out for me."

"So you'll go back on your pledge for the sake of tooth?" Mrs. Sullivan said. "That's not like you, John Sullivan."

"Ah, but did I say I'd be spending the half crown on myself?" Mr. Sullivan answered.

Tom burst out laughing, spewing tea all over his plate. "Tom!" I said. He wiped his mouth on his sleeve, still laughing.

"It came out his nose," Kevin cried pointing. Jane rolled her eyes. Mick poked Tom in the ribs and shushed him, but Mick too had caught the laugh and was turning bright red holding it behind his closed teeth.

"Do it again," Kevin said. "Da, say something else funny." Jane rolled her eyes again.

"See what you started, John," Mrs. Sullivan said, a barely suppressed grin on her own face. "I don't know why I keep you."

* * *

The boys were out jostling about in the lane. Angela and Jane were washing dishes in the washing vat atop the table. I moved to help them, but they held me off with a look. I was about to go outside to take my chances with the boys, when Mrs. Sullivan laid a hand on my shoulder.

"You can help me, Clareen," she said. She pulled a couple of chairs up to the fire, poking Angela in the behind to get her to make room. From beneath the bed she pulled a great bundle, all wrapped in an old sheet. She opened it, and out fell dresses, trousers, shirts, shawls, gloves—more clothes than I had owned in my entire life together.

"Are these all yours?" I asked in shock and amazement, then thought better of it. "I'm sorry," I said. "But I've never seen such a thing."

"My tugger just brought them," Mrs. Sullivan said, beginning to sort the garments into piles. Then I understood. I remembered Mama talking about how the last few years Mrs. Sullivan had done quite well for herself selling in the market.

"And you'll be selling them at the quay," I said. Mrs. Sullivan nodded. "Saturday," she said. "Things always sell better after payday."

Now perhaps I should explain that in those days, in the tenements, we didn't have money for new clothes. The well-to-do could go to the shops and buy a new dress or a new pair of trousers when they needed them. But we had to make due with second-hand. So tuggers, young women in tattered skirts mostly, would make the rounds in the respectable neighborhoods asking for donations of clothes for the poor. The rich would give them whatever things they no longer had use for, and the tuggers would pile it up in the wicker carts and tug it back to the city. There they would meet up with their dealers and sell them the booty. The dealers would wash and mend the garments and bring them to the market. There they would pile them high on great tables. "Rag fairs," the respectable people would call them. But for us it was our haberdashery. Sometimes you could find quite the bargain at these rag fairs.

"All rags and jags this time," Mrs. Sullivan commented, sifting through the pile. "I told Margaret those north-side folk got a hard drop in them, every one. Wouldn't ask a starving man if he had a mouth on him." She handed me a pair of boys' boots, and reached into a basket by the fire for a tin of blacking.

"When Mr. Sullivan and I were first married, I used to go abroad into the country to pick cabbages and such. Cabbage money paid for part of this house. But it was a long walk, and after I had Roddy and Jane, I had to bundle them up every day and take them with me. And, of course, the money only came in so long as the cabbages did. So Mary, Mary Doolan, my sister's husband's sister, and I decided to take over her mother's table at the Coal Quay. Her daughter— Mary's daughter Margaret—is my tugger, and Mary and I take turns minding the table. How are the insoles on those boots?" I put a hand inside. They were missing and I said so.

"No mind," she said. "I can get a Player's carton from Connor. The only thing cigarettes are good for if you ask me." She picked up her sewing kit, and bit off a length of cotton. "Can you thread this?" she asked, handing me the needle. "I've picked cabbages. I've cleaned houses. I've dealt clothing. I've scrubbed toilets. I've worked at your sack factory itself. I have to say none of it was as good a job as dealing clothes."

I looked up from the needle and cotton. "You worked at the sack factory?"

"I did," she said. "When I was about your age. Things were," she paused, "different then."

"My grandmother worked at a sack factory," I said. Mama always said that's why she died of the consumption."

I handed Mrs. Sullivan the threaded needle, and she set to work on a pair of trousers, patching the knees with some corduroy from another pair beyond fixing.

"The factory won't give you consumption," she said. "But if you have consumption already, the factory can give you the devil's own time of it." Mrs. Sullivan was never short on words, but it was clear she didn't want to talk about the sack factory. Or maybe she did, but couldn't.

Around my ankles I felt something soft and nudging. I looked down to see a grey cat winding its way around and around my leg.

"Shoo," Mrs. Sullivan said to the cat. "Don't you go bothering Clare when she's working. A perfect nuisance they are," she said. "But nothing is better for the rats," she added, looking up at me. Plenty of people back then didn't much like cats, but I had no real opinion one way or the other, never having had much to do with them myself.

The lean little creature left off its journey around my leg and hopped up on Mrs. Sullivan's lap. It tested the softness of the trousers with its paws and then unceremoniously dropped itself into a furry pile. Mrs. Sullivan smiled, scratched it about the ears, and let it sit. "I'm no great lover of cats, myself," she said, gently stroking the fur. "But I can't abide rats."

I held the boot I was working on up to catch the light of the paraffin lamp, and continued to work the blacking into the toe. "How long did you work at the sack factory?" I asked.

"Two years," she said briefly. The awkward silence fell again. I decided to drop the matter, held the boot up again, then set it down to pick up its mate. The cat began to purr.

"It wasn't so much the factory," Mrs. Sullivan said after a bit. "It was the men who worked there. In those days, if you worked in a factory, your employer owned you, or so it seemed. Times were hard and people did what they had to do to keep food on the table." She fell silent again. Wally came bursting through the door.

"Do you have an old sock in your bundle that we could take for a football?" he asked.

"You outgrew the word 'please,' did you?" Mrs. Sullivan replied.

"May we please have an old sock from your bundle?" Wally replied.

"No you may not," she said. "Now get on with you. Get out of our hair."

Wally's shoulders fell. He spun on his heel and left. Angela and Jane had finished the dishes and followed him out into the night air.

"Clare," Mrs. Sullivan said looking up from her stitching, "at the sack factory, if any of the men ask you to do something . . . " She paused. "You're there to sort and mend sacks, no more. If any of the men want you to do anything else, you don't have to." She looked deep into the fire, as though she was trying to make out some pattern, some memory held in the glowing coals. "If they want you to do something you know you shouldn't, you walk away. We'll find you some other way of earning the money for America."

I looked up at her. "I don't understand," I said.

"That's fine," she said. "If the time comes, you will. If the time comes, you remember what I said, won't you?"

"I will," I replied.

<h1 style="text-align:center">Eleven</h1>

I don't believe I had ever seen tonsils quite that size and color before. Mrs. Sullivan held Jane's mirror for me, and in the light from the front window, I peered down my own throat. They were huge, nearly meeting each other halfway, and they were spotted all over with tiny white spots. They say the sack factory doesn't give you consumption or even the croup. But in the three weeks I'd worked there, I was hard set to remember a time when my throat hadn't ached. The last few days had been worse than ever.

"Lay yourself down, Clare," Mrs. Sullivan said. She nodded at Jane and Angela's bed. I hesitated, looked over at Jane, who was peeling potatoes at the table. Her eyes narrowed.

"I'll do," I said, and sat in one of the chairs pulled along the fire.

"Nonsense," Mrs. Sullivan said. "You have fever on you. Lay yourself down, now. Maybe you can get a few minutes sleep before supper." Jane whacked into a potato at the table. The knife went all the way through and hit the table. She pushed her chair away from the table with a loud creak and went over to the cupboard for a carrot.

"Jane," Mrs. Sullivan scolded, "can't you be more quiet? Clare won't be getting any rest with you banging around like a bird in a box." Jane shot me another look and decapitated the carrot with such force that the greens went bouncing off the table and onto the floor.

"I think I just need some air," I said. "'Tis a fine evening." Actually it was a chilly, grey evening, but not nearly so chilly as it was before the fire with Jane. I rose from the chair. The room suddenly went dark. My head swam. I sat again, heavily.

"That's it," Mrs. Sullivan said. "You have fever. Get to bed with you." She put a hand beneath my elbow and brought me to a standing position. I walked gingerly to the bed and sat. My throat felt like raw meat. Raw meat covered with a layer or two of barley dust. I laid myself back on the mattress—a straw mattress, like we all had, but one with fine thick ticking and a flour-sack sheet that was long enough to tuck in at the edges. It may have been the bed, or it may just have been my own exhaustion, but I marveled at how comfortably Jane and Angela slept.

"It looks like only a touch of the quinsy at the moment," Mrs. Sullivan said, but if we don't catch it now, it could be much worse. You're lucky the nettles are growing." She dug under her bed for a handful of rags and went into the yard looking for Kevin.

"I'll thank you to get out of my bed," Jane said when Mrs. Sullivan was out of earshot. I ignored her. "Did you hear me?" she said. "I said, get out of my bed.

I'll not have you get it covered in your dust and filth."

"I don't take orders from you," I said. "It's your mother and father's house, and I'll take my orders from them, if you don't mind."

"Ah, but don't you see? I do mind," Jane replied. "I mind a great deal."

"What ever did I do to you?" I said, sitting up again on the edge of the bed. "I pay my way around here. I work hard. I help your mother with her mending, with the cleaning. You yourself have less work since I came here."

"You think you have her fooled, don't you," Jane said. "She thinks you're holy Saint Clare, or some such thing the way she fawns over you. Well you don't fool me. You're only a filthy laner like the rest of us. And a stupid, uneducated one at that. I don't want you in my bed."

I lay back down and turned to the wall. The movement shook loose some of the dust in my throat and I began to cough.

"That's disgusting," Jane said. "You're disgusting. And so are your brothers. We should never have taken you in. I wish that gentry man had hauled the three of you off to that industrial school where you belong." I continued to ignore her. "Where you belong with all the other orphans."

Orphans. I hated the word. I hated all it reminded me of. The hatred on me must have been obvious. "Orphan," Jane spat the word out, baiting me with it. "Orphan."

I rolled over and sat up yet again, glaring at her. "I am," I said. "And please God you never know for yourself just what that word means. For as much as you are a thorn in my side, Jane Sullivan, I'd not wish what I went through these three months on my worst enemy." I lay down again, then turned my back so she couldn't see what was on my face.

"If you leave for America tomorrow it will be too soon for me," she said and set about to her carrot massacre again.

I didn't go to work the next day, nor the day after that. I knew full well it would be a near miracle if I still had a job by the time I was fit for it again. Mrs. Sullivan dosed me with nettle, onion, and sage tea. I slept by day on Jane's bed, by night on the floor with my brothers. I coughed and I barked for days, and I brought up not only the products of a nasty tonsil infection, but also bits of dust and husk. Already it seemed I carried the sack factory not only in my nose and mouth, but also in my chest, my belly. After no better than two months there, the kinks of coughing and the gritty sputum already marked me as a veteran of the factory. We all knew it—the quinsy would come and go, but the cough would stay. For factory workers, the cough always stayed.

* * *

Mrs. Sullivan pulled a jacket from the bundle, a finely made tweed, it was, with the sleeves barely worn and the lapels as crisp as the day they were made. She flipped it inside out, and checked the lining, then held it up by the shoulders. "John," she said. Mr. Sullivan looked up from his paper. "What do you think?"

He surveyed the jacket. "'Twouldn't fit you. 'Twould be a bit tight through the chest parts." He grinned and bobbed his eyebrows.

"You filthy-minded creature, you," Mrs. Sullivan said. "Not for me. For you. For Mass."

"Is it the way you want me stolen on you, or what?" Mr. Sullivan said. "If I were to strut down any one of these streets in such a jacket, sure every woman on the south side would be snatching me away from you."

"Maybe so," Mrs. Sullivan said, "Maybe so. But only if I pinned a five-pound note to the lapel." She stood before him, the jacket in the heel of her fist, arms akimbo. The look in her eyes was a challenge, or an invitation, or something I couldn't quite read.

"Five pounds is it? Show me some credit, woman," Mr. Sullivan exclaimed, dropping his newspaper into his lap for emphasis. "Sure wouldn't I be unlikely to go for less than ten?"

Mrs. Sullivan laughed. She held the jacket up to his chest and surveyed the result. "Not half bad, I dare say. I wouldn't give them more than a lop to take your filthy self off my hands."

Mr. Sullivan wrapped an arm around her waist and drew her close. "And what would you give to keep me?"

"Well now," Mrs. Sullivan said, tucking a lock of is hair behind his ear, "if you'll chase the last of your chicks out into the yard, you and I can do a bit of bargaining."

* * *

We were out of the house, as we were many evenings. Jane and Angela had claimed the stoop of the tenement. They sat with their schoolbooks and their smug attitudes. I decided to wander across the bridge into the center of town. All too often, Cork was a wet and soggy city. But when it dried off, it did have its moments. I positively basked in the long light of a summer's evening.

Jane was right. I was a laner. I had four years of education and a job nobody else would do. I had two changes of clothes, and that only because of my time as a maid, when I needed a special one for work. I lived off potatoes and tea, slept on a straw mattress, lived with more lice and ticks that I cared to think about. But more than that, I was a laner because that's what people saw when they looked at me. When I walked down Patrick Street and looked through the windows, nobody expected me to enter the store and buy. When I walked down Front Douglas Road, everyone knew it was the tradesmen's entrance I'd be heading for. My shawl marked me. The lice and tick bites that dotted my body marked me. My skirt with its frayed hem and patches on patches marked me.

Jane might climb out of the lanes, Angela too. They might get a decent education, learn to speak like respectable folks. Then they might, if they were lucky, marry a tradesman or a shopkeeper. But I was a laner, and nothing short of packing up my life and moving it to another country would ever change that.

The lamplighter walked past on the other side of the street. In his blue serge suit with the city crest over the pocket, he stood out against the rags and jags of the lanes. He carried a long pole with a torch on top. He had it over his shoulder like a rifle, and with military precision, he lit lamp after lamp. Beneath the lamps, the men were already gathering to chat, play cards, sing. The children, with what little supper they were likely to get already in their belly, danced behind him chanting: "Billy with the Lamp/Billy with the light/Billy with his sweetheart out all night."

It was the nightly ritual in the lanes, where life took place in the in between. Between work and sunset. Between the dark walls of the tenements. Between hard days on the docks and in the factories. And in the short time between birth and an untimely death.

Twelve

"M rs. Sullivan, Mrs. Sullivan," a little boy boosted himself up to peer over the bottom half of the front door. His elbows strained through holes in his jacket as he hung by his arm pits over the door. "Mrs. Sullivan, Mama's having her baby. She needs you this minute."

Mrs. Sullivan looked up from the lunch she was packing. I looked up from my mending. It was Saturday, and we would presently be headed for the quay.

"Isn't that just the way?" Mrs. Sullivan said under her breath. She finished wrapping the chunk of bread, dropped it into the basket, and turned to the six-year-old glowing quite red with the effort.

"Stop hanging on that door, Davie," she said. "'Tis on the push. Come in here and talk to me." Davie dropped to the ground, opened the door and entered. He was a fine-boned boy with a chin that looked just a little too small for his face and a head that look just a little too small for his body.

"Where's your father?" she asked.

"Mama sent him to the pub," the boy answered. "She wanted a gill of porter to help with the pains."

"When?" she asked. The boy looked at her puzzled. Davie was a little slow, you see. All the Purcell men—seed, breed, and generation—were a little slow. Everyone in the tenement knew it. "When did your father go to the pub?"

"Just before sunup," Davie said.

"The pub wouldn't be open before sunup," Mrs. Sullivan said, gathering up a stack of newspapers and a large tin vat.

"Maybe just after sunup?" Davie looked at her hopefully.

"I suppose he could be down in the Coal Quay." Then she turned to me and whispered: "Trust Purcell to know every pub in the county with a special license to open at 7:00 in the morning."

"Maybe she sent him at 7:00 in the morning," Davie offered. There was surely nothing wrong with his ears.

"And was I talking to you?" Mrs. Sullivan said. Davie dropped his chin.

"No matter," Mrs. Sullivan replied. "You go down and see if your father is at the pub. Tell him the baby's coming." The boy dashed off into the lane, his bare feet slapping against the stones.

"Purcell will be no use at all, of course," she said to me. "Not fit to mind mice at a crossroads, that man. Show me the scissors from the sewing basket, will you, Clare? Still I figure 'tis partly his fault what his wife is going through. The least he can do is sit on the stoop and worry. Good," she said checking the scissors' edge and adding them to the vat. "And some strips." She tore a couple of strips of fabric from a shirt she was using as patch. "Good."

"Will I come with you, then?" I asked.

"No," she said. "I need you to go next door and find Mary, Mary Doolan, and tell her she will have to mind the table at the quay. Then go find my sister Nora and tell her Maura Purcell is due, and I may be needing her help. Maura had five babies already, none of them easy. You'd think she'd have the hang of it by now, but she doesn't."

"She has difficult births?" I asked, rising to hold the door open.

"'Tis not so much that the births are difficult," Mrs. Sullivan said, lugging the vat into the yard. "'Tis herself that's difficult."

* * *

Mrs. Doolan was on her way to the quay. But Nora was off on the annual trip to the seashore with her husband and the rest of the families from the Beamish brewery, where her husband was a carter. She wouldn't be back until late this evening, long after dark.

I climbed the stairs of our old tenement to give Mrs. Sullivan the news. When I reached the top, my mind on what I was going to tell Mrs. Sullivan, I turned right not left, only out of force of habit, mind you. It wasn't until my nose was already inside the open door of our old room, that I snapped to and realized I was in the wrong place.

The smell of soup wafted out of our old room onto the landing. I glanced about to see an unfamiliar table and chairs, and an unfamiliar baby crawling about in front of the hearth. Other people lived there now, ate there, slept there. People I had never met laid their head at night on the very spot Mama died. I paused for a moment, riveted by the sight of the baby patting its hand into the ashes of the fireplace, each pat sending a tiny cloud of dust into the air. He was a handsome baby, all in all. I would have to stop by sometime to ask his name.

As I stood lost in my thoughts on the landing, a sharp cry rang through the air. The Purcell's door was on the push, but even if it hadn't been, a cry like that would have carried as clear as day through the paper thin walls. The cry was the sound of bloody murder, part pain, part rage.

"Ned Purcell, you worthless scoundrel," the voice said, "if you ever come near me again I'll give you a shirt full of sore bones, by herrings so help me I will." Mrs. Purcell shouted loudly enough that I wouldn't be surprised if everyone in the yard could hear. Everyone knew Mrs. Purcell was a rip, but she was in especially rare form today.

To be honest, Mrs. Purcell hadn't many bad swearing days. Even on a slow day it was grand to listen to her when she was in a rage. She could roll out with a magnificent threat or bloodcurdling curse that could whither the pelt right off you. Yet she could always stop just shy of full blasphemy. It was a rare talent, it was, and everyone on the yard agreed it was a privilege to be cursed by someone so skillful. I paused outside the door, knowing that if I entered I would interrupt her flow.

"Ned Purcell, do you hear me? I'll take the carving knife to your trousers, I will by goats."

Then Mrs. Sullivan's voice: "Just keep walking. Keep walking."

"By all the goats in Kerry, I swore I'd never go through this again." Mrs. Purcell said, more quietly. "After all the trouble last time, I . . . " she paused, the rest of her thought clearly unspoken.

"Well now," Mrs. Sullivan said. "'Tis a bit late to be making that choice, isn't it?"

"And if I say no to him, what will the priest be saying? 'Tis a wife's duty, is what they'll say. And what will they know about it, them in their long black man-skirts and their shiny shoes, never having had to take care of family, never having done a hard day's work in their lives? What do they know? Never trust a man who wears a dress—that's what I say." I pushed the door open a bit, called in.

"Don't be shy," Mrs. Sullivan responded. "Come in here." I entered. "You're alone?" Mrs. Sullivan asked. Mrs. Purcell was red-faced and sweaty, leaning heavily over the table. Mrs. Sullivan was rubbing the small of her back, making small deep circles. "Where's Nora?"

"At the shore," I said.

"With the Beamish families," Mrs. Sullivan said with a grimace. "I forgot completely."

As for me, my eyes were locked on Mrs. Purcell, sweaty and wilted Mrs. Purcell, standing huge, bent over the table in her shift. The look in her eyes—a look of worry, anger, exhaustion—seemed to focus right through the table to something beyond, something unseeable by the rest of us. I watched her, studied her, tried to divine from her eyes, her posture, the single bead of sweat rolling down her cheek, what it was like to be in labor. But I had no way of telling. Here was a woman in labor, standing right before me, but I still had no way of telling.

I looked up and realized that as I had been watching Mrs. Purcell, Mrs. Sullivan had been watching me. She scanned me up and down as though I were one of her used dresses and she was appraising my value. I dropped my eyes.

"Would you like to help me?" she finally asked.

No, I thought. No I don't want to be here. I want to be outside with the men and boys, oblivious for a while longer. But I nodded; I'm not sure why. All I know is that if Mrs. Sullivan had asked for help spring-cleaning hell itself, I would have agreed.

"Good morrow, Mrs. Purcell," I said, with as much confidence as I could muster. She didn't answer but raised herself from the table, paced across the floor in her bare feet, her hands braced against her back in a way that made her full belly cant slightly upward. In the far corner of the room, she reached out to the bed frame and prepared to lower herself onto the lumpy mattress.

"Stand up, Maura," Mrs. Sullivan said. "Keep walking. You don't want the baby to go back to sleep, now do you?"

"'Tis my back," Maura said.

"And you think a lie down is going to help your back?" Mrs. Sullivan said. "It isn't and you know it. Up with you now. The faster the baby falls, the sooner you'll be finished."

"I'm tired of walking," Maura said.

"You'll be far more tired before you're through," Mrs. Sullivan answered. "Besides, we need to spread the newspapers, and we can't do it with you on the bed, now can we?" She handed me a stack of newsprint, then reached to take Maura by the elbow to lift her from the bed. "Take the sheet off. Then spread them nice and thick. Put the sheet over the top of them clean side up," Mrs. Sullivan said. "And if you have any left over, spread them here beside the bed." She motioned with her toe as she led Maura back to the center of the room.

I removed the pile of old coats and dumped them onto the pile of straw and sacking in the corner that served as the second bed. Beneath the coats was an old sheet made from ripped out flour sacks. The side closest to the wall was a dingy yellow. Maura Purcell was obviously no martyr to the washboard. But the side nearest me had passed yellow, passed tan, and was shading into a mature chocolate brown. I picked at the sheet with my thumb and forefinger, lifting it to see if it had a clean side. If it did, I couldn't tell which it was.

Now to be fair, I should say that in those days most people didn't bathe every day. They believed frequent bathing was bad for the back, or brought on the croup, or some such thing. Most bathed on Saturday evening so they would be clean for Mass in the morning. Ned Purcell, a docker who worked at unloading dirty old cargo on the quay, rarely made it to Mass.

I began to spread the newspaper over the old, stained straw mattress. A low growl came from the other side of the room. Maura was bent over the table, her teeth gritted and her face red.

"Just let me have a quick lie down, Sarah," she said. "The pains are murdering hard when I'm standing."

"In a little bit," Mrs. Sullivan replied.

"Then send her off for some porter." She looked up at me. "Only a bit of a gargle."

"You know porter's no good for you at all at a time like this," Mrs. Sullivan replied.

"You're a gallows hard one, you are, Sarah Sullivan. I knew you'd show me no pity. But you," she looked across the room at me, her face flushed and damp, "you wouldn't spare me a bit of comfort, now would you?"

I wasn't sure what to say. "Mrs. Sullivan said," I began.

"Now you leave Clare out of this," Mrs. Sullivan said, taking Maura's elbow again. "Clare, we'll need another two or three buckets of water."

I quickly scattered the rest of the newspapers on the floor beside the bed and almost tripped over myself reaching for the bucket by the hearth. Both Mrs. Sullivan and Maura smiled and laughed. "You needn't run," Mrs. Sullivan said, "only don't dally."

"I won't," I said, finding my way out the door.

"She's terrible young for this, don't you think Sarah?" I heard Maura say quietly as I closed the door behind myself. Mrs. Sullivan's reply was muffled. I pressed my ear to the door to hear it, but it was too late.

* * *

Now you have to understand that in my day, we didn't talk much about such things. That's what they would be called, too: "such things," never "sex" or "reproduction." You would think that living so tightly packed together in a single room, we'd know more than kids today. But the fact is that though brothers and sisters slept side-by-side, back to belly, they would never have seen each other in the all together. In fact, it was considered a sin for brothers and sisters to be too curious about each other. Sure we had seen couples intertwined in the shadows. We had heard their breathing get ragged in their niches in back alleyways or on stairway landings. But with the light from our poor gas lamps we couldn't begin to penetrate those corners. And imagination can only fill in so much.

Sex was simply not spoken of. Most girls didn't know much at all until their wedding night. In fact a girl might not know exactly where babies came from 'til after she was pregnant. I, myself, had a rough idea. I knew pregnancy meant a baby was growing inside the mother. And I knew that birth meant the baby coming out. I knew it involved a fair amount of pain, or at least a fair amount of groans and shouts that sounded like pain. Mrs. Purcell had labored with Davie all through the middle of the night some five or six years ago. I remember lying in bed, listening to the sounds from across the hallway, wondering what they meant. Now that I had the opportunity to find out, I wasn't sure I wanted it.

* * *

I poured the second bucket of water into the kettle and set it to boiling over the fire. The vat on the table already contained cool water. Mrs. Sullivan unpacked her kit—the knife, the scissors, the strips of cloth, and a small jar of something that looked like dried herbs. She set to scrubbing her hands with black soap and a small brush.

"'Tis something my mother taught me," she said. "And her mother taught her, and her mother her. You always greet a new baby with clean hands. The baby will see enough sorrow and filth in his life. He shouldn't have to greet it in his first minute." She motioned at soap, and I joined her at the wash basin.

Mrs. Purcell was lying on her side atop the clean side on the sheet. Mrs. Sullivan walked over to her, and sat on the edge of the bed, which crackled with the sound of newspapers. She laid a hand on Mrs. Purcell's belly, then reached over and began stroking her back again.

"Soon," Mrs. Sullivan said. "The baby's coming fast this time."

"I don't need you to tell me that," Mrs. Purcell replied, reaching back to brush Mrs. Sullivan's hand away.

"Hmphh," Mrs. Sullivan said. "It can come none too soon for me. You aren't the best of company when you're giving birth, Maura Purcell."

"And what woman is?" she replied.

"Some are," said Mrs. Sullivan. "Some are."

"Ppfft." Mrs. Purcell made a dismissive gesture with her hand. "Any woman who thinks childbirth is Sunday afternoon tea with the Lord Mayor of Cork is probably too soft in the head to bring up the child once 'tis born. I'm not here to chin wag. I'm here to push this baby out. Will you be catching, or should I send you home and tell young Clare here to hold out her hands?"

"I *should* go home," Mrs. Sullivan replied. "Then we'll see how you like it." She walked across the room to the table where I sat, and lowered herself with finality into a chair. It was obvious she wasn't going anywhere.

* * *

The sound of boots on the stairway brought me out of my thoughts, the random thoughts and speculations of a mind trying to figure out a puzzle for which it hasn't all the pieces. Davie burst through the door first, then Mr. Purcell.

"Is it here?" Mr. Purcell said. "Did it come yet?" His words were slurred. Davie had obviously found him at the pub.

"And would I be lying on by back with me legs spread from here to Killarney if it came already?" Mrs. Purcell called from her place on the bed.

Davie ran to the bed and jumped up beside his mother, jostling the springs and peering into his mother's face. "I think you should have a boy," he said.

"Purcell," Mrs. Sullivan said. "You best take the boy down to the yard."

"And take your worthless self with you," Maura added. "What were you thinking, bringing the boy up here at a time like this?"

"And what did I do to deserve such abuse?" Ned replied.

"Come stand here at the foot of the bed," Maura said. "Stand right here, and I'll show in a few minutes what you did. For the sixth time in my life, I'll show you what you did, I will Ned Purcell, you . . . "

"Go wait on the stoop," Mrs. Sullivan interrupted, steering him by the elbow. "We'll call you when we have news."

"Grrrr!" Another pain swept over Maura, she clutched at her knees, which doubled up to her chest.

"Mama," Davey said in alarm, laying a hand on his mother's arm.

"Get out of here," Maura said between gritted teeth. "Get out, or by the hole in my shoe I will get up out of this bed, wring the heads off both your necks, and pitch them out the door myself."

"Mama," Davie said as Mrs. Sullivan snatched him off the bed and handed him to his father.

"Aaahh," Maura gave a half scream, half cry as Mrs. Sullivan hustled the men out the door.

"I have every right to be here with my wife," Ned said, clutching at the door jam to steady his sodden legs.

"You have the right to *leave*," Mrs. Sullivan said. "This isn't the place for you. Go down to the stoop and worry like a husband should."

"Aahhh, aahh." Maura's cries had changed. They were more visceral, more urgent. I got up from the table where I had been watching the show and went to her side.

"Get out," Maura cried. "Get out. Get out." I wasn't sure if she was talking to Ned or the baby. I laid a hand on her shoulder. She snatched it up and squeezed so hard I thought the bones would break. "Sarah, get over here," she said.

Mrs. Sullivan placed a hand on Ned's chest and shoved him out the door, closing it with a slam.

"It feels as though my back is about to break," Maura said. Mrs. Sullivan waited for the pains to pass, then lifted Maura's shift to feel her belly. I sat at the head of the bed, my hand still on Maura's shoulder, close to her but out of her sight. I sat there and I looked. I'd seen pregnant women before, of course, but never the belly there in plain view and uncovered. The dome of it was almost too much for me to take in. It was beautiful, but it was also frightening, unreal. My head swam.

"Breathe, Clare," Mrs. Sullivan said. Then addressing herself to Maura, "The baby's facing to the front, I think. It shouldn't be a problem, but your back is going to hurt."

"Going to hurt? And it isn't killing me entirely already?" Maura said. "What can you do about it?"

"What do you want me to do?" Mrs. Sullivan replied. "There's nothing to be done."

"Write that on my tombstone, won't you?" She rolled away from us and stared unseeing at the wall.

* * *

Once the baby started moving, it came quickly. Maura might have disagreed, of course, but to Mrs. Sullivan and I it seemed Maura's labor was moving very quickly. Mrs. Sullivan had shifted Maura so she lay crosswise on the bed, her head to the wall, and her feet on the edge. The pains came like waves on the shore, one after another, pounding down then receding. Maura bore down until her face was red, as red as blood. I have never seen such a color before. It was as through her face was going to pop with the effort of it. She groaned and growled and screamed and cried her way through pain after pain.

"Kneel here," Mrs. Sullivan said, motioning at a place on the bed at Maura's side. Wrap your arm around her knee like this. Then take her foot. Hold her tight. Give her something to push against. I held tight as another pain took her, squeezed her like a large fist.

"Keep pushing, Maura," Mrs. Sullivan said from her place at Maura's feet. "The head's coming. Keep pushing."

I looked down at the foreign landscape. The furry patch between Maura's legs stretched large, the tissues red, the skin straining. It bore no resemblance whatsoever to my own body. Or so I told myself. Maura strained against me. Mrs. Sullivan held her other knee tightly to the bed. I was acutely aware of my own thighs, my own growing tuft of fuzz. Someday I would be the one being held to the bed. It seemed impossible.

"The head's coming," Mrs. Sullivan said. "Don't stop now."

First scalp appeared, then forehead, eyebrows, eyes and nose. The mouth, the chin, the head. The pains eased. Mrs. Sullivan reached for a clout to wipe the baby's head, caressing it gently, then easing it to the side. A slippery goo oozed from the baby's mouth. The baby sputtered, then opened its eyes for the briefest of seconds, looked right at me, and cooed.

"This one's already talking," Mrs. Sullivan said.

"Must be a boy," Maura replied.

They chuckled together. As for me, I barely heard them. I knelt there on the bed, Maura's thigh pressed tightly to my chest, looking with wonder at the tiny bodiless head nestled there between Maura's thighs. That tiny face had looked at me. Its first glimpse of world was of me.

"Oh, no," Maura said. "Here it comes again."

"Push gently," Mrs. Sullivan said. "Push gently for the shoulders."

"Aaaahh," Maura said.

"Not so hard," Mrs. Sullivan said.

"I can't help it," Maura gasped.

"Whistle," Mrs. Sullivan said.

"What in herring's name do you mean, 'whistle'?"

"Blow out, whistle. Don't push, not so hard." Mrs. Sullivan had one hand under the baby's head and another on Maura. "Don't push, blow," she said. "Here come the shoulders. Blow."

"You blow," Maura snapped.

The skin gave way, and the shoulders popped through. The baby landed in Mrs. Sullivan's hands in a tumble of arms and legs. Maura cried out. She neither blew nor whistled.

"A girl," Mrs. Sullivan said, quickly wiping the tiny girl's face.

She was a pinkish blue and the slipperiest thing I ever did see. Trailing between her and her mother was a pale blue grey cord. She sputtered and then let out a great cry.

"Now that's the way," Mrs. Sullivan said, wiping her shoulders and her chest streaked with lines of blood. "That's the way."

I released Maura's leg, and Mrs. Sullivan held the tiny little animal out, head flopping, arms and legs reaching and tumbling each to its own rhythm, and laid her on Maura's belly.

"Not a bad day's work," she said.

Maura didn't reply. Her eyes were on her daughter, eyes streaked with tears from the effort, but also tears from the relief of effort. She reached up a hand and laid the back of a single finger gently on the baby's face.

"She'll have Mama's hair," she said quietly. "The same red-brown. And my eyes."

I climbed quietly off the bed and tiptoed to the hearth to check the kettle. Mrs. Sullivan looked over her shoulder at me and smiled.

* * *

The floor was scrubbed and the papers burned. The afterbirth hissed and popped in the grate, smelling for all the world like burning meat. Maura and the baby were cleaned and tucked in, the baby with her breast and Maura with a bowl of stirabout. A pot of soup was simmering on the hearth, and the smell of cooking potatoes, carrots and beef bones seemed to draw the Purcell family in dribs and drabs through the door. After getting Maura's promise that she would stay in bed for at least the next few days, we packed up Mrs. Sullivan's kit, and made our way down the stairs, now dark and cool.

"May can cook breakfast for the lot of them tomorrow morning," Mrs. Sullivan said, stepping out the front door into the night air. May was Maura's oldest girl. "But you and I will need to see to suppers until Maura is churched and can start cooking again." She paused at the foot of the front steps. I paused, too. "You did well," she said. "I'd hold that neither of my two girls would do as well."

"Thank you," I said quietly, meaning more than just "thank you for the compliment."

"You're tired?" she asked.

"A bit," I said.

"But you'll manage?" It looked as though Mrs. Sullivan wanted to say something.

"I will," I said, waiting.

"Let's sit a bit," Mrs. Sullivan said. Jane and Angela will tend to supper. She set the vat down on the stones of the yard, and lowered herself with a great sigh onto the front steps. I sat next to her, enjoying the cool air. The breeze was gentle so the smell from the toilet wasn't too bad. And most people were in eating supper, so the yard was empty. Occasional snatches of voices drifted down through open windows, but for the moment, it was only me, Mrs. Sullivan and our thoughts.

"Did your mother tell you?" Mrs. Sullivan spoke quietly. She pulled her shawl up about her neck and gazed intently across the yard at the brick of the tenement across the way. I wasn't sure what she meant.

"Did your mother tell you about . . . babies, birthing. You know."

I shook my head. Mrs. Sullivan sighed. "Well," she said, "you know more than most now." I nodded. We sat. A boy about Tom's age dashed up the lane in front of us, tugged at the brim of his cap on the way past. He paused at the tap, splashed some water about, gave his face no more than a cat's lick and a promise, and then dashed up the steps and through the front door. Mrs. Sullivan smiled.

She looked over at me. "I wanted you to know. Before you leave, I wanted you to know. Who knows if in America you'll have anyone to talk with when the time comes. So I wanted you to know." I wasn't sure what she was talking about, but it did seem serious. I nodded.

"You know now how babies come out. Do you know how they get in?" she asked.

"Inside their mother?" I said. Mrs. Sullivan nodded. "Not exactly," I said. I scraped together in my mind all the bit and pieces I had learned. They were far from intelligible. "No, I don't," I said simply. Mrs. Sullivan nodded again.

"Well then," she said. "I'm waiting with Jane and Angela, waiting until they are about to be married. But I suppose I won't be around when you meet your man." She smoothed her skirt over her knees, then pulled a handkerchief from her pocket, licked the corner, and began working at a wee stain in her lap.

"Babies grow from seeds, a bit like flowers do." She paused, as though thinking. I added this new bit of information to the things I already knew. Together they made even less sense than before.

"You know what men have that we don't?" she asked. I nodded. I'd seen baby boys. "Well that's where they keep the seed. They plant it inside the mother, in the same place the baby comes out from. It grows into a baby." She stopped working on the stain and began tracing the hem of the handkerchief with her fingers. "I'll hold you that you can figure out the rest."

Man, woman, seed, baby, childbirth. It was more than I had before, but still not enough to get any kind of clear picture.

"You'll understand when you're married," she said. "That's the most important part, mind you. You need to make sure that only your husband plants the seed." I looked up at her, and I must have looked puzzled. She laughed gently. "Men are great farmers when it comes to their seed, Clare. Some will want to be planting as much seed as they can in as many fields as they can. But when a man plants a seed in a field other than his wife, 'tis a great sin. 'Tis a sin for him and a sin for the woman who let him."

I thought about the woman at the kiphouse, Polly, the woman who had gone to the sisters to have a baby. A man forced himself on her. She went to the sisters to have the baby. That's what Tom had said.

"Something I heard . . . ," I said. I wasn't sure how to say what I was feeling. "I heard. I heard that a man can force himself on a woman and she had a baby. Is that the same thing?"

"Where did you hear about that?" Mrs. Sullivan asked.

"I don't really remember," I said. It was a lie, but it was easier than explaining. "Is it the same?"

Mrs. Sullivan stared out into the yard. Her face was suddenly drawn, her eyes empty-looking. I was sorry I brought it up.

"'Tis no great matter," I said. "We can go in for supper if you'd like." I rose and reached for the vat.

"No, sit, Clare," Mrs. Sullivan said touching my arm gently. "Let you sit for a bit while I think." I sat back down. Mrs. Sullivan's hands resumed their journey round and round the hem of her handkerchief.

"Clare," she said, "when a man and a woman love each other, they join. The man plants his seed, and 'tis a wonderful thing. Some women don't like it much, that's true. But between a husband and a wife," she paused. "It can be a powerful fine thing. You need to remember that." I nodded. "But some men are so crazed to plant their seed, they will do it when they don't love the woman herself, when they aren't married to her. They will plant it when the woman fights him and tells him not to. That's what it means when people say 'a man forced himself on a woman'."

I sat quietly, fragments of images swirling in my mind. Behind us the doors of the tenement opened. We shifted over, and Ned Purcell stepped down the steps.

"Maura's sleeping," he said. "So's the babe." He pulled a small packet of snuff from his pocket, and drew out a pinch. "I do want to thank you for your help," he said, stuffing his finger into his cheek.

Mrs. Sullivan nodded. "She needs to stay in bed for a week or so," she said. "And you need to keep the children off her. She needs to get her strength back, and she can't do that with your brood climbing all over her. Give her some peace," she said.

"I will," Ned responded. He touched the brim of his cap and made his way down the lane.

"Probably on his way back to the pub," Mrs. Sullivan said. "When you marry a man, make sure he's taken the pledge. Make sure he has a steady job and doesn't touch so much as a drop. A drunken husband is worse than no husband."

"I will," I said.

"Clare," Mrs. Sullivan said, turning to face me and laying a hand on mine. "A good man is a blessing. A bad man can give you more pain than you can possibly imagine. I'm certain America has both. Be careful."

"I will," I said.

Mrs. Sullivan patted my hand. "Let's go see what Angela and Jane are cooking, shall we?" I stood, gathered up the vat, and we walked arm in arm across the yard.

At the Sullivan house, Angela and Jane were tied to the listening half of the front door, surveying the yard and whispering between themselves. The boys were huddled on the stoop beneath the window box, nursing an argument over one of Tom's books. Inside the house, the smell of soup filled the air. Mr. Sullivan was seated at the table reading the *Echo*.

"A girl," Mrs. Sullivan announced, hanging her shawl over the back of one of the chairs. "Maura has herself another girl."

Mr. Sullivan looked up from the paper, and before he could say anything, Mrs. Sullivan bent over him and met his lips with hers. The kiss was long and sweet, and I felt it from across the room deep inside me in a place I hadn't yet named.

* * *

Early Monday morning when I arrived, Maura sat abed in her shift, the baby in the crook of her arm. Davie bounced about at the foot, playing dogs and cats with his little sister. She was a blond, thin-haired two-year-old, with the tiniest eyes I had ever seen on a child. I searched my mind for a name, but if I had ever known it, I didn't remember it now. It wasn't easy keeping track of the toddlers who played by day in the tenement yard. If they lived to see their school days, to develop a preferred style of mischief, well then they became somewhat more memorable.

"Mrs. Sullivan sent me up with tea and bread," I said. "She'll be up at midday to make you something warm." I set the tea pot on the table and searched the area for a clean cup. The rest of the children had obviously done for themselves before leaving for school. Dirty cups and breadcrumbs littered the table, and an oatmeal-encrusted pot still hung over the dying fire. I removed it, thinking I would set it to soaking before I left.

"How's the baby?' I asked. "Did you choose the name?"

"The baby's a great deal better than I am," Maura said, shifting her over to the other arm. "They are hot little animals, babies are. I had Sally here in July, and I thought I would die of the heat. 'Tis like hugging a hot little stone to your breast." Sally recognizing her name climbed her mother to the top of the bed.

"Get off," Maura said. "Get off. Get off." She nudged at Sally with her free hand. "I can't have you kneeing and elbowing me, you little monkey. I need my rest." Sally rolled off onto the bed.

"Take these two," she said to me. "I'll never get a wink's sleep with them crawling, and climbing, and bouncing me to distraction." She looked up at me. I was emptying a dirty cup into the slops. "Take them," she said. "Take them."

"Now?" I said.

"Of course, now," she said. "Now is when they're bouncing holes in me, isn't it?" I set the cup on the table, and approached the bed, thinking I'd take Sally and sit her next to me while I poured tea and sliced bread. Sally had other ideas. She scampered over the top of her mother, and lay down with the most beatific look you did ever see in your life. I decided to go for Davie instead.

"Come here, Davie," I said. "You can help me."

"I'll not have him doing women's work," Maura said.

"Of course not," I said, somewhat taken aback. "I simply meant he could sit next to me while I cut your bread."

"Mmmph," Maura said. "She looked at Sally. "Can you sit there quietly?" she asked. Sally nodded.

"Come now, Davie," I said. Davie looked at his mother for a second opinion.

"Go," she said. Davie slunk off the bed like a dog being whipped. He made his way to a chair, climbed atop and sat, his hands playing with the hem of his shirt. He rested his chin on the table, his nose inches from a dirty oatmeal bowl. I moved it aside.

"Clare," Maura said. "I wonder if you could do me a favor." Davie began kicking at the leg of the table with the side of his foot. I could see the steady thump, thump, thump in his top of his head as the impact traveled from the table up into his chin.

"A favor?" I said. "Of course." I looked out the window. From the height of the sun, I expected the Angelus to ring any second. I'd need to leave for work soon.

"I wouldn't ask, but the kidgers got a late start this morning, and I can't do it myself, that's for certain." She paused. I picked up the cup of tea I had poured for her and walked to the bed. "I was wondering if you would go down to one of the pubs on the Coal Quay and get me a little something to keep body and soul together."

"Mrs. Sullivan said porter's no good for you, tea's better, until after your churching," I replied. "I think . . . "

"'Mrs. Sullivan said.' 'Mrs. Sullivan said'." Maura mimicked me. "The two of you are cat of a kind with your smug, self-righteous tone. You'd not show me only a bit of comfort after all I went through?"

"After all you went through, the porter can't be all that good for you," I said. I would need to be leaving soon and didn't have the time to run to the pub even if I had been convinced it was the right thing to do.

"Well," she said, "it wasn't exactly porter I had in mind." She fished between the bed and the wall and pulled out an empty whiskey bottle. She set it down on the bed next to the baby to accept the tea from my hand.

I was stunned. I stood there trying to think of what to say. Maura broke the silence.

"I know Sarah thinks it might be bad for the baby," she said. "But my old grandmother used to swear by whiskey after childbirth. She said it killed the soreness, and helped the baby to sleep."

"I need to get to work presently," I said. "I'll cut you another baat of bread before I go." I returned to the table and began to spread a thin layer of butter over the bread I'd sliced. "There's more tea if you'd like."

"It's not bread and tea I'm asking you for," Maura said, her teeth on edge. "Am I going to have to go fetch it myself?" She set the tea cup on the wash stand and the baby on the bed. She pulled herself up and sat at the edge of the bed, making like she was going to get up.

"Mrs. Sullivan said you were to stay in bed for another week," I said.

"Do you really believe that I care what you and your precious 'Mrs. Sullivan' say?" She stood, then froze. The blood drained from her face, and she reached out to the bed frame to steady herself. I set down the knife and went to her, tucking a hand under her elbow.

"Curse it all," she said. "Curse it all into the very bowels of hell then poke it with the devil's own fork." She shook loose my hand, then sunk to the bed, sitting with her head propped on her hand. Davie's steady tattoo on the table leg had picked up both in speed and volume. It was beginning to get under my skin.

"Clare, girl," Maura said, "Clare, I don't think you understand. I *need* a drop of the creature to get me through this, only a drop. 'Tis a hard thing. You saw. The pains killed me entirely, they did. And the ache of it now. As God is my witness, I don't know how I'll get by without a bit of help."

Through the window I heard the Angelus. In the room beneath us, the legs of a chair groan across the floor as someone pushed out from the table.

"I have to be leaving now," I said. I went to the table, and returned with the bread. I placed it on the washstand next to the tea cup. Sally perked up from where she had been huddled on the bed and eyed the buttered bread with obvious hunger. Davie's kicking was hard enough now that the teapot lid rattled and the plates were beginning to travel. I heard the sound of men on the lane as they greet each other on the way to work.

"I'll talk to Mrs. Sullivan about getting you a little something," I said, placing a hand on Maura's shoulder.

"Get out," she said quietly. Then more loudly: "Get out now. Get out, get out, get out or by goats I will do you some serious harm, and don't think I won't."

I snatched away my hand. Sally had oozed off the end of the bed, and was making her way out the door. Davie's drumming had also stopped, and when I turned to look, he was gone.

"I'll talk to Mrs. Sullivan," I mumbled as I snatched up my shawl. The teacup sailed past my head and shattered against the door. I dashed down the stairs and into the yard, where the neighborhood was well on its way into the new day.

Thirteen

I hit the door of the sack factory on the run. Gasping for only a bit more air, I pushed open the heavy door and scanned the room. Bluebell herself was already hard at work. I had to be very late.

With as few wasted movements as possible, I hung up my shawl and slid my smock over my head. Out of the corner of my eye, I saw Mrs. Houlihan giving me "the look." She knew I saw her—I probably glowed the usual shade of florid pink that always accompanied either embarrassment or heavy exercise. I pretended not to see though, but rather trotted over to the sack pile and immediately began shaking the nearest sack.

"Well, Buttercup, my girl," Bluebell said with a wry grin on her face, "did you get back late last night from your night on the town?"

I thought about last night. Mrs. Sullivan and I had cooked up a pot of soup for the Purcells after finishing our own supper. Then we'd both fallen into bed early, completely exhausted with the effort of caring for two families instead of one. By the time the boys got back from whatever they were doing that evening, they had to climb over my already inert body. A night on the town? I shook my head. No, it wasn't exactly a night on the town.

"Now then," Bluebell said. "You can tell me. I'd hold you were walking down Patrick Street, strolling along the south side, just doing Pana with your chums when you found a boy who fancies your company more than life itself. He would be finely made, but not too tall, with a shock of blond hair and nice eyes. And you talked and walked, and then he bought you a lemonade, and you told him you'd like to see him again."

I looked at her. "What are you talking about?" I said.

"Oh, no, wait," she responded. "That wasn't you. That was me." She clutched the sack she was holding tightly to her chest and almost bounced with the pure bliss of it.

"You found a boy!" I said, looking up from the pile of sacks that I had been working through furiously since coming in.

"Well, no," Bluebell said. "'Twas more like he found me. Yes, I'd say that was how it was. He found me. Not that I wasn't looking as well, mind you. Do you want to hear about it?" She laid a hand on my shoulder and looked both ways.

I looked up and joined her in scanning the room. Mrs. Houlihan was bent over her machine, stitching a long piece of canvas. Nobody seemed to be paying attention to me or the fact I had been late. I let out the breath I had been holding, and let my shoulders drop from their place up about my earlobes.

"Well," Bluebell said, "do you? Or should I take my story to someone else?"

"Of course I want to hear," I said. "Tell me. Tell me all about him."

"Well," she said "I got off work Saturday and went to the baths. Not the ones over by the quay. They're always so dirty." She wrinkled her nose in distaste. "I love the baths," she said. "All that hot water, as much as I want. And all this dust seems to just melt off." She had a far away look on her face.

"What about the boy?" I said. "Surely you didn't meet him in your bath tub." I laughed a little at my own joke.

"Don't be vulgar, Buttercup," Bluebell answered. "A lady's bath is her own."

"Well, pardon me," I said in mock apology, keeping the joke rolling. She stopped shaking the sack in her hands and looked up at me, puzzled. I met her gaze, then felt my smile slip from my face. I could never seem to tell when Buttercup was serious. "Sorry," I murmured.

"'Tis no matter," she replied and laughed. "People don't think I have a sense of humor, but I do. I understand jokes. They think I don't, but when they think I don't, I do, don't you know?" I nodded.

"We decided to do Pana, you know, look for boys in Patrick Street," she said.

"Who did?" I asked.

"Why me and the girls I met at the bath, of course," Buttercup replied. "They wanted to go dancing. They're older than I am, most of them, at least. But Mama had my pay, all but threepence, so I said no let's go do Pana, and they decided to go dancing anyway. So we went there after Mass, of course."

"Mass is on Sunday," I said.

"I know that," Buttercup said. "You don't think I know that?"

"But you went to the bath on Saturday," I said.

"And Mass on Sunday," Buttercup said. "I couldn't very well do it the other way around, now could I?"

"I suppose you couldn't," I said.

"Of course I couldn't," she said, a look of satisfaction on her face.

"So we went over to St. Patrick Street after Mass, and we were walking and looking in the windows and telling which of the dresses we would buy if we had the money. And that's when Daisy saw this group of boys only standing there on the corner across the street, looking for all the world like they didn't notice us at all, at all. But if we noticed them, they surely noticed us, don't you think?"

"Surely," I said.

"Of course they noticed," Bluebell said. She tested the seams of the sack she was holding, then tossed it into the mending pile.

"So did you go over and talk to them?" I asked.

Bluebell looked at me in disbelief. "'Tis little wonder you spent the weekend alone," she said, "if you're the type to just go up to a boy and start talking. Mmph!" She shook out the next sack for emphasis. "No, we walked down the street almost the bridge. Then we crossed over to their side of the street, and strolled past them as though we hadn't a care in the world."

"Then they talked to you?" I said.

"Well," Bluebell said, "not right away. But soon enough. One of them was the boy I met. But then I think I told you that. Finely made, he was. With a shock of blond hair that kept falling down into his eyes. And he went, 'cush, cush.' You know, that sound they make with their lips. And I went up to him, and I said, 'you should use some hair oil on that hair.' That's what I said, I did. Can you imagine? Then he said, 'I do. Gob oil.' And he took his cap off and licked his hand and smoothed his hair down with it. And I laughed. People don't think I have a sense of humor, but I really do, you know."

"And he bought you a lemonade?" I said.

"Not right away, of course," Bluebell replied. "We walked some, me and my chums and him and his boys. His name's Conan, and he said he was a messenger boy, was for three years. Do you think that makes him too old for me?"

"How old is he?" I asked.

"I don't know," she said.

"Did he look too old?" I said. "Was he old like an older brother, or old like your father's younger brother, or old like your father?"

"Or old like your grandfather?" The voice came from over my shoulder. It was Doolan.

"And what makes you think my private conversations are something you can just sneak up and listen to, Andy Doolan?" Bluebell turned and faced him down, hands on her hips.

"Well they couldn't be all that private if you're having them here in the middle of the floor where every dog and divil can walk up and listen." Doolan picked up the sack Bluebell had just thrown onto the pile. He shook his head and tisked. "If you don't put a little more elbow grease into these sacks, I'll have to report you to Mr. Doolan."

"Don't you mean 'Daddy'?" Bluebell asked.

"I mean Mr. Doolan, your supervisor," Doolan replied. "Mr. Doolan, the man who can give you the boot if you don't start doing your job better." I picked up a brush and started attacking a bit of dried malt on one of the sacks. "You should be more like sweet Mary Malone, here." Doolan came over to where I was standing and leaned with practiced nonchalance on the counter. "Look how well she's working." I kept my eyes glued to the sack, which by now was more than clean enough. "Pretty hair and a good worker. I like that in a woman." Out of the corner of my eye I saw him appraising me. He'd said my hair was pretty. I glanced up and gave him a half smile. He smiled back. "How about I buy you a lemonade after work, Sweet Mary Malone?"

"Her name is Buttercup," Bluebell chimed in. "And if you don't quit sweet talking the help when you should be working, I'll have to report you to Mr. Doolan. You know Mr. Doolan, don't you? He's your supervisor and the man who can give you the boot if you don't start doing your job better."

"What do you say, Buttercup?" Doolan leaned in, his elbow on the sack I was working on. Quietly he slipped his other hand out of his pocket and began drawing it up and down my arm.

"I'll have to think about it," I said. My voice shook slightly. I wondered why.

"Meet me outside beneath the sign after work," he said. "No need to fear me, sweet Mary Buttercup. You can ask any of the girls who work here. I know how to keep the girls happy." He winked as he pushed himself away from the counter and spun his cart around with what I guessed he thought was a certain flare. Looking over his shoulder at me, he disappeared through the double doors.

"'I know how to keep the girls happy'," Bluebell mimicked Doolan's honeyed tones. "'Ask any of the girls.' He's a bounder, he is. A bounder and a cad. Don't meet him, Buttercup. Don't do it."

"Bluebell," I said. "When you met Conan, did your belly do strange, floppy things?"

"Well, sure it did," Bluebell answered. "But I don't think that's what you're feeling. I think what you're feeling is the churning you get when you eat a bad piece of meat."

"I don't know," I said.

"I do," she said. "Stay away from him." She cast a quick look at the door. My eyes followed hers. Doolan was nowhere to be seen. "Listen to me, Buttercup." She paused. "You know, I hope you don't take offense, but you don't look much like a Buttercup. I think maybe Pansy would be a better nickname." She shook a sack. Reflexively, I squinted my eyes and held my breath as the dust cloud settled. "Listen to me, Pansy," she said, "when I first came here, Doolan asked me out for lemonade after work. He said I had pretty hair, and a nice smile, and he asked me to meet him under the sign after work. Well, I did, and he bought me lemonade, and then while we were walking home he took my arm and led me into one of the lanes when nobody was around."

I looked up at her. "What did you do?" I asked.

"Well, nothing at first," she answered. "But then he took his hand and he put it here." She turned her back to the rest of the floor and motioned discretely in the general direction of her breast. "And then he tried to kiss me."

"He didn't!" I said.

"He did," Bluebell replied. "Well I gave him a good, hard shove, I did. And I told him he was a cad, and that if he had a lick of sense, he would never ask me out for lemonade again."

"And did he?" I asked.

"Did he what?" Bluebell replied.

"Did he ask you out for lemonade again?"

"Of course not," she said. "Not after what my Da and my older brothers did to him."

"You told them?" I asked.

"Don't you know anything about how to handle boys?" Bluebell replied in astonishment.

"I, um, didn't ever walk out with a boy," I said.

"Well, then you definitely want to stay away from Doolan," Bluebell replied. "Of course I told my big brother, and he told my Da, and my Da told my other brothers. And they asked me what Doolan looked like, and then the next day when we got off work, there was Da and the boys waiting around the corner. Now Da was still covered head to toe with flour as he just got off work at the bakery, and the boys, well they looked enough like me that Doolan took one look at them and saw the handwriting on the wall." Bluebell laughed. "You should have seen him. His face went whiter than Da's, and him with all the flour covering him. And Da steps up to him, and says, 'Are you Andy Doolan?' And Doolan is wondering if he should change his name on the spot, but he squares his shoulders and he says, 'I am, sir.' And Da says, 'My daughter, Bluebell, says she never wants you to walk out with her ever again. And well, I'm here to give you a little something to help you remember that by.' And he lays heavy hands on Doolan, grabs him by the front of the shirt, and the boys they surround him, and Jimmy holds Doolan from the back, and the rest of them take their turns giving him socks, in the belly and the ribs mostly. And Doolan looks like he wants to double over on the ground, but they hold him up, and give him a couple more good ones just for a fare thee well. And when they let go, he falls to the ground, to one knee just."

I looked at her in shock. "They did that because Doolan tried to kiss you?"

"Of course, that and touch me like that," Bluebell said. "Wouldn't your Da and older brothers do the same?"

"Well, my Da passed on years ago, and my brothers," I paused and thought about Mick beaning Murphy with the wooden slat. "My brothers might have some trouble taking on someone like Doolan. They're ten and twelve."

"Then you should surely stay away from him," Bluebell said. "Surely."

* * *

As I hung up my smock that evening, brushing my skirts and running a hand over my hair to work loose the chaff, I made up my mind. I'd find a way home that didn't involve passing the sign. It was the coward's way out, and I knew I would have to see Doolan the next day at work, but better on the factory floor than in the street, where lanes and alleys and doorways offered far too many places to hide.

I walked out the door and quickly turned to my left into the factory yard with its horses and carts and men in aprons. I hugged the building, hoping Doolan wouldn't see me from his place beneath the sign. But he wasn't beneath the sign. He was right outside the door. He fell into step beside me.

"Well, sweet Mary Malone, Buttercup," he said offering his elbow. "I'm delighted you decided to join me."

"I'll not be joining you, Doolan," I said and picked up my pace.

"Why not?" Doolan said. "'Tis only a lemonade and maybe a little talk. You aren't telling me you'll marry me, after all."

"Thank you for the invitation, Doolan," I said. "But I need to go home now."

"And I'll walk you," he said again offering me his elbow.

"I'll be fine by myself," I replied. He was beginning to make me nervous.

"Bluebell filled your head with her nonsense, didn't she? What did she tell you? She's a liar, you know. A terrible liar." His voice was quiet because of the workers finding their way home though the yard. But it was tinged with anger, and that was enough to turn my nervousness into a growing panic.

"Well," he said, "did sweet, young Bluebell also tell you what happened to Mary Margaret?" He looked hard at me. I could see the hardness of his eyes out of the corner of my vision. But I pretended not to see and kept walking. "No?

She forgot that part?" he said. "Well let me tell you the story, so at least you get the truth about this one." He walked out of the factory yard with me, and taking long strides to match my own short quick ones, leaned in as though telling me a secret.

"It was a couple of months ago," he said. "Mary Margaret said she'd let me buy her a lemonade. Then just like you did, she changed her mind."

"I never said I'd let you buy me a lemonade," I interjected.

"And is this story about you, then?" Doolan replied. "'Tis about Mary Margaret. And she said she'd let me buy her a lemonade, and then she told me to go away, without so much as a by your leave, she just up and told me to leave. Well, I thought that deathly bad manners." He paused. "So I had her sacked."

I stopped in my tracks. Doolan stopped, too, right in front of me. He turned to face me. "That's right. I had her sacked."

"How?" I said. "You can't sack anyone."

"I have my ways," Doolan replied. "She came up to me before she left and said she thought it over and decided maybe it was the best thing for her to go out with me. But by then it was too late, you see. I only wanted to make sure you didn't make the same mistake."

"Are you saying that if I don't let you buy me a lemonade, you'll have me sacked?"

"No, no," Doolan replied. "I'm only telling you a story about Mary Margaret. But if you don't want to go for that lemonade, I'll just be on my way." He turned, stuffed his hands in his pockets, and strolled away from me.

Now, I have to say that I thought about catching up to him. The idea of looking for another job weighed heavy on me. But then I thought of Murphy, and Mick, and the way that we were no more than hop, skip, and jump from finding ourselves inside the industrial school. I didn't need trouble, and either way, Doolan was trouble. I crossed over to the other side of the street and took the long way home.

* * *

"What in heaven's name did you do to Maura?" Mrs. Sullivan was seething like a tea kettle at full boil. I walked through the front door and was hit full in the face with it. Mrs. Sullivan didn't offer me so much as a good day but only stabbed her broom into the corner by the sofa, attacking the dirt as though engaged in mortal combat. "How difficult can it be to bring tea and bread?" she said. "Hmm?"

It was more than I could take. I spun on my heel and launched myself through the door, stumbled off the stoop, and handed hard, palms first on the stones of the yard. I paused for a moment, not daring to lift my head. Life, it seemed, had penalties for such impudence. I sat back, right there on the stones and checked my palms. Both were skinned raw, with tiny bits of dirt and stone worked into the wounds. I dropped them into my lap, and right there in front of God, a half dozen scampering toddlers, and a three-man toss school, I burst into tears. It was as though I had a mere quarter drop of fortitude left, and that had just seeped out of me with the drops of blood oozing from my palms. I deflated right there on the stones.

"Clare," Mrs. Sullivan poked her head out the front door. "Clare?" She propped her broom against the front of the house, and squatted low to sit next to me on the stoop. I wanted to stop crying, but to do so would have taken a certain amount of strength, or will, or some such thing, and I simply did not have it in me. Mrs. Sullivan didn't say anything but simply sat. I could see her struggling to put down the anger I'd seen on her. I wanted to run from it, run from her, run from everything, but I couldn't, not just then. So that's the way it was—me in the dirt, her on the stoop. Now and then, she shooed away the occasional bluebottle or toddler, or assured a neighbor that the episode was nothing serious. Mostly we just sat as I cried.

The body, though, only has so many tears within it at any given time. No matter how trying the situation, no matter how weighty the pain, the body has a limited number of tears it can lend to the circumstance. When they've been exhausted, the mind and will are left to pick up where the tears left off. Eventually, my tears dissolved themselves. I wiped my eyes, my nose on the back of my hand. I sniffed and examined my palm again.

"Nasty scrape," Mrs. Sullivan said.

"A matched set," I said holding my hands side by side.

Mrs. Sullivan patted the stoop beside her. I scooted over and sat beside her. I felt I owed her some kind of explanation. And since she was simply sitting, waiting, I assumed she too felt the same way. I sighed.

"If I needed Mr. Sullivan and Roddy to beat someone bloody for me, do you think they would do it?" I said.

Mrs. Sullivan's eyebrows fairly levitated. She shifted to face me. "What happened with you and Maura?" she asked.

"Not Maura," I said. "A boy at work."

"Oh, well," Mrs. Sullivan said, "I suppose John and Roddy could warm up their knuckles on Maura and then take on your 'boy at work'." She stood. "I'm assuming this is a story you won't want the rest of the neighborhood to be talking about tomorrow." I nodded. "Well, then," she said. "Rinse your hands off under the tap and come inside. We can talk about it there." She handed me her handkerchief. I wiped my eyes, tucked the handkerchief in my sleeve, and went to wash my hands gingerly at the tap. I could see in the windows of the tenement the shadows of neighbors who had been watching. Even the men in the toss school were looking without appearing to be looking. I finished washing quickly and then walked with as much dignity as I could muster into the house.

Mrs. Sullivan had poured some hot water from the kettle into the wash basin. It was steaming on the table. "Sit you down," she said, moving the paraffin lamp from the mantle to the table. Gingerly she fished a needle from the bottom of the basin and sat next to me. "Let me see," she said. I held out my hands into the circle of light cast by the lamp. Mrs. Sullivan took the right one in her own and immediately set about digging out little bits of rock and dirt with the needle. "Tell me," she said, "why would you be wanting John and the boy to beat someone at work?"

I told her the whole story, pausing now and then to wince at the needle, now and then to sob back some previously uncried tears.

"Some day you're after having," Mrs. Sullivan said when it was over. "First Maura, then this. There," she said, "I think that's the worst of it. Wash them good. And use soap." I stood to dip my hands into the nearly scalding water. My palms screamed with the heat, but somehow it felt almost good. It was at least a clean, focused pain, not like the knot my throat had tied itself into.

"I don't think a fist fight is the best thing for your problem," she said. "Not that John wouldn't being willing, mind you. And Roddy, well, I'm afraid Roddy has developed quite a taste for the feel of flesh against his knuckles. He'd love to get his hands on the cad, I'm sure. But breaking the supervisor's son is not the best way to get on at your job."

I took the towel Mrs. Sullivan handed me and patted my hands dry. "It worked for Bluebell," I said. "Her Da and her brothers laid into Doolan one day after he, um, touched her. And she said that she's never had problems with him again."

"Hmm," Mrs. Sullivan commented. "And is this Bluebell one you can trust to tell you the truth of the matter?" I thought for a moment. Despite Doolan's protestations, it had never occurred to me that Bluebell may have made the entire story up.

"She said he was a cad, and he is," I said.

"I have no doubt of it," Mrs. Sullivan replied.

"I wish someone would beat him up," I said.

"'Tis a convenient solution to the problem," Mrs. Sullivan said. "It takes very little thought and even less planning to simply wade into a situation fists flying. Any fool can do it. Maybe that's why so many of them do." She reached outside the door for her broom, and picked up where she had left off in her sweeping.

"Would you go yourself for that lemonade?" I asked. "If Bluebell told you what she told me, would you go?"

Mrs. Sullivan stopped sweeping, sighed and leaned on her broom. "'Tisn't a question I can answer, really," she said. "'Tis more a question for the heart than anything else. What does your heart tell you about him?" She looked at me, then took up her sweeping again, probably to allow me the time to think. I did.

"He said I had nice hair," I said, finally. "I liked that."

"Mmhmm," Mrs. Sullivan said quietly.

"But he threatened to have me sacked."

"A bully's way, to be sure," Mrs. Sullivan commented.

"And I didn't like him touching me," I added.

"You didn't say that he touched you," Mrs. Sullivan said.

"On the arm," I said, "Only a little, kind of light, like this." I imitated Doolan's touch on my own arm. It seemed like an innocent gesture when I did it to myself.

"Maybe we should have Roddy pay him a call," she muttered to herself.

"Is that wrong?" I asked. "To let a boy touch me like that?"

"Probably not," Mrs. Sullivan replied. I noticed she had been sweeping the same patch of floor over and over. I looked down at the floor. She followed my eyes, smiled and shook her head, then propped the broom against the wall.

"Clare," she said, taking a seat at the table beside me. "Most boys are nice enough fellows. They like girls and they want to be around them because, well, that's what boys like. Girls too, truth be told." She took my hand, and examined it again, gazing into the palm like a palm reader, as though she could find the right thing to say somewhere there amidst the lines and the scratches. "But some boys," she paused, "some men are cruel. They don't want to be with a girl. They want to hurt girls, to lord it over them." She paused, then looked me in the eye. "Is Doolan that kind of boy?" she asked.

"I don't know," I said. I wasn't sure I knew what she meant. "How do you know?"

"I didn't," Mrs. Sullivan said quietly. She set my hand down, patting the fingers gently. She sighed, then in a voice that seemed to come from someplace long ago and far away, she spoke.

"When I was working at the sack factory, the supervisor there—it wasn't the same man as now, I'm sure—well, he took a shine to me, or so I thought. He always seemed to be looking over my shoulder, admiring my work. He was older than I was, a good ten or fifteen years probably. But still it made me feel good. Do you know what I mean?" I nodded. "Then one day he asked me to go out to the yard with him to bring in a cart of sacks. Well, now that was strange because the boys used to bring the sacks in and then we would clean and sort and mend them."

"'Tis the same now," I said.

She nodded. "But he was the supervisor, and so I went with him. Well, the boys were all gone, all away from the yard for some reason, and the yard was so quiet it made me nervous. But I kept following him to a big wagon full of sacks all loaded up and ready to go off to the brewery or some such place. And he turned to me, and I said 'these sacks are ready to drive out.' I could see it wasn't the sacks he was thinking about. He grabbed me and picked me up off my feet. He threw down into the pile of sacks and then threw himself on top of me." Her eyes looked unseeing at the needle still laying on the table. In them I could see the scene, the supervisor, the sacks, the weight of him. She looked up at me.

"Breathe, Clare," she said. I let out the breath I'd been holding and sighed a great sigh. I could feel my belly quiver inside me.

"Too much," she said. "I said too much." She sat back in her chair and stroked her lips with her fingers, as though trying to seal them closed, to seal in the memory that had begun to pour out of them. "I didn't mean to . . . "

"What did he do?" I said quietly.

"That's what my father asked," Mrs. Sullivan said quietly. "'What did he do? Did he force himself on you?'" There was that phrase again. My mind flashed to what Mrs. Sullivan had told me the night before. "I didn't know what to say," she said. "I didn't know what it meant. So I said 'no.' It turns out that was the right answer."

"He didn't then," I said. "He didn't force himself on you?"

"He did," Mrs. Sullivan said. "But that wasn't an answer my father could hear. I only said that he pushed me down into the sacks and pawed at me. That much was true. And for that my father took a hurley to the man's skull and his belt to me. If I told him everything, he might have killed the man, or me, or both. He had a temper, don't you know." She sighed. I sighed, too.

"Clare," she said finally, "do you think this Doolan is the kind of boy who might do something like that?"

"I don't know," I said. "Maybe. I don't think so. Maybe."

Mrs. Sullivan sighed. It seemed we were doing more than our share of that. "You can walk away," she said. "If he asks you to do something that makes you uncomfortable. If he asks you to go somewhere with him and it doesn't make sense to you, you can walk away." I nodded. "Do you understand what I'm saying?" she said. "You can leave the job on the spot, not finish out the day. We'll find another way for you to make some money. Do you understand?"

"I do," I said.

"You understand? 'Tis important that you understand."

"I do," I said.

"Good," she said. "Now help me with these carrots. John and Roddy will be home in no time at all." I stood. "And Clare," Mrs. Sullivan said. "You can talk with me about this any time, but I'd rather you not mention anything I said here to anyone else. Not everyone would understand."

"You have my word, Mrs. Sullivan," I said. I wasn't sure I quite understood either.

* * *

We made extra stew that night. It was a simple matter of a few extra potatoes and a good deal more water. Mrs. Sullivan sent half of it up to Maura and her brood. She sent it with Jane with the instructions that Jane wasn't to say much more than a simple good evening.

"The woman has a mean streak," she said. "After all I did for her these ten years." The anger was starting to rise again, and Jane seemed positively relieved to be able to scoot out the door with the pot of stew.

The boys came through the door just as Mr. Sullivan was seating himself before his plate and newspaper. The boys had that uncanny way of sniffing out their own food from halfway across town. Someday modern science will figure it out—how a boy can lift his nose, and through hundreds of stray smells discern the scent from his mother's own cooking pot. Someday they will isolate the precise center in the brain that can time a boy's arrival with the moment food comes off the hearth. Until then, I'll only say that Wally and my brothers were miracle workers in their ability to detect supper time on the breeze.

We said the blessing and pounced. It had been a hungry day for all of us. For the longest time there was little more than the clink of spoons on bowls. As the last of the stew was being ladled from the pot, Mrs. Sullivan broke the silence.

"Well, John," she said. "How would you like to bloody someone for Clare and myself?" I swallowed hard. I wasn't sure I wanted the story of Doolan and what happened that day told in front of Mick and Tom and the others. I tried to catch Mrs. Sullivan's eye, shaking my head softly. She looked up at me and smiled.

"Who exactly are we talking about, here?" Mr. Sullivan replied.

"I can help," Roddy said.

"I can, too," Mick chimed in.

"No, you can't," I said.

"Who is it?" Mick said, ignoring me.

"Maura Purcell," Mrs. Sullivan said. "And nobody is bloodying anybody up. Though I can't say the idea of seeing her put back in her box troubles me too badly."

"I'd say Ned should be left to handle any beatings that might be necessary there," John said.

"More like the other way around," Roddy chimed in. "I heard Ned showed up to work one day with a bloody eye and a stiff jaw, and he wouldn't let on how it happened. But Thomsy downstairs said her heard the two of them going at it like cats and dogs the night before, and he thinks Maura was the one who clipped him good."

"Roddy," Mr. Sullivan said, locking eyes with the boy, who dropped his own to his bowl and continued to decimate the stew inside. "She's still abed?" he said to Mrs. Sullivan.

"Supposed to be," Mrs. Sullivan replied. "But she sure gets around for someone whose feet aren't supposed to touch the floor."

Mr. Sullivan licked his spoon and dropped it into his bowl. He pushed back from the table and settled in to listen.

"It seems that when the doctor came by this morning to stitch her up and check on the baby, she filed a formal complaint against me." Mrs. Sullivan's shoulders tensed, and the anger started oozing out from the edges of her again. No wonder she'd been in the state she was when I got home.

"She didn't like the way you delivered the baby?" Mrs. Sullivan asked.

"She didn't like Clare helping," Mrs. Sullivan replied. "But she's a cow," she added, turning to look at me. "You did just fine. I've no cause for complaint."

"What's she complaining about," Mr. Sullivan asked.

"She said I let Clare deliver the baby, and that Clare is too young and unregistered and didn't know what she was doing."

"But you delivered the baby," I said.

"Don't I know that?" she replied. "And the doctor knows that too. He stopped by on his way out from Maura's. He told me I was one of his best bona fides. But he would have to follow up on Maura's charges because that's the way things are done."

Mr. Sullivan sighed. "It doesn't seem right beating up a woman. But sometimes I can see the use. Maybe I'll go beat up Ned instead."

"I'll help," Roddy said.

"Nobody's beating up anyone," Mr. Sullivan replied. "Roddy, one of these day's you'll have to get it through your thick skull that wanting to and doing are two entirely different creatures. Do you understand?" Roddy went back to wiping the last drops of his stew from the bowl with a piece of bread.

"I could lose my license," Mrs. Sullivan said simply.

"Any idea what set her off?" Mr. Sullivan asked.

Mrs. Sullivan looked at me. "She was already in a foul humor when I went up there this morning," I said. "I poured the tea, cut her a baat of bread. We talked for a bit, then she gave me dog's abuse, threw the tea cup at me, and I left."

"She threw the tea cup at you?" Mrs. Sullivan said. "Why?"

I looked over at Tom and Kevin. "Well," I said, "'Tisn't something I'd want every, um, every boy in the neighborhood to be knowing."

Mr. Sullivan dismissed the boys with a wave of his hand. Tom, Mick, and Kevin stood with a great scraping of chairs and furniture. Scavenging the last bits of bread from the table, they trotted out the front door.

"You, too, Roddy, Jane, Angela," Mrs. Sullivan said. Jane stood, murder in her eyes. She glared at me over her shoulder as she went out to sit on the stoop in the hopes of catching some of the conversation.

"Maura—Mrs. Purcell—asked me to run a little errand for her, and I told her I wouldn't," I said when everyone had finally left and the door had been closed. "She, um, she had an empty whiskey bottle behind her bed, and she said she wanted another one, a full one. And I said you didn't believe in taking any kind of drink so soon after a child was born, and she said her grandmother used to swear by it. And I had to get to work. And, well, she was a bit put out."

"I'd say she's more than a *bit* put out if she's throwing cups at you," Mr. Sullivan said.

"No," Mrs. Sullivan said, "When she's more than a bit put out, she starts throwing furniture." Mr. Sullivan laughed. "Is that all?" she said. "You wouldn't buy drink for her?"

"That was it," I said. "I think that was it."

Mrs. Sullivan shook her head. "I had images of you trying to sew her up before the doctor came, or some such thing."

"I wouldn't," I said.

"I know you wouldn't," she replied. "Just with Maura screaming murder and the doctor coming in with that deadly serious air of his. I just didn't know what to think."

"Am I in trouble?" I asked.

"No," Mr. Sullivan said. "Maura's in trouble. She had no call to ask you to fetch the whiskey, it being against the law, you know."

"But she said she has her boys fetch it for her all the time," I protested.

"I have no doubt of it," Mr. Sullivan replied. "Plenty of people do. But if she wants to file formal protests with the doctor, we can get formal just as easily."

"Still," Mrs. Sullivan said, "I think 'tis best if you not come with me to any more birthings until all this settles down. And I think you best stay clear of Maura for a bit."

I had no problem with the latter, but I had hoped Mrs. Sullivan would continue to invite me to help her. The whole episode with Maura's delivery was frightening to be sure. But I had the feeling that it was something I might want to do with my life. It was something satisfying, something that made my heart pump and my blood flow. I liked it.

Fourteen

I hate to say it but rats, you see, were a normal part of life. We didn't like them, to be sure, but we were accustomed to them. Most of the walls in the tenement were filled with horsehair insulation, that or straw. And the rats and the ticks and the lice all thought that they had never seen such a fine place to settle down and raise a family. Every now and again, the health department would come by and paint the hallways with a foul-smelling pink paste that was supposed to keep the beasties in the walls from coming through the walls. It was supposed to kill rats—or maybe lice, or ticks depending on who you asked. Mama said the only thing it killed for certain was her appetite.

Mama's philosophy was simply to keep the room as clean as possible, to keep meal and other things that might draw the vermin in metal boxes. Her idea was if you don't feed them, they will eventually realize that they'd worn out their welcome. But still we would hear the sounds of little rat feet in the walls or scurrying across the boards of the ceiling. We would see their droppings outside near the toilet, and now and then someone in the tenement would emerge with one dangling by the tail from a thumb and forefinger. It's safe to say that we in the Keane household treated the rat problem like we treated the rest of life—one day at a time, one rat at a time. Most people in the tenement did.

Wally Sullivan, however, had other opinions. I have never seen anyone with such a hatred for rats. I saw him once pelting a dead rat carcass in the yard with stones. Over and over again, he heaved the pebbles, bouncing them off the inert carcass. The look on his face was almost otherworldly in its rage or terror, or something I couldn't quite name. All of us hated rats. For whatever reason, Wally loathed them, despised them, burnt with a slow steady rage against them.

* * *

It was night, not long after we had begun staying with the Sullivans. As always, I was sleeping beside my brothers on our mattress on the floor near the front door. I woke to the sound of scurrying, close scurrying, on the floorboards near my head. It took me no time at all to figure out what it was. I rolled over to face the center of the room. The light was dim—a bit from the window and less from the hearth. I couldn't see anything. The scurrying had stopped. I raised myself up on my elbow for a better look. Nothing. Then the sound again, over by the hearth. Everyone seemed to be asleep. The chorus of breathing was steady, even. Roddy snored lightly. I lay back down, my eyes heavy. I heard a brief click of claws against stone, then nothing again. I must have drifted off.

"Mother of God!" The shout woke me up. "The filthy thing walked right over my face."

Mick bolted upright. "What?" he said. I laid a hand on his shoulder, as much for my own racing heart as for his benefit.

Over by the hearth, Wally was up and dancing, clutching the old coat that had covered him, shaking it fiercely, and looking frantically around him.

"Aw, shut it, would you," Roddy growled from his place on the sofa.

"A rat," Wally said. "A damn big rat."

"Wally, you, me, and my belt, are going to have a little chat in the morning about your language," Mr. Sullivan said from behind the curtain.

"It walked right over my face," Wally said. He threw the coat down on the mattress, and stood in the low light of the hearth clutching himself.

I heard a rustling from behind the curtain. Mr. Sullivan pushed it aside and came out in his shirt. He threaded his way between mattresses over to where Wally stood.

"Where is it?" he said.

"I don't know!" Wally snapped back at him.

"Then go back to bed," Mr. Sullivan said.

"He's here, though," Wally said, his voice tight. "The blackguard walked right over my face, damn his filthy pelt."

Mr. Sullivan cleared his throat noisily. I shivered under the blanket, feeling the sensation of tiny paws walking all over me.

"Find it, Daddy," Jane said.

"Maybe it will shut his gob," Angela added, her voice heavy with sleep. "All this foostering over a little rat." It was easy for her to say. Her mattress wasn't on the floor.

Mr. Sullivan sighed, and reached for the stub of a candle. In the light of it, Wally and Mr. Sullivan began the search—in the hearth, behind the wardrobe, under the bed. They rousted Roddy, who rose only after ample complaints and minor threats, and together they tipped back the sofa for a quick look beneath it. The rat, it seemed was long gone.

"Satisfied?" Mr. Sullivan said to Wally.

"No," Wally said. "I'm not."

"And is that my problem?" Mr. Sullivan said and blew out the candle with a quick puff. "Go back to bed."

Wally apparently knew better than to argue. He dropped like a sack of potatoes to the mattress on the floor. I could hear him and Kevin jockeying for position on the tiny straw mat. The curtain around the bed swished closed and after a bit of shuffling, the room fell silent again.

"Rat boy, rat boy, rat boy," the chant was coming from the foot of the bed. Mick whispered it quietly, almost inaudibly. "Rat Boy. Rat Boy. Wally, Wally, Rat Boy."

"Keep it up, Keane, and I'll stuff a rat up your arse," Wally hissed back.

"I'm not worried," Mick said. "You'd have to touch it to stuff it, Rat Boy."

"Mick," I said. "Leave him alone and go to sleep."

Mick rolled over. "Rat Boy, Rat Boy, Rat Boy," the whisper continued. I gave a light kick with my foot. Mick grunted, then settled back. He was soon snoring.

* * *

The next morning, a Saturday morning, Mrs. Sullivan and I tugged our bundles of clothes to the quay. I loved Saturday mornings. I loved not having to go into the factory. I loved working with Mrs. Sullivan. I loved the walk with her to the quay. I loved talking with her, listening to her quick, dry wit as she observed the life that set Barrack Street and the Marsh to buzzing. I would say that she reminded me of Mama, but the two weren't anything alike. Mama was fine-boned, small-breasted, pretty, with the possible exception of her nose. I inherited my nose from my mother, I'm afraid. It's a long prominent nose with a bit of a hook to it just below the place my glasses rest today. On Mama it could look classic, aquiline. On me it merely looks hooked. No one could miss the fact that Mama and I were mother and daughter. We both had the same build, the same strawberry blond hair with the same bit of wave to it, the same pink freckled skin. We also had the same voice, so much so that Mrs. Quillan used to hear me singing in the kitchen late in the evening and call in "Hannah, are you still here?"

No one would mistake Mrs. Sullivan for my mother, though. Mrs. Sullivan was either an amazingly petite large woman, or a small woman who filled much more space than she needed. I always thought of her as tall, imposingly tall, but when she and I stood side by side, I looked straight over at her, eye to eye, and I couldn't have been more than five foot four at the time. I thought of her as large-boned, but my arms went easily around her when she pressed me to her ample bosom. She had fine yellow-white hair, and soft, finely-wrinkled, ivory skin to match it. That was Mrs. Sullivan—she was soft and pale on the outside. But she had a layer of sharp wit just under the surface, the outermost layer of a strength, some might say hardness, deep inside.

"Could I ask you a question?" I said that morning, laying out the boys' shirts one atop the other.

"And what's to prevent you?" Mrs. Sullivan said, still rummaging in the bundle.

"Why don't Jane and Angela come with you to the quay?"

"Did you see that silk skirt anywhere?"

"I didn't," I said.

"I want it someplace where I can keep an eye on it." Mrs. Sullivan opened the second bundle. "'Tis just the sort of thing that could grow legs and walk off on its own." I finished the shirts and started stacking the trousers.

"I'll tell you if I find it," I said.

"Good, good," Mrs. Sullivan said, shaking out another more heavily patched skirt and draping it over the table. "Could I tell you a story?" she asked.

"And what's to prevent you?" I said, grinning at her from across the table.

She laughed. "A few years ago," she said, "word came down from London that all the handywomen were going to be replaced by midwives. For birthing, that it. We could still lay out the dead, of course. But for birthing we were going to be replaced by midwives. I didn't think much of it until one day a public health worker came by nosing around. She asked in the neighborhood and didn't take long to find out I was the handywoman. She came knocking on my door and told me I had to prove that I could deliver babies. Can you imagine that? If I could prove that I could deliver babies, the government would give me a piece of paper, make me a midwife, and that would make it legal. Well, I pointed to Nora's two that were out in the yard playing, and I said to her, I said, 'there's your proof. I delivered those two and most of the other children you might see on your way out.' She didn't take well to that and said that without the paper, I could be locked up for delivering any more. I could be put in jail for doing what I did just fine these twenty years."

"They could lock you up for being a handywoman? That sounds like foolishness to me," I said.

"It sounds like the government to me," Mrs. Sullivan said. "Not that the two aren't cat of a kind, mind you." She winked at me. "So I took a bath on a Tuesday, put on my Sunday dress, went into the public health office, and said I wanted to prove I could deliver babies. The man behind the desk looked down his nose at me, then pushed a form across the counter and told me to go over to the civic buildings this day week for the test and to bring a pound for the fee and they would give me the license. Ah, here it is." She pulled the skirt from a bundle, and shook it out. "I do like the material of it. If I were twenty years younger and a few pounds lighter." She sighed and shrugged.

"So John and I raided the dead money, and I came around Nora and Tom for a few shilling. And I had Roddy help me fill out the form. Roddy's not much for the books, but he writes with a fair hand, better than I do. The test was the next week. Roddy said I needed to study because that's what you do when you have a test coming up. But I hadn't the foggiest how you could study for a childbirth test. I mean 'tis not the kind of thing that lends itself to practice runs, if you know what I mean. Well, the next week I went to the test, form in hand, sweating great stains onto my best dress. When I got there, they led me into a large room with long tables and a handful of other women, and they gave me a pencil and a fistful of papers and told me I had two hours. It was a paper test, you see, and I was never one for paper tests, even when I was in school."

"What did you do?" I asked.

"What could I do? I sat down and I started to read. They were questions, and I was supposed to write the answers in the blank spaces—I could tell that much. But I didn't recognize half the words. So I brought the paper and pencil up to the woman who was sitting at the front of the room. I laid them on her desk, and I asked for my pound back. She said no refunds, and I said I didn't once use the pencil and the paper was clean as the moment I got it from her. She said no refunds and would you please be more quiet so the others could take the test. Well, by that time I was greatly tired of whole affair, and so I gave her the devil right then and there." Mrs. Sullivan tossed a pair of shoes onto the table and looked up at me. She locked eyes with me as though I were the woman at the test.

"I said I didn't see what papers and pencils had to do with bringing babies into the world, that my mother caught hundreds of babies, and she couldn't do much more than spell her name. And the woman at the desk told me to lower my voice, but by that time everyone in the room looked up from their tests and were staring at us. And when I saw that a few of them were smiling, I thought, Sarah Sullivan, you haven't a thing to lose, so I opened up and told her just what I thought, so I did. And she told me to get out or she would call the guardai, and I said, 'you don't have to ask me twice to leave a place like this'." She paused. "They didn't give me the license, wouldn't you know," she said, then threw back her head and laughed.

"But you still deliver babies," I said.

"Well the next year, they decided there were many more babies waiting to be born than there were women willing suffer the nonsense of their tests. They couldn't very well ask the babies to wait until they got their paperwork in order. So they fixed it so we could get a statement from the priest that said we were of good character and were a year at least delivering babies. And if we brought the statement to the right office, they would make us *bona fide* midwives. That's the government way of saying a handywoman, which is what I was all along. They wanted me to buy a kit, a fancy bag with a bunch of fancy equipment to put in it, but I wouldn't know what to do with all those things even if I had the money to waste on them. So I only nodded at them and kept making do with the same things I always use." She folded up the old sheet she was unpacking and stashed it in her basket.

"Do you want to unpack this one, too?" I asked, hefting the last bundle. "The table is close to full."

"Maybe later," she said, and sat on the stool she pulled from the cart. "In another three or four years, they'll come and put the test under my nose again," she said. "I'll deliver God only knows how many babies by that time, but I'll know no more about what the test means than I did the last I saw it. There will come a time, when they'll say I can't deliver babies any more. That's the way of things in the modern world. By then I might be old enough that I'll want to stop anyway. But Jane and Angela, well they'll be only starting out." She looked up at me. I was straightening the piles on the table, trying to arrange them so they look nice. "So will you," she said. I nodded.

"I walked the streets the night after the test," she said. "I thought about my girls, how I wanted them to be able to live in a world where you prove yourself with a pencil, not your hands and your back. I walked home, snatched John from his paper and his chair by the fire, and we went out to the yard to talk. That's when I told him I wanted the girls to stay in school."

"How long?" I asked. The Sullivan girls were fifteen and sixteen, older than I was. I had never met girls that age who were still in school.

"Until they finish the secondary school," Mrs. Sullivan said. "John was against it at first, of course. He wanted them to find work, make some money, help us put some meat on the table. He said if anyone should be allowed to stay in school it was Wally or better, Kevin, who seemed a bit more taken with the books than Wally. But I got around him in time. Some time after you're married and living in America, write me a letter, and I'll tell you how I did it." She winked and laughed again.

The quay was beginning to get a bit more crowded. Across the way, a woman in full brown skirts and a long, formerly white apron hoisted a peck of potatoes from her husband's cart. He had the leathery cheeks and pale brow of a farmer, and she hoisted the potatoes like she did it every day of her life, which she probably did.

"Remind me, Clare," she said rummaging through the basket. "Remind me to check to see if John O'Keane has any pork cuttings before we go on off home. A little pork would be nice for a change, so it would. Did you see the scissors?"

"I didn't," I said. "They aren't in the basket?"

"Jane was using them last night," Mrs. Sullivan said. "Bless her pointed little head, I'll hold you that she left them by the hearth." She sighed and dropped her hands heavily into her lap.

"I could go check," I said. "'Tisn't far."

"Ah, well, when a body's fourteen, I suppose it isn't far," she said. "Would you be a dear?"

I nodded. "Do you want anything else?" I asked.

"No, only the scissors." She patted my arm lightly, and I set off.

* * *

Wally was sitting in the chair by the hearth, his elbows on his knees and his head bent.

"Shouldn't you be in school?" I said.

"Sshhh," he said. He was looking down at the floor as though he were trying to stare a hole right in it. I came closer and bent to see what interested him so. It was a knot hole in the floorboard, a circular hole about an inch and a half across from which Wally had pried the knot.

"What's down there," I said.

"Sshhh," he replied.

"Sshhh, yourself," I whispered. "What are you looking at?"

"Rat," he said simply. "The same bugger from last night, I'll hold."

"Can you see it?" I asked. "Is it down there now?"

"Not yet," he said. "But it will be." He reached behind him to a loaf of bread on the table and pinched off a hunk. He appraised it for a moment, took a small bite and poked the rest through the knot hole. I got down on all fours and peered through the hole, a small pile of bread bits lay at the bottom.

"And if you make friends with him, he'll not crawl over your head at night?" I rose and began searching for the scissors Mrs. Sullivan needed.

Wally shuddered, a visible tremor passing through his shoulders and back. "That dirty blackguard'll never crawl over anyone else ever again, I swear it. So help me God, I swear it."

"Swear all you want," I said. "But you'd better not let your mother hear you do it. She doesn't take lightly to casual oaths."

"Nothing casual about it," Wally said. His hand squeezed down on the rag he clutched. "Sshh," he said in a coarse whisper. "Don't move. Do you hear him?" I froze and listened. A faint scratching came from the edge of the room. I tiptoed to the knothole. Wally glared at me and motioned for me to be still. He reached back with the rag and pulled the teapot off its hob. Tea pot in hand, his elbow braced on his knee, he bent again over the hole.

"A thousand welcomes, Mr. Rat, you filthy bugger," he whispered. "Care to take a bit of tea?"

"What are you doing?" I asked.

"Sshhh," he said.

I bent over the hole, trying to see around Wally's head and the teapot. First a tiny paw, then a brown nose came into view. The rat dragged a bit of bread away from the hole and out of sight.

"Damn," Wally said. He spat the word out like someone accustomed to using it.

"Wally!" I said.

"Shh," he said. "Here he comes again." I looked down the hole. First whiskers, then a nose, then the ears came into view. Wally upended the teapot, sending the boiling water down the hole.

"Take that, you filthy, miserable, louse-ridden creature." The boiling water splashed across the floor. I leapt back as a few stray drops hit my stockings. A terrible squeal came from under the floorboards.

"I got him," Wally shouted. "I got him." He set the teapot on the hob and tiptoed through the rapidly cooling water to peer down the hole. I could hear thrashing and the occasional squeak from roughly the middle of the floor. The rat wasn't dead, not yet. Wally had an air of triumph about him as he snatched his cap from the peg and fairly danced out the front door. I grabbed the scissors from the box and followed him out.

"You're just going to leave him there?" I asked.

"Under the floor is better than on top of it," he said and trotted off across the yard.

He was right. Rats' main purpose in life was to be killed by people, or so it seemed. But still I couldn't get the image of that scalded little beastie dying in the dirt beneath the floor. It was a terrible way to go, even for a rat.

* * *

As I closed the door behind me, I caught sight of a young man, eighteen perhaps, maybe younger, trotting across the yard in my direction. He was wearing a navy blue uniform and pushing a nearly new bicycle. Clearly he was not from the neighborhood.

"Clare Keane?" he called from halfway across the yard. He slowed, walked his bike toward me, and tipping his hat said in a more official sounding voice, "Are you Clare Keane?"

"I am," I said.

"The woman upstairs told me you moved?"

"We did," I said.

"You should have informed the Cunard office," he said.

"Cunard the steam ship company?" I said.

"And do you know another Cunard?" he replied, digging through the leather bag he wore on a strap over his shoulder. "I have a memorandum for you," he said.

I remember thinking that I hadn't the least notion what a memorandum was, but that it did indeed sound official, official enough to warrant a man in a navy uniform and a shiny-brimmed hat. More importantly, though, I remember wondering if "memorandum" was another way of saying "good news" or "bad news." Perhaps "memorandum" was a fancy way of saying "tickets."

The man finally found what he was rummaging for and handed it to me with a tip of his hat before turning and disappearing down the lane. It was an envelope with "Miss Clare Keane, 16 Walsh Lane, Cork" written in a fair hand across the front. I wiped my hands on my apron, then walked unseeing to the steps of the tenement, where, smoothing my skirts and adjusting a pin in my hair, I sat and opened the envelope. The paper inside was a rich ivory with a bold script letterhead that read "The Cunard Steamship Company (Limited). Corner Third Street and Second Ave. South. Minneapolis." In the upper corner was an emblem, a lion wearing a crown, playing with a checkerboard ball. It all looked mortally official. The typed message read:

Dear Miss Keane:

We have sent to the Cunard S.S.Co.Ltd., Cunard Wharf, Queenstown, third class Prepaid Certificate M/O 5368 issued in favor of yourself, Michael and Thomas Keane, for passage from Queenstown to New York, N.Y., and requested forwarding via S.S. "CARONIA" from Queenstown August 1st. In addition we have instructed our agents to pay you $10.00 in cash upon arrival in Queenstown and $50.00 in cash upon arrival in New York, to be used for transportation to St. Paul. We have also been instructed by Ronan Keane of St. Croix Falls, Wisconsin to request that you wire him at the Eclipse Lumber Company in St. Croix Falls when you arrive in St. Paul.

Our Queenstown Office will give you necessary information with reference to sailing, etc. We think it would be well if you would communicate with them at address given above with reference to your transportation, giving number of same, etc., and advising them when you will be ready to travel.

Wishing you a pleasant voyage, we are

Yours truly,

THE CUNARD S.S.CO.LTD.

It was indeed an official sounding letter, so official I wasn't quite sure what it was asking of me. It sounded as though we would be leaving on August 1st, almost exactly a month from now. But I wasn't sure what it meant by St. Croix Falls, Wisconsin. But whatever it meant, it was certainly official looking. I folded it carefully, tucked it into the envelope, and tied it into my skirt pocket.

* * *

Barrack Street was bustling when I stepped out onto it. Something about the letter in my pocket, or the knowledge of what the letter held, suddenly made life on the street jump into sharp relief. I breathed in the air, tried to imprint the smells and sounds onto some deep place within me.

People chattered, and horse hooves echoed off the brick walls of the building. People made their way in and out of shops. The pawn shop, always busy it seemed, had a line of women outside, each bearing a coat, a pot, a piece of jewelry. Up and down the street, horses drew carts laden with cabbages, cucumbers, onions, and young carrots from the countryside. A woman bundled in a deep blue shawl sold cherries at the bottom of the hill. She huddled as though bundled against the cold, or so I thought until I came more closely upon her. It was then that I saw the tiny feet of the babe she had at her breast under the discrete cover of the shawl.

I wondered if women in America wore shawls. The women in Barrack Street all wore them. American women probably didn't. The rich women of Cork could afford coats and capes. Surely American women could as well. But Barrack Street women, the women of the lanes, myself included, all wore shawls. Our shawls were protection against the cold, the wet, the world. We bundled packages in our shawls. We reared babies in them.

We even used them as weapons against the young boys where were always underestimating the fortitude of the "shawlies." I once saw a boy about eight or nine years old steal an apple from the bin of an old woman selling apples in the Coal Quay. The boy snatched an apple, then turned to run, supposing, I would imagine, that we could outrun the old woman. But he was no faster than her shawl, which she snatched off her shoulders and whipped at his arm with such force that he dropped the apple. I've seen boys with welts from teasing the wrong shawlie.

Mrs. Sullivan wore a shawl, so did my mother, so did I. I used to think it marked us as poor, and that it did. But I now think it also marked us as resourceful, versatile. When all you have is a square of knit or woven wool between you and the world, you learn to make do with what you have. Whatever else you could say about the shawlies, you could say that.

* * *

Mrs. Sullivan was on the Coal Quay where I left her. The tidy stacks of shirts and trousers I left were now piles and bunches strewn in no particular order all about the top of the table. I approached with a smile, a smile that was a bit forced perhaps at the sight of that unholy mess. Mrs. Sullivan laughed at the look on my face.

"You always were a tidy one, weren't you Clare?" she said. "So was your mother, God rest her. But folks like to pick. And I can't very well tell them to go away for doing so, now can I?"

I reached into my pocket and pulled out the scissors, which I handed to her. Then I untied my inner pocket and pulled out the letter and handed that to her as well.

"What is this?" she asked.

"From the steamship company," I said. "I think we finally have the fare."

Mrs. Sullivan opened the letter and looked at it briefly before handing it back to me. "Read it for me, won't you?" I pulled up a crate beside Mrs. Sullivan's chair, and began reading, slowly, laboriously. The nuns didn't exactly have memoranda in mind when they taught me to read. Between the two of us we puzzled out most of the words and the general gist of the letter.

"August 1st," she said, clipping a patch from a pair of hopeless trousers.

"August 1st," I replied. I sat holding the letter, watching the people on the quay walk by, watching them purchase the potatoes one by one from the large bin across the way, watching them tug loads and herd children.

"You could stay," Mrs. Sullivan said, breaking the silence between the two of us. "If that was what you wanted. I mean, I'm delighted you have the chance to go. But if it isn't what you want, you could stay. You and Tom and Mick could keep living with us."

I wasn't sure what to say. I looked up at her, looked into her eyes. She met my eyes for the briefest instant, then dropped them to the table and began picking through the clothes, tossing the odd gansey up into the pile at the center. I looked at her, the softness of her profile, the liquid softness of her eyes, and I lay my head in her lap. It was the only thing I could think to do. There we sat, one of her hands on my shoulder, the other continuing to fuss with the table.

* * *

Kevin came by the table in the late afternoon. He was carrying a library book slung on a strap over his shoulder. It was hard to say who had his nose in a book more—Tom or Kevin. He stepped to the end of the table, and dragged his hand lightly over the silk skirt as he waited for his mother to look up. She finally did and smiled.

"Do you have anything to eat?" he said without so much as saying hello. "Anything leftover from lunch?"

"'Tis grand to see you, too, son," Mrs. Sullivan said. Kevin smiled and blushed—Kevin was fair and towheaded and could blush with the best of them. "No, I haven't a thing left from lunch," Mrs. Sullivan said, stroking the color on his cheek lightly with her forefinger. "You can't wait for supper?"

"I only thought . . . ," he said, as he folded his legs under him to sit on the stones beside his mother's chair, the book in his lap.

"Kevin," I said, "do you know where Mick and Tom went after school?" The letter was a steady presence in my pocket. I wanted to show it to them as soon as I could. Maybe they could figure out the parts Mrs. Sullivan and I couldn't make out. "Are they home?"

Kevin blushed furiously, a deep blush that started at the ears but lit up his entire head, even the scalp that showed through his fine, pale hair. "They, they aren't, they aren't at home," he said.

"Kevin," Mrs. Sullivan said, fixing her eyes on him as only a mother can. Kevin glanced up, then quickly dropped his eyes.

"I don't know where they are," he said, his eyes riveted to the cover of the book in his lap. The back of his neck glowed hot pink. 'Tis a cross for a boy to blush like that, to have such a barometer to the soul written all across his face.

"I'm sure you know that lying is a sin," Mrs. Sullivan said casually. "And I'm sure that you also know that if you lie to me, confessing to the priest will be the least of your worries."

I was sorry to see Kevin getting into trouble. But I was more curious to hear what he was trying not to tell us. "Where are they?" I said.

"They told me not to say," Kevin said.

"And why would that be?" Mrs. Sullivan replied.

Kevin was silent.

"If they are getting into mischief, and you don't tell me what they're up to, you'll share your father's belt with them. You know that, don't you?"

"They went someplace called 'Becky's.' Wally went with them. They wouldn't let me come," he said. "Are they going to get a flaking?"

"Becky Butler's?" I asked. Kevin nodded. Mrs. Sullivan looked at me with a shrug. "Oh, yes," I said. "They're going to get a flaking."

I stood, brushed down my skirts, and without so much as a by-your-leave, marched straight off for Becky Butler's.

* * *

Most of the men I saw on the way were still hard at work. But outside the door of Becky Butler's, there was no shortage of male bodies lounging, gabbing, and gambling. A huddle of tweed backs bent over a card game. Others stood talking, waiting for friends to get off work at the docks and come spot them a drink.

I picked my way along the least populated route I could see and was nearly to the door when I heard a familiar voice. I couldn't quite place it for some reason.

"The reason Guinness is more expensive is because 'tis a better stout," the voice said.

"A pity when a man's sense of taste dies so much sooner than he does," his companion said.

"You think drinking naught but Beamish day in and day out your whole life long makes you an expert?" the familiar voice said. It was coming from a pair of men sitting, elbows on knees on the edge of the walk. They were no more than fifteen or twenty feet from me, but I couldn't see either face. I kept walking.

"I may not be an expert, but I know that I'll not be paying extra for a stout that is no better than Beamish. I know that much to be sure."

"Ppft," the first man said. He took off his cap, ran a hand through his hair, then snugged the brim down again. A whiff of his hair oil floated out on the breeze. It was then I recognized him. Murphy. I stopped dead in my tracks. Something about the abruptness of the movement must have caught his eye because he turned to look. A wholly unsettling smile spread across his face. At that moment, I wanted nothing more than to cave that smile in and with it his oh-so-smug face. I could feel my fists knot up with the desire of it.

"Be damned if it isn't sweet Sister Clare," he said, rising and tipping his cap.

"Crawl back into the sewer you crawled out from," I said, moving quickly to get around him. He was too quick and stepped in front of me, blocking my path.

"Oh, my," he said. "You wound me. I do understand, truly I do. We parted on such terrible terms, and now you bear me ill will. I understand. But I don't know if my heart can bear it." He sighed a deep sigh, eyes downcast, then looked up at me, a leer on his face.

"Let me pass, Murphy," I said.

"Why Sister Clare, you'd leave before giving me a chance to make amends?" He raised a hand toward my face. It was a gentle movement, but I took a sharp step backward.

"Why do you call me that?" I asked. "Why do you call me Sister Clare?"

"Well, it suits you, now doesn't it?" He backed off a bit, leaned nonchalantly against the front wall of Becky's. "The piety, the scruples, the . . . " He paused. "I always had the belief," he said, "that what the good sisters of our beloved church need, every last one of them, is a night each with a good man, myself for example. It would revolutionize the schools, maybe the entire church itself." He cocked his head as though waiting for my response.

"That's blasphemy, and you know it," I said.

"Is that what you call it?" he said. "Well, now, I suppose that's as good a word for the act as any. I myself prefer screwing, humping, the old jig-a-jig leg over, whatta ya say?"

"Murphy." The man Murphy had been arguing with rose from the curb. He was a tall, lanky man, with unruly blond hair, that stuck out in every direction from under his cap. "Stop your gob, man. Is that any way to talk in front of a girl?"

"I suppose that depends on which girl, now doesn't it." He pushed himself away from the wall and began walking toward me again. "Just what are you doing here, sweet Sister Clare? Had a change of profession maybe? Found out you can make more money on your back than you can on your feet all day?" I dashed to the curb, trying to get around him again, but he was too fast for me, his arms too long. He herded me back onto the walk, his arms spread wide like a man herding cattle.

"Murphy, leave her alone." The lanky man, laid a hand on Murphy's shoulder. Murphy shook it free. The lanky man grabbed for a fistful of jacket but missed. "Andrew, let the girl pass," he said.

Andrew. His name was Andrew. I had always just thought of him as Murphy.

"Stay out of this, James." Murphy fixed his eyes on me. I felt my skin crawl with the film of filth his gaze left there.

"You know I won't do that, Spud," James said.

"This girl cost me a job, James. A good job." Murphy took another step toward me. I took another couple of steps back. I began to think it would have been wiser to have sent Mr. Sullivan or Roddy in to get Mick and Tom. But it was too late for that now. "Sweet Sister Clare, here is teasing me since I first laid eyes on her, and I think 'tis time she made it up to me." Murphy reached out. I turned to run, but he pounced, wrapping both arms around me from behind. His grip was like a vice. I froze.

"Murphy." I heard James' voice just over my shoulder. Then I felt a lurch as Murphy took a couple of steps back and then let go of me. James had him by the back of the belt, and was dragging him kicking and stumbling into the street. "I'll not let that go with you," he said simply. He let go of Murphy and stood between him and me.

"Do you want to have a go?" Murphy said, his eyes flaming. "Is that what you want?" He stripped off his coat and started undoing the top button of his shirt. "I'll give you the devil to eat, I will. 'Tis none of your affair, James."

James nodded, then gestured with his head toward the alley. Murphy popped open the rest of the buttons of his shirt, and strode toward the alley, his face red with rage.

"Go," James said over his shoulder to me.

"Thank you," I said. James nodded and followed Murphy to the alley. A parade of men followed them, some already laying their bets.

* * *

The publican was standing behind a line of glasses, each partly filled with a deep chocolate-brown porter. He picked up the one at the end, filled it to the top, and placed it in front of a customer who was leaning heavily over the bar watching his every move.

"Is the bishop in town, then?" the man asked, pointing at the thick white "collar" of foam atop the deep brown pint.

"Just take it and don't complain to me," the publican said. "If you could wait long enough for me to pour you a proper pint, it'd not have such a head on it."

"I can wait," the man said, drinking down a third of the glass in one long draw. He wiped the foam from his upper lip with the back of his hand. "I can wait."

"You were halfway over the bar, you were," the publican replied. "If I let you, you'd be back here suckling my tap like a teat, and you know it, Jerry."

"Still, 'tis no excuse for giving a man such a pint." He drained the glass, and leaned over the bar again. I walked up beside him, and standing on my toes, addressed myself to the publican.

"Beg your pardon, sir," I said.

He looked up from his tap, and his eyes widened. "Did you take a wrong turn somewhere, lass?" he said. "Surely you're not here to see Miss Becky."

"I'm not," I said. "I'm here for my brothers, Mick and Tom Keane, and for their friend Wally Sullivan. I was told I could find them here."

"Good," the publican said. "That's good. I was hoping you weren't here to see Miss Becky about, um, 'work'. I think Mick and Tom are in the back stacking crates." He pointed over his shoulder at a door. "Don't you be dawdling back there, though. It's supposed to be employees only."

I nodded and made my way around the end of the bar. I paused at the door, then pushed it open a crack and listened. It was Mick's voice I heard first.

"She said he made her take a bath first," Mick said.

"While he watched?" Wally asked.

"Nah, you dead head, he didn't want to watch," Mick replied.

"Oh," said Wally.

"He made her take a bath. Then when she came out, still in her pelt, he handed her two bunches of scallions. What he wanted was for her to chase him around a table, whipping him with the scallions."

"Naked?" Wally asked.

"Of course, naked," Mick said.

"And for that she got two pounds," Mick said.

"Go on with you," Wally said. "Two pounds? My Da would have to work," he paused, "a long time to make two pounds."

"How much does your Da make?" Tom asked. So Tom was in there with them. I'd see Mick hurt for this.

"Scallions, you say," Wally said. "Why scallions?"

"Are you going in or not?" the publican asked. The voice came from just over my shoulder. I jumped with the sound of it and pushed the door all the way open.

Tom was seated cross-legged atop a large wooden cask. Wally and Tom lounged on the floor, their backs to other casks. Mick was handing a pint of porter to Wally, laughing liquidly. He spotted me in the doorway and quickly slapped his palm over his top lip wiping way the evidence.

I had nothing to say, everything to say. More importantly, I still hadn't let the steam out of my fists after my encounter with Murphy. I walked over to where Mick was scrambling to his feet, and slapped him as hard as I could across the face. He stumbled and fell. Tom rolled forward to his knees and looked down at him from the top of the cask. I grabbed at the back of Mick's collar and hauled him to his feet. Mick looked at me in shock, his eyes not quite focusing.

"Clare," he said. "I didn't . . . " I let go his collar, took a step back, and slapped him again. Mick staggered, then without so much as looking at me swung, a huge round punch with no shoulder whatsoever behind it. I stepped inside it and shoved him. He landed in a pile amidst the casks.

"Clare," Tom said. I raised my hand again and stepped toward him. Tom scrambled off the cask, and positioned himself carefully so the better part of the barrel was between him and me. I shoved the cask, but it wouldn't budge. I kicked it, then kicked it again. The pain shot up my ankle and I stopped the third kick in midswing.

"Clare." Tom leaned over the cask and looked down at my foot. "Are you hurt?"

Mick by this time had scrambled into a corner. Wally merely sat where I found him, his mouth hanging open in shock. The pint in his hand shook ever so slightly.

The rage was dying down, being replaced with hurt, and ever-rising pain from my ankle.

"I should pack you both up and send you alone to Uncle Ronan. I should pack you off and stay here in Cork myself. Let him try to talk some sense into you," I said. "I don't know what to do any more. I ask you not to come here, but here you are. If the guard catches you, we'll all be hauled off."

"The guards aren't a problem," Mick said, his words slightly slurred. "Becky pays them back hand, gives them a free ride every now and again. They don't give her any trouble."

I looked at him, looked but didn't really see for the rage that had risen again before my eyes. I closed the gap between us in a couple of large strides, then drew back and kicked him as hard as I could. Then I kicked him again. My ankle screamed with the pain, but somehow I welcomed it. Mick tried to get away but he was boxed in by the corner. He wrapped himself in his arms and whimpered.

"Clare," Tom said, his hand holding a large fistful of my shawl. "Clare, stop." He tugged, laid his other hand on my chest. The touch of it brought me back.

"I want you all home, now. Before I get there. When I get home I want to see you all waiting for me." I turned to leave, but my ankle gave way beneath me. I caught myself on one of the casks.

"Are you hurt?" Tom said.

I tested my ankle. It was weak, could barely support me. I tried to walk, but the pain from it shot up my leg and stopped me cold.

Tom put a hand under my elbow. "We'll help you," he said. He wrapped my arm over his shoulder. "Wally," he said. "Get on the other side." Wally rose, setting the porter atop one of the casks. Mick scrambled to his feet and elbowed him aside.

"She's *my* sister," Mick said. He slipped under my other arm. "She's my sister."

* * *

I sat before the hearth. My ankle, smothered in a poultice of water lily root and goose grease, was bound tightly by rag strips and raised to rest on the coal box. I was miserable with the throb of it, but not nearly so miserable as Tom, Mick, and Wally looked. They leaned heavily against the wall by the door, sour looks oozing from their faces. It would be a while before they would enjoy sitting again.

Mr. Sullivan had a system when it came to boys and whippings. When he gave the signal, they all dropped their trousers and leaned over the table. Mr. Sullivan then arranged them in order, based on the severity of their offense. Once he was content with the arrangement, he would swing his belt crosswise, drawing it across the lineup of waiting cheeks. It was an efficient method, developed over many years of raising boys. It both saved time, and ensured that the boy with the most to regret would catch the snap at the end of the swing.

This evening that boy was Mick, who was still not quite sober by the time Mr. Sullivan came home. By the time he and Roddy finished scrubbing the coal dust from their hands and faces, Mrs. Sullivan was already flowing freely with a powerful temperance lecture. She handed off to Mr. Sullivans, whose work with the belt leeched the last of the alcohol from Mick's system. The three boys watched us eat supper that night, then were handed a few leftover crusts, but only after Mrs. Sullivan extracted the promise that they would stop selling peanuts and never set foot in Becky Butler's ever again as long as they lived.

Once the promise was made, normalcy began to settle again on the house. Angela and Jane set to work on the dishes. Mr. Sullivan settled into his chair with the *Echo*. Mrs. Sullivan and I reached for the sewing kit, and the boys retreated to the yard to bait and accuse each other beneath the gas lamp that lit the lane with a flickering yellow light.

I knew by now that the letter would have to wait until after the dishes were done, after Mr. Sullivan finished his paper. It was part of the order of the Sullivan house, an order that I had grown to cherish despite the itch to draw out the letter and begin puzzling over it. I settled back, my mending on my lap and my foot on the coal box, and I quietly surveyed the scene before me. The cat hopped up on Mr. Sullivan's lap, and he swept it off again with brush of his hand and a rustle of newspaper. Mrs. Sullivan clucked and patted her lap, and the cat strolled over in its own sweet time before hopping up and settling in amidst Mrs. Sullivan's ample skirts and petticoats. I myself settled in as well, content to stay there in that one room for the rest of my life.

* * *

"We have train fare," Tom said. He was leaning heavily over the table, where Mr. Sullivan, Mick, Wally, Kevin, and I were bent over the letter. "Look, it says we have passage all the way to St. Paul."

"It doesn't say anything about a train," Mick said.

"But it does say we have passage all the way to St. Paul," Tom replied. "Sixty dollars. How much do we have in the tin?"

I reached back to the mantle. When we'd moved from our room to the Sullivans', the tin moved with us, from one mantle to the other. I pried off the lid, and spilled the contents. A pound, two shilling, and six pence. The Sullivans had been letting me save a full half of my salary since we moved in. The money had begun to add up.

"And sixty dollars is ten pounds," Tom said, "so we have thirteen pounds, two shilling, and six pence."

"Add to that what we can get for the furniture," Mick said. Our furniture had been moved to Nora's house. She and her husband were using the bed frame and the chairs, and her neighbors across the hall had the table. We planned to pawn them all as soon as we knew we had fare.

"So fourteen pounds," Tom said. "Maybe more." It was a great deal of money. We all sat in awe.

"Do you know what I'd do if I had fourteen pounds?" Kevin said.

"You don't," Wally replied. "They do." He was still in a bad humor after the whipping.

"But if I did, I'd buy a horse and dray. And I'd charge people to haul things for them."

"I know what I'd do if I had fourteen pounds," I said quietly.

"You can't buy a horse for fourteen pounds," Roddy interjected from his place on the sofa. He was paging through his dad's copy of the *Echo* but clearly not reading it.

"You can on time," Kevin answered. "Fourteen pounds down and pay off the rest with the fares."

"What would you do with fourteen pounds, Clareen?" Mrs. Sullivan asked, looking up from her sewing. I didn't think anyone had heard me. The quietness of her voice brought Kevin and Roddy and their argument up short.

"I'd quit my job at the sack factory," I said. "We can live off what we get from the furniture until it's time to leave. Can't we?" Mr. Sullivan nodded. "And we don't have to earn train fare," I added. "And, well, we have fourteen pounds. I want to quit at the factory."

"I think that's a grand idea," Mrs. Sullivan said. "You can work with me."

"Hmpph." It was Jane. She was sitting outside on the stoop. I should have known she was listening.

"I think it's a grand idea," Mrs. Sullivan repeated.

"I'll tell Mr. Doolan tomorrow," I said.

"There's one thing I don't understand about this telegram," Tom said. "I don't understand why would Uncle Ronan would want us to contact him in Wisconsin."

"Are you sure that's what it means?" I asked.

"I'm sure," Tom responded. Mick and Wally both nodded agreement.

"First Lindstrom," I said, "then, what was it?"

"Wyoming," Tom replied.

"Wyoming, then St. Croix Falls. We don't know where the man lives himself."

"I didn't ever hear of a saint named Croix," Wally said.

"Maybe he's an American saint," Mick said.

"Or maybe your uncle made him up. Maybe there is no such saint. Maybe your uncle's a filthy liar."

Mr. Sullivan glared and Wally and lightly stroked the buckle of his belt with his thumb. Wally fell silent.

"How much do you know about your Uncle Ronan?" Mr. Sullivan asked me.

"He's Da's brother," I said. "He's tall, like Da was, has dark hair like Da and Tom." I thought about the letters Da had received before he died, the picture of Da and Uncle Ronan taken when they were in their twenties. Frankly, I didn't remember much.

"What does he do for work?" Mr. Sullivan asked.

"He's a fishing guide," Mick said.

"A fisherman?" Mr. Sullivan asked.

"No," Mick replied. "He takes rich people out and shows them where they can catch fish."

"Hmmpph," Mr. Sullivan said. "And in America this is a job?"

"It says in the telegram that he's at the Eclipse Lumber Company. Maybe he found a different job. As a logger maybe, or sawing lumber."

Mr. Sullivan reached for his cup and took a sip of tea. "Is he a good man? Does he drink too much? Does he gamble?"

"He used to drink too much," I said. Tom and Mick looked at me in surprise. "I think Mama said that's why he left for America, because he couldn't keep a job here."

"That's not true," Mick said.

"Mama said so," I replied.

"Why didn't you tell us?" Mick asked.

I shrugged. "Drunken family is still family. Besides he left Cork fifteen years ago. A man can change in fifteen years."

"Not all do," Mrs. Sullivan murmured from her place by the hearth. I looked over my shoulder at her. She had a tight frown on her face. I was sure she saw me turn to look, but she never lifted her eyes from her needlework.

Mr. Sullivan sighed and pushed himself back from the table. "You know you're welcome to say here," he said. "You don't have to go to America if you don't want."

"Thank you," Tom said. "But we do want to go." I looked over at him. He met my eyes. "At least I want to go."

"'Tis a most generous offer," I said, addressing myself first to Mr. Sullivan, then to Mrs. Sullivan. "But we'll have to think it over."

Fifteen

I was thinking," I said.

"You're pulling my leg," Mrs. Sullivan replied. I hadn't done much but think over the last couple of days since the Sullivans offered to let us stay with them.

"And would I do that?" I replied. She grinned. Mrs. Sullivan and I were on the back edge of the crowd, nearly out of earshot of the Barracka, the Barrack Street band, who were leading the way through the south side to the chapel. It was the feast of St. Oliver Plunkett, and as many as could joined the procession. Barrack Street was a human river, flowing with people in their best clothes, people carrying bits of red crepe, people humming or singing along with the band.

"I was thinking about what kind of situation I might want if I stay here," I said. "I think I might want to be a handywoman. And I can't think of anyone I'd rather learn from. And, well, could you teach me?"

Mrs. Sullivan didn't answer right away. I fiddled with the rosary I carried in front of me, my fingers searching out the rough edges of the beads. "Could you teach me?" I asked again. Perhaps the question had been carried away into the sounds of the band and crowd.

"I could," Mrs. Sullivan said, "I could. But little good it would do you if what you want to do is deliver babies. You'll be needing the license before you can practice. I could teach you to be a handywoman, but in this day and age you'll only be able to practice if you're licensed as a midwife. And I don't see . . ."

"I'd be needing some more time in school before I can get the license," I said. She nodded. "And it's too late for me to go back to school."

"How many years did you get?" she asked.

"Four," I said.

"You'd need to finish primary school," she said. "And then secondary, and then the training classes."

"And there's little chance of me getting that kind of schooling," I said.

"I don't see how you could," she replied.

Myself? I could see only one way, and it was a long shot. "It would take money," I said. I was thinking about the twelve pounds. Most of that, though was waiting for us in New York. I doubted the Cunard people would be so kind as to put it in an envelope and send it to me, it being earmarked for train tickets in America, not schooling here in Cork.

"It would take money," Mrs. Sullivan said. "Money and time. You could live with us, work with me after school in the market. But the money. You know we'd help you if we could, but . . ."

"I know," I said. "I couldn't begin to thank you for all you did for us already."

We continued to walk. All around us was the chatter of folks enjoying a day off. All around them the sidelong glances of people who considered chatter in processional to be the height of rudeness. Not that the St. Oliver Plunkett processional was really a processional. In time it might become one. But when I lived in Cork, it was more like a parade, with the band playing hymns, and the people enjoying the summer air on their way to the chapel for a sermon and a blessing.

Down Barrack Street I could see the band turning off onto Evergreen. I spotted Roddy's lanky form easily among the crowd. The brown cap beside him was probably Mick. Tom was still further down the hill with Wally, Mr. Sullivan, and the girls.

"Is that what you want?" Mrs. Sullivan asked. "To catch babies?"

"I did so admire the way you helped Maura," I said. "'Tis a worthy thing to do with one's life."

"'Tis," Mrs. Sullivan replied. "If they'd only let you be one. God only knows why they think catching babies takes a diploma. They'll still let you lay out the dead, of course." She seemed to be talking as much to herself as me. It hadn't passed my mind to that point just how much of Mrs. Sullivan was wrapped up in her status as handywoman for the tenement. It was sad thinking of her losing something so important to her.

The clouds parted a bit, and the sun came through. I picked at the front of my dress. The weather wasn't so much hot as it was sticky. It had rained all night. Then the sun came out, warming the damp stones and steaming all who walked them. But still, sticky was better than rainy, and more than a few St. Oliver Plunkett processions had been walked in the rain.

"You could learn to be a dealer," Mrs. Sullivan offered. "You could take over my table when I get too old for that sort of thing. God knows Jane and Angela have no head for it." She sighed. "They'll need to marry well, those two. A more worthless pair never walked this green earth."

"Jane has the looks for it," I said. We rounded the corner onto Evergreen street, and again the band could be heard clearly a couple of blocks ahead. I found my steps falling into time with the music.

"Would you want to be a dealer?" Mrs. Sullivan asked. "You can make good money at it if you're willing to work. Maybe enough to keep Tom himself in school when the time comes."

"Mama would be pleased," I said. "I think she always wanted him to become a priest."

"I can't see Tom as a priest," Mrs. Sullivan said. "Though if God should choose him, of course . . . " She crossed herself quickly. I followed suit. "But he just doesn't seem like a priest to me."

"Nor me," I said.

"I could teach you to be a dealer," Mrs. Sullivan said.

"I would be grateful," I answered with less enthusiasm than I'd hoped to manufacture.

"If you'd like," Mrs. Sullivan added. "You don't have to decide now."

"If I have to decide before August, I think I do decide now," I replied. "If we want to go to America, now is a grand opportunity. We may not get one so good ever again."

Mrs. Sullivan simply nodded. "If that's what you want to do."

I wished I had even the slightest clue what I wanted to do.

* * *

I sometimes wonder what would have happened if Mick had been able to control himself, or if Wally hadn't been such a sheep. Would I be sitting this very moment at a table on the quay selling rags as clothes, wearing rags as clothes? Or would I be dead and buried, eaten up before my time by the consumption or the typhoid, or some such thing?

It began with a cap, Wally's cap confiscated from its place on a peg by the door, one Saturday in mid-July. It was an ordinary cap, with a slouch top and a grimy brim. It had sprung another hole and, as she was on a patching spree, Mrs. Sullivan had bundled it up with the clothes for the quay, intending to patch it in her free time. But as she tossed the bundle over her shoulder that morning, she'd felt a scratching in her back.

She unbundled the clothes and found it. A blade. A blade hidden in the brim of Wally's cap.

She hid the blade beneath her mattress, dropped the cap back on the peg, silently bundled the rest of the clothes, and with me in tow began the trudge to the quay.

* * *

It was a quiet walk. Unusually quiet given how much Mrs. Sullivan had to say about most subjects. I walked silently beside her, helped her set up the table with only the talk needed to perform the task. Then we sat, her with her needle, I with mine, waiting for the market to set itself up, waiting for the right mix of women to gather.

"Clare," she said after several minutes of painful silence. "I was thinking about what we should do with Mick." The statement surprised me. It was Wally's cap, after all. Though I supposed if I'd asked myself, I would have known exactly why we were talking about Mick.

"He is a handful, so he is," I said.

"Wally is a handful. Roddy was a handful. Mick is terrible trouble all together."

The assessment seemed a bit harsh. But that didn't mean it wasn't true. "Mama's passing was hard for him," I said. "He wasn't like this . . . before. Her passing was . . . hard."

"Don't you think I know that?" Mrs. Sullivan replied. "Your mother was as good a friend as I had in this world. It's been hard on all of us."

Then there it was, the old weight, the weight that had been halved since coming to live with the Sullivans, now back in full force, pressing down between my shoulder blades, pressing on my chest, my eyes, my heart.

"Especially hard on you and the boys," Mrs. Sullivan said, reaching out a hand to pat my knee. "I know that."

We sat again for a bit, needles dipping in and out. "Clare," she said. "My boys aren't what you would call good boys. They aren't what you would call bad boys either. They are boys with a powerful mix of good and bad within them. Now I believe that a boy like that can become a good man if he has the good in him fed and the bad in him beat out at every opportunity. When he was young, Roddy was like Wally is now. But now he's nearly a man, working hard beside his father, going to Mass every Sunday, and thank God not a slave to the drink. He'll make some woman a good husband some day, but it's not for want of effort. Some nights John and I would lie awake nights worrying about him, about the fights he'd start, and the rowdy friends he'd keep, and the way he was always a wee bit slow in school. But he's growing into a fine man if I do say so myself."

"He is," I said.

"Clare," Mrs. Sullivan said. She looked at me. "I need to know. Will you be going to America?" It sounded like she was asking for a decision right then and there.

"Tom wants to," I said. "Mick. . . ," I paused. "I don't know what Mick wants anymore. He talks about America, then the next minute he talks about not wanting to leave his friends. He actually said yesterday that he wanted to stay. It surprised me to no end."

"I think you should send Mick," Mrs. Sullivan said. "Tom, too, if he wants to go."

"'Send them'," I echoed`. Was she asking me to stay?

"Or go with them," Mrs. Sullivan added. "Though God knows it would be like sending my very own daughter to lose you." Her voice caught.

"True enough," I said quietly.

"There's naught but trouble here for Mick," Mrs. Sullivan said. She dropped her eyes back to her sewing. "The animal gangs. The troubles brewing. The underground groups taking them younger and younger every year. A boy like Mick could find a belly full of trouble without looking."

"And a boy like Wally could follow him into that trouble without so much as a by your leave."

Mrs. Sullivan nodded. "You could send Mick to America, to Ronan. Alone."

"Tom would be killed by it all together," I said. "Mick leaving. Himself not having the chance."

"You could send them both," she offered.

That's where we sat. In the midst of the knowledge that Mick couldn't stay. We both knew it. We'd known it for some time. But living with the knowledge is one thing. Unpacking it and setting it out on the table to look at is quite another. So it sat. So we sat. And the market hummed around us as though it were an ordinary day.

* * *

That night before supper Mr. and Mrs. Sullivan chased us all out into the yard with warnings that if we either entered the house or left the yard we would remember the consequences 'til our dying day. I sat on the stoop next to Jane, hoping to catch a few words out of the quiet hum of voices inside.

"So are you leaving?" Jane said.

"I don't know," I replied. "I didn't decide yet."

"'I didn't decide yet'," she said. "'I didn't decide yet.' Don't you mean 'I haven't decided yet'?" She shot a quick burst of breath from her nose. "May you leave and soon, please God," she said. "That's what I say." Her voice was full of venom. But then her voice was always full of venom when she talked to me, those few times she felt it absolutely necessary to talk to me.

"You may just get your wish," I replied. We both fell silent. I listened, hoping to catch a word or two through the cracks in the door. The voices inside were too low to hear. I could feel Jane's contempt for me oozing out and filling the space between us. "Why are you so filthy to me?" I asked quietly, not really expecting an answer. "I was never anything but kind to you."

"You call bringing your dirty laner brothers into our house 'kind'?" There it was again, the contempt, the condescension.

"You're a fine one to talk about dirty laner brothers," I said, matching her tone. It seemed the only way to hold a conversation with her, if you could call it that.

"If you all left tomorrow, I'd be so happy you'd hear me laughing all the way in America," she said. "I'd be so happy they'd look up in New York and wonder who that was laughing all the way across the ocean."

"You haven't the least notion the blessings you have here," I said. "None at all, at all." I rose into the yard. The area around the tap was muddy. I waded in, washed my hands, splashed still more water on my face. It was cool.

It was then I knew. We had to leave. All three of us. I couldn't bear to send the boys alone. I couldn't bear to live here alone, living among the Sullivans girls like the only potato in a bowl of fruit. I was tired of people looking at me and seeing nothing but a laner. It wasn't just that Mick had to go. I had to go.

I walked past Jane and opened the front door. Mr. and Mrs. Sullivan looked up startled from their conversation at the table.

"We'll be going," I said. "All three of us. As soon as we can arrange things with the steamship company." They simply looked at me. "I know you said not to disturb you, but I thought it might make your conversation easier," I added. Then I turned and went back to the yard.

A few minutes later, Mr. and Mrs. Sullivan waved me, Tom, and Mick into the house. In those few minutes something happened inside me. The doubt dropped away. I was suddenly resigned, like a prisoner mounting the scaffold, or a soldier wading into a hail of bullets. It was decided. In my mind it was decided. We would go.

"We did the best we could by you," Mr. Sullivan began. "For the sake of your dear mother, we did the best we could." The three of us stood silently. I think the boys knew, too. "But we aren't your true family. Your only family is America now. That's where you should be." I looked up. Mrs. Sullivan's eyes were welling as she bent over the supper pot to test the potatoes inside. She blinked deliberately.

"We'll take you to the emigration agent tomorrow," he said. "He'll know what else you need to do before you leave."

"Thank you," I said.

"Thank you," Tom echoed. I could feel the excitement oozing off him. I looked over at Mick. His jaw was set.

"It's not your decision to make for us," he said. Then he tugged the cap over his head and dashed for the door. Mr. Sullivan jumped to his feet and lunged, but Mick was slippery. He bolted off the front steps and down the lane.

"Call the rest of them," Mr. Sullivan said to me. "It's time for supper."

* * *

Mick didn't come home that evening, nor the next. When he stopped by for breakfast on the third day, Tom and I snatched him up, and with the help of Roddy's muscle, hauled him to the emigration agent to confirm passage and pick up the three tickets. The process was surprisingly simple—a few questions, a bit of paperwork, a quick medical exam, the assurance that someone was indeed waiting for us in America. Before we knew it, we were emigrants. Nobody cried too many tears for the loss of the likes of us.

Jane was delighted, of course. Mr. Sullivan simply looked relieved. Mrs. Sullivan withdrew. Our chats on the way to the quay dried up. And in the evening, she'd give me the boot, along with Jane and Angela and the boys, and she and Mr. Sullivan would sit alone before the fire. I'd sit under the lamp at the end of the lane and listen to Tom read library books aloud. He was taking them out of the Carnegie library by the arm full, almost as though he were trying to finish the library before leaving.

As for Mick, he was gone as much as he was home. He got caught sleeping in the church one night, came home with the scruff of his neck in the priest's fist. The priest stood in the Sullivan's doorway lecturing Mick about the road to hell. Mick took it, his head bowed, but the next day he was gone again.

And me? Mostly I just went about my life, doing what needed to be done, trying not to give in to either too much excitement or too much fear.

* * *

Now you should know that we Irish have a long history of doing what needs to be done, be it pleasant or not. My grandfather, Thomas Brody, the man who was my mother's father, was born to be a farmer. He and his family had a small patch of ground in County Clare. No more than a couple of acres and a cot. But 'twas enough to live on. Or at least so the story was told to me throughout my childhood.

Thomas's father taught him the art of squeezing from the rocky ground enough for both the landlord and the family. And Thomas's mother rightly assumed that someday he would marry, take over the land, and provide for them in their old age. It was the way of things.

Or so it was until 1846.

It was a wet, stormy summer, riddled with lightning. That's what the old folks recall. Grandpa was thirteen. The first sign of trouble was the smell, a rotten, sulphury smell that hung in the air like a specter. When the time came, Thomas and his family dug the potatoes, only to have them rot in the cellars. That winter they ate the seed potatoes, and in the spring they sold the cow to gamble on the next year's seed.

The new seed withered in the ground no sooner than it was planted.

Cellars were empty, the yard and fields bare. The landlord went unpaid, and before the first frost, Thomas and his family found themselves eating grass and bark, sleeping beside the road, huddled with dozens of their neighbors who found themselves in the same straits.

The very young and the very old died first—Thomas's baby sister, his youngest brother, his old aunt and her husband. Then went the ones who stared the situation straight in the eye and saw no other reasonable course than to give up all hope. But soon even the strong—the fighters and the lovers, the bonny and the blest—all were succumbing. That's when Thomas's mother did what needed to be done.

She bundled all the food she could beg or borrow into a wee cloth, stuffed it into Thomas's pocket, and set his face toward the south. Rumors had filtered up from refugee to refugee that there was work to be had in Cork and Dublin. So Great grandma bundled up the last of her hope for her family's future and placed it on her oldest son. He walked the hundred miles to Cork, arriving with empty pockets and an even emptier belly. The rumors of work were greatly exaggerated.

Thomas lived on the quays and begged work from the foreign sailors who docked their ships amidst the desolation that was then Ireland. One day as he was scavenging food behind a dockside pub, a small shroud was off-loaded from a British merchant ship. The cook's boy had died in port of a throat ailment, and the cook was desperate to replace him before the ship set sail. Thomas was in the right place at the right time, and for that he found himself drafted into a life of virtual slavery.

About his new life, Thomas knew one thing to be true above all others: even slaves are fed. He curled up in his greasy hammock deep in the bowels of the ship and prayed heartfelt prayers of gratitude. Though his belly was never full, neither was it empty. Moreover, a grimy hammock was better than the wet and cold of a stony ditch. So he offered up his gratitude along with dual prayers for his family—prayers for their deliverance, miraculous though that seemed, and, barring that miracle, prayer for the repose of their souls, souls that had known far too little repose in the last two years of life.

Gradually, Thomas learned to cook. And when one spring the ship's cook disappeared among the exceptionally attractive women of a certain Spanish port they visited regularly, Thomas was promoted to ship's cook. It was a strange life for a farmer's son from County Clare. But Grandpa found it comforting to have the huge pots of food passing beneath his hands each and every day. A farmer can only eat what the earth deems fit to bless him with. He can break his back working all summer long and still starve. But a cook has food as long as he has work. Standing all day in the cramped, suffocating galley of a ship made him ache for the fresh breeze of his boyhood farm. Yet that ache was much to be preferred to the ache of hunger, the ache of impending starvation. Grandpa, like all of us, did what needed to be done.

Mama used to tell us his story often when we were young. It was a curious bedtime story for children, but I think she meant it as comfort. She took comfort, I know, in being the child of such stock. Her father had survived. Mama had survived.

We would turn our faces west, and we too would survive.

Sixteen

July thirtieth was a soft day, a friendly, partly-sunny-partly-cloudy, mostly warmish day—one of those rare days in Cork that remind you just why you love the city. The air was clear and crisp, air washed to spotlessness by five or six months of rain.

I was not the only one walking through the streets soaking up the weather. Grand Parade was shoulder-to-shoulder with people who had found an excuse to get out, to run a quick errand, to get a bit of sun on their heads.

I, too, was on an errand. For me my errand was one last look. One last goodbye.

I walked past St. Finbarr's Cathedral, "St. Barry's" to everyone on the south-side. The church wasn't ours, to be sure. I had never been inside—had never been inside any Church of Ireland church, for that matter—and it didn't occur to me to go inside that day. But I did feel the need to say goodbye to the spire. The great stone spire of St. Barry's towered over the lanes of the south side. No matter where you went through the twists and turns and narrow alleys, you could always look up and set your bearings to the spire of St. Barry's. Today that spire stood hard against the blue sky and puffy clouds. Before the softness of the clouds, it looked almost too real, as though it were trying to force itself into the soft flesh of my mind and ensure I would never forget. I pressed the image to my mind, then turned and let St. Barry's go.

The brewery was humming, its dock teaming with men unloading sacks and loading kegs. The smell of it traveled heavily on the breeze, a deep murky smell that was a steady undertone in the concert of smells that was the south side.

I bent over the rail of the Main Street bridge and watched a barge laden with kegs float below. The Lee, green and quiet, ambled past. I would miss that river something terrible. More than anything else, the Lee defined Cork, split it into north and south sides, brought in goods, and hauled off butter, and stout, and all the other products of Irish hands. Today, as every day, the water the south channel, our channel, flowed easily along the banks of the south side. Downstream it would join with the water from the north side, then further still, with water from all over the county, all over the country. Then all of it together would flow through Queenstown and out to sea.

* * *

The bakery wagon driver knew he was being followed. I watched him eye the boys behind the low stone fence. He reached under the seat of the wagon, snatched up a small stone, and flicked it at one of the youths. The boy—about Mick's age, I guessed—dodged easily. He hopped over fence and started walking the sidewalk, following the wagon down the street. From my vantage point across the street and a half block down, I could feel the trouble on the air.

"Can you spare a crumb or two?" the boy called out. His companion, a bit more reticent, kept the fence between himself and the vanman. The vanman didn't answer.

"Only a crust?" the boy called, sidling up beside the horse. The horse drifted away, into the center of the road. The vanman reined him back.

"I'm warning you, boyo," the vanman said. He slowed the wagon nearly to a stop. Still leaning on the rail of the bridge, I watched the boy reach up to grab the horse's harness. The vanman reached under the seat again. The boy let go.

"Only a crust is all I'm asking," he said. "Is that too much?"

"I was robbed by the likes of you for the last time already," the vanman said, pulling a stick from under the seat. The cocky grin dropped from the boy's face and he backed off. The vanman looked as though he might follow. The boy snatched up a stone, cocked his arm back. That was enough. The vanman bolted from his wagon, taking a wild swing for the boy. The boy scrambled back, tripped and skidded on his hip over the stones. The vanman's stick landed hard on his shoulder. The boy cried out and scrambled out of range again. The vanman lowered his stick.

That would have been the end of it, I suppose, had the boy's eyes not betrayed him. He looked up from his place in the dust to the back of the wagon, where his buddy was handing loaves of bread to two other boys I hadn't seen until just then. The vanman followed his line of sight, then spotting the theft, bellowed and took up pursuit, brandishing his stick. The boys set off at a dead run, bread tucked under their arms. Rather than leave his wagon, the vanman turned again on the boy clutching his shoulder in the dust. He raised his stick, and with a swing powerful enough to do in any lad that size, brought it down hard. The boy, still clutching his shoulder, rolled out of the way at the last second. Still clutching his shoulder, he ran for his life. It seemed a terrible price for a crust of bread. But I suppose the price of having no bread at all was just as high.

My eyes followed the lad until he disappeared behind the church yard. I wondered if he had parents, or maybe a sister, at home to question him about his shoulder.

* * *

When I was a child, death was not a stranger. Loss was not a stranger. I grew up on Irish wakes and Roman funerals. Our lane was forever losing people and gaining people. Birth and death, birth and death, birth and death. I thought I knew it. I thought I knew loss.

But when Mama died, I was introduced something that went so far beyond mere loss that I don't think the language has a word for it. "Loss" makes it sound like a piece of the jigsaw puzzle dropped out of the box and under the sofa. The picture is incomplete because of it. Every time you look at it, you see the gap, the hole that mars the whole. That's loss.

But when Mama died, I lost more than a piece of my life, I lost all the connections. It was as though with that one piece missing, suddenly none of the connections fit. The loss changed me, jarred me, altered me down to my very marrow. My connections to my community no longer fit. My connections to Tom and Mick chafed. Even the connections within myself, the way I had always seen my life, even they no longer linked up.

I was loose. I no longer fit anywhere. I went back to the old places for comfort, only to find them strange, alien. The puzzle was no longer a picture, certainly not a picture of my life. The puzzle was now only a collection of pieces, individual pieces that if they could ever form themselves again, would do so without me.

When Mama died, I lost everything. Everything, that is, but the moment— the sights, sounds, smells that passed in front of me one by one. I lived them as they came. I became the steady parade of duties and chores. I became all the things that demanded to be done, all the things that filled my life, even if they couldn't possibly fill me.

So on that day, on July 30, 1906, as I walked the streets and said goodbye, I was saying goodbye to a life that no longer existed, a life that had already slipped over the horizon out of sight and out of reach. Goodbye, I said. A woefully inadequate and somewhat belated goodbye.

* * *

The grass over the grave was patchy still, coming in little tufts here and there. But the dirt was packed down by the rain and weather, no longer the clumps of mud and loam that had landed with hollow thuds in the empty grave three and a half months earlier.

I knelt, prayed my beads for a while, but that felt so formal. So I sat down on the grass and laid a hand on the cool stone, remembered.

The headstone was simple by Irish standards:

May God have mercy on the soul of
Joseph Thomas Michael Keane
1858-1902
and his wife
Hannah Elizabeth Mary Keane
1868-1906

I could see him in my mind—Papa in his butcher's apron, the carcass of a sheep resting heavily on the leather pad slung over his shoulder. He was dark-haired, like Tom, but lithe and slight like Mick. I had his eyes, blue-green, with a little wrinkle in the corners. In my mind he was frozen into scenes, behind his table at the market, playing on the floor with Mick in front of the fire, seated at the head of the table presiding over the ham at Christmas, feeding the ducks at the Lough dressed in his great coat, the coat long since pawned. I saw the images of him like photographs, like portraits taken at weddings and christenings lined up one after the other on the shelf of my mind. I looked at the headstone and thought of him lying in the soil beneath me. And the grave seemed no more than another photograph, something I might see in my mind years from now as I stood on American soil thinking back to my childhood in Ireland.

I wondered if I would feel that way about Mama some day, too. I wondered if the immediacy I still felt would fade. I clutched her shawl snugly around me and remembered her arms around me in bed at night. I remembered the smell of her, the solid presence of her as we conquered the washing each Monday, side by side, our arms up to our elbows in wash water. Her name on the headstone told me that she was gone, she was a part of the past as was Papa. But the ache inside me was a part of the present.

"Mama," I said, "We're leaving. Tom and Mick and I are leaving tomorrow. We have tickets on a boat called *Caronia*, and we're going to go to America to live with Uncle Ronan."

I brushed a stray clump of dirt from base of the headstone, pulled a thistle growing above where I imagined Mama's face to be. The soil that clung to its roots was good. The grass would be covering the grave in no time.

"Tom is already talking about going to an American school," I said. "He talks about going to secondary school and about all the great libraries there must be in America. I keep thinking about what you would say to such hard dreams. But then I think that maybe in America you would simply give him your blessing."

A cloud passed overhead, chilling the air slightly. I heard the sound of horses' hoofs on gravel as the hearse passed through the gates and entered the cemetery.

"I'm glad Uncle Ronan will be able to take Mick in, Mama. He's gotten to be a bit of a handful. Mr. Sullivan had to whip him three times last week. I'd be blessed if it took, though. He's gotten hard to it. I feel I don't know him sometimes. But . . . we're going. All of us together. I'm keeping us together. I thought you'd want to know that."

I looked at the headstone, trying to fix it in my mind, trying to burn the photograph of it deep into myself where I would carry it always. Hannah Elizabeth Mary Keane 1868-1906. My mother. Joseph Thomas Michael Keane 1858-1902. My father. I felt I should do something before leaving. Before leaving never to see this place again.

A mere two days from now, we would be gone entirely. We would be the last of the family to leave these shores. We the living would go on with our lives in a new place. The dead would remain behind in the soil of the old. But in a sense, the past was already buried, already gone. I couldn't return to it if I wanted to. Ireland would never be the same. Our apartment would never be the same. I was propelled out of my past by a stiff boot to the seat.

I stood, ran a hand over the top of the headstone. "Goodbye," I said simply. "I love you." And I turned and made my way out through the gate.

* * *

When I arrived at the Sullivan's that evening, the air in the lane was filled with an utterly foreign smell. Children milled around the Sullivan's door. Tom, Wally, and Kevin leaned against the corner of the house, holding a half-hearted conversation. Even the clutch of women sitting on the stoop of the tenement angled themselves to catch a whiff of it on the breeze. For a moment I didn't recognize it, though I had smelled it hundreds of times at the Quillans and the Goods. I elbowed my way through the children and into the house.

There it was, hanging over the hearth, an entire joint of beef. Juices dripped down from it into a pan set in the coal fire below. Potatoes and swedes bubbled in the kettle. And on the table in a bowl, were two beautiful ripe peaches. I breathed in the air, the smell of the joint, then bent over the table to take in the honey fragrance of the peaches. Mr. Sullivan sat in his chair, the *Echo* unread in his lap, his eyes closed, a look of utter contentment on his face.

"Are the boys in the yard?" Mrs. Sullivan asked.

"They are," I said.

"Mick, too?"

"I didn't see him," I said.

"His loss," Mrs. Sullivan replied. She lifted the kettle off the fire, and set in on the stones of the hearth. Gingerly she touched the surface of one of the potatoes to test for doneness. "Roddy and I took your furniture to the pawns this afternoon," she said. "The money is in your tin."

"Thank you," I said. I reached for a spoon from the cabinet and handed it to her.

"Don't you want to know how much?" she asked.

"We have enough to leave," I said. "That's what I need to know."

"And here I could be spending it and you'd never know the difference," she replied.

"You'll not tell her?" Mr. Sullivan interjected. "We did spend it. And some of our own as well."

"Hush, now," Mrs. Sullivan said. Mr. Sullivan grinned at her. "Go get the girls," she said to him.

"And the boys?" he replied.

"I'd hold the boys already know we want them."

Just then Wally peered around the side of the door. "Can we come in yet?" he asked. "We washed already. Twice."

"Then get your clean self in here," Mrs. Sullivan replied. "We have a farewell dinner to eat."

* * *

Dinner was quiet. The boys ate like wolves. Mick showed his face halfway through the meal. For a short while his anger and defiance gave way to a meal better than any he had eaten in his life.

I myself ate my fill, but don't remember a taste of it. Mrs. Sullivan finished half of her plate, then pushed the rest over to Roddy.

"I would imagine we'll have to leave early tomorrow," I said in an attempt to break the silence. "Queenstown is ten miles if it's a foot."

"More like fifteen miles," Roddy said. "I rode there with a friend last year."

"Seven or eight hours then," Tom said. "If we leave at six, we can be there by mid afternoon."

"Go on with ya," Mr. Sullivan said. "The trip shouldn't take you better than an hour."

"It took me nearly an hour just to walk to Douglas," I said.

"True enough," Mr. Sullivan replied, "but then you didn't take the train to Douglas." He reached into his jacket pocket and drew out a small packet wrapped in newspaper. The newspaper was covered in coal dust, as was the pocket it was drawn from. Mr. Sullivan unwrapped the packet and drew from it three train tickets. "I wish we could go with you all the way to Queenstown, but these things don't exactly grow on trees." He handed the tickets to me. I cradled them in my hands gingerly.

"Thank you," I said. I don't think I'd ever seen train tickets before.

"Thank you," Tom echoed. He reached for them.

"We best put them with the boat tickets," I said, "so they don't get lost."

"Well, then," Mrs. Sullivan said. "You can put them in this." She fished behind the sofa and drew out a large basket, a shoonaun. It was a deep basket, made of rushes. From under its lid, I could see the edges of the calico lining. Mrs. Sullivan sat it down on her chair and undid the tie holding the calico closed. She beckoned me to stand next to her and pointed into the basket.

"See here." She pointed, then undid a smaller string tie. "I sewed in a secure pocket for tickets and papers and the like." She took the rail tickets from me and tied them into the pocket.

"And those?" I pointed to a small stack of clothes at the bottom of the basket.

"Well those are what's going to make you look like respectable Americans," Mr. Sullivan said. Mrs. Sullivan drew out a new shirt, a nearly new shirt at least, and a pair of short trousers, and handed both to Tom. He held them up to himself, then quickly pulled his gansey over his head.

"Not until you take your bath," I said. Tom stopped, then carefully refolded the shirt.

"One more thing," Mr. Sullivan said. He stood, reached behind the coal box and drew out a pair of newly blacked shoes, not boots, real shoes. In them was tucked a pair of stockings.

"They may be a bit big for you," he said, "but they're nearly new and shouldn't wear out before you grow into them."

"Thank you," Tom exclaimed. His eyes fairly devoured the shoes entirely. He traced a finger along the blacking. It was smooth, not a bit worn. I was a bit jealous.

Mick was silent. Still munching a potato, he tried to hide the anticipation in his eyes.

"I think the little maneen thinks we have something for him as well," Mrs. Sullivan said.

"The touch of my belt," Mr. Sullivan said, smiling, "only that."

"I think we have more than that," Mrs. Sullivan said. She drew a white shirt and a pair of trousers from the shoonaun. Mick made no move to take them from her, then changed his mind and held out his hands. He held the shirt up for inspection, then shook out the trousers. They were long, the kind of trousers men wore. His eyes got big.

"I expect you to wear them like a man," Mr. Sullivan said. "I expect you to see your family safe to America. If you begin behaving like an unruly child again, Clare has my permission to take them from you, if you have to enter America bare-arsed yourself." Mick nodded. "Starting tomorrow, Mr. Sullivan said. "You will need to be a man whether you like it or not. But until then," he said, "you are still a boy, and you still answer to me. Me and your new shadow." Roddy lifted himself off the couch and went to stand behind Mick, a hand on his shoulder.

"Think of me as your personal escort to the train station," Roddy said with a malicious grin. "In case you had any thoughts of taking your new trousers and going missing."

"And for you, Clare," Mrs. Sullivan said as she drew something pale and yellow from the shoonaun, "I thought maybe you'd like to enter America looking like a lady. It was a pale yellow shirtwaist with tiny tucks up and down it. Mrs. Sullivan put it in my hands, then drew out a long black skirt to go with it. "The skirt was Mrs. Grove's," she said. "Mrs. Grove told Margaret that it's what all the fine ladies are wearing these days. The shirtwaist I made myself. In the evenings."

I was struck speechless, simply looked into Mrs. Sullivan's eyes. I saw there what I supposed was in my own eyes—love, sadness, a deep connection. Tom elbowed me. "Say thank you," he hissed.

"Thank you," I said finding my tongue and nearly enough breath to balance it. "Thank you for everything."

Mrs. Sullivan nodded.

"Ah, but then you didn't see everything," Mr. Sullivan said.

"True for you," Mrs. Sullivan added. She stepped behind the curtain that hid their bed. From behind it she brought a brown bundle. She handed it to

Tom. It was Da's coat. Tom clutched it to his chest. Mrs. Sullivan reached out and took my hand. Into it she placed something cool and hard. Mama's wedding ring.

"They were still at the pawns," she said. "A body shouldn't have to leave everything behind and her going all the way across the ocean to America." I clutched the ring tightly.

"Thank you," I said.

"'Tis sore we'll miss you," Mrs. Sullivan replied.

Seventeen

The world whizzed by at a pace I'd never seen before. The deep purple lilacs that dotted the rural landscape were a mere blur outside my window, a blur with no scent, no texture. A small herd of cows appeared on a nearby hill, then just as quickly receded into the distance.

Before I'd set foot on the train that morning, the fastest I'd traveled was at the speed of a carriage. We'd seen cars, of course. A handful of the richest people owned one. Young Michael Good owned a motor bicycle, a noisy, soot-belching terror that he drove full-throttle up and down the driveway at the expense of his mother's nerves. When once he laid the contraption down on its side, having hit a pile of road apples at a good thirty miles an hour, Mrs. Good made him promise to trade the evil thing in on a motor carriage once he was married. But it was only rich people, and then only young rich people, who traveled in the things.

I, on the other hand, rarely traveled faster than my feet would take me. I was a child of the premotorized world, and that suited me just fine. Out the window of the train, just as I would get interested in something, it would disappear from view. I grew fairly dizzy with the effort, and the bread and tea I'd eaten that morning flip flopped menacingly in my belly. I leaned back in my seat and closed my eyes.

"You look at bit green, Clare," Tom commented from his seat across from me.

"I feel a bit green," I said.

"Is it the train?" Tom asked. I nodded. "Can I help?" he asked. I shook my head. Tom fell silent, a worried look on his face.

"If you had endless pockets full of money, what would you do?" Tom finally asked. I could see he was trying to distract me, to take my mind off my stomach and my spinning head. I was grateful to him for it, though I suspected it wouldn't work. I shrugged. He looked at Mick.

"If I had endless pockets full of money? That's easy," Mick said, warming immediately to the topic. "First I would buy a fine house. I'd hire servants to clean it and care for it. And I'd have a horse, maybe two or three, and a carriage, and a man in starched linen to drive it. And whenever I wanted something to eat, the servants would fix it for me, anything I wanted. And I'd eat and eat to my heart's content."

"You'd get too fat to walk," Tom said.

"When a man's rich, he should have a little meat on his bones," Mick replied. "Maybe I'd take up smoking and have a big collection of pipes, and whenever I wanted a smoke, my servants would fetch my pipe and fill it for me."

"You'd get lazy," Tom said.

"It's not laziness if a man can hire servants to keep busy for him," Mick said. "He's still getting a great deal of work done. He's just not dirtying his hands to do it."

"So a rich man can sleep all day and still not be lazy?" Tom asked. "That's rubbish."

"It is not," Mick replied. "Think about it. Who's the richest man you know?"

"Andrew Carnegie," Tom replied.

"Andrew Carnegie?"

"Andrew Carnegie, the Yank who built the new library in Anglesea Street."

"What about James Murphy from the brewery?" Mick said.

"Carnegie's richer," Tom replied.

"But you don't know Carnegie," Mick countered.

"I don't know James Murphy. Besides Murphy's dead."

"Fine, then. We'll say your precious Carnegie," Mick said. "What did he do to make all that money?"

"Andrew Carnegie built a great steel empire," Tom replied.

"So do you think he's ever handled the steel himself? Do you think he's ever worked a full day in the steel mill, manning the furnace or lugging the steel rails? Of course not. He has laborers to do that for him, but he gets the credit for it because he's rich. He's not lazy; he built great mills and factories. Yet he probably doesn't have to put his own coat on in the morning. He has servants to do it for him."

Something about the way Mick said "servants" dropped a great chunk of ice into my belly.

"'Tis a 'servant' who's put food in your mouth all these years," I said quietly. "And I'll thank you to remember it."

Mick fell silent. "But," he finally asked, "wouldn't you rather be the lady of the house rather than the servant if you had the choice?"

"Ah, but I didn't now, did I?" I said. "I didn't have the choice."

We sat a while in silence, but the silence was more difficult to stomach than Mick's loose talk. "Tom," I said, "What would you do if you were rotten with money?"

Tom grinned and perked up. It's clear he had thought about the question. But then which of us hadn't?

"I'd buy us a fine place to live, of course," he began. "But then I'd buy one of those fancy blue blazers the rich boys wear, and I'd go to school at a good school. And then when I finish there, if God spares me, I'll go off to university and study bridges and dams and ships and factories. I want to know how to build them."

"You want to own a factory?" I asked. I thought of young Michael, young Michael with Tom's face ordering around laborers at the mill. The image didn't seem right somehow.

"Not own," Tom said, "I want to build them. And maybe not a factory. Maybe a bridge. I want to learn how to build a bridge. Or maybe a ship. I want to be an engineer myself."

Mick was silent. We were both silent. In our world, boys aspired to be butchers, or carpenters. They aspired to be something other than pack animals and shovel jockeys. They didn't aspire to be engineers.

"Where did you learn about engineers?" I asked.

"A book," he replied. "A book in the library."

"And this book said you have to go to university to become one."

"It did."

"And if you had all the money in the world, 'tis what you would be?"

"'Tis," he replied.

I wanted to tell him that being an engineer was a fanciful a dream as having all the money in the world. I wanted to tell him that the best he could hope for was maybe to be a priest, or a mason on some bridge somewhere. But more than that, I wondered if it might be possible. I wondered if in America it might just be possible.

"What would you do, Clare?" Tom broke into my thoughts. "What would you do if you had all the money you ever wanted?

"I believe I'd hire a carriage to carry us to Queenstown," I said. "I don't like this train much at all."

* * *

By train it wasn't far at all to Queenstown—a half an hour, maybe a bit more, but it was the longest half-hour my stomach had ever lived through. Soon the town, built between a hill and the ocean, slid into view. The train slowed and we traveled past inns, and hotels, and simple homes, many sporting signs offering lodging and food. The train laden with emigrants—along with the road, equally laden—squeezed its way between the signs and the Queenstown harbor. Everyone it seemed carried a bag, a basket, a suitcase, a trunk. The city streets teemed with emigrants, like a chunk of bread left out during the ant season.

Aboard the train, all around us, our fellow passengers rose to their feet as we slipped into the Queenstown station. I too stood, calculating that they were far more likely than I to know what to do in the situation. Beneath us our car lurched and thunked and the squeal of wheels on track split the air. I staggered briefly, then sat heavily back into the seat. The train came to a stop and I stood again.

"Queenstown," the conductor called. "Queenstown station." Mick gathered the shoonaun from its overhead rack and clutched it tightly to his chest. We joined the mass of people moving down the aisles. Very few people remained seated. Queenstown was by far the most popular destination on this run.

We stepped out onto the cement platform, and the crowd carried us like a river through the station. All around us porters loaded baggage onto hand carts. A conductor shepherded the first class passengers down the steps and into the melee. Ragged boys pushed their way through the crowd soliciting business for the various inns and hotels. The filtered light from overhead skylights gave the whole scene a rather unreal tinge. I moved with the crowd, with one hand clutching Mick's sleeve, and the other tightly in Tom's grip.

We flowed through the exit and found ourselves immediately on the quay. The crowd scattered in every direction, and without the steady current of the human river, we were left to figure out where we needed to go.

"Can you see anything?" Tom asked me, fairly shouting to be heard over the chaos all around us. He was no more than a half a head shorter than me. That half a head did me no good at all.

"I can't," I replied. A man with a huge trunk bending his back split the link between Mick and me. I scrambled for another a handful of Mick's coat, but he was already out of reach.

"This way," he called back to us and headed toward the water.

"Do you see something?" I asked. He didn't reply, but continued to forge a path through the crowd to the edge of the dock. Tom in tow, I followed.

"Look," he said, pointing out over the water. There at anchor, out in the harbor, was a large liner. The black hull was topped by several storeys of windows set into a brilliant white superstructure. Over them towered two large smokestacks painted bright red with black tops. The ship was huge. It dwarfed the tender roped to its side, and the men aboard the tender looked like mere specks by contrast.

"The *Caronia*," Tom said. "Our ship. You can tell by the smokestacks she's a Cunard ship. Red on the bottom, black on the top means Cunard. I'd hold she's the *Caronia*."

"How do we get out to it?" Mick asked.

"*Her*," Tom replied. "Ships are called 'she' and 'her,' not 'it'."

"How do we get out to *her*?" Mick repeated.

"I can help you." A boy about Mick's age sidled up beside us. He was dressed in the uniform of the lanes—short grubby trousers, a shirt with a frayed collar, a heavily patched jacket. He was bare legged and barefoot. From the looks of his grubby ears and the smell of him, I'd guess he probably hadn't had a bath in a good long while.

"I live here in Queenstown," he said. "I can show you around. I know the best places to stay, the best places to eat. I can carry your bags. I can tell you what you need to do to get out to your ship out there." He gestured with a jerk of his head to the *Caronia* and smiled. His teeth were a mess, worse, if anything than our own, and that was saying something indeed.

"For a fee?" I said.

"Threepence," he said. "'Tis how I earn my bread," he added.

"We don't need help carrying our bag," I commented.

"I'll deduct that from my bill, then," he replied, still smiling.

"And we have our own food," I added.

"But you still need someone to show you where you check in, where you check your bags, where you stay the night."

"We do," said Mick. "You're hired." He stuck out his hand and the boy took it. "Mick Keane, from Cork, bound for St. Paul in America. My sister Clare, my brother Tom."

"Edmund Brick," the boy said. "You can call me Eddie."

"Well, Eddie," Mick said, "where do we go first?"

"First," Eddie said, taking the basket from Mick, "if you're traveling on the *Caronia*, you check in with the Cunard office. That's down the street." He poked a thumb roughly in the direction of town center. "After that, you have to find someplace to stay." Not waiting for a reply, he headed off through the crowd on a beeline for the street. I trotted after him, a wave of terror washing through me as I lost sight of the shoonaun in the crowd. But Mick was able to keep up with him, and just down the street, in front of an official-looking red brick building, we found the two parked in a long queue, talking animatedly.

"First you check in here, hand them your papers," Eddie said. "Then you go find some place to stay the night."

"We thought we'd stay on the boat," I interjected.

"You won't be able to get on the boat until tomorrow," Eddie replied. "Maybe not then. Sometimes people get stuck in Queenstown for a week or more waiting for a boat. And the guards won't let you sleep on the docks. You have to find a room."

"How much?" Mick asked.

"Well that depends on what kind of room you want," Eddie replied. "If you were wearing silks and satins, I'd suggest the Queens Hotel. 'Tis right there." He pointed at a building just up the street. It was fronted with a brilliant red canopy and doormen in fine blue uniforms. "It's as fine a hotel as any in Europe," he said with pride. "Then there's the cheaper hotels up the street." He wave a hand in the general direction of the center of town. "But I'd say you want something cheaper still." Mick nodded.

"Then you can't do better than Ginny O'Rourke's house," Eddie said. "A hot meal and a bed for a bob a piece. You have to share the room, of course, but you can have your own bed. Ginny has eight of them. She's my Da's sister," he added.

"Is there anything cheaper?" I asked. Three shillings took a sizable bite out of our small stash.

"Cheaper? There is. Cheaper but still safe? If you find anything, tell me and I'll recommend it to you." Eddie stepped a bit out of line, the shoonaun still slung over his shoulder. He assessed the queue, which was moving slowly, but steadily toward to office. "Half hour," he estimated. "I wouldn't stay at the really cheap places myself," he said. "You drop off to sleep and wake up to find your basket gone and your money missing. Or worse." He paused for a while to let the image sink in. It did. I considered taking our shoonaun from him then and there. I wanted very much to feel it in my hands, to assure myself that it was indeed still going with us to America.

"No, the best thing you could do is to get a room with Aunt Ginny. She'll take good care of you."

* * *

We crept forward with the line and through the front doors of the building. The line ended in front of a high desk at which sat an official-looking gentry man in a Cunard cap and dark suit. He asked for our letter, tickets, and emigration documents in a tone that said he had asked for the same documents from hundreds if not thousands of people before us. He examined the documents, dumped the tickets into a pile on his deck, copied our names onto a roll, and without even looking up at us instructed us to be outside the Cunard office at 6:00 a.m. tomorrow. He then called for the next person in line, and we were herded out the far door by another bored official, who too looked like he was only biding his time before gaining enough seniority to be bored by a much better caliber of job than the one he had now.

"That's the first step," Eddie said when we stepped out again onto the quay. "Will you be stowing this basket in the hold?" he asked, hefting the shoonaun in his arms. I shook my head. "Any other goods?" I shook my head again. "Then you certainly won't be staying at the Queen's," he said with a wink. "Let my show you Ginny's."

We crossed the teeming street, passed the hotels with their well-dressed doormen, passed the hotels without doormen, passed a few inns and lodges. Eddie pointed out all the sights—gave us a running commentary on the hotels, the places to eat, and all the local gossip. Then we started up the hill. In Queenstown you can take the main road up the hill. It wends and winds its way past shops and houses and gets you up the hill in all good time. Or you can take the goats' route up lanes that pass grubby single-room houses and find their way up the hill following the shortest distance between two points. Eddie led us up the lanes. It was all I could do to find purchase on the slick cobblestones. I slipped and skidded and climbed for several minutes before Eddie stopped.

"Here's Ginny's" he said, pausing before a two-storey house sporting peeling aqua paint and a door so small that I would probably have to duck to enter. I stopped, then doubled over, hands on my knees, out of breath from the climb.

"Where did you say you were from?" he asked. "Someplace flat?" He grinned at us, barely breathing hard.

Mick steadied his own heavy breathing and replied. "Not that flat," he said, then drew a deep breath. "But, no, not this hilly." I straightened up and looked out over the hill we had just climbed. Below me lay the lanes, but before me stretched a grand vista of the harbor with its docks mooring tenders and tugs. The great liners, three of then, were anchored out in the harbor. An island bore barracks and warehouses and docks at which a huge British warship was moored. And far out, on the other side of the harbor, a channel of water led to the open sea and eventually America.

"Well, then," Eddie broke into my thoughts. "I'll be going. That will be one shilling." He held out his palm.

"A shilling," I said. "You said threepence."

"I did," Eddie replied, "and that's only what I charged you. Threepence for carrying the goods. Threepence for leading your through check-in. Threepence for finding you a room. And threepence for the tour of Queenstown. That makes one bob even."

"As I see it, we owe you the threepence you said you'd charge us minus a penny because you didn't need to help us check baggage. And we could have carried the basket ourselves."

"But you didn't," Eddie said. "One shilling. That's my going rate for the services I gave you. You'll not find a better rate anywhere in town."

I doubted that. I dug in my pocket, pulled out a threepenny bit, and held it out for him. "You were very helpful," I said. "I'll give you the extra penny and my thanks."

Eddie made no move to take the coin. "A shilling," he said. "You owe me a shilling."

"Take it," I said, still holding out the coin. "Take it or take naught." Eddie handed the shoonaun to Mick, spun on his heels and slipped through the front door of the house, leaving me standing with the three penny bit still in my outstretched hand. I dropped it back in my pocket.

"We may want to find another place to stay," I muttered to Mick and Tom, not wanting to be overheard. "If his aunt is no more honest than Eddie . . . " The door opened, and out stepped a man with a large, knotted stick in his hand and a stern look on his face.

"My son says you refuse to pay him," the man said.

"Only a misunderstanding about the fee," Mick replied stepping between me and the man. "Of course we meant to pay."

"How much do they owe you?" the man asked his son.

"One shilling, sir," Eddie replied.

"That seems reasonable," the man said. He looked me up and down, all the while continuing to slap the large stick into the palm of his other hand.

"You'd hit a girl with that?" Mick said, puffing out his chest. I'd seen that show of bravado before. It was likely to get us all beaten to a bloody pulp.

"Mick," I hissed.

"Let me handle this," he whispered back over his shoulder. "I think you're too much a man to take a great stick like that to a girl or a little boy." He gestured over at Tom and myself. "So why don't we just sit down and talk this over."

"What do you take me for?" the man said. "I had no intention of using this on children." He hefted the stick in his hand. "But you. You're a right little maneen. Surely you wouldn't object if I used it on you?" He jabbed the end of the sick lightly into Mick's chest. "A man's responsible for his own debts, now wouldn't you say?" He jabbed Mick again, harder this time. Mick took a step back. "Well, maneen, are you going to pay your debts, or do I have to take it out of your hide?" He poked again. This time Mick stumbled and fell. Quickly he scrambled to his feet. He balled up his fists and raised them, a look of defiance on his face.

"Mick," I said. "Don't be an eejit."

"Get back, Clare," he responded. The man raised his stick, waving the end in Mick's face. Mick swatted it away.

I dug in my pocket and pulled out a shilling, one of sixty-two that had to hold us until we got Uncle Ronan's advance. I held it out and walked into the thick of the impending massacre.

"Here's the shilling," I said. I handed it to Eddie. "We don't want trouble."

Eddie examined the shilling, then pocketed it with a tug of his forelock. "I thank you," he said. "A pleasure serving you." His father laid a hand on his shoulder and gave him a stiff shove toward the door. He muttered something. Eddie whimpered softly. Then the two ducked into the front door of the house, and closed it tight behind them.

I looked out at the *Caronia*. We were out a bob and without a place to stay. But come morning, that grand ship was ours.

Eighteen

Back on the quay, we found a rail to prop ourselves against, no small matter given the shortage of leaning space in Queenstown that day. I pulled the loaf of bread from the shoonaun and broke off a hunk for each of us.

"I think we should stay on the quay tonight," I said. "We'll sleep just outside the Cunard office, so when they open in the morning, we'll be there."

"I can keep watch while you sleep," Mick said, "then I'll wake you up, and you can watch while I sleep." I nodded. It was a good plan, and it would save us some money.

I ran the calculations in my head once more. Three pounds, two and change. Sixty-two shillings: seven in my pocket. Eight in Mick's. Five in Tom's. One already spent. The rest in the basket. We would probably need five or more for food between here and St. Paul, and another four for a telegram to Uncle Ronan from St. Paul. I wondered if we would have to find a room in New York or St. Paul. I wondered if we would have to find transportation between St. Paul and Lindstrom, or Wyoming, or wherever Uncle Ronan was at the moment. Sure we had money coming to us both here and in New York, but I hadn't the least notion how to collect it. More than that, I hadn't the least notion how far a shilling stretched in America. It was best to pinch every penny, at least until we knew better what we were facing.

"I don't think the guard will allow us to sleep outside," Tom said. "That's what Eddie said."

"Devil take Eddie," Mick said.

"We should know better," I said. "We don't have the money to let our guard down with the likes of Eddie roaming the streets."

"We may have to find an inn," Tom said.

"I'd rather not spend the money," I said.

"I can show you where to check your bag." A grubby little kidger about half my size was tugging at my skirt. "I can show you the line offices and where to stay the night. Four pence."

I shook my head. He drifted off into the crowd looking for another customer.

"I have a scheme," Mick said.

"God save us from your schemes," I replied.

"Grand," he replied. "Grand. Just for that I won't tell you what my scheme is." He handed the basket to Tom, and waded into the crowd pouring from the station.

"Mick," I called after him. Several people looked at me. I had half a mind to just let him go, but in this crowd it would be far too easy to lose him entirely. I hoped his scheme didn't involve spending more money.

We lost sight of him as Tom and I swam upstream against the current of people exiting the station. Another train had just arrived. The passengers were the same diverse bunch we had traveled with—farmers, shawlies from the lanes, children in newly washed and patched clothes, but also merchants in new trousers, grand men in suits sporting bowlers, and women in long full skirts and towering hats resplendent with feathers and fur.

We swam upstream against the lot of them, and finally found Mick, cap in hand, speaking to a grand woman with a tiny dog tucked under one arm. The dog was one of those wrinkled-faced little brutes with no nose on him. He nestled under her arm looking out sourly at the world around him as though the entire planet existed only to inconvenience his nasty little self. The woman was clearly wealthy and wore an architectural marvel of a hat that was a good three times larger than the scowling little beastie she bore under her arm.

"Six pence, Ma'am," Mick was saying. "And when I say six pence, I mean six pence and not a penny more. For that I'll carry your bags, show you the line office, and get you settled into a hotel for the night. You'll not find a better price in all of Queenstown."

The woman assessed him carefully, and nodded. Mick snatched up one of her bags, tucking it under his arm. The second bag he grasped by the handle in his right hand, the third in his left. The bags came to his waist and they were obviously heavy. Mick staggered and limped under their weight as he led the woman to the exit. Tom handed me the shoonaun, and dashed to help.

"My brother and, um, associate," Mick explained. "No extra charge." Tom tipped his cap to the lady, and grasped one of the bags. The parade—Mick in front, the woman and her dog following, and Tom bringing up the rear—marched out the station exit. I did the only thing I could think of. I followed.

I have to allow, the scheme was a good one. Or so it seemed until we got out the door, out the door and straight into Eddie Brick, who barred Mick's path, hands on his hips and eyes full of challenge.

"Out of the way, young man," the rich woman said sharply.

"You heard the lady," Mick echoed, "out of the way."

"Ma'am, there's something you should know about this boy holding your luggage," Eddie said, his head inclined slightly. He did have a way of looking trustworthy when he turned on the charm. "This boy here is no local boy. He has no notion how to show you around the town."

"Is that true?" the woman asked Mick.

"Everything you'll need, I can help you find," Mick replied. "And I'm not a cheat and a scoundrel like this, this . . . "

Mick had no chance to finish his sentence before Eddie's fist buried itself in his belly. Mick dropped the bags and doubled over gasping for breath.

"I had my hands full," he choked out between gasps. "If my hands were empty, you wouldn't land that punch. You're a cheater and a coward, just like your father." Eddie's fist found Mick's nose. Mick sprawled on the ground.

"I never!" the rich woman exclaimed. She scanned the crowd and flagged down a uniformed porter, who hurried toward us with a cart. "It doesn't pay to be kind to unfortunates," she said, pointing out her bags to the burly young man who promptly stacked them. Mick groaned from his place on the ground. I was afraid he was going to be trod on, so I moved between him and Eddie and offered a hand. Mick ignored it.

"My late husband, God rest him, always said that the poor were more trouble than they were worth." The woman assessed the state of her baggage, as she preached to everyone and to no one in particular. "He said it doesn't pay to be kind to them, that they would always find some way to repay your kindness with ill will." Her dog, sensing either her mood or the electricity jetting between Mick and Eddie had begun to bark in high, choked yips that split the ear and wormed their way into the brain like tiny corkscrews. I glared at the little beast.

"You're upsetting Buster," the woman exclaimed, glaring back, first at me, then Tom. She probably would have glared at Mick too, but he was still kneeling, bent double on the ground. I doubted she could see him well through all the trouser legs milling about us. The rich woman stroked the animal's nearly nonexistent nose, but the yips continued.

"Which line, ma'am?" the porter asked.

"Yes, of course. Buster will be fine once we quit the company of these young ruffians. White Star, of course. I'm traveling the White Star line." The porter began tugging the cart down the quay. The rich woman shot one more parting look of disdain at all of us before turning to follow him.

I reached a hand down to Mick again. He ignored it and stood of his own accord.

"Piss pot," he spat in Eddie's direction.

"Ass's arse," Eddie shot back.

"Cheat," Mick added.

"Shite face," Eddie fairly shouted. "Do you know how much money you can make off a woman like that?"

"I know I was about to make six pence before you stepped in," Mick added.

"Six pence!" Eddie exclaimed. "A rich woman like that! You get the porter to carry the baggage to the check in, then you show her all the places the rich folks like to visit, and you make yourself a couple of bob without lifting a finger. Six pence! I made double that off you lot, and you look like something they'd scrape up off the bottom of the docks." Mick charged him, bumping into a man with an umbrella who gave him a good swat with it as he passed by.

"Mick," I said. He was already swinging wildly at Eddie's head, though Eddie was doing a fair job of staying out of his reach. "Mick, do you want to get us sent back to Cork? What if the guards see you fighting out here in front of God and everyone?"

Mick shot a fist out at Eddie's gut, and though it wasn't much of a shot, it was enough to make Eddie step back sharply, clutching his ribs. That was apparently enough for Mick as well. He backed off.

"Tell me," Eddie said, "do you know where White Star baggage check-in is?" Mick stood silent. "How about the best place for a rich woman like that to get a respectable supper?" Mick stuffed his fists into his pockets. "I didn't think so," Eddie replied. "Keep your filthy hands off my customers," he said, and still clutching his ribs, he disappeared into the crowd streaming out of the station exit.

Mick stood watching him, then turned and pushed through the crowd to the rail. I followed, Tom right behind me.

"I need to find White Star baggage," Mick muttered, half to himself.

"Mick," I said, "drop it. It was a good scheme, but 'tisn't going to work."

"Maybe if I followed a few rich people from the train station, I could find where they go." He talked through his sleeve, which he had pressed tightly to his nose. I wondered if it was bleeding. If it was, he would just have to enter America with blood on his cuff. I wasn't going to clean it for him.

"Mick, drop it," I said.

"Or I could ask the porters."

"You're not going to drop it, are you? Thick-headed . . ."

"Why should I?" he wheeled around a look of pure fury in his eyes. His fist was still wadded up. "Why should I drop it? Just because you say so?" I took a sharp step back. "Sorry," he mumbled. I leaned on the rail, trying to get interested in whatever it was they were doing on the Navy dock out in the harbor. The air coming in from over the water was fresh, a welcome change after the pungency of the crowd.

"We have the time," Mick said. "And you and I both know we need the money." He leaned back against the rail, his arms crossed across his chest. "I'm going to take a quick look around."

"Go, then," I said. He looked at me, surprised. "You never do anything I ask you. If I asked you to stay here with us, you'd only ignore me and leave anyway, so you might as well go." He looked away, his jaw tight. "Only know, Mick Keane, when that if the boat leaves, and you're nowhere to be found, I'll not ask them to wait. Go on with you."

Mick turned his back to me, then without looking back waded into the crowd.

"Shall we wait for him here, then?" Tom asked quietly.

"No," I said. "I think I want to wait up there for a bit." I pointed to the top of the hill, where the cathedral sat overlooking the town. I was suddenly feeling the need to get up and out of the crowd, away from emigrants and bags and trains and all the chaos that swirled around me. The huge cathedral atop the hill seemed a refuge.

* * *

The walls of the cathedral had been erected, as had been the roof. She was a church—a church and a grand one, no doubt about that—but she was still clearly a work in progress. Scaffolding covered the side of the building, and the base of what would be the spire teemed with workers.

Outside the front door, masonry dust all about her feet, a woman ran a cloth over the brass of the door. For only a moment, I thought it was Mrs. Sullivan. She had the same yellow-white hair, the same soft shoulders, the same ivory skin. But then she turned to look at us, and the illusion crumbled into the dust. The feeling of loss hummed to life inside me again. The woman smiled as we entered, then returned to her polishing.

Inside the cathedral was a magnificent place, everything I imagined St. Barry's back in Cork to be. But this cathedral was ours, and that made it more than St. Barry's could ever be. Rose-colored columns rose from grey stone footings to a high vaulted ceiling. Dark walnut confessionals lined both sides of the nave. On an impossibly high scaffolding, far above us, workers were covering the ceiling with the same dark wood.

I dipped a finger in the holy water at the entrance and blessed myself. Tom shifted the shoonaun to his left shoulder and did the same.

"I think we should make our confession before getting on the boat," I said. Tom murmured assent. His neck was bent all the way back, and his eyes were fixed on the workers hauling a bundle of wood laths to the top of the scaffolding on a rope.

"They would have an easier time of it if they used a pulley," he said.

"Why don't you tell them?" I said. "If you think you know their job better than they do."

"Truly?" He looked at me. "Do you think I should?"

"No," I said. "I do not. They know their job. They don't need help from someone whose only knowledge of building comes from a book."

Mrs. Sullivan's "twin" entered behind us. She picked up another rag from a pile in one of the back pews.

"If you'd like to make your confession, I can go for Father Michaels. He'll see you," she said.

"How did you know we were here for confession?" I said.

"If I was the one going off onto the ocean in one of those Belfast-made ships, wouldn't I be here for confession?" she said. "Made by Protestants, they are, every last one of them. In Belfast and Liverpool. You can't sail to America in a ship made by good Catholics. 'Tis a crime, it is."

"Do Protestants build them differently, then?" Tom asked.

"Well, I'm sure I wouldn't know about the ships themselves," the woman said. "But a friend of my second son worked there in Belfast, at the shipyard don't you know. And he said one time he saw one of those Protestant fellows write something on one of the inside parts of a ship, inside where nobody could see it once the ship was finished. Well, I'll not say what it was he wrote—God forbid such words ever pass my lips—but it was the vilest slur against the Blessed Mother that ever rose on sulfur smoke out of the very depths of hell itself." She crossed herself quickly. Tom followed suit. His eyes were big, and he hung on her every word.

"Well that ship," the woman continued, "that ship was no better than an hour out of port when it sank—turned over and sank right down to the bottom of the sea, it did. And everybody said they couldn't imagine why such a grand ship would sink like that, but my son's friend said it was because of the slur, he would stake his very life on it." She ran her rag across the back of the pew, then leaned in a bit closer. "Now if you ask me, I'll tell you what I think. I think those Belfast men will never find that ship on the bottom of the ocean, not if they look the rest of their lives. If they want to find it, they'll need to look in the very mouth of hell, they will, because that's where it deserves to be." She nodded her head sharply for emphasis.

Suddenly my knee felt a bit watery. I sat heavily in the pew beside me.

"You say the Father will hear our confession," I said, changing the subject— or getting straight to the heart of the subject, one or the other.

"If he knows you're going abroad in one of those great beasts, he will," she said. "I'll go find him if you'll bide here." I nodded. The woman took another swipe with the rag across the back of the pew and headed off for the sacristy.

Tom sat next to me. "Do you believe her?" he asked when the woman was out of earshot.

I shrugged. "I want you to make a good confession, though," I said.

"If I learn to build ships," Tom said, "I'll hire all Catholic workers."

We sat in silence for a bit. I pulled out one of the kneelers and lowered myself onto it. I'd never seriously considered the possibility of our ship sinking.

Surprisingly enough, the thought didn't frighten me, or at least not much, though I imagined drowning to be a fairly miserable way to go. Beside me Tom knelt, his eyes raised heavenward, though his heart was more likely involved with the nature of scaffolding than the mysteries of God's hand in the world. Behind us a family entered the church. Each wore their best clothes. Each bore a bundle or a basket. They scanned the confessionals, looking for one that might be occupied. We would not be the only Christians on the boat. God knew his own. Or so I hoped.

* * *

We descended the hill just before sunset. The quay was still crowded, the trains were still arriving, still pulling out. The tenders continued to make their way out to the ships moored in the harbor. We watched them for a while, then found a place out from under the milling feet to sit. Mick was nowhere to be seen. For all I knew he had set his feet on the road and was halfway back to Cork by now. But I wouldn't know for sure until morning at check-in, or until he found us again. When he did, I would usher him up the hill to have a little talk with Father Michaels, no mistake about that. I closed my eyes and began to rehearse in my mind what I would say the next time I saw him.

I woke to a hand shaking my shoulder lightly. It was twilight. Tom too was sleeping, his head resting on the shoonaun. I hadn't realized how tired I was.

The hand pulled away, and my eyes focused on a pair of neatly pressed trouser legs. I looked up. The guard.

"You can't sleep here," the handsome young man in a peaked cap said. I looked around. Mick was nowhere to be seen.

"I'm waiting for my brother," I said. "He should be here shortly." I hoped it wasn't a lie.

"You can't sleep here," the guard said simply.

"We'll be going out to the boat in the morning," I offered.

"Cunard?" the guard asked.

"Cunard it is," I replied.

"They didn't tell you?" the guard said cryptically.

I looked at him, puzzled. "They didn't tell you about the hostel, the immigrants' home?" he asked.

"They didn't," I said.

The guard sighed. "I'll show you," he said. "Get you up, now." He offered me a hand, which I took.

"But my brother," I said.

"Tell me what he looks like, and I'll watch for him," he said. "You can't stay here."

* * *

The hostel was not far from the Cunard office. It was a large building, milling with people bearing baggage of all shapes and description. The lobby reeked of crowd, and of a vague chemical smell that clung to the back of my throat. The man at the front desk asked for our paperwork.

"How old is the boy?" he asked, eyes still examining our tickets.

"Ten," I said. "Eleven in September."

"Your parents?" he said. "In America?"

"Dead," I said, "both are."

"All right," the man said. "You can both stay in women's rooms. If he were twelve, we'd have to place him in the men's rooms. As it is, he can stay with you."

I thanked him.

"One ten," the man said cryptically. "Up the stairs, to the right, then about halfway down the hall."

I thanked him again, though at the time, I wasn't sure what I was thanking him for. I'd never been to a hotel, or hostel, or inn. In fact I'd never slept anywhere but home and my employers' houses. But I understood "upstairs, to the right, halfway down the hall," so that's where I headed.

The hallway was long and straight and filled with the sounds of voices. Many of the doors were open, and the breeze from open windows mingled with the smells of crowd and stout. We walked slowly, taking it all in. On one side, a woman just inside her doorway bent over her bed changing her baby's clout. On the other side, a round-faced man in wire-rimed glasses sat on the floor propped against his door, playing a slow air on a penny whistle. About halfway down the hall, we came to a door just barely ajar with 110 painted on it in large black letters. I paused. Tom placed his hand on the door and gave it a shove. It swung open and we walked inside.

The room was not a large one, but ten beds lined the walls. Between them was enough room for a bit of baggage but not much more. A couple of washbasins sat on long tables on the far wall. The bare walls and board floors were Spartan but clean. And aside from us, the room was empty.

Tom chose the bed closest to the window, and lay the shoonaun on it. The linen on the bed was fresh and white, like the linen I used to scrub and pound for the Quillans. The pillows were fluffy, and the dark blue blanket embroidered with the logo of the Cunard line lay smoothly over the bed. I went to the window and opened it. A breeze came in from the harbor and gently puffed the yellow curtains. Tom walked down the center aisle between the beds, running a hand along their smooth metal frames, taking it all in.

"Did you see the enamel on this basin?" he said. He ran his hands over the basin, over the thick white enamel without so much as a chip or dent in it.

"How much do you suppose this is going to cost us?" I asked. Tom shrugged.

"Did you ever before slept on a pillow like this, Clare?" he asked, returning to the bed. I shook my head. "It's better than the one at Mama's wake," he said, pressing it to his face.

I looked out over the town. I could see the Cunard office, and if I got really close to the window and looked sideways I could see most of the street.

"Tom," I said, "I need to talk to the man downstairs. Stand you here and see if you can spot Mick anywhere in the crowd out there." Tom moved to the window. I stepped out the door, leaving it open.

It was more to think about. Mick was not with us. We were not any place he could find us easily. And a room like the one I had been in would likely cost us more than we could afford at the moment. Why did it seem that all my problems seemed to center on Mick or money or both? As I found my way back to the lobby, I gave myself a good talking to. I told myself that even if Mick didn't find us tonight, he would find us tomorrow when we checked in at the

Cunard office. I told myself that at the very least he would find us when we boarded the boat. We were, after all, traveling on the same boat, and how far could he get on a boat?

I knew, though, that I wasn't telling myself the half of it. Mick could disappear back into Cork, or into God-knows-where in Ireland. He could work himself into more trouble than his mouth could talk him out of. He could come back to us, and a bloody mess. I couldn't tell myself truly, but I was worried we'd never see him again.

It's a strange thing, worry. It's born of love for a person. But when it's through with you, it can make you hate that person for all the pain that love costs you. Still, just then, I would gladly set that hate aside in a mere second were Mick to walk up the stairs toward me, were he to tell me he was at my side for the rest of the journey.

The man at the desk was talking with a young couple—him a thin, short man with no more than a hair or two for his cap to rest upon; her a sinewy woman, two or three inches taller, clearly in a family way, six or seven months gone, maybe more. The man was explaining to the desk clerk that his son was going to be born a Yank. He beamed with pride over his wife and their child. She looked at him as though every morning the sun rose up from the very heart of himself. The clerk, bored and busy, was caught up despite himself in their glow. He handed them back their documents and with all sincerity wished them the best on their journey. The man shook his hand energetically before leading his wife to the stairs.

When they had left, I approached. "Beg your pardon, sir," I said. "You told my brother and me to go to room 110. I was wondering if you'd be so kind as to tell me how much the room is going to cost us. You see . . . "

"The line pays for the room," the man said.

"The line?"

"The Cunard line pays for the room," he said. "It won't cost you anything. Neither will breakfast or the shower and examination in the morning. The line pays for it."

"Thank you," I said. I was stunned. I felt like I should say something more. "Thank you," I said again. I was halfway up the stairs, still pondering our good fortune when I remembered the other reason I wanted to talk to the clerk. I turned around and made my way back.

"Sir," I said, again at the desk. The clerk looked up from whatever he was writing. If he recognized me, he didn't show it. "I'm traveling with my two brothers. One is upstairs waiting for me. The other," I paused, not quite sure how to tell him Mick was out working on some new scheme. "The other is separated from us for this minute. If he comes looking for us, would you tell him where we are?"

"Umm," the clerk replied. I took it as a 'yes'.

"His name is Mick Keane, Michael Keane. He's about this tall." I motioned with my hand. "And hair about the same color as mine."

"If he comes in, I'll send him to you," the clerk said. "He's alone, you say?" I nodded. "I'll send him to you." He went back to his writing. "Why the line allows children to travel alone is beyond me," he muttered to himself.

* * *

The mattress was full and comfortable. The rest of the beds had filled in with women, children, and baggage. Tom and I lay in ours side by side. The bed was a big one, bigger than we had slept in at home. But we lay close, sharing the lovely pillow, the blanket pulled up to our chins despite the warmth of the night. The sheets were clean and soft against my freshly scrubbed feet. Both Tom and I had washed as thoroughly as modesty allowed before making any contact with those lovely sheets. Lying between them, I felt like good news tucked into a fresh, clean envelope.

I awoke deep into the night, after midnight probably. Mick had still not arrived. Earlier, Tom and I had taken turns watching at the window until the light was too poor to see anymore. Tom had offered to go find him, but I didn't want another brother roaming the streets of Queenstown loose. We would simply have to meet Mick in the morning at the check in. He was probably fine. It wasn't the first night he'd been out on the streets. But still I lay awake, wondering, worrying. I'd give him a piece of my mind in the morning if I thought it would do any good.

* * *

Back in Cork, when I pictured getting on a boat for America, I figured it would entail mostly getting on a boat and staying there until it reached America. I had no notion at all of the troubles that would be required of me before I left.

Tom and I stood outside the Cunard office the next morning in a light drizzle. The crowd, freshly fed in the great Cunard dining room, was huge. Several hundred people it was, each carrying bags and baskets and suitcases they refused let out of their sight. They nudged, and crowded, and milled, each jockeying for a position just a wee bit closer to the rostrum. There was little hope of finding Mick in such a mass of people, but we tried anyway, milling, wandering, oozing past people of all shapes and classes. When a uniformed official mounted a small rostrum with a megaphone, we were no more than twenty feet from the front of the crowd. I was relieved to be able to hear every word.

Tickets in hand, he began to call names, familiar names, names from all across the country—Brennan, Reagan, McCarthy, Walsh. Finally I heard my own, "Clare Elizabeth Keane." I waved a hand and shouted. The official made a tick mark on his paper. "Thomas Joseph Patrick Keane." Both Tom and I acknowledged his call. The official marked his paper. "Michael Finbarr Joseph Keane." I strained my ears but heard nothing. I looked up at the official. He scanned the crowd then made a tick on his paper. I tried to look where he had been looking, but couldn't see much over all the bodies in the way.

As instructed, we made our way through the crowd to the table beneath the rostrum. A long line of men in blue uniforms, eight or ten perhaps, sat hunched over stacks of paper. We stood before one of them.

"Name?" he said.

"Clare Elizabeth Keane," I replied. He ran a finger down a list of names until he found mine. Placing a small check beside it, he reached for a wide sheet of paper with numerous columns and rows, the passenger manifest.

"Age?"

"Fourteen," I said.

"Married?"

"No," I said, wondering just how many fourteen-year-old, married women he'd seen.

"Occupation?"

"Well, sir, that's not a simple question," I replied. "You see I was in service for three years, but then . . . "

The official scribbled "servant" on the paper. "Able to read?" he asked. I nodded.

"Last residence, nearest relative, final destination, by whom passage was sent, whether been in U.S. before, place of birth, and color of hair and eyes." The questions came in rapid fire, curtly, efficiently. I answered all of them. Some, like hair color, would have seemed to have been obvious, but I gave him a thoughtful answer to that question as well. It was the way I was raised, I suppose, not to question my betters but simply to do as I was told.

"Are you an anarchist?" the official asked as he reached the bottom of his list of questions. He asked it without a trace of irony, not that irony would have helped me answer one way or the other.

"I don't understand, sir," I said.

"Do you believe in the violent overthrow of the government of the United States or assassination of its public officials?"

I thought about what he was saying. I recognized some of the words, but still was unable to piece together what he was asking.

"I'm sorry, sir," I said. "I still don't understand."

"I suppose you wouldn't," the official said, then wrote "no." "We do have to ask, don't you know?" I nodded.

When he finished with me, he asked the same questions of Tom, simply making ditto marks beneath my name for many of Tom's answers.

When our entries in the manifest were completed, the official stamped our tickets, shuffled some more papers, then grabbed three cards and scribbled on them. He handed two to me. They said 24/8. Tom's said 24/9. Both had "Cunard" printed in large block letters at the top.

"Pin one to your dress, and the other to your basket," he said. "Then follow the line to the immigrant's home for your examination."

Beside us, the roll continued. The *Caronia* had room for well over two thousand passengers. Many of them boarded in Liverpool before the boat reached Ireland itself; but hundreds, maybe even a thousand, would board with us, here in Queenstown. I craned my neck. Among those hundreds, Mick was nowhere to be seen.

* * *

The crowd around me surged. I reached for Tom's hand and let the current carry us away from the rostrum and table and back toward the immigrant's home. Blue-uniformed gentry men herded and shouted instructions. We joined the line, the line that the gentry men said would lead to the examination.

"Did you see Mick?" I asked. Tom was carrying shoonaun, jostling against me now and then in the crowd. I knew the answer before hearing it myself.

"I didn't," Tom replied.

"But surely he was there. The official ticked off his name."

"Did he?" Tom said. "I thought he was ticking off the name of the person after Mick."

"I think it was Mick's name he ticked," I said.

Tom nodded. "Will we leave without him if we can't find him?" he asked. I was caught off guard by the abruptness of the question. Not that the question itself had surprised me—I'd been asking myself that very thing ever since Mick disappeared into the crowd on the quay. Mick made no secret of his reluctance to leave Cork. His behavior had been so erratic in those last days before we left that I wouldn't put it past him to leave us and find his way back there. But would I leave him? I can't say it wasn't tempting, but sometime just before the dawn last night I had made up my mind. No. I couldn't leave him. We would have to find him or miss the boat trying.

"He'll be back," I said. "We'll find him."

"Find who?" Mick sidled up beside us, his hands stuffed nonchalantly into his pockets.

"I was just telling Tom how I was hoping to leave without you," I said, shortly. Now that he was beside me, all my worry had suddenly been replaced by anger.

"Hmmph," he said. "No doubt you were."

He reached across me and took the basket from Tom. He had dark circles under his eyes, and his face looked drawn. He reached into the pocket of his jacket and pulled out a fist. A jumble of coins lay in it.

"Not a bad night's work," he said. Tom held out his hand, and Mick dumped the coins into it. Tom began counting.

"You were there earlier when the official was calling roll?" I asked. "You got yourself checked in?"

"I did," Mick said, jiggling the tag pinned to his shirt. "Don't you want to know how I made the money?"

"I don't," I said.

Mick held out his hand. When Tom continued to count, Mick snapped his fingers impatiently. Reluctantly, Tom handed back the coins. Mick's fingers closed tightly around the coins, and stuffed them back in his pocket. The line moved into a large room. Officials began separating the men from the women and children.

"We were worried," Tom said quietly. Mick didn't respond. "We didn't know where you went. And then the guard told us to go to the immigrants home, and we weren't sure you'd know where we were." Mick said nothing. Ahead of us the crowd continued to part, men to one side, women to the other.

"So you were worried about me," Mick addressed the question to me.

"And would worrying do me a bit of good?" I replied.

"I'll take the shoonaun," Mick said. "Tom and I can take turns watching it. You take this." He pulled the handful of coins from his pocket and dumped them into my open palm. I pocketed them.

"I'll see you on the other side," Mick said. "We'll stay together from now on."

"Seeing is believing," I said.

"We will," Mick said. "I promise."

* * *

The shower was cold, but I nearly didn't notice. I think that was their plan to take your mind off the iciness of the shower by filling you up with pure humiliation. Even if that wasn't their plan, I do have to say the scheme worked.

The line I was in led into a large room filled with women in varying states of undress. I quickly dropped my eyes. You'd think that growing up in a tenement would have prepared me to see all manner of body parts. But quite the opposite, the overcrowding of the tenements drummed into us the need for modesty. I'd never seen my brothers unclad, never seen my mother in less than a shift. So when I was led into a room filled to overflowing with women, girls, young boys, all reluctantly undressing, a great panic flooded through me.

"Remove your clothes," a woman attendant said, handing me a large white sheet. "Pin your garments together, and attach your tag to them. You'll then be shown where to shower."

"I washed myself quite thoroughly last night," I said, but the woman had already moved on, and the line continued to push from behind, propelling me into the center of the room.

"Remove all your clothes for fumigation," another attendant said, as she wended her way through the room as casually as a lady out for a Sunday stroll. "Your clothes will be deloused, then returned to you after you finish with your shower."

I stepped to one of the long benches that ran from end to end along the walls and down the center of the room.

"I do not have lice," a woman shouted loudly enough to be heard over the general din. "I do not have lice, and I find it deeply insulting that you believe that I do." I looked up, spotted the woman, assessed her patched clothing, and knew enough not to believe her. The attendant apparently did as well.

"That's all well and good, ma'am," the attendant said wryly. "But nobody gets on the boat without a shower and fumigation. Even those without lice." The corner of her lip curled in an unsuccessfully suppressed smile.

"And what kind of rule is that?" the woman complained.

"A rule that you will have to follow if you ever want to see the sweet shores of A-mer-I-kay." The attendant turned her back and continued to make her rounds. The woman huffed and sat to remove her shoes.

One by one, I undid the buttons down the front of my shirtwaist. I looked around, nobody seemed to be watching, though a number of others were looking around for watchers just as I was. A woman with a three-year-old boy set down a bundle of shawl on the bench beside me. I looked up and smiled. The woman smiled back, a forced smile that said she would rather be almost anywhere else but here. She fumbled with the neck button on her little boy's gansey. I dropped my eyes to give them some privacy.

"Mama," the little boy said when his face popped out from under his sweater again. "That lady has a shift just like yours." I looked up. The little boy was pointing at me. I felt the color rise up the back of my neck. His mother muttered an apology and picked the boy up and reoriented him toward the wall. I draped the sheet over my shoulders and began to remove my undergarments beneath it.

The shower was, as I've said, cold. On the way in, the attendants stripped us of our sheets, and handed us bars of foul-smelling soap. They instructed us sternly to scrub ourselves head-to-toe with the stuff, taking special care to work it into our hair. So there in a large, tiled room with faucets and nozzles all around, surrounded by blue bodies and children screeching from the shock of the water, I took my first ever shower. It was cold, it smelled like pesticide, and I refused to take anything but baths for a good ten years.

* * *

After the shower, we were given sheets again. We were seated in the clean room, a long narrow room, lined with tile and benches. We clutched the sheets about us as a female attendant explained what would happen next.

The American government, it seems, had some very clear ideas about who it did and didn't want setting foot on its shores. If the Cunard line transported an immigrant who didn't meet government standards, the line would have to transport that immigrant back to their home without any further remuneration. It was, therefore, in their best financial interests to examine each passenger carefully.

The attendant gave us stern instructions, solemn instruction. We were to wait in the clean room until we heard our names called. We would then proceed to the examination room where we would be checked over by a doctor.

Now, I understand that the American government had the right to decide who could enter its borders. And I understand that the Cunard company was only looking after its interests. But that examination was one of the most terrifying experiences of my life. I had never been examined by a doctor before. I'd never had a vaccination. I'd never been naked in front of anyone other than my mother, and that not in several years. Perhaps more terrifying, I had never had so much riding on a single examination. They took everything. I went into that room with nothing more than a sheet and blind terror. I came out with an inspection card all officially stamped and signed. Only then did I get my own clothes and possessions back.

To this day I would rather not speak of it any more than to say that the Cunard line handled each of those hundreds of passengers like the efficient emigration machine it was. Pity the poor emigrants were far less than machine-like.

Nineteen

I had heard the horror stories of transatlantic travel in days gone by—the cramped conditions in steerage, the long months at sea, the merciless North Atlantic waves, and the gooey piles of barely edible food handed down into the bowels of the ship in metal buckets. As a girl, I grew up on stories of the famine ships—coffin ships they were called—on which the odds of reaching dry land were sometimes a great deal less than fifty-fifty. If I had traveled a mere fifty or sixty years earlier, I would have been telling a very different story, or perhaps I would not have survived to tell the story at all.

As it was, I traveled the Atlantic during the age of the great liners, those floating cities that offered accommodations that could only be called "grand," no matter what standard of life you were accustomed to. Palaces they were—glorious, floating monuments to the segregation of the classes.

Now, it is true that we in third class were not invited to the grand balls of first class. Uniformed wardens barred the door to the snow-white linens of the second class. Our crowded "promenade" had winches and hatch covers, not shuffleboard courts. And we listened to band music float on the breeze from first class, or, more likely, we make our own music. We were part of Cunard's no-frills, volume business, part of the herd Cunard ferried to improve its cost-to-benefit ratio. But for most of us, the bulk-rate accommodations that were home for the six to ten days upon the ocean were still nothing short of grand.

Cunard's was certainly far better than anything in the lanes of Cork and Dublin, better than anything we could aspire to as servants and laborers. And though we would spend our week encased in windowless steel-walled cabins, like meat in a tin, most of us who lined the docks of Queenstown were happy. Our bellies were full, and, perhaps more importantly, we were being given the chance to become one of those Americans who could afford to send the nearly unimaginable twenty-dollar boat fare across the Atlantic to poor relations.

* * *

Our ship was the *Caronia*. It carried 2650 passengers, more than three-quarters of them third class. On that much-awaited day, the first of August, 1906, she lay at anchor far out in Queenstown harbor. We, the herds, fresh from our encounter with the Cunard doctors and their showers, trampled the docks. We were shepherded by Cunard officials. We were funneled and channeled by fences and ropes strung between poles. In volume we were directed through a final ticket checkpoint and onto a small tender. Then shoulder-to-shoulder, back-to-belly, we were ferried, surrounded by baggage and postal sacks out into the harbor to the waiting *Caronia*.

A huge, glorious, great cathedral of a boat she was, with red and black smokestacks already oozing deep grey smoke. All heads rocked back on their hinges as the tender approached and the great liner grew to fill all our vision. Tom's face was in rapture. "Do you see the size of that anchor chain?" he said. "It's bigger around than I am." Even Mick seemed pleased. He grabbed my elbow and pointed at the tiny crewmen busying themselves in the bow.

The stairway from the tender to the *Caronia* was nearly as long as the stairway in the old tenement—two stories, maybe a bit more. The metal of its steps clanged under the feet of the herd, who continued to crane their necks as they climbed, trying to take in the magnificent expanse of the ship. On deck, still more dark-suited officials checked our tickets and assigned us to stewards, who led us down the third-class stairway. Again the clang, clang of feet echoed off the walls, as the herd made its way down, down, down into the belly of the ship. On either side of us were freshly painted metal walls, above a tidy lattice of metal pipes and conduits, below bare board. The corridors seemed to go on forever. Third class on the *Caronia* was a world all its own.

The herd was led haltingly down a narrow corridor. In front of us, family after family peeled off, each heading into one of the metal doors. In a tight clutch, not daring to lose physical contact with each other, Mick, Tom, and I waited. We waited, shuffled forward, swiveled our head from side to side, waited some more, took it all in. Finally it was our turn. The steward checked our tickets, then asked me for my inspection card. Where it said "berth number" he scribbled 1/145, then made a note on his list. He handed the card back and motioned toward a room. Our room. Our cabin.

Now by modern shipboard standards it wasn't fancy. It was third class, after all. But by the standards of the lanes, it was pure luxury. A bunk a piece, narrow bunks with soft mattresses and butter-soft sheets. Like the beds in the immigrant home, they bore navy-blue blankets emblazoned with the crest of the Cunard company. Between the two sets of double-decker bunks was a sink. A can of water was bolted to the metal wall above it, and a tap released the water on command. I'd seen sinks before, of course. The Good's had had running water; so had the Quillans. But I, myself, had never had a sink right there in my own bedroom. I ran a hand over the smooth steel of its lip, ran a hand over the thick blanket on one of the bunks, ran a hand over the shiny metal frame provided to keep passengers in bed during heavy seas.

"Which one's mine?" Mick dropped the shoonaun and kicked it under one of the bunks. The board floor was freshly scrubbed.

I scanned the tickets in my hands. "It doesn't say," I said. "I guess you can choose your own."

"Then I'll take number three," he replied, climbing the metal frame and settling with a bounce into the top bunk marked three.

Tom eyed the top bunk, then sat on the lower one, the one just below Mick. "I'll take this one," he said, and punched through the mattress up at Mick. Mick squirmed then made himself comfortable again. Tom picked a new place and punched again.

"When I get my own room in America," Mick said, his hands laced behind his head on the pillow, "I'm going to put in beds just like these, one on top of the other. And maybe a sink like that one there." He pointed his chin at the sink. "What do you suppose all these pipes do?" I looked up at the ceiling. A maze of iron pipes, painted grey like the board walls of the room, stretched above me. I shrugged.

"Which bunk do you want Clare?" Tom asked.

"I think I'll take this one," I pointed at the other lower bunk. The upper bunk looked like fun, but maneuvering into it wearing long skirts looked tricky.

"Where do you suppose the privy is?" Tom asked.

"They make you hang your arse over the side of the ship," Mick responded. Tom ignored him. I did, too.

I scanned the floor, under the bunks, in the corner behind the door. "No under-bed vessel," I said.

"They make you hang your arse over the side," Mick said again.

"I heard you, Mick," I said. "Tom, why don't you go see what you can find?"

Tom stuffed his inspection card into his pocket and stuck his head out into the hall.

"Don't lose that," I warned him.

He nodded, and finding a lull in the stream of people that flowed through the hall, he stepped over the lip of the doorway and went out. Mick considered for a second, then hopped down from the bunk and joined him.

I sat on the edge of the bunk for a few seconds, my hands idle in my lap, then rose to examine the room. The towels hanging from hooks by the sink were well-worn but clean. The drinking glass sitting atop the water can had far more heft to it than the jelly jars I was used to. It sparkled, was probably new, or close to. Above me hung an electric light, a bare bulb in a wire enclosure. I scanned the empty, grey walls and found the switch by the door. Gingerly, I put a finger on it and pressed it down. The bulb went out. I pushed the switch up; the bulb lit. Down, up. Down, up. No trimming wicks, no cleaning globes, no filling bowls. I wondered if Uncle Ronan had electricity.

That was our cabin—bunks, sink, towels, glass, mirror, light bulb. That and enough room to turn around. It was all clean. Suddenly I found myself with nothing to do. So I sat on the edge of my bunk and surveyed it all once again.

"You should see the toilets," Mick said, charging into the room some minutes later. "They have flush toilets and real loo paper." Mick drew his hand out of his pocket and with it a large wad of toilet paper.

"And sinks with salt water coming out of them," Tom said. "You're not supposed to drink it," he added. He squeezed past me and put his mouth under the tap and opened it. "This is the drinking water," he said.

"Use the glass," I said. Tom stood on his tiptoes to get the glass and filled it.

Mick hopped up onto his bunk again. "I think I'm going to like it here," he said. "This must be what America is like—running water in your room, flush toilets, sheets and blankets. I think I'll make a good American."

"Did you see?" I walked to the light switch and flicked it off and on again. Mick bolted from his bunk and elbowed Tom out of the way. He flicked the light off and then on, off and then on.

"It's not a play thing," I commented. Mick took his hand off the switch, and Tom quickly grabbed for it.

"I wonder how it works," Tom said, his ear close, listening to the click of the switch. "When we get to America, I'm going to learn how things like this work."

* * *

The flow of passengers through the corridor slowed. After a bit of remedial inner instruction, I taught myself how to lie back on a bunk in the middle of the day. I lay there on the butter-soft pillow, feeling the knots in my shoulders untie themselves. I listened to the sounds of families getting settled in their rooms, of children scampering through the corridor, of stewards discussing amenities with my neighbors. The bunk above me remained free. I imagined a girl about my age introducing herself before hopping easily into it. It would be nice to have company during the voyage.

The steady din in the hall bounced in a tangled mess from open doors to metal wall to metal wall. Gradually, though, my ears began to focus in on a particular conversation, the sound of two women ganging up on a poor steward not far from our door.

"The women's section is completely full," the steward said. "You can take these berths in the family section, or you can wait for the next ship. I have one berth here and another down the hallway. Do you want them?"

"I want you to find me a room where my maid and I can stay together," a voice responded.

"I'm afraid that's not possible," the steward responded. "If you'd boarded earlier . . . "

"Fine," the voice said. "Fine. We'll take your rooms until you can find us a better arrangement."

"Very good," the steward said. "This is one berth." I watched as he came into view outside our door. "This is the other." He gestured at the spare bunk, then hurried down the hallway.

An older woman, well into her sixties I would guess, a frail wisp of a woman covered on every available surface with spots and blotches, stepped briefly into the room. I stood to greet her, but she merely eyed us, and as fast as her stick would carry her, strode out into the corridor again. I sat back down on the bunk.

Moments later she returned. "It's immoral, it is." She was backing another steward into our cabin, poking him over and over in the chest with her cane. "It's immoral to ask a young, unmarried woman to share a cabin with two men." I reassessed my opinion of her frailty.

"A family," the steward commented. "A married man and a young lad no more than eight. And the man's wife is present as well."

"And that makes it respectable?" The woman continued to back the steward across the room. "Young man," she said, "I was married for thirty-seven years. I know what married couples do, especially when they're confined to a tiny room with beds for days on end. I'll not have a girl in my care exposed to such things before her time."

"Perhaps you would like to wait for the next ship?" The steward's backside found the sink, and he stopped, the old woman and her cane nose-to-chest with him.

"I would not," the woman said. "I would not care one little bit to wait."

"I'll see what I can do," the steward replied, slipping between the woman and my bunk and making a quick retreat.

Now that she had no one left to poke, the woman seemed to realize for the first time that she wasn't alone in the room. She looked me over, then examined Tom and Mick in their bunks.

"Is this your bunk?" she asked me.

"It is, ma'am," I said.

"That means this one is mine." She patted the edge of the upper bunk. It was a good two inches above her head. "I swear this shipping line is incapable of ferrying cattle let alone paying passengers. What kind of idiot would assign a top bunk to a sixty-three-year-old woman?"

"I could take the upper bunk if you'd like, ma'am," Tom said.

"You're a true little gentleman, you are," the woman said. "But I'll be taking your bottom bunk and my companion this top." She rapped Mick's bunk with her cane.

I stood, a bit shocked. The woman broke into my thoughts.

"I know what the steward said," she said. "But once the idiots who run this company get the cabin assignments straightened out, we'll be taking these two. She shooed Tom off his bottom bunk and sat heavily. Mick hopped off the top bunk and climbed into the bunk above me.

"Tell me something . . . " The woman paused. "What did you say your name was?"

"Clare Keane," I said, "and my brothers Mick and Tom."

"Bridget Keane," she said. "Kin maybe, at least by marriage. And this is my lady's maid Patricia Phelan." A young woman in her early twenties appeared in the doorway.

"Pat," Patricia said.

"And didn't I tell you a dozen times already that Pat is no name for a girl?" Mrs. Keane said. "Sure why would you be wanting a man's name? Patricia is a perfectly good name, and you'd be wise to use it."

Patricia stood silent, barely disguised defiance in her eyes.

"No sense, that one," Mrs. Keane pointed to Pat. Pat made a deep sound in her throat, something between a sigh and a growl. "So tell me something, Clare Keane. If you owned a shipping company, would you put a nineteen-year-old unmarried woman in a cabin with two men?"

"I'm sure I wouldn't know anything about shipping companies," I said.

"But then you don't have to to answer the question, now do you?" Mrs. Keane said.

"I wouldn't," Mick said.

"Thank you," Mrs. Keane said. "Now if yon wee maneen knows that such a thing is wrong and no mistaking, and him most likely without the sense God gave a goose, don't you think a shipping company would know better? Don't only stand there, Patricia, you stupid creature. Make yourself look handy and bring in the bags. You'll take this top bunk." Patricia ducked out the door and began muscling one of two heavy suitcases.

"Where am I going to sleep?" Tom whispered in my ear. I glanced up at Mick. He shrugged his shoulders and scooted over.

* * *

Beneath us I could feel the engine rise. The power of it set the floorboards to humming, and the small cabin filled with the heavy rumble that was to be our constant companion during the voyage.

Suddenly the reality of what we were doing struck me, hollowed out my belly with the knowledge of it. We were moving, pulling steadily out of the harbor. Soon we would ride out onto the sea, and my last glimpse of Ireland would have faded over the horizon.

"I want to go upstairs," I said.

"On deck," Tom said. He was studying the wires that led into the light switch. Mrs. Keane had warned him on pain of dismemberment that she would tolerate no further flicking of the switch, so Tom merely stood, eyes glued to the wires, examining, thinking. "On a ship," he said, "'upstairs' is called 'on deck'."

"Grand," I said. "I want to go 'on deck'."

"I'll go with you," Tom said. Mick hopped down from his bunk. Pat leaned over from her top bunk. Mrs. Keane nodded. She climbed down and the four of us found our way through the crowded corridor, wove our way up the crowded stairs to the third class promenade.

The rails were lined with people, three and four deep. From above us I could hear cheers spilling off of the first and second-class rails. All around us I could hear not only cheers but also sobs, some quiet, some loud and unashamed. That's what I heard. What I could see was people, the backs of people craning their necks to catch a glimpse over the side. From somewhere forward I hear the sound of a woman keening, the long soul-wrenching wail for the dead. The man in front of me slapped his companion on the back over and over again. "We're on our way now, John," he said. "We're on our way now."

I stood on my toes and tried to see over the men's shoulders. But in front of them were more shoulders, heads, large hats. I took a deep breath, my last breath of Irish air, and went below.

* * *

I wasn't used to sitting idle. Since Da died and I went into service, I hadn't really had much free time. During the day, I'd clean the house, cook, clean up after cooking. In the evening, I'd sit by the fire and sew, simple mending usually—I never was much of a hand with the fine sewing. Or I'd pray my rosary once through before bed. On the ship, though, the staff did the cooking and cleaning, and all my mending had been finished before leaving home. An exploratory expedition that first afternoon had told us that one could go up on deck and sit, or one could stay in one's cabin and sit, or one could go to the dining hall, which between meals doubled as a lounge, and there one could sit. Or stand if one preferred. Or walk, if one didn't mind stepping over the legs of those sitting.

After dinner that first night, I went back to my cabin, and there I discovered the chief form of amusement aboard ship—exchanging information about America. Mrs. Keane, I found, was not only Irish, she was Butte Irish, a genuine Irish-American. Mrs. Keane loved to talk. She had opinions about everything, and one of her foremost opinions was that it was her duty to share her wisdom freely with others. I soon learned that she was an encyclopedia of information about America.

All that first evening, we sat in the cabin, the two of us. The boys were still exploring the ship, and Pat had gone elsewhere, anywhere to get away from Mrs. Keane and her steady stream of opinions. So the two of us sat on the edges of the two bottom bunks, me leaning against one of the metal rails, Mrs. Keane leaning forward onto her stick, and we talked. Actually she talked. I listened.

Mrs. Keane, it seems, had just buried her husband in Waterford. That nonsense completed, she was now headed home to Butte to live out the rest of her life in the house that was part of her husband's mine pension. She had two sons and a daughter in Butte, and another son in New York City, working the "high steel," whatever that was. She was Irish, no mistake, but she could be Irish in Butte just as easily as Waterford, and so was making her way home.

Mr. Keane had been a copper miner in Butte, Montana, which, I learned, was farther from Ireland than St. Paul itself was. He had started as a laborer but over the years had risen through the ranks to become mine boss. Like many of the Irish miners in Butte, he was a sentimental soul about the old country. Unlike most of the miners, he was able to save a bit of money. One evening, a little worse for the drink, he spent that money on two ticket vouchers to Queenstown—one of them round-trip, the other one-way. The next day, he dropped the vouchers on the kitchen table and announced to his wife that his final wish was to die in Ireland, in Waterford to be precise. His wife, like most Butte women, was of a more practical bent. But on this matter she couldn't dissuade him.

It took him no better than a few months to decide it was time to redeem the vouchers. His chest was bad enough that he figured he wouldn't last another Butte winter. So they lent out the house, and left Butte to make the return journey. The whole way across, Mr. Keane was on his last leg, sure to be dead in a matter of months, if not weeks. But once exposed to the fresh sea air and fed by the company of relatives he hadn't seen since his late teens, Mr. Keane had rallied, and much to his and his wife's dismay, he had lingered for another four years.

By that time she was able to leave, Mrs. Keane's health was also failing, and for that very reason she quickly boarded a liner and started the trip back to America. Nearly forty years earlier she had sold everything and hopped a rickety old sailing ship to America fleeing the misery that was all around her in Ireland. She had fled Ireland looking for a new life. Having found one, she'd be swallowed sideways if she was going to turn her back on that life only to die in Ireland. No, she'd die in America. She'd be buried not with her husband and his old-world ways. She'd die in Butte, and from then on, her children and their children after them would be buried with her.

* * *

Beneath us the great engines roared as they powered us farther and farther out to sea. At first the gentle rock of the ship was merely curious, disorienting. With my head and belly both, I struggled to adapt to the new fluidity of my environment. When that didn't work, I thought to put my tipsy brain out of my mind. I settled into Mrs. Keane's stories of dry American land, hoping to find in them the stability my body craved. When Mrs. Keane decided to go for a short walk before bed, I lay down on my bunk. Despite the ruckus just outside the cabin door, I promptly fell sound asleep.

The rolling of the cabin picked up sometime in the middle of the night. I woke to the feel of my arm bumping rhythmically against the rail of my bunk. The not-quite-right feeling spilled from my head down the back of my throat. It was then I realized that I might feel this way for the rest of the voyage. The prospect did not enthuse me.

The cabin was as dark as you'd expect from a room with metal walls and no windows. The door was open a crack, and a thin line of light from the corridor split Mrs. Keane top to bottom in the bunk across the aisle. Above the rumble of the engines I could barely make out the sound of Tom snoring above me. The air was August warm and stifling close. I kicked off the blankets, and tried not to think about my stomach.

Less than an hour later — around four in the morning, I'd guess — the rolling and pitching started in earnest. The crack of the bow hitting the waves echoed in the cabin, and the pitch of the deck rolled me like a log back and forth in my bunk. It was all I could take and a little more beside. The mild dizziness blossomed to a gut-churning, brain-turning, green and clammy case of seasickness. I woke Tom up, and he went out and found me a bucket somewhere. I spent most of my first full day at sea hanging over it.

* * *

"This is nothing," Mrs. Keane pronounced from her place on the edge of her bunk late the next morning. One hand had a white-knuckle grip on the rail of the bunk, and her feet, which did not quite touch the floor, swung and bounced like a pendulum in the motion of the waves. She and I were alone in the cabin. Mick had disappeared shortly after the vomiting started. Tom had been chased out when Mrs. Keane wanted some privacy to wash and get dressed, and he hadn't come back since. Pat had gone to check on lunch.

"This is nothing," Mrs. Keane repeated. "When I came over the first time in sixty-five—1865 that is—the seas were so rough that we had to tie our baggage to the bunks. It wasn't like this with the private cabins and the high-class dining hall. We all lived and slept in one great room, ate there, too. And when the seas got rough and people started puking, and the baggage worked its way loose and started slamming into bulkheads with every wave, well then you'd just have to mind your soup, huddle over it and eat it anyway because as miserable fare as it was, it would be all you got. Why I saw seas so rough that a body couldn't stand and never mind walk. If you wanted to move about the cabin, you'd have to get down on your hands and knees and crawl through the puke and hope none of the great trunks flying back and forth knocked you silly. This sea, this is nothing."

I wondered if lunch was ready. Not for me. For Mrs. Keane. For me, the thought of eating was way down on my list of things I wanted to be doing. Lunch was slightly more appealing than being trapped in a cabin listening to Mrs. Keane talk about sea sickness that happened forty years ago, but it was noticeably less appealing than curling up into a ball and dying.

"In '65," she continued, "it took us nearly a month to make the crossing, and a good twenty days of that was in rough seas. I never seemed to get sick myself. When I felt like I might be, I just put it out of my mind. Willpower, my girl, that's the key, don't you know. My poor husband Jack—well he wasn't my husband just then, we'd only just met on the boat—Jack never could seem to get the hang of it. He rolled over and turned a sad state of grey just after we left port, and he didn't pink up until we were through Castle Garden and out the other end to a priest in New York. We were married a full day before I knew the man could blush." She laughed. The laugh bounced off the cabin walls and mingled with the smell emanating from my bucket.

"Lunch is ready," Pat said, entering, then closing the door to the cabin behind her. "They strung up ropes to help people keep their feet in the dining room. And I found the third class smoking lounge. It's not much more than a dozen benches bolted to the deck, but it smells a powerful lot better than this place." She wrinkled her nose in disgust. "You can smoke there, too," she added.

"We didn't have smoking lounges in my day either," Mrs. Keane commented as she rummaged eagerly through her bag and to my amazement pulled out a pipe and a pouch of tobacco. "Why you couldn't smoke at all below deck, and they only let you above deck for a short time every afternoon, not that I smoked back in those days."

"Well, then I guess we're lucky we *aren't living in your day*," Pat said brusquely.

"Pshaw," Mrs. Keane exclaimed as Pat handed her her stick for one side and offered an arm for the other. "You wouldn't last a month in my day." The two swayed back and forth, back and forth. My gorge began to rise and I clamped my eyes shut.

I could hear them arguing all the way down the hallway, even with the door mostly shut. But soon they were gone, completely gone, and I settled back into the steady drone of the engines and the ebb and flow of voices and footsteps. Tom checked on me a couple of times. But most of the day was only me and the slop bucket and the steady roll of the waves.

* * *

The sea quieted during the night. I must have fallen asleep because I woke around noon the next day feeling nearly human. The cabin was empty. A cut of white bread rested on the shelf above the sink. I ate it slowly despite the gripping demands of my empty stomach. Then I waited, my bed sheet wrapped around me, monitoring the movements beneath the boards, the movements inside me. The bread stayed where I put it quite nicely. So I washed and dressed, then gingerly made my way through the narrow hallway, up the metal stairs, and onto the deck.

The smell of vomit, and not all of it mine, clung tenaciously to the inside of my nose. Concentrating on keeping my legs under me, I walked to the bow rail, to the far outside of the press of humanity on deck. The wind hit me full in the face, and I breathed deep of the cool sea air, taking in the fresh saltiness of it. Beneath me, the prow of the ship sliced through water as smooth as glass. I whispered a quick prayer of thanks and another for smooth water the rest of the journey.

All around me, slightly rumpled folks lounged on the deck, leaned on the rails, chin wagged with new friends. Laborers and laners they were, servants and social ne'er-beens like myself. This was our "promenade"—the very bow where the movement of the waves was most pronounced and the deck space was the most cluttered. We shared our leisure space with equipment, with bollards and anchor chains, hatch covers and winches. We didn't, however, share it with the first and second-class passengers. More importantly, they didn't share theirs with us.

The superstructure of the ship, hidden mostly from our view by rails and decks, was where the respectable people lived and played. Up there was another ship entirely, a ship of deck chairs, shuffleboard, and fourteen-piece bands that played requests. Its well-aired cabins, replete with four-poster beds, private baths, and large windows, looked out on pristine white decks with grand names like "promenade," and "bridge," and "shelter." Its entrances and exits were jealously guarded—guarded against the likes of us—by uniformed wardens. Yet even if its doors had been thrown wide open, it would never have occurred to me to enter that world. Theirs was a world of gilt and mahogany, of silk and furs. Mine was a world of bare bulkheads and frequently patched wool. Any fool could tell the difference.

On the wind I caught a whiff of sweat and tobacco from the clutch of men just up the rail. They smelled like the laborers of the lanes, like honest work, and too much of it. Still their smell, though strong, wasn't nearly as oppressive as the smells below deck had been. Below deck, the smell had already become offensive in every sense of the word. The mix of vomit, over-taxed toilets, coal fumes, and unwashed humanity reached out and slapped you across the face, made your eyes water and your nose recoil. Escaping the soup of smells below for the moving air of the deck did me no small bit of good.

I turned around, leaned back against the rail, my arms hooked around it for security. Not far away, two men sat propped against a great pile of rope, their caps pulled down over their eyes. Just down the rail a small handful of women clustered, talking quietly, their shawls wrapped loosely around their shoulders despite the heat of the sun. I let go of the rail and walked aft, making my way around men's legs, women's skirts, and boys playing cards on the decking. A girl in heavily darned stockings cradled a homemade doll, whispered something in its ear, then pointed out to the already unimaginably unbroken expanse of water.

* * *

My stomach, I found, was far better outdoors. I had been enjoying that fact while surveying the sea, marveling at the sheer expanse of it, when the corner of my eye caught something odd, a six-foot flash of pure white from over by the steerage entrance.

Now that much white may not have turned a head in first class, but in third class, it was as exotic as tropical plumage. So was the man wearing it. He was a fine doorful of a man with a large handlebar mustache and crisply pressed white trousers. His white knit shirt conformed to his chest and exposed his finely made arms. He held himself carefully, like a heroic statue come to life, always angling his jaw to its best advantage. Under one of his arms was a small black package, carried in the crook of his elbow.

As he moved forward through the crowd, all eyes turned to look. A gentry man he was, or perhaps a gentry wanna be. He clearly belonged in second class, maybe even first. I smiled to myself, waited for the expression on his face when he realized his error.

He strode into the crowd like the deck was his very own. It was only when he'd chosen a bare patch of board and stopped that I noticed that he had a young woman and two girls in tow. The girls were my age, or no more than a few years older. Around the hem of their grey, knee-length dresses were bright red stripes. On their legs were finely knit grey wool bloomers, and on their feet matching slippers, each held snugly with a single strap. Strangest of all, though, were their hands, which were encased in huge black leather mittens.

The man removed the black package from under his arm. It wasn't a package at all but his own pair of mittens. He slipped them on his hands and then held them out to the young woman who quickly did up the laces. She and the girls giggling together at something he said, something the murmur of the crowd covered before I could hear it.

The mittens tied securely, he raised his hands to chest height, and feet firmly planted against the deck, he thrust his jaw forward. It was then that all the pieces came together to form a picture for me. The man was a fighter. A fighter or something like it. His posture was stiff and artificial, not nearly as calculated or mobile as that of the men I had seen fighting outside pubs and throughout the lanes of Cork. I couldn't imagine fighting in all white with mittens tying up fingers and knuckles.

One of the girls faced the handsome man and took up a similar posture. The man nodded, then corrected her stance gently.

"Hey, boyo," a man called out in a Dublin accent. "If you want to have a go, I'll do ya. I can probably give you a bit more of a go than your little girl there." The man's companions laughed loudly.

The handsome man ignored him. "See if you can hit me on the chin," he said to the girl in a distinctly English accent. The wind blew his words toward me so it sounded as though he were standing right next to me. "See if you can hit me." He jabbed and feinted, never letting his punches get very close to the girl opposite him. She swung timidly, throwing the punch from her elbow. Her mitten bounced lightly off the man's shoulder. He laughed in a condescending way. I had never seen a girl fight like that before, and the timidness of it embarrassed me.

"Come on lad," the Dublin man said. He stripped off his jacket. "I'll wear your wee mitties if you'd like. You and me. Let's have a go."

The man dropped his hands and turned to face the Dubliner. "I, sir, am a gentleman," he said. "I would not 'have a go' with you or any other ruffian."

"Oooo." The Dubliner's companions elbowed each other in the ribs.

"I fought a gentleman once," the Dubliner boasted, "I kicked him in the shin, then gave him a glorious crack to the jaw that he'll remember to his dying day."

"A gentleman does not kick," white shirt commented.

"A 'ruffian' like me does," the Dubliner said. "And quite hard at that." His friends laughed and punched at his shoulders from the back.

"I would imagine you do," white shirt replied. "Now if you will excuse me, I have a lesson to give to my daughters." He turned back to the girls.

"Lesson?" said the Dubliner. "You teach little girls how to give each other sock?"

White shirt turned again, sighed with obvious impatience. "I am a boxing instructor," he said. "I teach boxing, Marquis of Queensberry rules. I have some very influential clients waiting for me in the United States, and yes, some of them are young ladies. Now if you will excuse me."

"Marquis of Queensberry?" one of the Dubliners interjected. "I think I saw him board on the first class ramp. Are you sure you're on the right deck there, boyo?" The crowd, who was warming to the baiting, guffawed.

"Ignore them," white shirt commented to his daughter. "See if you can hit me on the chin." The girl swung a pathetic punch. It skidded off the man's arm.

"Good," white shirt said. "Again." The girl punched again, this time missing him entirely.

The other girl stood a few paces away, her gloves raised, imitating the man's every move. She looked a bit more confident, but still utterly small in comparison to the able, strong man she shadowed. I felt embarrassed for them, and in a strange way embarrassed for myself as well.

"English women shouldn't try to fight," a young man's voice came from just over my shoulder. I jumped in shock, not aware that he had been there. I spun around to see a nicely made young face, a lad about my age in a crisp blue shirt, long trousers and a cap.

"English women just don't have the heart for a good fight," he said. "Fighting isn't about dressing up in sporting clothes and dancing about tapping each other with padded leather gloves." He shifted in beside me. The first girl had stepped aside allowing the second to take her shot at the Marquis man.

"Fighting is about heart." The lad tapped his chest. "English women shouldn't try to fight."

"And what of Irish women? Should we try to fight?" I asked, surprising myself. It was a cheeky question of someone I had just met.

"Irish women don't need to try. Irish women are fighters by nature," the boy said. "Sure, 'tis the Irish men who square off behind the pubs. They boast about how handy they are in a fight. But when those men go home, they tremble before their wives and daughters, and so it should be. Irish men are some of the best fighters in the world, but Irish women are stronger than the whole lot of them." He squared off against me, taking up the ridiculous stiff-limbed, jaw-first posture of the Marquis man. Atop the stiff jaw, was a barely stifled grin twisting its way from his lips. I laughed, and he shot short jabs at me. I raised my hands and thrust out my jaw, grinning back at him.

"Punch me," he said. I dropped my hands and shook my head.

"No, go on. Punch me." He danced around me, flicking little jabs my direction. He'd begun to draw a bit of attention away from the Marquis man and his daughters. I shook my head again. "Come on," he said. "For Ireland. Show me that I'm not wrong about Irish women being strong and fierce and a fair match for any Irish man." He continued to dance and jab. I tried to turn away, and one of his fists clipped me on the shoulder. I turned to face him, locked eyes with him.

"Don't," I said simply.

"Isn't that just what I was saying?" he said. "Come on. I'll teach you how to really use your fists, how to really take care of yourself."

"I take care of myself just fine," I said.

"So you do," he said. "So you do." His fist reached out and clipped me gently but firmly on the jaw.

I turned and glared at him. Something told me I should just walk away. But his sandy hair falling into his dancing eyes, his grin, his way of getting just a little too close, all fascinated me, held me as tightly as if he had reached out a hand and grasped me by the wrist. "That was uncalled for," I said.

"Then hit me back," he said. "Hit me back. I'll warrant you can do it."

I felt my hand ball into a fist. Could I do it? He jabbed at me again, I moved back ever so slightly to avoid contact.

"Good," he said. "Good instincts." He threw another jab, then a cross, then another jab, all short, playful. I smiled and raised my fists.

I raised them just in time to see my opponent collapse onto the deck, and without so much as a tap from me. He disappeared into a tangle of arms and legs. Atop him were Mick and Tom.

"What do you think you're doing?" Tom shouted into the lad's face. Mick was atop him, straddling him, landing punch after punch on his arms and shoulders as the lad curled up onto his side. "That's our sister," Tom said, standing over the fight, landing kicks on the lad's thighs and seat. The lad's cap fell off and began to blow away. Quickly I stepped on it, pinning it to the deck. A group of girls scrambled back. The Dublin men angled themselves for a better view.

"I didn't do anything," the lad protested, covering his face with his hands and forearms. "Tell them," he shouted at me. "Tell them I didn't do anything."

"Mick," I said. "Mick, get off him."

"Let me finish," Mick said.

"You do, and I'll finish you," I said and grabbed him by the back of the collar. Tom stepped in, and I pushed him off with a glare. Mick threw another punch, and I slapped him across the back of the head. He cocked his arm again, and I slapped him across the ear.

"Ow," he said, turning to glare at me.

"Get off," I said, still gripping his collar. Reluctantly he got to his feet and backed away. The lad scooted out of range before getting up, brushing his now rumpled shirt, in the hopes of working loose a stain the deck had put on the sleeve.

I let go of Mick's collar, and he rolled his shoulders settling the shirt back onto them.

"We'll talk back in the cabin," I said, glancing around at the crowd that had by now completely forgotten about the boxers.

Mick glanced around, too. He locked eyes with me with a look I had never seen before, a look that surpassed anger, that oozed over into hatred. "Don't ever do that again," he said, his voice tight, raspy. He turned to the lad still brushing at his shirt. They locked eyes, and for a moment I thought they would start throwing fists again. "I'm watching you," Mick said quietly, then turned and made his way through the crowd. Tom shot a glance at me and at the other lad, and followed Mick.

"My brother," I said, stooping and handing the lad his cap.

"Who else would it be?" the lad said.

We turned to look again at the boxers, but they had moved away. Small clutches of passengers talked, shooting occasional glances our way.

"You prove my point," the lad said. "No one in their right mind should ever fight an Irish woman, least of all an Irish man."

"Hmpph," I answered.

"My name is Colum O'Moran," he said, glancing around for Mick, then offering his hand.

"Clare Keane," I said, shaking it for the sake of politeness, no more. Or so I told myself.

"My parents and I are emigrating to Bellingham in Washington. I have uncles and aunts and cousins there," he said. "How about you?"

"Minnesota," I said, being intentionally vague.

"Do you have family there?"

"Yes," I said, turning to make my way back to the cabin.

"I'd like to see you again," Colum said taking a place at my side.

"You may well," I said. "How would I be going anywhere?"

Colum laughed. "May I call at your cabin?"

"No," I said. "But you may walk out with me here on deck. Tomorrow. About this time."

He tipped his cap and smiled.

"One thing," I said. "No more fighting lessons."

"And what would I teach the likes of you?"

Twenty

All evening long I could feel Colum O'Moran's hand shaking mine. I roamed the corridors, then the deck, half hoping to see him, half dreading that he would see me, would see written on the very flesh of my face how much he occupied my thoughts. It made no sense. Never had a boy's face affected me like his did. After no better than ten minutes on my eyes, the memory of it filled my mind, pushed memories of Ireland to the far back corners. I half-heartedly tried banishing it, but had no luck.

As for Mick, he didn't return to the cabin at all that evening. I asked Tom where he was, but Tom only shrugged, mumbled, and drifted out of the cabin himself. When it came time to turn in, Tom had the bunk above me to himself. All night long I started at every little noise from the corridor, anticipating Mick's return. The air was thick and warm, too warm. I twitched and tossed until my sheets knotted about me, all the while dreaming strange, grey dreams of boxing first Colum, then Mick, then Colum again, them in their white shirts and me with soft, black mittens binding my hands.

* * *

"He can't get far," Mrs. Keane offered as we were dressing for breakfast that morning. "He can't very well swim to America, and if he could, I doubt he'd willingly get that far from the dining hall. Besides, boys need their freedom."

"Boys the likes of Mick don't need freedom," I replied. "They need a heavy boot in the backside to keep them in line."

"True enough for you," Mrs. Keane said holding her arms out so Pat could slide her dress over her head. "My Bryan was that way. Best thing for a boy like that is work, hard work and plenty of it. Let 'em breathe mine dust for ten or twelve hours at a stretch. That'll screw their head back on straight."

"Your Bryan works in the mine, then?" I asked.

"No," she said. "Frank and Fred work the mines. Bryan's the one that's in New York 'working the high steel,' or so he says. Moved there after Jack and I went to Waterford. Wrote and said he wouldn't be grubbing the dirt the rest of his life, said he wanted to make something of himself. As though he couldn't do that in the mines. His father did. The boy has a stubborn streak, he does. Always has to do things his way. Still having family in New York gives me a place to stay for a few days when we reach America. Beats having to go from the ship to the train directly. I don't think my old bones could take that any more. Your Mick will be fine. Be careful with your buttoning, there, Patricia. You're pinching my neck."

"Sorry," Pat mumbled. She shifted her fingers a bit, succeeding only in making the buttonhole pinch even more.

"You'd think you'd never buttoned a button before, you ham-handed creature," Mrs. Keane said spinning around and slapping away her hand. "Let me do it." She raised her arms, but stretch as she might, she couldn't reach the button behind her neck.

"Blinking sea air has my rheumatism biting down like a dog on a bone," she said, dropping her hands to her sides in resignation. "It was never this bad in Butte." She again turned her back to Pat, who gingerly reached again for the button. "'Twas Waterford, so it was. All that damp air rusted me solid. And now this blamed boat is making it all that much worse. Patricia! Would you stop before you rub my neck raw!"

Patricia quickly pushed the button through the hole and stepped back like someone who had just set a trap and was pulling her fingers back before it could spring back. "Sorry, Mrs. Keane," she said. The tone of her voice said she wasn't sorry at all.

"You'd think there would be a proper lady's maid somewhere in Waterford, but could I find one?" Mrs. Keane wrapped her shawl around her shoulders and sat heavily on the bunk. Pat knelt to put on her boots.

"One willing to travel all the way across the ocean and the better part of a continent in your company?" Pat held open the right boot. "I'd say you'd have to search halfway across Ireland to find such a creature," she said. I startled a bit at the cheekiness of it.

"So I should have," Mrs. Keane replied. "Maybe I would get better than a kitchen maid for my trouble." She swatted Pat's hands away from the boot and reached to pull it on herself. Her arms reached roughly to her knees before she sat back again. Pat gave the boot a tug, then reached for the buttonhook.

"I never called myself 'a proper lady's maid'," Pat said, eyes still on the boot. "You said you'd pay my way to America if I saw you and your goods safe from Waterford to Butte. And that's what I'm doing. No more. No less."

"Jack should have hailed from Dublin like I did," Mrs. Keane said, holding out her other foot. "I'd hold there would be a lady's maid there who would jump at the chance for a free ticket to America. But, no, he had to be from Waterford. The back of beyond, it is. The back of beyond filled with ham-handed louts. Patricia!"

Pat's shoulders stiffened. She opened the second boot wider, and eased Mrs. Keane's foot inside. "What kind of service did you do, Clare?" she said, changing the subject.

"General service," I said. "Cleaning, kitchen work, whatever the mistress wanted."

"Small house?" Pat asked.

"Only my Mama and me in the first situation," I said. "Then me, two other women and two men in the second. The master there owned a mill."

"I was a kitchen maid," Pat said. "For a family filthy with crystal money. But those days are over." She finished buttoning Mrs. Keane's second shoe, and gave it a pat. Or was it a swat? "In America, I want to work in a big store or maybe an eating house. I'm tired of service, tired of always being short of cash, tired of having my hand so deep in the dog's mouth that I can't ever say an honest word to the lady of the house. It was always, 'very good ma'am, of course ma'am, that'll do ma'am,' though her schemes be the most clot-headed things you ever heard in your life."

I glanced over at Mrs. Keane. She was still seated on the bunk, powdering her face in a small pocket mirror, apparently ignoring every word Pat said.

Pat turned to the mirror above the sink to comb her hair. "I swear," she continued, "there is nothing like money to chase any kind of sense out of a person's head. The second you have enough of it to hire a servant is the second you become completely useless. Show me someone with five servants and I'll show you someone who hasn't the sense to feed themselves on their own. Show me someone with ten servants, and I'll show you someone with all the brightness of an overstuffed divan." She set the comb in the sink and gathered up her hair, twisting it into a knot. "Hiring servants rots the brain," she said, "no mistake. It rots the brain. And who's the one to suffer for it? The help. The able serve the clot-headed. We're the ones to suffer." It was a challenge, no mistake. I held my breath.

Mrs. Keane looked as though she hadn't heard, continued to pat the powder over the mosaic of spots that was her face. Pat threw a glance her way, then began to hum, then sing,

This girl was poor.
She hadn't a home.

Or a single thing she could call her own.

Drifting about in the saddest of lives.

Doing odd jobs for other men's wives.

As if for drudgery created.

Begging a crust from a woman she hated.

Pat wasn't much for carrying a tune, and what ability she did have was being sacrificed to volume as she made sure none of the words were lost to the sound of the engines.

I shot a nervous glance at Mrs. Keane, then at Pat again. I'd heard folks speak badly of their employers before, of course. You don't spend three years in service without hearing considerable venom. But where I came from, it was always whispered, spoken quietly behind closed doors, or perhaps loudly in pubs no respectable person would frequent. Never would I think to say such things aloud in front of my mistress. I glanced at Mrs. Keane. She was poking at her spots with the powder puff, as though she were trying to chase them off her face rather than cover them. Finally she stopped.

"You think you know what it is to be ill used?" she said, her voice quiet but barbed. Pat continued to study herself in the mirror, but I could see her face twitch slightly. She'd heard. "You think you know what it is to be ill used?" Mrs. Keane repeated more loudly. "Once you're after surviving a famine, then you'll know the saddest of lives." She snorted, snapped her pocket mirror closed and stuffed it into her handbag. "You haven't the least notion what it is to be poor, girl, what it's like to think yourself as blessed as the Pope himself if you had so much as a crust to your name. I may have a couple of extra pennies to rub together today, but that's only because I worked hard for forty years. I had nothing when I stepped off the boat in '65. Nothing. Nothing in my hands, nothing in my pockets, not a decent layer of fat over my ribs themselves. 'Saddest of lives'? You have no notion. No notion at all."

"Maybe I don't," Pat replied, still studying her hair in the mirror. "But I do know I wasn't made for service. I know that much. When my feet touch American soil, I'm walking away from that foolishness entirely. I know that much."

"You mean when your feet touch the soil of Butte, don't you?" Mrs. Keane locked her in a gaze that was the essence of the reason I never back talked my mistress. The look sent a shudder through me, and it being aimed at someone else entirely. Pat, on the other hand, didn't flinch. She only turned from the mirror and returned the gaze.

"Butte," she said. "Of course I meant Butte."

Mrs. Keane shot a burst of air through her nose. "Until then, your ladyship, I don't suppose it would be too terribly cheeky of me to ask you to show me my stick. Listening to all this foolish talk worked up an appetite in me. Maybe there's someone in the dining hall with the sense to carry on a reasonable conversation." Pat handed Mrs. Keane her cane, and then offered an arm to help her stand. Her touch was surprisingly gentle given the defiant look on her face. Mrs. Keane leveraged herself off the bunk, then brushed down her skirts before taking Pat's arm again.

As for me? I followed them out the door and down the hall to breakfast.

I was speechless myself. But Pat's words rang in my head. "I wasn't made for service." Who could think such a thing? Until now, it hadn't occurred to me to choose a job based on what I was "made for." It was bright, shining new idea, it was. I turned it over and over in my mind, feeling a touch guilty for doing so.

Still, in America, who could say?

* * *

Mrs. Keane was right. She had raised three boys, so I suppose I shouldn't have expected less. We found Mick in the dining room, hunched over his breakfast like a greedy dog over a joint.

"Where were you last night?" I said.

"Try the bread," he said, handing me the plate full of thick slices.

"I don't care what you do during the day," I said, "but you need to be back at the cabin at night. I was worried about you." Actually, "worried" wasn't quite the right word. I knew he was on the boat. I knew the stewards and the wardens kept order. And I think, to some degree, I'd simply given up. Mick was going to do what Mick was going to do; my worrying wouldn't change that one scrap. But as much as I had told myself not to worry, I *had* tossed and turned all night.

"I can take care of myself," he said. "And you don't seem to need me to take care of you."

"Do you think we can get more eggs?" Tom asked. The egg he was peeling was the last one in the bowl.

"Go talk to one of those men in the white suits," I said. Several were squeezing between the tables, between benches of hungry passengers, carrying bowls, baskets, fresh plates. Tom rose, and with a hand on Mick's shoulder worked his way behind him to the aisle.

"Do you think you could find a way of taking care of me that doesn't involve breaking heads?" I asked.

"Who was he?" Mick asked.

"A boy," I said. "Just someone I met on deck."

"He was beating on you," Mick said.

"We were playing," I replied.

"And how was I to know that?" Mick demanded. "How I was I know that the dirty little cur beating on my sister was only playing?"

"The fact that I was smiling might give you some clue," I replied.

"A man should not pretend to beat a woman," he said. "It goes against my blood just to think of it, and all the more if she's my sister." He crushed a bit of egg shell into his plate by way of punctuation. "It's sinful, so it is."

"Maybe you're right," I said. "Maybe you're right." Somehow I couldn't think of the Marquis man and his silly little girls as too grave a sinners.

Tom returned with a bowl of eggs. "We're having beef with potatoes for dinner," he said. "And ham soup for supper." He was elated, fairly floated past Mick to his seat, where he added a second egg to his plate. He was in paradise. The food on the ship was plain fare, but there was plenty of it. It would be a cliché to say that Tom ate to his heart's content, but to watch him was to leave no doubt that he ate with heart as well as mouth. But then we all did. After five months of famine fare, how could we do otherwise?

*　*　*

"There you are so." I looked up from my breakfast. Colum's hands were stuffed in his pockets. He swayed with the motion of the ship, his thigh bumping gently against the edge of the table in rhythm with the waves.

"So it would seem," I said, glancing his direction, then looking down again to spread a thick layer of butter on my bread. For nearly five minutes, in the presence of breakfast—white bread, as white as the shell of the egg that sat beside it on my plate, as white as the milk that swayed from side to side in my glass—in the presence of all that bounty, I had nearly forgotten about Colum O'Moran. But now as I watched that well-made thigh go bump, bump, bump against the calico tablecloth, I knew that my forced casualness was unlikely to hold. The boy unnerved me to my very core. I worked the butter to the very corners of the bread, then evened it out a bit in the center.

"Much good may it do you," Colum offered, gestured casually at the breakfast. Could I be mistaken, or was his casualness a bit forced as well?

"You're a nervy beast," Mick said. He set the egg he was peeling back on his plate. It rolled to the edge and back again. Mick stood, lifted a leg out to straddle the bench, and drew his shoulders back. "Didn't I tell you I didn't want you talking to my sister?" he said.

"No," Colum replied. "No, you didn't. You told me never to box with your sister again, and you told me that you would be watching. I'm not here to box, and if you'd like to watch me eat, I have no trouble with that." Mick scowled at him. "My name is Colum O'Moran," Colum said extending his hand.

Mick ignored it and began poking again at the eggshells on his plate. "Leave then, Colum O'Moran," he said. "I'll not tell you twice."

"My brother, Mick," I said. "And my other brother, Tom." Tom nodded, barely looking up from his third egg.

"Mick," Colum said, "I'll leave you to your breakfast, if that's what you want, but first I wanted to apologize if I was too forward yesterday." His hands were jammed back into his trouser pockets. "I have nothing but respect for your sister. And if that weren't true, I now have nothing but respect for your right fist itself. I would never do anything to shame your sister or your family."

Mick looked up. "How are the ribs?" he asked.

"They've seen better mornings," Colum confessed with a wry smile. Mick's lip curled slightly in satisfaction.

"Did you eat yet?" Mick said. Colum shook his head. Mick sat back down and motioned with his chin to the seat beside me. Colum sat, keeping a respectful distance between his thigh and my own. Tom passed down the plate of bread he had been keeping in front of him. Just like that most of the tension drained from the air. I doubted that I would ever understand boys.

"Where are you from?" Mick asked as he resumed picking at the shell of his second egg.

"County Down," Colum replied. "But we're going to Washington. My uncle's a logger there, and he said he could find work for my father, my older brother, and me."

"Our uncle is a logger too," Tom said. "In Wisconsin. St. Croix Falls."

"He might be a logger," I said. "He might be doing something else for the lumber company. We aren't sure."

"There's good logging in America," Colum said. "My uncle sent a picture from Washington. It was him and three other loggers sitting on top of a tree they chopped down. Four men could sit abreast on the stump and still have plenty of elbow room. One of the men in the picture wasn't much older than I am. My uncle says the logging company will take a man who's only fifteen. If he's able enough, that is. I'm going to apply when I get to Washington. Da wants me to keep in school, but in America if you have a strong back you can make a good living without the schooling."

So he was at least fifteen. Fifteen and still in school. I looked out of the corner of my eye at him. He had a tiny razor nick on his jaw and not a bit of stubble. It probably hadn't been necessary for him to shave. I wondered if he did so because he knew I'd be sneaking looks at him.

"My uncle says that an able man can make nearly fifteen dollars a week," he continued. "I wouldn't make that much at first, but maybe by the time I'm twenty, by the time I'm old enough to have a wife and family." My eyes were on my egg, but for an instant, out of the corner of my eye, I thought I caught him glancing in my direction.

"That's three pounds a week," Tom exclaimed. "A laborer in Cork would think himself the luckiest man in the world if he made a third of that and no more."

"Do you think they'd have a job for someone thirteen?" Mick asked.

"I don't think they'd let you chop down trees," Colum replied. But my cousin, my uncle's son, works in the stables. He's younger than I am."

"I always did want to drive horses," Mick said. If he had, it was news to me.

"My uncle says that the horses they use are bigger than dray horses in Ireland. When the loggers cut the trees down, the horses haul them to the river. And then the men bind the trees together and float them down the river to the sawmill. They do most of the cutting in winter, so the horses don't have to haul through the mud; they can haul along hard-packed, icy ground."

He went on, with Mick and Tom hanging on his every word, talking of trees and log rafts and saws and axes, and jobs they would and wouldn't want to do. I must say that I, too, hung on his every word. Yet I doubt I could have told you more than a bit of what he said. For me it was the voice itself that was captivating. He had the silver-edged accent of a northern man, and the innocent tenor of a boy whose voice had changed only recently. The words flowed out of him like music from a flute, slipping and dancing through the air. I floated along on them, barely tasting the bread and egg, wondrous as they were.

That's when I noticed it. Colum picked at his breakfast, ate in nibbles in between stories, left a bit of underdone egg on the rim of his plate. So he was used to having food in his belly, could afford to leave some just because it wasn't to his liking. He wasn't a laner, then. I wondered if he could tell that I was. The shirtwaist and skirt I wore could have belonged to someone middle class, but my accent said both Cork and laborer through and through.

"What work does your father do?" Tom said, as though reading my mind again.

"He's a clerk," Colum replied, "or at least he was. When the shop started having troubles and dismissed half its staff, Da decided to join Uncle Sean in Washington."

A clerk, then. Well, so it began—the fine sifting of the underclasses. With that one tiny piece of knowledge, I learned he was too good for me. Simple as that. He would be leaving soon. The son of a clerk wouldn't associate with a common housemaid.

"What about your father?" Colum asked.

"Our father died," Mick said. "Four years ago." He reached for another cut of bread. The bowl that held the eggs was empty. "Are you going to eat that?" Mick motioned at the bit of underdone egg on Colum's plate. Colum shook his head and shoved the plate over to Mick.

"Your mother?" Colum said.

"Died last spring," Mick said, then stuffed a large hunk of bread in his mouth, too much to talk around.

"Clare's been taking care of us," Tom offered. "She's the best. She worked and cooked for us and took care of our clothes as well as Mama did." He sounded like a newspaper advertisement for soap cakes. "Extra thick bar, washes out stains without harming your most delicate fabrics, guaranteed to make your laundry work lighter."

"She's going to make someone a good wife," he said. I looked up with a start and glared at him sternly. "You are," he said, and dropped his eyes. He scanned his empty plate, then in one large draw finished his milk.

"What did you work at?" Colum asked, shifting a bit on the bench to look more directly at me.

"I was in service," I said quietly, more quietly than I intended. I wondered if maybe the answer had gotten lost in the rumble of the engines. It didn't.

"Honest work," Colum said. I knew that that was what people say about work they consider beneath them. Hauling and scrubbing and digging are "honest work." Grubbing and mucking? "Honest work." Tell someone you're a doctor or a mill owner, and they never say "honest work."

We sat quietly for a few minutes while Mick finished the last of his breakfast. Colum had shifted back to face the center of the table again. He ran his finger back and forth over a chip in the rim of his plate. He was clearly thinking, and I knew what he was thinking about. He was charting the quickest way away from the three of us. Without knowing it, he had eaten breakfast with three children he probably wouldn't have been allowed to speak with back in Ireland. Well, it served him right. He should have known by the accent that we were laners. I glanced over at him. His hair was hanging over his forehead, and from where I was sitting I couldn't see his eyes. I didn't have to. I knew what was in them.

"Mick," Colum said finally. "I'm going for a walk. Just up on deck and about the ship. If I could get your permission, I'd like to ask Clare to join me." I looked over at him in surprise. He smiled back. His teeth were straight and white.

"On deck and through the corridors?" Mick asked. Colum nodded. "Fine by me," Mick replied. Colum stood and offered me his hand to help me climb out over the bench. I took it. It was smooth, far smoother my own. If he noticed, he made no sign.

* * *

The corridors were close—crowded with people, heavy with air that had been breathed too many times already. But the deck was too crowded to walk, and we wanted to do more than just stand. So we roamed the hallways, went up and down the stairs, covered the same territory over and over. Each time we met a cluster of people, Column would put his hand lightly on the small of my back and direct me through the narrows. Then when we'd passed them, he'd take his place again at my side.

I asked him about County Down. He asked me about Cork. I told him about the river, Grand Parade, the brewery. I didn't tell him about the south-side, or the tenements, or the closet I'd lived in for three years at the Quillans. If he noticed the omissions, he was too much of a gentleman to mention it.

"If only Bluebell could see me now," I said when we'd reached the end of the corridor for perhaps the fourth time. Somehow I had gotten comfortable, and the filter I'd always kept between mind and mouth had dropped. As soon as the words were out, I regretted them.

"Who's Bluebell?" Colum asked. A round-faced man sitting in the corridor playing his tin whistle pulled his legs in. Colum shifted slightly to get around him, and his shoulder brushed lightly against my own. I could have moved a bit to give him more room, but I didn't.

"Bluebell is a girl I worked with at the sack factory," I replied. I paused. How could I say that if she could see me now, walking side-by-side with as finely made a boy as ever tread Irish soil, if she could see me now, she would be torn up with envy? How could I say that to the very boy himself?

"And why do you wish she could see you now?" He asked the question. I suppose it would have been too much to ask of the saints to see to it that he didn't. I felt a blush rising up my ears.

"Well," I said, thinking fast and coming up with little of use, "for one thing, this boat. 'Tis a grand sight, no mistake?"

"'Tis," he said.

"A grand sight," I repeated. I looked at him. He was smiling, and the look of the smile made me a bit weak in the knees. I wondered if it showed.

"And this Bluebell," he said. "A great lover of ships, is she?" His lip curled a bit too tightly, just on the right side. He knew. He looked in my eyes and he knew. I knew he knew.

"I think Bluebell would like it," I said. "She was a great lover of beauty in all its forms."

"And you?" he said.

"Some forms more than others," I replied, then brazenly looked him in the eye. What I saw there made me relax, settle into his gaze. Colum O'Moran at fifteen years old had to have been one of God's most magnificent creations, and just then he had eyes only for me.

* * *

We walked the corridors until we met a bulkhead or a stern-faced warden guarding a second-class compartment. Then we'd turn around and walk the same hallway again. Up the stairs, down the corridor, down the stairs, up the corridor.

It was near the end of one of those nameless corridors that a sound broke into our conversation. It was the sound of a woman, but not a normal sound. It was enough to make Colum stop in his tracks. But I knew the sound, and hurried toward it.

The sound, a deep moan, oozed out from a partially opened door. I peeked in. The woman was lying on the lower bunk, her knees pointed at the bunk above her. She was sweating, disheveled, stroking her full belly gently.

I recognized her immediately. She was the woman from the immigrant home back in Queenstown, the woman whose child would be born an American, or so her husband boasted.

I walked right in. She was alone in the cabin, and I was there. So I walked right in, assuming there was something I could do for her. Even then I thought like a nurse.

"I'm Clare Keane," I said. "I can help you."

The woman looked up at me in surprise. I may have thought like a nurse, but I certainly didn't look like one.

"My husband went for the doctor," she said simply.

"Don't worry yourself," I said. "I delivered babies myself. I worked with a handywoman back in Cork." It was only a small lie, after all. "I'll stay with you until the doctor comes. Your water broke then?"

The woman nodded. "A while ago," she said, "a couple of hours. I was having pains since last night. But they weren't bad, at least at first. I'm not due for four weeks, maybe five. I thought if I just stayed in bed they'd stop." Another pain bit down. I ran some water over one of the towels and pressed it to her forehead. Eventually, the pain eased. She sighed and looked up at me again.

"My name is Rose," she said.

"If you'd like, Rose, I could see how close the baby is to coming," I said. "Whether the head is coming or not."

She nodded. Apparently she'd decided I was more than just a girl. I moved to the end of the bunk, and began to lift her skirts.

"Clare." It was Colum's voice from the door. "Is she . . . ?" He paused. I looked up to see him and a handful of other passengers peering seriously through the open door.

"She's having a baby if that's what you're asking," I replied. I dropped the skirt. "Rose," I said. I think if you'll turn so your feet are toward the wall, it might give you a bit more privacy."

Rose looked up at me, then at Colum and the door and the other passengers. She blushed a deep red and nodded. I helped her sit, then rewet the towel so she could lay it over the back of her neck.

"Colum," I said, wanting to say something, wanting to explain myself, to ask him to wait. "Keep watch for the doctor, won't you? And close that door. This isn't a hurling match. Rose doesn't need an audience."

Colum also looked like he wanted to say something more, but instead he just closed the door. I helped Rose out of her dress and back onto the bed, feet to the wall this time. When she was comfortable, I lifted the skirt of her shift and looked beneath. The head was beginning to show. I dropped her shift back into place.

"Soon," I said.

"Are you certain?" she replied, raising up off the pillow. Her voice shook. I patted her knee and nodded. "I didn't think . . . They say your first . . . Is the baby all right?"

"Everything looks perfectly normal," I said. "It's going to be all right." She sighed again and lay back down. Even then, I suppose, I must have had "it," that power to project confidence in the midst of stress, the power to say a word and find people trusting me with their most frightening situations.

"When the pain comes," I said, "you go right ahead and push. Please God, you'll have a brand-new baby before supper time." Rose smiled weakly.

"Thank you," she said. "I was afraid Davy wouldn't be able to find the doctor, afraid I would be alone, when . . . " I nodded and took her hand.

The pains came again quite quickly. Rose bore down, red with the effort. I held her shoulder, whispered, "good, good, good" over and over again. Finally the pain subsided. Rose lay back on the pillow, her hair drenched. I could see her lips moving.

"I'm sorry," I said, "did you say something?"

"I was counting," she said, "counting my breaths. It's something my grandmother taught me. She said when she was in the middle of a bad time, she would stop, slow herself down, and count each time she drew a breath. I remember it as clear as day how she would just breathe and count, and breathe and count. She would do that for twenty, thirty breaths. Then she would announce, 'well, that's thirty more the good Lord gave me. I guess it's not time for my end yet.' I picked up the habit. When things get bad, I start counting. It always calms me down." I smiled. She drew a deep breath and sighed.

"That's one," I said quietly.

"One," she replied with a faint smile, then drew another slowly, deeply. I drew one with her.

That's the way it was, the pains coming every few minutes, me holding her hand, talking to her, counting with her, doing instinctively all the things that years later I would be trained to do. It couldn't have been more than twenty minutes. But in those twenty minutes a bond formed, the same bond I've felt hundreds of times since with other women doing that most womanly task on the face of God's good earth. I think she felt it too as we sat, we two women—though saying so may have been stretching the point a bit in my case—until the door to the cabin opened.

"And just who would you be?" A balding man, fortyish, in a dark grey pinstriped suit and crisp linen shirt stood in the doorway. A stethoscope hung from his neck. Off his right elbow, I could see Colum and the woman's husband peeking in cautiously. The doctor strode into the cabin as though it were his own, and dropped a black leather bag on the bunk opposite.

"She's been having pains since last night," I said. "They're coming every few minutes now. Her water broke a couple hours ago, and the baby's head is beginning to show, about an inch, maybe a bit more. She's too far along to move, I'd say. Should I go to the galley and get some hot water?"

"Who *are* you?" the doctor said again, looking me over. "Are you her daughter?" A port-wine birthmark over his right eye dipped to the center as he furrowed his brow at me.

"I'm not," I said. "I'm," I paused for a second, trying to figure out just who I was in this situation. Could I tell him the truth, that I was passing by, walked in on a woman giving birth, and knew immediately that it was my place to help not only her but other women like her? Could I tell him that I was a future handywoman or whatever it was that America called those women who caught babies and comforted the women who had them? The doctor waited, still looking down at me as though I were a dirty little animal he found curled up at the foot of Rose's bed.

"I guess I'm only a friend," I said.

"A friend," he repeated as he turned to rummage in his bag. "In that case, I'll have to ask you to leave." Just like that: "I'll have to ask you to leave." Never mind that I knew for a fact that it was my place to be at Rose's side.

I laid a hand on her shoulder, smiled at her. She smiled back.

"Can you stay?" she asked. "Please stay."

The doctor turned. "No," he said over his shoulder. "There's no room in these cabins to turn around. I certainly can't have . . . " he paused, "*her* getting in my way."

"But she wants me here," I replied. "Surely that should mean something." He didn't reply but rather grasped me by the elbow, and without so much as a by-your-leave hustled me out the door.

Since that time—over the years—I have thought of a hundred things I should have said to that doctor. I should have told him that the ignorable little immigrant girl he so easily dismissed might someday be the nurse who saves his life in the emergency room of some hospital. I should have told him that we laners might not have the fancy linen and rich leather medical bags, but when it comes to caring for a mother in labor, a *woman* in labor, we could certainly teach him a thing or two. I should have told him that patients are people, that friends of patients are people, that we laners are *people*. But instead I scowled. I locked eyes with him and I scowled, and that in itself was a milestone, the first time I had ever scowled at a gentry man telling me what I needed to be doing.

I joined Colum in the hallway. Tight groups of people had sprung up, lining the corridor, talking and listening. The cries of the poor woman inside were, after all, the best entertainment to be had in third class that afternoon. We pushed past them and made our way up the stairs to walk the hallway above. I was still fuming, but I believe I hid it just fine. One doesn't live through three years of service without learning a few things about hiding strong emotion. Colum was quiet as well, too quiet. He continued to steer me through the small clusters of people, but the flow of conversation between the two of us had been stopped up tight by the events we'd just been through.

"When did you know that it was a logger you wanted to be," I said, breaking the silence between us. Perhaps if I changed the subject the storm inside me would quiet.

"I grew up on letters from my uncle and my cousins," he replied. "They'd talk about the beauty of the place, the money a strong man can make if he's willing to put his back to good use. I've always wanted to see the trees they talked about, trees so big that five men holding hands could barely reach around them." He stuffed his hands in his pockets and looked long down the musty corridor, as though he were looking past the steel bulkheads all the way to Washington. "I guess I always knew," he said.

The silence fell again. We continued to walk, up the stairs, all the way to the end of that corridor and then back, stepping over the legs of passengers sitting in corridor chatting, dodging children who saw the long straight corridor as a racetrack, the legs as hurdles.

"What do you want to do in America?" Colum asked. I realized it was the first time he'd asked me anything about my future. We'd talked about his future, his past. We'd talked enough about me to establish that in Ireland I would have been much more likely to be serving at his table than sitting at it. But I'd never realized before that we hadn't talked about what I wanted, my future. I felt a sudden annoyance with him, then brushed it aside.

"Back when I was working for the Quillans, they never had any complaints," I said. "I know I could make a living in service."

"You want to be a maid, then?" He eased in behind me as we came to the stairs. A bit of a draft worked its way down from above. It was a welcome bit of air. I clearly wasn't the only one to think so. The stairs were lined, top to bottom with passengers lounging, talking, getting out of the tight, stuffy cabins. When we'd descended to the next deck down, he resumed his place beside me as we started again down the narrow hallway. I could see at the end the small crowd of people still milled outside Rose's door.

"I did factory work, too," I said.

"I don't think I'd like working in a factory," Colum said. "I like being out in the air."

"Well," I said, "it's not a matter of liking or not liking when you work in a factory. It's a matter of regular money and taking what you can get."

"In America I'd say there are better jobs to be had," he said. The crowd thickened again. Above the sound of their voices, above the rumble of the engine, came a cry. Rose. My mind flashed back to Maura, to the red of her face, the look of intensity, desperation, of pure pain. I heard the voice ring through the hallway and saw in my mind's eye as clear as could be the face that went with such a cry.

We passed the door, propped part way open, enough to let in some air, but not so much that the people in the hall would have a show to watch.

"Back in Cork," I said to Colum when we'd passed through the thick of the crowd, "back in Cork I stayed with a woman, Mrs. Sullivan, after my mother died, don't you know." He nodded. "Mrs. Sullivan was a handywoman, and she let me help once at a birth. She said I kept my head, that I was a big help. And do you want to know something?" He nodded again. "I liked it. It was a terrible thing that Maura, the woman, was going through. And she was screaming sometimes like she was passing through the very flames of hell itself. And part of me felt for her, felt for her pain and her worry. But most of me was just excited, thrilled to be doing something so important, something I could do and do well."

Another cry came down the hall. A shudder ran through Colum's shoulders. "I don't think I could do it," he said.

"Men probably shouldn't," I said.

"Men who are doctors should," he said. "It's part of their job."

"From the looks of that one," I tossed my head back at the cabin behind us, "maybe what we need then is some women on the job."

"Women doctors?" he said, a smirk on his face. "And then what next? Women loggers? Women dockers? Women draymen? Or is that 'draywomen'? 'Drayladies'?"

"You were the one who said Irish women were stronger than Irish men," I said. "Why not women doctors? Why not women loggers if they can handle the job? Why not . . . "

"What I said," Colum interjected, "was that Irish women are better fighters than Irish men, not that they were stronger."

"Then are you going to fight this Irish woman if she says that maybe what she wants is to be a doctor and deliver babies? Are you going to tell me I can't?"

"And risk a bloody eye or worse? I don't think so." He backed away from me, palms out, eyes dancing.

"Bright man," I said. He laughed. We walked, again back through the hall, again up the stairs, this time on deck where a good sized crowd was standing at the railing, scanning the horizon for some point of reference within the miles and miles of water that lay before us.

"Clare," Colum said, when we'd found a place along the rail that was no more than a person or two deep, "do you really want to be a doctor?"

"I don't know," I said. "Maybe. Or a handywoman."

"Or a logger's wife?"

I turned to look at him. "I never really considered it," I said.

* * *

One might argue that falling in love is no more an emotion than falling is. It is what happens when aesthetics, or interlocking neuroses, or hormones bring a body into another body's orbit, and the mind doesn't fire thrusters to break it free. Falling in love is simply a matter of attracting forces—action and reaction. A body in motion tends to remain in motion. A body at rest tends to remain at rest. A body in love tends to remain in love. Without any outside influence to break it free, it merely spins, round and round, covering the same territory over and over.

Falling in love, then, is little more than a happily acquired rut.

Loving someone is a different matter. Loving someone can be more an act of the will than a reaction of one body to another. I loved Mick, sometimes only by pure brute force, but I did love him. I loved Mick, and the effort of it tired me to my very marrow.

Perhaps that was the reason falling in love was such splendor. The sheer ease of that kind of love was pure bliss. It was like the food in the dining room, served to us already cooked on freshly washed white plates. It was like the commodes that emptied themselves with a flick of a switch. It was like lying on one's bunk in the middle of the day for no particular reason at all. No struggle, no work, no worry. After Mick, meeting Colum was good food and clean sheets and my very own sink in my very own room. Without even knowing it, I fell into his orbit, relaxed there basking in the glow of his light.

* * *

I was orbiting quite cleanly that evening. Colum had joined Mick and Tom and me for dinner and then had stood with me at the bow rail, at the place we had "boxed" a mere day ago. There, shoulder lightly brushing shoulder, we talked as we watched the sun set. We must have stood there for hours given how far north we were. But when we went below at 10:30 or after, we found still more to talk about outside my door. At one point Mrs. Keane must have wondered about the steady the murmur of voices outside her partway-opened door. Her shawl clutched tightly around her bare shoulders—she was already dressed for bed—she stuck her head into the corridor. First she looked at me. Then she looked at Colum. Then smiling a knowing smile, she ducked back into the cabin, closing the door behind her.

It wasn't that Colum and I talked of anything important. We talked mostly of small things—dinner, the ship, his childhood, my family. Every word we spoke, though, hammered another nail into the bridge we were building between our two hearts. So when he left my side, I continued to play his words through my mind to keep me company.

"That boy has a soft eye for you, no mistake," Mrs. Keane said from her bunk. The light from the hallway must have awakened her. Either that or she had stayed awake for me. She adjusted the blankets over her chest. "Anyone with an eye in his head could see it." Well, I thought, she had raised three boys and a girl to adulthood. If anyone would know the look, she would.

I left the door ajar for the sake of the light and dropped into the shadow to undress. I could hear Tom's light snore in the bunk above me. The uneven shape in the other top bunk must have been Pat.

"He's nice," I replied quietly, unbuttoning my shirtwaist.

"I met my husband on a ship, don't you know," Mrs. Keane commented.

"So you said," I replied.

"Got married in New York, less than a day off the boat." She propped herself up on her elbow to get a look at my face.

"Mhmm," I said, folding my shirtwaist carefully. The talk of Colum and marriage in the same breath made me feel bare.

"Is he a good man, then?" she asked.

"He is," I said. The word "man" lodged just inside my ears. He was fifteen, old enough to begin plying a trade. I was in love with a man. Not only sweet on a boy, but in love with a man. The feel of it was new, foreign but wonderful.

"If he's a good man, Clare . . . " She paused. I had turned my back to step out of my skirt. Mrs. Keane reached for her stick, which she kept hooked over the bed frame, and poked me soundly with it in the thigh. "Are you listening to me, Clare? This is important."

"I am, Mrs. Keane," I said, taking a seat on the edge of my bunk, my skirt in my lap.

"Good," she said. "This is important. Good men are as scarce as roses in a mineshaft. If you find one, one you care about and one who cares about you, and if he truly is a good man, you would be a fool not to keep him. Do you understand me?"

"I do," I said.

"A fool," she said again. "Do you believe that?"

"I do," I said again.

"Good," she said. She lay back on her pillow. "And that soft-eyed pup of yours is no small joy for the eyes either." She smiled, winked, then rolled over, and closed her eyes.

"He is at that," I said quietly. "He is at that."

Twenty-One

I was barely awake, barely dressed when the knock came at the cabin door. My heart jumped a bit, hoping it was Colum, there unbidden to escort me to breakfast. His voice had continued to reverberate through my dreams, and I couldn't think of anything I would rather see to start my day than the image of his smiling face. Pat opened the door.

As it was, what stood just outside the lip of the cabin was exactly what I least wanted to start my day with. A stern-faced, hard-eyed warden filled the doorway, a fistful Mick's shirt in his grip, and a look in his eye that said he considered Mick, me, every immigrant on board to be the height of inconvenience for his poor beleaguered self.

I sighed and stood.

"I'm looking for this boy's parents," the warden said abruptly.

"Well, then I hope you're prepared to search the halls of heaven," I said. "For you'll not find them here." My words surprised me. I don't think anything quite so cheeky had ever come out of my mouth, and I wasn't sure why it did just then. The warden glared. I considered apologizing, but only for the briefest instant. I had reached "enough" with Mick and his shenanigans. I had reached "enough" with gentry men who kept bringing him back to me, as though I had any control at all over the boy. The anger I felt far outweighed any civility I may have held myself to.

"And who would you be?" the warden asked, matching my abrupt tone, note for note. He gave Mick a bit of a shake as punctuation.

"My name is Clare Keane," I said, "I am this boy's sister."

"I need to speak to a responsible adult," the warden said. By this time Mick was squirming. The collar of his shirt was surely biting into his neck. Good, I thought. I was about to tell the warden that I was the closest thing to a responsible adult in this family, when I heard Mrs. Keane clearing her throat behind me.

"You can talk to me, then," she said from where she sat at the edge of her bunk. I shifted out from between her and the warden.

"Might I ask who you are?" he said, trying to shed the tone he was using on me, but not quite succeeding.

"I am your responsible adult," Mrs. Keane said. The warden frowned. "I am the boy's aunt, Bridget Keane. He and his sister and brother are traveling with me."

"Well, then," the warden said, loosing Mick's shirt, and giving him a tiny shove toward Mrs. Keane, "I caught this one stealing bread from the kitchen before breakfast. If he would have just waited two hours, he could have had his fill of bread, but he took it upon himself to sneak in behind the cooks' back and pinch a loaf that wasn't his." He waited for Mrs. Keane's response. She sat at the edge of the bed, her feet dangling, her chin resting on her cane.

"Where's the bread?" she asked.

It was clearly not the question the warden was expecting. He worked his mind free from the glitch that had snagged it and answered. "I returned it to the kitchen," he said.

"Good," she said. "Good. That takes care of the bread. And the cooks, too, I would imagine?" The warden nodded. "That only leaves this miserable excuse for a boy here, and we'll take care of him. I think you can call the matter finished." She plumped her pillow and made ready to lie back again.

The warden simply stood in the doorway, watching her hook her cane over the bedpost. She pulled her legs up onto the bunk, then looked up again at the door. "Are you still here?" she asked.

"Ma'am . . . ," he said.

She interrupted him. "You have your bread," she said. "I have the boy. I'll deal with him; don't you worry about that. Go," she said simply. "Go, go." She made dismissive moves with her hand. The warden, still not sure what had happened, tipped his cap, stepped over the lip of the door and exited. Mrs. Keane smiled quietly to herself.

Mick waited a second for the warden to be out of earshot, then sunk heavily onto the edge of my bed. "Aunt Bridget," he said, in his voice the tone of a boy who appreciated a good lie. "Can I call you that? Aunt Bridget?" He chuckled a bit. "Thank you, Aunt Bridget. I was sure he was going to put me off the boat, send me back to Cork."

"If it were up to me, he could do just that," Mrs. Keane said, swinging her legs back over the edge of the bed. "Any boy foolish enough to steal bread he was about to be given freely deserves to be put on the next steamer back to Ireland. You're given a ticket on this great fancy liner. You're fed, and clothed, and transported in luxury to a new country. You're even given a shining new chance to make a life for yourself. What do you do? You steal your own bread. Foolish. Foolish!" She sighed a great, heavy sigh, a veritable grunt of a sigh. She retrieved her cane and motioned with it at Mick's trousers. "Drop 'em," she said.

Mick stared at her questioningly. "Your trousers. Drop 'em," she repeated. "This bunk will do just fine," she added, testing the mattress, assessing the height. "Drop your trousers, and bend over here." She hauled herself to her feet.

Mick's face finally registered what she was asking. He took a step back. Mrs. Keane hooked the handle of her cane into Mick's shirt, just above the waistband of his trousers and tugged. Mick jerked away. A button popped loose and fell to the floor.

"Listen to me, boyo," Mrs. Keane said, "you can drop them now, or I can turn you over to the warden again, and we can see what he and the captain have in mind for you." The look on her face, though calm, could wither the pelt right off you. The corner of Mick's nose twitched a bit as he assessed his options. Finally, he fumbled with his trousers, and dropped them to his ankles. With one hand covering his privates, he bent double over the bunk and flipped the tail of his shirt off his bare buttocks. He obviously had some familiarity with the move. Mrs. Keane, her technique also informed by long years of practice, took up a position beside him.

"How old are you?" she asked.

"Thirteen last week," he said. "Barely thirteen. Actually twelve," he amended. "I'm twelve, ma'am."

"Thirteen it is," Mrs. Keane answered, then raised her cane for the first blow. It landed with a crack rather than a thud, a deeply stinging clout that made me cringe from my place beside the door. Mick jumped, then quickly stood. He glared at Mrs. Keane, his fists tugging down the front tail of his shirt.

"Twelve more," she said calmly.

"No," Mick answered.

"Twelve more," she repeated.

"No," Mick said, reaching down for his trousers. I could see the welt beginning to rise on his behind. He fastened his trousers, and turned. I barred the door.

"Twelve more," I said. "Then we'll forget the whole thing." He glared at me coldly. I laid a hand on his shoulder. "Mick," I said, "just take the rest of the caning, and we'll move on." He grabbed me by the wrist, then squeezing with a strength that shocked me, dragged me to the bunk, and shoved me down.

"No," he said with a cold resolve and bolted out the door.

* * *

I was redoing my hair for the third time. My arms shook. No matter what I did, the braiding just didn't look right. Mrs. Keane sat on the bunk, rapping her stick against the bed frame in time with the waves. Every now and then she'd snort a blast of air from her nose and shake her head. Tom, who had watched the aborted caning from the top bunk, had simply rolled over, his back to the room. He'd been pretending to sleep ever since.

Pat folded Mrs. Keane's nightdress and laid it on my bunk. She then pulled the heavy suitcase from beneath their own bunks, bumping Mrs. Keane's foot in the process. Mrs. Keane snorted another blast of air from her nose.

"When I was in service," Pat said, muscling the suitcase onto my bunk, "the butler at the house I worked at used to cane the boot boy until his arse all but glowed with it." She undid the buckles on the suitcase straps and opened it. "He'd take him down to the kitchen and take a cane to him, or a shaving strap, or a wooden spoon, or whatever he could lay his hand to, and he'd lay into that little weasel until the gardener would swear he could hear the crack of it all the way out into the yard. And the boot boy, well, he'd scream like he was being flayed alive because he knew the butler wouldn't want to make so much noise that it would disturb the household. And the butler would stop, and he'd put a hand over the boy's mouth. And he'd be trying to swat him with one hand and hold his mouth with the other. And the boot boy would squirm so the blows would glance off his arse. And the kitchen maids, well we'd get the giggles because the butler would either lose the mouth and the screams would come out again, or he'd lose the arse with all the squirming. And he'd finally get so frustrated he'd stop . . . " She chuckled a bit to herself at the memory.

"Patricia," Mrs. Keane said quietly.

Pat stopped and looked up. "Hmm?" She said.

"Shut your gob, Patricia," Mrs. Keane said. "Shut your gob or I'll take this cane to you, don't think I won't."

I stopped braiding my hair.

"What did I do?" Pat asked. "I didn't do anything." I cringed. Mrs. Keane stood, with effort. Then leaning on her cane, and refusing Pat's elbow, she opened the door and, in complete silence, left.

* * *

I'd given up on my hair. I'd be lucky if the braid held half the day. I decided I didn't care. It could all fall out, and I didn't care. My whole life could all fall out for that matter. I didn't care. Really.

I was tucking the edges of my blanket under the bunk when I heard a knock at the door. Pat answered it, looking through the crack in door that was almost always there for the sake of the air. She said something to someone in low tones, then turned, closing the door behind her.

"It's your shadow," she said quietly. "He's here to escort you to Mass."

My heart jumped. Mass. It was Sunday. How could I have forgotten it was Sunday? The fact that I had shocked me. But then I realized something that shocked me more. I hadn't known if Colum was Catholic. I hadn't asked the question itself. That omission frightened me, appalled me, rattled me to my shoes. I sat heavily on the edge of the bed. I should probably talk with the priest about it next time I went to confession. Somehow I had missed confession as well.

He was, though. Colum was Catholic. I relaxed a little, but not much. Still, this boy who had so filled my world yesterday evening, who had become as all encompassing as the ocean we floated on, this boy was in many ways still a stranger.

"Tell him I'll meet him directly, on deck, at our spot," I said.

"'Our spot'," Pat repeated with a mocking grin on her face. "You have a spot?"

"Tell him," I said.

Pat stuck her head out the door, relayed what I had said, then taking up her chaplet, stepped into the hallway herself. I reached a hand to the top bunk where Tom was still feigning sleep.

"Tom," I said. "Mass. Rouse up, or you'll be late." Tom rolled over and moaned.

"I'm tired," he said. "I want to sleep."

"You didn't do enough in the last few days to be tired," I answered. "I want you out of that bed before I leave."

He rolled over and looked down at me through bleary, red eyes. "When will you leave then?" he said. "Do I have time for another forty winks?"

"Rouse," I said. "Rouse. Now. I'll not have you missing Mass."

Tom scooted to the edge of the bed and dropped to the floor with a groan. While he pulled on his clothes, I dug Mama's shawl from the basket and laid it over my shoulders to serve as a head covering later at Mass. Then with Tom dragging along behind, I went up on deck to meet Colum.

* * *

Mass was held in the third class dining room. Neither Colum nor I had remembered to make our confession the night before, so we found ourselves kneeling for a good while as the other passengers went to receive the Body of Christ. Kneeling on a ship is a strange experience. The waves, even the light waves of that morning, are a challenge to the balance, and the bench in front of us was little use as stability.

Kneeling beside Colum was no less strange. The night before at the rail, as we watched the sunset, the nearness of him had nearly melted my heart. Then afterward in the corridor, as we huddled together, whispering over the sounds of the engines, the confidences we shared had been quiet, intimate. But I must say that neither could compare to the impact that praying beside him had. Whether it was the kneeling or the intimacy that is inherent in the act of praying itself, I don't know. But there was something so private, so soul-baring about the experience, that I felt myself quiver beneath its weight. I sat back on my heels, pressed my folded hands tight to my chest as a cool and trembling wave took over my belly. Had I not sat of my own will, I would have fallen back to be sure. Beside me, Colum sat back as well.

As the father laid the last bit of Host on the last tongue, Colum leaned toward me a bit, ever so slightly until his shoulder brushed mine. Ever so lightly, I leaned back. The ship rocked us back and forth, turning that electric space between us into a gentle caress.

"Thank you," I prayed, mouthing the words soundlessly. "Thank you. Thank you."

* * *

Now, I suspect that every fourteen-year-old feels somehow fundamentally defective. My body was not the same as it was a year ago: I no longer saw myself as a child, but neither was I a woman. When I looked into the mirror, what I saw was an assemblage of spare parts, none of which quite fit with the others. But my body wasn't the half of it. My mind and heart were even more defective, stripped bare for renovation, thrown into confusion not just by puberty, but by the events of the past months. I was changing. Everything was changing. And frankly, those changes didn't feel like much of an improvement. A year ago I had occupied my mind with matters like dusting and laundry. Now I worried about an entirely new country and whether I, a defective fourteen-year-old laner, could make a life there for myself and my brothers. Some days I thought perhaps it was possible. Some days I doubted my ability to manage the simple act of growing up.

Before Mass, the morning had been flooded with doubt. With my hair working its way loose from its pins, and the memory of Mick's anger still resting heavy in my belly, I had been certain of nothing so much as my own fundamental inferiority. But somehow, in either the familiar words of the Eucharist, or in the skin-flushing newness of Colum's presence, I had solidified back into a nearly normal person. That morning at breakfast, as we talked and ate and talked some more, the thought ran through my head over and over again. Colum didn't care in the least that I was defective. He didn't care that I was poor, that the clothes on my back were the only presentable ones I owned, that the teeth in my head were already grey with poverty and poor food. He didn't care that I was fourteen, and awkward, and a laner, and no great beauty on top of it all. If I didn't already love him for his lovely shock of blond hair and his sweet song of a voice, I would love him for his blind eye that saw not my defects but the heart of me. And I would love him for teaching me what a power of feelings could grow within that poor heart.

* * *

"God save all here." The voice came from just outside the cabin door. Colum's family had wanted to spend part of Sunday afternoon alone together, so Colum had dropped me off at my cabin for a nap before supper. "God save all here." The voice woke me from a far country of memories and dreams. I sat up and swung my legs over the edge of the bunk. A thin, short man stood just outside, his eyes on the floor, his cap clutched in his fist. He looked familiar, but I couldn't place him.

"God save you kindly," I said, rising to meet him at the door. I was alone in the room, and it wouldn't do for him to come to me.

"Davy Hanlon," he said. "I'm Rose's husband." His eyes were still downcast, and he mumbled, so much so that I wasn't sure I had caught his last name. But I did catch "Rose's husband." Suddenly the face came back to me.

"Rose's husband," I echoed. He nodded. "How is Rose?" I asked. "Did she have her baby?"

"She did," Davy replied. "A fine little girl. Tiny enough to carry in one hand, she is, but perfectly made, and with a wee shock of her mother's strawberry blond hair." The man was obviously in love, and twice over at that.

"God bless them both," I said. The man nodded his head briskly, then crossed himself, a tiny little cross, but not much smaller than his chest.

"Rose would like to see you," he said.

"And I would like to see her," I said. "Is she in your cabin?"

"Not this minute," Davy said. "The doctor thought it best if the two of them stayed in the ship's infirmary until we dock. It's cooler there, and the air's better."

"If you could take me there, I'll visit her now," I said. "It will only take me a moment to pull myself together."

"There's nothing I would like better than to take you there," Davy said. "But I'm afraid the sister won't allow it. You see I already sat with her and the wee one most of the day. And the sister finally threw me out on my ear, she did. Said my wife and baby needed some sleep. Said she didn't want to see my face again until morning."

"Maybe I should wait, too," I said.

"No, no," he said. "Rose asked for you by name, made me promise to go looking for you. She said she wanted to ask you something. She'll be wanting to see you today. I'm sure of that."

"Then I'll stop by and see her," I said.

"Thank you," Davy replied. "And thank you for being with her. Helping her. Yesterday in the cabin. I, I didn't want to leave her. On my soul, I didn't want to leave her there. But she needed the doctor, and," he paused. "Thank you." He smiled a timid smile at me.

I smiled back. "'Twas nothing," I said. "Only a bit of comfort, that's all."

* * *

An inquiry here, and another there told me that the ship's infirmary was in toward the center of the ship, deep inside second-class territory. To see Rose I would need to pass through the border lands, the least of which was a humorless warden ready to beat back any third-class passenger wanting to make an incursion into the space of their betters.

Colum wasn't supposed to pick me up at my cabin until supper, but if I was to go parading into the second class space, I was going to need a bit of moral support.

The door to the cabin was propped open a bit, as most of the doors were. Through the crack, I could see Colum stretched out on one of the bunks, a faraway look on his face. I called in. The man who rose and came to door could not have been anyone but Colum's father. The same shock of blond hair dangled over his forehead. The same long, straight back, gave him an air of dignity. He was nearly as striking as his son. He called Colum to the door. Colum blushed fiercely, hopped down from his bunk, and joining me in the corridor, shut the door after him.

"I was going to pick you up at your cabin," he said. "For supper." He emphasized the word *supper*.

"You were," I said, beginning to have second thoughts about coming there. "But Rose, the woman who had the baby, her husband came to my cabin. And he said Rose wanted to see me in ship's infirmary. I wanted . . . " I wasn't sure how to express exactly what it was I wanted of him.

"Wait here," Colum said, retreated into the cabin, and closed the door again. He appeared a minute or so later.

"Mam's not happy," he said. "We spend Sunday together. I'll have to make it up to her somehow." He laid a hand on the small of my back and steered me out into the corridor.

"I could explain to them if you'd like," I said. "I'd like to meet your family." Beside me I could feel Colum blanch. "If you're not embarrassed to introduce me," I added. Just because Colum didn't seem to mind walking out with a laner didn't mean his parents would be so open-minded. I guess I had always known that in the back of my heart.

Colum stepped in front of me and stopped, his eyes locked onto mine. "It's not that, Clare." He took me by the hands. "How could you think that? How could you think that I'd be embarrassed of you." His eyes were soft, pained. I immediately regretted my words. "It's not that," he said. "It's just so soon. It's not time yet."

"And what exactly makes for the right time in these things?" My tone was cooler than I intended. Part of me really wanted to know why he thought it the wrong time. It wasn't as though I had any great experience with meeting a beau's parents. Most of me, though, wasn't sure I believed him.

"We'll know when it's the right time," Colum said.

"Right time or wrong time," I said, "we're a little short of it. In a few days, you'll be headed for Washington. I'll be headed for Minnesota. We may never see each other again."

"Don't say that," Colum said. "We will. We will see each other again."

"And how do you know that?" I asked.

"I know," Colum said.

"And what will you do to see that it happens?" The question dropped between us. Colum slowly released his grip on my hands. He was silent. I slipped around him and headed back down the corridor.

"We have *now*, Clare," Colum said softly, his words dropping in from behind my ear.

It was my turn to be silent. All I could think was that soon he would be taken from me. Perhaps I might have been sad had I not been so angry. I could sense it as clearly as my own breath. I was about to lose one more person whom I loved.

* * *

The warden scowled in the manner of all gentry men. I met him, nose-to-nose, and scowled back. "I wish to pass through to the ship's infirmary. Our Rose is after having a baby, and I need to see them both safe."

"The infirmary is off-limits to all but patients and their immediate family."

"Well, then call me family," I said shortly, "but let me pass."

"You're family?" the warden asked, raising an eyebrow in that slightly dismissive gesture I'd seen from bosses, guards, all manner of authority figures. Usually the look intimidated me. At that moment it only made me angrier. I fought down the climbing rage and set about "handling" the gentleman. Handling gentry men was not as difficult as one might expect. I'd seen women of my class—Mrs. Keane, Mrs. Sullivan, Mrs. O'Rourke, my mother—I'd seen them all do it. The memory of it, combined with anger rising inside me, made me bold.

"I am indeed family," I said. "I am her sister." And now wasn't it true? Didn't all women who held each other's hands, saw each other through the pains of labor, weren't all such women sisters? Rationalization or no, I knew I would have to confess the lie next time I was before a priest. I hoped that knowledge didn't show on my face at the moment.

"Her sister," he said, with no small bit of skepticism. "And him?" he nodded toward Colum.

"Our brother," I said. I could feel Colum's ears reddening behind me, almost as if the heat of them could fill the air between the two of us.

"Your brother," the warden repeated.

"Isn't that what I'm after saying?" I said. "Now if you'll excuse me." I worked a shoulder between the warden and the door jam. He moved slightly to block my way, then looking into my eyes, saw something there that made him step aside. I passed unhindered through the second-class promenade to the door of the surgery. Colum, his ears glowing, followed close behind.

The good saints and angels must not have taken too much of an exception to my little lie because as I opened the door to the surgery, the doctor I'd met in Rose's cabin was nowhere to be seen. Behind the desk, a sister in a starched cap and long black skirts was making notes.

"I'm here to see my sister Rose," I said, suddenly realizing I hadn't the least notion what Rose's last name was. If the infirmary contained more than one Rose, I would soon be discovered. "She had a baby yesterday evening," I added.

"Rose Hanlon?" the sister asked.

"The same," I said, hoping Hanlon was indeed my "sister's" last name.

"She's in room three," the sister said. "I'll take you there."

* * *

Rose lay in a heavy metal bed bolted to the floor. The room was cool, much cooler than the rest of the ship, and she had a blue Cunard blanket tucked loosely around her legs. Her baby was in a clinical-looking bassinet between her and the wall. Rose lay quietly, her head turned, her eyes resting lightly on the child. She looked up as I walked around the end of the bed.

"Clare," she said, her face brightening. "Davy found you then."

"He did," I replied. I sat lightly on the edge of the bed, and laid a hand on her arm. "How are you feeling?"

"Tired," she said. "But good." She paused a moment. "Blessed," she said simply. She took my hand.

"Thank you," I said to the sister by way of dismissal.

The sister inclined her head in a quick nod. "Five minutes," she said, closing the door behind her. Colum propped himself up in the corner of the room, and set about crossing and uncrossing his arms. He was uncomfortable—that much was clear. But at the moment making him feel more at ease seemed less important than my time with Rose.

"The birth wasn't too hard, then" I said.

"No," Rose said. "Yes. I don't know. She's my first. How hard is too hard? I'm not sure I would know."

"I'm not sure I would either," I said with a little chuckle.

Rose smiled. I smiled back. Her hand rested lightly in mine.

"Would you like to hold her?" Rose asked.

Would I like to hold her?

Now this will sound strange, but it was then that I realized I hadn't held a baby since Tom was born, and me only four years old or so at the time. The memory was fuzzy enough I wasn't sure it was a memory at all. I'd seen Maura's baby born. I'd seen Rose's well on it's way. I had told myself that I had a certain amount of experience catching babies. But truth be told, I couldn't remember ever having held one.

"I wouldn't want to wake her," I said.

"'Tis no trouble at all," Rose replied. She let go of my hand and swung her legs over the side of the bed. "I'd like her to meet you." She reached into the bassinet and gently scooped up the little one, cradling her head ever so gently in the palm of her hand. I sat at the foot of the bed and with my heart racing, held out my arms.

She was warm, warmer than I expected, and just a little bit damp. She lay heavy in my arms, soft and fluid, still asleep and totally relaxed. I gathered her to me, lay her head in the crook of my arm. She made little sucking noises, tiny little noises that I could hear over the ship's engines only if I hunched over her. Somehow it seemed right to do so, noises or no. Holding her stirred something inside me, something frightened and protective both.

"She's an angel," I said.

Rose just smiled. And so we sat, both of us totally absorbed by the tiny little creature asleep in my arms.

"Mr. Hanlon said you had something you wanted to ask me," I said, finally looking up.

"I do," she said. "I know you said your name is Clare, but I was wondering if you had a saint's name, too."

"I do," I said. "Elizabeth. After the mother of John the Baptist."

"Elizabeth," she said. "I can't think of a better name." She reached out a finger and stroked the little one's cheek. "We plan to call her Doreen Alice— Doreen after my mother, Alice after Davy's. But then she'll need a saint's name. What do you think of Doreen Alice Elizabeth?"

"I like it very much," I said. I could feel my eyes get warm.

"Elizabeth was there with Mary, you know," Rose said. "When Mary was expecting Jesus." I nodded. "I think Elizabeth is the perfect saint's name."

"Little Doreen Alice Elizabeth Hanlon," I said. "What a start in life you made." I looked up at Colum. All the uneasiness had dropped from him and he stood, leaning ever so slightly toward me, his eyes soft. I smiled. He smiled back, a smile that looked like it was born of some wonderful ache inside him. The anger I'd been feeling toward him suddenly was no more than a memory.

* * *

"I could watch you forever," Colum said was we passed the warden and stepped again into the safety of the third class corridor. "You with the babe in your arms, the little of bit of tears in your eyes. I'm glad you came for me at the cabin."

"I'm glad too," I said.

"Just now, I saw sides of you I never imagined," he said. He steered me up the stairs.

"What sides?" I said.

"You with little Doreen," he said.

"Doreen Alice Elizabeth," I said.

"Doreen Alice Elizabeth," he agreed. "And you with that warden. Where exactly did you learn that?"

"Learn what?" I asked. The deck was full. We found a small bare patch where we could see a bit of the sky if none of the ocean.

"That look for one thing," Colum said. "That look you fixed on the warden." His eyes were full, searching my own. "That look that says you're about to eat the poor man whole if he stands in your way a second longer."

"Was it really that fierce?" I asked. I have to say, I was feeling rather proud of myself.

"That fierce and more," Colum said. "Like a great, black dog standing between her pups and danger, all fangs and snarling."

"It wasn't that fierce," I said.

"Well, perhaps not," Colum said. "But it was fierce enough to be sure. I would move."

"And you would be a bright man to do so," I said, pulling my shoulders back just a bit.

He looked at me. I looked back at him. The love on his face filled me from bottom to top.

"Colum," I said, "I want to meet your parents. Not later. Now."

"You're going to insist?" he said.

"I am," I replied.

"Then after supper, I will take you to them," he said. "I will say, 'this is Clare, the woman whose very presence makes my life worth living.'"

"You would say that to your parents?" I said.

"Maybe not just those words," he admitted. "True though they are."

* * *

'Twas after supper. And after three or four stories, which Colum told with great gusto. And after a good bit of time at the rail of ship with the wind in my hair and Colum's hand in my own. He was stalling. I knew as much. I finally turned to him and said simply, "now." He took my meaning, and we went below.

Colum's shoulders were riding up to his earlobes even before we reached the foot of the stairs.

"My father can be a little gruff," he said. "Don't take any notice. He doesn't mean anything by it. It's only his way."

I nodded. "And your mother?" I asked.

"As good a woman as ever walked this earth," he said. I recognized it as a standard Irish male response.

"Is she pretty?"

"Not as pretty as you," he said. I wasn't sure what to say. My first impulse was to offer my condolence. Not as pretty as me meant quite ordinary. But I don't think that was how he meant it, so I simply smiled.

The door was closed to his cabin. He put a hand on it, looked at me. I smoothed the front of my skirt, and nodded. He opened it.

In retrospect, when I replay the scene in my mind, as I have many times over, I feel myself screaming, "Knock! Knock first, Colum!" But, alas, that day he did not.

The door swung open and immediately revealed a man's bare belly. The belly of almost any middle-aged Irish man is not a sight to be fervently wished for. We all tend to have too little pigmentation to cover our flaws. But beyond that, Mr. O'Moran had the doughy look of a man chained indoors to a desk for most of his life. His suspenders were down around his hips, and his trousers sagged loosely. He was pulling his undershirt off over his head. When he heard the door open, half of him continued the movement, and the other half scrambled to cover himself again. The result was that the shirt tangled around his face and neck. When he finally succeeded in pulling it back down, his face was florid. He looked first to me, then to Colum, then to me again. I ducked back into the hallway, my back pressed hard to the wall.

"What do you mean to do, bringing people here at this hour?" he said.

"I'm sorry, Da," Colum said. "I thought . . . "

"You did not," Mr. O'Moran said. "You did not think. That's the trouble with you: you don't think. Your mother and sister are already in bed, and you bring people by?"

"I'm sorry, Da," Colum repeated. "It's only that I wanted you to meet Clare."

Mr. O'Moran stuck his head out the door, and when he didn't see me immediately, he craned it around left and right. I turned to face him, summoning up a weak smile.

"Wait," he said, disappearing back inside the door and closing it.

"Colum," I said, "maybe I should go."

"No," Colum said. "No, no. No. When my Da says 'wait,' he means wait. He would not be happy if we should go missing."

I nodded again, then reached for his hand. He squeezed mine briefly, then dropped it. His eyes were jetting nervously between me and the door. Finally, it opened. Mr. O'Moran, clad in a clean shirt, his suspenders back in place, motioned me in. Mrs. O'Moran was seated at the edge of the bed wearing a coat despite the heat. I could see the hem of her nightdress beneath it. Her hair was pulled back hastily. On the bunk opposite were two girls, neither of whom could have been older than eight. They snickered together as though they had just shared a joke.

"Mam, Da," Colum said, "this is Clare." Just that. I waited for them to speak. They didn't.

"Do you have a last name?" Mr. O'Moran said finally.

"Keane," I said. "Clare Keane. I'm from Cork."

"So you are," Mr. O'Moran said. "And doesn't the lilt of your voice say so as clearly as your words?" I smiled. "So you're the young lady who's taking Colum away from us this whole voyage."

"I'm sorry, sir," I said.

"Pffaw," Mr. O'Moran dismissed my words with a wave of his hands. "Better he spend the time with you than here moping around the cabin and tormenting his sisters. Do you have family in America, Miss Keane?"

"An uncle," I said. "In Minnesota. Or maybe Wisconsin."

"And you and your parents will be living with him until you get settled?"

It was a logical assumption. Most of us Irish did it that way.

"My brothers and I will be," I said. "My parents are dead."

"With whom are you traveling?" Mrs. O'Moran asked, leaning forward a bit.

"I suppose we're traveling with each other," I replied. I knew that wasn't what she meant.

"Alone," she said.

"We are," I said. "But Uncle Ronan sent us the fare for the boat and money for the train. We already found the boat. Now all we have to do is find the train, and it will take us right to him." I sincerely hoped it would be that simple, but I seriously doubted it would be.

"And how old are you," Mrs. O'Moran asked.

"Fourteen," I said.

"And your brothers are older?"

"Younger," I said.

"I have to say, Clare," Mr. O'Moran said, "I admire your resourcefulness. I doubt very much Colum could make such a journey on his own, and he's nearly sixteen."

Beside me I heard Colum's sudden intake of air. I felt for his hand. "There's nothing like need to breed ability," I said. "I'm sure Colum would manage just fine, pray that he never has to." Colum's hand tightened in my own.

Mr. O'Moran smiled indulgently. Silence filled the cabin, or what passes for silence on a ship whose engines never stopped pounding away. I suddenly became painfully aware of my smile, as though if I didn't balance it ever so carefully on my face, it would fall off entirely. I could feel my cheeks twitch with the knowledge. I looked over at Mrs. O'Moran. She seemed to be struggling with much the same predicament.

"These are my sisters," Colum finally said, breaking the silence. "Rosemary and Martha." The girls giggled and said hello. The silence fell again.

"I suppose Clare should be getting back to her cabin," Colum said.

"I should," I said.

"We won't keep you," Mr. O'Moran said. "It was nice to meet you."

I curtsied ever so slightly, and turned to Colum, who hustled me out the door and closed it behind us. His shoulders deflated.

"They hate me, I said, collapsing against the wall.

"They don't," Colum said. "It was just too soon."

"No," I said. "I think they hate me."

Colum didn't disagree this time. He took my hand, and tucked it into the crook of his elbow. "Let me tell you something about my father," he said. "Anything I like, he will deem not worth my attention. Anything I love, he will oppose. My father likes his books, his ledgers. I'd rather spend time with people. I like sport. He calls hurling and rugby a waste of good sweat. So the way he acted," he sighed, "it really couldn't be any other way. If I love you, he'll do everything in his power to keep me from you."

"So it's hopeless," I said. At that moment, I couldn't see life in any other terms.

"No, no, Clare," Colum said. "It will just take time. I can't tell my father how much I love you. That will just make him want to separate us. What I need to do is to persuade my father that *he* likes you."

"And how are you going to do that?" I asked.

"I can't say that I'm entirely sure," Colum said. "But I think it's going to take some time."

We were five days into the voyage. I bit my lip and kept myself from pointing out the obvious.

* * *

Tom picked his way up the stairs, threading between the folks sitting and leaning, and trying to catch a breath of moving air. Colum and I had parked ourselves there after breakfast, sitting tight together, allegedly so as not to block passage.

"I found Mick," Tom said, dancing a bit so as not to tread on the skirts of the woman on the step below us. He had something clutched in his hand.

"What's that?" I asked.

"'Tis a whistle," Tom said. "A tin whistle. Mr. Wisely gave it to me."

"Who's Mr. Wisely?" I asked.

"You know Mr. Wisely," Tom said. "We met him at the immigrant home. Or at least I did. He's the one who's always playing a tune in the corridor." Now that I thought about it, I had registered a face. "He's teaching me and some of the boys to play," Tom said. "I can play 'Down by the Salley Garden,' at least the first part. My second octave isn't very good yet.

I didn't know Tom even knew the word "octave." I began to realize that I hadn't spent much time with him since we boarded the ship.

"He gave you the whistle?" I said. "To keep?"

"He did," Tom said his voice sounded a bit scratchy, a bit deeper than usual. "Don't you want to know where I found Mick?"

"In the ship's jail?" I said. I meant it as a joke, but once it was out of my mouth it no longer seemed funny.

"I don't think the ship has a jail," Tom said. "At least I didn't seen one yet. No, he's in the open berth steerage quarters. The men's."

"They let him in there?" Colum said.

"They did," Tom said. "They let me in, too. If you're third class, you can go anywhere in third class, even the open-berth section. If you're second class, you can go anywhere in second or third. And if you're first class, you can go to first or second, or third, or anywhere you want. I didn't see any first class people down in the open berth section," he added.

"What is open-berth?" I said.

"Just one big room with bunks," Tom answered. "Maybe thirty of them, maybe more. No walls like we have. Mick found an open bunk there. He says he's tired of women, that he's going to stay with the men." He coughed. There was something wrong with his throat.

"The men can have him," I said. "Are you picking up a touch of the quinsy?"

"I think it's only the bad air," Tom said. "It's better when I'm on deck." The air was quite bad anywhere below deck. The ventilation system worked night and day, of course, but the job of changing air so tightly packed with bodies overwhelmed it. I myself had regularly begun to fell a tightness in my own chest that drove me onto the stairway or the overcrowded decks for most of my waking hours.

"Remind me to take a look at your throat when we get back to the cabin," I said.

Tom screwed up his face. "'Tis nothing," he said. "'Tisn't myself I worry about; 'tis Mick."

"Why so?" I asked. I wondered if he had caught the same thing Tom had. If the air was bad in third class, it had to be worse where Mick was. The fact that he had holed up there gave me a pretty good idea just how angry he was with me. "What is he doing down there? Besides getting away from women?"

"Not much that I can tell," Tom said. "Most of the men just seem to sleep all day. But Mick said one of the lads is teaching him to play a game called poker."

"So long as he keeps it to sleeping and games, I suppose he's all right," I said. "Let him be. That's what I say." I looked over at Colum for confirmation.

"Does he have any money?" Colum asked.

"Why?" I said.

"Well, poker is a betting game," Colum replied. "He could lose a power of money playing poker with grown men who know the game well."

"Does he still have the money from Queenstown?" I asked Tom.

"I don't know," Tom said. "He maybe put it in the shoonaun. I saw him digging around in there yesterday."

"More likely he *took* money from the shoonaun," I said.

"I don't think he would bet our train money," Tom replied. "Do you?"

"I think we need to pay a visit to the open-berth section," I said, sighing. It seemed I was always sighing during conversations about Mick. "Right now nothing Mick might do would surprise me, even betting our train money." I sighed again.

"Why don't you stay here?" Colum said. "Let me go down there and look around. I'd guess that Mick's a little like my father. If you tell him one thing, he may do the opposite just to spite you. I think he'd see you coming, and his back would go up, and you'd never get a straight conversation out of him after that. But maybe I can get 'round him, find out what he's doing down there."

It sounded like a good idea. But then anything that helped me avoid another confrontation with Mick would have sounded like a good idea. "Tom can show you where he is," I said.

"Will you wait on deck?" Colum said.

"Wait? For you?" I said. "And how could I say no? Waiting for you is the only thing about this whole scheme that should be no trouble." Colum raised my hand to his lips and kissed it lightly. Then standing, he followed Tom down the steps.

* * *

The wind off the water was coming in from the north. It was chilly, not icy but definitely chilly, enough to make me cross my arms and hunch over the rail. The coolness of it was welcome after the sticky heat below deck. I breathed it in, and the feel of it going down calmed me. It was something I'd noticed since that first afternoon on deck—air out on the ocean was fresh, clean in a way that I had never encountered before. In Cork, even out where the rich people lived, the air was always perfumed with the smoke of cooking fires. In the wealthy neighborhoods, the smell was one of coal smoke. In the poorer parts of town, it was a mixture of coal and turf, mingling with all the other smells of the lanes. Nowhere, though, was it completely clean like the air I breathed at the rail. I filled my lungs, hoping to clean out the anxiety that was building inside me. Despite Tom's vote of confidence, I had no doubt that Mick had it within him to spend our train money. If he smelled easy money, he wouldn't think twice about betting the cash that was supposed to see us safe to Minnesota. We could find ourselves on America's shores as broke as the day we were born. I inhaled again, a deep quivering breath. I sagged against the rail, and I waited.

By the time Colum stepped through the door from steerage, I had worked myself into quite a state. He spotted me, threaded his way between people, and inserting a shoulder between me and the woman standing next to me at the rail, delivered his report.

"Open berth steerage," he said, "is nothing more than a big room with bunks all around the walls. I found him. He met some older boys, and they told him about the empty bunk."

"And decided he preferred their company to that of is nagging sister."

"Something like that," Colum replied.

"Is he playing poker for money?" I asked.

"He wouldn't say," Colum replied. "But I saw several card games going on down there. Between that and Mick's tight lips, I'd guess he is."

"Then I need to go get him," I said. I leaned over the rail and watched the water rush past the sides of the ship. The thought of another confrontation made me tired. But it was unavoidable. I took another deep breath and pushed myself back from the rail.

"You can't go get him," Colum replied. "That part of steerage is naught but men, and foul-smelling men at that. It's off limits to women."

"And girls," I said.

"True," he said, "not that applies." He grinned at me. I'm afraid I couldn't work up much of a grin to offer him back.

"Where's Tom?" I asked.

"He went back to your cabin," Colum said. "He said his throat was paining him something fierce. But he told me not to tell you because you'd only worry."

I leaned over the rail again, watched the water stream past, wondered how much of it our bow had parted since we left Queenstown. A million gallons? Ten million gallons? "So I have one brother back in the cabin coming down with some kind of throat ailment, and another brother holing up in the bowels of the ship with a bunch of sweaty men because he prefers that to my company. And there isn't a thing I can do about either. Well, doesn't that just sound like my life?"

"What do you mean?" Colum said.

"If you think about it, no sane person would offer more than a shilling or two for the life I have right now," I said. "No money. No parents. No home. No job. I have you for now, but you'll soon be leaving. Besides your parents don't like me. Mick hates me." I could feel the tears stinging my eyes. "I can't say that it's a life I enjoyed living for the last few months."

Colum was silent beside me. He too just gazed down at the water. Finally he looked up. "Clare, don't take this wrong, but maybe you're living in the wrong part of your life," Colum said. I looked up from the water. His eyes were soft, but the corner of his mouth was twitching upward in that little half smile

I'd grown to love.

"I should emigrate from my own skin, then? Not that it's an all together bad idea."

"Don't you dare," Colum replied. "I'm rather fond of your skin myself." I blushed. He smiled softly at my coloring. "All I'm saying is that when the past is more than you can bear, and the present is no more than a weight around your neck, the only place to retreat to is your future."

"Pffaah, and what future would that be?"

"Any future you wish," he said. He removed his jacket, laid it on the deck, and motioned for me to sit. I did so. Self-consciously. Colum had a serious look on his face, an intense look, one that made me shake a bit around the edges. He sat down beside me.

"I'm in Washington," he said, "my ax in my hand. And my uncle cries out with a great voice, 'Timber!' and a great tree falls at my very feet." I looked into his face, his eyes gazed out at something as far away as the horizon.

"The crash of the tree breaks branches and crushes the small bushes, and the smell of the forest comes over me like a great flood. I hear the birds protest loudly and fly away. And I unshoulder my ax, and I start on one of the great branches. I swing and I swing, and the chips from the branch fly in every direction, bouncing off my legs, until finally I chop through. And I wipe my face on my sleeve, and feel my muscles tired in my shirt. And I know I'm making good money, money that will get me just that much closer to a house and a family of my own." He looked over at me, and his eyes focused again. He smiled and shrugged. "Your turn," he said.

I thought for a while. Any future I wanted. I had never been offered any future I wanted.

"I'm a handywoman," I said. "The woman I'm tending is about to give birth. I wipe her face with a soft cloth. Her face is red and damp from the effort. And when the pain takes her, she cries out and clutches at the sheet. Pure white sheets, they are, in a clean room with soft electric lights. And the baby comes out in a rush, a little girl. And I clean her nose and her mouth, and she cries out. I lay her on her mama's belly." I stopped, suddenly as much in the past as the future. I took a deep breath and dragged my mind back to where it belonged. "I know that this tiny wee lass has a good mother, a mother who will spend their money on food for her baby, not on drink, a mother who will live and be healthy, and see her baby grow to have babies of her own."

Colum reached out for my hand. I gave it to him.

"I am home," he said. "In a house I made with my own two hands. And my wife is there, and my babies." I felt his hand tighten around my own. "And I know that I would be skinned alive before I let anything bad happen to any of them. I know I would work to my last breath to feed them and keep a roof over their head."

"I'm home," I said, taking my turn. "And my husband comes through the door after work. And the smell of the bacon I'm cooking fills the air. And we have cabbage on our plate, and bread, and potatoes, and a great pile of bacon. And the floors are like butter, and the curtains white and billowy. And I kiss my husband as he sits down to eat. And I know that I would work to my dying breath to make a home he could come home to happily every night until we grow old together."

I could feel the flesh of Colum's hand warm to my own. He sighed. "Like I said, you were living in the wrong part of your life."

* * *

We sat for a while, suspended silently between the present and the future. As wonderful as that place was, I was too practical to think I could stay there forever.

I knew I had to confront Mick, and soon. I had to confront him before he had the chance to lose all our money. I thought for a while, then Colum and I talked things over and hatched a plan to bring Mick back to the cabin, and maybe keep him there for the rest of the voyage. I squared my shoulders and followed Colum down the stairs.

At the door to the open berth steerage there was no warden to contend with. I suppose I shouldn't have expected one. A warden's role in life was to keep the riffraff from trying to invade the space of their betters. As for the riffraff's space, well, nobody seemed to mind who strolled through it. Nobody but the riffraff themselves, that it.

The first thing we needed to do was to get Mick out into the corridor. Colum pushed the door open. "Wait here," he said. "I'll get him."

"No," I said. "I'll get him myself." We hadn't discussed that part of the plan. It wasn't that I didn't trust Colum. It was just that I had much more experience handling Mick. Colum's diplomacy and wishful thinking wouldn't get through the boy's thick skull. I knew that. I would have to confront him myself.

"You're not allowed," Colum said. I locked eyes on him. A faint smile crossed his lips. He stepped aside bowed, slightly, and motioned toward the door. I stepped over the lip, and entered.

One of the things the Cunard line had obviously cut to save money in open berth steerage was the ventilation. The air was moving. I could feel it. But the movement merely stirred the smells. So did the churning of the floor. We were in the very bow of the boat, probably beneath the waterline given the absence of windows. The waves cracked against the bulkheads. The floor heaved, more than it did in our cabin. That rough night at the beginning of the voyage, the one that had made me sick, well, it had obviously taken its toll here as well. Someone had made an attempt at cleaning the floor, but between the tightly packed bunks and the baggage stuffed into every available cranny, the attempt was obviously little more than a token. I breathed through my mouth, drawing the air between barely open lips, and scanned the room.

I didn't get much of a look before my view was blocked. Blocked by an enormous quantity of flesh covered with golden fur. A great bear of a man, dressed in nothing more than trousers and suspenders, had rolled out of the bunk by the door and barred my way. I was looking at him at barely above belly button level.

"Did ye take a wrong, lass?" the bear said in a thick burr. "Ye've stumbled into the men's barracks."

"Thank you, but I believe I'm in the right place," I said. "I'm here for my brother. If you'll only let me fetch him, I'll be on my way."

"I'm afraid I can't do that," the bear said. "There are sights here not fit for eyes as pretty as yours."

"I thank you," I said, "but I don't mind." I fixed my best "look" on him, fully expecting him to let me pass.

"Ah, well, you may not mind, but *I* mind," the bear said simply. He began walking toward me, backing me steadily toward to door. Sooner than I expected, I felt my heel make contact with the lip. Both Colum and the bear reached out to steady me. I stepped over and out into the hallway.

"Now. Your brother, you say?" the bear said. Here in the hallway, with the doorway between the two of us, he didn't look quite so imposing.

"It's important that I talk to him," I said. "His name is Mick Keane."

"Well then if it's important, I will go get him for you," the bear said, "*if* you will wait here." I agreed with a nod.

"Clare," Colum said to me. "Let me. I'll get him for you." He didn't speak to the bear, but to me. I think he was more than a little intimidated by the bear's size and overall furriness. He looked up at the bear, who gestured to the door, and Colum squeezed past him, his jaw set resolutely.

The corridor rose and fell with the waves. I wasn't sure if it was the more pronounced movement there in the bow or the thickness of the air down there in the depths of the ship, but as I waited, I began to feel that tight, green feeling climbing the back of my throat into my skull. I sincerely hoped Colum and the bear wouldn't take any more time than absolutely necessary. I was beginning to crave the open air of the deck.

I shouldn't have worried. In less than a minute, the door opened and the bear stepped out into the corridor. Tucked under his arm like a parcel was Mick, squirming futilely. Colum followed, his eyes wide.

"The lad said he didn't want to see you," the bear said, dropping Mick into a pile on the floor. "But I reminded him that a man has a duty to his sisters that isnna dependent on how he feels on any particular day." Mick stood and rearranged his shirt.

"Thank you," I said, casually I hoped.

The bear, smiled slightly, bowed his head slightly and returned to the cabin, shutting the door behind him.

"Were you gambling?" I said without preamble. Mick spun on his heel and made for the door. Colum cut him off. Mick turned to face me.

"Were you gambling?" I said again.

"Only a little," Mick replied, "not that it's any of your affair."

"If it's my money, it's my affair," I replied.

"It's *our* money," Mick said.

"How much did you lose?" I said.

"What makes you think I lost?" Mick replied.

"How much?"

"Not much," Mick said quietly.

"Right," I said, nodding to Colum. Colum stepped up and faced Mick, chest to chest. Mick's chin jutted forward. His hands balled into fists. It was what I hoped for. I slipped around behind him, and wrapped my arms around him, pinning his arms to his sides, clutching him tightly to me.

"We're here to collect," I said. "Do you remember how Mr. Sullivan said you got to keep those long trousers only if you behaved like an adult? Well, I'd call this pretty childish behavior, and we're here to collect."

Colum made a dive for Mick's fly. He had his hand in Mick's waistband when Mick wrenched himself almost loose from my grip. The force dropped Colum to one knee.

"Hands off, boyo," Mick said simply.

"Sorry, Mick," Colum said, not rising but reaching in for another attempt. Mick didn't wait for him to make contact this time, but simply lifted one knee hard and fast. The point of it caught Colum just under his cheekbone, and threw him back hard. He fell to one hip, clutching his face and moaning.

"Mick," I said. "How could you?" Mick wrenched himself loose and spun to face me.

"Someone tries to take a man's trousers by force, I'd say that man has the right to defend himself," he said. Colum rose to one knee. He seemed to be steady enough. But the grimace on his face and the way he clutched his cheek said he was hurting.

"Mick," I said. "I don't want your trousers. I only want you to come back to the cabin and start acting responsibly. I never know what to expect. First you steal. Now you gamble away our money. I don't want your trousers, but I don't know how else to keep you from sinking this family no less than if the ship itself went under. Tell me, Mick. What do I need to do to get you to start working with me, not against me?"

"I never meant to work against you," he said quietly. I could still see the rage bubbling up out of his chest, tightening his jaw.

"It's hard to tell," I said.

"Maybe it's you who needs to work with me," he said.

"To help you steal?"

"That was wrong," he said.

"It was," I said.

Colum had risen to his feet behind Mick and was standing outside arms' reach. I glanced over at him. His face was red, but it didn't look as though it was swelling much. I felt bad for him, but I couldn't take my mind off Mick that moment.

"Mick," I said. "We'll be arriving in America soon. I can't be wondering where you are when they let us off the ship. And until then, I can't be wondering what you're doing, whether you're losing all our money or doing something that's going to get you sent back to Cork. Mick, I need you to behave like the man of the family."

Mick sighed. "How long do we have before we land?" he asked.

"I don't know," I said. "Maybe a day, maybe a little more." I looked to Colum. He nodded in agreement.

"I'm staying here," he said. "Until we dock. I'll not share a cabin with that lunatic woman and her stick."

"Mick," I said.

"I'm staying here," Mick said, "and you cannot make me do otherwise." His eyes were hard. He was probably right. I wasn't sure how I could make him do anything against his will. "But I will give you my word that I'll stop gambling and that I'll not get myself into any more trouble as long as we're on the ship. I swear it," he said, his hand on his heart. "On our mother's grave, I give you my word. Is that enough?"

"Nearly," I said. "Now you'll give us all the money you have on you." I held out my hand. Mick looked away, his eyes flashing with anger.

"You don't trust me," he said.

"I'll trust you once I have the money back in my pocket," I replied. Mick looked at me, his chin raised, his nostrils flaring. Colum, behind him, drew himself up from where he had been leaning against the wall and made himself ready. Finally, Mick stuffed a hand into his trouser pocket and drew out a fistful of notes and change and slapped the money into my palm. Then without a word he retreated back into the cabin.

* * *

Colum didn't say much when we'd found our way back up on deck. In the noon sun I got a good look at his face. The cheekbone wasn't broken; I could tell that much. The skin was red, slowing becoming ever more discolored. It would probably turn into a black eye. I said so.

"And how am I going to explain this to my father?" he said. "He hates when I fight."

"Tell him the truth," I said. "Tell him you were helping me."

"Clare," Colum said, "that's not going to make him like you any quicker." He looked disgusted.

"I could explain," I said.

"You don't understand, do you," he said.

"I only thought . . . " I paused.

"I need to get back to my cabin," he said. "My mother wants us to eat together from now on."

"Just your family?" I asked.

"I need to go," he said. "It's nearly noon."

"Can I meet you this afternoon?" I said.

"If I can get away, I'll be on deck," he said. Then without waiting for a reply, he turned and headed for the stairs. I waited for a minute or two, then went down myself.

* * *

The door to the cabin was propped open. Tom lay on his bunk, his back to the world. Mrs. Keane sat beneath him on my bunk, her legs dangling, her cane propped in front of her. When she saw me enter, she hopped down and hoisted herself onto her own bunk.

"Change of scenery," she said. "I looked at that wall long enough I can tell you the name of every screw and rivet. So I thought I'd look at the other while for a while."

"Any better?" I asked.

"A bit," she said. "Most people would tell you they were identical twins, those two walls. But they aren't. The difference is that pipe there." She gestured with her cane at a pipe entering the wall above Tom's bunk. "On that wall, it's bolted down with six bolts. On the one behind me, it's bolted with seven."

"Good to know," I said.

"Pfff," she replied. "I thought you'd be out locking eyes with that young pup of yours. Where is he?"

"I came to check on Tom," I said.

"So you had your first fight?" Mrs. Keane replied, perking up considerably. "Was it about your family or his?"

"It wasn't a fight," I said, "and it's hard to tell whose family it was about. I wouldn't give you a lop for either right now. Speaking of fights, where's Pat?"

"You aren't the only one with a beau on board," Mrs. Keane said. "She didn't tell you?" I shook my head. But then when could she have told me anything? Between the two of us, we'd been out of the cabin so much that I hadn't seen more than ten minutes of her in the last few days.

"He's from Waterford," Mrs. Keane said. "It turns out they worked no better than a mile apart for the last three years. They went to the same church themselves. But she had to meet him on a ship hundreds of miles from home before she could take notice of him."

"Is it serious?" I asked.

"All shipboard relationships are serious," Mrs. Keane replied. "So long as you're on the ship. If you want them to last on dry land, you need to marry 'em before they get their land legs. So has that soft-eyed pup of yours proposed yet?"

"I'm fourteen," I said.

"Fourteen is old enough if you're sure he's the right one," she replied.

"It's not old enough for me," I said. "If I got married now, I could have five children before I turned twenty."

"I wouldn't bet on more than three," she replied. "And sure 'tis much easier to have them when you're young and strong."

I pulled the shoonaun out from under the bed and began rummaging around in it, as much for something to do as anything. The conversation was making me quite nervous. But while I was there, I pulled the wad of notes from the secret pocket and added them to the ones in my skirt pocket. It wouldn't hurt to see how much Mick had lost.

"You'll need to change those notes," Mrs. Keane said. "They can do it on the boat. Likely 'twould be easier than waiting until New York."

I counted the notes. Three pounds, three and six. Plus Uncle Ronan's ten dollar bill that the Cunard people had given us in Queenstown. Mick hadn't lost more than a few pence, then. A wave of regret swept through me. I'd made much more than six pence worth of fuss over things. Nonetheless, I folded the bills into a tight packet, and tied it into the pocket of my skirt.

"Would you like to join me for dinner?" I asked. "We can find the purser afterwards."

"It'll do me no good waiting for Patricia," she said. "The girl left me high and dry both yesterday and the day before. She knows I need help, the way this blamed boat keeps shifting beneath me. But I'm not thirty, handsome, and wearing trousers."

"Tom," I said. "Wake up. Dinner."

"I'll go later," he said. His voice was raspier than was justified by the grogginess.

"It's probably after noon already," I said. "The dinner bell rang some time ago. If you don't go now, you could miss it."

Tom rolled over to face me. He looked a bit pale. "Is your throat that bad?" I asked.

"Only a little sore," he said.

"Let me see," I said, stepping up on the bottom bunk to get a better view. I took his chin in my hand, clutched at the bed frame with the other.

"Get off," he said, swatting at me.

"Let me see," I said.

"It's only a little sore," Tom said. "Can't you mind your own business for once?"

I stepped down. Mrs. Keane, reached out to me. I offered her my arm, and she pulled herself up. "Let him be," she whispered in my ear.

"I heard someone in the corridor say dinner today was beef and carrots," she said, supposedly to me, but loud enough that Tom could hear easily. "I never turned down a good beef and carrots and I never will," she added. Tom rolled over again to face the wall. He had never turned down any food, never mind beef and carrots. If he'd rather sleep than eat now, his throat had to be more than just a little sore.

Twenty-Two

The metal railing of the ship was warm, almost hot. The sticky air was hotter. I leaned over the rail and looked down into the grey green water. A chunk of wood tangled with seaweed floated far below. The languid sounds of voices hummed in the stagnant summer air—the familiar Irish lilts, the foreign but familiar rhythms of the English passengers' speech.

Over the water, snippets of speech drifted between the ships bobbing in the bay. Four or five of them, there were, liners like our own. I could see the passengers, wilted like I was, hanging over the railings of their own ships. On the breeze I could hear their talk, some of it harsh and guttural, some fast and rhythmic like the beat of the bodhrán. It was too hot to pay much attention, though. All I wanted to do was hang limp on the rail and imagine the coolness of the water below.

* * *

Nearly two days ago just before breakfast we had steamed into Lower New York Bay. Tom, and I had joined the other passengers flooding the drizzle-moistened decks, hoping to catch a glimpse of New York City. We scanned the shoreline ahead for the familiar silhouette, the woman with the torch we'd seen in pictures for as long as we could remember. But before we could see her, the ship stopped short. The great winch that occupied such a large part of the immigrant deck creaked as it dropped the anchor. And there we sat beneath the grey, cloud-choked skies, listening to the far off rumble of a thunderstorm blowing in from the southwest. The winds buffeted the deep green trees that lined the shore of Brooklyn on one side and Staten Island on the other. Just off the port bow lay the industrial-looking quarantine buildings on Hoffman Island. The vast Atlantic was behind us. Before us was New York City, Manhattan, or so they told me. From our point of view these shores could have been anywhere—Ireland, America, we couldn't tell.

Here in the bay the waves were smaller, much more benign, not enough to be noticed by a ship as large as the *Caronia*. I hung over its rail and watched them until the clouds finally let loose with great sheets of water and forced me to the shelter of the stairway. Water above. Water below. I can't begin to say just how tired I was of water.

* * *

Night fell without so much as a twitch of movement in the boards beneath our feet. Since we arrived in the Narrows, Colum's family had kept him with them in their cabin. I saw him the second evening at supper. He sat beside his sister, hunched sullenly over his stew. In that context, he looked like a boy, not the man I had come to love. He caught me looking, looked back with longing in his eyes. But when I rose to go to him, he shook his head slightly. He and his family left without a word. That evening, most of the passengers went down to their cabins early. The deck was wet. The mood aboard was sodden. We weren't passing through Ellis that day either. Disappointment and anxiety hung in the air.

I lay back in my bunk coated in it—the smells of the voyage, the smells of a week of bodies pressed cheek by jowl had dissolved themselves into the sticky air. The thick syrup of it clung to bulkheads, sheets, us. All night we tossed with it, barely sleeping for the thickness of the air and the anticipation. Tom sat on the floor at the foot of my bed, trying to catch a bit of cool air from the door. Now and then he coughed, a thick rattle it was, one that came up from the depths of him. The rain seemed to make things worse for him. I worried, drowsed, then worried some more.

I must have finally fallen asleep, for the knock woke me with a start. It was the steward rapping on the door of our cabin, long before breakfast, before the usual morning sounds had begun filtering through the hallway. The steward knocked on our door, then moved on to the next door, and the next.

"Go to the dining room," he called over and over. "Bring your inspection cards with you."

They were simple enough instructions, but at that time of the morning, they seemed ominous. So when we dug our inspection cards from the hidden pocket in the shoonaun, pulled on our clothes, and joined the stream of sleep-rumpled people heading toward the dining room, we walked through an atmosphere of foreboding, of formless dread that probably would have been greatly diluted by a single ray of morning light.

"What is it?" Tom asked. I shrugged.

"Beg your pardon, sir," Tom tapped the man ahead of us on the shoulder. "Do you know what it is they want?" His voice scratched and grated, and the effort of talking brought loose something. He got caught in a kink of coughing that bent him over. I handed him my handkerchief.

"Nasty cough," the man ahead of us said over his shoulder. The line had slowed as it approached the stairway. We made our way halfway up, and then stopped.

"Terrible time for a cough like that," a woman behind us said. She spoke with an English accent, one of those that sound like something up in the back of her mouth was pinching and squeezing the words so they came out bent and slightly flat. "Terrible time for any kind of sickness. They send people back for less than that." She motioned at Tom, who was spitting something thick and nasty into the handkerchief.

"I had a brother go through," she said. "Ten months ago. Maybe a bit more.

He said that they make the whole ship load of people march past the ship's doctor, and they pull out the sick ones, and they put them on an island in the harbor. He said that a steward told him that once an entire ship load of Greeks or Germans, or something like that, got shipped over to the island only because one of them had a disease the doctors couldn't cure. They held them all there on the island, and one after another they all got sick."

"I heard," the man behind her said, craning his head around the woman to get a better look at Tom. "I heard that if someone on a ship has a bad contagious disease, they shave everyone's head and then hold you on the ship until everyone either gets healthy or dies."

"Just pray it stays out of your eyes," another man chimed in. "I heard that once you get onto Ellis, the inspectors take a buttonhook to your eyelids, yank them up and look under them. And if you have anything wrong in your eyes, they send you back."

Tom coughed again. His chest seemed looser than it was the day before. But still it sounded terrible.

"All I have to say," the woman chimed in, "is that if I get this close to America and can't get in because of some grubby lad with a cough, I will be very displeased. She glared first at Tom, then at me.

"'Tis only a touch of the croup," I said. "No more than that. He'll be right in a day or two." I looked forward. The line continued to inch up the stairs. We'd be in the dining room soon.

"I will be very displeased," the woman repeated, partly for my benefit, but mostly for her own, I think.

* * *

The stewards split the line at the door to the dining room. The men were sent farther down the hall. The women and children stepped through the door and around a fabric screen set up so we couldn't see what was going on until we were fully inside the room. Tom followed me as I made my way around the screen.

The ship's doctor was there. The same man who had delivered Rose's baby. He was dressed in a billowy white suit, with a mask over his face, but I recognized him from the birthmark over his eye. In the heat, the mark seemed more vivid, or maybe it was only the contrast to the white of his mask and bunny suit. He perched on a high stool, facing the head of the line, hovering over a woman, the front of her dress undone. So it was an examination, then. Mouth, ears, chest, nose—I watched the doctor assess each one. The procedure seemed simple enough. But memories of Queenstown still ran through my bloodstream, filling me with a deep undercurrent of anxiety that tumbled and mingled with my worry for Tom. My breath came short. I could feel the blood struggle to reach my face. The woman at the head of the line stepped aside and started doing up the front of her dress. Tom and I shuffled forward.

"I'm not seeing any lice in this lot," the doctor said to the woman beside him. A large woman she was, a monument of a woman in a blue striped dress and starched white apron.

"Not for want of trying on their part, I'm sure, doctor," the woman responded. I moved up in the line. The large woman instructed me to open my shirtwaist. She wasn't the kind of person one would be likely to say no to even if one were inclined, which I wasn't.

"But then, the lice we can cure," the doctor said. "I'd gladly treat five boat loads full of lice if I could avoid a single passenger with something more serious. Did you hear about that Italian ship a few months ago?" The nurse shook her head. "Typhoid. Two passengers. They hauled the whole lot of them over to Hoffman Island. Ship's doctor, too. The poor so-and-so was stuck there for weeks filling out endless forms and examining the stools of hundreds of 'em, all terrified of getting the typhoid themselves, begging to get out, all with the stink of fear and confinement on them." He shook his head and tisked. "No, thank you. I'd rather jump with lice myself than be put through that." He nodded the women in front of me over to the side. I moved to my place in front of him, looking down, hoping he wouldn't recognize me.

"Lift your head, girl," he said impatiently. I did. I lifted my head and looked him square in the eye. He obviously didn't recognize me. He wedged my mouth open with a stick of wood and looked down my throat. Satisfied, he then placed a cold disk of metal on my chest. It was attached by narrow hoses to his ears. With a faraway look on his face, he said simply, "Breathe in and out."

I did so. He moved the disk to another place. "Cough," he said. Removing the tubes from his ears, he grasped my head in both hands and tilted it forward. I could feel his hands rummaging through my hair, displacing the pins and setting free strands that fell down over my face in wisps. His hands then tipped my face up and his fingers pulled down at my lower eyelids.

"She's clean," the doctor said. "Next."

The large woman motioned for me to do up the front of my waist, and reached out a hand.

"Inspection card," she said. I handed it to her. With a large stamp and a pad of black ink, she marked a big X over the section of the card that said: "Passed at Quarantine. Port of ____."

I looked over my shoulder at Tom, who was standing in front of the doctor, his shirt open and his face pale, even paler than it had been the other day from the illness.

"Cough," the doctor said. Tom did so, and a loose rattle vibrated through his chest. The doctor moved the disk. "Cough," he said again, but the command wasn't really necessary. The first cough had loosened something in Tom's throat and his body seemed determined to be rid of it.

"He's had a touch of the croup," I said over my shoulder, hoping the doctor would hear. The large woman was scribbling something on the card. "He's getting much better," I continued. I wasn't sure the doctor was listening. "By next week, he'll be right as rain."

A sharp tug brought my attention back to the large woman before me. "Did you hear what I said?" She had a pinch of my shirtwaist between her fingers and was tugging it sharply. "Did you hear a word I said?"

I turned back to face her. She stood with my card in her outstretched hand. She fixed me with her gaze.

"I said," she repeated in a condescending tone, "keep this card in your possession until you have cleared all processing stations on Ellis Island. Without this card, you will not be allowed to enter the country. Do you understand?"

"I do," I said.

"Then go," she said. "I have too many others to see today to spend my time chatting with the likes of you."

I looked over my shoulder at Tom.

"My brother," I began.

"Go," she said simply. "Go."

I went, followed the stream of bodies that flowed through the corridors back to the cabins. Once there, I sat stiffly on the edge of the bunk, waiting for Tom. I didn't have to wait long. He arrived about five minutes later, a big smile on his face.

"The doctor said it was only a virus," he said. He drew his card from his pocket and handed it to me. It bore a large X, just as mine did. He said that at the rate the harbor inspections were going, I'd not only be done with it, I'd be lucky to remember I had it by the time it was our turn for Ellis."

"Thank you," I whispered, and crossed myself before tucking the cards into the secret pocket of the shoonaun.

"I told you 'twas nothing," he said.

"To bed with you then, Tommeen," I replied. "We still have some night left. And if the doctor said you'll be forgetting this virus, you'd better get a start doing just that." Tom nodded and climbed the bunk. Within seconds he was snoring a rattley, congested snore.

* * *

Tom was still asleep, and Mick was still missing when the next wave of inspectors arrived. I could hear them talking in the corridors, quick, official-sounding American accents. Mrs. Keane and I lay back on our bunks in the near dark. Breakfast would be in another hour or so. I figured I could catch up to Mick there. I needed a way of impressing on him that we needed to be together for these inspections. Who knows when we would be released to Ellis. I didn't want to have to go looking for him when the time came. I was deep into rehearsing the speech I had prepared for him, when the inspector spoke.

"Are you decent?" The voice came from the doorway.

"We are," Mrs. Keane answered, "and who would be asking?" I looked up. A squarish figure stood in the entrance to our cabin, backlit by the light from the corridor.

"Boarding matron for the Department of Immigration," the woman said simply. "You are Bridget Keane?" She flipped on the light.

"I am," Mrs. Keane answered swinging her feet over the side of the bunk. I did the same.

"You are an American citizen?" The woman asked, her eyes focused on her clipboard. She was bulky, a strong lump of a woman, her graying hair pulled back and tucked under the navy uniform cap she wore.

"I am," Mrs. Keane answered, "since July 4th, 1871."

The woman nodded. "I have a few questions for you then." She ran a finger down the clipboard. "Why did you leave the United States?" she asked.

"Because my great fool of a husband, God rest him, had some fool notion about dying in Ireland. And since he had his heart set on it, I couldn't very well let him go off and do it on his own, now could I?"

"You're a widow, then," the matron asked.

"Now isn't that just what I'm after saying?" Mrs. Keane replied.

"And is this your daughter?" The matron nodded vaguely in my direction.

"My daughter is in Montana," Mrs. Keane replied. "This is Clare, an orphan, saints preserve her and all orphans."

"An orphan?" the matron asked, looking up from her clip board to examine me. She seemed to have suddenly lost all interest in Mrs. Keane. I stood. "You have no family at all?"

"I have my two brothers," I replied.

"Older?"

"Younger," I said.

"And how to you plan to support yourself and these two brothers?" she asked.

"I was in service since I was eleven," I said.

"How old are you now?" the matron asked.

"I'm fourteen," I said.

The matron flipped a few sheets of paper and scribbled something on her clipboard. "Name?" she said.

"Clare Keane."

She continued to scribble. "Place of origin?" I wasn't sure what she meant. "Where are you from?" she demanded.

"Cork," I said. "Cork, Ireland"

"Has anyone brought you to America, offering you work or any other assistance?"

I wasn't sure what she was asking. But Uncle Ronan had sent us the tickets. "Yes," I said tentatively.

She looked up again, scanned me topped to bottom, then tucked her clip board under her arm. "Miss Keane," she said, "do you know what white slavery is?"

Tom by this time was awake. I heard him shift in his bunk to get a view of the proceedings. "White slavery?" he asked. I glanced at him over my shoulder. His face was a patchy mix of pink and grey.

"Your brother?" the boarding matron asked.

"He is," I said, "my brother Tom . . . Thomas."

I waited. She looked at me expectantly. "I ask again: do you know what white slavery is, Miss Keane?"

"Enslaving white people," I answered. It was obviously a guess.

"Well, yes," the matron replied, "but to what purpose?"

I shook my head. "I'm sure I wouldn't know ma'am."

"White slavery is when men, evil men, capture young white women for immoral purposes." I apparently still had a blank look on my face. "These young women service men," she added.

"Women of the unfortunate class," Tom whispered hoarsely.

"I know," I whispered back over my shoulder.

"Has any man made you promises, offered you work?" she said.

"Not like that," I said. "I would never."

"Most of the girls trapped in white slavery at this very minute would have said the very thing. But then they became lost in a strange country, hungry, with no job, no means of support, younger brothers depending on them for their very life," she fixed her eyes on me. I could feel myself getting light-headed. "Desperate girls do desperate things, Miss Keane."

"Yes, ma'am," I said, sitting heavily on the edge of the bunk. I knew it was impolite, but I didn't think my legs would stand for any more standing at that moment.

"If you don't mind," Mrs. Keane said, stepping between the two of us, "Before you jump to any conclusions. I said Clare was an orphan, not that she was without family. She has an uncle in Minnesota, the good and generous man who sent for her. And she has me, not the closest of relatives, grant you, but I would never let her be on her own like that."

"This uncle," the matron said, "mother's brother?"

"Yes," Mrs. Keane replied.

"He's married?"

"Soon to be," Mrs. Keane replied. "A fine woman and a good Christian."

"It would have saved both your and my time had you mentioned this uncle when I asked you about your family." She was glaring at me again.

I wasn't sure what to say, so I only nodded. The boarding matron turned her attention again to Mrs. Keane. "Mrs. Keane," she said, "as an American citizen you will not be required to pass through immigration on Ellis Island. You will, rather, be inspected here on the ship. Please report to the third class smoking lounge." Then as abruptly as she had entered, she left.

"Cow," Mrs. Keane whispered after her. The woman made no sign she heard. Maybe she didn't. I cringed nonetheless.

"Uncle Ronan is Da's brother," Tom said, once she had gone.

"Shh," Mrs. Keane said. "And does that matter one scrap now that she's gone?"

* * *

Every immigrant, it seems, has their story about the Statue of Liberty. They speak of standing on deck, shoulder to shoulder with the others, seeing it come into view, rising out of the mists of the harbor. They speak of the tears, the hopes, the apprehension. They are all wonderful stories to be sure. I have a story, too. It may not be as wonderful as most, but it is mine.

After Mrs. Keane left for her inspection, I lay myself back on the bunk, thinking about the boarding matron, about Becky's, Polly, and all the other unfortunate women of my acquaintance. Above me Tom coughed, and turned, and moaned, then coughed again, then moaned. I listened to him anxiously. Finally, I climbed up and laid myself down beside him. His forehead was warm—whether from the heat of the cabin or from fever I could not tell you. Strands of his dark hair lay pasted against the white of it. I stroked the nape of his neck and that dark hair that reminded me so much of Da's. As I lay watching him sleep, thinking of all I would give for him to have a good life in America, the great engines beneath us roared to work. Outside the door, people scrambled through the halls, calling to each other in excitement. We were moving, moving up the Narrows to the great city of New York.

"The boat's moving, Tommeen," I said quietly. "Do you want to go upstairs . . . on deck?"

Tom muttered something, then rolled over and curled himself into a ball. I curled myself around him, laid a hand on his shoulder and began to pray my beads. In my mind's eye I could see the statue of the great lady rise from the horizon. She stood in the early morning light just outside the bulkhead that Tom pressed his forehead to. In my mind's eye I saw her. She wore a blue cloak, her eyes cast down piously. And I prayed with all my strength that she would let us enter.

* * *

It was well into the afternoon. I stood at the rail again, shoulder-to-shoulder again with all the other wilted bodies, trying again to catch whatever breeze the afternoon might offer. The engines that had powered us into motion early that morning were now, a couple of hours past dinner, back to a low growl beneath us. We'd come up through the Narrows, headed for the piers lining the edges of the great city that rose out of the water off our starboard bow. But before we could dock, the ship stopped. And once again we waited.

We were not the only ones. Other liners bobbed beside us. And still others, ferries, cargo ships, airy little sailing vessels, and great muscular barges wove their way through the nautical obstacle course that lay between New York's rivers and the sea.

To port, lay the island, Ellis Island. A castle it was. A great red brick and white stone castle poised on a tiny scrap of land. America must be a rich land indeed if could afford to lavish such opulence on the likes of us.

Every now and then, smoke would billow from one of liner moored just off the island, and that liner would inch slowly toward the piers of the city. Every now and then a ferry would send up a puff of smoke as it pulled away from Ellis and also made its way to the piers. An hour or so later the ferry would pull away from the pier, riding lower in the water, ferrying yet another load of human cargo to the island. In the meantime, ships and barges and tugs and ferries crisscrossed their way across the harbor, weaving their way between the liners. Their wakes splashed gently against the side of our ship, oh so many feet below. Until our turn, we would settle in and wait, anchored unmoving between Ellis Island and the Statue of Liberty, between the tall forest of buildings that was New York City and the mainland that contained, somewhere in its depths, St. Paul, Minnesota.

I hung on the rail for a while, then napped below in the sweaty confines of my cabin, then made my way up top, chatted, waited and watched some more. Around me scores of others did the same. A sea gull circled overhead, watched by hundreds of bored immigrant eyes. Another ferry fired up its engines at the dock, pulled away slowly and headed out for the harbor. We all crowded the rail, held our breath, hoping we would be the one to meet it at the wharf. But as one-by-one the liners around us powered up their engines, the vibrations in the boards beneath our feet remained unchanged. I turned away from the rail to pace a bit, not that I was likely to find the room on the crowded deck.

In the great pile of humanity covering the deck, Colum was nowhere to be seen. I hadn't seen him—even at a distance—for nearly a day. I considered going to his cabin, but after the meeting with his parents I was flooded with embarrassment every time I thought about it. Besides, it did a girl no good to be too forward with a boy. No, Colum knew where to find me. He knew I would be either in my cabin or here on deck. I would wait for him to find me.

Tom was sitting cross-legged on the boards with Mr. Wisely and a couple of other of the gang. The breeze was a bit too stiff for whistles, so for a change they were bent over a chessboard, trying to understand the game Mr. Wisely was trying to teach them. Tom rubbed his eye with the back of his hand, screwed up his nose at the itch, then with an intensely serious look on his face, moved one of the white pieces to replace one of the black ones.

"Good!" Mr. Wisely said.

Tom grinned at the praise, then began to cough again. It sounded as though his chest was less full than it had been. That was good. But he was still pale, a bit grey instead of his usual pale pink. The sleep this morning had done him good, but not as much good as I'd hoped.

Mick, still asserting his independence, sat leaning against a ventilation shaft. Since we'd moved up the Narrows, Mick had been aloof, but generally within eye fall. He had even spent a few minutes after breakfast with Tom and me in the cabin. I had decided to postpone my lecture. Mick might be headstrong, but he knew what was at stake here, of that I was fairly certain. Since we'd come up on deck, he had been working his way through Tom's American book.

"You must be powerful bored if you're reading to pass the time." I picked my way between through the maze of seated figures and stooped to sit beside him. He made a face and scooted over to make room. I wedged myself between him and another passenger napping with a cap pulled over his face.

"Did you know," Mick said, "New York has 942,292 people? 942,292 people!"

"It has more than that, now," I said, smoothing my skirts.

"Look," he said, "942,292." He pointed at a line in the book. "And that's only New York City."

"Yes but look," I said making a sweeping motion with my hand, motioning to the packed mass of sweaty bodies surrounding us. "I'd wager a couple of thousand people are biding their time on this ship. And each of those ships abroad surely has another thousand or two more. I'd say your wee book is out of date."

"Perhaps," Mick said, falling silent, burying his nose again in the book. His shoulders were stiff. He wasn't reading. I laughed at my own joke. His shoulders tightened all the more. He looked as though he wanted to stand and disappear again.

"I didn't mean anything by it, Mick," I said, laying a hand on his arm, partly by way of apology, partly to make sure he didn't disappear again. "Tell me what else the book says. It would do us no harm to learn what we can about this country."

"Well," he said cautiously, "look here. Father Brynes—that's who wrote the book—says, 'Young persons from the ages of 12 to 20 years can select in America almost any trade or profession for which they consider themselves fit.' Any trade at all. I could own my own shop. Or I could be an inspector or a doctor if I wanted to." He fingered the health inspector's card through the fabric of his shirt pocket.

"I don't suppose Father Brynes explains how it is we're going be to paying for you to learn to be a doctor."

"Well, I don't know that I'd want to be a doctor," he replied. "A shopkeeper maybe."

"It will still cost us," I said.

"It will," Mick said, flipping pages. "But look here. It says 'Servant-girls in America get from eight to sixteen dollars a month—sometimes they get as high as twenty. Now if they save half of that amount every year, and place it at interest, they will have a considerable sum at the end of ten years.' In ten years I'll be twenty-two, old enough to go to have my own shop. If we save half of what you earn, we can have the money by then."

"How much is a dollar again?" I asked.

"Five dollars is a pound," Mick replied. "You would be earning about two pounds a week. We could almost certainly save twenty-five pounds a year, put it at interest. In ten years we could have over £250."

I did the arithmetic. Ten years. In ten years I would be twenty-four. An adult. The image of Colum, me, a child or two floated again into my mind. Suddenly, sitting beside Mick in the clear light of day, I felt exposed.

"What kind of shop would you want?" I asked. I wasn't quite ready to share the image with him.

"It doesn't matter what kind of shop," Mick replied. "What I'm saying is that I can choose any trade I want. I could be one of the respectable people. I could be as wealthy as the Quillan boys, maybe as wealthy as Mr. Good himself."

I pictured Mick in a blue blazer, spilling egg on his tie. I pictured him strolling through the front door of the house, handing his coat to me as though I were nothing more than a coat rack in the corner. I pictured him sitting in his easy chair, puffing on his pipe, calling for is supper.

"I suppose it is possible," I said. "Mama and Papa would be glad of it." I shifted as much as the tight quarters would allow, rested my head against a ventilation shaft and closed my eyes. Through the boards of the deck I heard the engines rumble to life. My eyes snapped open. We were headed for the pier.

And for another wait.

* * *

We stood on deck, Colum and I, angling as best we could to catch a breeze, any breeze off the water. At supper that evening, he had found me. We had walked the ship again, then in search of cool air, had climbed the stairs to the deck. Even in the open, the air was heavy with humidity, with the smells of the boat and the city. It was even heavier with all the things we felt but for one reason or another could not say. We had arrived in New York, arrived in America. That meant our time together was nearly over. The knowledge of it was thick and more than a little bit choking.

Night fell gently. As the sun faded behind us, the city began to sprout lights, one after another, blinking on, speckling the tall buildings, lighting the streets that led to the pier. We leaned against the railing, and ever so lightly against each other. For a moment we lived only in the magic of it, in a world where the sadness of our parting did not have to be spoken.

Behind us the sound of a pennywhistle floated over us. A waltz it was, sweet and high on the night air. Colum stepped back, away from me, and held out his hand.

"Would you care to dance then?" he said with forced casualness.

"I would love to," I said, laying my hand lightly in his. "If I knew how. I never did learn." My hand trembled in his. I tried to still it, but the effort made it tremble all the more. "I'm sorry," I said, pulling my hand away, clutching it to myself in an effort to still the tremors. "I'm afraid this night air has given me the shakes."

"'Tis nothing," Colum replied, reaching again for my hand. "You should feel what the night air has done to my heart." He took my hand in both of his, then placed it on his chest. I could feel within, the strong beat of his heart. "I can teach you to dance."

I nodded. On the other side of the railing the pier lights flickered on, casting a delicate light on the boards of the deck. Colum took my hand from his chest and placed it in his own. He placed my other hand on his shoulder, then ever so gently, as though I were made of china, he laid his other hand lightly on the small of my back. A tremble rolled through me, and to my wonder, an answering tremble rolled through him. He smiled a broad smile and chuckled. "'Tis the least of what you do to me, Clare Keane," he said. "You must promise me to love dancing, so I can have you in my arms like this forever."

I blushed. I don't know if it was the newness of the electric lights, the faint sway of the ship at its moorings, or just the utterly alien feel of Colum's body, but the night suddenly became not quite real. The crowd around us was populated by specters. The music came not from Mr. Wisely's whistle, but out of the air itself. We didn't merely stand on the deck; the deck held us.

"Follow me," Colum said.

"Anywhere," I thought, and for just that instant I meant it.

I'm not much of a dancer. But the crowd on deck—the other couples dancing, the children playing, the families hanging over the rail, talking of the future—all these left little room for movement anyway. So we mostly held to each other and swayed. He pressed his cheek to mine. And the electricity that jumped the slight gap between his body and mine was even more potent that the power that lit up our tiny corner of the pier. At that moment I decided I loved dancing.

* * *

"Come to Washington," Colum said. The music had deteriorated as Mr. Wisely's students joined him. Colum and I had found a bare place on deck and were sitting propped against a hatch cover. He still held my hand, still looked at me as though life were me and nothing but me in an otherwise empty world. Every now and again, I summoned the courage and looked back.

"Come to Washington," he said again. "My uncle will find Mick work in the stables or some such place. I'll work as a logger. And every Friday evening we'll go dancing. I'll save, and you'll save, and when we have enough money for our own house, we'll get married."

"I'm fourteen," I said.

"So you are," he replied. "And I'm sixteen."

"You aren't," I replied.

"Almost," he said. "Sixteen next month. That's plenty old enough to know that I found the sweetest girl ever to walk this earth. Say you'll come with me to Washington."

"What did your parents say about me?" I asked. There I was being practical again. A small voice told me to fall into his arms and pledge to never leave his side. Instead I asked, "Did you talk to your father about us? Did you tell him I'm from the lanes?"

"In America that doesn't matter any more," he replied. "What matters is that you are willing to work. We'll work hard. We'll have a house, and a family. And every evening I'll come home, and you'll have dinner, and we'll eat and then sit by the fire. And I'll sit there and watch you in the glow of the fire, your hair down about your shoulders, my baby son at your breast, and I'll think that no man could possibly be as lucky as I am." He brought my hand to his lips and kissed it gently. I blushed, a deep blush I could feel in my breasts, my belly.

"Will you come?" he said.

"Do you mean it?" I asked.

"I mean it," he said. "Will you come to Washington with us?"

"I'd have to talk to my brothers," I said, "and Uncle Ronan. And we'd have to change the train ticket."

He dropped his hand and mine into his lap. "You couldn't just say 'yes'?" he said. I looked at him, his head hanging, his soft hair falling again into his eyes. And I knew just then I would never find a man so handsome, so willing to make a good life for me.

"Yes," I said. Only that, "yes." He looked up, looked deep into my eyes, then cast his gaze a bit lower, to my lips. He leaned in, and we kissed. It was a tiny, awkward kiss, a kiss of two people whose only practice had been on mothers, maiden aunts, grandparents. But I knew then in my heart it would be the first of many, that I would spend the rest of my life kissing this man.

Colum sat back, leaned against the hatch, my hand in his on his lap. "Don't worry yourself," he said. "I'll arrange it with my parents." I nodded. He would arrange it. I had nothing to worry about. "We'll change your tickets and wire your uncle after we go through Ellis."

"Washington," I said, getting used to the sound of it.

"Um hum," Colum said. "Washington. It will be a good home for us. You talk to Mick and Tom. I'll talk to my parents." He leaned in again, and nuzzled his nose in my hair. I could hear his breath so miraculously close to my ear. "Meet me here tomorrow morning. Meet me in this very spot, and we'll go through Ellis together, hand in hand."

"I will," I said.

"Marry me, Clare Keane. Say you'll spend the rest of your life with me."

"I will," I said. "I will, Colum O'Moran."

* * *

The only problem with feeling, it would seem, is that once you start, it's hard to stop. Not that I hadn't felt a great ocean of feelings back in Cork. I'd felt the sadness, the anxiety, the loss, and, well, of course, the hunger pains. But now, floating as I was on this great city moored at the gates of an even greater city, my belly full, and my chapped hands healing, I was feeling things I'd never felt before.

That evening, when he left me at the door of my cabin, I undressed with the sound of his voice still in my ears. I lay down holding great conversations with him in my mind, wondering if he was thinking of me, knowing somehow that he was. When I was with him, I felt comfortable, snug in his company. Our eyes would lock, and I would gaze upon him without shame. He knew me for what I was, and fine man that he was, he loved me all the more for it. And for that I loved him back with all that I was, and more than that, all that I ever hoped to be.

But the problem with feeling is that it's like a river. Once the river inside me had cut its channel, the water flowed there, and as it flowed the channel grew deeper and deeper, until I found myself so full with it that I could hardly bear it. I rushed with tenderness. I flowed with intimacy. I gushed with desire, roiled with love, bubbled, and burbled and broke with that unnamed feeling that burst forth inside me at the slightest touch of his hand. Long after we lay alone in the dark, each in our own narrow bunk, the river churned its way through the center of me. "Thank you," I had found myself saying a hundred times a day every day of our voyage together. "'Twas nothing," he would reply, quite honestly. "You don't need to keep thanking me." But I couldn't help myself, for the river rushed with gratitude, gratitude for these feelings I never knew existed.

I must say, that on that evening, the evening Colum first proposed to me, I feared myself drowned in it all. But never would a body go to her Maker more willingly than one drowning in such a river as this.

Twenty-Three

A bump and a rumble traveled through the decking. It was late morning, and I was on deck leaning against "our" deck hatch. I hadn't seen Colum at breakfast, but then he hadn't promised to meet me for breakfast. After we ate, Mick and Tom had gone looking for him. Mick said he wanted to talk with him man-to-man about his intentions and whether Colum as a provider could do right be me. Mick liked the idea of living in Washington. Tom, I think, liked the idea of having a family with adults again. But when they went looking for Colum, he was no longer in his cabin, and he didn't appear to be on deck. Still, I wasn't worried. It was a big boat, easy to miss someone. He would come for me.

I took up a position against our hatch, and I waited, played the night before again and again through my mind, looked up every time someone rounded the corner from the stairs. Rumor had it that today was the day, so I had made sure Mick, Tom, and the shoonaun were on deck with me. Between the warm morning air and the fact that I hadn't slept much that night, I must have fallen asleep because the bump and rumble jolted me awake. It was the sound of feet on the decking, feet on the stairs, feet milling all about me. I stood so as not to be trampled by it all, by all the people squeezing past each other for either the rail or the stairs.

"A ferry," someone shouted. Then everyone took up the call, "A ferry. A ferry. A ferry came for us."

I looked around. Mick and Tom were at the rail, trying to see through the crowd of people in front of them. I made my way to them, and reached for Tom's hand. Mick reached for mine. All around us, the mass of people poured out of the lower compartments and flooded the decks. I checked Mick's other hand. He had the shoonaun.

"Everything is in there?" I asked.

"It is," Mick answered. "I checked before I came up top. Everything is out of the cabin."

Bundles and trunks bumped against us. The brown tweed of men's jackets and the black serge of women's full skirts closed in around us. Everyone, it seemed, had changed into their best clothes for the day. The mass of people teemed and sweated and shifted, but didn't seem to be going anywhere. I scanned the crowd for Colum. I couldn't see him, but to be fair, I couldn't see much in the press of bodies. But still, I began to worry.

Finally, a man in a dark blue uniform made his way to one of the first class rails. From there he called down upon us through a megaphone.

"Please do not push. Do not rush. You will be disembarking shortly to the Cunard pier. There you will be sorted by manifest number and met by barges that will take you to processing at Ellis Island. The barges will have room for you all. Please make sure you have your inspection card in your hand. Immigration officials will not allow you to pass without your inspection card. Please remain where you are until we begin the disembarkation process. Again, please do not push. Do not rush. And please check to make sure you have your inspection card." He stepped down, and another official took over the megaphone and began the same message in Gaelic.

I let go of Mick's hand, fingered my inspection card. It was still in the deep pocket of my skirt. I glanced over at Mick and Tom. They too were patting their pockets for confirmation. More and more people made their way up the stairs onto the crowded deck. Even if Colum were nearby, he couldn't make his way to me. There was nothing to do but wait.

* * *

It has always amazed me how quickly one's life can veer off in an entirely new direction. When I stepped aboard the *Caronia* back in Queenstown, I pictured the boys and me traveling the ocean, making our way deep into America, arriving on Uncle Ronan's doorstep ready to begin a new life with him. But as the voyage had progressed, that image changed, replaced by Colum's alternative futures. The night before we disembarked, all sorts of images danced in my head—Colum and I traveling with his family and the boys on the long train trip to the opposite coast, Colum and I walking beneath huge trees, Colum and I dancing in a large hall with other loggers and their beaus, Colum and the boys kicking about a football on a Sunday afternoon while I watched from my place in a warm patch of sun. Washington. That would be my home.

Or so I thought last night. Today, as I jostled my way across the deck, I did so with Mick on one side and Tom on the other. Colum was nowhere to be found. I knew what had happened. Or at least I strongly suspected. He had told his parents that he wanted to marry me. They had pointed out the obvious— that he was still a boy, that I was beneath his station, that they didn't need the responsibility for three grubby orphans they didn't know from Adam. I had heard of shipboard romances, two people who meet, fall in love, disembark, and then never see each other again. I'd heard of them. I just never thought I'd be a part of one.

I readjusted the images in my mind. Mick, Tom, me. The train. Uncle Ronan. Minnesota. Alternative futures were for people of leisure, not for the likes of me.

* * *

The metal stairs they pushed up against the side of the ship led down to a long wooden pier that jutted out into the Hudson River. A weather-beaten building with "Cunard" lettered on the sides and end stretched the full length of the pier. Mick muscled the shoonaun down the stairs, then through the crowd bumping and shifting on all sides of us. We were all getting our land legs again.

The rock-steady pier seemed to rise and fall beneath us.

We staggered, swept along by the river of bodies. On either side of us stood two columns of somber men in dark blue uniforms and splendid caps, each with a golden eagle on the crown above the brim. The men said nothing, but motioned us to several lines of immigrants and baggage—it was our first line of many on American shores.

As we neared the front of the line that led to our table, we could see two Cunard men bent over stacks of paper on a table. The first man was in charge of a till. Behind him were three guards with pistols strapped to their belts and nightsticks in their hands.

"Inspection card," the man at the table said. I handed it to him. "Clare Keane," he said.

"I am," I replied. He shuffled through his papers.

"Fifty dollars," he said. "Sign here." He made an X on the piece of paper in front of him and turned it so I could see. The line he pointed to had three boxes: one box said "Clare Elizabeth Keane." The second said "$50." And in third, was the X he had just made. He handed me a pen. My tongue pushed its way into the corner of my mouth as I carefully drew my name into the tiny box.

"Twenty, forty, fifty," the man said as he counted the bills into my hand. It was more money than I had ever held in my life. Mick elbowed up beside me, reached out, and touched the bills. I pulled my hand away. The man at the table motioned us to the next line. I made my way to the back.

"I can hold some of it," Mick said. "We shouldn't have all our money in one place." I ignored him and took the ten and one of the twenties off the stack and tied them into my skirt pocket. The other twenty I tied into the shoonaun. Mick reached for the shoonaun, but I waved him away, keeping it in front of me the whole way up the queue to the second man.

"Inspection card," the Cunard man said when it was our turn at the front. I handed him mine. He shuffled one of the stacks of paper and made a check mark on one of the sheets. "Queue twenty-four," he said. Tom handed the man his card. Again the man shuffled, checked, and announced, "queue twenty-four." Mick handed the man his card. Shuffle, check, "queue twenty-three."

"Pardon me," Mick said. "If I might . . . "

"Address questions to that gentleman over there." The man jabbed his thumb at an older gentleman in a navy uniform and bushy, white, mutton-chop whiskers. The gentleman rocked back and forth, heel to toe, his hands clasped behind his back, surveying the crowd.

We stepped out of line and approached him. "Beg your pardon," Mick said. The man rocked to a stop. "I'm in queue twenty-three. My sister and brother are queue twenty-four." He paused. The man simply waited.

"We were wondering if there was a mistake," I said.

"Cards," the man replied. We handed them to him. He glanced at them quickly, then handed them back. "No mistake," he said. "Line twenty-four." He handed my card to me, and Tom's to him. "Line twenty-three." He handed Mick's card back to him, pointing to the manifest number stamped on the front.

"We'd like to be in the same queue, um, line," Mick said.

"Sorry," the man said. "Passengers are processed by manifest number. If you're in the wrong line nobody on Ellis Island will know who you are."

"No exceptions?" Tom asked.

"None," the man replied.

We worked our way through the crowd and then around the back of the table to where the lines were forming. All three of us were silent.

"I'll find you on the island," Mick said as we approached the back of the lines that had already begun forming.

"If you can," I said.

"I will. I'll find you," Mick repeated.

"Tom and I will take the shoonaun," I said. "Do you need anything?"

Mick shook his head. He looked frightened.

"Here's the way we'll do it," Tom said. "The first time they let us out of the lines, we look for the pillar closest to the center of the room, and go stand there and wait for each other."

"What if we're not in a room?" Mick said. "What if we're on a dock?"

"Then we go to the center of the dock and look for each other there," Tom said.

"The center," I said. "And if any of us see Colum, we tell him to meet us there, too—at the center of whatever room we're in." Mick shot me a dirty look. He was obviously annoyed with me again. Almost as annoyed as he was frightened.

"The center," Tom repeated.

"The center," I said. I would have felt much more secure if I had some image of what center we were talking about.

"The center of, wherever," Mick said. His face was pale as he made his way toward the line marked "twenty-three." Given the hollow feeling in my belly, I imagined I was roughly the same color myself.

* * *

They herded us line by line toward the waiting barges. The barges were dwarfed by the great liner beside us, but when well-packed each could hold a hundred or more people—roughly three lines worth—in the long, wooden cabins that covered their decks. The sun was hot, but given the humidity, the puffy clouds that occasionally darkened the pier did little provide relief. Some of the herders removed their navy jackets and performed their tasks in amply-soaked white shirts. The immigrants moved up the lines foot by foot, sitting now and then on their luggage, then rising to rock nervously from foot to foot.

Mick's line was well ahead of us, and I craned my neck to see if I could see him among the people walking up the gangplank. If he was there, he was lost among the bags and skirts and adults much taller than he was.

A couple of men stopped the stream of people, grasped the end of the gangplank leading up to the barge, pulled, and dropped the ramp onto the dock. The barge steamed off, its life boats swaying from their brackets on the roof. A mass of faces crowded the open windows. Mick had to be in there, but his face was nowhere to be seen through the windows that were slowly pulling away from the pier.

Within seconds, another barge pulled into place, this one smaller, shorter, apparently older. The large wheel on its side slowed, then stopped as workers secured lines and positioned the ramp. The flow of people began again, this time taking us with it, down the pier, up the gangplank, into the long nearly windowless cabin.

The moment we entered, it hit us—a wave of mixed smells. Sweat, vomit, urine, coal smoke, seaweed, and dozens of other smells too brutal to be identified. The column of passengers began to drag, to lag, as though everyone were trying to decide if they wanted to push their way through the sticky-hot wall of stench.

"Move to the back of the cabin," a man in a blue uniform called out.

"Phew," Tom said wrinkling his nose and burying it in his sleeve. The column of people continued forward, pushed on by others in the rear who had not yet reached the "wall."

Tom coughed. "It smells like a privy," he said.

"No, it doesn't," I said, grabbing his sleeve and dragging him as quickly as I could toward one of the back windows.

"Yes, it does," Tom replied loudly. "It smells like a dead dog sitting in a privy in Mr. O'Connor's room with smelly boots, and . . . "

"Shh," I said. "Do you want to get us thrown off the boat?"

Tom's mouth snapped shut. "Would they?" he whispered.

"Maybe," I said, glad he was quiet. I didn't think so, but I didn't know for sure. "Still it's rude to say such things about their boat."

"But it's true," he said, still whispering. "I think I'm going to gag."

"I know," I said. "Me, too. Breathe through your sleeve and try to ignore it." I knew the moment I said it that this was some of the most senseless advice I'd ever given. The smell was not ignorable. But neither was it deadly. We would live. There was nothing we could do about it. Consequently, it was not worth complaining about.

The reluctant wall of people continued to press. I leaned a hip heavily against the wall beneath the small, open window. The air outside was still, and the window was not much help. But it was better than what the people in the center of the barge had. For them a single skylight, propped open with a stick, let in some light and even less air. I staked my claim on the window and determined not to let it go until we reached the island. Tom, his nose in his sleeve, leaned in heavily beside me. He obviously had the same idea.

The barge was filling rapidly. Tom stood on his toes, clutching at the windowsill with his free hand. The sill came to roughly his hairline, too high for him to be able to see anything. I could barely see myself. The air outside smelled like coal smoke and the sour, unwashed worker tending the mooring line. With a little luck that would change once we got out on the water.

"How long," Tom asked. "Do you know?"

"No," I said. "But it shouldn't be long once we start moving. The island isn't that far." He nodded, then coughed hoarsely and heavily.

"I think I'll sit for a bit then," he said, sinking down on the shoonaun. His shoulders slumped and he rubbed his eyes, then settled his head into his hands.

I reached down to place a hand on his forehead. A little warm, perhaps. But that could just be the sun we stood in before boarding. I tried to remember if Tom had been this warm when the doctor on the ship stamped his card. A virus, the doctor had called it. Only a virus. Long forgotten before we set foot on the island. I removed Tom's cap, and smoothed down his hair, stroking it lightly. He inched over on the shoonaun and leaned warmly against me. Sweat trickled down between us.

Eventually, the engine chuffed. The sweating, coughing crowd murmured. The deck lurched beneath us. People lurched with it, struggled to catch their balance. The barge was packed tightly enough that they probably wouldn't have hit the ground had they indeed fallen, but none of them did. The engine behind began to growl in earnest, and through the window, I could see our ship, the faithful *Caronia*, swing into view, then slowly recede.

* * *

The air on the dock was anything but cool, but by comparison to the inside of the barge it was welcome fresh. For what seemed like an eternity, the barge had hung at anchor, its engines quiet, a mere stone's throw off Ellis Island. Inside the barge, the mass of people breathed the foul air and contributed to it. A few fainted and were left to sit on the soiled decking, propped against sacks and trunks. The barge had no seats, no place else for them to lie. Some people sat on their suitcases, but most stood, packed back to belly, cheek by jowl with the rest. There at anchor we waited, probably no more than twenty minutes, but long enough to drain us of any energy we may have had boarding the barge.

Now as we climbed the ramp onto the dock, a slight breeze revived us. I drank it in. In my hand, Tom's elbow shivered. I reached out a hand to his forehead. It was hot, very hot. How could it have gotten so hot so quickly? I wrapped an arm around his shoulders then took the shoonaun from his grasp. He surrendered it easily.

"'Twill be over and done with soon enough, Tommeen," I said.

"Mmm," he replied. "I suppose it will."

The footfalls of dozens of pairs of shoes thudded step-by-step across the wooden dock toward the great steel and glass awning and, beneath it, the front door. The sweat rolled down the small of my back. Again we merged ourselves into the river of bodies.

"Form a line here," shouted one of several men in white shirts and white aprons. The others in similar garb were grasping passengers and bodily moving them into a line that formed behind a small hand cart. "Form a line for food," they repeated over and over again. Tom and I edged into the line.

"Can you eat?" I asked him.

"When couldn't I?" he said with a half-hearted smile. I smiled a feeble smile back at him.

"The inspectors have all gone to dinner," a white-aproned man in a paper cap said, moving down the line to straighten it. "They'll be back at one. In the meantime, we have a lunch for you—bread, pickled herring, and coffee, all courtesy of the people of the United States of America."

The man with the cart began making his way down the line. I stuffed a hand into my pocket and untied the secret pouch. Inside were a handful of crisp notes and a couple of coins. I wondered how much lunch was going to cost us. I still had no intuitive feel for the value of the money in my pocket. I could tell you exactly how far a threepenny bit would stretch on the quays of Cork. But these strange green bits of paper? A clerk could ask me for triple the amount something was worth; I would know no better. I fingered the notes, wondering how many I would have to part with for lunch.

The cart moved down the line. A boy perhaps a year or two older than I was stacked a piece of pickled herring on a thick cut of white bread, and handed it to a red-haired immigrant who tipped his cap and took it. The immigrant stuffed his free hand in his pocket and pulled out a copper coin.

"No charge for food," the boy said slowly. "Do you understand? No charge for food."

The man grinned. "Aye, Yank," he said. "Ye talk a bit queer, but I understand you just fine."

The boy blushed. "Most of the people who come through here . . . ," he said. The man shifted his bread to his left hand, and extended his right. The boy took it.

"Ye talk a bit queer," the man said, "but I was never a one to hold that against a man offering me free food. I thank ye." The boy nodded.

We collected our bread and herring and a cup of coffee and leaned against the railing to eat. The bread was softer than I was used to, the herring tart and pungent, unlike anything I'd ever eaten before. I wondered if this was what all Americans ate.

Beside me Tom took a bite, and screwed up his face as he swallowed.

"You don't like it?" I asked. Tom coughed heavily, too heavily to talk. "I wouldn't like it every day," I said, trying to mask my concern at the sound of Tom's chest. "But it's food sure enough." Tom stroked his throat. "Still sore?"

He nodded. "Worse," he said.

"Maybe some coffee will make it feel better," I said. He handed me his bread, and took the coffee cup from the ledge under the rail.

"If you want my bread," he said, "I can do without."

"One piece is fine for me," I said, biting into my slice while holding his in the other hand.

"Just the same," he said, "why don't you eat mine anyway?" He sipped slowly at his coffee. "Stronger than tea," he said. "Feels good on my throat."

"Remind me to look at your throat when we get a free moment," I said. He nodded. I could see the worry on his face.

* * *

We had no more finished the coffee when the entrance doors opened and a half dozen men strode out. They were dressed in navy uniforms and flat navy caps with shiny brims. One of them paused to chock the door open. Another dropped a stack of papers onto a high desk, which he then maneuvered to a place just inside the doorstep. A third, picking his teeth with a small stick, made his way past the line to the dock.

"Manifest number twenty-four," the man at the desk called out, and three others fanned out into the crowd asking to see inspection cards. We were herded into a straight line beneath the awning. The groupers wasted few words, but rather checked our inspection cards and pointed, giving our elbows a bit of a nudge if we were slow. We took our place, and inched forward with the rest toward the great front doors.

When it was our turn, we paused before the desk. On it was a stack of tags and a box of safety pins. The inspector behind the desk took our cards and ran his finger down a list.

"Keane," he said.

"We are, sir," I said.

The man nodded, wrote something on a few tags, then handed back our inspection cards. Another official stepped forward. Grasping a pinch of my shirtwaist, he pinned one of the white tags to my shoulder. It was white with

"Manifest Sheet No." printed on it in black, and a large red "24" stamped below that. Beneath was my name written in a fair hand. As I inspected it, he tied a similar tag to the shoonaun and pinned still another on Tom.

"Don't take this card off," the official said smiling at us.

"We won't, sir," I said.

"We won't, sir," Tom echoed.

"Good lad," the man in the navy suit said and turned to tag the next passenger. The line inched forward.

"Please proceed to the baggage room," another official called out from the main entrance. He waved us into a large room. "Please check your baggage at the baggage room." The line moved haltingly forward.

We'd passed the first hurdle easily enough. We were inside.

Twenty-Four

The baggage room was a high-ceilinged room, a huge warehouse of a room lined on either side with great stacks of bags. Baskets and sacks sat atop suitcases, which sat atop trunks, some of them big enough for both of us to climb into. Some of the bags were locked with great, heavy locks. Others were tied shut with rope. All around us people milled and grouped and lined up, and milled some more. The noise bounced off the walls, a steady din of voices, and bags scraping the floor, and officials shouting commands. I scanned the room looking for Mick. I saw a number of boys his size, but none of them were Mick. Then I realized I was also scanning for Colum. So I hadn't given up on him entirely, then. The thought surprised me a little, but no more than the surprise surprised me.

"Leave your basket here," a man shouted at us, reaching for the handle. His booming voice went off like a bomb just over my right shoulder. I jumped.

"It has all of our things in it," I heard Tom say behind me. He reached for the basket, his hand colliding with my own and that of the official.

"You'll get it back," the man said, loudly enough to be heard over the din.

"It has our money, and all our things in it," I replied. "We'd like to keep it with us, please."

"You are not allowed to keep your baggage with you," the man said. "You must leave it here."

I looked at Tom. It was true we had next to nothing. But without the shoonaun we would have nothing entirely. The distinction between the two suddenly seemed huge.

"Your name and manifest number is on your bag," the man said, pointing to the card tied to the basket's handle. He leaned in, but still had to talk loudly to be heard. "It's the same information as you have pinned to you. When you want to reclaim your bag, you show your tag to an official, and he will give you the basket."

"May we take a few things out first?" I asked, my voice straining to be heard. It seemed nothing in comparison to the booming voice of the baggage man, who was undoubtedly selected for the job because of is ability to make himself heard over the constant din.

"Be quick," said the man, turning to the next person in line.

Together we muscled the shoonaun out of line, barely out of line, to a place we could open it with less fear of being trampled. The official was reaching out to the next family in line. I undid the laces, and opened the lining to expose the contents. Everything lay in a pile at the bottom. Everything we owned lay there in that small basket. Tom and I knelt beside it and removed the coats and jackets that lay atop everything else—a couple of books, the dog Da had carved Mick, Tom's whistle, our old clothes, which looked no more than rags now that we had been wearing respectable clothing for a week or so. It wasn't much.

As I rummaged, bent double, nearly up to my shoulders in the basket, I suddenly felt a knee push up against my shoulder. I looked up just in time to see the official with the loud voice stumble backward. He tripped over his feet trying not to trample us, and landed in a pile a foot or two away.

"Try to take my bag," a man shouted. "I'll bloody your nose if you try." That bit of the crowd nearest the incident hushed for the briefest moment.

The official scrambled to his feet, shooting us a dirty look before turning his attention back to the loud man.

"You may not carry your bag through registration," the official said with forced calmness. He approached the angry man who stood defiantly in front of his trunk and his family. His wife laid a hand on his shoulder. Tom stood, took me by the elbow, and pulled me up. Then he took a step forward, placing himself between me and the angry man. I smiled despite myself. The gesture struck me as something Mick might do. I laid a hand on his shoulder.

"You're not taking it," the man said.

"You won't be able to carry it through the inspection line," the official said calmly. "It's too big. It won't fit through the gate even if you were allowed to carry it, which you aren't."

The man took a step forward, his hands balled into fists at his side. The official waved over a pair of guards with nightsticks.

"Wallace." A woman, probably his wife, spoke the name, and it called him up short. "Wallace, it will be fine."

"My mother's jewelry is in there," he responded it in a strained voice, perhaps a bit louder than he intended. "And the plate your grandmother gave you."

"I know," she said. "But if you make trouble, we'll likely be carrying your mother's jewelry and my grandmother's plate back on to the boat. Would you like that?"

The man's shoulders sagged, but his fists remained clenched.

"This ticket will remain on the trunk until you yourself remove it," the official said. "No one but you will be able to claim it." The man continued to hold his ground. The guards removed their truncheons from their holsters.

"Stand aside, Wallace," the woman said, stepping around her man. She locked eyes with first the guards, then the official. "These are honest men. They have the look of it about them." She moved to stand before the official who took a step back despite himself. "And as honest men they know that God takes a dim view of anyone who would steal from the poor." She looked hard into the official's eyes.

"Yes, ma'am," he said. "We do know that."

She nodded and taking her husband's elbow moved him away from the trunk. The official dragged the trunk over to a pile. The man unclenched his fists and stuffed his hands into the pockets of his jacket. Then muttering something inaudible, he turned to follow his wife. The baggage man rolled his shoulders and adjusted suspenders, then turned his attention to the next immigrant.

I watched him for a moment, to assure myself that the excitement was over, then bent again over the shoonaun open on the floor. The pile of things inside seemed so small, so insignificant. But they were all we had, everything we owned in the world.

"We should take only the things we might need," I said. "I don't want my arms full in a crowd like this."

"I want my books, then," Tom said, then coughed, his face screwing up in pain. The coffee hadn't helped him much then.

"You don't need your books," I replied.

"What if they ask a question about America?" he said. "I might be able to find the answer in the books."

It was a flimsy explanation. I knew the real reason was that he couldn't bear to part with something that important to him. I handed the smaller of the two books to him.

"And my whistle," he said, stretching out his hand.

"Leave the book, then," I said. He handed the book back and peered over the lip of the shoonaun searching for the whistle. I found it and handed it to him. He dropped it into his trousers pocket. The top few inches stuck out at an awkward angle.

"We need to take the coat, too," Tom said. I nodded and handed him the coat, wadded into a bundle. Tom straightened it out a bit, then taking the whistle from his trousers pocket, stowed it in the inside pocket of the coat. It wasn't as though we would need the coat, not in this heat. But I don't think either of us could bear to be apart from it. Tom held the coat to his nose. I knew what he was doing. He was trying to catch a scent of home, of Mama, of Ireland.

"And the money and the telegram from Uncle Ronan," I added, opening the secret pocket. There was Mama's ring. I'd almost forgotten about it. I slipped it onto my finger and snuck out the small wad of notes. I looked around. Nobody seemed to be paying any attention, but the crowd, the noise, the foreign-looking faces all made me uneasy. I pulled a five-dollar note off the pile and tugged Tom's shirtsleeve a bit.

"Put this deep in your trouser pocket, I said. "I don't like the idea of having all our money in the same place." Tom looked both ways, then snatched up the note and stuffed it into his pocket. Twisting around, so I could see better, I picked the strings to the secret pocket in my skirt, untied them, and added the wad of notes to the money already in there. I snugged the strings tight and tied them in a tight square knot. If we lost that money, we would be stranded with no fare for the train, not even any money for food. I patted the small bump, pressing it into my thigh, reassuring myself that it was secure.

"Can we leave the rest?" I asked.

"It's too hot for jackets," Tom said. "Leave the rest."

I tightened the strings of the shoonaun. Tom lifted it and handed it to the official who stacked it with the rest. I fingered the ring on my right hand, draped Da's coat over my left arm, and thus fortified, set out to meet whatever Ellis Island had in store for us.

* * *

"Follow the line up the stairs," yet another official shouted from his place over by the wall. His voice could barely be heard over the din. "Follow the line up the stairs. Be sure you have your manifest cards pinned to the front of your garment." He then shouted something in a foreign language, Irish I think. The words were different, but the tone was the same—businesslike, perfunctory. His voice pushed its way over the top of men shouting, feet shuffling, women in shrill arguments. I kept a hand on Tom's shoulder in front of me. Behind me I could feel the press of the crowd on my very heels.

"Right this way, little lady." Another man in a blue jacket, shouted as he motioned me toward a long staircase, teeming with people, all of them going upstairs, none going down. His directions were hardly necessary. Trying to go anywhere but the staircase would have been like swimming upstream against an irresistible current. We shuffled forward, carried along by the steady push behind us.

A minute or so later we were finally in position where we could see directly up the stairway. On either side inspectors in blue uniforms gazed at each of the people who passed. One by one, they looked them up and down, pulling the occasional person aside to mark something on their jacket or dress. I scanned the line. Suddenly my eyes came to rest on a man in a puffy white suit. A doctor. They were the medical inspectors.

"Wait," I said, tightening my hand on Tom's shoulder. "Before we go up there, I want to see something." I took Tom by the hand and pulled him out of the line, over to the side, trying to get out of the push of the crowd. My heart was pounding.

"Let me see you, Tom," I said, bending down in front of him. He looked at me, his face a question. I handed him the coat. "You have something in your eye," I said, pulling out my handkerchief. I licked a clean spot and dabbed at the corner of his eyes. They were still a little bloodshot, slightly swollen, with tiny clots of shraums clinging to the lids. I worked them loose, and smoothed the eyelids straight. Tom's face was still warm, almost hot, to the touch. So it hadn't only been the ferry. It really was a fever.

"How do you feel?" I asked.

"I'll do," he replied. I frowned at him. "Not so good," he said. "Weak."

"Do your eyes hurt?"

"A little, but my throat hurts more," he answered.

"Let me see," I said.

He opened his mouth. Around me I scanned for blue uniforms. I grasped his shoulders and angled him so I could see in the light from one of the large windows. His throat was red, covered with tiny white spots. A shiver seized me, shot through my body. It looked bad. Unmistakably bad. I knew he wouldn't pass a close inspection.

I stood and took Tom by the shoulders. "If anyone asks you how you feel," I said, "you tell them you feel fine."

"I feel fine," Tom repeated, trying the lie on for size.

I nodded.

"It's a lie," he said unnecessarily. "I'd be lying to a guard, to an American guard."

"I think we have to," I said.

Tom nodded. His forehead was creased. He understood what was at stake. I had kind of hoped that he didn't. It might have been easier on him. But he understood.

"Let's have this done with," he said. "Can you carry the coat and my whistle?" I nodded, took our things from him, put an arm around his shoulders, and together we joined the line that led up the grand stairway.

Inspectors, arms crossed on their chests, looked up and down as we passed between them. None touched us with the chalk. I breathed a sigh of relief as my foot landed on the top stair. One more hurdle crossed.

* * *

At the top of the stairway, the crowd split into several queues. Each queue had it's own fenced off-chute that channeled it into the back half of the room. I quickly scanned our surroundings. A huge room it was, but without a single pillar in its center. Its floor was covered by a maze of rails and chain link fences, like cages, pens for animals. I would never be able to make my way to the center of it to meet Mick. A tremor of panic rolled through me. With all my heart I wished Mick were with us.

"This way." An inspector grasped my elbow and directed us to one of the chutes. Its wire mesh sides were almost as tall as I was. I made my way through the metal gate, Tom in front of me. Almost immediately we stood before the first of the inspectors.

"Turn this way," he said." I turned to face him. He looked into my eyes and waved me on to the next inspector.

I looked at Tom. The inspector had his hands on Tom's face, and was looking into his eyes. He took a piece of blue chalk from his pocket and marked Tom's shirt with a large blue C, then motioned him to the next inspector. The next inspector looked him up and down.

"I feel fine," said Tom. His voice shook slightly. The inspector smiled.

"That's good, boy," he said and motioned him down the line.

"C," I thought. "What could C mean? C for child. C for Clare. C for cargo." What could C stand for?

Tom edged up beside me. "C for consumption?" he whispered in my ear. The blood drained from my face and I reached out for the metal rail. I looked at Tom. In his eyes were the same fear that was washing over me.

* * *

At the end of the chute, the immigrants spilled out before the final health inspectors, the eye men.

"It's the button hook men," Tom whispered.

"I know," I said.

"It can't be that bad," Tom said. " Look at that man." He pointed to a small man with a large bushy black mustache who had just finished being inspected.

"He's fine." The man stepped into the exit chute rubbing his eyes. "Don't worry," Tom said. It was too late for advice like that. I was already about as worried a body could get. I nearly told him so, but then thought better of it.

An inspector waved Tom to him. Another further away motioned to me. I walked over, stood before him.

"Look at me," he said, lifting my chin with his hand. I turned to try to get a glimpse of Tom. "Look at *me*," he said again.

"Do I have to?" I looked at the hook he held in his hand, close, too close to my face.

"You have to," the man said smiling. His accent was that of a Munster man. It surprised me to hear my own accent coming from the lips of this obvious American. "We have to check for the trachoma and the favus. We can't have a country full of blind, bald Americans now can we?" He seemed like a nice man, despite the hook he wielded.

"Just relax," he said as he reached out a hand, grasped my eyelashes, and rolled the lid of my eye back over the buttonhook. "That one looks good," he said, and grasped the lid of the second. "Good," he said. "Now tip your head forward." I looked down at the floor. The inspector parted my hair with something hard, searching my scalp systematically. "Good," he said. "You're fine, lass."

"Thank you," I said, looking over to the station where Tom had been. He wasn't there. I ran my eyes down the exit chute but I couldn't see much around all the people. "He's probably waiting at the next checkpoint," I thought.

"Inspection card," an official seated at a table at head of the exit chute said. Still scanning I handed it to him. He stamped it. "Next," he said.

"Beg your pardon, sir," I said. "I'm looking for my brother. He seems to be lost."

"He can't get far," the inspector said. "He's either made his way into the registry lines or he's in detention. Those are the only two places. Next."

A herder took me by the elbow and herded me into the front half of the registry room. The panic inside me crowded out everything else, the smells, the heat, the noise. Suddenly, none of it mattered. The only thing that mattered was that I was in a foreign country and I was utterly alone.

* * *

Once I reached the front half of the registry hall—and I could hardly reach any place else given the cage that flanked the walkway—still another grouper came up behind me, took me by my now-well-used elbow, and spun me around so he could see the tag pined to my shirt waist. "Sheet 24," he said. "Row six." He steered me to one of the mesh-lined pens. Tom wasn't there. Neither was Mick.

"My brothers," I said. "I need to find them." My voice was shaking.

"Row six," he said, nudging me through the gate.

"My brothers," I said, stepping out of the pen. The panic was rising in me. I scanned the adjacent rows frantically but caught no sign of either of the boys there either. I made my way out of the row. Tom wasn't there. He had to be in detention.

"I need to find detention," I said to the herder.

"You need to wait here," the herder replied, again taking me by the elbow.

"You don't understand," I said. "My brothers. They're younger. I need to find the central pillar." I realized I wasn't making much sense, but the panic was getting tangled up in my words, keeping them from coming out straight. I tried to push it down. "My brothers went missing," I finally said.

"Probably in that cage." The voice came from behind me. A comforting voice with a Cork accent. "That's where they put the ones who didn't make it." I turned. He pointed in the general direction of the back corner not far from the eye men. I couldn't see anything for all the bodies between me and it. "Poor blighters," the man muttered.

I climbed up on the bench that ran the length of row six and tried to see back into the shadowy back corner. The bench wasn't enough. I could see the cage, could see the taller people in it. But I needed a few more inches to be able to see someone Tom's height. I grabbed at the tall metal pole that held the row number. If I could only hoist myself up a bit. My hands were sweaty, though, and slipped. I kicked at the pole in frustration and tried again to climb only a bit higher.

"Looks like you got a loony on your row, Masters." The grouper came up and loosened my hands from the pole. I brushed him away and tried again to make the climb. "Want me to run her over to the head-check room?"

"Come down from there now, girl," the grouper said sharply. "You can't be climbing that."

"I'm not coming down until I see my brother," I replied. It was a knee-jerk answer and I thought better of it almost immediately. The tears started to fall. The two men were grabbing at me. I swatted at the one trying to loosen their hands. I only wanted to be able to check the detention pen. That's all I wanted. I only wanted to find my brothers. They didn't have to go grabbing at me.

"Come down, I said, or I'll have to have you arrested," the herder grabbed me by the elbow.

"Couldn't you take me to see my brother?" I asked, letting go of the pole and stepping down from the bench. The herder marked an X on my shirtwaist with blue chalk.

"The doctors are supposed to do that," Masters said.

"But they didn't, now, did they?" the herder replied. "I'll save them the trouble. Do you want to take her over or should I?"

"Go ahead," Masters said. I'll need to bring these lot over to the desk rows soon enough."

"Come with me," the grouper said, digging his fingers deep into my elbow. I twisted with the pain of it.

"I'm sorry about climbing on the benches, sir," I said. After lecturing Tom on good behavior, how was I to justify that I was the one being hauled into detention for being cheeky beyond my station?

"Be a good little loony and I'll ease up a bit, all right?" I nodded and relaxed. "That's good," he said and began hustling me toward a detention pen. Tom wasn't in it.

* * *

They sat along the back of the room on six rows of pew-like benches. I took my place among them: women sobbing quietly, men staring blankly into space, and a boy about my age who sucked loudly on his two center fingers. The window was open, and through it blew a hot, wet breeze from off the harbor. We sat, sweat dripping off us, inspection cards clutched in our clammy hands. A grouper pulled the leftmost person in our row off the bench. We all shifted down and still another grouper—Ellis Island seemed to have no shortage of men whose sole job was pushing immigrants through chutes—added another body to the right end.

Each person pulled off the bench was led to one of four tables clustered in the center of the room. Over each of the tables bent an inspector, an immigrant, sometimes a translator. They looked very interested in something, though from the benches, I couldn't see what it was. The grouper pulled the boy to my left off the bench, and I slid to the end.

I picked at the manifest number pinned to my dress, stared at the number. I was restless, couldn't stand sitting, couldn't seem to keep my hand quiet. I kept running it through my mind. Tom—he was there beside me; then he was gone. Surely they would tell us if they planned to deport him. If they could find us. How were they to know Mick was his brother with the difference in manifest numbers? And how were they going to find me, stuck here in this room, out of sight, out of earshot. I looked back at the door I'd come in through. A uniformed man—a large, burly uniformed man—stood square in the middle of it. So much for sneaking out while no one was looking. The only way out, it seemed, was the official way, and God only knew what that entailed.

An immigrant at one of the tables stood. His chair made a loud scraping noise against the floor, and everyone looked up. A guard took him by the elbow and led him out the door at the far end of the room. The grouper standing beside me put a hand on my shoulder and motioned for me to stand. I did, and he led me to the open table.

"Inspection card," the inspector said, motioning at the now soggy piece of paper clutched in my hand. I handed it to him. He smoothed it out on the table. "English or Irish?" he asked.

"Irish," I said. The inspector motioned for one of the men lined up on high stools under the windows. The man made his way to the table and sat in the empty chair beside me. His suit jacket was draped over his arm, and I could see on it a bright gold badge. Guard, I thought, or whatever the American equivalent was. Maybe I was in trouble for climbing the pole in the great hall.

"Name?" the inspector said.

The guard looked at me and said something in a language I didn't understand.

"Do you want my name or his?" I asked the inspector.

"You speak English?" the inspector said.

"I do, sir," I said.

"Then why did you say you speak Irish?"

"I never did, sir," I said. "I'm sorry, sir," I added, figuring when something went wrong in the presence of one's betters, it never hurt to apologize.

"Pftt," the inspector blew through his teeth in disgust and waved off the man with the badge. "Name," he said.

"Clare Elizabeth Keane," I said.

"Occupation?"

"Servant, sir," I said.

"Well, then, Miss Keane, let me ask you a few questions." I nodded. "Can you count from one to twenty?"

"I can, sir."

"Please do so," he said. I did. I then counted from twenty to one and told him all the months of the year in order. I was beginning to think this was not about the little infraction at the pole.

"Now, Miss Keane, if you were cleaning a flight of stairs for your employer here in America, would you clean them from the top down, or from the bottom up."

"I don't have an employer here yet, sir," I said.

"Of course you don't, but let's imagine, nonetheless, that a few months down the line you find a job as a general maid and are cleaning a flight of stairs. Will you clean them from the top down or the bottom up?"

"Well I hoped I could find work as a cook's assistant," I said, "if I go into service. I might want to try my hand at something else."

The inspector sighed. "Your own stairs, then girl. I don't care whose stairs they are or how you come to be cleaning them, I just want to know how you would clean them."

"Well, I suppose I'd use a bit of black soap and a brush and I start at the top and I work my way down from there," I said.

"All right, then," the inspector said, "was that so difficult?"

I wasn't sure what he was asking, so I held my tongue. He then reached under the desk and pulled out a wooden box, a puzzle it was, with a star, a circle, a square and a rectangle that all fit in their own slots in the box. He dumped out the pieces on the table and asked me to put them back in place. I did so.

"Good," the inspector said. He once again smoothed out my inspection card on the table and wrote something in one of the boxes. He handed it to me along with a small grey card, and motioned for one of the groupers. And that was that. I was herded past the guard and back into the pandemonium of the great hall.

It was only later that I discovered I'd been at that moment pronounced sane. I think back on the anxiety welling inside me, the confusion, the feeling of utter rootlessness. I suppose sanity is a relative term.

* * *

It took a bit of doing, but eventually I was sorted into a pen with still more worry-bent women, still more men staring into space. This pen was for relatives of people who had been taken for medical examination. I sat, squeezed shoulder to shoulder with a woman in a bright red and orange striped dress. The dress was worn, as was the bundle at her feet, but she herself sat with dignity, straight, tall, with the tears on her cheeks running straight down the clean planes of her face. I took a deep breath, determined the tears would not be contagious, and pulled myself up to sit just as straight and proud as she was. She felt the change in posture and looked over at me. She smiled sadly. I smiled back.

"Clare." I heard the voice from behind me. It was Mick. Even over the din of the hall I could tell it was Mick. I stood and turned. There he was, two rows behind me in the same pen.

"Mick," I said, craning my neck around. "Are you all right?"

"I'm fine," he said. "They took Tom."

The tears I had been trying so hard to hold back started working their way out. "I know," I said, my throat tight.

"Stay there," Mick said. "I'll come to you."

Relief at finding Mick. Worry over Tom. The heat. The crowds. The tears I'd been fighting began spilling over. I pawed at them with the back of my hand. The woman beside me leaned forward. She pulled a handkerchief from her bundle and handed to me. She said something in an odd language, one filled with flips and trills of the tongue. Looking into her eyes, I only shrugged. She looked back at me. For the moment her tears had stopped.

"Thank you," I said, dabbing at my eyes. She answered. I had no idea what she said. Oddly enough, that was not a problem.

* * *

The door at the end of our pen opened now and then. Men and boys stepped out adjusting their suspenders, tightening the knot of their ties. Each came out the door, then paused to scan the room for familiar faces. Among those waiting in the pen, every head would look up and swivel each time someone came out. Then when we saw it was not our loved-one, we would sink back onto the bench to wait some more. Packed in as we were, it was almost as though we inflated and deflated as a group, as one large beast. I don't know how long Mick and I sat, our eyes on the door—hours, maybe. It seemed like days. I needed to use the toilet, but I didn't dare ask for fear I would miss Tom when he came out.

From the front of the row, an official called out a name and a number. Nobody responded, and the official began to comb the hall, looking at tags. Some of the immigrants had removed their jackets, and the inspector had to repin the tags to their shirts. The sun was beginning to dip toward the horizon, but the temperature showed no signs of dropping in the muggy Great Hall. All around me folks were shedding—jackets, shawls, some even extra layers of clothing they'd put on because wearing them was easier than carrying them in a bundle. The floor between the benches was thick with it. Da's coat sat heavily atop my feet. I reached down to check that Tom's whistle was still in the pocket. It was. Together we sat, shoulder tight against shoulder, and we sweated. I listened for someone to call "Keane" but no one did.

All around me were people. Some of them could have been neighbors back in Cork. Most of them were obviously not Irish. In the detention cage a small man with a sharp hump on the back of his left shoulder talked to a dark-haired four-year-old whose nose streamed with a dirty-colored matter. Some of the caged immigrants didn't look at all sick to me. But all of them stood, self-consciously marked with Es, and Ns, and Cs, waiting to be pulled from the cage and herded through the door at the end of the hall. Mick sat beside me, head in his hands. For a little while I think he might have even slept, miraculous as that seemed.

I squeezed my legs together, glanced across the room to the sign that said Ladies. The official called out "Malcolm McBride. Robert Atkinson. Michael Dunn. Thomas Keane."

I jumped to my feet. The woman in the red and orange dress startled beside me, then smiled and laid a hand on my arm. She said something in a language I didn't recognize. I smiled back. I worked my way to the end of the row, Mick on my heels.

"Do you speak English?" the official asked.

"I do, sir," I said.

"And you're with Thomas Joseph Keane, Cunard line, manifest number twenty-four?"

"We are," Mick and I said together.

"Thomas has been transferred to the hospital island," the official said. "He has an infection and will need to be treated."

"He's not going to be deported, is he?" Mick blurted the question out. It was as though it had been bottled up so tightly inside him for so long that he couldn't have held it in a second longer if his life depended on it.

"I can't really say," the official said. I must have whimpered, at least the small moan I felt on my chest seemed to come from my own throat. The official squatted down beside us and laid a hand on Mick's arm. He was a kind-looking man, or so I saw once I got a good look at him. I could picture him with children of his own.

"Right now," the official said, "all we know is that he was taken to the hospital. The doctors there will do everything they can for him. In the meantime, you will be staying here as our guests." His eyes were soft, small reassurance, but even that was welcome. "Harris," he called rising to his feet again. "Take these two to the detention room."

Twenty-Five

Harris steered us first to the toilets, then to a second set of stairs.

"Come on," he said, motioning up the stairs. "I'm going to do something for you two I don't do for just anybody."

"Thank you," I said without a clue what he was talking about.

"No problem," he said. "I have two kids about your age. My boy is fifteen and my little girl eleven. The boy wants to be Mayor of New York when he grows up. Can you imagine that? What do you want to be, boy?"

"I'm not sure, sir," Mick said.

"'S okay," Harris said. "You don't have to know yet." We were only halfway up the stairs, and he was already puffing. Harris may have had an English name, but he had the physique of a well-fed American. "Stay in school, though. Be sure you get all the education you can." He exhaled hard and drew in a deep breath. "My grandfather. Came from England. Sheep farmer. Not much schooling. Came to America. And spent the rest of his life with a shovel in his hands. Father laid bricks. Me? They made me finish high school, and now look at me. Got a good job. Make at three times what my father did." We reached the top of the stairs. Harris rummaged in his pocket, took off his cap and ran a handkerchief over his brow. "Hot enough to melt a bloke's hair right off his head," he said. "Like breathing split pea soup. Even hotter up here, I'm afraid." He took another deep breath.

I peered over the rail at the top of the stairs, past the huge American flag that hung out over the edge. We stood on the balcony that wound its way all the way around the room we'd just been in. Below us the great registry hall teamed, almost as though it were itself alive. Between the patchwork of rails, hundreds, maybe thousands, of people shifted, moved, waited, shouted to make themselves heard.

"Anyway, like I was saying, my grandfather spent his life in ditches. But he saw that my father finished eighth grade. And my father got a good job as a mason. He helped build the bridge, you know."

"What bridge is that, sir?" Mick asked.

"What do you mean, 'what bridge?' *The* bridge. The Brooklyn Bridge." He paused for a moment to look down over the balcony rail. "It gets more crowded every year," he said and shook his head. "People know a good thing when they see it. You mean to tell me you've never heard of the Brooklyn Bridge?"

Mick shook his head.

"Hmmph," he said, "you must really be from the sticks. The Brooklyn Bridge is one of the great wonders of the world. My father took me to see it the day it was opened. We walked out on the road—the bridge road—climbed and climbed, then once we got to the top, I looked out, and there was New York, all of it. Can you imagine? I'd never seen such a thing in my life. I'd never been so high in my life. And I thought, 'my father helped build this bridge.' A man can take pride in something like that."

Harris opened one of the doors and motioned us through. We entered a long narrow room, crisscrossed, as was most of the island, with iron rails and poles. The sound of clanking chains stopped as we entered.

"Ain't you finished yet?" Harris demanded.

"No, sir," a young man in navy work clothes answered. "Johnson flushed out a rat. So we checked out that hole we patched up last week, and sure enough the little buggers had chewed through again. So we walled it up, this time with a piece of metal we found down in storage. Let's see the buggers chew through that." He grinned a flawless smile at Harris, who glared back.

"And you're telling me it took all four of you to wall up a rat hole?"

"Well, no sir, but,"

"Just finish the bunks, Toohey," Harris said.

"Yes, sir," Toohey said.

He and the other three men went back to unlatching chains, dropping the canvas bunks into position, and relatching the chains so the iron-framed bunks hung in long rows from the lattice of iron poles and rails.

"Are there many rats in here, sir?" I asked.

"Nah," he said. "But if I were you I wouldn't put any food on the floor. In fact, if I were you, I'd take a top bunk, one over by the windows. You might be able to catch a bit of a breeze. I don't think it's going to cool down much tonight."

I looked at the bunks, three of them stacked one on top of each other. The top bunk had to be a good six feet off the ground, almost up to the bottom of the windows that ran along the outside wall. I supposed we could climb that high.

"You do need to see the bridge before you go off to, where did you say, Cincinnati?"

"St. Paul," Mick said.

"St. Paul. My father built that bridge, you know. He died a couple of years ago. But he told me when I was a kid, 'Stay in school. Get an education.' He made me finish high school, and now look at me. I have a good steady job that I don't have to break my back for. I'm not even forty yet and I have twelve men working under me." He raised his voice. "Even if they are lazy, rat-chasing louts who deserve to be put out onto the streets." The men setting up the bunks picked up their pace a bit.

"You can stay here," Harris said, taking out his handkerchief to mop his brow again. "If they tell you that you should be out on the roof with the other detainees, you tell them Harris told you that you could stay. You got it?" We nodded. "Now, I've got to go check on the other rooms. Grab a couple of those top bunks over by the window. The rest will be coming in shortly, and it looks like a crowded night. Grab your bunks while you can."

"Thank you, Mr. Harris," I said.

"'S nothing," he said. "You're good kids. Remind me of my two. Grab those bunks now." He stuffed the handkerchief in his pocket, replaced his cap, and strode of the door.

Mick began climbing up onto a bunk by the window. I gathered up my skirts, and put a foot onto the outside rail of the lowest bunk.

"Wait," Mick said hopping from the bunk straight down to the floor. "Not this one."

"Why not," I said. He craned his neck to look up underneath the bunk and pointed. I grasped the edge of the bunk and leaned under. The smell of ammonia assaulted me as I spotted the faint outlines of a large stain in the olive drab canvas.

"I'd hate to be the poor bugger in the second bunk last night," he said.

"Mick!" I chided him. "Watch your mouth."

"It's a good American word," he said.

"It's vulgar," I replied.

Mick scooted onto the bottom bunk and made his way through to the next row. He climbed easily to the top, and looked out the window. "This one's good," he said. "You can see the ships out in the harbor and a little bit of the city."

"Can you see the bridge?" I asked.

"I don't think so" he said. "Though I can't say I know exactly what I'm looking for."

"Can you see the hospital?"

"I can't," he replied and sat down cross-legged on the bunk, his back against one of the poles.

I gathered my skirts around me and climbed up to sit next to him. "You can take this one," I said patting the bunk on the other side of the pole. He nodded but didn't move.

"What do you think it is?" he asked. "What Tom has. Do you have any idea what it is?"

I shook my head. "I thought it was only a touch of the quinsy. But I wouldn't think they'd put him in the hospital for the quinsy."

"Maybe that's what the C was for, 'quinsy'. Is that how you spell it?" I shrugged. It wasn't a word I had ever spelled. Still, I liked the suggestion. It certainly was a better alternative to consumption. "I suppose it could only stand for the building they took him to, 'hospital C.'" Mick shrugged.

"Maybe it stands for 'contagious.' Maybe they just didn't want him giving the quinsy to all the other people in the hall," he offered.

"C for croup. C for contagious. C for consumption. I don't know," I said.

"C stands for conjunctivitis," Toohey said as he made his way down our row of bunks. He was making a final check to make sure they were all hooked to the poles correctly. "C. Conjunctivitis. Better than Sc for scalp. That's what they put if you have favus. Sc means you get sent back, no questions asked."

"What's conjunctivitis?" I asked.

"Eyes," Toohey said. He paused for a moment to lean against the bunk opposite us. "Red and mucky eyes. I think it's different from trachoma, that other eye disease they're looking for. Why do you ask? Someone got a C on their jacket?"

"Our brother," I said. "They took him to the hospital. Do you know where that is?"

"Sure," Toohey said. "It's the building on the other side of the island, ya know, the little spit of land on your left when you came in on the ferry."

"Can you take us there?" Mick said.

"Only if I want to lose my job," he said. "If they want you on the other side of the island, they take you there. If they haven't taken you there, it's a good bet you could get into a lot of trouble by showing up unannounced. Nah," he said jiggling the bunk he had been leaning on, "I got work to do, or Harris will be coming down on me with both feet again. Sorry."

"'S okay," Mick said, doing a perfect imitation of Harris.

"Did you get your kit yet?" he asked over his shoulder as he made his way back down the row.

"I don't think so," I said. I wasn't sure what a kit might be.

"When the rest start coming in, make sure you get it. It's just soap, a towel, and a blanket, and it's hardly likely you'll need the blanket. But, hey, you're entitled, so why not?"

"Thank you," I said again.

"Sure," he said. He jiggled a few more bunks and nodded to us as he opened the door to leave. "Good luck with your brother," he said.

"Sure," Mick replied.

"'Sure'?" I said when Toohey had stepped out. Mick shrugged.

* * *

The sun was nearly down when the press of immigrants pushed into the room, women and children all of them. It looked like Mick was one of the oldest boys in the room. The women made their way with dispatch to the various bunks, where they dropped their black blanket, soap and towel.

"Mick," I said, "why don't you get the soap while I hold the bunks?" He was lounging on his bunk with his cap over his eyes and his feet propped up on the chains at the end of the frame. "Mick," I said, poking him in the ribs. "We need to get ours before they run out." He sat up, kicked his legs over the edge, and dropped to the floor. I put the coat on his bunk to hold his place.

All around us the bunks were filling up fast. The air was also filling up with the smell of bodies that had been stewing outside in the late afternoon sun. Mr. Harris was right. It was a welcome evening for a window.

* * *

I lost sight of Mick swimming upstream through the crowd to the door where the blankets were being distributed. Very few open bunks were left, but the crowd continued to push in. A small woman in a garish striped skirt and flowered shawl made her way up the next row. She paused for a moment before Mick's bunk, then reached up to remove the coat.

From my side of the bunk, I pounced, landing on the coat with my hands, my knees striking the rail hard. I winced but managed to grasp enough of the fabric to pull the coat out of her hand.

"Beg your pardon," I said, leaning in to be able to see clearly over the side. "This is my brother's bunk. He just went to fetch our blankets."

The woman rattled off something in a sharp, staccato language, then set her blanket on the bunk and began to climb. I scrambled over the rail onto Mick's bunk, and stared the woman in the face. What caught my eyes first was single black hair grew from her chin and a small crop of similar hairs darkening her upper lip. Wisps of black and grey had worked themselves free from the bright blue scarf she had tied tightly around her head. I had never seen anyone who looked remotely like her. Still, I set the coat down on the bed, staking my claim to it.

"This bunk is taken," I said slowly and clearly.

She responded, again in the rat-a-tat language, and swung a leg over the side onto the canvas. Her ample skirts and petticoats swatted me in the face, and a cloud of garlicky air climbed into the bunk with her. I backed away to my bunk, leaving the coat. The woman pointed at the coat and at me.

"The coat is mine, and the bunk is mine," I said, still holding her eyes with mine.

"She doesn't understand," a woman with bright gold hair and a severely pockmarked face said as she rose from the bunk below Mick's. I could see by the way she towered against the bunks that she was a good head taller than the woman next to me. The accent said Ireland, though I couldn't place just where in Ireland. "She sounds like she's Italian, maybe Spanish, either that or a gypsy of some kind. From the look of that skirt, I'd wager gypsy. You wouldn't believe what some of them wear. I know a language she'll understand, though."

The gold-haired woman stepped up on the bottom bunk, and reached for the gypsy. The gypsy now kneeling on all fours atop the bunk, lurched away, but the gold-haired woman managed to snatch a handful of blouse and shawl. She balled up her other hand in a fist, cocked it back to her ear, and aimed it square at the single hair on the gypsy woman's chin.

"This bunk is taken. Do you understand now?" The two remained like that, frozen for a second while the gypsy woman thought things through. The sinews on the gold-haired woman's forearm bulged beneath her rolled up sleeve. Her pockmarked jaw was clenched tight beneath a malevolent smile. I'd never seen a woman do anything like that before—a man, yes, but never a woman. Finally the gypsy slowly lifted her hands in front of her, palms out. She mumbled something, and gently removed the gold-haired woman's fist from her blouse. The gold-haired woman backed off, her fist still cocked, while the other gathered up her blanket and bundle and made her way down from the bunk. When she hit the ground and had backed off a few paces, her demeanor changed. Her open hand clenched, and she shot a quick, jerky gesture, a gesture I had never seen before, but instinctively knew was something highly unflattering.

"I'll bet your Mama taught you that," the gold-haired woman said.

"*Something-something-something* Mama," the woman said. With a movement so quick I nearly missed it, she dropped her bundle and snatched her slipper-like shoe from her foot. Taking a step forward, she brandished it, then repeated the gesture. The gold-haired woman jumped off the bunk with a thud, and the other woman spun and bolted, nearly running down Mick who was just arriving with the blankets.

"Refugee from the lunatic asylum?" Mick said. The gold-haired woman tousled his hair roughly.

"Her only problem was that we Irish take care of our own," the woman said. "Niamh Kane." She extended her hand. Something about her manner said "man," though she was clearly a woman. Her ample bust, if nothing else, announced that fact.

"Mick Keane," Mick replied, shifting the blankets to one arm and taking the offered hand. "My sister Clare."

"Thank you, Mrs. Kane," I said.

"Miss," she said. "Miss Kane. No great matter. Like I said, we Irish take care of our own. Have to," she said, tucking a stray curl back with her ample hand. "It's not like anyone else will."

I was silent, thinking of Mr. Wisely, Mr. Harris, and the woman who had offered me the handkerchief back in the Great Hall. Mick nodded. "Are you here with family?" Mick asked.

"No," Miss Kane said. "I made the trip alone. My man, bless his worthless hide, said he'd be coming straight from Amsterdam, but only between you and me, I'm not holding my breath if you know what I mean."

"Your, um, 'man' is from Amsterdam?" Mick asked.

"Andy? Not bloody likely," the woman said with a snort. "Dublin bred, Dublin born. And it was in Dublin he found himself enough trouble that he had to stow away on a cargo ship bound for Amsterdam. Left me to explain things to the guardai, the worthless clot. I told the buggers I wasn't the woman they were looking for, and that Andy was as innocent as the day he was born, but they didn't believe me, so, well chicks, here I am. Looking for that new life everyone keeps telling about. Who would think the guardai had such long arms? Those American guardai put me in here until I prove I'm not the Niamh Kane the Dublin guardai have a warrant out for. Good time to be born with an Irish tongue, don't you think?" She winked dramatically. "How about you? Are you here with your father, or do you have other family?"

"Clare is my family," Mick said. "Clare and my brother Tom, who's over in the hospital. So tell me, Miss Kane, how do you plan to persuade the officials you aren't the woman they have a warrant for?" I shot him a look. I could scarce believe some of the things Mick would say without thinking.

She laughed. "I do suppose I'll have to think of something before the hearing," she replied. "Otherwise I'll be back on that ship and out on that ocean all over again. And when my Andy gets here, he'll never be able to talk his way out of his own warrant. The worthless lout." Her eyes bore a softness that belied her hard words.

"Mick," I said, "you had best come sit on your bunk before someone else tries to take it from you. Thank you again, Miss Kane."

Miss Kane nodded. She climbed back into her bunk while Mick tossed the blankets up to the one above. I looked out over the milling crowd with what I hoped was a forbidding demeanor. I wasn't anxious to see another display of Miss Kane's communication skills.

"How did you meet her?" Mick asked. "Isn't she something?"

"Later," I whispered.

* * *

The bunks had filled in. Anxious women herded children and muscled bundles through the narrow aisles in the hopes of seeing an opening the others had missed.

Among them was a pale specter of a woman, who shuffled the aisle slowly, her hand on the shoulder of a small girl who walked one step ahead of her. The woman hugged a small bundle with her other arm. Her eyes cast back and forth from bunk to bunk as she made her way down my row. Reaching the end, and seeing every bed full, she paused, scanned me, then scanned the woman in the bunk below me and those occupying the bunks across the aisle. Bending down, she whispered something in the little girl's ear, then, gathering her skirts around her, she sat down on the floor of the aisle, her back to the wall. The girl, who looked to be about four or five, climbed into her lap. The woman held her tight, swaying slightly. Tears began to roll down her cheeks. She looked stunned, like a woman who had reached her limit of new sensations and now could do no more than sit and overflow from the shock of it all.

I lay on the bunk and gingerly peered over the edge. From above I could see the woman's pale yellow hair, braided tightly and looped into coils around the crown of her head. Her tear-shiny cheeks were pressed into the little girl's hair, also pale yellow, also braided, but hanging free over her shoulders. She kissed the back of the girl's head, lightly, gently, over and over again as the tears fell.

"Mick," I said. He was already stretched out again, feet up, blankets and hands behind his head, watching people get settled in the fading light. "Mick, move over. I'm going to share your bunk." He looked at me. I sat up and looked down over the edge.

"Ma'am," I said. The woman didn't look up. "Ma'am." She continued to sway, to hold the little girl. I swung my legs over the edge, twisted, and searched with a toe for the bunk below me.

"Ma'am," I said, reaching the floor and squatting beside her. "If you'd like, you can have my bunk."

She looked up and shook her head. She responded quietly in a language I didn't recognize.

"You," I said pointing to her, "and your little girl," I pointed to the girl, "can have my bunk." I turned looked up and pointed. Mick was directly above me, looking down at us.

"You," I said pointing at her and at the bunk.

"Ja," she said. "Ja, tack." She stood the girl on her feet, rose, and picked up the bundle beside them. "Tack så mycket," she said again.

"Tack så mycket," I repeated after her. Her face lit up in a smile.

"Anna," she said pointing at herself. "Lena." She laid her hand on the girl's shoulder.

"Clare," I said, laying hand on my chest.

"Tack så mycket, Clare," she said, nodding her head slightly.

I made my way around to the other side of the row. There in the bunk below Mick's, Miss Kane lay, her hands behind her neck, shaking her head. I shrugged my shoulders and smiled. She scowled back. Quickly I climbed the bunks and fell in next to Mick. The canvas sagged, and I tumbled over into him. Mick grabbed my elbow to steady me.

The woman was already in the next-door bunk. She looked at Mick, at me, then began shaking her head.

"*Nej*," she said. She pointed at me, at Mick. "*Nej*. No." I wasn't sure what she meant. She pointed again at me, at Mick, then laid her head on her hands and closed her eyes as though sleeping. She opened them, wagged at finger at us. "No," she said.

"I don't think she wants us to sleep in the same bunk," Mick said.

Suddenly I understood. I smiled.

"It's fine," I said. "He's my brother. Brother." I tried to think of a way to pantomime "brother," but came up with nothing. "Look," I said, grabbing Mick's sleeve and hauling him in close. I leaned over and put my face next to his. I pointed to his hair, the same light reddish blond as my own, his mouth, my mouth. Our mother's mouth, I thought. "Brother," I said.

She smiled. "Brother. *Broder*," she said, nodding. "Brother," she tried the word out on her tongue, then nodded. "*Syster*," she said pointing at me.

"*Syster*," I said, trying to mimic the strange pronunciation.

"*Ja*," she said. "*Bra! Syster.*"

"*Syster*?" I said, pointing at the little girl who leaned heavily against her.

"*Nej*," she said. "*Dotter*." He stroked the girl's hair lightly. The girl smiled up at her.

"*Dotter*," I said.

"*Dotter*." She pointed at the girl. "*Moder*." She pointed at herself.

"*Moder*," I repeated.

"*Ja, bra! Bra!*" The woman, her face still streaked with the tears was now beaming brightly at me. Somehow we had created a small island of our two bunks, an island where the noise, the smell, the anxiety didn't seem to make as much difference.

Anna, grasped the small bundle that lay beside her. Picking with her fingernails at the knotted ribbon that held it closed, she opened it and laid it out flat on the bunk between us. Within the dingy outer fabric was a fine linen, embroidered with small, painstaking stitches in a deep blue pattern. Small birds sat on stylized trees. Apples and pears hung on branches with flowers and leaves. It was magnificent work, truly a treasure. I looked up at Anna.

"It's beautiful," I said.

"*Min moder*," she said, pointing at herself. "*Sverige*. In Svee-dan." Her eyes took on a faraway look.

"It's beautiful," I said again. She folded it carefully, wrapped it in its cloth, and retied the ribbon.

"*Moder*?" she said, pointing at Mick and me. She looked around at the adjoining bunks. "*Moder*? *Fader*?"

"Dead," I thought. How would one pantomime something like that? "Dead," I said. She looked into my face. "Dead," I said again, not knowing what else to say. Not much else could be said even if I had the words.

"*Fader*," Mick said, bringing the coat out from behind him and laying it across his knees.

"*Moder*," I said, touching Mama's ring on my middle finger. I looked into her eyes and shook my head. I could feel the old sadness rise again behind my eyes.

Her smile faded and she reached a hand out to touch mine. She said something softly, something vaguely musical, something comforting.

"Ja," I said. "Thank you, Anna. *Tack så mycket.*"

* * *

The moon was nearly full. Its light streamed in the window, fell gently on Mick, on me, on Anna and Lena in the adjacent bunk. The night had added to the crowd of bodies and smells, a new crowd of noises. Beneath us, Miss Kane snored steadily. All around us snores and snorts, moans and sighs mixed with the muffled sounds of people talking quietly or shifting noisily in the muggy air. Mick shifted, rolled onto his side. His feet pushed into my belly, an improvement from where they had been, almost in my face. I rolled over too, tucked my knees into the back of his. The sway bottom of the bunk pushed the two of us together, closer than I would have liked, given the heat. But there was something reassuring about having the physical presence of my brother beside me. I propped myself up on one elbow and studied his face in the moonlight. He was nearly thirteen. His face was still smooth, still beardless, but it had lengthened, had lost the boyish roundness of two years ago. He slept soundly, untroubled by the heat. I laid a hand on his ankle briefly, then lay back down, bunching the blanket into a ball beneath my head.

Beside me Anna lay on her side, Lena curled up in front of her, their bundle sandwiched safely between them. I looked into Lena's face. It was beautiful, innocent. Well, perhaps not completely innocent. One could not make such a journey without leaving some of one's innocence on the other side of the ocean. But still, Lena's sleeping face bore none of the lines, none of the tension of life. She lay secure in her mother's arms, safe in her mother's protection.

How strange it was—Mick beside me as always. But Tom somewhere in an unseen hospital in a still foreign country. I wondered if I would see him again. Where I came from infections and fevers were never innocent. The lanes bred fevers that could turn deadly seemingly overnight. Quickly I banished the thought. Tom will live, I thought hard to myself, willing it to be true. Tom will live, and get better, and the three of us will climb aboard a ferry and leave this island and travel to Minnesota or Washington, or somewhere where we would find people waiting for us.

I pictured Tom lying alone in his bed. Tom alone in a hospital bed. Mama and Papa lying beneath the earth on the other side of a great ocean. And me, lying in a room with a couple hundred strangers who were fleeing from God only knows what. The whispers of two young women on the top bunks just across the aisle drifted through the moonlight. I strained to hear a familiar word, but the unfamiliar syllables fell senselessly like the rustling of leaves on my ears. Despite Mick's knees against mine, despite the press of people all round me, I suddenly felt alone, utterly alone in the world.

I stuffed my hands into the itchy wool of the blanket and bit my lip. The tears—the tears again—came in a rush to my eyes. This time they were not entirely unwelcome. I settled into them. This time they were not tears of sadness exactly, not tears of frustration or anxiety, not even tears of loss—these were tears of "too much." Too much change, too much heat, too much worry, too much foreignness assailing my ears and nose, too much to deal with and no one to turn to for help. The tears made the wool around my eyes itch all the more. I wiped them with the back of my hand, then rolling onto my back held the hand up to see if I could see the tears on it. Instead of tears, there in the moonlight, I saw another hand. It reached out and took mine. Anna stroked the back of my hand, wiping away the tears, then took my fingers gently in her own.

The sleep that had eluded me seemed to travel into my body through her fingers. I rested my hand in hers, and drifted off to sleep, safe in the care of a woman with whom I shared a half a dozen words, and a bond that language could never express.

* * *

The night never cooled. The sticky heat of the previous day clung tenaciously to the walls and ceiling. When the sun rose, it merely warmed over the already sultry air.

Women lowered themselves from the bunks and squeezed past each other on their way to the toilets. Blue-suited officials began stowing the beds, transforming the dormitory into a huge waiting room. Across the aisle one of the two young women who had whispered half the night away curled up on herself, a corner of the blanket shielding her eyes against the sunlight streaming in the window. An official stood beside her, spoke, then nudged her with a billy club. The woman uttered a low word, no better than a growl really. The official nudged her again. I leaned, my back against the wall and watched. The day was starting unlike any other in my entire life.

"Listen up," a loud voice shouted through a megaphone boomed from the doorway. "We will now issue detention cards." We all turned to look. A few, those who could speak English also turned to listen, but from the looks of things, we were in a minority. All around me, women chattered with puzzled looks on their faces.

"I will call your name. When you hear your name, reply by saying 'here,' and raise your hand. You will then receive your detention card. Immigrants will not be allowed into the dining room for breakfast without a valid detention card." A second official took the megaphone and made the announcement in a second language, then a third. The hum of voices continued, nearly drowning out the man's voice despite the megaphone.

"Maggie King," a guard shouted into the crowd.

I pushed myself away from the wall, and strolled toward the door. The aisle was crowded, even with the bunks raised into their daytime position, no more than three people could stand abreast in the aisle. I pushed forward with the crowd and listened.

"Eunice Evans." A woman on my aisle raised her hand and called "here." An official near the door moved sideways along the wall as close as he could to the voice. Then when he could move no further he lifted an arm and tossed a card over the heads of the women. What with the pack of bodies, it would have been impossible for the card to hit the floor. It landed in the crowd then was passed from hand to hand until it reached Eunice.

I lost track of how many women and children received cards before I did. It's hard to say how many people were packed into the large, airless room, but the number was well into the hundreds. After an hour or so of waiting, I finally heard my name called. I raised a hand and shouted "here," and the card came sailing over the top of the crowd, landing no more than two or three hands from me. I clutched it tightly and worked my way to the back wall.

At the top was written: "United States Immigration Service. Ellis Island, New York Harbor. Detention Card," all in crisp gothic letters. Below that was a handwritten bit: "Name: Clare Keane," it said. "Vessel: *Caronia*. Cause of detention: family medical detention, LPC." The LPC was written in large loopy letters, obviously by someone who had scrawled those particular letters time and time again.

Mick was perched atop the folded up bunks, studying his own card. He removed the tag pinned to his shirt and using the point of the pin to puncture the detention card, pinned it with his manifest number back onto his shirt.

"They did say they'd give us breakfast, didn't they?" he asked. I nodded. "I know," he said. "I'd hold they bring the food in here and then just toss it over our heads into the crowd like they did with the cards." He laughed at his own joke. "Raining eggs and bread and tea. I'd be in the middle of it all with my head back and my mouth wide open."

* * *

They fed us in a large dining room with long tables covered with pure white paper. Bread and butter, crackers, milk and coffee, lots of it. We sat on dark wood benches, shoulder to shoulder. And we listened to voices speaking dozens of languages, hundreds of languages it seemed.

Across the table a black man sipped his coffee, clutching the mug tightly in both hands. It may seem strange to anyone who grew up in America, but I, a child of the lanes of Cork, had never seen a Negro before. Most of my neighbors were not only white, they were very white even by Caucasian standards. We were a race of pink-skinned, freckled, pale-haired folk. I found myself shooting surreptitious looks over the top of my breakfast, examining the skin of his hands, which, when he was not drinking, cupped the coffee mug on the table before him. The backs of them were a beautiful chocolate brown color, the edges of the palms creamy, a bit reddish, perhaps from the warm mug. Once I got past the foreignness of it all, I remember thinking what a beautiful color that was for human skin, a richer, deeper color than my own. I wondered if he thought of me as a pale imitation of the people he had left behind.

After breakfast we were chased out onto a flat rooftop, fenced in—like everything else at Ellis Island—with steel rails and wire mesh. The crowd, men and women both, paced and leaned. I spent a large chunk of the time gazing over the top of the ferries coming into the hospital building on the other side of the island. Now and then someone would be wheeled in a wheelchair or on a gurney. Once I saw something that may have been a body being loaded under a sheet onto one of the ferries.

Mostly I thought of Tom, wondered, prayed. And I waited. We ate dinner—beef stew and bread—then waited. Then we ate supper—baked beans and stewed prunes, and we waited some more. All the while, officials were pulling immigrants, one by one, family by family, from the herd. They would wade in among us, call names, check tags. Then someone would gather their things and exit. But all that first day, Mick and I just waited. Waited and wondered and prayed.

* * *

That's what I did my first full day on American soil. On the second, I did much the same. On the third morning, our names were called.

Twenty-Six

We followed obediently — Mick, a half a dozen other people with worried looks on their faces, and I. The grouper led us outside, past the ferries waiting at the dock, past the kitchen and the ferry house bustling with workers, then up the stone steps of the hospital building.

The corridor smelled of strong soap and that vague something that one only smells in hospitals. At the time the smell was a new one — I hadn't been in a hospital before, unless one counted the ship's infirmary. The smell settled into the back of my throat, lingered there, introducing itself. Nurses in white caps and long white aprons hustled through the corridors, ignoring our small herd. From the wards we heard the sounds of low voices punctuated by the occasional moan. Mick reached over and took my hand.

"It's all right," he said. "It's only a hospital." His face was pale.

"I know," I replied. Though I was worried about Tom, the hospital stirred more curiosity in me than fear. For Mick's sake, though, I held his hand tight.

The grouper stopped us in the corridor outside one of the wards. We waited while he disappeared inside for a moment, then returned with a nurse.

"Thomas Keane," the nurse read the name from a clipboard without preamble.

"Yes," I said. "We're here to see Thomas Keane."

"Follow me," she replied. She pulled open one of the double doors, and we followed her into a long room.

All along both walls were child-sized beds, white beds with white metal frames and pristine white sheets and pillows. Head to the window, foot to the aisle, one after another after another, dozens of them — they covered the full length of the room. In the center aisle between the two rows were two more lines of beds, these arrange head to foot, head to foot in tidy ranks. Even in the hospital at Ellis Island, one could not avoid standing, or in this case lying, in lines.

In each bed was a single child, each dressed in an identical white gown. Side-by-side, end-to-end they lay. The hospital was not nearly as packed as the dormitories, but one still got the impression that this island could accommodate more people only if its administration put a boot in and packed us all down.

Several of the children looked up as we entered. I scanned faces looking for Tom. What I saw instead were faces like mine. Thin as death upon a wire, some of them were. Faces showing signs of poor diet and too much worry. Faces holding a scant mouthful of poor teeth. A small boy waved at me as I passed. His head had been shaved, showing yellowish patches of scaly skin. One of the patches crept down his face dangerously close to his left eye. I had seen ringworm before, of course. But somehow in the lanes, set against the backdrop of poverty, and dirt, and dozens of other ailments, it didn't seem as stark as it did here on that tiny shaved head laying on a spotless white pillow case. I waved back, and the boy grinned.

The nurse, without so much as a break in stride, scooped up a bent wood chair from beside one of the beds and carried it with her. Making a crisp left turn, she dropped the chair beside a bed and announced in a voice that would brook no disagreement, "fifteen minutes." It was only then that I noticed that the boy in the bed was Tom.

He was curled up on his side, his back to us. The steadiness of his breathing told us he was asleep. I bent quietly over the bed and looked. His face was pale against the white pillowcase but he seemed whole. I watched his chest rise and fall, rise and fall, reassured by the familiar rhythm of it.

Mick stood for a second at my elbow, then vaulted up onto the bed. The springs bounced beneath his weight.

"Yo, boyo, rouse up now," he said, shaking Tom's shoulder vigorously. "We go to all the trouble of visiting you, and you try to sleep your way though it."

Tom rolled onto his back and opened his eyes. A big smile spread across his face as he woke enough to realize it was us. I laid a hand on his forehead. It was cool. Nonetheless, I lingered there for a moment, then smoothed Tom's hair from his face before withdrawing.

Mick bounced a bit on the bed, then ran a hand over the sheets. "If I knew the hospital was such a fine place to spend the night, I'd fake an illness myself," he said. Tom only smiled back.

"How are you feeling?" I asked.

Tom opened his mouth, and the sound that came out was thin, a little hoarse. "Fine," he said. "A wee bit sore."

"Let me see your throat," I said. Tom swallowed heavily, then opened his mouth. I had expected to see the same swollen tonsils, perhaps the same red streaks and white spots themselves. Instead, I saw two raw patches, deep red with white streaks rising up from them. "Turn," I said, angling Tom so I could get a better look in the light coming in from the window. Where the tonsils had been was now just two angry patches of raw skin.

"They took them out," Tom said in a whisper.

"Your tonsils?" I said.

Tom nodded.

"Let me see," Mick said, hopping off the bed to stand beside me. Tom opened again, and Mick's face went pale. He sat heavily in the chair. "They *cut* them out?" he said. Tom nodded again. "With a knife?" Mick said. Tom nodded again. "Poor bugger," Mick muttered under his breath.

"Mick," I hissed. "That's the last time I want to hear that word." But I felt a bit sorry for Tom myself.

"How did they do it?" Mick said. "Just stick the knife in and . . . "

"Mick," I said, "it hurts him to talk. Can't you see that?"

"It's not so bad," Tom said. "I'd rather talk . . . now that you're here." He latched on to us with his eyes. I could see in them the same relief that I was feeling inside me. It was good that the three of us were together again. It was good.

"So tell," Mick said. "How did they do it?"

Tom smiled. He sat, grasped the pillow, punched it into a ball, and stuffed it behind himself against the bed frame. I scooted Mick over and sat gingerly on half the chair.

"One of the guards brought me here, from the cage in the great hall," he said. "Do you know the one I mean?"

I nodded. "I didn't see you there," I said. "I looked." I didn't mention I had climbed a pole and been labeled a loony in my attempts to get that look.

"I wasn't there long," he said. "They brought me out, took me to a room with a power of doctors and most of the men in nothing but their pelt. And a doctor looked down my throat, then listened to my chest. And he wrote something on my card, then sent me with one of the guards to this place."

"So we'd guessed," Mick said. "I want to hear about the tonsils. Did they use a carving knife, then?" He grinned maliciously at Tom. Tom grinned back.

"They had a big leather chair," he said, "with a cupped rest for my head, and a foot rest for my feet, though my feet didn't quite make it to the foot rest. It was a fine, comfortable chair. The nurse sat me down in it, and put a heavy rubber apron over the front of me. Red, the apron was, and hot as blue blazes. And she dropped some tools into a big pot of water she had boiling over a gas flame on the counter. And we waited there, me in the apron and her with one eye on me and one eye on the tools. I didn't know what was going on, so I asked her. She only said the doctor would explain everything."

Mick leaned in, elbows on the bed. Tom shifted a bit on his pillow, paused for a second, swallowed hard again.

"Are you sure you're good to talk?" I said.

"I'll do," he said.

"He'll do," Mick said, "just let him talk." Tom smiled. He was clearly enjoying being the center of attention.

"The doctor came in with his long white gown and a round mirror strapped to his forehead. He told me to open my mouth, and he held my tongue down with a stick of wood. 'They'll definitely have to come out,' he said to the nurse. Now I didn't know what he meant by 'they.' I thought maybe he meant my teeth, and I have to say that I didn't like that idea one little bit. Doctor or no, I told him as much. Well the doctor only laughed and said he wasn't a dentist; he was a surgeon, and he was going to remove my tonsils, not my teeth. Now I wasn't entirely sure that was any great improvement on the matter, but never having had a tonsil removed, I decided to give him the benefit of the doubt."

Tom gestured toward a glass of water that was sitting on the window sill. I handed it to him. His voice wasn't as raspy as it had been now that it was warming up. But the face he made when he swallowed the water said he was far from comfortable.

"It's worse when my throat's dry," he said. "But it's not as bad as it was. They gave me ice cream to make it feel better, but that itself was no great joy to eat."

"You got ice cream!" Mick said. Tom nodded. We'd heard of ice cream, but where we came from it was a dish for rich folk. The thought of any old laner biding his time in the hospital eating ice cream caused me to revise my estimate of America's riches up one more notch.

"Do you think they'd do my tonsils, too?" Mick said.

"I think you'd be bright not to let them within an arm's length of your tonsils," Tom said, handing me the empty glass. I set it back on the sill. He got a look on his face, just for a moment, that belied the casualness with which he was telling the story. Then the look faded, and he launched back into the tale.

"It was a team effort, you see," he said. The nurse held a curved enamel bowl under my chin. Another man in a white jacket went behind me and laid hands on my shoulders. Then the doctor took a tool from the boiling water, and said simply, 'open your mouth'. Now the tool was about the size and shape of a pencil, but instead of a point, it had a tiny little blade on it, you see. And when I opened my mouth, the doctor dove in with that blade and made two or three little cuts so fast I hardly knew what was happening. The blade likely set off something in the back of my throat because I started gagging, and that brought a rush of blood out my mouth and into the basin. When I looked down, there was a lump of flesh right in the middle of the puddle of blood. Where that lump was in my throat was now only a screaming sore, like the roof of my mouth was on fire."

Mick sat there, his chin propped on his fist, leaning heavily on the bed. He was silent, his eyes wide.

"But you know," Tom said, "that wasn't the worst part."

"It wasn't?" Mick said weakly.

"It wasn't," Tom said. "The worst part was when he asked me to open my mouth again so he could do the second one." He chuckled, then shoved Mick's shoulder so his chin fell off his hands.

"A small thing to go through for ice cream," Mick said casually, but I could see the respect in his eyes.

"It would be a small thing if it were your tonsils and my ice cream," Tom countered.

* * *

And that was my first visit to a hospital. The next day they released Tom to detention. Before breakfast, I was standing at the rail of the "roof garden" watching the boats come in. The dormitory had been so packed that the groupers had opened up the roof earlier than usual. Mick and I had escaped the heat and stench of the interior to await our breakfast chit in the early morning air of the roof. We were straining our eyes, looking out over the bay, following the progress of a liner with Cunard colors, when suddenly I looked over and there was Tom standing beside me, a big smile spreading across his face.

"So they let you go," I said.

"They did," he said. His voice was nearly back to normal.

"That means they'll soon be letting all of us go," Mick said.

"None too soon for me," Tom said.

* * *

The late morning sun from the tall window behind the desk cast a shadow across my lap. As I looked down at my skirt, I could see there the outlines of the three or four wisps of hair the man in the center had combed over his bare pate. The three men at the desk were talking quietly among themselves, shuffling papers, nodding gravely. I couldn't hear them, not clearly at least.

"Please stand," the man in the middle said. We did.

"Protestant or Catholic?" the man said.

"Catholic," I answered.

"How old are you, Miss Keane?"

"Fourteen, sir," I answered.

"Do you know what an oath is?" he asked.

"I do, sir," I answered.

"And you know that if you swear an oath to tell the truth and then lie, you will answer to both God and the United States government."

"I surely do, sir," I said. "I understand."

The man nodded to the official by the door. The official took a crucifix from where it lay next to a Bible on the table, and brought it before me. "Place your right hand on the cross," he said. I did. "Do you swear to tell the truth?"

"I do," I said.

"Be seated," he said. I sat. Beside me Tom and Mick did too, in their eyes something new, a new respect perhaps.

"Miss Keane," the man in the center spoke, "you have been supporting yourself and your two brothers for how long?"

"Since our mother died," I said, then counted quickly on my fingers. "Nearly five months, sir." I glanced up at him tentatively. He looked as though he wanted to smile, but didn't. He sat in his fine grey suit, flanked on either side by stern men in navy blue uniforms. He looked like a man used to bearing the fate of families in his hands.

"You plan to continue to work once you have entered the United States," he said.

"I plan to, yes," I said.

"As a maid?" he asked.

"A maid, yes," I said. "Or perhaps someday when I'm a little older as a cook, or maybe something better." My mind flashed back to the infirmary on the ship, to Rose, the baby. I wanted to say that someday, God willing, I would be a handywoman. The oath, though, prevented me. I knew how to become a maid in America. But a handywoman? For all I knew America had replaced all its handywomen with doctors, and becoming a doctor seemed to be far too much of a stretch even if I hadn't been under oath. For now, the closest thing I could find to the truth was to say that I would be a maid.

"Mmm," he said, flipping through the papers once again.

Tom shifted in his chair beside me. I could see out of the corner of my eye that he was biting at the skin around his thumb. I reached out a hand and placed it on his elbow gently. He looked over at me, thumb between his teeth. I shook my head slightly. He nodded and carefully dropped his hand into his lap.

"You plan to live with Ronan Keane, an uncle, in . . ." he paused. "Minnesota is it?"

"Yes, sir," I said. "Ronan Keane. Minnesota or Wisconsin. We do, sir."

"Mr. Keane has not arrived yet to pick you up," the man said. "The paperwork is in order, and we plan to release you to his custody when he arrives, but so far he has not checked in with the immigration bureau in New York."

"In New York?" I said. "But he's in Minnesota or Wisconsin."

"Near St. Paul," Mick said by way of amendment.

"Well, yes," said the man. "But surely he realized that he had to come here to pick you up?"

"He sent money for train tickets," I said. "From New York to St. Paul. He said to contact him in St. Paul when we arrived."

"Mmm," said the man in the grey suit. He leaned over to whisper something in the ear of the uniformed man next to him. The man nodded gravely. "Always," he said and shook his head.

"Will we be able to contact Ronan Keane at this address in . . . " I ran his finger down the sheet of paper, "Lindstrom, Minnesota?"

"Well, sir," I said, "I think, this address might just work a bit better." I reached in my pocket and drew out the letter from the Cunard Company. "He's in St. Croix Falls this minute."

"St. Croix Falls, Wisconsin," he said, reading the letter quickly. He pronounced it "Saint Croy." I made a mental note. "He didn't know that he needed to pick you up in person? He didn't know that we won't release minors without a proper escort?"

"I suppose he didn't, sir," I said.

"The steamship company in Minneapolis should have informed him," he said. "They didn't?"

"I'm sure I wouldn't know, sir," I said.

He sighed. "No, I suppose you wouldn't. All right, then," he said, "we'll wire him in St. Croix Falls." He nodded to the guard by the door who moved to pull out my chair. I stood.

"So we'll be staying another few days, then?" Mick said.

The man looked up from the notes he was making. "At least that," he said shortly, and returned to his writing.

"And if Uncle Ronan doesn't come for us?" I asked.

"Then you'll be sent back," the man said simply.

We followed the guard out of the room and back to the detention area.

* * *

The bunks in the dormitory had filled long ago. The bunks in the temporary building were also brimming. We clutched the blankets to our chests and made our way through the narrow aisles between them. The temporary building was, if possible, more stifling than the dormitory itself. At least the dormitory had the thick stone walls to hold in whatever coolness the night air bestowed on them. The temporary building was bare board all around, and the wood seemed to sweat with the humidity in the air.

"There's nothing here," Tom said. I didn't reply. The comment was so obvious it didn't really need a reply. Still we continued to shuffle between bunks, between drippy women trying desperately to make themselves comfortable in the canvas bunks. Suddenly, the woman who had been walking the aisle ahead of us stopped. Without so much as a word or a pause, she stopped and sank heavily onto the floor. There she sat, a look of resignation on her face. In front of me, Tom stopped so as to avoid treading on her. I stopped, too. Mick, behind me, bumped into my back, then stopped. I turned and motioned for him to work his way back down the aisle.

The hallway in the main building was not much better. Dozens of sweaty immigrants muscled bundles, looking as we were for a place to spend the night. Others sat on benches, rails, the floor. A uniformed guard stepped up from the stairs, worked his way around two children playing with a kerchief on the landing, then addressed the crowd.

"Ladies and Gentlemen, may I have your attention," he shouted. "Attention please." His words set off a flurry of talking and mumbling in dozens of different languages as those who didn't understand consulted those who might.

"Ladies and Gentlemen," the guard said. "The dormitories are full. Those of you who do not already have a bunk will need to spend the night in the registry room or here in the corridor. If you do not have one, you may still pick up a blanket. In this corridor, women will stay at this end. Men will need to move to the other end outside the men's dormitory." The herders began sifting through the crowd, taking the men by the elbow and nudging them to the other end of the corridor. Another blue-suited man took his place at the head of the stair and began what I can only assume was the same message in some other language.

I myself found a spot by the wall. Mick and Tom, elbowed their way to stand beside me.

"I slept in worse," Mick said.

"I can't say that I'd like to hear about it," I replied.

"Fine," Mick said, "but I did."

I spread my blanket out on the floor, and sat. Mick and Tom did the same. We sat and watched the herders work the crowd. And we watched, the crowd— some restless, some obviously annoyed, most merely resigned as we were— slowly took on some semblance of order, women and children bunched around us, men and older boys further down the hall. A tall, obviously Irish youth, stepped over my outstretched legs on his way to the other end. He reminded me of Colum. And apparently not only me.

"Where do you suppose Colum is by now?" Tom said, reading my mind again.

"I'm sure I wouldn't know," I replied.

"Almost to Washington, I'd hold," Tom said. When I didn't reply, he fell silent.

Once again, as I had for six days now, I found myself scanning the crowd. It was an involuntary response, autonomic almost, as though I had no choice in the matter. Every shock of sandy young hair lifted my heart. Every glimpse of a strange face caused it to plummet again. Colum was gone by now, little doubt of that. He was gone, had boarded a train, was riding the rails west into a land so large I pictured him as nothing more than a tiny speck moving across its face.

That's when the feeling flooded through me. There in the corridor, with legs and ankles milling all about me, I felt it. Utter destitution. I was utterly alone. That hard reality had been held back by my worry for Tom, but now, with my brothers on either side of me, both safe for a time, now the stark knowledge bubbled up and broke the surface. I may never see Colum again. I had met my one love, the man I wanted to spend my life with. But now, with every second, he was steaming his way farther and farther from me.

I leaned back heavily against the wall and saw it all in my mind. Him a speck on the great continent of America. Me a speck on the great ocean, being sent back to Ireland, back to a life of cleaning other people's dust, back to a life where the best I could hope for was sewing sacks instead of cleaning them, marrying a sober husband not a drunk. I could feel it down to the very marrow of me. I would never see him again.

I pulled my knees to my chest, smoothed down my skirts, then sunk my forehead into my folded arms.

"Are you crying?" Tom asked quietly, whispering his still deepened voice into my ear.

"I wish I could," I answered.

* * *

The next two days were uneventful. Days on the roof watching the steady stream of bodies flow into the building. Nights in the corridor. Beans, bread, bananas. Now and then someone would pull out an instrument, others might sing or dance. Saturday it tried to rain, but didn't.

We'd listed to the names being called each morning, each afternoon. But ours was not among them. Not until Monday afternoon.

* * *

The man at the desk was not the same man we had talked to earlier. In fact the desk wasn't the same desk either. This one sat in a small windowless room, and the man at the desk was flanked by one uniformed official and a dour looking woman of about fifty years. The woman wore a simple white shirtwaist and a full navy blue skirt. I suppose it might have been a uniform, or it might just be the dress of a woman far more interested in other matters than she was in clothing. Either way, it was clear that her current interest was us. She followed our entrance into the room with a hard stare. I glanced up at her, then down at the floor again. The guard who brought us in motioned to the chairs, and we sat.

The man in the center shuffled some papers, then spoke. "My name is Henry Burr," he said. "You are Clare Elizabeth Keane, Michael Finbarr Joseph Keane, and Thomas Joseph Patrick Keane?"

"We are," I said. The boys echoed me: "We are."

"I have been assigned to your case," he said, gesturing at the folder full of documents in front of him. "I have here a telegram from one Karl Larson of St. Croix Falls, Wisconsin, and, unfortunately, a warrant for your deportation."

"Deportation?" I said.

"We don't know a Karl Larson," Tom said. Mick just groaned, as though he had been punched in the belly. I knew exactly how he felt.

"We wired Ronan Keane," the center man said. "We were unable to reach him, but received this instead." He handed a telegram across the desk. I rose and reached for it.

"Keane no longer works here," it says. "Went east. Hayward." It was signed Karl Larson, foreman, Eclipse Lumber Company in St. Croix Falls, Wisc.

"Did you try wiring Hayward?" I asked, not sure if it was a person or a place.

The man in the center looked over at the woman. She stood, walked around the desk and put a hand on my shoulder. It was a firm, cold hand, and I wasn't sure if she meant to comfort me or simply to control me should I be on the edge of hysteria or some such thing.

"Clare," she said, taking her hand away and crossing her arms over her ample bosom, "we are not allowed to release children unless we have some evidence that they will not become wards of the state. Do you understand?" I didn't and shook my head. I didn't quite trust my voice given the fiery lump that was rapidly rising in my throat.

She sighed. "Your uncle Ronan has had three addresses in four months. He didn't come to pick you up. He didn't make arrangements for someone else to pick you up. He didn't send you a train ticket, just money, and that not enough to pay for both food and the fare to Minnesota. He didn't even leave a forwarding address so you could find him once you arrived. The only thing we can assume is that he is not a responsible enough individual to assume care for three minors. We cannot allow you to enter the country if you have no one to care for you." Her voice had a softness to it, but her eyes and face were still frozen in a scowl.

"I can care for us," I said. "I can get work. I did back in Cork. I found work all by myself, and I supported us."

The man in the center sighed. "It's not a matter of ability," he said. "It's a matter of law. The law says you are a minor, and you must be released to the custody of a family member or legal guardian. I see no family member. I don't even see a train ticket and address to which you may be sent. I'm afraid we have no choice but to send you back to Ireland."

"A family member?" Mick said. "Can it be any family member?"

"It must be an adult who can prove he has means of support and will take the responsibility for caring for you until your majority." Mr. Burr set down his pen and leaned back in his chair. "Talk to me, son. Do you have another relative who might be able to take you in?"

"Well," Mick said leaning in. "There's Aunt Bridget and her family." I whirled about to glare at him. He silenced me with a look. "Do you have her address, Clare?" he said evenly.

I fumbled in my pocket for the scrap of paper Mrs. Keane had given me aboard ship. I handed it to him, and Mick handed it to Burr. "She more a great aunt by marriage," Mick explained. That's why my sister didn't think of her when you said "relatives."

Burr copied the information onto a fresh form, then handed the paper back to Mick. "We'll get back to you," he said. He looked a little put out.

"Thank you," I said.

"Thank you, sir," the boys echoed.

* * *

I looked around. The waiting room was packed with people talking, napping, amusing themselves with games and music. I grabbed Mick and dragged him through the crowd to the far wall. Again I looked around. The only blue uniforms were near the entrance, but still I couldn't allow myself anything louder than a hoarse whisper.

"What were you thinking, lying like that?" I said, whispering as loud as I could, straight into his ear.

"I didn't take the oath," Mick replied.

"And that means lying is no longer a sin?" I said. "They'll find out and then they'll send us back. As sure as we live they'll send us back."

"Hmm," Mick answered, backing himself away. "And what were my choices? Well now, let's think about that. I could be sent home right away, or I could lie and maybe get in or maybe get caught and be sent back later."

"You can't lie to the United States government," I said.

"It seems I already did," Mick answered.

"If he did, I suppose that means that he can," Tom said astutely, a big grin spreading over his face. "So it seems he can indeed lie to the United State government."

"You just shut your gob, Tom," I said. "It was wrong what he did. Immoral and sinful." The smile vanished.

"Don't you think they'll find out that Mrs. Keane isn't kin?" I turned again on Mick. "And when they do, what do you think they'll do to her, and herself watching out for us like she did?"

"They won't find out," Mick said. "Mrs. Keane will stand with us. I know she will. And if they do find out themselves, I'm the one who lied, not her."

"I'm getting tired to my very bones of your lies and schemes, Michael Keane," I replied. I sank onto one of the benches along the wall. Only then did I realize just how tired I really was. I sank my head into my hands. "Maybe it would be better if they did send us back. Maybe the brothers in the industrial school can do something with you." The tears started welling in my eyes. I cupped my hands around them, elbows on my knees.

Mick sat down next to me and leaned his head back against the wall.

"The fighting, the scheming, the lying, the boys you associate yourself with." I sobbed in spite of myself. "The kiphouse, and the drink, and the money earned God only knows how. The money you gambled away God only knows how. I don't know what to do with you, Mick. I can't do anything with you."

Tom wandered off toward the roof garden, his hands stuffed hard into his pockets. Between my fingers, I could see his feet shuffle away. Mick sighed deeply beside me.

"I feel like I failed you—you, and Tom, and Mama," I paused, realizing once again just how far away Mama was, an ocean away, a life away, an eternity away. "Especially Mama," I said. "We should never have set a foot on that boat. We should be back in Ireland where we belong. Let them take us back. Let the industrial school take you. I can't do anything for you any more."

"But you're a wonderful sister, Clare," he said. It was the same silky tone he'd used on the immigration official only moments before. He touched my shoulder gently. I shrugged it off.

"I'll have no more of your charm, Michael Keane. No more at all. You, and your charm, and your slippery tongue can go to hell." He started, jerked his hand back as though he'd laid it on a hot stove. Then quietly he stood, and left.

* * *

I wasn't sure how long I had been sitting, thinking, dozing, crying. My seat was numb from the hard wood of the bench. I shifted and stretched. Tom, napping on the floor, his arm draped over the bench beside me, woke when he felt me move.

"Mick isn't back?" he asked. I looked around and shook my head.

"Supper soon," he said. Already people were wandering out of the waiting area. I nodded. "We could join the queue," Tom added, "maybe find a seat before they run out." I nodded, unfolded my legs a bit, trying to stretch the ache out of them before rising.

"Are you going to tell them?" he asked. "About Mick and his lie?"

"I think so," I said. "It's the Christian thing to do."

"And they'll send us back," he said.

"I think so."

Tom shifted. I pulled my feet in, and he knelt down before me. His face was tight, but blank. He took my hand in his. "Don't," he said. "Don't tell them."

"I can't lie," I said.

"Don't lie," Tom said. "Just don't tell them."

A woman in a flour sack shawl edged in and took the spot on the bench where Tom's elbow had been. She glanced over at us, watched us out of the corner of her eye, but her face showed no evidence that she had understood the word "lie." She spoke no English then. I leaned in toward Tom. Tom did the same, his forearms on my knees. He inclined his head toward me, as though he wanted to say something, but he said nothing, just rested his forehead against mine. We sat there for a good long time.

"Clare," he whispered finally. "I want to stay. I want to stay in America. I want to live with Uncle Ronan and go to the university. I don't want to go back. Please don't tell them. For me. Please don't tell them."

He sat back on his heels again, his eyes still focused in my lap. The bell for supper rang. The woman beside me stood and smoothed down her skirt. She cast a quick glance at us, then made her way to the door.

"Promise," Tom said. "Promise you won't tell them."

"I can't promise," I said. Tom's eyes began to fill. "But I will think about it," I added.

* * *

Mick didn't find us until after the bunks had been lowered for the night. Tom was in a bottom bunk. I was in the middle one above him. We had tried to save the top one for Mick, but the dormitory filled in fast, and we lost it to a dark-skinned woman with a son a few years younger than Tom. They both climbed the bunks and fell promptly asleep above me. I too was drowsing by the time Mick returned. When he did, it was a huge grin on his face. He tossed first Papa's coat and then a handful of notes and coins into the bunk beside me. I sat up, gathered them together, and handed them back.

"Don't you want to know how I got all this money?" he asked.

I lay back down, turned my back to him. Tom slipped out from the bunk beneath me.

"How much?" he asked.

"Three dollars, a half dollar, two dimes, and six pence," he said.

"Six cents?" Tom asked.

"These are cents?" Mick said. "I thought they were pennies."

"They are," Tom said, "but six pennies are worth six cents, not six pence. Three, seventy-six," he added. I rolled over to face them.

"Where did you get that kind of cash?" Tom asked.

"Poker," Mick said. "Cards. Now aren't you glad I learned to play on the boat?" I rolled back away again. Cards. Again. If I had any energy at all, I would have gone to Mr. Burr right then and turned us in. Maybe they would put Mick in the ship's jail for the trip home and I wouldn't have to look at him anymore. Almost as a reflex, I slipped a hand into my pocket to check the wad of notes there. They were intact, still tied into the secret pocket. I still had all the cash. That was when I realized it: Mick hadn't had any cash to gamble with. I was puzzled, but I wasn't about to ask him how he managed to play without money.

"You won $3.76 playing cards?" Tom exclaimed. I could feel him waiting for me to weigh in on the matter. Apparently, he hadn't realized yet that Mick didn't have any of our money to play with.

"I did," Mick said, sitting on the edge of my bunk. "$3.76." Tom sat beside him. I could feel the small of their backs against me as I lay curled, my back to them. "And against men a good bit older than myself."

"$3.76," Tom said. "That's ten, maybe twenty bob."

"And I can make more tomorrow," Mick said. "They invited me to play again tomorrow."

"Maybe I should go with you," Tom said. That did it. I rolled over to face them.

"Where did you get the money to bet with?" I asked. A look of realization crossed Tom's face.

"Clare has all the money," he said.

"Not anymore." Mick grinned, hefting the cash in his hand.

"Where did you get money?" I repeated.

Mick didn't answer, but his eyes rested on the coat beside him on the bunk.

"You bet Papa's coat?" Tom said. Mick didn't reply. Tom stood to face him. "You bet Papa's coat?"

"I needed a stake," Mick said. "I knew I could win, so it wasn't like I'd lose it. I only needed a stake to get me started. Now that I have money, I won't need to bet the coat tomorrow." I rolled back, my back to the both of them. If I had had any chance of finding a free bunk, I would have moved entirely.

"You won't be gambling tomorrow," Tom said. "Clare's right. If you got what you deserved you'd be locked in an industrial school this very minute. That or jail. If you got what you deserved, you'd be in Mr. Burr's jail right now waiting to be sent back to Ireland. If I wasn't your brother, I'd turn you in myself. But since I am, I'll only tell you this: you'll not do any more gambling, not tomorrow, not at all. You'll give us the money you won, and you'll behave like an altar boy under a priest's nose until we reach Uncle Ronan's house. And if you don't, I'll make you hurt, so help me I will. Give me the money," he said.

"I won't," Mick answered.

I'm not entirely sure what happened next. I heard a scuffle, then felt a jar, a body falling into the edge of the bunk. I turned over and quickly sat just in time to see Tom's fist connect with Mick's left eye and all of Mick's money fly out of his hand all over the floor. Mick quickly dropped to his knees to pick it up. Tom kicked him in the ribs. Mick curled reflexively into a ball. Tom bent over him, his fist clenched.

"Stop, Tom," I said quietly. He looked at me, then at Mick, then back at me. "Stop," I said. He silently straightened, never taking his eyes off Mick, who was again scrambling to collect all his money.

"If the guards see you fighting, it will do our case no bit of good," I said. Tom climbed silently into his bunk. I climbed back into mine. I felt the bump as Mick reached under me to fetch some stray cash.

"I did it for you," he said and climbed into the bunk beside me.

* * *

The next morning I felt an irresistible need to count our money again. It wasn't that I expected any of it to be missing. It's just that I needed to be sure it was all here. When Mick got up to go to the lavatory, before the guards came through to chase us all out and bolt up the bunks, I picked open the knot in my pocket, removed the notes and a small handful of coins. Sixty-one dollars and some change. Plus the five Tom had, plus a pound still in Irish money. I didn't even count the $3.76 Mick had announced last night. As far as I was concerned it was gone already.

To my surprise, Mick stayed close that morning. We didn't talk, but he was never out of my sight. Things were strained between him and Tom. The two didn't speak at all. Tom was favoring his right hand, and Mick's eye was blossomed like a great purple flower. After breakfast we sat together in the waiting room. We listened to the roll, the names being called one by one. Women worked their way through the crowd to receive documents or to be led off by herders.

When the roll was finished, we went out to the roof garden. Mick propped himself against one of the walls, legs outstretched, pulled his cap over his eyes, and settled in for a nap. It was as good a place as any. I sat beside him. Tom on the opposite side of me from Mick, pulled his whistle from the pocket of Papa's coat. He fingered it quietly, the mouthpiece resting on his chin, not in his mouth. He blew gently over the blade, and the notes came out as a whisper. "Down by the Salley Garden." If I concentrated, I could hear it over the steady drum of noise. Over and over it again. "Down by the Salley Garden." Even the same song over and over again was better than trying to hold a conversation. I couldn't nap. I didn't have Tom's whistle to keep me occupied. All I had were my thoughts.

What I thought about was the meeting that would be coming soon with Mr. Burr. I thought about my options. I couldn't lie. I wouldn't enter America riding the back of a sin. But if he didn't ask for the truth, was silence a lie? I rolled a half dozen different scenes through my mind. And I decided that I would answer any questions put to me truthfully. If they simply released us to Mrs. Keane, I would not stand in their way. But if they asked straight up if Bridget Keane was our aunt, I would tell them the truth. Then I would take the boys back to Cork, put them in the industrial school, and find myself a job, a factory job in all likelihood.

I reached into my pocket and pulled out Mama's rosary. With the ease that came from practice, I began to finger it bead-by-bead and to pray. God help me; I would tell them the truth.

* * *

Our names were called about mid afternoon. The guard led us this time into a small conference room. The man at the desk was the same Mr. Burr we had met yesterday. He motioned for us to sit, shuffled some papers, then spoke. "My name is Henry Burr," he said. "You are Clare Elizabeth Keane, Michael Finbarr Joseph Keane, and Thomas Joseph Patrick Keane?"

"We are, Mr. Burr," I said.

"We still are," Mick muttered under his breath. I wanted to slap him, but I pretended not to hear. So did Burr, if indeed he did hear in the first place.

"Bridget Keane of New York is your aunt?" he said.

I paused, took a deep breath, made ready to speak the truth. But that pause was only long enough for Mick to speak up. "The relationship is more like a great aunt through marriage, or something like that. Our mother's father's brother's wife. Or is it our mother's mother's brother's wife. I'm not entirely sure of the exact relationship."

"We call her aunt, though," Tom chimed in.

"I see," said Burr.

"And Bryan Keane," he said, looking square at me.

"Our cousin," Mick answered.

"All right," Mr. Burr said. As far as he was concerned Mrs. Keane was kin. I opened my mouth, but no words came out to disabuse him of the notion. He nodded to the guard who opened the second door, and in walked Mrs. Keane on the arm of a man in his early thirties. The man had a shock of reddish-brown hair and as near perfect teeth as I had ever seen on a body. He led Mrs. Keane to a chair then smiled at me.

"You are Mrs. Bridget Keane?" the official asked.

"I am," she said, never once looking at me.

"And you are these children's aunt?"

"So they call me," she said. "Though the reality is a bit more complicated."

"So I understand," Burr answered. "And you are gainfully employed?"

"When I get back to Butte, I'll be living off my husband's pension, and I take in laundry now and again. But here in New York, I stay with my son, Bryan" she said.

"And you, Bryan Keane?" He looked up at Bryan, who was still catching glimpses of us out of the corner of his eye. "Are you able to take financial responsibility for these three children?"

"I am a riveter," he said. "On the Manhattan Bridge Perhaps you've heard of it?"

"I have," Burr replied evenly.

"And how could you not?" Bryan said. "It'll be the finest bridge in the city when we're through with it. Don't you worry about me. I probably make better than most of the blokes around here, and them with their cushy government jobs. I probably make better than you, even." He closed his arms on his chest, and pushed himself up a bit. He was, without a doubt an impressive looking man.

"Congratulations," Mr. Burr said coolly. "But that's not the issue we're discussing at the moment. The issue is whether you are willing to assume financial responsibility for these children until their majority?"

"We are," Mrs. Keane said. Bryan nodded. I was shocked. I had just assumed that we would be released to Mrs. Keane's custody, and that she would see us onto the train. But here she was agreeing to care for us for years. I felt the need to say something, but I wasn't sure what it was.

"And you'll sign a bond to that effect?" Burr said, pushing a piece of paper across the desk. Mrs. Keane took the pen he offered and without hesitation signed, so did Bryan.

"Well, then," Burr said. He ran a finger down a sheet of paper. "I believe everything is in order. Welcome to the United States." He tucked the signed paper into a folder and handed it to the guard.

"But, sir," I said, hardly believing. "Mr. Burr." He looked up at me. "Is it that easy?" I finally asked.

"That easy," he said with a smile. "We're not ogres. Despite what you hear. We just wanted to make sure you weren't going to be alone. Now that we know that you're not, yes, it's that easy." He smiled at me. I smiled weakly back at him. That easy. And I hadn't really lied. Not really.

"The guard will take you to the desk for your entry tag," Mr. Burr said.

"Thank you," I said. Tom and Mick echoed me: "Thank you." Mick was fairly bouncing with joy. But for me, after all the dread, all the worry, the meeting had been rather anticlimactic.

"You're most welcome," he said, motioning for the guard.

Our final herder took our baggage check information, then led us to a line forming in front of a table. By the time we had moved to the front of the line, our shoonaun was waiting for us. We were tagged, our paperwork was stamped, the last of our Irish money was changed, and when we finally made our way out the great double doors, it was in the custody of our "aunt" Bridget and "cousin" Bryan. Just that easy.

* * *

"They never suspected a thing," Bryan said quietly as we made our way out to the dock and the waiting ferries.

"Bryan, hush," Mrs. Keane said. "Your gloating could still get them sent back." She turned to me. "Do you have your train tickets?"

"I have money," I said. "Uncle Ronan didn't send tickets."

"Money will do," she said. "Well, then, I suppose we'll need to be finding which station you belong in."

"For the train for St. Paul?" I said.

"Well, yes, for St. Paul," Mrs. Keane responded. "That is where your uncle is, isn't it?"

"We're not sure," I said. "We thought he was in Lindstrom. Then he moved to someplace called St. Croix Falls, but the telegram Mr. Burr sent to St. Croix Falls didn't reach him. His boss thought he might be somewhere called Hayward. I don't know where that is," I added.

"Well," Mrs. Keane responded, "Well. Well, well. That's a cat of a different color, then isn't it? Is that why you needed us to come fetch you off the island? I thought you only needed someone to see you to the train."

"I don't know," I said. "All I know is that they said they couldn't release children without an escort. But now . . . ." I paused.

"That's what they told us, too," Mrs. Keane said. "That they wouldn't release you without an escort. But I only thought that your Uncle Ronan couldn't make it, so we would be standing in for him."

So she hadn't signed to take us on as her own. She had merely signed to set us loose to travel west to Uncle Ronan.

"We still plan to go to Minnesota," I said. "We just need to figure out where."

"Well, then," she said. "It looks like you'll be staying with us until we can contact your uncle."

* * *

Though I wasn't eager to reenter the building, Mrs. Keane led us back through the double doors. I clutched my release papers tightly in my fist as she asked one of the guards where the telegraph office was. It wasn't far, but the line was long. While standing in it, we formed a plan.

We weren't sure where to send the telegram. Larsen had suggested Hayward. Lindstrom was also a possibility. Uncle Ronan had lived there long enough to make friends. Maybe those friends knew where he was. In the end, we decided to send two. The one to Hayward we addressed simply "Ronan Keane, Lumber Company, Hayward, Wisconsin." In it we gave Uncle Ronan Bryan's address and asked him where we should go to meet him. The other one we sent to the manager at the Lakeside Inn in Lindstrom, Minnesota. It explained that we needed to find Uncle Ronan and asked them to wire us if they had information. The telegraph official thought we would have a better chance of getting a response if we sent money for the return telegram, so that's what we did.

* * *

"Where do you live?" Mick asked Bryan as we again made our way across the dock to the ferry.

"Gashouse district," Bryan said. Mick looked puzzled. "East side," Bryan said by way of clarification. Mick shook his head. "There," Bryan said, pointing at the city. "On the other side, a few miles up."

"New York City," Mick said, bit of awe in his voice.

Bryan laughed. "Yeah. New York bleedin' City," he said.

Twenty-Seven

As the bright red ferry dropped its gangplank onto Ellis Island's departure dock, I couldn't help but notice just how much it paid to be in America's good graces. The ferry was twice the boat we'd come in on, newly painted—red with white trim and "Department of Commerce and Labor U.S. Immigration Service" painted down the side. Perhaps more to the point given the stickiness of the weather, it had ample windows, and inside those windows were benches to sit on.

We loaded the shoonaun and ourselves quickly, moving ahead of the small crowd that pushed in behind us. Bryan quickly assessed his mother's ability to climb the gangplank on her own, then scooped her up into his arms, and despite her protests and the dull blows she landed on his chest, carried her up the ramp and onto the boat. Tom and Mick immediately dashed up the stairs to the top deck. Bryan deposited his mother on one of the benches inside the cabin, and rather than sit in her icy presence, trotted up the stairs to join the boys.

"Will you be all right here?" I asked Mrs. Keane. I wanted very much to go out to the rail.

"Grand," she said with a grunt. "It's the problem with being small, you know. Everyone thinks they can just walk up to you and pick you up. Not so much as a by-your-leave. Rude, it is. Rude."

I was listening; really I was, but my mind must have been on the engines kicking in beneath us and the scenery beginning to shift outside the window.

"Go," Mrs. Keane said. "If you want to go out to the rail, go on with you. Me? I had more than enough of this canker of a city already. Wild horses couldn't keep me here a minute longer than I have to. But if you want to go see it, you go right ahead."

"Thank you," I said, and dashed off to the rail. A quick glance up to where Bryan was showing Tom and Mick the sights told me that the top rail was already packed shoulder to shoulder, so I took up a spot near the bow.

Once clear of the dock, the ferry driver kicked in the engines, and we were away. The river was packed with traffic. We swerved a bit to avoid another barge load of immigrants that had cut its engines and taken up station just off the island. We weren't close enough to see the anxiety on the faces of its passengers, but I do believe I could feel it, oozing off the barge and across the water. I scanned the line of piers edging the city, looking for the dock where the *Caronia* had been. The liner was gone, of course. Headed back to England. Another stood in its place, this one with three huge smokestacks painted in Cunard colors. A liner off to the south made its way steadily toward us, steaming slowly up the harbor. A coal barge peeked out from behind the city, then headed up and around to where the steamships were moored.

A light drizzle began to fall. Some of the passengers around me ducked into the cabin, but I wasn't about to trade my first real glimpse of America for a dry shirtwaist. I shifted into place at the very bow of the ferry, and took it all in.

"Excuse me, Miss." The voice came from behind me. I turned to see a navy uniform, actually, on second look it was a navy suit with a white shirt. But the cut was very similar to the uniforms on Ellis Island, his cap nearly identical, and the brightly polished brass buttons looked highly official. "Do you speak English?" the man asked.

"I do, sir," I said. My stomach flip-flopped. We weren't on American soil yet. I fingered the landing card in my pocket.

"Good," the man said. "Very good. So many don't you know." I nodded. The man removed a leather wallet from his pocket and opened it to show me a large brass badge. "I'm with the Department of Commerce and Labor," the man said. "We've been told that some of the immigrants coming through Ellis Island have been given the old currency. May I see any American money you've been given either by the money exchange on the island or by your steamship company?" I fingered the safe pocket inside my skirt; the notes were still there. I hesitated.

"Old currency, you say?" I asked. Something about the situation seemed wrong. I looked up to the second deck. Bryan and the boys must have moved around to the back.

"Yes, Miss," the man in the blue suit said. "It's currency from the McKinley era. It was, of course, replaced when President Roosevelt came into office, but some of it is still in circulation. The problem is that it's now five years old, and so quite worthless. That's why the Commerce Department has posted agents on all the ferries, to make sure you immigrants don't start your life in your new country with worthless money in your pocket."

"You can replace old money with new?" I asked.

"Yes, Miss," the official said, removing a large leather wallet from his inside breast pocket. I can replace it right now if you'll show me the money you were given.

I rummaged in my pocket to undo the string and pull out the wad of notes inside. Tom had five dollars. Mick had whatever he had left over from his last card game—I was too disgusted to ask how much. The rest was here in my pocket. I pulled it out and showed it to the man.

"Just as I thought," the man said. "I hate to see this happen, Miss. You've been swindled. This is old money. It won't buy you so much as a cup of coffee in New York, or any place else in America for that matter." He shook his head. "If you can tell me exactly where you were given this currency, I'll replace it, and my department will prosecute those who gave it to you." He reached out to take the money.

"I don't want to get anyone in trouble," I said.

"They'll only get the trouble they deserve," the man said, quickly snatching the notes from my hand. He counted with the practiced efficiency of someone used to handling large piles of cash. "Sixty-six dollars," he said, tucking the money into his wallet. From a second pocket he pulled another stack of notes, larger than the ones I'd given him, and with not just green, but accents of red, blue and yellow. He counted out sixty-six dollars, then counted the stack again. "There you go," he said. "Now, if you will tell me who gave you this worthless tender."

"I got it on the boat," I said. "The *Caronia*."

"Cunard Line," the official said. "We've had trouble with them before. Well, thank you, Miss. We'll follow up on this." He tipped his cap. I smiled, thanked him, and buttoned the new notes into my skirt pocket. I was about to turn to watch the skyline of New York again, when I caught sight of the man. Rather than approaching any other passengers, he had taken up station right next to the gangplank. Hoping he wouldn't see me, I quickly climbed the stairs to the top deck.

"Tom," I said when I found them clustered in the stern of the boat. "What do you know about the new American currency?" I held out the stack of notes for him to see.

"Where did you get this?" Bryan said abruptly.

"From a government man, down on the lower deck. He replaced the money I had with this, told me it was the new currency."

"Show me which man," Bryan said.

I made my way around to side of the ferry, Bryan and the boys in tow, then pointed down toward the gangplank. "The man in the blue suit with the flat-topped cap."

Bryan leaped over the railing in one smooth motion and landed with a thud on the lower deck. Within a second, he had the man by the collar of his jacket. Mick assessed the jump, then dashed along the railing to the stairs. Tom and I followed.

By the time we got to the lower deck and had pushed our way through the growing crowd, Bryan was rummaging through the man's wallet.

"Road apples," he said, pulling out a fist-full of red and blue notes. He waved the fist in the man's face, then tossed the notes overboard into the water. "Not worth the ink to print them." He rummaged through the wallet and pulled out a second fist-full of notes, these green. "Clare," he said. "How much did this skunk take you for?" I gave him a blank look, trying to decipher what he had just said. "How much did he steal from you?"

"Sixty-six dollars," I answered. Bryan quickly counted out a stack of notes and stuffed them into his pocket. The rest he pulled from the wallet and tossed into the crowd. Mick quickly pounced on a stray note that blew our way. The rest of the passengers scrambled for what they could gather up of the notes that danced on the breeze off the harbor. Bryan tossed the empty wallet into the water.

"That's my wallet," the man shouted. "You have no right."

"Well, now," Bryan replied. "If it's your wallet, maybe you should be the one to go diving for it." He grabbed the man by the lapels and shoved him toward the railing. The man grasped the railing to keep from going overboard. Another passenger stepped forward from the crowd, and attacked the man's hands, peeling them from the railing. A third grabbed the man's feet, and together the three of them tossed the man struggling and grunting into the harbor. He landed with a splash, disappeared, then bobbed to the surface. I assessed the distance to shore. The man in the water did the same, then with a half-muffled threat began to swim.

Bryan grinned and shook hands with the two men who had helped him. "Not a bad day's work," he said. He pulled the money from his pocket, looked it over, and then put it back. "Not bad at all."

* * *

It was at the Battery that it first dawned on me that America might not be what I had always pictured. I had pictured a large spacious land, with huge trees, and happy Americans, all speaking the clipped, to-the-point dialect I'd heard from the few Americans I'd met in Cork. These happy Americans worked good jobs, made good money, and were able to make a good life for their families. That was the America I'd held in my mind.

The Battery was an entirely different place. The Battery was, in a word, chaos. Now that I think of it, that should not have been surprising to me. The Battery was, after all, a meeting of worlds. To the south was the harbor and ships from all over the world. On the north was the great city of New York, its tall buildings looking down on us as our ferry landed. From the water came immigrants of all descriptions, speaking a great stew of languages, sporting a kaleidoscope of clothing. From the land came the tracks of the elevated train, spilling out workers and relatives, street hawkers and gawkers. And they all spilled into the Battery. In the chaos, it was no trouble at all to spot which were immigrants. They dodged horses and wagons, mingled with peddlers wheeling their carts through the crowd, met relatives waiting to pick them up, and wandered trying to adapt to a city whose customs and sheer dimensions were unlike anything they had ever seen before. Mostly, they stared, taking in the city with the look of a deer caught in a rifle sight. And me? I was no exception.

The five of us walked slowly from the ferry to the el, matching our pace to that of Mrs. Keane and her cane. Mick, Tom and I craned our neck this way and that, taking it all in. In the near field it was very much like Ireland. In the sticky summer air, the crowd smelled like a crowd, the horses like horses, and the ocean had the same musky, fishy, salty smell we had left in Queenstown. But here the air was also filled with the exhaust of motor cars, the burnt smell of brake linings, and the aroma of foods whose creators had clearly traveled much farther than I had. Here the buildings towered, the streets teemed, the quays were packed cheek by jowl with steamers and sailing vessels from every point on the globe. We were in America and it seemed half the planet had joined us there.

* * *

Somewhere in the midst of the crowd, about halfway to the el platform, we caught sight of him—a skinny little man in a too-tight suit, elbowing his way the crowd toward us. In his mouth was a stub of a cigar as thick as his forearm. In his hand was a tattered envelope with scribbling on the back. Somehow around the stub he managed to call out to us, to Bryan in particular.

"Nice day, huh, buddy?" His accent was pinched, as though the words had been pushed out somehow between his back teeth. "You speak English?"

"Better than you," Bryan said, not slowing down, not that we could slow down much more without coming to a dead stop.

"I'll be damned if you don't," the little man said with a forced chuckle. "Are you looking for work? I have work to offer. Good work. Six dollars a week. You won't find that in—where did you say you were from?"

"East twenty-second street. New York City," Bryan replied. "Save your lousy job for the greenhorns. I make three times that. Do you make three times that? Huh?"

The man muttered something, tossed his head, and wandered off scanning the crowd for another person to approach. Bryan's rudeness surprised me, especially to someone who was offering him work. Back in Cork a laborer would never have been rude to someone offering him work. Even if he hadn't needed the job, he would have figured that anyone offering was a person to be reckoned with, a person to be respected. I replayed the conversation in my mind as we walked, searching for the key that would make it make sense.

"What's a greenhorn?" Mick asked as we dodged a wagon load of baggage.

"That's a greenhorn," Bryan said, gesturing at a man in the bushes. I could barely see him, just that he was rustling the branches, and his head was bobbing up and down as though he were hopping about on one leg. Then I caught a flash of white, a bare buttock. I turned away.

"Need a pair of Lithuanian worker's trousers?" Bryan said. "He'll probably just leave them there in the bushes." I scanned the bushes. Sure enough they were littered with scraps of clothes—a pair of trousers here, a hat there, tiny piles of them draped over branches and piled on the ground. My first impulse was to go and collect them, to see if I could find a dealer who could sell them.

"Yup," Bryan said, "and that's a greenhorn." He pointed at a young, stringy fellow who was listening to the skinny man's pitch. The skinny man pantomimed digging with a shovel, then rummaged in his pocket and pulled out a wad of notes. The greenhorn's eyes brightened and he nodded vigorously.

"That's a greenhorn," Bryan pointed at a dark-haired woman with a toddler clinging to her skirts. The woman's eyes were round, and she clutched at the hand of the man beside her like a shipwreck victim might clutch at a piece of debris bobbing in the ocean.

"And look," Bryan said with mock theatrics. "Look at the bright shade of spring green on those three!" His lip curled, and he stared at the three of us. I blushed. Mick glared back at Bryan. Bryan laughed. "I didn't mean anything by it," he said. "It's just that the three of you are going to have to be careful. The whole city would need nothing more than a casual glance to know you're just off the boat. Easy marks—that's what you look like. Apple?"

"Apple?" I said.

"Do you want an apple? Or an orange?"

I looked over at Tom and Mick. I hadn't needed to. They were never ones to turn down food. Bryan strolled over to a white-haired woman in a shawl, presiding over a large flat basket balanced on a rail at the foot of the stairs to the elevated.

"Three apples. Three oranges," Bryan said. He reached into his pocket and pulled out a wad of money, our money, and stripped off a note. "Keep the change," he said. The woman beamed as she pocketed the note. She handed over the three apples, three oranges, and added a small fried cake to the pile. Bryan pocketed the cake and a couple of the apples before distributing the rest to us, one a piece.

I'd say it was just like back home, just like when Mama and Da and the boys and I would buy an orange or two and go down to the Lough to watch the ducks. Actually it was nothing like that. But the sweet taste to the orange brought it all to the front of my mind nonetheless. Once there, the memories tumbled over and around all the new sensations surrounding me. It wasn't long before all of it—past, present, future—all took on the feel of a dream, of something not quite real. I linked my arm through Tom's and let him and the tide wash me up onto the platform of the el.

* * *

An el is a train, nothing more. I could see that as the cars pulled into the station high above us on a platform. Having ridden the train from Cork to Queenstown I considered myself something of an authority on trains. I knew about the tickets, the conductors. I knew about standing up before the train came to a full stop. I also knew that trains tended to make me motion sick if I rode in them backward.

What I didn't know is that els didn't have tickets; they had gates where you paid before getting on. They didn't have conductors but rather security guards. Furthermore, at this time of day, they didn't even have room to sit down.

"Keep your basket in front of you," Bryan said to Mick. "Never let it out of your hands. And put your money in your front pocket, not the back. Is your money in your pocket book?" he asked me.

"Um, no," I said, "I don't have a pocket book, and, um, you have my money."

"So I do," he said. "It's probably safer with me. I'll just hold on to it for a while then, shall I?" I nodded my head hesitantly. The money was probably safer with Bryan. But *I* would have felt safer if it had been with me.

"As soon as the doors open, we need to step on and find Mama a seat right away," Bryan said. "The el is on a tight schedule, and it doesn't wait for greenhorns."

* * *

The sun was low on the horizon as the Second Avenue el pulled out of the Battery station. Bryan had paid for our tickets with our money. He now stood, one hand hooked onto an overhead strap, in the other the second of the two apples.

Fulton Street, Franklin Street, Shatham Square—we made our way up the line. At each stop, workers boarded. Men rose to allow the women to sit in the few free seats. I positioned myself so I could see out a window. The great Brooklyn Bridge. Shops, factories, and everywhere I looked, the tenements. On a balcony, a toddler in nothing more than a diaper played with a wooden spoon. The dying light shining through the iron railing cast stripes up and down his body. A housewife in a wilted shirtwaist sat with her shirtless husband and an idle tin washtub on the fire escape of their tenement. Another labored over something just below the windowsill of her small apartment. With the back of her hand, she pushed a damp strand of hair from her face and watched the train pass, mere feet from where she stood in the kitchen of her own home.

The train rumbled through the sultry city. Houston Street, Ninth Street, Fourteenth Street. At Nineteenth Street, Bryan helped his mother to her feet, and motioned for us to follow. As we descended the platform, the tenements continued to rise on either side of us. They were, perhaps, not as squalid as those in the neighborhood we had just ridden through. But as a child of the tenements, I knew full well what I was looking at. I recognized the hand-me-down clothing on the children. I knew instinctively that the women seated on the front steps were waiting for their husbands to come home not from a lucrative desk job, but from the factory, the construction site, the foundry, the stable.

More than the look of the place, though, I recognized the smell. Well, it wasn't so much that I recognized the smell, but I recognized the fact that this was a place with a smell no wealthy person would have tolerated. Back home, the smell was the smell of the brewery, the privies, the stables. Here the smell was not nearly so earthy. I sniffed the air, trying to decide what it was that was assailing my nose.

"Gas works," Mrs. Keane said, reading my mind, or more likely my puckered face. "They turn coal into gas. For lighting and cooking, don't you know. The tanks are all over this part of town."

"You have gas in your apartment?" I asked Bryan. Perhaps the area was not as poor as I had estimated.

"Sure," Bryan said. "It's twenty-five cents an hour by meter, so I can't very well afford it, but yes I have it."

"Do you have electricity?" Mick asked.

Bryan laughed. "Of course," he answered, "I was talking to John D. Rockefeller one day at the club, and he said how much he liked his electric lights, so I said to myself, 'you know Keane, you really should have them installed in your mansion'." He snorted and shook his head. "I don't know what they told you back in the 'old country,' but not everyone in America is a bleedin' millionaire."

We walked for a while in silence through the gassy air. Mrs. Keane was tiring.

"Are we close?" I asked.

"Another half a block," Bryan answered. We fell silent again. "I tell you what," Bryan finally said as we turned down Twentieth Street. "How about I take you to a show this evening? I'll take you to see the Russells, and then we could get something to eat. You've never seen anything funnier in your entire life."

"The Russells are children," Mrs. Keane replied. "And obscene children at that. I don't know what you see in them."

"You don't have to come with us," Bryan said.

"You couldn't drag me with you," Mrs. Keane replied.

"I'll go," Mick said.

"Me, too," Tom added.

Bryan looked at me. I nodded my head.

"Good," Bryan said. "Hot dogs then vaudeville, then maybe a soda afterward. I'll see if the lads want to join us."

* * *

The stairs of the tenement seemed to never end. Bryan's apartment was on the fifth floor. By the fourth, I was uttering a small prayer of thanks that he didn't live at the top. The air I drew heavily into my lungs was thick and scratchy, laden with coal smoke from cooking fires and with that terrible gassy smell that hung thicker than the worst stench of the nastiest privies ever to grace a backyard in Cork. Tom coughed. Mick screwed up his face. I breathed through my mouth until it burned.

We reached the landing of the fifth floor, and Bryan pulled a key attached to a long string from his pocket and unlocked the door. He swung it open for us, then bowed with a flourish.

"It's not much, but it's home," he said. Mrs. Keane hobbled in and made a beeline for the bed on the other side of the room.

I entered. Gingerly. The floor was littered with bits of this and that—newspaper, dirty rags, a pile of frayed blankets. That and old scraps of food, if the smell was any indication. The large main room served as kitchen, dining room, sitting room, and bedroom, just as ours had back in Cork. A bit of an archway separated the kitchen from the living room with its murphy bed, but to call the living room a separate room was more than a little generous. Unlike our room in Ireland, though, here a door led to a second room, a bedroom, judging by the two disheveled mattresses lying on the floor. They were laden with dirty clothes and what I thought at the time might have been a body. The sink held dirty dishes. The table was covered with newspapers, which in turn were covered with spots of crusted potatoes and grease. The place was a sty.

Mick kicked aside a pair of grubby work boots and dropped the shoonaun by the door.

"Go ahead and kick aside anything that's in your way," Bryan said, dipping a glass of water from a bucket on the table. He drained the glass and then filled it again for his mother. It was pretty clear he had no plans to ask if I had a mouth on me. The walk through the heat and the gas had put a powerful thirst on me. But I decided against asking for the moment.

"That mess in the bedroom is Joe," Bryan said, strolling into the living room and dropping himself onto a corner of the bed. "Joe's a night watchman, and he doesn't live here, so you won't see much of him. He just warms a bed now and then when his wife's sewing machine keeps him awake all day. Alan and Rick work on the bridge with me. They'll be home when the pubs close. Now and then a few other fellows take the floor. Five cents a spot. It's not a bad deal."

Five cents a spot. Did he mean five cents a night? Five cents a week? I tried to remember how much a cent was. It was so much easier to figure out whether we could afford something when I was calculating in shillings and pence. Bryan apparently saw me working the numbers in my head.

"Don't worry," he said. "I won't charge you. Friends of Mam's stay free."

"Thank you," I said. "I'm sure we won't be here long."

"Pfft." Bryan waved his hand dismissively. "No matter. If you can find a clean spot to lay a blanket, it's yours." He looked at me meaningfully. I caught the hint.

"I could help you with the cleaning if you'd like," I said.

"That would be mighty kind of you," Bryan answered. "It's not always this thick. It's just that we clean when the weather is bad and we can't work." He surveyed the disarray and shrugged. "The weather's been good lately."

* * *

Bryan had gone down the street to call on "the lads," to see if they wanted to join us for an evening "on the town" as he said. Tom and Mick had gone to explore the neighborhood. Myself? I sat for a moment or two, listening to Joe's snores from the bedroom before the mess all round me sucked me in. It started with a dried-up bread crust in the doorway. I couldn't just let it sit there where it would be trampled and eventually tracked through the house. I picked it up, then stacked some newspapers, then carried all the dirty dishes to the sink. Before I knew what was happening, I had found the tap in the hallway the broom in the corner, and was scrubbing and sweeping.

Mrs. Keane sat silent while I worked. In the corner of the living-room half of the long room, under a picture of the Sacred Heart, she sat on the edge of the bed, the only piece furniture other than the table and chairs in the kitchen. She was surrounded by a small oasis of tidiness, undoubtedly her own doing. Her chin in her hand, she gazed out the window, eyes focused on nothing in particular. Her silence was so unlike her that it unnerved me a bit.

"Can I make you a bit of tea then? Or cut you some bread?" I said, making my way into the living room and laying a hand on her shoulder.

"And wouldn't you be the first to ask me that in the week and more since I arrived?" she replied, patting my hand. "No, dear, I'll make myself a little something while you're at the show."

"Are you feeling well?" I asked, propping myself against the windowsill.

"As well as these old bones ever feel," she said. Her eyes were still resting on the air outside the window.

I sat for a moment. "You don't seem quite yourself," I said.

"Nothing a day in my own house in Butte won't cure," she said.

"When will you and Pat be leaving?" I asked.

"I'll be leaving tomorrow afternoon," she said. "As for Patricia, may she be halfway to hell by now."

"She left," I said unnecessarily.

"She did," Mrs. Keane confirmed. "She had to go through Ellis. So I took a ferry from the city to the island and waited there at the island for her. Ten hours, it was. Ten hours of noise and heat before she finally came through. We arrived here at the apartment, and Patricia left her bags at the foot of the stairs. She said she'd see me to the top and then go back for the bags. When Bryan opened the door, she went back down, and that was the last I saw of her. I knew the girl was misery the moment I laid eyes on her back in Waterford. What kind of girl would be willing to leave her home and family on a moment's notice like that? A good Christian wouldn't do such a thing to begin with."

"So will you go to Butte alone then?" I asked.

"It's not as though I had a son to accompany me," she replied. "'I have a job, Mam.' 'I can't afford to leave New York, Mam.' 'I would if I could, Mam.' I asked him straight out to come back with me, to join his brothers in the mine. It has to be better than living here in this pile of horse turds they call a city. But, no, he won't leave. He won't spare so much as a month to see his own mother safe to the house she raise him in, and her likely going home to her death." She sighed. I wasn't sure what to say, so I just sat. "Never grow old, Clare," she said quietly. "Never let yourself get so frail you have to depend on the aid of children and servants." She sighed again. I stood and laid a hand on her shoulder. Her jaw hardened. "Don't you have work to do?" she said.

Twenty-Eight

The queue stretched halfway down the block. Men in dark jackets. Women in crisp shirtwaists and hats so piled with feathers and furs that you could mistake them for a new and magnificent creature all their own. A clutch of ragged newsboys, papers still tucked under their arms, conspired together as they waited their turn at the ticket booth.

"The wages here must be grand if newsboys can afford the theater," Mick said. I could feel the cluster of ratty boys tugging at him.

"And isn't that why we made the trip?" I replied.

"I can ask them," Mick said, "whether there's good money in selling papers."

"We need to get into the queue," I said. What I was thinking was that I didn't want to lose him, not in a city this large, this foreign.

"It won't take but a minute," Mick said.

"It won't take any time at all if you stay here with us," I said, grabbing the sleeve of his shirt in my fist. Mick shook me off, and made his way toward the newsies.

"Mick," Bryan called out. "We can't hold a place in line for you if you're not with us. Where do you want to meet us after the show? If you're too far back in line to buy your own ticket, I mean." Mick looked back over his shoulder, then trotted over to take his place in line beside us.

"I'll talk to them after we get the tickets," he said.

"Smart lad," Bryan commented.

The line inched forward slowly. The sun was low on the horizon. Soon the city would blossom with electric lights, just as we'd seen from the ship, just as we'd seen from the windows of the detention room on Ellis. Only this time, for the first time, we'd be standing beneath those lights. For the first time, they would be our lights.

A young couple took their place in the queue behind us.

"Did you see John and Jimmy yet?" the young man asked his girl. His voice was pure Cork, working class Cork. "Jimmy reminds me of an aunt I have back in the old country." It seemed an odd thing to say, but I wasn't so much concerned with what he'd said as they way he'd said it. I turned.

"Pardon me," I said. "Are you from Cork?"

"I am so," the man said. "Born and reared in the shadow of the spires of St. Anne's Shandon." A north-side man, then. But still from Cork. I was positively delighted.

"We're from the south-side," I said, "near St. Finbarr's. My brothers and I."

"Good for you," the man said, and turned to face his lady friend again. That was it.

"He was Irish," I said to Bryan, "from Cork, not more than a mile or two from our old tenement."

"And with no great effort, I could find another five like him in this line alone," Bryan replied. "This is an Irish vaudeville, after all, and New York City has more Irishmen between its shores than the entire city of Cork itself."

"Go on with you," Mick said. "More Irishmen than Cork?"

"More than Dublin," Bryan replied. "The Irish, you see, don't leave home, they bring home with them. First all their relatives, then their favorite pubs, their music and dance, even their theater. The only difference between New York and Ireland is that in New York Cork lies cheek by jowl with Dublin and Belfast. That and the fact that Italy and Germany lie just across the street."

"Is it that way in Minnesota, too?" Tom asked.

"I'm sure I wouldn't know," Bryan said. Nor care, or so said the look on his face.

The line inched forward. I listened on the muggy night air to the voices around me—Cork, Dublin, Galway, the occasional snatch of Gaelic. It felt familiar. The smells, though, were anything but familiar. The raspy scent of automobile exhaust, the aroma of a food I didn't recognize wafting down from a restaurant on top of the building. Perfumes and toilet water, aftershave and cologne all milling with the crowd. The sights were also foreign. The traffic made its way down the wrong side of the street. The buildings that surrounded it rose to impossible heights, heights that caused the sun to dawn just before noon and set soon thereafter. A Jewish man in side curls with tassels hanging below his limp jacket wheeled a push cart up to the front of the theater. One by one, the theatergoers left the line to pick through the fruit stacked in great piles on the two-wheeled cart.

"Do you want a banana?" Bryan asked. I shook my head. Surely bananas were expensive, even here where fruit seemed plentiful. "How about a peach?"

"I could eat a peach," Tom said.

"You could eat a dead dog," Bryan said. "Not that yon sheeny would sell you one. Mick, Clare? We won't get a chance to eat until after the show. It's on me." Mick and Tom nodded vigorously.

"A peach, then," I said. "Thank you."

He pulled a wad of notes from his trouser pocket and pulled a single from them. Unless I missed my guess, they were our notes. He smiled a big smile at us. "Hold my place in line," he said.

"Is that our money?" I asked Tom.

"I'll hold that it is," Tom replied.

"We need to get it back," I said. He nodded.

"I know how," Mick chimed in.

"We just ask him for it," I said.

"I doubt that'll do the trick," Mick said. "Trust me."

I sighed. Bryan came back with the peaches. They were small, but they smelled heavenly, and when I bit into mine, the juice immediately filled my hand and dribbled down my forearm. I pushed my sleeve back and savored.

"Say, Bryan," Mick said.

"Mmm," Bryan said, taking a big bite from his banana.

"I was thinking," Mick said. "Why don't we pay for the tickets to the theater? It's the least we could do after all you did for us already."

"That's mighty charitable of you, Mick," Bryan replied.

"My pleasure," Mick said. He reached a hand into his right trouser pocket, then transferred his peach and rummaged through the left. With a puzzled look on his face, he patted his jacket, then his shirt. Then with what I thought was a grossly overacted look of recognition he said, "Oh, I remember, you still have our cash from the to-do on the ferry. I can't thank you enough for that, by the way. If you can show me the cash now, I'll pay for the tickets at the window."

"Ah, Mick, now why don't you allow me?" Bryan said. "New York is not the safest place for greenhorns with cash in their pockets. Your money is safer with me just now. Safe as a babe in arms it is." He patted his pocket for emphasis.

* * *

I don't have to say that my mind was not on the show. I may have left the tenements of Cork behind me, but the money worries I'd lived with in those tenements had traveled the ocean with me. They were, at the moment, sharing my seat in that very theater. I listened half-heartedly as an Irish tenor sang "Foggy Dew " then something I had never heard before, something called "My Wild Irish Rose." Everyone joined in on the chorus. I hummed along and swayed back and forth with Bryan, who moved partly out of the sentimentality bred into every Irish male, partly from the effects of the flask he had been sneaking in and out of his breast pocket. It worried me that he had our money. It worried me even more that he seemed the sort who could hold his money no longer than he could hold his breath.

A man in a boater hat introduced the acts: A fellow with a monkey in a cap and coat. A woman contortionist who wore significantly less than the monkey. A man in a white muscle shirt and handlebar mustache that reminded me of the Marquis man on the boat. The man threw a few dramatic jabs before beginning to sing:

'Twas down at Dan McDavitt's

On the corner on the street

And there was to be a prizefight

And both parties were to meet

To make all the arrangements

Make sure everything was right

McClusky and the Negro

Were to have a finish fight.

He was no more into the second line of the song before I was back there, back on the boat. Colum with his dancing eyes, his fist raised stiffly in front of him, jabbing playfully at me. Colum and I standing shoulder pressed to shoulder at the boat rail, pointing out anything that happened to break up the interminable expanse of water. Colum's lips on mine. "Marry me, Clare Keane. Say you'll spend the rest of your life with me." I wondered if he was in Washington yet. I pictured him amidst tall trees, trees so big four men could sit abreast on the stump. There he sat in my mind, alone on that stump, waiting for me to arrive.

It was a rude awakening to be jolted back to the vaudeville. A great crash of a noise echoed through the hall. "Throw him *down* McClusky." The audience sang along, pouncing on the word 'down' with all their might. Men stomped the floor. Women clapped; some stomped a bit themselves. And the newsies hefted their stacks of papers and with all their might slammed them to the bare board floor. "Throw him *down* McClusky." Beside me Mick leapt into the air, coming down hard, if a bit off beat. Bryan grinned, and on the next chorus, he too jumped into the air and landed his big boots with a thud on the floor. Swaying a bit, he caught himself on my shoulder and grinned again.

The crowd called for an encore, and the singer, knowing his audience would stand for nothing less, began the final verse one more time. By the time he left the stage, the barker in the bowler had to say nothing more than, "And here they are, the act you've all been waiting for: John and Jimmy Russell." The crowd erupted. The curtains parted.

John was on his hands and knees, up to his elbow in soapy water, scrubbing the floor. Jimmy flicked a ridiculous feather duster over a cabinet door. The duster was huge but not likely to do much more than rearrange the dust. Still that was not the most ridiculous thing about the scene. Not by a fair sight. Both men were dressed in women's clothes, the dresses of a maidservant in the old country. John's cap was nearly identical to the one Mrs. O'Rourke used to wear. Jimmy's dress was made of a fabric so close to my old one that I would need to see them side-by-side to tell the difference. Jimmy turned to face the crowd, a day's growth of beard on his face. The audience howled. I could feel the color rise in my cheeks. I can't say why I felt such shame, but I was glad the house lights were dim.

Jimmy continued to dust, and John to scrub, both with exaggerated swishing of their bottoms. A grand movement of the duster knocked a key from the top of the cabinet. John tried it in the lock. It opened. Inside were bottle upon bottle of whiskey. The audience ooed in anticipation.

I won't say any more. To this day the memory of it raises feelings inside me. Suffice it to say that if I had ever behaved like that when I was in service, I would have been out on the street so fast I wouldn't have known what hit me. God knows I was sacked for far less.

Beside me Bryan chuckled. Mick leaned over, whispered something to Tom, and pointed, a big grin on his face. I just sat, my arms folded on my chest, my thumb stroking my lips, as though trying to persuade them to silence. I sat and I thought of Mama, of Mrs. O'Rourke, of my room beneath the stairs, of the backbreaking work that made my hands bleed.

*　*　*

The night air had cooled some when we left the theater. A breeze somehow found its way down the canyon between buildings. It was a welcome thing after the close air of the theater.

"What did you think?" Bryan asked.

"Throw him *down* McClusky," Mick chanted as he stomped his foot on the sidewalk. "What a grand song!"

"I liked the monkey," Tom said.

I held my tongue. "Clare?" Bryan said. I looked up. "What did you think?"

"I never saw anything like it in my whole life," I said. I was still in a contrary humor and thought it best I stayed noncommittal.

"And so you haven't," Bryan said. "New York has the best theater in the world. How about a soda?"

"Never had a soda," Mick said.

"Never had an ice cream soda?" Bryan said incredulously. "How about a hot dog?"

"Is that something to eat?" Tom asked.

"Green, green, green," Bryan said, shaking his head. "Hot dogs and ice-cream sodas it is." He glanced over his shoulder, and waded out into the street. "Come on." We followed, dodging carts and horses, cringing a bit when a police officer halfway down the block shouted and waved his night stick at us.

"Bryan," I said when our feet were safely on the sidewalk again. "We need to be a bit more careful about our money. "We still have to buy train tickets. And I'm not sure how much food costs here. And . . . "

Bryan interrupted me with a wave of his hand. "And what kind of a host would I be if I didn't buy you a hot dog and soda on your first night in America? Don't worry about the cost. I have plenty of money right here." He patted his pocket again for emphasis. I could practically feel all our hard-earned money there beneath his palm.

"Bryan," I said. "We need that money. I worked hard for that money. So did Mick and Tom. It's ours. I think you should give it to me now."

"Clare, now don't you go spoiling the evening," Bryan said. "I've said it before: your money is safer with me until we get off these streets. You don't know how many gorillas there are out there just waiting to steal a greenhorn like you blind. When we get home, you'll not even need to remind me. As soon as we cross the threshold, I'll give you the money. How's that?"

I nodded. I wasn't sure what recourse I had. I couldn't very well wrestle him for it, certainly not there in the middle of the street in front of God and everyone. And he had taken us in. And saved me from the swindler on the boat. Even if I didn't completely trust him, I did feel a certain sense of obligation. I nodded and decided to wait.

"You know,' Tom said, changing the subject, "I think I used to know someone who had a dress just like Jimmy's. If I could just remember who it was."

"Did she have a mustache like his, too?" Bryan said, nudging Tom with his elbow.

Tom staggered a bit. "I believe she did," he said with a laugh.

"No women in the world more beautiful than Irish women," Bryan said. Mick burst out in a huge guffaw.

I held my peace.

We came upon an ice cream parlor before a hot dog vendor. Bryan motioned us through the front door and parked us on high chairs at the counter where we could watch the soda clerk work.

"Four ice cream sodas," he said.

"Chocolate or pineapple?" the clerk said.

"What do you think?" Bryan asked.

"Chocolate," Tom said.

"Chocolate," Mick echoed.

"And chocolate for me," Bryan said. He looked at me. So did Tom and Mick.

"Pineapple," I said. I don't think I'd ever had pineapple in my life. But at that moment, all I could think was to distance myself from the three of them. I couldn't very well go somewhere else in a completely foreign city, so pineapple it was.

"Three chocolate, one pineapple." the clerk said. He pulled four glasses from the shelf, gave each a quick swipe with a towel, and began spooning something thick and syrupy into each glass.

"So," Bryan said, "how long do you suppose you'll be staying with me?" He addressed the question to Mick.

"Just long enough to track down Uncle Ronan," Mick said. "I can't imagine it will take that long. What is that he's doing?" Mick pointed to the soda clerk, who was opening a valve of some kind and spraying some kind of liquid into the glasses.

"That's the soda water," Bryan said. "Why do you think they call them ice cream sodas?"

"Hmm," Mick said. The clerk took four long spoons from a jar and stirred the soda water into the syrup. "How long does it take to get a telegram to Minnesota from here?" he asked.

"I wouldn't think any time at all," Bryan said. "It just goes right across, you know."

"So it does," Mick said. "Maybe a day or two to respond then. Not long."

"They have to find him, don't they," Bryan said.

"They do," Mick replied. "I guess I can't really say, then. Not long, though. I can't imagine it would be long." The clerk was scooping ice cream into the glasses. Mick's eyes were drawn to it. I looked at Tom. His face was animated by pure desire. Despite the peach we'd had before the show, my stomach growled. We must have looked quite a sight, the three of us lined up at the counter, grasping at those glasses with our eyes and our hearts.

"Would you want a job in the meantime?" Bryan asked, hitting on the one thing that could have drawn our minds from the food. "You and Tom. Earn a little money?"

"We would," Mick said. "What do you have in mind?" The sound of the clerk drawing more soda filled the shop, but Mick turned to face Bryan, his eyes straying only slightly to the nearly finished sodas.

"We can always use a good water boy on the job site," Bryan said, "or two. You fill the water buckets, add a bit of salt, a bit of lemon, take it out to where the fellows are working. It's hard work, hot work. But the money is better than you'd make hawking papers, and sometimes if you really hop to it, the fellows will give you a little extra."

"We'll take it," Mick said.

"Good," Bryan replied. "I'll introduce you to the foreman tomorrow. He owes me one, so I'd say you're as good as hired." The soda clerk spooned a bit of cream over the sodas, topped them with cherries, slipped in straws, and slid them across the counter to us.

"Where is it you said you worked?" I asked. I pulled the spoon gingerly from the glass, and licked the handle. The flavor was completely foreign, but quite wonderful. Tom was looking at his straw. He slid it out, gazed down its length, then reinserted it. Looking around, he was obviously trying to glean clues as to its use. Bryan grinned at him, leaned in and sucked on his. Tom did the same. His face brightened.

"I work on the Manhattan Bridge," he said. "Riveter. No one works harder, but then no one gets paid better."

"Is it dangerous work?" I asked.

"If you call the possibility of falling three-hundred feet to your death 'dangerous'," he said. He stirred the scoop of ice cream in his soda round and round the glass. "But that's only likely to happen if you don't know what you're doing. I do."

"And Mick and Tom, would they be climbing to three-hundred feet?" I asked.

"Them? No, no," Bryan said, "not nearly that high. Granted, on a construction site there are perfectly good ways to die with your feet on the ground. But everybody watches out for the water boys. Nobody's going to put them in too great a danger. We do that, we die of thirst." He smiled. I guessed that he was kidding and smiled weakly back.

"Ah, Clare, now if you aren't just like my own sister with your worrying," Bryan said. "Mick and Tom will be fine. I can assure you of that. But no matter what I say, you'll still worry. That's the way of things. The women worry. The men make do. It's been true ever since the first man built the first building ever." He took a deep draw of his soda.

"We'll be fine, Clare," Mick said. "It'll be a chance to earn a bit of extra cash. That way it will be all right if we don't find Uncle Ronan right away."

* * *

My teeth ached. From the way Tom was walking one hand on his jaw and his left eye squeezed shut, I guessed his did as well. Mick and Bryan walked ahead, both with their hands bulging in their pockets, both with their caps pushed back on their heads. If either of them were hurting, I couldn't tell by looking at them.

The hot dog vendors had all called it an evening by the time we got to the edge of the park, where Bryan expected to find them. So we ended up at a confectioners, where we stuffed our faces with sweets. Bryan stressed that these were *American candies* as we stood arched over the glass display case filled with cream filled chocolates, and toffees and caramels. His implication was clearly that they were superior in some crucial way to anything we had eaten before. The thing about American candies that made the greatest impression on me, however, was that it took American teeth to eat them. The poor, rotten teeth of an Irish laner were no match for the sticky, creamy sweetness of the American candy store.

As we walked out onto the park again, watched the police officers nudging the bums from the grass with truncheons, I began to wonder what place America had for the likes of me. Was America so rich a place that she would do no more than laugh when I came to her looking for work with nothing more than scrubbing floors and sorting sacks to my credit? Was it true that any boy could grow up to be a riveter, or a grouper at Ellis Island, or Mayor of New York? Or could folks like me only taste opportunity before finding it hurt our teeth too much to swallow?

The cop nudged a bum out from under a bench. Lying there, he looked like a pile of rags. The cop herded him from the park, swinging his truncheon in circles before him. As we passed him, he tipped his hat.

*　*　*

On the front steps of the apartment, a man with a thick brown mustache and canvas worker's trousers hailed us. Bryan trotted up to him and stuck out a hand.

"George," he said. "Long time no see."

"That's just what I told that worthless roommate of yours," the man said.

"Ah now, George," Bryan said, "you'll need to be clearer than that if you want me to know who you're talking about, and me with two, sometimes three or four, worthless roommates."

"You haven't changed at all, Keane," the man said. "These aren't yours, are they?" He motioned at us.

"Not that I know about," Bryan replied. The man laughed. "They're just some kids my mother came home with. Got time for a drink?"

"That's also what I said to your worthless roommate. Rick, I mean," the man said. "And do you know what he said? 'I have work tomorrow and can't afford to be hung over.' Work! What have you been teaching that boy, Keane, that he'd allow work to stand between him and a pint with an old friend?"

"Shocking," Bryan said. "Shocking! How about I buy you one instead?"

"And your mother's, um, friends?" George asked.

Bryan turned to us. "You should be asleep, shouldn't you? It's late."

"Should we just sleep on the floor then?" Mick asked.

"Or pull together a couple of chairs," Bryan said. "Stay out of Alan and Rick's room and stay out of my bed—that's for Ma and me—but other than that, you can sleep in the sink for all I care." And with that he slapped his friend on the back and headed off down the street.

We had climbed the interminable staircase and were up in the apartment, assessing the futility of trying to turn two kitchen chairs into a bed before I realized that all our cash had gone with Bryan to buy George a drink.

Twenty-Nine

I slept below the window and awoke the next morning covered in a sticky sweat and a thin layer of soot. My teeth were throbbing in my head. Mrs. Keane was already up, bumping about the kitchen pulling together breakfast from the meager stores Bryan kept in his pantry.

"Not so much as a drop of milk for my tea," she said, slamming the door of the empty icebox. "I come all the way from Ireland to visit my son, and he can't be bothered to pay the milkman so I can have a drop of milk for my tea in the morning." She dropped the kettle onto the range with a clank. "Bryan," she said. "Give us two bits for the meter now." Not so much as a sound from him. "Bryan. Wake up. The meter needs money. You wouldn't send your old mother off without a bit of tea in her belly, would you?"

Bryan looked like a pile of dirty clothes in the corner. Mrs. Keane had spent the night on the murphy bed. Bryan, who I assumed would share the bed with his mother when he got home, had slept on the floor. He was still in his clothes from the night before. In fact he was still in his cap and shoes. He had apparently bedded down where he fell the night before. From the looks of him, I doubt he had slept any worse for the disaccommodation.

"Bryan!" Mrs. Keane had stridden with purpose into the living room and was beating the floor with her stick mere inches from his head. I heard Alan and Rick stir in the bedroom.

"Stinken bowsie," Mrs. Keane muttered. "Mick, boyo, come help your aunty, won't you?" Mick rose from the floor beside me. "Reach down into his trouser pocket there and see if my drunken lout of a son has a quarter for the gas meter." Mick looked hesitant. "Go on then, boy," she said. "Unless you want to wait until noontime to get something in your belly."

Mick bent down over Bryan's inert form, and gingerly slipped a finger into his trouser pocket. Above me on the chairs, Tom shifted for a better look.

Frankly, I wouldn't have believed Bryan could move that fast, what with the state he was in. His hand darted out from under his head, and I heard a sharp slap as it locked over Mick's fingers.

"Hold off there, boyo. There's nothing in there I'd like the likes of you pawing at," he said.

"He lives!" Mrs. Keane exclaimed. Bryan grumbled as he extracted Mick's hand and fairly threw it back at him. Mick withdrew to the kitchen, and dumping Tom from one of the chairs, sat heavily. "Get your worthless bones off that floor, and come feed the meter. I have a train to catch, and I'm not about to climb alone onto one of those smoke-belching beasts without my tea."

So she was leaving. I knew she would be soon, but I had hoped she would at least stay as long as we did. In my mind, I pictured staying here with Bryan until the telegram arrived. Without Mrs. Keane in the picture, the image shifted radically. I felt the sudden desire to get myself up, fully awake, ready to meet what the day might throw at us.

"Your train doesn't leave until 1:00," Bryan said, glancing out the front window. "It can't be later than six now. We have hours."

"I want my tea," Mrs. Keane said. "And I want to see a priest. Then I want a decent meal with my son. You been promising to take me to that cafeteria you always go to for creamed oyster on toast. If you're going to send me all the way across the country alone, the least you can do for me is feed me right for a change."

Bryan removed his cap and scrubbed a hand through his greasy hair. "Yeah, sure, Mam. Tea, priest, meal, train. We can do that." He reached into his jacket pocket and drew out a small purse. He dug with his fingers around the edges of the bills until he found a quarter, which he dropped into his mother's hand.

"I'll tell them that next time they say you're a worthless lout of a son who would never so much as lift a finger to see his mother safe and happy." Mrs. Keane hobbled back into the kitchen and dropped the coin into the meter. "I can't take another day in this penance of a city. Heat, smoke, more heat. And that stink. It's enough to curdle the food in your mouth, that stink is. All I do is sit alone all day, sweat and retch."

"I'd stay home with you, Mam. You know I would. But I have to work," Bryan said. He had pulled off his boots and was changing his stockings. "It's a good job, Mam, and I don't want to lose it. I had to cash in any number of favors just to get the day off to see you to the train."

"Ah yes, a good job. The 'high steel'. So I heard. If it's such a good job, why do you still live in this hole?" She drew a pinch of leaves from the tea box and dropped it into the pot.

"I have three rooms, three windows, every one of them opening onto free air. I have water and a flush toilet on the very floor I live on," Bryan said evenly. "It's a good apartment."

"Your brother has a house," Mrs. Keane said. "A house, and a family, and a fair sight more than three windows. He's a respected man already."

"Well, fit him for a halo, then," Bryan grunted. "Just don't put the cost of it on my bill." He was pulling his boots on again. "When do you want to leave the house?"

"Soon," Mrs. Keane.

"I'll be back 'soon,' then," Bryan slapped his cap onto his head and strode out the door.

* * *

We drank the tea without milk and ate what little bread was still in the box. Halfway through breakfast Rick and Alan emerged from the bedroom like bears from a cave. Alan flipped open the lid of the breadbox, shook the tea pot, then muttering a good morning, shook his head at Rick. They were out the door in no more than a minute. Mick and Tom gulped the last of their tea and followed.

"Be back in ten minutes," I called after them.

"Ten minutes," Mick shouted from the stairs.

I rose to start work on the breakfast dishes. Between the ungiving boards of the floor, my teeth, the heat, the unfamiliar stink, and Bryan's stumbling in sometime in the wee hours, I had slept quite poorly. My neck hurt. My arms and legs felt lazy, reticent.

"Clare," Mrs. Keane said to me as I was gathering the tea cups, "I would like to ask you something." She was brushing the crumbs on the table into a little pile.

"Go right ahead," I said, setting the cups in the sink and sitting down again at the table.

"How would you like to go to Butte with me?" she asked.

"Butte," I said finally, when I had found my breath again. "Me?"

"You," Mrs. Keane said. "Patricia is nowhere to be found. I have the money for her ticket left. And Lord knows I could use the help, what with my worthless lump of a son doing nothing more than shoving me onto the train then turning his back."

"Only me," I said. "Not Mick and Tom."

"I can't really afford to bring Mick and Tom," she said. "I could afford a bit extra to send you on to the soft-eyed pup of yours in Washington. It's not that much farther, you know. And Bryan could put the boys on a train to their uncle when they find him."

"Only me," I repeated to myself. She nodded.

"You do want to go to Washington?" she said.

"I do."

"He'd welcome you?"

"He asked me to marry him," I said. "But he's only fifteen, well maybe sixteen by now. And I'm not that myself."

"My Anne was just barely sixteen when she wed. Her man was a year or two older, of course. I think marrying early is a good thing. I married when I was nineteen, and by that time I was already set in my ways. So was Jack. We fought like dogs for the first two or three years. My Anne never went through that. I think it was because she married young. Besides when you marry young, you still have some life left in you when your children are grown and gone."

"I don't know," I said. "Marriage is . . . "

"Now, am I asking you to marry this minute?" Mrs. Keane said, nudging me gently from my thoughts with her cane. "All I'm asking is, will you see me safe to Butte? That's all. What you do when you get there or to Washington is your decision."

"Let me think," I said, rising from my chair. If my legs had been heavy a minute ago, they were doubly so now. They barely carried me to the sink. Were these the same legs that were supposed to carry me to Butte? To Washington?

"Think all you want," Mrs. Keane said. "But do it quickly. We leave in an hour or two."

An hour or two. I rinsed the teapot, dipping water from the bucket into the pot and pouring it down the dry sink. Going with Mrs. Keane would solve some of our money worries, what with me not having to buy a ticket. And I could be with Colum again. And I would like to help Mrs. Keane. After all she did for us, I felt as though I owed her a bit of help.

Mrs. Keane shuffled up behind me, and laid the bread knife in the sink. She seemed to be leaning a bit heavier on her cane this morning. I wondered how much it hurt her to walk. The problem was going to be Mick and Tom. Bryan would see them onto the train to Uncle Ronan. If they could find Uncle Ronan. We still hadn't heard anything from the lumber company in St. Croix., though it had been less than a day since we sent the telegram. Of course, there was always the matter of money—in this case, how much Bryan had already spent, how much Mick would spend without me there to watch him. I wasn't sure I trusted Bryan with the boys. And did Mrs. Keane need me on the train more than the boys would? If I traveled with her, they would travel alone. Every bit of intuition said I should see the boys safely to Uncle Ronan before heading further west. But when I closed my eyes, all I saw was Colum's face.

I glanced into the living room. Mrs. Keane was seated on the edge of the murphy bed looking out the open window. How I wished she wouldn't leave. She had been an aunt to us, as much as Ronan had been an uncle, and he was our own kin.

When it came right down to it, though, there was only one real issue: family. Not extended family, not future family, not adoptive family, but *my* family. The boys and me. I told Mama I would care for the boys, that I would keep us together. The three of us had been through the very flames of purgatory in an attempt to keep that promise. I couldn't very well leave them now, now that we had finally made it to America. I could feel Colum tugging at my heart, but, no, I had to keep us together.

"The boys need me," I said. It came out far too quietly. I cleared my throat and tried again. "The boys need me."

"And I don't?" she answered, not taking her eyes from the window.

"I promised my mother," I said. "I promised I would keep us together."

"You keep your promises, then."

"I try," I said.

"I wish my children did," she said.

I didn't know what to say to that. "I'll see you to the train," I said. She didn't answer, just continued to stare out the window.

* * *

It must have been close to 10:30. The boys were down on the front stoop. Mrs. Keane and I were sitting quietly. She was smoking her pipe. I was trying to ignore the soot on the windowsill. We were both watching life unfold out the window. Children too young for school played on the front stoop across the way. Now and then a vendor would make his way through the streets: "Rags to give, rags to give, any old clothes." "Knives to sharpen, scissors to grind" "Peanuts. Fresh roasted peanuts." Every now and then Mrs. Keane would consult her watch, snort, and shake her head. I was beginning to wonder if maybe we might have her with us a bit longer. I suppose that secretly, I hope it would be true. That was when we heard a knock at the door. Mrs. Keane motioned with her cane, and I rose to answer it.

"I'm looking for Mrs. Keane," the man in the doorway said. He held his cap meekly over his belly. He looked as though he were afraid someone was going to hit him. Given that that was a fitting response to having met Mrs. Keane's bad side, I assume they knew each other and invited the man in.

"Who would you be then?" Mrs. Keane said, shifting a bit on the bed for a better view. The man walked into the living room a bit farther to spare her neck, which was craned around about as far as it would go.

"Henry, ma'am, Brennan Henry."

"Mr. Brennan," she said. "What can I do for you?"

"The name is Henry, ma'am," the man said.

"I understand, Mrs. Keane replied, "but since I just learned it a second ago, I can't very well call you by your Christian name, can I?"

"No ma'am," he said. "But it's Brennan Henry. Henry is my last name."

"Sounds like it should be the other way around," Mrs. Keane pronounced with finality.

"I've always thought so too, ma'am," Mr. Henry said.

"So what can I do for you, Mr. Brennan Henry?"

"Well ma'am," Henry ran a hand through his thinning brown hair. He had bad news. I could tell it. He set his eyes on something out the window, shooting nervous glances at Mrs. Keane out of the corner of his eye. "I have a message from your son, from Mr. Keane." I took a seat in the kitchen. "He hired my wagon for the rest of the day, said I should take you anywhere you wanted to go."

Bryan was alive at least. Not that he would be for long once Mrs. Keane got her hands on him.

"And did 'Mr. Keane' say where he was going to be?" Mrs. Keane said coldly.

Mr. Henry's shoulders tightened. "Well, that's just the thing. He said he wasn't going to be able to see you off. He said a business opportunity had presented itself, one that he couldn't walk away from." He paused. "He said he knew you would be upset, but that he hoped you would understand."

Mrs. Keane said nothing, just swung her cane in a wide arc. The jug that had been sitting on a wash stand beside the window crashed to the floor. I wondered if Bryan had mentioned to Mr. Henry to stay out of range of the cane. He cringed a bit at Mrs. Keane's outburst, but didn't seem too surprised. Mrs. Keane cranked back and backhanded the tip into the window. It cracked but didn't shatter.

"Ass," she spat the word out like something bitter and nasty in her mouth. "Ass." Leaning heavily on her cane, she stood. "Ass." Mr. Henry stepped back to give her a wide berth. "Don't only stand there," she said. "Start loading all this." She motioned at the trunk and the bags lying beside the bed. She reached for her hat and set it atop her head. She wielded her hat pin in a way that made me reassess the number of her potential weapons. "I raised an ass for a son," she said. Mr. Henry was already nearly out the door with the trunk, as heavy as it was.

"Clare, I have three bags, the trunk, and that hamper beside the icebox. See that he doesn't miss anything. I'm going to make a start on those flaming stairs—if I never see them again I'll count myself blessed."

"I'm still coming with you to the station?" I asked.

"Didn't you say you would?"

"I did," I said.

"Well, then you best move your feet," she said. "Unless you'd like to go back on your word as well."

* * *

With Mick and Tom's help, we loaded the wagon and set off through the streets. It had to be nearly eleven o'clock. I was glad to be out in the air. I was equally glad to be riding in the back with the boys and the bags. Mr. Henry apparently worked for a brewery as his wagon was half-full of hops sacks. We sat back against them, outside cane range, but that didn't mean any of us relaxed. Tom fidgeted with some loose strings hanging from one of the sacks. Mr. Henry sat rigid on the seat beside Mrs. Keane and her principal weapon, talking gently to his horse. The soothing words, I guessed, were as much an effort to calm himself as the beast.

As the sun climbed the sky and began lighting the streets between buildings, we cut over to Fifth Avenue. To my amazement, within blocks we passed from tenements to the streets of gold I had heard tell of back in Ireland. As we turned north onto Fifth, driving past Madison Square and the Waldorf Astoria, we shared the street with shiny motor cars and beautiful carriages. The shop windows bore jewel and clothing the likes of which I had never seen. The houses we passed were great mansions built on wide tree-lined sidewalks. Mick came alive, his head swiveling to and fro. Myself? I felt a bit like a trespasser, as though I had entered this glorious part of town through the front door and not the tradesmen's entrance. Not that I would turn back, of course. Mrs. Keane was determined to see a priest, and not just any priest, a priest in the cathedral. None of us were about to tell her she couldn't.

Appropriately enough, in New York, the cathedral sat just down the street from the Vanderbilt mansion. Contrary to the rumors, the Vanderbilts were obviously not "as rich as God." The cathedral, brand new and gleaming in its glory, outshone every mansion on the block as though they were just so many poor sisters. This cathedral was greater than the one in Queenstown, greater than Ellis Island, greater than anything I had seen in my life. The great gold-colored front door was three times my height and then some. That door was set into an arch that was twice its size. And that great arch was no more than a small part of the front facade, which, in turn, was dwarfed by towering gothic spires. A body could lose herself just making her way into the church. Perhaps that was the point.

Inside the stone floors gleamed as did the gold of the altar. The great vaulted ceilings terrified me and called to me both. I would have liked to have walked, explored—for in a cathedral this huge one would have to walk and explore to see the half of it. But Mrs. Keane sat us firmly in a pew with strict instructions not to go disappearing, as she had lost enough people for one day. The echoy air hummed with life—tourists with their necks bent back as far as they would go, priests ducking in and out on business, folks like me sitting or kneeling in the pews, waiting for someone or something.

As we sat, a woman caught my eye, an elderly dark-haired woman in a plain dress and apron. With a rag she polished the wood of a pew. From the look on her face, I could see that she polished not only with muscle, but with her heart, her whole self. I watched her, a feeling of gratitude welling inside me. She must have felt my gaze, for she looked up, meeting my eyes immediately. I smiled and nodded a bit. She smiled and nodded back. I didn't recognize her race, but I did recognize a kindred spirit. I think maybe she did, too. The hurry and turmoil inside me settled a bit, enough for me not just to pray but also to be still and listen. I drew my attention from the grandeur of my surroundings and set them on their Owner. It was a relief of worry just to sit in his company and pray my beads.

When she returned, it was clear that Mrs. Keane had received no such grace. She was, if anything, more unsettled after her confession. I wondered if it were possible to make "bless me, Father, for I have sinned" sound like a threat. She motioned with her cane, and without appearing to take in any of the beauty of the building, she walked, and limped, and hobbled toward the door.

* * *

The station was not far. But when we got there, we found ourselves dodging construction wagons, barricades, and dozens of other people like us weaving their way through workmen and machinery. It was too late to visit a restaurant, that much was sure. Mrs. Keane would go off to Butte without her creamed oysters on toast. Instead, we ended up with bagels from a pushcart for lunch. We ate them in the wagon wishing for something wet to chase them down with. We didn't dare ask, though. Mrs. Keane had stopped talking beyond sharp, single word instructions to the pushcart operator and to Mr. Henry. "Twelve." "Train." "Go." Beside me Tom sighed two or three times every minute.

At the front door to the station—which was, I should say, another massive stone building with no shortage of adornments—Mrs. Keane looked at us, her face a stone mask, and said simply, "stay." Mr. Henry hopped out to find a porter. Once they had eased Mrs. Keane down from her seat and loaded the bags onto the porter's cart, I realized that was it. I had expected to see her onto the train, at least onto the platform. But she was heading toward the front door on the elbow of the porter, and we were still sitting atop the hops sacks in front of the building. Mr. Henry stood motionless, clutching the edge of his driver's seat. He too appeared to be watching for clues about what to do next.

"Wait," I said, leaning over the side of the wagon and touching Mr. Henry's shoulder lightly. "Wait for a bit, will you?" He nodded. I hopped out the back of the wagon. It was no trouble to catch Mrs. Keane and the porter. But once I'd caught them, I wasn't quite sure what to say. That's when I felt Mick behind me, nudging his way around me.

"Aunt Bridget," he said, opening his arms for an embrace. Mrs. Keane released the porter's elbow and took him in. Mick planted a kiss on her stiff cheek. "Thank you," he said. "Whenever I think about how I entered America, I will think about you. You made it possible."

"True enough," Tom said. He leaned in and added his kiss to Mick's.

"I would be coming with you," I said, "if I could. You know that, don't you?" Mick looked over at me, a question on his face. Mrs. Keane nodded slightly.

"You're good children," she said, the mask crumbling only the slightest bit. "It's nice to know there are still a few left in the world."

"Let us come in with you," Mick said. "Just to see you onto the train safely."

Mrs. Keane shook her head. "I'm on my own. 'Tis best I get used to that idea right now. Go," she said. "Go. God bless." She caught the porter's arm, and turned her face to the station.

* * *

"The floor could use a bit of going over," Bryan commented offhandedly the next morning during breakfast. He slathered butter on a cut of bread, stuffed it nearly whole into his mouth and chased it down with a swig of coffee. "The stove, too," he mumbled around the mouthful that wouldn't go down on the first swallow.

I assumed he was suggesting that I do some major cleaning while he was away at work. It was fair, I supposed, after he went out on a limb for us, took us in without asking us to pay.

"And you can tell Mrs. Lotti across the hall that we won't be needing her to cook as long as you're here."

"You want me to cook, then?" I asked.

"You said you could, didn't you?" Bryan responded.

"I did," I said.

"Well then it doesn't make any sense at all to pay Mrs. Lotti to cook so long as you're here," Bryan said with no small amount of irritation.

I decided to hold my tongue and simply nod.

"Do you know what I'd like?" Bryan said. I shook my head. "Cod," he said. "I haven't had cod since I was a boy. Every now and then a fresh load would come in on the train, and Mam would bake it with bacon and onions. I asked her to fix it like that when she was here. She said she was too old to be traipsing off to some fish market through streets not fit for a dog. That's what she said. My own mother. Can you bake cod?"

"I believe so," I said. I'd baked other meats, why not cod? Then something dawned on me. "Is it Friday?" I asked.

"Wednesday," he said, "Here." He pulled a few coins from his purse and dropped them on the table. "You need to go down to Hester Street. That's where the best fish is. The sheenies bring it in on pushcarts. Don't pay more than thirteen cents a pound, no matter what they tell you."

"Thirteen cents," I said. "And where would Hester Street be?"

"It's down below Houston," he said. "Lower East side. Not too far from the bridge."

"Below Houston," I said. I hadn't the slightest idea what he meant.

"Just take the elevated, the one outside the window?" He looked at me. I nodded. It was hard to lose a train that rattled the windows at all times of the day and night.

"Get off around Chatham street, then . . . " He paused, obviously trying to picture the route in his mind. "Then just ask someone. Everyone knows where Hester street is."

"Is it far?" I asked. "Not that I mind the trip. It's just that I wouldn't want to miss the telegram boy when he comes."

"It's not far, and Mrs. Lotti can catch the telegram boy. Leave the tip with her before you leave. Just how difficult is it for a man to get some cod for his supper? You'd think I was asking for pâté de bleedin' fois gras. Is that too much trouble?"

"It's not," I said. "But, uh, just one more thing?" Before he could respond, I blurted out my question. "Is this enough money for the train?" The pile of coins in my fist were beginning to look familiar, but I still had no instinctive feel for their worth. Bryan sighed, dug into his purse again, and dropped another two into my hand.

"While we're on the subject of money," Mick said. "Do you suppose we could have the money you're keeping for us now? We could keep it here in the apartment until we leave." I cringed. The boy had no sense of timing whatsoever. I knew the answer before he finished asking.

"With Rick and those other blokes coming and going?" Bryan said. "I don't think that's a good idea."

"Just the same," Mick said. "We'd like to hold our money ourselves."

"I have to be getting to work," Bryan said. "You coming? You want the water boy job?"

"I do," Mick said. "But about the money . . . "

"Trust me," Bryan said. "It's safe. Oh, and Clare, when you do the bed sheets, bring the water in here. The landlord doesn't want us using the tub in the hallway for washing."

"I will," I said. It appeared I had a job as well.

* * *

Things were different back then. Today if a woman was asked to do the things we did back then, she would revolt, declare that she wasn't anyone's slave, wouldn't be put upon in that fashion. But you have to remember that this was before automatic washers and dishwashers, before blenders and electric knives.

If the carpet was going to get cleaned, someone, usually a woman, would have to take a broom to it, or would have to haul it on her shoulders to the yard and beat the dirt out of it. If the wet clothes were going to get dry, someone had to hang them in the yard, take them down from the yard, heat the iron on the fire, press them, and finally fold or hang them. Food was chopped by hand, fires were stoked by hand, water was carried by hand, anything roasted, toasted, broiled, dried, beaten, pressed, packed, or pickled, was done so by hand. Our version of a laborsaving device was called a spouse. If a man had a woman by his side, he didn't have to clean and cook for himself. If a woman had a man by her side, she didn't have to go out, earn a living, then come home and wrestle the house to the ground in the evening.

I think it was just such a laborsaving arrangement that Bryan had in mind. Perhaps not the spouse part, but certainly the coming home to a clean house and a hot meal part. In retrospect, I think maybe he had certain spousal privileges in mind as well. I was too young, too inexperienced to read the signals if they were there. It was enough on that day that I had a cod to find and kitchen to scrub. And if Bryan made me a bit nervous, the housework did settle me. I'd talk to Mrs. Lotti, find the cod, wait for the telegram. We'd see about the sheets after that.

* * *

Bryan's door was straight across the hall from the Lotti's. We shared a landing and water closet with them. Given that, not to mention the heat that forced all the doors in the buildings open for ventilation, I felt I already knew a good bit about the Lottis, though I had never really met them.

When I stepped across the hall to knock, a ragged-haired boy of nine, maybe ten, years met me at the half-open door. Were it not for the dark eyes and olive skin, he could easily have been a boy from the lanes of Cork. His grubby feet were bare. His shirt tail, the hem patched with two different colors of thread, hung out over his nondescript short brown trousers. He opened the door, then stood there looking at me, then over his shoulder at a woman and a young girl huddled over a table by the window, then at me again.

"Come in, come in," the woman at the table said. "Sit." She motioned at a chair. "Timeo, don't you close that door. Do you want them to find us all dead in here of the heat?"

"It won't stay open, Mama," Timeo said. Mrs. Lotti sighed and gave him a look that said "deal with it." Timeo propped the door open with the skillet from the stove, returned to the table, and picked up a mallet.

"I'd offer you some coffee, but Louie doesn't get paid until tomorrow, and we drank the last of it this morning." She held up a small scrap of silk she was painting and examined it in the low light filtering in from the window. Bryan was apparently accurate when he bragged about having better windows than most. The Lotti's view looked out at a brick wall mere feet away. Satisfied with her painting, Mrs. Lotti laid the bit of silk out with a couple of dozen others to dry.

"We have some tea left, I think," she said. "Would you like a cup?"

"Thank you," I said. "But I don't have time to stay."

"Suit yourself," she said. I was a bit surprised. Her accent was minimal and she spoke in the same American idioms I'd been hearing since I arrived. Bryan referred to the Lottis as "the dagos across the hall," and complained bitterly he never understood what Mrs. Lotti was saying. But to me, Mrs. Lotti looked and sounded far less foreign than most of the New Yorkers I'd seen on the streets.

"You'd be the boss's sister then," she said. "Or some relative of Mrs. Keane."

"Well, no," I said," "I don't believe he has a sister in New York, or, well, if he does, I'm not her." I picked up one of the little scraps of silk. A tiny vein of purple split the pink in two. That little line turned the scrap of fabric into something else, something that looked almost alive. "I'm not a sister," I said, "only, um, a friend." I hesitated a bit on the word "friend." Bryan was doing a friend's favor for us, but I wasn't sure if that's what one would call a man who could still rob us blind. Still I supposed "friend" was as good a public description of the relationship as any. "He helped us out with some trouble we were having with immigration," I added.

"Oh?" Mrs. Lotti said, raising an eyebrow. The air around her chilled. "Do you have business with me?" It might have been just my imagination, or it might have been the sudden tenseness in Mrs. Lotti's face and shoulders—whatever it was I suddenly sensed that I was no longer welcome around her table. Just then Timeo brought the mallet down hard on the die he'd been fussing over. The table jumped. I must have too because my chair skidded back with a screech.

"I have a message from Bryan, um, Mr. Keane," I said, feeling the need for a bit of formality. I could feel her eyes cold upon me. I wanted nothing more than to scoot out from under them and continue on with my errands. "He said he would no longer need you to cook for them as long as I'm here."

"You cook, too?" Mrs. Lotti said. "That has to be convenient for him."

"Yes ma'am," I said, rising from the chair. I wished I knew what I had said or done. "I'm sorry . . . to . . . trouble you." I bent over to shift the skillet out of the way.

"Wait," Mrs. Lotti said. "Wait. I'm the one who's sorry. You seem like a good girl, maybe you found your way into Bryan's bed purely by accident, but I have to tell you . . . "

"Bryan's bed?" I said. "No, ma'am. No. I'm not. . . . No, not that."

"So you're really just a friend, not, um, his 'friend'?" Mrs. Lotti said.

"Didn't I say so?" I replied.

"Yes, I suppose you did," Mrs. Lotti said, "but I thought . . . " She paused. "Well, never mind what I thought," she picked up another scrap of silk, and with a flourish traced a purple line across its front. "It's just that, um, one hears things. One sees things. Those three gorillas you have been staying with have been fuel for more than one good gossip among the women of the building. They don't exactly spend all their spare time in church, if you catch my drift."

I didn't, not entirely, but I did catch it enough to know I wanted to find out more. "Does Bryan have many friends, then?" I asked.

Mrs. Lotti looked up from her painting, stared at me for a moment in surprise, then burst out laughing. "Why do I think you aren't the innocent young thing you appear to be? You've either seen it all or you're no more than a day from your Mama's womb, I can't tell which." She handed me a fine bit of wire, and pushed several of the petals she'd painted across the table at me. "You might as well work while you listen," she said. She showed me how to thread several of the petals onto the wire, fan them out more or less evenly, then tack them into place with a bit of paste. A small silk flower took shape.

So there we sat. While we worked, she talked, told me a story of strange women entering and leaving Bryan's apartment at odd hours, a story of drunken fights between Bryan and his roommates nearly every payday. Mrs. Lotti speculated that the fights and the women were why Bryan couldn't keep a room in a respectable boarding house and had to take a room in this tenement, whose landlord allegedly would take anyone with cash. A picture began to take shape. I wondered if Mrs. Keane knew about her son's habits. Perhaps she did, and that's why she felt the need to leave so quickly.

"And you're staying with him?" she asked. "On the kitchen floor?" I nodded. "How long?"

"Until we hear from my Uncle in Minnesota. Then we'll go out there."

She twirled her brush in the paint a bit to sharpen the point at its tip. "Well then, do be careful," she said.

Be careful. As though care had made one bit of difference to my situation thus far. No, if there was one thing I had learned in the last few months it was that being careful sometimes made no difference whatsoever.

"I will," I said, to be agreeable more than anything else.

Timeo brought the mallet down again with a crash.

* * *

The telegram never did come, and I never did get to the fish market. Mrs. Lotti, Timeo, and I sat and worked until dinnertime. Little Gina, who could not have been more than four, got a dispensation from her mother after a few hours that allowed her to stop separating petals. She retreated to a place by the window where she fed paint chips to her dolly. When the sun had reached its peak and was finally shining, but now quite without mercy, on the kitchen table, Mrs. Lotti pulled from the ice box a huge pile of little pillows. The pillows, it turns out were noodles stuffed with cheeses and crumbs and spices I couldn't begin to identify. We ate them cold with bread and cool butter.

After dinner we worked and talked some more. She talked about New York and the Lower East side where she had grown up, about her parents who had come from a small town outside Rome, who never spoke a word of English but who insisted their American-born children be as American as they were Italian. I talked about me, Mama, my closet room under the Quillan's stairs, and the miserable work of the sack factory. Mrs. Lotti was nothing like Mrs. Sullivan, but sitting beside her, working beside her, made me ache for my place at Mrs. Sullivan's second-hand table on the quay. I missed her. I missed Mama. I even missed Mrs. Keane. I missed how I felt when I was at their side.

When the sun had long since climbed out of the dark chasm outside the window, we packed away the day's flowers and headed down to the corner, where a man with a thick black mustache and a pushcart filled the Mrs. Lotti's oilcloth bag with potatoes, onions, and carrots. The butcher across the street cut her a great hunk of beef and wrapped in brown paper. She paid for half, and I paid for half from the money Bryan gave me. Then when we returned to her apartment we divided everything up. I worried some about not getting the fish Bryan had asked for. But Mrs. Lotti dismissed that worry with a sweep of the hand.

"He'll forget about the cod before he gets home," Mrs. Lotti said. "Bryan doesn't care that much about food. Every now and then he'd ask me for fish, too. 'Just like Mama used to make.' But I never did go to the fish market for them. For my own family I might make the trip, but for that crowd, give them a good stew, and they won't complain."

It turned out she was right. The five of them—Bryan, the boys, Alan, and Rick—strode through the doors that evening, sank into the chairs, and had half of my fresh soda bread stuffed into their faces by the time I had the stew ladled into their bowls. Mick and Tom paused long enough to bow their heads and cross themselves perfunctorily, but none of them slowed enough to notice that it wasn't cod they had on their plates.

After shoveling a couple of spoonfuls of stew into his face, Mick dug into his pocket and dropped a small handful of coins on the table.

"A day's wages?" I said. He nodded. "How much is it?" I asked.

"A dollar and five pence," Mick said. "For the two of us."

"Cents," Tom said. "A dollar and five cents."

"Same thing," Mick said.

"How much is that?" I asked.

"About five shillings," Tom said. As much as I made in a week, then, and the two of them had made it in a single day.

"Good money," I said, "for the work." Tom mumbled assent.

"Water boy's wages are nothing," Alan said around a mouthful of potato. "We make twenty times that, more than twenty times that."

"Pff. It's a good thing you aren't a bookkeeper," Rick said, then addressed himself to Tom: "We don't. We don't make that much."

"We do," Alan said. "Twenty times fifty-two cents is—what?—ten dollars or so. We make more than that. Lots more."

"A week," Rick said. "Not every day."

"Oh," Alan replied. "Right. Maybe not twenty times then. But an experienced man working the high steel can make twenty dollars a week. That's good money. A lot better than a water boy."

"Four pounds a week?" Tom said. "For labor? That is very good money."

"You don't start making that, of course," Alan said. "Got any more of that stew?" He handed me his bowl and I refilled it. "You start by hauling and fetching for maybe seven or eight dollars a week. If the pushers—that's the bosses—like what they see, they might make you an apprentice. That's where you learn the job. Bryan and I apprenticed together on the Times Tower. Twenty-five stories. We worked like dogs."

"Is that when you learn to walk out on the beams like you do?" Mick asked.

"Yeah," Alan said. "That's when you start to learn. They teach you that when a big gust of wind hits you, and you jump down from the top of the I-beam to the bottom and grab the top with your hands. Keeps you from falling off."

"Or you could just do what Alan did when he was first learning," Bryan said. "He used to crawl from one end to the other gripping the beam with his teeth so he didn't fall." I was surprised to hear Bryan say something. His method of eating, which involved hunching over his bowl and shoveling, didn't seem to leave much room for dinnertime conversation.

"With his teeth?" Mick said. "You used to grip the beam with your teeth?"

"No," Alan said, "not with my teeth. That was Bryan's idea. I was just cautious; that's all. You can't learn the trade if you're nothing more than a wet spot on the ground below. I don't think people understand how difficult and dangerous it is to build these tall buildings and bridges. They climb the stairs, ride the elevators, look out their glass windows, and never stop to think that some bloke walked the very beams that hold them up. People don't think. A lot goes into building those things. We earn every penny of our money; I can tell you that much." Alan reached for the peppershaker and sprinkled its contents liberally over his second bowl of stew.

"Mhmm," Tom said, he picked up the peppershaker Alan had set down, sniffed delicately at it, then added some to his own stew. "Someday, I'm going to learn how to design skyscrapers," Tom said.

Rick snorted.

"I am," Tom insisted. "I'm going to go to university, and I'm going to become an engineer, and I'm going to design skyscrapers. Maybe bridges."

"And some day I'm going to become the queen of France," Rick said.

"Don't listen to her majesty there," Alan said. "If that's what you want to do, you go right ahead and do it. Somebody's gotta design the things. Why shouldn't it be you?"

"Maybe because he doesn't know the first thing about skyscrapers?" Mick said.

"Well, then maybe he could learn," Alan replied. "You want me to teach you all you need to know about tall buildings?" he asked. Tom set down the peppershaker and his spoon both.

Alan stuffed a large chunk of potato in his mouth to fortify himself as he talked. "First of all," he said, gesturing with his spoon, "building a skyscraper isn't like building, say, a cathedral. Cathedrals were built like walls, brick on brick, block on block." He picked up a couple of slices of my soda bread and stacked them. "A skyscraper, though, would have so much weight on the bottom blocks that it would crush them." He pushed down on the top slice, and the two mushed into crumbs. Alan considered the crumbs for a moment, then scooped them up and added them to his stew, stirring the mixture into muck.

"So you find something stronger to build the skyscraper on, stronger than stone," Tom volunteered.

"Not exactly," Alan said. He shoveled a lump of soggy soda bread into his mouth. I wondered if he tasted it. Real meat, fresh potatoes, but to him it was no more than fuel. That more than his bragging told me that these men were well paid.

"Tell me something," Alan said to Tom. "What holds up your body?"

"Feet?" Tom answered tentatively.

Alan smiled. "True," he said. "Feet and legs. But what give feet and legs their stiffness?"

"Bones," Tom answered.

"Bones, it is," Alan replied. "And that's what holds up skyscrapers, too. Steel bones."

"More like I-beams," Rick muttered.

"I-beam bones," Tom said.

"Exactly," Alan replied. He held his spoon end-on on the table, then snatched Rick's from his hand. "We build the bones from steel." He held the two spoons side-by-side. Rick reached for his spoon, Alan hit him with it.

"Can't you see I'm trying to teach the boy something?" Alan said.

"Teach him with your own spoon," Rick replied, pushing his chair away from the table with a loud screech. Tom handed Alan his own spoon. Alan shrugged and tossed Rick's spoon back at him.

"We build the bones from steel." He held the two spoons end to end at a right angle. "Then the masons can come and cover the bones with a skin of brick or terra cotta, or anything else they have a mind to using." He scanned the table for some "skin" for his spoon building. Finding none, he handed the spoon back to Tom. "The whole building is lighter, so it doesn't crush at the bottom. But it's stronger because it has not only skin but also steel bones."

"Who thought of this idea?" Tom asked. Alan shrugged. "An engineer?" Tom prompted.

Alan shrugged again. "I just build 'em," he said.

* * *

Rick and Alan finished their stew, polished off the last of the soda bread, drained the teapot. Then without comment or hesitation, they dropped their caps on their heads and strode out the door. As a servant I had never expected anyone to comment on the food I'd prepared. Sometimes my employers did say something, but I had never expected it. Here, though, I thought maybe someone might say something, perhaps just a thank you. The fact that they didn't said more about my place in the house than anything else that had happened so far. I carried the dirty dishes to the sink and set to work on them.

The evening was hot, muggy. Not that saying so wasn't redundant. A bit more than two weeks ago the *Caronia* had moored itself in the Narrows. Four of the subsequent nights had been spent floating in the bay. A week's worth we'd passed at Ellis Island. The night I stood doing dishes in Bryan's sink was my fifteenth night in America. Every last one of them had been hot enough that I couldn't have imagined sleeping until I dropped off from exhaustion. I rolled my shoulders, trying to work out some of the stiffness. Between the day making flowers and the evening cooking stew in a steaming apartment, I doubted exhaustion was going to be a problem that night.

Bryan gathered up his soap and towel for a wash in the hallway sink. I insisted Mick and Tom join him, making a mental note find time for a quick bath tomorrow when the men had left for work. The three of them came in damp and headed immediately for the fire escape, Bryan claiming it was the only real air in the apartment.

I put the last of the bowls in the cabinet, brushed the crumbs from the table, then strolled to the window and stuck my head out. Bryan was right: the breeze did make the heat a bit more bearable. If Mick and Tom squeezed together, they could make room for me. I was hitching up my skirts when I heard a noise above. The woman in the apartment above us was clamoring unceremoniously out onto her own escape. Through the dirty slats, I had a full view up her skirt and what she was and wasn't wearing underneath. Bryan looked up, too, and whistled. The woman shouted something down through the slats. I didn't have to speak Italian to know it was highly unflattering. Bryan laughed. I glanced down at a couple of youths watching the show from the escape below, and contented myself with leaning on the sill with my head out the window, at least until the sun was down.

"Damn," Bryan said. He was leaning back against the hot brick of the wall, his legs stretched out and his feet hanging over the street. "Damn, damn, damn." He cranked his head around to look at me. "I forgot my beer, Clare. Would you be so good?"

"Beer?" I said, "Um, I would but, well, I'm only fourteen. Can children buy beer in this country?" Bryan just looked at me, his neck craned at an extreme angle. "In Ireland," I continued. Bryan's guffaw interrupted me.

"In the icebox, Clare. In the icebox. This is America. We have bottled beer here. We have iceboxes here. This isn't your precious "old country" where a man has to walk two miles in the rain both ways just to pour a decent drink into himself." Mick and Tom laughed. I have to say I didn't find either Bryan's tone or what he said particularly funny. But I did open the icebox, and sure enough there was the beer. The label read "Hell's Gate Brewery." I couldn't argue with the choice of name. I handed a bottle out the window.

"Just one?" Bryan said. "After a hard day's work? Lass, you'll make a powerful cruel wife for some man some day."

"How many would you like?" I asked.

"Three should do the trick," he replied. I returned to the icebox, then handed out a couple of more bottles.

"That's more like it," Bryan said, popping the top from the second bottle. "You two can share, can't you?" he said to Mick and Tom. Mick nodded eagerly. Tom glanced at me.

"They're too young," I said.

"They worked a full day's work," Bryan replied. "In the hot sun. They worked their arses off." He handed the bottle to Mick. Mick looked at me, then took a long swig. He got a thoughtful look on his face.

"What do you think?" Bryan asked.

"They use a bit more water in American beer?" Mick replied. Bryan laughed.

"The man knows his beer," he said. Mick beamed, then took another swig and handed the bottle to Tom. Tom looked at me. I shook my head. Tom nodded is assent, and handed the bottle to Bryan.

"Come on, Tom," Bryan said, handing the bottle back. "It'll put hair on your arse. Granted, this may not be the best weather to be sproutin' fur. But I do have to say that after a hard day a cold beer goes down so smooth I think I might be willing to take the chance." Tom shook his head and tried to hand the bottle back. Mick intercepted it and took another long swig.

"You start liking that stuff too much, and I'm going to start calling you fuzz butt," Bryan commented, taking another deep draw himself.

That was when I knew that we had to leave. I went back to the kitchen, spread Papa's coat out on the floor, lay back, and began praying for a telegram first thing the next morning.

* * *

About an hour later, Mick stumbled through the window to fetch a few more bottles. A few minutes after that, I heard Mick and Bryan cheering Tom on as he took a drink. They didn't come in after that. Mick and Tom slept on the fire escape with Bryan. Just as well. I couldn't trust myself to be civil to Mick just then. Sooner or later I would have to talk with him, but at the time, I wished with every ounce of me that I'd taken Mrs. Keane up on her offer.

It was late—or early depending on how you look at it—when the door to the apartment opened. Rick and Alan stumbled in. I think they meant to make a beeline to their room to pass out, but given their state, a straight line was not really within their capabilities. I could see Rick's outline in the dim light of the kitchen. He was veering toward me. I sat up and pulled in my feet. He heard me.

"Is that you, Mick?" he said.

"Clare," I said.

"Where's Mick?" he said. His words sounded slurred.

"On the fire escape," I said.

"Oh," he said.

"A young lady like you shouldn't be sleeping on the floor," he said. "It's not right."

"I don't mind," I replied.

"I have a mattress," he said. "Not a proper bed, I'm afraid, but at least a mattress."

"No thank you," I said.

"It's big enough for two," he commented.

"No thank you," I said. "I'm fine." Mrs. Lotti's words came flooding back through my mind.

"It's not right," he said. "It's not right." His voice was rising. From his silhouette, I guessed he might be close to reaching out to me. I scooted back a bit on the floor and wondered if I could make it to Mick and Bryan out on the fire escape. On the other hand, I wondered if Mick or Bryan would do me any good. I guessed Mick had had a good bit to drink. And whether Bryan would help me or would help Rick, well, that was something I didn't really want to think about.

"Let me bring the mattress out here," Rick said. I could sleep on the coat there, and you could have a bed."

"No, thank you," I said.

"I could sleep on Bryan's bed," he said.

No," I said.

"Rick!" The voice came from outside the window. I looked up. Bryan's forehead was visible over the sill. I could hear Rick stumble a bit, trying to get a bearing on the voice. "Rick, you great horse's arse," the voice said, "go to bed and stop bothering the girl."

"I just wanted . . . "

"Sleep it off, man. We have work tomorrow. The last thing I want is you pitching me hot rivets with your eyes fogged over. Go to bed, would you?"

Rick stood for a while, then turned unsteadily and headed into the bedroom. I went to the living room, and spent the rest of the night beneath the window.

Thirty

Seventy-two hours and a bit more had passed since we sent the telegrams from Ellis Island. Certainly three days was enough time for them to get to their destinations. Or so it should have been if someone had actually been there to receive the telegram on the other end. I was restless with the waiting, but

I didn't dare leave the gassy air of Bryan's apartment for fear of missing the Western Union boy.

Mick has skulked out of the house soon after waking, hoping I think to hide what a fat head he had on him. Tom was a bit bleary-eyed, but then he always was in the morning. If I had to guess how much he had drunk the night before, I'd say it wasn't much. Bryan, Rick, and Alan, amazingly enough, seemed no worse for the night's debaucheries. Even sinfulness, it seems, grows easier with practice.

The morning I spent scrubbing. The sink and table responded well to a bit of boiling water. The kitchen floor, though, took me a couple of hours. In some places the dirt and food scraps were so caked on, I wondered if it had ever been scrubbed. When the floor was finished, I tried washing the windowsills, but the thick black soot only streaked and smeared. Given the looks of the air outside, I doubted the cleaning would hold for long anyway. I washed the sheet on Bryan's bed and hung it to dry on the fire escape. The smells emanating from Alan and Rick's room would have persuaded me to leave theirs alone, even if I had been feeling disposed toward helping them out, which I wasn't.

At the very least, one could now walk from one end of the apartment to the other without kicking aside rubbish. It was still not a place I wanted to stay for long, but it was an improvement. I brought in some fresh water just after noon for a bit of a wash. Bathing was futile in the heat that hung around the apartment like a soggy blanket. I was ripe again before I even finished dressing. I dumped the water down the dry sink and scanned the apartment. There wasn't much else to do.

So come afternoon, I stepped across the hall again to make silk flowers and listen to Mrs. Lotti's tales until it was time to begin cooking again. We left the door ajar to listen for the delivery boy, but when the men paraded through the front door looking for supper, the telegram still had not arrived. By that time, though, I'd made up my mind.

* * *

"We have to leave," I whispered that evening. Mick lay beside me on the kitchen floor beneath the window. Very little breeze seeped in, and what did was nearly as muggy as the kitchen was. The bare board of the floor had not completely dried, and I could feel the vapors of it rising up to coat my skin. Tom hung draped over one of the kitchen chairs, a beam of moonlight forming a stripe across the back of his head. From the other side of the paper-thin bedroom wall, I could hear Rick and Alan snoring in the bedroom. Bryan's bed was empty. It was apparently his turn to disappear until all hours.

"We can't stay here," I said.

"But you said the telegram didn't come yet," Tom said.

"It didn't," I replied. "But we can't stay here."

"You're dreaming of Washington, I suppose," Mick said. "You want to go to Washington and find Colum."

"I do," I replied.

"We can't," Tom said. "We have to go to St. Paul. Uncle Ronan paid for our tickets. We can't just decide we're going somewhere else now that we used them. We have to wait for the telegram."

"What if there is no telegram?" Mick said, "Uncle Ronan might not be in Hayward or Lindstrom. He might be in another place entirely, or he might be on his way here. For all we know, he might be dead. Logging is no Sunday picnic, you know. What happens if we go all the way to St. Paul, use up our tickets and all our money, and then can't find him? I think we should stay here. We sell the tickets if we can. Then you and I get jobs to pay Uncle Ronan back for the rest when he finally contacts us."

"We could do that in Washington, too," I said. "We could get jobs in Washington."

"Do you know how much Bryan makes here?" Mick asked. "Sixteen dollars a week. That's over three pounds. I start as a water boy, work up to laborer, then apprentice. By the time I'm twenty, I could be a riveter just like Bryan."

"And where will we live while you're chasing your money?," I said. "You never think of things like that, Mick. At least in Washington we'll have people to watch over us."

"You'll have your precious Colum, you mean," Mick replied sourly, "sweet, wrinkle-free Colum, never-did-a-day's-work-in-his-life Colum." I gave him as dirty a look as I could manage in the dim moonlight from the window.

"It's not just me," I said. "We'd all be better off there. We'll have Colum and his parents. They may not be family, but least we know where they are. At least we know they'll help us; they'll see we don't starve. I'm sure of it."

"And isn't that what Bryan did for us these last days?" Mick said.

"Bryan?" Tom said. "Bryan's spending our money like there's no tomorrow. Spending it on that beer you were guzzling last night, I'd hold. Do you want to know what Bryan's been doing? Wasting our money. That's what Bryan's been doing." I was surprised at the anger in his voice. Had the frustration been building inside Tom all this time as it had in me? Or had he somehow caught my mood again. I wasn't sure, but I approved. Anyone who wasn't frustrated in a situation like this wasn't paying attention.

"Tom's right," I said. "We stay here any longer and all our savings and all of Uncle Ronan's money will be gone. I say we go to Washington. Tomorrow."

"I say we go to Wisconsin and find Uncle Ronan," Tom said. "Tomorrow," he added.

"Fine," I said. "How about this—we get our money, what's left of it, from Bryan. We go to the train station tomorrow. If we have enough for Washington, we go there. We get jobs and send money to Uncle Ronan to pay him back. If we don't have enough money for a ticket to Washington, we go to St. Paul, and we see if the Cunard office can find Uncle Ronan."

"And if we don't have enough money for either, we stay here," Mick said.

"We can't stay here," I said. Tom nodded.

"But if we don't have the money we can't very well leave, can we?" Mick replied.

I sighed. "Mick," I said, "If I tell you something, will you promise me you won't go off breaking heads?"

"Whose head needs breaking?" he replied.

"Nobody's," I said. "Just promise me."

"I promise I won't break anyone's head," Mick said.

"Promise you won't try," I said. "Promise you'll leave him to God."

"I promise," Mick said. "Now tell me whose head I'm going to regret not breaking."

"Rick," I said. "It's not that he's done anything. It's just that," I paused, "he talks. When he's drunk. And I heard things myself. About him, Rick, Bryan. From Mrs. Lotti. I don't think it's right for me to be here with those three, and them unmarried men."

Mick sat quietly. His eyes were focused out the window. In the light of the moon I could see the set of his jaw, that set of his jaw that told me he was thinking about something both he and I would live to regret.

"You promised," I said.

"I promised," he replied.

"Mick," I said. "Bryan, Alan, and Rick are three grown men. And you and Tom are only two, and two not yet fully grown. If they get improper notions in their heads, you may not be able to protect us. I don't think we should stay here. Not now that Mrs. Keane is gone."

Mick stared hard at the floor, ran a hand through his hair. "I suppose I could always come back to New York and find an apprenticeship once I'm grown," he said.

"You could," I replied.

"But now I need to get us someplace safe," he said.

"A good run is better than a bad stand," I said.

"I hate that saying," Mick replied. "I wish you would stop repeating it like it were some nugget of golden wisdom."

"Sorry," I said.

"We have to get our money," he said. "Tonight. When Bryan gets home. I'll talk to him."

"Thank you, Mick," I said. He nodded.

* * *

The moon had passed overhead. Its light no longer shone in the kitchen window. The apartment was dark—too dark to negotiate—when I heard Bryan fumbling with the doorknob. The hinges creaked open, and then I could hear the rustle of a box of matches before one struck and lit the lamp beside the door. Bryan struggled to replace the lamp's chimney. It took considerable doing on his part to find the space between the three brass prongs that held the glass. I had little doubt just where he had spent his evening.

Bryan ambled unsteadily into the living room, gave the murphy bed a tug. It landed hard. He staggered out of its way, then landed hard himself on top of it. I had serious doubts about whether he noticed the clean sheet and whether the sheet would stay clean for long. Beside me Mick stood.

"This may not be the best time, Mick," I whispered. He ignored me, pulled his shoulders back, and headed into the living room.

"Bryan," he said. His voice was loud. Or it might just have been the contrast to my own struggle to make as little sound as possible. "Bryan, might I have a word with you?"

"Have two, three even," Bryan said. "Then when you're finished, bugger off. I have to work tomorrow. I need my sleep."

"Bryan, we'd like our money."

"Sorry," Bryan replied. "That was four words. 'Bryan . . . we'd . . . like . . . our . . . money.' Oops, five words. Now bugger off."

"'Tis our money," Mick said. "Give it to us."

"No," Bryan said. He draped an arm over his face. "Gawd, I hate when the room won't sit still. Does my gullet no good at all. Now let me get some sleep, will you. We can talk about money in the morning."

"Fine," Mick said, returning to the kitchen. I could hear Tom stir atop his bed of chairs. Mick sunk to the floor beside me.

"He's not going to give it to us," Tom whispered. "Not tonight. Not tomorrow. It may already be gone, already drunk by him and whoever he bought drinks for tonight."

"Then we'll have to take it," Mick said. He sat against the wall, then shifted over a bit so he had a clear line of vision into the living room. The kerosene light still burned. Bryan had probably already forgotten it. I had a fair idea what Mick was planning to do, so I simply lay there, quietly, watching Mick watch Bryan. Soon the snores from the living room joined the snores from the bedroom. Mick stood silently. I wanted to whisper, "be careful," but didn't for fear I'd wake Bryan again.

Mick tiptoed across the floor. Above me Tom shifted on his chairs to get a better look. Between the rungs I saw Mick pause beside the bed. Bryan was curled up on his side, face to the wall, making noises halfway between snores and snorts. Gently, ever so gently, Mick reached toward the dark lump on the bed.

"Can you see?" Tom whispered to me.

"Ssshh," I replied. I couldn't, at least not very clearly. I waited, listened. Finally I heard the clasp of a change purse snapping shut.

Mick turned. Between his thumb and forefinger was a wad of bills. A big grin spread across his face. I sat up against the wall. Mick headed back for the kitchen, a bit of a swagger in his step.

"Hear me good." The snoring had stopped. Mick startled, then spun on his heels. Bryan rolled over to face him. "If you three aren't out of my house by the time I wake up in the morning, you will leave by way of the window. Do you understand?"

"I do," Mick said. Tom scrambled to his feet, knocking over a chair in the process. From Bryan's throat came a low growl. I don't think I'd ever heard a sound like that from a human being before. He bolted to the window, hung his head out and vomited onto the sidewalk three stories below. A baby's cry split through the night air. "Who did that?" I could hear a man's voice rise up from the street through the open window. The tone of Bryan's voice, the anger of the man below, the sudden break in tension. I move like one shot from a gun, scrambling into my skirt, doing up my shoes with quivering fingers.

Mick pocketed the wad of cash. Tom slipped into his trousers and grabbed the shoonaun. I snatched up the coat, which I had been using for a pillow, and we hurried into the hallway. At the top of the stairs I paused.

"Did you get all of it?" I said.

"All of it and a bit more for our trouble," Mick replied. "Or so I'd guess. It's a fair sized wad of notes."

"I don't want 'a bit more for our trouble'," I said. "I want the money we came with, maybe a bit less to pay for our room and food for the last few days." I thought for a second, tallying the numbers in my head. "Sixty-four dollars," I said. "Sixty-four of that is ours. We give the rest back."

Mick stared at me. For a moment I thought I would have an argument from him. But instead he nodded, and turning to catch the light from the single lamp on the wall of the floor below, he counted out the sixty-four dollars and handed it to me. The rest he slid under Bryan's apartment door. I peeled five dollars off to give to Tom, pocketed a few myself. I was planning on tying the rest into the secret pocket of the shoonaun. But the sight of Mick returning without argument from doing the right thing did my heart good. I peeled off five dollars and handed them to him. "You keep that," I said. "We'll put the rest in the shoonaun."

"Best not to have all our money in one place," Mick commented.

"'Tis," I said. And with that we made our way down the stairs.

We stepped out into the night—the sodden, sooty New York night—orphans again, or orphans still, depending on how you looked at it. Not so much as a roof over our head, everything we owned packed into the shoonaun and our pockets. That's how we arrived at the train station. It was three in the morning.

* * *

The bustle we'd seen two short days before had quieted, but not completely. Even at this small hour of the morning, we were far from the only ones there. I strode up to the window. The night clerk was half asleep, kicked back in his chair. He tipped forward and assessed me suspiciously.

"We would like three train tickets to Bellingham, Washington," I said. Behind me I could feel both Mick's and Tom's muscles tighten. To their credit, they said nothing.

The clerk hauled a thick book onto the counter between us. "Immigrant rates?" he said.

"Is anything cheaper?" I asked.

"Not hardly," the clerk replied.

I took that to mean "no" and nodded my head. "Immigrant rates, then," I said.

The clerk licked his finger and paged through the book. "Bellingham, Washington," he said. That's when I realized I'd been holding my breath. Bellingham, Washington. His finger came to rest on the table. "You'll have to change trains in Chicago. He jotted down a couple of numbers and did some quick addition. That'll be $72.75," he said.

I ran some quick calculations in my head. The money we'd gotten back from Bryan, the boys' wages for the last two days, the money Tom had kept in his pocket since the island. We had enough. Barely. We had enough, and the train went to Bellingham. We were going to Washington.

I fumbled in my pocket, laid my notes on the counter, then extended a palm to Mick and Tom, who both surrendered the contents of their pockets as well. The clerk counted. "You're $43.75 short," he said.

"I know," I said. "We have more."

Mick unloaded the shoonaun from his shoulder, and I opened the secret pocket. All the money we had in the world was in there. I peeled off forty-four dollars and handed them to the clerk. The rest of the money, a bit less than three dollars, I tied back into the shoonaun.

The clerk scribbled something onto three tickets, stamped them, and handed them across the counter with a quarter's change. I glanced at them, then tied tickets into the basket and dropped the quarter into my pocket.

"The train leaves at 3:15 this afternoon. Wait in the immigrants' waiting room around the corner. You may leave and return in time to catch your train, but if you're late, there will be no refunds. You may not wait in the main waiting room. That room's reserved for Americans."

"Or foreigners who can pay," Mick muttered under his breath.

"Exactly," the clerk said. I was surprised he'd heard Mick.

"Thank you," I said. The clerk scanned over our heads like we weren't there for other paying customers. Not finding any, he kicked back again in his chair and closed his eyes.

* * *

Mick shouldered the basket, and we worked our way around the corner to the waiting area. It was a simple room, benches like church pews ran most of the length. The ceilings were bare girders, the floor cement. It reminded me a little of third class aboard the *Caronia*—basic, utilitarian. It was also just as stifling. The air, filled with the smells of a dozen countries, moved not a bit. The few immigrants who stretched out on the benches, tossed and sweated. Many more simply sat, eyes glassy with the early hour, staring at the windowless walls.

"We should get some sleep," Mick said. I nodded. Tom selected a bench and stretched himself out. Mick and I took the bench opposite him, and with the basket on the floor just below our noses, lay down head to head. Tom was out within seconds. I craned my neck. Mick's eyes were still open.

"Thank you," I said quietly.

"For what?" he replied.

"For agreeing to go to Washington," I said.

"Right, so," Mick replied. He fell silent. Actually, I suppose he didn't exactly agree to go to Washington. But neither had he protested. Maybe that's what I was thanking him for. "I like trees," he said quietly, breaking into my thoughts.

"I do too," I replied.

* * *

The morning brought an ever-growing crowd into the waiting room. We sat up to make room for them all. My stomach growled and tumbled. I reached into my pocket, fingered the coins there. Not having food was bad enough. Not having food after having it for a couple of weeks was grief on top of hunger.

"Are we going to find some bread, then?" Tom asked, again as though reading my mind.

"I was hoping they would feed us on the train," I said.

"I'm hungry now," Tom replied.

"And will a little hunger kill you now?" I said. "We're not exactly made of money these days." Tom fell silent.

"Do we know they'll be feeding us on the train?" Mick asked. Frankly, I hadn't considered that they might not. The fact that I hadn't disturbed me.

"They did on the boat," I said. "And they did on the island."

"But we don't know about trains," Mick said. "Maybe they're different."

"I could find out," Tom said.

"Take Mick with you," I replied. The two of them trotted off, and I put the shoonaun between my feet to guard until they came back.

How long could a train trip across the country take? A week? Two weeks? Three dollars was about twelve shillings. I could keep us from starving for a couple of weeks on that. But we'd arrive in Washington like newborn babes, without a cent to our names. I wished there was some way of contacting Colum. But if I sent a telegram saying we were coming, he would have no way of responding: We'd likely be on the train before a reply could reach New York.

While I waited, a family of three settled in on the bench across from me. The father removed his hat to reveal blond hair, thinning, close cropped on the sides, imprinted by the damp and the band of his hat. He leaned in to his wife and said something in a language I didn't understand. She nodded and opened the knee-high basket at her feet. I didn't mean to spy, but I doubt I could have not looked, not under the circumstances. Inside was a great pile of sausages. And breads. And cheeses wrapped in cloth. The aroma was powerful enough that I could smell it over the increasingly full waiting room. My stomach lunged inside me. My mouth watered.

The woman balanced a flour-dusted loaf of brown bread on her knee and drew out a knife to cut it. A boy a little younger than Tom snugged into her skirts. I knew the look on his face. It was the look of a boy in love with his breakfast.

So why would a family planning on being fed by the railway, bring such a basket on a trip? I figured there was one way to find out.

"Beg your pardon, sir," I said. The man looked up.

"No speak English," the man replied, his tongue thick with some other language. "Little English. *Sprechen Sie Deutsch*? Ger-man?" I shook my head and shrugged. I was about to take my seat again when I remembered Anna and her daughter in the bunkroom back on Ellis. There were ways of communicating that didn't involve words.

"Train," I said. "Chug, chug, chug, whooo!" I worked my hands like pistons in front of me. "Train?"

"Train," the man said. "*Ja*, train."

"Food," I said. I pantomimed eating, then pointed to the basket.

"*Ja, ja*, food," the man said.

"Do they serve food on the train?" I asked, trying to figure out how to pantomime the question. The man looked at me, puzzled. His wife leaned over to him and said something in German. The man replied, also in German. They appeared to be disagreeing. Finally the man nodded. The woman reached into her basket, and pulled out a small loaf of brown bread. She held it out to me.

"You. Food. Train," she said.

"No, no," I said. "No. Wait. I'm sorry. That wasn't what I was asking. I couldn't." She thought I was begging food. I put my hand on my heart, then shook my head. "Thank you," I said. "But no."

The woman continued to hold the bread out. I raised a hand to hold it back and shook my head. The woman dropped the loaf in her lap. She held an arm out for the boy, who walked into it. The woman untucked his shirt with a tug, lifted it, and ran a finger over his ribs. The skin over them was pale and even. Perhaps more to the point, it was full. The boy was well fed, no doubt about that.

"Good, *ja*?" she said. I smiled and nodded.

"Good," I said.

"Good," she said, running a finger over her own ribs. "You, no good."

She pointed at me, then her finger traced a path through the air, as though exaggerating each rib. She inclined her head to me. "You, no good, *ja?*"

I nodded. There was really no point denying it. The woman picked up the loaf and held it out again. "*Für Jesus,*" she said, then followed it with a stream of German. I looked at her blankly and shook my head. "Give us this day our daily bread, and forgive us our trespasses," she said in English, in a nearly impenetrable accent. But still the words were unmistakable to someone such as myself who had grown up saying them. She transferred the bread to her left hand, still holding it out to me, then quickly crossed herself with the other. "Für Jesus," she said.

I nodded, reached out and took the bread. "Thank you," I said, and quickly crossed myself with the practiced hand of someone who had done it thousands of times before. "God increase you."

The woman beamed. Nudging her husband with her elbow, she rattled off something in German. "Give us this day our daily bread," she said again.

I smiled back.

* * *

The boys returned with long faces. I had already guessed the news.

"They won't feed us," Mick said.

"Where did you get the bread?" Tom asked. His eyes had already devoured half the loaf.

"The family there," I nodded at the German couple. The man was picking his teeth with a fingernail. The woman had pulled a well-pressed, white handkerchief from her pocket and was cleaning the boy's scrunched up face.

Mick looked over at the family, then looked at the bread. He straightened his shoulders and walked across the narrow aisle. Standing before the man, he extended his hand.

"My name is Mick Keane," he said. The man took his hand and Mick shook it. "I thank you for the bread you gave my family. I can't repay you right now, but if we're on the same train, and if there is anything you need during the journey, I am at your service."

The man smiled back at Mick. "No English," he said, then reached out and clapped Mick on the arm. "Good boy," he said. "Good boy." Mick tipped his cap and grinned before returning to sit with us.

I pulled off a piece of bread and handed it to him. Tom took another. "We have to go out and buy some food, then," I said.

"We have at least six hours," Tom said. "I think we should be back by noon."

"At least noon," Mick said. "Earlier would be better."

"We should be able to find a pushcart and get a few things, then." I said.

"Could we go see if we could find one up near 33rd Street?" Tom asked, talking around the bread in his mouth.

"Why?" Mick asked.

"Where is that?" I added.

"It's a bit west of here," Mick said before Tom could answer. "Ten blocks maybe." He pulled another hunk of bread off the loaf.

"It's where they're building the new Pennsylvania Railroad station," Tom said. "Alan said the tunnel they were building was a sight not to be missed. A huge hole in the ground where they're only now starting to pour foundation. It's big enough they run trains through it to haul out the dirt. He and I were going to walk over there this Sunday, but now . . . " He shrugged.

"We have the time," Mick said, looking up at me.

I looked at the clock on the wall. It said 6:00, shortly before 6:00 a.m. We had time. And who knows when we'd have a chance to stretch our legs again. I nodded. "We can go take a look," I said to Tom. "But since it's your hole in the ground, you're carrying the basket."

* * *

A crowd of bystanders stood on the bridge and peered over a rough wood fence. We had found a peddler who gave us a good deal on bread—several loaves were wrapped securely and packed into the shoonaun. I was happy to still have a one-dollar note tied into the basket's secret pocket. Mick was happy that we had been able to get a bit of cheese in addition to the bread. And Tom was absolutely delighted to find the big hole just where he thought it would be.

Below us, carts on small tracks hauled off loads of dirt. A steam shovel puffed and groaned as it gouged into the embankment. I peered over the railing, a railing that came nearly to my nose. The noise and commotion of it all was exciting. I could see why Tom was fascinated by it. Tom, himself, was having a bit more trouble seeing the action. He first tried looking through a knothole in the fence. Then he found a small pile of debris beside the rail, kicked at it some, then tried to climb it to get a better view of the men with picks chiseling away at the rock face below. It was a tough climb with the basket slung over his shoulder.

"Would you like me to hold your basket?" a man asked. He was a young man, a wiry man with equally wiry brown hair sticking out at all angles from under his cap. He smiled a mess of crooked teeth first at Tom, then at me.

"Thank you," said Tom, "but I have it just fine." Tom took the strap of the basket from his shoulder and grasping in his fist, tried again to make the climb. Something about the man made me nervous. "Mick," I said, looking over to where I had last seen him. Mick had moved a little way down where the fence was lower and was craning his neck to get a better look at the steam shovel. He apparently didn't hear me over the construction noise.

"Thank you for your help, sir," I said, stepping in to intervene. "But I'll hold the basket for my brother."

"No need, little lady," he said. "I may not be much of a gentleman, but my mother wouldn't have raised any kind of man if I let you carry such a burden when my hands are free." He reached out, and with the deftness of someone who has practiced the movement many times, snatched the strap of the shoonaun from Tom's grasp.

"Give me the basket," I said, stretching out a hand to take it from him.

"Sorry," he said. "No can do." With that he turned and strode quickly through the crowd. I lunged at him, but snagged a toe on some of Tom's debris, and the man slipped away.

"Stop," I said. "Someone stop him. That's my basket."

A couple of the men standing on the bridge turned to look. The thief caught a glimpse of them and bolted through the crowd at a dead run.

"He took my basket," I shouted. Mick finally heard me. He scrambled down from the rail, and took off, bouncing off people right and left. A couple of the men in the crowd followed on his heels. I leaned against the rail. Panic gripped my belly, pulling the blood from my face.

"Are the train tickets in there?" Tom asked quietly.

"Of course they are," I snapped. "You saw me put them in the pocket. The tickets. And our money. And the bread. And Da's coat. And Mama's ring. And your books. All but this." I pulled a quarter—one quarter, the change left over from our purchasing our tickets—from the pocket of my skirt. Suddenly the loss seemed nearly overwhelming.

Tom shrank, sinking to the filthy ground beside the rail. "I'm sorry," he said. "I'm sorry. I shouldn't have let him take it. I'm sorry." He took off his cap and dragged a dusty hand through his hair.

"It looked to me like you didn't have much choice," I replied. "He was obviously a thief, and a good one at that." I bent down to offer him a hand. "There now, stand yourself up." He ignored the hand. I brushed a smudge of dust from his cheek.

"Mick might be able to catch him," Tom said, batting my hand away, and dropping his head into his palms.

"I hope so," I said. Below us the sound of the picks on rock ticked off each individual second as we waited.

* * *

"He's gone," Mick said as he arrived back at the bridge. He was on the verge of tears, though I could tell they were tears of anger.

"What's done is done," I said. The tears started to rise in my own eyes as well.

"What are we going to do?" Tom asked.

"We're going to go back to the train depot," I said. "We're going to see if they can give us another set of tickets."

* * *

The clerk was a different one from the clerk who had sold us our tickets the night before. He had no time for the likes of us. He simply pointed at the sign that declared "No Refunds" and called for the next customer.

I suppose shock set in at that point. I remember sitting again in the immigrants' waiting room. I remember scanning the benches for the German family, not that I could ask them for any more than they'd already given us. I guess I was seeking something familiar, something comforting. I remember sitting, listening to the boarding calls. Mick left to talk to someone else about the tickets. But soon he was back, sitting as I was with a shocked look on his face. Tom simply lay his head in my lap. I could feel his tears soaking into my skirts. He felt responsible—I knew as much. I did to.

"We can't stay here," Mick said.

"They won't notice if we sit for a while," I replied.

"But there's nothing we can do here," Mick said. "I should go to Bryan's building site and see if I can earn us enough money to buy some more food."

"We should go back to Bryan," Tom said. "Apologize to him. At least it would be a roof over our head."

The thought gripped my gut like a hand. Even when we had money, living with Bryan had made me nervous. The thought of being at his mercy—it did cold, unspeakable things to my belly.

"We'll not go back to Bryan," Mick said. "We'll not. I'll find us a roof. I'll take care of us."

Thirty-One

The plan sounded sensible enough when we came up with it. We had limited resources, needed a place to stay until we could contact Uncle Ronan, or the Sullivans, or Colum, or somebody. We needed to learn to live on nothing in a foreign city where we knew next to nobody. It was that simple.

Who would know better how to get by on nothing than those who did it every day? And where would we find such people? In the parks. On the streets. We headed south again. I could recognize a landmark or two in the Gashouse district, and in that fact was some small comfort. I knew a park just down the shore from Bryan's where I'd seen the down-and-out bide their time in the mid afternoon when other men were working or home sleeping off a night job. We would spend the afternoon talking to those men. We would bed down wherever they recommended for the night. Then in the morning, Mick and Tom would go to Bryan's job site to find work, and I would talk with Mrs. Lotti about finding some piecework of my own. We'd scrape together enough money to send a telegram, enough to keep food in our bellies until someone could send for us.

We followed the third avenue elevated south, walking in the track-striped shadows until a train came along. When we heard the rumble approaching, we'd duck out from under the tracks, pausing to watch the cars whiz by. I understood that the trestles were made for trains to pass over and pedestrians to pass under, both no worse for the close encounter. But it looked like being run over to me, and, God help me, I was already feeling too run over to want to go through the experience in fact.

As we walked, I realized that we must have sat for a good bit of time in the station—I don't think I could have said just how long—but it must have been hours. By the time we began smelling the Gashouse district's trademark stench, we were sharing the sidewalk with workers freed from their jobs for the evening. We trudged the steamy sidewalks slowly, all of us, some of the men carrying their jackets slung over their shoulder, some of the women actually carrying their hats instead of wearing them. Propriety dictated we remain properly dressed, arms and legs clothed, buttons fully buttoned. But as we pushed through the sticky, smell-laden air, I fervently wished for a girl's short skirts.

We followed the tracks to 24th street, then cut east to the river. The recreation pier was filled with families spreading picnic suppers and individuals angling themselves on the rails trying to catch just a bit more breeze from off the river. A small brass band, four mustached men in navy blue uniforms sat with their back to the rail, arms draped limply over their knees waiting for their time to play. Their instruments—a coronet, a clarinet, a drum, and a tuba—sat in cases beside them. I would have liked to have stayed to listen to them play, but my rumbling stomach reminded be we had a task before us.

We headed down to the river, staying as close to the cool of the water as we could. Young boys in just their shirts, just their drawers, some in less than that, splashed at the water's edge. I could feel the river's edge tugging at Mick, beckoning him to get wet, to get cool, to become just another bare-arsed boy with nothing more on his mind than soaking his chums. To his credit, he squared his jaw and continued on to the park.

By the time we reached the two-square block patch of grass, the sun had sunk well beneath the tops of the buildings, the light was beginning to fade, and the street lamps sprang to life. To my amazement, the park was covered with sheets and blankets, whole families getting ready to bed down in the open air. They lay there in patches of streetlight, in full view of the police officers and security guards strolling round and round the block. The otherwise zealously guarded grass lay flat beneath makeshift beds.

As we strolled the sidewalk around the perimeter of the park, I began to make out what we had come for. There, in and amongst the families, were the ragged few, the men whose claim to the street air long preceded their temporary neighbors. Some sat knees to chin, curled tightly into a ball, making themselves as small as possible. Some stretched out on their backs, caps pulled down over their eyes. Most were asleep. One sat on a bench not far from us. Mick and I spotted him at nearly the same time.

He sat hunched over his bread. Though most of the benches were full and a bit more, the space beside this man was empty for a good two feet. The laborer who sat at the other end of the bench angled himself away, his nose pointed to the river and a hope of fresh air. I looked at Mick. He looked at me. With Tom in tow, we approached.

A ragged scrap of a man he was. His trousers were triangled with wrinkles. His jacket bulged and sagged over his lean shoulders. On his head a straw boater spoke of better times, but the once-white hat was now sweat stained, spotted with the rain, smudged with one too many nights on the street. Tufts of barely graying hair hung raggedly below it.

As we drew closer, something in his eyes drew me up short. He had the look of a hungry dog with a bone as he ripped hunks of bread off the loaf with his teeth.

"Maybe we shouldn't bother him," I said.

Mick ignored me, and hands in his pockets, strolled over to where the man sat. Mick tipped his cap.

"A good evening to you, sir," he said. The man looked up. He looked confused, as though we had snapped him back suddenly from some far distant place.

"I was wondering if you could help us," Mick said.

"I'd very much doubt that, sonny," the man said. The man's voice was airy, as though he had no words to balance the breath within him. He appraised Mick from head to toe. On his cue, I did the same. Mick was looking more and more like the young "street Arabs" that populated the streets of the city. I supposed anybody would look a bit worse for a night on the fire escape followed by a day of hard labor, followed by several hours on the benches of a train station. I wondered if I had the same hard-bitten look myself.

"I'd like to help you, lad," the man said. "I really would. But I don't make enough money to feed myself these days. Sorry." He stuffed the bread he was munching on back into his inside breast pocket, where it contributed to the bulge he had sagging there on his chest. He began smoothing the creases in his trousers, stroking them ineffectually with his fingers, over and over again.

"It's not money we're asking for," I said. The man started. Could he have not seen me, and with me standing right before him all the time?

"We're looking for a place to stay, a room, maybe, or maybe only a bed," Mick said.

"And food," Tom added.

"A room? In this heat? You'd be better off here in the park," the man said.

"They'll let you stay here in the park?" Mick asked.

"Until the heat breaks, they will," the man said. "They've had a couple dozen people die on them this summer. Hospitals are full. The cops know which side their bread's buttered on."

"And after the heat breaks?" Mick pressed the man a bit. I was glad for his persistence. We had walked all the way from the station in search of information, and it seemed wrong to settle for nothing more than a patch of grass to spend the night on. "We haven't much money," he added.

"Where are your parents?" the man asked. "Your father run out on you?" His eyes didn't quite meet Mick's, but rather stared out just over Mick's left shoulder at the park that lay beyond.

"Our parents are no longer alive," Mick said simply. "We have no family, only us."

"No family," the man said. "That's tough. That really is. That's tough." It looked like he was struggling to haul his mind back from wherever it had been, struggling to latch on to what we said.

"A room?" Mick prompted.

"Right, a room. Well, a bed'll cost you fifteen cents a night," the man said. "On the Bowery. You can find them cheaper, but not in places I'd send children."

A dollar and five cents a week, then. Plus food. I already had a rough idea what food cost. A dollar a week would keep us in famine fare. So two dollars and a bit more just to keep body and soul together.

"Do you know where we can get food cheap?" Tom asked. "Maybe some tonight." He looked first at the man, then at me. I knew he was hungry. To his credit he hadn't complained during the long walk here.

"There's the bread of charity at some of the bakeries in town. They hand out the pieces that didn't sell. End of the day. Or when the baker comes in at 4:00." His hand went absently to his chest and rested on the hunk of bread he's stashed there. He'd given up staring off into space as he talked, but was gazing at the ground, though there was nothing beneath him but sidewalk. "There's fruit and vegetables on Rivington Street. They throw it out if it's too rotten to sell. But there's good bits on it if you're hungry enough."

"Where did you get the bread you had?" Mick asked. The man's hand went again to his chest, protected the bit of food he had there. "We don't want yours," Mick added quickly. "We just want to know where we can get some for ourselves."

"You know that big Grace Church on Broadway?" Mick nodded. I hoped he did indeed know. "Right in the shadow of that church. Good baker. Gives out good bread. Doesn't make you feel like less of a man for taking it. If you know what I mean."

"I do," Mick said. "Sometimes a man has no choice. Sometimes he has to do things he never thought he would just to keep his family fed."

The man looked up. His eyes were beginning to look a bit clearer, like he was beginning to see the same world we were seeing. "You said it sonny," the man said.

He looked around a bit, then extended his hand to Mick. "Name's Harry."

"Mick. This is Clare and Tom." Harry tipped his cap slightly.

"You from Irish Town?" Harry asked.

"Irish Town?" Mick repeated.

"Yeah, Irish Town," Harry said. "In Brooklyn." Mick shook his head. "I thought maybe. You sound a bit Irish."

"We are," Mick replied. "Just over from Cork, Ireland. No better than a month on American soil."

"Greenhorns, huh?" Harry said. "Well, seeing as how giving advice to greenhorns is kind of a favorite pastime in these parts, let me give you a bit myself. You three really shouldn't be out on the streets walking up to strange men and asking them advice. You don't know who you're going to meet on these streets."

"True enough," Mick said.

"But since you met me, and I'm obviously as meek as a newborn lamb, why don't I show you a night on the town?" Harry said, hoisting himself to his feet. His voice was stronger. And he smiled a smile that was directed directly at us. Maybe we had just caught him waking up from a particularly disorienting dream earlier.

"We appreciate the offer," I said. "But you don't have to do that. We're just thankful for the advice."

"We don't really have any money for a night on the town," Mick added, "and you said . . . " He paused.

"I said I was broke as a stone," Harry finished his sentence for him. "No matter. I'll show you how to enjoy a drink at a little sidewalk spot I know about, how to bed down on a nice soft bed, then how to get yourself a nice satisfying breakfast—all for no more than you'd make sitting on a park bench gazing out at the river all day."

I looked at Mick. He nodded. I didn't need to look at Tom. I knew we had him at the mention of the word "breakfast."

"Well, then Harry," Mick said. "I think we'll accept your kind offer."

Harry bowed with a flourish, and motioned toward the sidewalk.

* * *

The summer twilight was most welcome as we walked through the canyons that divided one tenement from the next on the Lower East side. The streets teemed with pushcarts finding their way home, horses hauling their drivers back from a day of deliveries, and insects—perhaps more flies than people, if that were possible. But more than that, the sidewalks teemed with residents whose better judgment told them to stay out from the steaming boxes that were their homes. Some perched on the stoop watching the world pass. Others made ready for a night on the sidewalks or the fire escapes. Tenements that were barely livable on their best days, belched forth their tenants on hot, sticky nights like this one.

I had always noticed back in Cork that the wetter the evening, the more the smells of the streets rose and hung in the air. Here I added the observation that the hotter the evening, the more the smells reached out and wrapped themselves around you. In the hot, muggy air, the smell of horse manure rose from the gutters. The smell of urine crept along the sidewalks. Onion, garlic, fish, and cabbage—all the day's cooking smells tumbled over each other as they wafted from the windows. And each person we passed added their own scent to the mix, the scent of men who had stood on factory floors all day; the scent of women tied to piecework, or a kitchen, or an infant, all in the heat of a single tenement room. It was the smell of effort and neglect mixed. I recognized it as the smell of the lanes.

We wove our way through the maze of bodies on the sidewalks. The park, when we finally reached it, was no less crowded. Police officers in tall hats and sweat-heavy navy-blue uniforms paced the sidewalk half-heartedly. The "keep off the grass" ordinances they typically enforced had been sacrificed in the name of heatstroke prevention. So had the public loitering laws, even some of the public decency standards. The police, instead, found themselves breaking up fist fights brought on by too much sweat and too little space.

"Harry was right," Mick said, leaning in to me. "I don't think we needed to worry about finding a room for the night." He led us out on to the street for a moment to dodge an altercation spilling from the park onto the sidewalk. The grass was filling rapidly with sheets, blankets, jackets, and other makeshift beds. Tom spotted a bare patch and pointed. We made a beeline for it.

"Ah, the dream of the down and out," Harry commented wryly. "Soft grass for a bed, and the chance to sleep the entire night through without once being rousted for vagrancy. It's almost enough to make up for the heat."

I lowered myself to the grass. Only then did I realize how footsore I was. From Bryan's flat to the station, to Tom's hole, to the station, to the riverside park, and then here. We'd covered a good bit of the east side. Yet as far as we'd walked that day, we'd traveled even farther. A mere twenty-four hours ago, we had been on our way west, west to Washington, to Colum, to trees and clean air. Now we were just three more vagrants with no place to go and no means to get us there if we did. Our bellies were empty, and our fortune was tied to a stranger—save his first name—who was a bit "disconnected," to be charitable about his situation.

"Best get some sleep," Harry said, stretching out his sparse frame on the grass. "Breakfast is at 4:00. We'd best get there at 3:00 to be sure of a place in line, and it's about a five-block walk."

"One of us better stay awake," I said to Mick. "I'm so tired I'll likely sleep until sunrise." Mick nodded.

"How do we know when it's time leave?" he asked.

"No problems," Harry said. He pulled a watch from his pocket. It was a beautiful gold piece. He flipped it open. A photo of a young woman adorned the inside of the cover. It's 7:30 now. I'll be awake before 2:30."

I stared at the watch. For such a wealthy piece to be drawn from such a poor pocket—I couldn't help but stare. Harry caught me looking. He quickly snapped the watch shut and stuffed back it into his pocket, the pocket of his trousers this time. His hand he left there with the watch.

"That's not why I was looking," I said. He looked so ill at ease, I felt I needed to say something.

"Habit," he said, a small smile just barely rippling over his wary features. "If you're going to survive on the streets, you need to keep a sharp eye out. Guard yourself tonight. Even here in this crowd."

I nodded.

"More's the pity should someone strip our pockets bare," Mick said, turning the pockets of his trousers inside out. A bit of lint fell from one of them. A wry smile danced on his lips.

"Or steal our last scrap of food," I said, catching the irony of his mood myself.

"Or drop us alone into the center of a big city with no one to watch us," Tom said, he was straining a bit to reach for Mick's attempt at humor.

"Or leave us with only the clothes on our backs," Mick said. "Cold and alone." He chuckled lightly, getting into the game.

"Alone at least," I said. "I'm not exactly cold. But if you are, I could see if I could borrow a blanket." Mick laughed. I was smiling too, despite myself.

"What I wouldn't do for a hot bowl of soup this minute," Tom said. "Something to warm my belly and stand between me and the icy gale."

I began to snicker.

"We best be careful," Mick said, "hang onto our riches with all our might. It's a cold world on this side of the ocean."

"It is," I said, lying down on the grass and wrapping my fist around the quarter in my pocket.

* * *

The sun was still well below the horizon when Mick shook me awake. "It's time," he whispered. I sat up slowly, rubbing the crick in my neck. The park shifted and moved. Though most of the people were sound asleep, enough tossed and turned to give the impression of a large undulating organism spreading itself out over the grass. Mick shook Tom awake. Harry was already standing, brushing the grass and bits of this and that from his trousers.

"Are you ready?" he asked. He seemed more alert, more lifelike than he did last night.

"Almost," I said. With the poor sleep I had gotten the night before and the long walk through the city, I slept like the dead. Most of my moving parts were the worse for it. My hip hurt almost to the point of numbness. My neck was stiff, and my shoulder didn't seem to want to move like shoulders should. It took me a moment of stretching and shrugging and taking inventory just to get moving. It was in the middle of that inventory that I began to get an idea of what we looked like. I had grass stains all down one sleeve. Both Mick and Tom still had fire escape stripes on their shirts from two nights before. My skirt was dusty from top to bottom, and the hem on one side was beginning to fray. We all were a spider's web of wrinkles from top to bottom. Back on the ship we may have been mistaken for middle-class. Just then, nobody with an eye in their head would have made that mistake.

Harry pulled his watch from his pocket and opened it. "We need to move quickly," he said. "You three overslept."

"I'll wait for you here," Tom mumbled. He was still curled up in the grass.

"You do, and you go without food for the day," I replied. "We'll not bring you any." Tom considered this and rolled himself into a sitting position.

"Let's go," Harry said, picking his way between sleeping bodies to the sidewalk. I offered Tom a hand, and with him in front of me so I could steady him if I needed to, I followed Harry out.

The first stop was a public fountain where we washed our face and hands and drank a bit of water. Harry explained that the fountains in the wealthier areas were better for drinking. The poor tended to use theirs as bathtubs. He scrubbed a bit behind his ears and encouraged us to drink a bit more.

We then cut across town on Ninth Street. The sky was beginning to get light. When we arrived at the bakery—in the shadow of the great stone spire of the Grace Church, just as Harry said it would be—I saw why Harry didn't want to dally.

The ragged line was made up of men mostly. Ragged men. But a few children, and now and then a woman, stood huddled and waiting. From the looks of them, hunched in on themselves, arms crossed on their chests, you would think the weather was chilly, not early-morning warm and dewy. But I supposed there were other things in life to huddle against besides cold. In fact as I stood among them, I found myself adopting a very similar posture.

The bread was cut in thick slabs, good bread, white and pure. I ate most of my piece before stashing a fistful in my skirt pocket for later. Harry showed us the subway, where a body could get out of the sun for a bit. The cool air of the trains rushing through the tunnels was a welcome thing, or so it was until we were rousted by a guard. Harry showed us pushcart alley, where the peddlers sometimes tossed half rotten fruit on the ground. "Half-rotten," Harry explained, meant half good. And so for lunch we feasted on brown peach and grey plum courtesy of a man in a black coat and side curls.

As we roamed the city, Harry pointed out the sights. Here was a Jewish bakery where we could get bread on a Sunday. There was a restaurant that didn't guard its trashcans. Here was a park that wasn't so fussy about people flattening the grass. There was a bathhouse that charged only three cents, not the usual five.

* * *

It took a bit more walking to find a cool place to sit. That did seem to be the one flaw in Harry's system for survival. Going from "bed" to bread to fruit to cool required a good bit of walking. Early that morning we had washed off the streets at the fountain, but by the time we arrived at the bakery we were feeling coated with them again. We ate the bread at the bakery, but by the time we found a cool spot to rest in the subway, we were hungry again. That hunger required another walk to pushcart alley, which found us tired and hot. As we sat for a moment by the river, I realized that I was more tired, hungrier, hotter, and grubbier than I had been before we started our education in subsistence living not quite twenty-four hours ago. It did seem that just getting by was nearly as much work as working for a living.

"So do you want to follow us to the job site tomorrow," Mick asked, "or do you want to go look for work on your own?"

"I thought I'd stop by Mrs. Lotti's apartment, to see if she's seen the Western Union boy yet."

"That's a good idea," Mick said. "Go in the late morning while Bryan's at work. I don't know if he meant what he said about throwing us out the window, but I don't think I want to find out."

"I don't think I would want a job that made me work on Sundays," Harry said. He fished his piece of bread from his pocket, gnawed off a tiny bit and chewed. "Day of rest, don't you know. Man has to have one every now and then."

"Is tomorrow Sunday?" Mick asked.

"All day," Harry replied.

"I lost track," I said.

"Me too," Mick replied.

"We ought to go to Mass," I said. "It's been too long."

"Know of a good church in the area?" Mick asked Harry.

"When it comes to churches," Harry said with a dismissive brush of his hand, "you name it, we got it. We got Methodist. We got Catholic. We got Presbyterian. We got a good dozen brands of Baptist—never could keep them all straight. We got Jewish. We even got your Mohammedan and Chinese church temple thingummies. You name it, if God lives there, we got it here in New York."

"Catholic," Mick said.

"Catholic?" Harry said. "Lots of Catholic churches. Some are more generous than others. Some of the priests will take you in and feed you if you hit a particularly tough spot. Some will help find you some new clothes if you wear out the ones you've got. Some, though, sweep you out the door like you were just so much trash. I can tell you which are which. Save you some time."

"I think just a close one will do fine," I said.

"Close," Harry said. "Hmm. You being Irish and all, I'd say Old St. Patrick's. The priest there is a nice bloke. Let me sit in one of the pews for a while once when I got caught in the rain. It's not far. I can show you."

"We're just looking for Mass in the morning," I said. Both Mick and Tom nodded.

"Well then," Harry said, "why don't I show you the church, and then we can part company. I'm a Methodist myself. I got nothing against Catholics yourselves, but your churches inside give me the willies. All them statues of skewered people. I mean it's one thing to believe in it, another to build a statue to it, am I right? Since it's not raining, I'll let you do your church on your own."

And so we parted company at the gate to St. Patrick's Old Cathedral, just outside the fence built at a time when a lot fewer people could say they had "nothing against Catholics." I thanked Harry sincerely. Thanks to him, we had a chance.

Thirty-Two

Things would have been very different, I suppose, had I been Protestant. But as it was, I felt the need for the Mass. I was always taught that there was great power in that wee piece of bread, that it was strength for the journey, all that a Christian needed to rouse herself and do what needed to be done. Given that I was hardly sure what the journey entailed at that particular moment, and given that most of my strength had left me, no less than had it been packed with my worldly goods in the stolen shoonaun, I felt myself in sore need a new infusion.

Old St. Patrick's would be celebrating a number of Masses that Sunday, no problem there. As for the required fast, I hadn't been counting the exact hours, but the dull rumble in my belly told me it was empty enough that evening, never mind the next morning. That just left one more detail. Receiving the Body of Christ meant going to confession first. After the events of the last few weeks, I figured confession would do all three of us no small bit of good.

It turns out that by the time we reached the church that evening, Saturday confession was over. So early the next morning, we found our daily bread, stuffed it into our pockets despite the temptation to eat it on the spot, made ourselves presentable at a public fountain, and arrived at the church about the same time as the priest. A trickle of people in their Sunday best was already beginning to flow from the tenements and lanes.

Unlike the parishioners we'd seen at the new St. Patrick's, none of these folks looked rich. Most of them, though, looked a fair sight better than we did. Kneeling beside Mick, I noticed how worn the cuffs of his shirt had gotten. I marveled at how fast a suit of clothes could go from riches to rags when one lived in them around the clock. I ran my fingers over Mrs. Sullivan's even tucking on the front of my shirtwaist. I felt as though I ought to confess the grass stains and worn spots I had superimposed over her loving work.

A woman who could well have been straight out of the lanes of Cork opened the confessional door and stepped out into the side aisle. She covered her head with her shawl, just as the shawlies back at St. Finbarr's had done. I smiled a bit to myself as I stood and took her place in the confessional.

"Bless me, Father for I have sinned," I began. "It's been three weeks since my last confession."

Had it been only three weeks since I'd knelt in the cathedral in Queenstown, unburdening my soul before stepping out across the water? Three weeks ago I had been on another continent. Three weeks ago I never knew Colum O'Moran existed. Three weeks ago I had money in my pocket, a telegram from Uncle Ronan tucked away safely in my shoonaun. And perhaps most importantly I had a plan for the future, foggy though it was, stretching out before me. Now I had none of that. Now I would unburden myself of the sins of the journey here, and I would set my face toward America. And I would hope that great continent wouldn't swallow our bones before we set so much as a foot on the mainland.

"Go on, my child," the priest said. His voice was an older voice, tinged with grey and experience.

"Since that time I accuse myself of the following: Once I used the Lord's name in vain," I began. "Once I lied to immigration agents and once I lied to a ship's warden. And at least twice more I let the immigration men think things that weren't true."

"Letting someone believe a lie is the same as lying," the priest said.

"Then three times I lied to immigration agents," I said. "And a couple of times I hated my brother, though I do love him, Father."

"With family, it's easy to do both," the priest said.

"'Tis," I said, "'Tis at that."

"But you must try to love your brother as you love yourself," the priest said. "It is, after all, what our Lord taught us."

"I will, Father," I said.

"Once I kissed a boy," I said. "But that isn't a sin, is it?"

"Just a kiss," the Father said, "no more than that?"

"A kiss, and holding his hand," I said. My mind was already back to bow of the ship, to Colum's lips on mine. When I thought of it, I could still feel them, still feel the heavy night air, still see the magic sparkle of the lights from the dock.

"Are your thoughts about this boy pure?" the priest asked.

"I want to marry him," I said. "To raise a good Christian family."

"And your parents agree?" the priest asked.

"My parents passed on," I said. "My brothers and I are alone."

"Living with family?"

"No alone," I said. "I'm not sure where we'll be living. We were going to go to Minnesota to live with my uncle, but now we don't know where he is. Then we were going to live in Washington with Colum, um, the boy I kissed, but then we lost him on Ellis. Then Mrs. Keane left for Butte. Then the shoonaun, the basket, was stolen." I paused. None of these were sins. "I'm sorry, Father," I said.

"You're alone, then," the Father said. "Are you living on the streets?"

I nodded, then remembered he probably couldn't see me nod. "We are, Father," I said.

"My daughter," he said, then paused. "What's your name, my daughter?"

"Clare," I said.

"Clare," he said, "I can help you. I'll be hearing confessions until after Mass. Find me then, and I'll help you."

"I will, Father," I said.

"Now do you have any more sins to confess?"

* * *

That was how we found ourselves being driven like three calves before a very young priest who had been drafted by the older priest to the task. What precisely the task was, none of the three of us could say. All we knew was that the young man in the black cassock, after waking us from our night's sleep on the floor of the rectory lobby, had stuffed a clump of bread each into each of our fists, and was now herding us the two blocks to the elevated.

The bread went down well, but far too quickly. The look on the young priest's face said we'd be wise not to ask for more. The crease between his eyebrows said he could think of things he'd rather be doing than tending to the likes of us.

So we rode the el-train in silence, and in silence we walked the five or six blocks after we'd reached our stop. In silence we entered the door of what looked like a shop. "Catholic Children's Protectory of New York" it said on the front window.

The wall by the door was lined with shoes. We made our way between shelves of men's shirts and trousers, women's shirtwaists and skirts. A cluster of caned chairs and a couple of bed frames stood along the far wall. Perhaps we were here for new clothes. It stood to reason. If I was to look for work, I would have to have something respectable to wear. I began leafing through a stack of shirtwaists that looked to be roughly my size.

"Don't touch anything," the priest said. The sound of his voice surprised me a bit. He hadn't said so much as five words since we left the cathedral.

"Yes, Father," I replied, immediately interlacing my fingers in front of me. The Father stepped up the counter, conferred quietly with the clerk, who nodded vigorously, then motioned toward the back stairs. The priest, who had fallen back into silence, indicated with a jerk of his head that we should follow.

At the top of the stairs was a large door with a smoked glass window. On the window was lettered "Catholic Children's Protectory of New York, Receiving House." The priest turned the knob and motioned for us to enter.

"Bob!" the man behind the desk called, jumping to his feet, "or I guess I should say 'Father'. How long have you been back in town?"

"A few days," the young priest said. A smile lit his face. He hardly looked like the same man. Or I should say he looked like a man for the first time, not like a generic priest, a stiff, place-holder face atop a stiff white collar.

"Sorry I missed your ordination," the man behind the desk said. "I wanted more than anything to be there."

"I know, Ken," the Father said.

"And who would these three be?" The man motioned at a chair and sat himself. There was only the one chair, and I assumed, rightly it turned out, that he wasn't motioning to one of us to sit. The Father lowered himself onto the padded leather seat and crossed his legs beneath his cassock.

"Do you have room for three more?" The priest straightened the line of his cassock over his knee, then brushed a bit of lint from it.

"As much room as we ever do," the man said. "Though if you folks over at St. Pat's were to mention our work from the pulpit more often, it would do us good. We could use the extra cash."

The priest smirked. "Is that the price for taking these three off my hands?"

"Take it or leave it," the man said. He too had a playful smile on his face.

"Deal," the priest said. "One mention for three inmates. Quite a bargain if you ask me."

The man behind the desk laughed. "I don't suppose you can stay for dinner," he said. "Greta makes chicken on Mondays."

"No," the priest said, "Father Connery has me scheduled for visitation in," he checked his watch, "a little over an hour. Remember me to her, though."

"I will," the man said, standing. "It's been good to see you again, Father." He extended a hand. The priest shook it and nodded.

"All the best to you, Ken," he said.

"To you, too, Bob." He worked his way around the desk and held the door. The priest made a quick sign of the cross over Bob's bowed head and then exited. I looked for some clue what we were to do. I got none, so I simply stood where I was, rooted to the spot, waiting for instructions. Tom did the same.

Mick, however, was never one to wait and watch. The boy had his virtues, I suppose, but patience wasn't one of them. He strode over to where the man stood watching his friend descend the stairs, stuck out his hand and introduced himself.

"Ken," he said, "my name is Mick Keane. This is my sister Clare, and my brother Tom. Quite pleased to meet you."

The man turned from the door and stared at Mick, his hand still outstretched. "You will address me as Mr. Brent. All our inmates are required to treat the staff with respect. You will address us as 'mister' or 'miss,' or in the case of the religious 'brother' or 'sister'. Do you understand?"

"I do, Mr. Brent," Mick said. He withdrew his unshaken hand. "But if you don't mind, Mr. Brent, would you be so good as to tell me just what an inmate might be?"

Mr. Brent ignored the question. He pulled a form from his desk, covered it with a piece of carbon paper, then laid a second form atop it. "Name," he said, looking up at me. I told him my name. "Are your parents deceased?" I nodded, then remembered my manners. "They are, Mr. Brent," I said.

"Age?" He began a long list of questions, painstakingly copying the answers onto the form in a slow, tidy hand. When he'd finished filling out forms, three of them, one for each of us, he separated the sheets and sealed one copy of each in an envelope.

"You can ride with Mr. Flannagan when he drops off today's load. Wait for him at the foot of the stairs, and show him this when you see him." He handed me the envelope. "Then keep it someplace safe; don't lose it," the man said.

"I won't sir," I said.

He stepped around to the door again and opened it, motioning for us to exit.

"One small matter, Mr. Brent," I said, "if you'd be so kind." He stopped waving us down the stairs and looked at me impatiently. "Just where is it we would be going with Mr. Flannagan?"

"Well, to the Protectory, of course," he said, "in Westchester." I must have still had a puzzled look on my face. "The orphanage," he said by way of clarification.

"The Catholic Children's Protectory of New York is an orphanage, then," I said.

"Of course it's an orphanage," he said. "What did you expect? Coney Island?"

I was silent. I hadn't known what to expect. Now that I had a name and the word "orphanage" I still wasn't sure what to expect. But I did know two things: First, I was frightened. And, second, all things considered, it was probably our best chance.

* * *

Mr. Flannagan was a great mountain of a man, a well-fed American with a thick strawberry blond beard covering what was probably a double chin. Tom and I sat behind him in the empty van, our back to his, washed over by the thick smell of him that seemed to fill the air like rancid honey despite the breeze generated by the wagon's brisk movement through the street.

"Do you work for the Protectory, then?" Mick said. He had settled into the seat beside Mr. Flannagan, immediately striking up a conversation.

"I do," Mr. Flannagan said, removing his cap and wiping his forehead on his sleeve for probably the fifth time since we'd met him. The sleeve of his jacket was several shades darker than the rest of it, the rest except for under the arms, of course. "Did now for some eight years."

"Do you like the work?" Mick asked.

"Well enough, I suppose," Mr. Flannagan replied. "Why do you ask? Are you thinking of being a van driver?"

"Well, now, I can't say I considered it," Mick said, "though I'd say it looks a fair enough life. Sun. Air. And you don't have to be breaking your back all day like you would, say, on the docks."

"True for you," Mr. Flannagan replied. His accent said south of Ireland, though I couldn't be sure just where. The sound of it had been so familiar I hadn't realized I was hearing it in an unfamiliar place. "It's not shoveling coal either," he said. "Thank God for that. But the van doesn't exactly load itself, don't you know."

Mick laughed. I craned my head around and caught a glimpse of Mr. Flannagan's face. He was smiling, too.

We rode for a bit in silence. I watched New York City fall away behind me—the wagons, the occasional motor car, women in tall hats, men and boys in dark jackets despite the summer heat, pushcarts manned by dark-clothed men in side curls, and shops, more shops than I could ever have imagined living back in Cork. Some of the windows had signs bearing words I'd never seen before. Some even contained alphabets I'd never seen before. We worked our way north, through the tenements, then through streets of brownstones with their fine windows and beautiful clean steps. Now and then we would pass a hotel guarded by men in crisp dark uniforms or grand houses of white stone or marble. Without knowing I was doing it, I found myself scanning for the servants' entrances.

Gradually the houses thinned. The road narrowed. Brick buildings gave way to board, small shanties with ragged children playing in front of them. We even passed through a section of town where every face was black. The faces stared at us, as we stared back at them. And with each clop of the horse hooves we got further from the train station, further from bakeries we knew, further from Bryan, who appallingly enough was the closest thing we had to family in this town. With each turn of the cart wheels I lost days, months, years and no less. I went from being the head of my household to an orphan girl. I went from being the breadwinner—not that I had been on much of a winning streak lately—to being under someone else's authority and care. It was a weight off my shoulders to be sure. But the weight was replaced by another, the insecurity of having one's future days summed up in one small phrase: Catholic Children's Protectory of New York. I felt my belly pressed with the uncertainty of it.

"Could you tell us something, then, Mr. Flannagan?" Mick said, breaking the silence.

"Well, if I can, I will," Mr. Flannagan said. "What is it you'd like to know?"

"What kind of a place is it we're going to?" Mick asked, just as straightforward as you please.

"Ah, so there it is then," Mr. Flannagan said. "I was wondering when it was you'd ask." He chuckled to himself. "They all do, you know. They all ask eventually."

"Do they, now?" Mick replied, a forced casualness in his voice.

"They do, boyo," Mr. Flannagan said. "They do indeed." He stripped his cap off, and once again ran his sleeve over his forehead. The motion seemed almost a conversational thing with him, a mark of punctuation perhaps, like a comma, or an ellipsis. "Well, let me tell you, boyo, if you're an orphan, you couldn't ask for a better life. Good food. A bed all to yourself. And they teach you a trade. If you learn well, you can do better than driving a van the rest of your life. You could be a carpenter, or a metal worker. Good money in that."

"Is that so?" Mick replied.

"'Tis," said Mr. Flannagan.

Mick fell silent. I could tell he was thinking, could feel it in the space of air between his back and mine.

"And the brothers," Mick said, "the brothers who run the place . . . " He paused. Mr. Flannagan made an encouraging noise, little more than a grunt really. "Well," Mick said, "I suppose the brothers have to beat the kidgers, at least sometimes."

Mr. Flannagan turned to look at Mick, then craned his neck around to examine me. "Not as much as you think," he finally said. "The director doesn't approve of such things. Though now and then I'd imagine there's a boy who leaves the brothers little choice. Now and then the switch is the best thing that could happen to a boy's soul. The boy just has to accept that, just has to accept he'll understand once he becomes a man."

"To be sure," Mick answered, though his tone lacked conviction. "And if you don't like the place, will they let you leave?" I shifted in my seat, craning in to hear the answer. It was the question I'd most been wondering myself.

Flannagan considered the question. Beside me I could feel Tom holding his breath. "We don't always get what we like most out of life," he said finally. "But I know a dozen kidgers if I know one who would consider themselves the luckiest Christians on the face of God's green earth if they got half the opportunities the Protectory offers."

"We don't get to leave when we like then," Mick said.

"No," Mr. Flannagan said quietly. "You don't."

* * *

The clatter of paving stones beneath the wheels of the cart gave way to the crackle of gravel. Trees overhung the roadway. Grass along the sides was mowed short by goats, sheep, and cows. Just as the city let loose its grip on the land, Mr. Flannagan reined the horses onto a side road, which led up a hill to a busy cluster of buildings. A large brick, four-storey building dominated the campus. Topped by a mansard roof and a central clock tower, it said not "home" but "institution." A couple of dozen boys were spread out over a dusty baseball diamond. A small group of girls in a field drew long, curved bows, loosing arrows at flimsy targets mounted on tripods. A trio of boys bent over a book on the step of a low stone building. Everywhere I looked there were children— children playing, children walking between buildings, children standing in neat lines headed by dark-clad religious. Dozens of them, hundreds maybe.

"I need to be seeing to these fellows," Mr. Flannagan said, reining up the horses. The cart rolled to a halt. "The stables are yonder, on the other side of the campus. You'll do as well as to get out here. Do you have your papers still?" I pulled them from my pocket, smoothed them out against my thigh, and held them up. "Good," he said, "good. Take them through that door there, into the main office."

"Thank you for the ride," I said.

"'Tis nothing," Mr. Flannagan said. "The best of luck to you, so. 'Tis a good place to live. If you have to be an orphan, 'tis a good place indeed."

We jumped out of the wagon, and Mr. Flannagan clicked the horses into a slow walk.

"Looks fine enough," Tom commented. "At least we'll have regular meals. That alone makes it a world better than the streets."

"'Tis at that," I said.

"But we need to choose now," Mick commented. "If we want to leave, we could. We could leave now and nobody would be the wiser. But once we walk through that door, we'll be on their books, and then we'll have the devil's own time leaving if we want to."

"I like it better than the streets," Tom said. "I wonder if they have a library. I'd hold a place this size has a good library."

"We don't know that it's better than the streets," Mick answered. "We can still walk away."

"Nobody's walking away," I said.

"You can't make that decision for all of us," Mick said.

"Nobody's walking away," I repeated. I turned my back to him, and headed at a brisk walk for the door Mr. Flannagan had pointed out.

"I didn't say I wanted to walk away," Mick said to my back, trotting to catch up. "I only said that if we wanted to walk away, now would be the time."

I didn't answer, just kept walking for the door. In some ways I was glad Mick was being Mick. I needed a push to send me face-first into that new life.

* * *

It didn't take long before one of the brothers peeled the boys off, leaving me to wait for my escort, a promised Sister of Charity who would, as the office manager promised, "get me settled."

I have to say the sister who finally arrived was not a bit what I expected. In Ireland I was used to sisters with pale—even grey—faces, sisters with green eyes, with long ivory-colored hands, sisters who looked, well, "Irish." This sister most emphatically was not Irish. Her face was dark, vaguely coppery. Her eyes were black, not just the pupils, but the large irises, too. Beneath her arched brows, her eyes looked liked the bull's-eyes of the targets we'd seen outside. Despite her flowing habit, I could sense that her body was wiry, strong, built like a short coiled spring.

"Choo ta noo curl?" she asked in a staccato accent. At first I wasn't sure what she said. "Choo ta new girl," she repeated more slowly. My brain sorted through what I'd heard. A couple of beats later it came up with a translation. "Are you the new girl?"

"I am," I said.

The sister pulled my file off the desk and glance at the tab. "Clar Keen," she said. I had never heard my short last name so abbreviated before. In her mouth it was barely a sound at all. She looked me up and down. "Choo need clothes, Clar Keen." She turned on her heel and walked to the door with a stride that chewed up each step and spit it out behind her.

"Will I come with you, then?" I said.

"Chess," she said, spinning quickly on her heel. "Chess, chess, of course." She waved a beckoning arm with a movement that looked like a slap. I rose and followed her.

"I'm Sister Xavier," she said tossing the words back over her shoulder. She pronounced it Havyair, with a curious little flip of the tongue on the r. I tried the new American sound out quietly on my tongue as I trotted my way down the long hallway and out onto the quad.

* * *

Sister Xavier pushed open a heavy door and held it for me. The sound coming from inside was familiar but oddly out of place somehow. It tightened my shoulders, turned my shoes to lead. Almost against my will, I dragged myself through the door and entered the long, high-ceilinged room. There they were. Sewing machines. Dozens of them in long ranks from one end of the room to the other. The air was relatively clear by contrast to the hops-laden atmosphere of the sack factory, but the clacking sound in the air brought a wash of memories over me. I rubbed my nose reflexively.

Sister Xavier was talking to another sister, a tall, thin woman with a pale face, who seemed to be trying to slide out from around Sister Xavier's words. Even conversation with Sister Xavier was an intense matter. She stood close to the skinny sister, backed her down with each word. Through my mind flitted an image of Sister Xavier at prayer, storming the bulwarks of heaven, angels and saints scattering like puppies before a trolley car. I wondered if God was as relieved as I was that she was on our side.

The tall sister pointed to the far end of the room, and Sister Xavier with a quick nod of her head, turned to me, snatched me by the sleeve, and charged off in the direction she was pointed.

The eyes of dozens of girls rose from their machines as we passed, girls about my age, some of them younger, all in tidy print dresses, all wearing matching ribbons in their hair. They sat at the machines confident of their place there, looked up to see who had entered their territory. I tried not to meet their eyes, focused instead on Sister Xavier's brown hand, still clutching my sleeve. Never had I felt more an alien than I did at that moment.

At the other end of the long room, on racks and shelves and hangers, were the products of all the sewing machines. Sister Xavier rifled through several dresses hanging on the rack before coming up with a teal green one. She held it up to me to try the size. I ran a finger over the lace that adorned the large collar and pointed yoke.

"For the eyes," she said, then followed the comment with a burst of some language I didn't understand. She pointed at the teal fabric then at my eyes. I understood.

"Yes, sister," I said. She smiled and handed me the dress.

"Choo need drawers, too," she said, holding a set of underwear against me for size. I could feel the blood rise into my ears and cheeks. Sister Xavier, smiled, tisked and said something in a dismissive tone. I couldn't quite catch it. She folded the drawers, piled them on top of the dress. I quickly tucked them underneath.

"All girls," Sister Xavier said with a laugh and a sweep of her hand. "No watch choo." I looked out at the girls at the sewing machines. All I saw were backs. I smiled back at Sister Xavier. She tisked and waggled a finger at me, then went back to the shelves.

"Underskirt," she said, adding one to the pile. "Estockings. Choos. Ribbons for hair. Nightgown. Chool look just like a **Gibson girl**."

I had no idea who a Gibson girl was, but I assumed Sister Xavier meant the comment benevolently, so I smiled.

"Choo wash now," Sister Xavier announced, and again grasping a bit of the fabric of my sleeve in her fist, hauled me back down the line of sewing machines and out the front door. I followed, arms laden with new clothes, not merely new to me, but *new* clothes, and new clothes I had not worked for at that. I held them gingerly, arms outstretched like a shelf, and without even knowing I was doing it, braced for the inevitable reckoning I could not help but believe would soon come.

* * *

The dormitory looked nearly new. The stone floor of the entryway was unscuffed, the stone stairways we climbed to the second floor, unworn. Sister Xavier brought me into a large washroom. Along the wall were a series of hooks. Most had towels hanging on them and hairbrushes and toothbrushes in the cubby above. Sister Xavier first scanned the hooks, then the clipboard she had tucked under her arm.

"Choo are 231," she said. "Choo understand? Two. Three. One." She held up first two fingers, then three, then one.

"Two, three, one," I said. She nodded, scribbled a note on her clipboard, then turned to a cabinet and pulled out a marking pencil. Taking first my new dress, then the rest of my new things, she wrote on labels sewn into each "231." She even printed the number in a fine hand onto the center of each of the hair ribbons. Then she scanned the wall of hooks, grabbed me by the sleeve again, and stood me before the hook marked 231. On it was hung a clean towel with 231 lettered onto the corner. I couldn't see the hairbrush and toothbrushes above me on the shelf, but it wouldn't surprise me if they too bore that number.

"231," Sister Xavier repeated seriously.

"231," I said, matching her tone.

"Good," she said, brightening. "Choo wash now. Change clothes." She strode over to a large donut-shaped sink and pressed a bar near the floor with her foot. From dozens of spigots all around the sink, small jets of water flowed. "Soap," she said pointing to one of several bars scattered along the rim of the sink. "Gets the street off." She rubbed a hand over the sleeve of her habit for emphasis.

"Yes, sister," I said, gingerly undoing the top button of my blouse. Sister Xavier smiled, then like a woman on a mission, which I suppose she was, strode out the door, leaving me alone, silence echoing off the tile walls.

* * *

I was standing next to that great sink, half-in and half-out of my new set of drawers, when she entered. I hopped a bit on one foot, glanced over my shoulder to see who it was. And that was how I first met Annette, the girl who to this day sticks in my mind as being the most tormenting of all the creatures to walk the face of God's good earth. On that first day, in less than thirty seconds' time, I knew she and I were destined to make each other miserable.

"Hey, new girl," she said "I could introduce you to a gorilla who could get you thirty cents a bang for that."

"A gorilla? What do you mean? Thirty cents for what?" I said, taking the bait without even knowing it was bait, not that the one ever does.

"For that," she said, stepping up and dragging the back of her fingernail up the length of my buttock. She then added by way of clarification something that should never said aloud let alone put into the permanent medium of print. I jumped back like one bitten. She laughed. It wasn't a laugh of amusement, but a laugh to press salt upon the wound she knew she had opened.

"What kind of accent you got there?" she asked. She had stepped back and was leaning casually against the sink.

"Irish," I said, "County Cork." She herself had a touch of something in her voice, something not quite American, though to say what was and wasn't an American accent in New York of the time was no small matter.

"Well, County Cork," she said, "you're no longer back in the 'old country'." She released the words as though they were a bad piece of meat she'd bitten into. "And since you're clearly as green as they come, I'll give you a little advice." She pressed down the foot bar with her toe and stretched out her hands under the running water. "First, the sisters may think they run things here, but they don't know the half of what goes on under their noses. If you want to get along, you have to make nice with the sisters, but you have to make even nicer to the people who are really in charge of this place."

I stood silent, buttoning my drawers, making just enough eye contact that she would know I was listening. I wondered if Sister Xavier was within shouting distance if it came to that.

"Don't you want to know who's really in charge?" Annette said. She'd finished washing her hands, and was toying with the foot bar, turning the water on and off and on and off. I looked up and assessed her. She was about my age, close to my height, probably not quite as strong as I was. The hair ribbons tying her brown hair into pig tails made her look like a young girl, but there was nothing girlish about her face, her expression. I decided to hold my ground.

"I suppose you're going to tell me you're in charge," I said. My tone was pleasant, but I wanted her to know that I wasn't about to jump away again. "I'm sure Sister Xavier would find it very interesting to hear that."

"For that bit of cheek I'm not going to give you the rest of my advice." She slid her foot off the bar, and the taps closed with a thunk. "Well, maybe only one piece." She took a step forward. Feeling a bit exposed in nothing but my drawers, I took a step back despite myself. She smiled a half smile that curled her upper lip up around the side of her nose. "Ask around, County Cork," she said. "Ask anyone what happens to people who cross Annette. That's all I have to say." She turned, hands still dripping, and left.

* * *

In order to understand the phenomenon of the Catholic Children's Protectory of New York, one needs to understand something crucial about the turn of the century. Back then we didn't have nearly the extensive a catalog of pathology as folks do today. Back then the children who ended up in the Protectory were simply called "down and out." In general, the label applied to anyone who was not a productive member of society. Those without jobs were down and out. Those convicted of a crime and sentenced to prison were down and out. The mentally disabled were down and out, too, but only if they didn't have family to care for them. You were down and out if you had slipped through the hole in society's pocket and were currently being kicked about on the sidewalk under foot.

The Catholic Children's Protectory of New York was a place for down and out children. That list included, but was not limited to: children whose parents themselves were down and out, so much so they could no longer care for their families; children in trouble with the law; children pulled off the streets, child prostitutes, thieves, and scroungers; children of prostitutes, thieves and scroungers; and, of course, orphans.

Today, we wouldn't think of putting someone who had recently lost both parents in an institution with a child convicted of some kind of larceny. But back then, since both children needed to be pulled out of their unfortunate past and set on a path to being respectable, institutions thought nothing of lumping them together in great institutional-style buildings.

And that was how I came to share a dormitory room with pickpockets, con artists, chain smokers, and girls with sexual experience that probably outstrips my own today as a wife and mother of two children. In the eyes of the Catholic Children's Protectory of New York, I was just another member of the down and out.

* * *

That first evening in the dining room, I stood behind my place on the bench, one of dozens of orphans like me, lined up along a long table. That table, moreover, was one of dozens that stood in crisp rows from one end of the cavernous dining room to the other. I bowed my head, one of hundreds of heads bedecked with the same kind of ribbons, the same pigtails; and along with hundreds of girls, I murmured the amen and crossed myself. Supper was simple, but ample—beans, bread, carrots, milk. In a highly efficient manner, we ate, prayed again, then marched up the stairs to the dormitory. The sister in charge of our room read us a story, a story of one of the saints. Then she watched as we changed into our nightdresses, knelt for prayers, and hopped into bed. Finally, she walked the aisle, pausing at each of the gas wall lamps to turn them off. In true institutional fashion, she didn't so much tuck us in as she provided incentive for us to tuck ourselves in. As she approached each bed, we'd pull up the blanket, smooth down a wrinkle, put ourselves in order like soldiers making ready for inspection. From lamp to lamp, from bed to bed, she walked, shutting the day down bit by bit until finally she paused at the door.

"Sleep well," she said. "I commend you to the arms of God."

* * *

The night fell slowly. It was New York, and late summer after all. Gradually, the room fell into sleep. But as tired as I was, I was nowhere near drowsy.

This was my own bed now—so I found myself reflecting. The sheets were clean, if heavily darned. The blanket was a blanket, not a reincarnated coat. And not only did I have my own pillow, I had a pillow without someone else's feet resting on it. My belly was full, my face and hands were clean, and I'd stepped out of a new dress into a new nightgown. If Mick were here, I'd reassure him that life was good.

All up and down the aisle I heard the sounds of girls sleeping, not quite sleeping, listening to other girls sleeping. Springs creaked. Now and then someone coughed. Outside the open window were the sounds of the orphanage descending into night.

Life was good. That's what I told myself. You should be happy. No more than twenty-four hours ago you were looking at starvation on the malignant streets of a foreign city. Now your belly is full. But still I could feel it rise within me, the growing, steadily building distaste for this place. I couldn't quite figure out why but less than twelve hours after arriving, already I chafed against the Catholic Children's Protectory of New York.

The girl in the bed next to me rose, brushed down her nightdress, and padded off in bare feet to the toilet. An indoor toilet, it was. Clean, white porcelain, without a creak, without a smell. Life is good. So I told myself. I could feel a nameless tear tighten the back of my throat. Life was good, but I didn't like it. Not a little bit.

"Well, then, Clare Elizabeth Keane," I heard from deep in my mind, "maybe you're just living in the wrong part of your life."

I closed my eyes, and felt it—the boards of the *Caronia* beneath my feet, the salt air on my face, the smell of unwashed wool all around me. I felt his hand in mine.

"I am in Washington," I began, whispering the words so low I could barely hear them myself. "And the trees surround me, tall green trees, smelling of life and future. And from behind one of them steps Colum." I hesitated. From the end of the long room a low snore rumbled. I rolled over, pulled the pillow over my head.

"From behind one of the great trees," I continued, "steps Colum, my husband." The words sounded foreign, but right. "Colum, my husband," I whispered again. "He's carrying an axe over his shoulder. His face is damp with sweat, and his shock of hair lays heavy, pasted to his forehead. He's grown, or so it seems, from the work, from the months since I saw him last. And his shoulders are broad and his hands strong." The heat of the pillow grew. I shifted again, pushed it from my head and again heard the sounds of the crickets from outside the window.

"His shoulders are broad," I whispered, "And when he sees me, his smile lights his face. And I feel the spark of it in my belly, my breasts." I wonder if this is how Eve felt when she first saw Adam. I wonder if this is what it feels like to know that you have been made for another person. "I can't take my eyes from him," I whispered. "And I feel his eyes resting softly on me, my face, my hair, my own shoulders, and . . . " I paused, not really able to say it.

"He walks through the forest toward me, takes the axe from his shoulders. 'I knew you'd come,' he says. 'Now neither of us will ever be alone again.'" The whisper died back like the last breath of wind in my mouth. I clutched the pillow to my chest, and I felt his soft moist lips on my own.

I curled up upon myself, tightly, arms wrapping shoulders, clutching within my own embrace the aching need to climb into another's arms. I imagined Colum's body wrapped around my own, his head heavy on my shoulder. I imagined Mama's warm breast, a soft pillow for my cheek. I imagined smooth hands up and down the length of my back, soft hands smoothing a stray curl away from my face. I sank into it, into the feeling, let it take me, let it take me into tears and out the other side. In the muggy night, my arms were damp with my own sweat, moist with my own tears. And from deep within my own embrace, I ached for another.

All around me were the sounds of humans, stacked end to end, long warehouse shelves laden with human stock. And I wondered how on my own little shelf, surrounded by others, how I could be so completely, utterly alone.

Thirty-Three

I was too old to sit in a classroom, or so Sister Xavier told me. I was to learn a trade or perhaps the skills I would need to function as a wife and mother—not that there was much distinction between the two in those days. Sister Xavier suggested embroidery. I told her I was willing to try, but that in the past I'd displayed a chronic inability to handle fine needlework. She suggested machine sewing, but the memory of the sack factory must have shown on my face, so she asked me what I wanted to do. I said I wanted to learn to cook. It was the only other thing I could think to say given that I doubted the orphanage had much use for handywomen.

Upon hearing my choice, Sister Xavier proclaimed with characteristic enthusiasm that it was a good one. She then grasped me by the sleeve and hauled me at athletic speed to the door of the kitchen, where she dropped me off without ceremony, like a box of potatoes ordered, expected, but no more worthy of special handling than any other shipment.

The kitchen was huge, a great white room with electric lights hanging from the ceiling and tall windows all down one side. Worktables ran down the center, stoves and ovens down the side. In the back, in a part of the room shaded from the windows by what was probably a pantry, were the boilers and sinks. I noticed immediately that the room, everything about it, was spotless.

I wasn't sure I should just enter unannounced, so I scanned the kitchen for whoever might be in charge. It was not difficult to find her. She must have felt my eyes, for she looked up from the floury pile of dough she had been kneading, wiped her hands on her apron, then motioned for me to enter.

She was a large woman—a head and then some taller than most of the girls around her. But more than merely large, she was solid, massive, with hips that were as deep as they were wide and breasts that rode large on a broad chest. She was muscular, but in no way masculine. It was more like she was a woman and then some—larger, stronger, softer, and just "more" than any woman I had ever seen before.

"I'm Clare Keane," I said, making my way around the end of the table. "Sister Xavier sent me."

"*Sprechen Sie Deutsch*, Clare Keane?" the woman said.

I looked around at the other girls working in the kitchen. None of them looked up to help me.

"*Deutsch*?" the woman said more slowly. "*Sprechen Sie Deutsch*?"

"German?" I said. It was a guess.

"Ja," she said. "Ger-man. Speak you German?"

"No," I said, searching my mind for the German word for no, and coming up blank. I don't think I had ever heard it, let alone used it. "No," I said again with a shrug.

She sighed. "Kristie," she called over her shoulder. A girl, maybe my age, maybe a year or two older, made her way between the lines of girls chopping and peeling. She was wiping her hands on a white towel.

"*Ja?*" she said.

The woman rattled off a spate of German, and Kristie nodded.

"Are you assigned to work here?" she asked.

"I am," I replied.

"Have you ever worked in a kitchen before?" she asked.

"I did," I said.

"Good," she said. "You're lucky. That means you don't have to start washing dishes and scouring pots."

"Luck of the Irish," I said. But then thought of all the Irish I'd known who had made their living washing and scouring.

"Are you from Ireland?" Kristie asked. I nodded. "My best friend—before she was shipped out west—was Irish. Her name was Maisie," she said.

"Grand," I said, not sure what else to say.

"Grand," Kristie repeated after me. "You don't speak English like Americans."

"We don't," I said.

"Well, that doesn't matter," she said. "We speak mostly German in the kitchen, anyway. I'm Kristie. This is Mrs. Riezler."

"Margarethe. Riezler," the large woman said slowly enough that I couldn't fail to catch every sound. She said something to Kristie. Kristie replied. I listened hard, trying to catch a word or two, but German was quite unlike either English or the hundred or two words of Gaelic I knew. I got none of it.

Kristie turned to me. "I explained to her that you've worked in a kitchen before. She said you can help with the potatoes."

"*Ja*, potatoes," Mrs. Riezler said. "*Kartoffeln. Schäle die Kartoffeln.*" She motioned toward four girls who stood at one of the counters peeling their way through a large sack of potatoes.

"*Schäle die Kartoffeln*" I repeated after her. She smiled a big smile at me then nodded vigorously.

"*Ja, ja, Schäle die Kartoffeln,*" she said, then motioned with her hand that I should leave her and begin immediately.

"I'll get you an apron and a knife," Kristie said, indicating with her head that I should follow.

"Why do you speak German here?" I asked.

"Well," Kristie replied, "I suppose because Mrs. Riezler does."

"Doesn't Mrs. Riezler speak English?" I asked. It had never occurred to me that someone had been in America long enough to be in charge of a kitchen might not speak English.

"She speaks English," Kristie said, selecting a paring knife from a drawer and testing its blade against her thumb. "At least some English. The sisters wouldn't have hired her if she couldn't speak with them. But she doesn't like speaking English. She says it's a flimsy language. So here in the kitchen, *her* kitchen, she speaks German, and so do we."

I took the knife. Kristie selected another for herself.

"There's not much to know here," she said. "Follow instructions. Keep everything clean—Mrs. Riezler can't abide clutter or dirt. We can talk if it doesn't get in the way of work. Kitchen duty's a lot better than sewing. Those girls can't talk at all while they sew. You'll pick up the German you need pretty quickly."

The girl across the table from me tossed another potato into the pot in the center. It was larger than any pot I had ever used before. I wouldn't be surprised if it took two people to lift it to the stove.

"Have you been in America long?" Kristie said.

"Three weeks," I said.

"And you're in this place already?" Kristie shook her head. "What happened?"

"I'll tell you about it sometime," I said. I was finally starting to relax. The familiar feel of potato skin beneath my fingers was beginning to settle me. Or maybe it was just being around food. I didn't really want to trouble the waters inside me all over again. "How long have you been here?"

"I came over from Sweden when I was five," she said. "I don't remember much about it, just that the ocean seemed to go on forever."

I nodded. I had meant "how long have you been in the orphanage?" But I didn't really blame Kristie if she didn't want to talk about that.

Mrs. Riezler, who was presiding over the stove, glanced over her shoulder and said something to Kristie.

"She wants us to slice some bread when we're finished."

"*Brot*," Mrs. Riezler said.

"*Brot*," I repeated.

"*Brot*," Kristie said. "That means 'bread'. It's just like English, almost." She said something back to Mrs. Riezler, who nodded and motioned with her hand to the back sinks.

"We need to rinse these and put them on to boil," Kristie said. "Take the other side." I grasped the handle and together we hoisted the pot over off the table.

"How many of these do you cook each day?" I asked.

"I don't know," Kristie said. "Mrs. Riezler would know if you want to ask her."

"'Tisn't important," I said. "I was only curious. I never saw so many children in one place before. In Ireland, the schools themselves weren't this big."

"Is Ireland much different from New York?" Kristie asked as we hefted the pot onto the rim of the sink.

"'Tis," I said. "'Tis, indeed."

"'Tis," Kristie echoed me and chuckled.

"The way people speak," I said. "That's different. In Cork, people speak with a fine melodious accent. It's like a song, really, much more like a song than the way Americans speak. And the buildings aren't so tall. And there's no electric light, except at the brewery. And we have covered cars, which I've never seen here, and a sport called hurling." We dumped the potatoes into a huge colander. Kristie began running water over them, and handed me the pot to rinse.

It was talking about it, I suppose, that brought it all back. Or maybe working in a kitchen. There as I stood listening to the water ringing in the pot, the sights of Cork, the sounds of it, the smell of it, all washed over me again. First I saw my mother's face as she did dishes by the light of the kerosene lamp in the Quillan's kitchen. Then I could see Mick charging down the lane with Wally and Roddy, chasing a makeshift football. I could feel the brilliant green of an Irish spring day at the Lough. I could see the slow amble of the Lee, could smell the thick sweetness oozing out from the gates of the Murphy's plant.

"Do you miss it?" Kristie said, breaking into my reverie.

"It was home," I said. "And why shouldn't I miss it?" I was hoping for a more casual tone, but the memories, though trivial, were far from casual. My voice caught a bit.

"Is that clean?" Kristie motioned to the pot.

"'Tis," I said.

"'Tis'," Kristie repeated. "Just like Maisie. I'd like to see Ireland. When we're grown, when we've gotten good jobs and are making a lot of money, why don't you and I go to Ireland, just travel the country? You can show me around. What do you say?"

"I'd like that," I said.

"Good," Kristie said. "Then it's settled. Let's get these potatoes back in the pot before they grey. First we make dinner. Then we grow up. Then we see Ireland."

* * *

During my first week, I learned the rhythms of the place. Prayers in the morning. Then work, then the noon meal, then religious instruction, then a break, then more work. Eat on schedule. Wash on schedule. Play on schedule. Sleep on schedule. I wondered how Mick was doing.

I asked around a bit, trying to find out as much as I could about the boy's side of the protectory. One of the girls in the kitchen told me that the boys had a wider range of trades they could learn. Some did printing, some made shoes or caned chairs. Others apprenticed with wheelwrights, tailors, blacksmiths, farmers, carpenters. A couple of times I had seen Tom in chapel, but I didn't get the chance to talk with him. Each day during recreation, I scanned the yard for him and for Mick, but to no avail. Instead I watched dozens of boys I'd never met play baseball, kick a ball around. They seemed happy enough. I chose to believe Mick and Tom were, too.

* * *

It had been two weeks, maybe a bit less—working, settling in, wondering about Mick and Tom—when one afternoon Sister Xavier swept into the kitchen, snatched me up by a pinch of blouse, and hauled me off to one of the offices. She told me what it was all about, but between her accent and my trying to keep up with her, I didn't really catch much. Something about a train.

When she deposited me in front of an open door, Mick and Tom were already sitting across the desk from a man in black habit, one of the brothers probably. A gentry woman in one of the finest silk shirtwaists I'd ever set eyes on stood at his side, towering over him. The brother stood briefly as I entered, then motioned to the chair. I sat and took Tom's hand. We would probably not have a chance to talk, but I was grateful for the contact. Both he and Mick looked good in their new white shirts and knickers. Both looked healthy and well-fed. But on their faces were the same questions I myself wore.

"How would you like to go out West?" the brother said without preamble.

"To Minnesota?" Mick said. "Did you find Uncle Ronan?"

"Your uncle has been deemed unsuitable," the brother said simply. "And I can't say if it will be Minnesota. Perhaps. Or perhaps Missouri or Oklahoma. A farm, maybe. Many of our children go to live on farms. Wherever we send you, it will be a new life, a better life than you'd have in the city."

"So we're not to stay here?" I said. I had just assumed that we were here for the rest of our childhoods, until they could teach us a trade and send us out into the world.

"No, no," the brother said. "The three of you are adoptable. You work hard. You're well mannered. It's not like you were street Arabs or, um, an 'experienced' girl when we found you. I'm sure we can find families happy to take you."

Families. Not "a family" but "families." That's what he said.

"We'd like to stay together," I said.

"Of course," the man said. "We make every effort to place brothers and sisters as close as possible to each other, but you have to understand that it will be difficult to place all three of you in the same family."

"We'll try," the woman said. It was the first time she'd spoke.

"This is Miss Paris," the brother said. "She'll be asking you some questions." He rose to leave. Miss Paris took his place behind the desk.

"You have family in Minnesota?" she said.

"We do," Mick replied. "Uncle Ronan is the one who sent for us. All we really need is a bit of help getting to Minnesota. Then we could live with him." Suddenly I pictured a repeat of the interview on Ellis Island. I decided then and there that I would not let Mick skate through the interview on half truths and false impressions.

"We're not sure where Uncle Ronan is," I said. "He sent us the money for the boat ticket, and then we, um, lost him. But he is family, really the only family we have. If you can find him, we'd like to go live with him."

"He might be in Wisconsin," Tom chimed in. "Working for a logging company."

"Uncle Ronan. Would that be Ronan Keane?" Miss Paris asked. She flipped through the file folder on her desk.

I nodded. "Our father's younger brother," I added.

"I have a letter from a social worker on Ellis Island here," she said. "It says they were unable to contact Ronan Keane, and that you were released into the custody of Bryan Keane. We have an address here, on Twenty-second Street, New York, but a case worker we sent to find him says he is no longer at that address. Is he also an uncle?"

"No," I said. "That was a misunderstanding."

"Oh?" Miss Paris said, her eyebrows arching.

"We aren't related," I said. "We can't stay with Bryan Keane. In fact we wish never to see Mr. Keane again."

"I see," Miss Paris said.

"We like to go to Minnesota," Mick said. "Uncle Ronan will take us in once we find him."

"I'm afraid that's not possible," Miss Paris said. "Your uncle didn't meet you in New York. He didn't reply to telegrams sent to contact him. He has left at least three jobs in the last few months. In addition, he's a bachelor with no permanent place of residence. I'm afraid he's been deemed unsuitable. What we can do is find you new families—maybe in Minnesota, or maybe Wisconsin—who will take you in. We screen all our families, make sure they're good Catholics, make sure their priests believe they're suitable parents for our children. They're good Christian families, all of them. You would be better off with one of them than you would be with your uncle."

We sat silently, even Mick, who was not naturally given to silence, sat closed-mouthed, his eyes glued on an ink spot on the floor at his feet. The news was a bit of a shock—yet one more shock in a long series of shocks.

When Mama died, it had taken quite some doing to adjust to the thought of a future with Uncle Ronan. After that, it was a bit easier to consider a new life with Colum. And after the streets, it was still easier to adjust to a future in the orphanage. Now I was being told that I would be allowed none of those futures, that I would have to piece together still another future in my mind, one with a family I had never met, in a state I had never been to. You'd think that with all the practice I'd had, that new adjustment would have been simple. But once again I found myself missing crucial pieces I needed to form a clear picture of where my life was going. I found myself again hanging loose in time.

"I just need to ask you a few questions, and then I can begin processing the paperwork," Miss Paris said. "Clare first. How much schooling do you have?"

"I started school at seven, left when I was eleven, when my father died," I said. Miss Paris jotted a few notes.

"Vocational training?" she asked.

"Work, do you mean?" I asked.

"Training for work, yes," she said.

"My mother taught me to do for the rich people—to clean, cook, serve at table, that sort of thing. And I work with Mrs. Riezler here."

"Don't forget the sack factory," Tom said.

"I don't want to work in a sack factory," I said quickly, with as much force as I could without being rude.

"You made sacks," Miss Paris said.

"Cleaned sacks," I replied. "For the breweries. I'd rather go back into service that do that kind of work again."

"We're not placing you in a job," Miss Paris said. "We're placing you in a family. They might ask you to work in the family business like any other member of the family would. In fact, we expect the foster families to teach our children Christian virtues and the value of hard work. But one of our purposes here is to allow children the chance to have a childhood before they're forced into full-time work and adulthood."

Yet another piece of the puzzle that didn't fit. I wondered if it would be possible for me to go back to being a child again. It seemed like years since I last felt like one.

Miss Paris went through her list of questions—education, ethnicity, whether we had ever been in trouble with the law. Mick squirmed a bit at the last question, but to his credit, he confessed to his few minor brushes with delinquency. I drew the conclusion that living with the brothers had been good for him. Tom mentioned that he wanted to be an engineer, asked if Miss Paris could perhaps place us with a man who made his living as an engineer. Miss Paris said that placement was rarely that exact, but that she would see what she could do.

All together, we spent about a half hour in the office asking and answering questions. In that short time, Miss Paris assembled on her bits of paper, a sketch of our future. Our new future. Or perhaps I should say our *newest* future. I hugged Mick and Tom before a young brother took them back to the boy's side. As for myself, I was eager to get back to the kitchen, to the familiar present. Juggling my ever-shifting future just made me tired.

* * *

When I returned to the kitchen, the girls were off on break. Every afternoon when it wasn't raining, the sisters chased us outdoors. For the younger girls the half hour outdoors was recess from school. For the older girls in the kitchen it was a bit of time off between cleaning up after dinner and starting supper. These breaks were practically sacrosanct. The sisters who ran the protectory were great believers in fresh air and sunshine, as though the wind and the sun were as crucial to the moral rehabilitation of the down-and-out as prayer and work were. Sister Xavier often joined us for our break, trotting from girl to girl like a cheerleader, encouraging us to breathe deeply. I knew better than to stay in the kitchen when I should be outside.

That afternoon, Sister Xavier was elsewhere. I was a bit relieved. I was feeling a bit battered after my interview with Miss Paris. I didn't really feel as though I had the energy to manage anything more than the most rudimentary breathing.

I strolled the grounds alone, replaying the details of the interview in my mind. Some of the younger girls were skipping rope along the road. With each jump, puffs of dust rose up to settle on my sticky skin. The girl on one end of the rope looked up as I passed by, then just as quickly went back to her twirling. Two girls shared the center of the rope, their pig tails bobbing and leaping with each jump.

I watched them for a couple of minutes, then strolled across the road toward the ball field where a half dozen boys lobbed the ball around the bases, waiting for a fuller complement to begin a game. I scanned faces. Mick and Tom weren't among them. I was disappointed. I would have liked a chance to talk with them about, well, everything—the protectory, the interview, the chance we could be adopted. I began systematically surveying the grounds for them, hoping they might also have been released on break.

That was when I noticed a clutch of older girls huddled apart, over near the fence at the edge of the ball field maybe fifty feet away. Two of them I recognized from the kitchen. But they alone wouldn't have caught my eye. What caught my eye was that Annette was among them.

Since the first time I met her, Annette had me marked as someone to torment. Rarely did I see her in our dormitory when she didn't have some snide word, some little jab for me. A couple of days ago she had smeared soap down the back of my dress in the lavatory. A few days before that, she had used my blanket to clean her shoes. Each time, with unfailing accuracy, she had managed to time her assault so that the sisters were no wiser. I had learned to dread even the sight of her.

That afternoon she was leaning against the ball field fence. The girls who were with her hung on her words. All of them wore either pig tails or a long braid down their backs—the sisters saw to it that each morning we were properly braided and ribboned before we were allowed to leave the dormitory.

But even with the pigtails and pink ribbons she wore, even with her calico dress and clean-scrubbed face, she exuded a street corner air. Quickly I looked away, began moving steadily back toward the dormitories, hoping she wouldn't notice me. Unfortunately, I wasn't quite invisible enough.

"Hey you," Annette called, closing the distance between us at a trot. "Hey, County Cork!" That was her name for me and had been since our very first meeting. "Gotta fag? I'm dying for a smoke." The other girls trotted after her.

I shook my head. Annette laughed. The other girls chimed in, laughing and elbowing each other. I'd seen hints of it in the dormitory and the kitchen, but here out from under the noses of the sisters and other adults, it was plainly obvious. The other streetwise girls hung just off her shoulders, followed her when she moved, took their cues from her. At the time, I didn't have a term for her role in the group, but I knew instinctively that she was at the heart of the new danger I felt myself in.

"I'll bet you've never smoked, hey, County Cork?" She talked loudly enough that I was sure the boys on the ball field would soon stop to look. They didn't. "Is that so, County Cork? Is it true you've never smoked?"

I continued to back my way toward the dormitory. I didn't want to give them the satisfaction of making me run away, so I just walked, half backward, half forward, always keeping at least one eye on the pack. Annette led them in, a smirk on her face as she steadily closed the distance between us. As I walked past the rope jumpers, a couple of them looked up, first at me, then at Annette and her gang. Right in the middle of "Mary Mack," they all missed a beat. The rope fell silent for a second, then resumed, the song half-hearted, the jumper shooting occasional nervous glances in our direction. I could feel it in my shoulders—everyone on the playground, everyone within a fifty-foot radius went on alert.

"Cat got your tongue, County Cork?" Annette's voice was not only loud; it was penetrating. "So have you?" Annette pressed the issue. "Have you ever had a drag?" I shook my head. A couple of girls split off the jump ropers and huddled in quiet conversation near the dormitory door. They reminded me of two tiny rodents huddled near the entrance to their den, nervous at the shadow of a hawk overhead, ready to dive for safety at a second's notice.

"Ever had a man, then?" Annette called. The girls in the pack snickered. I turned, looked over the playground to the east, the swings flowing back and forth on their great metal frame. A cart had pulled onto the main drive, and was making its way slowly along the dusty road. A tarp covered the bundles in the back. That wasn't what I was looking for, though. I was looking for black. Black and white. A sister. Any sister. I saw nothing but colors, children. Fellow prey.

"Are you deaf, County Cork, or just rude?" Annette and her pack continued to move in slowly. So she was going to force the issue. The issue was, of course, not whether I had "had a man" but whether or not I would be bullied.

I didn't recognize the sifting process at the time, but since then I've seen it wherever children gather with only moderate supervision. I saw it when my girls were in junior high. I saw it on the beaches in the summer where they waited for swimming lessons. The process, a primal, Darwinian-selection thing, goes something like this: Introduce a new child onto a playground, a lunchroom, a junior high hallway. Within minutes, the weak move aside, and the strong move in. They test and worry the new beast, seeing if it will roll over and play submissive right away, or whether it will need to be "taught a lesson" first. Sometimes, of course, the new beast will refuse to be taught a lesson. Sometimes she will go nose-to-nose with the leader and back her down, maybe even steal a few members of her pack. But most of the time the new beast will roll over, and the pack will mark her: "toady," "outcast," "cheap labor," or, if the new girl is particularly unlucky, "victim." Being the designated victim in the playground jungle meant scars, sometimes even physical ones. But then so did challenging the leader for top slot. The best an early adolescent could hope for was anonymity, a comfortable slot someplace in the middle of the pecking order.

Of course, I didn't know all this then. Annette and her pack moved in, and I was aware only that I had a choice. I could face them down, or I could run and hope I could make it to the door of the dormitory before someone caught up to me.

"Deaf, I think," Annette said. "Are you deaf?" She shouted even louder, though I wouldn't have thought it possible.

"Only when what I'm hearing isn't worth listening to," I replied. I stepped off the road onto the walk that led to the dorm. Suddenly, I wished Mick was here. If he were, it would probably only mean that we both get pounded. But still I wished for him.

"She thinks she's better than us," Annette said. "Holier than us. Don't you, County Cork, or should I call you 'Sister Cork'?"

"I *think* I want to be alone," I said. I knew immediately that it was the wrong thing to say. But then I'm not sure there would have been a right thing. Annette moved in. The rest of the pack fanned out. I did what any other prey would have done in my circumstance. I bolted.

A hand clutched at my sleeve, but I swatted it loose and hit the stairway at a dead run. Throwing myself at the door, I fumbled for the knob. It turned. I pulled the door open, slipped through, and slammed it after me. The crack of it echoed down through the hallway. Never have I been so glad of a girl's short skirts as I was then, dashing down the corridor, listening to the wild laughs bouncing off the walls behind me.

I have to say, at just that moment, I thought about leaving. I thought about slipping out a side door, hunting down Mick and Tom, and making our way to Minnesota as best we could. I would leave Annette, leave Miss Paris and her plans to send us to some stranger's home. I would leave it all behind. No more than halfway down the corridor, though, the flaws in that plan screamed out at me. I knew from first-hand experience that failure in such a plan could do me far more damage than Annette and her girls ever could.

* * *

I made my way up the stairs at a dead run, scuffling and shuffling and coughing as loudly as I could the whole way up. The corridors of the dormitory had an industrial feel to them and tended to magnify the sounds of footsteps. The sisters used those sounds to track children who weren't where they should be. Since I was definitely someplace I shouldn't be—and that in more senses than one—I figured noise might draw one of the sisters. I knew full well that encountering an adult could well mean both help and punishment. I prayed for the former. The latter I would deal with when the time came.

As I turned the corner to ascend the last flight of stairs, from below me in the main corridor, I could hear the low voices of Annette and her pack. "County

Cork, County Cork, County Cork," they chanted in a stage whisper. The sound carried up the stone stairs as clearly as if the predators were right on my heels. It made the back of my neck go all cold and quivery.

Reaching the top of the stairs, I looked right, then left. My heart sunk. The corridor was empty. The voices were now coming from somewhere on the stairs. I was going to get pounded, and on the marble floors of the dormitory, not the soft dirt of the playground.

That's when I decided to take a chance. Rather than turning left to the dormitory, I turned right. Right toward the infirmary. Annette could find me easily in the dormitory. But the infirmary? She was highly unlikely to stick her nose into the infirmary.

* * *

The infirmary was inhabited by a specter the inmates called simply "Nurse." Going to visit Nurse was a dreaded thing. Not only did Nurse dose you with patent medicines that were designed to strip the insides from you along with any ill-fated virus that was unfortunate to be harbored there; but she dosed you fast and hard, with jerky movements that made you wonder whether she was planning to cure you or to slap you silly with a swat to the side of your head. Or at least that was the story the inmates told. They all avoided the infirmary as though it were haunted.

Haunted or not, that day the infirmary was my best hope. I bolted through the door and skidded to a stop, my breath coming fast and raspy. There, seated at the desk hunched over a stack of paper, sat the specter herself.

"Are you sick?" Nurse said. It didn't sound so much like a question as a challenge to someone who had stepped across the border into a forbidden world. I shut the door behind me and cowered against the wall beside it. I shook my head. Her eyes assessed me, deep brown eyes, set into a stark skull of a face. They were dark, those eyes were, and they seemed to swallow up all light, even the tiny glint that most people have to their pupils. I looked deep into them, and found no welcome at all in their depths. Just as I expected to be ousted back into the hallway, Nurse instead returned her attention to the papers on her desk. I waited. She continued writing as though I weren't even there. I wondered if she was waiting for me to say something, do something. I really had nothing to say. I wasn't sick. I didn't belong there. But I couldn't very well leave. So I simply stayed, simply stood beside the door waiting. For what, I had no idea.

I scanned the infirmary. A glass-front cabinet stood in the corner, filled with vials and bottles. An examining table stood next to it. A sink. A table. Two iron beds with a small table between them over in the corner. At the desk and chair, sat Nurse, her pointed shoulders still hunched over her papers. Those shoulders seemed to shake a bit, and her hand was unsteady on her pen. I craned my neck around to see if the rest of her shook as well. That's when I saw it, my salvation. In a shaft of sunlight streaming through the window, a dust bunny lay at Nurse's feet, beside one of the legs of the desk.

"Do you have a broom?" I asked. When in doubt, I figured it was always safest to go with the things I knew. Perhaps if could prove that I knew how to work, she would let me stay. "A wee broom," I said, "or a bit of a cloth?" That did the trick. She looked up.

"Are you sick?" she asked. It truly seemed like a question this time.

"I'm not, thank God," I said. "If you have a broom, I could clean this floor for you, maybe knock down a few of those cobwebs." I gestured at the dust bunny and at a soot-covered web that darkened a corner of room.

"You live here?" Nurse replied.

"I do," I said. "For now."

"You're one of the inmates?" she said

"I am," I replied.

"And you're not sick," she said.

"Not sick," I said, "no, thank God."

"You do know that this is the infirmary?" she said. "A place for sick people?"

"I do," I said. I desperately wanted to change the subject, but I thought it best not to point out for a second time the dirt I was seeing in her infirmary. A brass badge pinned over her nearly nonexistent left breast bore the cryptic inscription "Lavender, M.D., R.N."

"What does 'Lavender, M.D., R.N. mean?" I asked. I knew lavender was a wild flower, but what that might be doing on a badge I had no idea.

"I'm not a doctor," she said, "if that's what you mean." She sounded a bit defensive. She pulled her glasses from her face, leaving them to dangle from the chain around her neck. Then suddenly she stood and walked swiftly to the closet. Her long striped dress and white apron hung on her shoulders as though they were a coat hanger.

"I didn't mean anything, to be sure," I said. "I only wondered what your wee badge stood for."

"People look at it and accuse me of trying to pretend I'm a doctor," she said, digging a broom from the closet. She walked back to the desk and began to stab at the dust bunnies beneath it. The inmates had a rumor that Nurse was prone to fits. Watching her handle the broom gave me some idea how the rumor may have started.

"I could do that," I said. "I'm not doing anything else at the moment."

She handed over the broom with a jerk. I took it, fished out the offending dust bunny, then began work under the bed closest to me.

"I don't know how things get so dirty," Nurse said. I nodded.

I strained my ears listening for footsteps in the hall. I heard none. It might be safe to leave, but it might not. And as odd as Nurse was, she was better company than Annette and her crew.

"Why do people accuse you of trying to pretend you're a doctor?" I asked in an attempt to keep the conversation alive.

"M.D.," Nurse said. "Medical doctor. But in my case it stands for Melody Day, my name. Melody Day Lavender. Have you ever heard anything so ludicrous in your entire life? I can't imagine what my parents were thinking."

"No saint's name," I said.

"Hmmph," she said, "as if that were the half of it."

"What about R.N.?" I asked, hoping it wasn't as touchy a subject as M.D. had been.

"Registered nurse," she said.

"Nurse means 'sister,' does it not?" I said.

"You're from England?" she said.

"Ireland," I answered.

"Then 'nurse' means 'sister,' yes," she answered. "Though I'm not a nun."

"How did you become a sister then?" I asked.

"A nurse," she said. "I studied, worked. Hard." She had dug a rag from the broom closet, and was running it over the windowsill. Her shoulders seemed to have dropped an inch or two, and unless I was mistaken, her jerkiness was less, too. "Bellevue Hospital in Philadelphia," she said. "R.N. means secondary school, then three long years of training at a hospital, then registration with the state board. If you want to earn the title "nurse" the right way, that is. Hardest thing I've ever done, bar none. But worth it."

"Is it book learning?" I asked. "Or work with your hands?"

"Both," she said. "Here." She set the rag down on the desk and walked to a bookcase and selected one of the larger tomes. It was a big, two-handed book with a blue binding.

"*Anatomy and Physiology for Nurses*," she said. She retrieved her dangling spectacles and put them on. I propped the broom against the bed, and went over to the desk. She flipped to the Table of Contents. "See, every part of the body is in here." She handed me the book. I gathered it into my arms, and looked down the list, tried to make sense of the words. Most were long. I squinted some at them. Certainly not what the sisters had in mind when they taught me my alphabet.

"I can't say I can read much of it," I said.

"Do you need glasses?" Nurse commented with a wry smile. She chuckled at her own joke, then took her spectacles from her nose and slipped them onto my face. "Here. Try mine." She chuckled again.

The rumors were true. She was an odd one. One minute she was a high-strung dog guarding a bone. The next she was joking with me as though she didn't notice I was an inmate and considerably younger than her at that.

"I never wore spectacles myself," I said. "Thank you, though. 'Tis the words. That's all. I never was much for book work, never was able to make much sense of long words."

Nurse, however, wasn't ready to let go of the joke. She stood before me and adjusted the spectacles on my nose, hooking the temple pieces behind my ears. "There," she said. "Now don't they make you look intelligent?" She leaned back against the desk, surveying me, the book, the spectacles.

I nudged the nosepiece higher on my nose and smiled back at her politely. The lenses made her look a bit blurry, sitting maybe six or seven feet away, there on the on the edge of her desk. But then I looked down at the book, and if it were not such a cliché, I would say that the scales fell from my eyes. The long words that had always just been long, unidentifiable strings were now series of letters, crisp, clear letters. "Bones of the hand," I said aloud. That's what it said, as clear as could be. "Sternocleidomastoid." I couldn't pronounce it. I had no idea what it meant. But there it was, a series of letters, suddenly decipherable letters. "Structure of the eye," I read aloud. I took the glasses off, and the page became shapeless strings again. I put them on and everything jumped into focus. I took them off, put them on again, all the while staring at the contents of *Anatomy and Physiology for Nurses*.

"I think maybe I do need glasses," I said finally.

"Well now," Nurse said her eyebrows arched. "Put that down for just a moment and come here." She opened the door of a cabinet to reveal an eye chart. "Stand there by the bed," she said. "Cover your right eye." I covered my right and read the letters she put before me. I covered my left and again read the chart with no problems. But then Nurse held a small chart just eight inches or so off my nose, and that chart was another matter. I puzzled over each letter before announcing my verdict. Nurse handed me her glasses, and again positioned the small chart a bit off my nose. I put the glasses on, and the letters jumped into focus. I read them easily. I had never read a book or newspaper easily in my life, but I read that chart like I was born to it.

"You're farsighted," Nurse said by way of diagnosis. "We'll have to get an optician—that's an eye doctor—in here if we're going to fix the problem. But you are definitely far sighted."

"Blessed Bride," I said in astonishment.

"Your teachers in Ireland never noticed?" she asked.

"I wasn't in school for more than three years," I said. "And before that, they only said I wasn't all that suited to book work."

"You might be surprised once you're fitted with glasses," she said.

"And me already so surprised I could drop my teeth," I remarked.

So there we sat, Nurse and I, looking at each other. Her shoulders were down where normal people keep theirs. And she was smiling. She looked nearly normal. I must have smiled back.

"I can get an optician in here probably by the end of the week," she said. This time next week you could be reading like a professor.

The end of the week. I fairly hummed with the anticipation of it. Perhaps it was that very anticipation that was the warning sign for me. I took a deep breath.

"And just how much would a pair of spectacles cost, um, roughly? I tried to make it sound casual, but I knew that if the price was too high, I might never be in a position to see just what difference glasses would make in my life.

"A dollar," she said. "Maybe two. But the protectory can probably fit you with a pair. You won't have to pay."

"And they can do that before the end of the week?"

"Probably," she said. "It makes me glad you stumbled in her today. Just what was it you wanted anyway?"

"Maybe I only took the wrong turn," I said.

"Or the right one," she replied.

Thirty-Four

As unlikely as it seemed, there she stood—Annette, her arms in soapy water to the elbows. She stood at the sinks, under the boiler, in the hottest, muggiest, nastiest part of the kitchen. She stood alone, surrounded by great mounds of dirty dishes from dinner, plates and bowls, spoons and pots. All of them grubby. Her dress was wilted. So were her pigtails. Had she been anyone other than Annette, I would have felt sorry for her. I unloaded my armful of serving bowls onto the rail by the sink.

"You couldn't hire yourself someone to do that for you?" I commented. Annette's pack was no longer with her, and she was on Mrs. Riezler's territory. I felt a sudden surge of boldness run through my bones. Annette looked up. Her face was flushed and sweaty. My comment did little for her expression, which was none too sweet to begin with.

"I'll feed you those words," she said simply.

"And your hands will be nice and clean when you do," I said. Annette spun to face me, her hands wadded into fists and dripping into puddles on the floor. I followed her gaze. It went first to my hands, then to my face, then back over my shoulder. I glanced in the direction she was looking. Mrs. Riezler had her eyes on us. Annette turned back to the dishes. I smiled a bit to myself and returned to the kitchen area.

"Don't rile her," Kristie said as I reached the stove, looking for more dirty dishes to bring to the back. Kristie was making pudding in a huge pot on the stove, stirring it with a wooden spoon as long as her forearm. "Annette's a miserable sort," she said, "and she has no qualms about taking that misery out on whoever gets in her way."

"And don't I know it already?" I said. "We met."

"A memorable meeting?" Kristie asked, her right eyebrow disappearing up under the bangs of her hair.

"Not as memorable as it could be, I'm sure," I said. "But enough to leave a sour taste in my mouth nonetheless."

"Then you know what I'm saying," Kristie said. I nodded. "She's been there for six months," she said.

"In the kitchen?" I asked.

"Hands in the sink the whole time," Kristie said. "She's just worked her way up from breakfast duty, scrubbing breakfast pots and pans at five in the morning. Lots of grease and stuck-on porridge. Miserable work. Mrs. Riezler likes to start the experienced girls at the breakfast sink. She says it builds humility."

"But she didn't start me at the sink," I said. "You asked if I had experience, and when I said yes, she put me here."

"Ah, well, now that's not exactly the kind of experience I was talking about," Kristie said, winking. "I'm talking about experience on the streets, a woman's experience. Do you know what I'm talking about?"

"Annette was a woman of the unfortunate class?" I said.

"Unfortunate class," Kristie said. "I don't think I've ever heard it put quite like that before. But if you mean she was a hooker, yes, that's the rumor. I talked to a girl who said she knew Annette back when she was selling herself to men on the Bowery."

I wasn't really sure what to say to that. My mind, however, wasted no time in its speculation, sending image after image across my imagination.

"Why do you suppose a girl would do that?" I said finally. "Why would she sell herself like that?"

"It's better than starving, I suppose," Kristie replied. It was pretty clear the question hadn't crossed her mind.

"I don't think I could," I said.

"Of course you couldn't," Kristie replied. "I think you have to have a sinful streak like Annette does before you'd ever consider doing such a thing."

"Or doing such a thing sets the streak into you," I said.

Kristie shrugged. "I wouldn't know," she said. "What I do know is that unless you have a liking for misery, you'll stay away from her." She pulled the spoon from the pot, and set it aside on the table. "Would you hold that bowl?" She tossed me a towel and nodded at a large metal bowl sitting empty on the counter. I covered my hands with the towel and grasped the sides of the bowl. Kristie muscled the pot off the stove and tipped the contents into the bowl to cool.

"Everyone with any sense walks the other way when she comes near," she said. "I do. I try not to get within twenty feet of her if I don't have to." As the pot emptied, I reached for the spoon and scraped the last bits off the sides.

"I suppose then it will be myself who carries that pot to the sink," I said.

"If you would so kind," she replied with a small curtsey and a big grin. "But take my advice and don't rile her. I'd hate to see blood on Mrs. Riezler's clean floors."

* * *

I really didn't mean to stare, but I suppose I did. When I think of that day, I do have a very clear picture of Annette, back to the room, working through the dirty pots one by one. I guess what I was wondering was whether it was possible to tell if a woman had been with a man just by looking at her. Mrs. Keane had seen Colum on me, and I had done no more than kiss him. I scanned Annette up and down, her hips, her legs. I wondered if she had ever had a child, if a pregnancy was how she had ended up on the streets, ended up as a fallen woman like the unfortunates at Becky Butler's.

"I know you're back there, County Cork," Annette said quietly.

"I'm only bringing this," I said, setting the pot on the rack. I must have done so too quickly for as I withdrew my hand, the pile of pots and plates that balanced there began to shift precariously. I reached out to steady it. I was frozen there for a moment, a pot under one hand and a pile of serving spoons under the other, looking to Annette to help me get things under control. I suppose that's why I didn't see the knife sooner.

It was a small paring knife, no more. Annette drew it from the soapy water. Before I could retreat, she grasped my apron tie at the waist, slipped the knife inside, and cut it cleanly. I jumped back. The pots slid to the floor with a clatter. The spoons landed on top of them.

All these years later, I can't tell you how many times I've played that scene over and over in my mind. Annette with the paring knife. Me pumping the shock through my body. The pile of dirty pots on the floor between us. I remember seeing a chefs knife on one of the tables, not too far away. I could have picked it up and faced her down. Or I could have called for Kristie and some of the other girls to help me. Or I could have walked away, shown Mrs. Riezler the cut string of my apron and had Annette ejected. Or I could have just screamed blue murder to see where that would take me.

What I did was turn and bolt. I went to Mrs. Riezler, hand discretely holding my apron together, told her in three or four broken German words that the flour in the kitchen bin was running a little low, and asked her for permission to go to the pantry to fetch more. Then without waiting for a reply, I dashed through the pantry door and closed it behind me.

Seated atop a pile of flour sacks, I tried to swallow my breath enough to get it to do me some good again. But for a good long while, as I tried to tie together the strings at my waist with shaking hands, I gulped air more than breathed it. I finally got the strings tied together, finally got myself to the place where I was reasonably sure I wouldn't burst into tears or pass out in front of everyone. I still had no idea how I was going to handle Annette, but I knew I couldn't hide in the pantry forever. I opened the door and ventured out.

The pots by the sink were again on the drip board. Annette was scrubbing one of them vigorously. Perhaps a shade too vigorously. The kitchen had settled back to its usual rhythms. I returned to the tables and tried to remember what I had been doing before the whole incident occurred.

Mrs. Riezler herself was the one to remind me. She had been standing near the flour bin, waiting for me to arrive with the sack. As I approached, I could see that the bin was indeed low. A lucky guess on my part.

"*Das Mehl?*" Mrs. Riezler said with considerable annoyance. "*Wo ist das Mehl?*"

"Sorry," I said. "*Das Mehl.* The flour. Sorry. I forgot." How did one say "I forgot" in German? I didn't know. I shrugged. "*Das Mehl.* In the pantry. *Vorratskammer.*"

Mrs. Riezler rattled off a fast bit of German. I didn't understand a bit of it, but reading the one hand drumming on the top of the flour bin and her other hand motioning me toward the pantry, I took her meaning well enough.

"I'm sorry," I said. "I forgot."

I went back to the pantry and began sorting through the flour sacks to see if any were already opened. My hands were still shaking, so much so that I could barely sort my way through the sacks. In frustration, I wadded up a fist, and punched it into one of the sacks. The sack puffed white. The feeling was so satisfying that I punched again, then again with the other hand. Over and over again I punched. The flour was a cloud around me settling on my arms and in my hair. I punched myself tired, and when I stopped and sat heavily atop a sack, I noticed something. My hands no longer shook. My gut was no longer knotted.

That's when the words began running through my head. "A good run is better than a bad stand. A good run is better than a bad stand."

"I wish you would stop repeating it like it were some nugget of golden wisdom." That's what Mick had said. Until that moment in the pantry, I had always believed that it was golden wisdom. But sitting there, my fists still stinging from the sack, I realized that while I was hiding in the pantry, punching sacks of flour, I could have been back in the kitchen punching Annette. That's why my hands had been shaking in the first place. They had really wanted to punch someone. They had really wanted to defend me. And here I had bled all that energy off doing violence to an innocent bag of grain.

A good run might be better than a bad stand. But a good stand was better than both of them put together. For the first time in my life I had a glimmer of understanding concerning Mick and his fists.

That evening, I snuck the apron out of the kitchen. While everyone else was at supper I slipped into the sewing room, found some white thread, brought it back to the dormitory, and mended the apron string. I stuck the needle into the collar of my old shirtwaist, thinking I'd return it in the morning. I then hid the mended apron under my pillow. Nobody was the wiser, or so I thought.

*** *** ***

Since that day, I have told a handful of people about my encounter with Annette and the paring knife. When I have, they all have invariably asked the same question, "why did you keep what she did a secret? Why didn't you just tell Mrs. Riezler or the sisters?" I have thought about that question for more than fifty years now, and I'm still not sure I have a good answer to it.

Part of the answer was that I knew what the sisters could and couldn't do. They were already doing what they could to keep me safe. They kept a close watch over all of us, stopped the fights they saw, punished bullies, bucked up victims. But it wasn't the attacks they saw that worried me. Annette had a rare gift for timing her attacks to be admired by her pack while slipping in beneath the notice of adults. The amount of damage she could do while the sisters' backs were turned was prodigious. The damage she was likely to do to me if I turned her in was equally so.

My reasons for not turning Annette in were not, however, merely motivated by self-preservation. I believe now that my reasons were born of something much deeper, much more primal. I knew instinctively that dealing with Annette was not a matter of crime and punishment. It was a matter of fight or flight. I could no more turn Annette in than the mouse could have the hawk arrested. I needed to find a way to survive for myself. And I needed to find it within myself.

*** *** ***

They were used glasses, that much was sure. The eye doctor, a grey man in an equally grey suit, drew a pair from his case. Holding them up to the light, he examined the scratches on the lenses.

"You need them to see close, you say." He picked at one of the scratches with a fingernail and, finding the flaw to be permanent, drew a handkerchief from his breast pocket and gave the lenses a quick going over.

"I do," I said. "I need them mostly to read and do close work." I was restless, eager. I forced my hands into my lap, where they refused to stop fidgeting.

A few minutes before, I had been called away from the kitchen and preparation for supper. When Sister Xavier tapped me on the shoulder and said I was wanted in the infirmary, my mind immediately flashed to the glasses. I was out of my apron and into the hall so fast that Sister Xavier herself had to work to keep up with me. Nurse and the eye doctor were waiting for me, Nurse with her shoulders flying at half-mast, the doctor fiddling with his case in the thick silence that filled the infirmary. He sat me down, and we got to business immediately.

"Not being able to see near is better than not being able to see far," the eye doctor said. I didn't see the distinction myself. Near, far, both meant you were missing part of the world. "If a girl can't see far," the doctor explained, "she needs to wear her glasses out on the street. I do hate to see that happen. You, at least, can limit your wearing to close work, things you'll do at home."

"I understand," I said, though I must admit I was anxious to wear my glasses as much as possible to see what I had been missing all these years.

The doctor held the glasses up again, then grasping them by the bridge of the nose, held them out for me. I took them gingerly by the temples and hooked them around my ears. I looked up. The world had gone blurry. I immediately felt the strain in my eyes. Wasting no time, I unhooked them.

"Not right?" the doctor said.

"They aren't," I replied.

"Too strong?" the doctor asked.

"Too blurry," I said.

"That doesn't tell me much," the doctor replied. He placed the glasses back in the case, and drew out another pair. They were two long ovals in wire frames. The frames along the temples had been etched to give a tortoise shell look. They were a fine pair of glasses, and I said so.

"For a man perhaps," the doctor said. "Glasses make a man look intelligent." He pressed his own higher on his nose and peered at me through them, as though to illustrate his point. "It's a shame, though, when girls as young as yourself need them. Spectacles are so disfiguring to women and girls. If it weren't for the serious eye trouble they prevent, I wouldn't even give them to girls. Granted, with a girl like you, the disfigurement is less an issue. But it pains me to place a pair on the nose of a beautiful young girl. It feels like spitting into a sunset."

"Is that so?" I said, not really sure how to reply.

"For you, though, they may actually break that long line you have down the center of your face." He gestured at my nose and handed me the glasses. "Couldn't do that much harm, I suppose. Still, if I were you, I would only wear them when I had to."

I set the nosepiece on my "long, center line," and hooked the temple pieces around my ears. They were better than the first pair. I looked over to Nurse Lavender, and she handed me a book from her shelf.

"*Notes on Nursing*" I read from the spine. I nudged the glasses further down on my nose and looked over them. The words blurred. I pushed them up and the words jumped back into focus. I looked up at Nurse. She smiled back at me.

"I know the feeling," she said, lightly patting the glasses that hung from her neck on a chain. "I take it those will suit you."

"They will," I said. I opened the book at random and looked back down at the page: "Shall we begin by taking it is a general principle that all disease, at some period or another of its course is more or less a reparative process," it said. I had no idea what it meant, or even if I pronounced some of the words correctly. But I would learn. Now that I could see the words, I would learn not only to read them, but to understand them. That much I resolved.

The doctor packed up his case. Nurse handed him a form, and he made a few notes. I put down the book reluctantly, just long enough to thank the doctor as he left.

"Do you want to see what they look like?" Nurse said, fishing into a drawer and drawing out a hand mirror. She passed it across the desk to me.

The glasses did change the look of my face; the doctor was right about that. I gave the bridge a bit of a push with my index finger. My nose did look a bit shorter perhaps. The glasses sat just above the hook, almost as though giving the hook a purpose, a reason for being there. I considered the possibility that maybe my nose had been made with a bit of a shelf purposely to rest glasses on. I held the mirror out at arms length and peered into it to assess the overall effect.

"Do you think they make me look wealthier?" I said.

"Wealthier?" Nurse replied, propping herself against the table and looking at me. "What do you mean?"

"I'm not sure," I said. "Maybe it's just that not too many people in the lanes could afford spectacles. Only those whose eyes were so bad they couldn't see to work. They were the only ones willing to part with the money it would take to buy spectacles. And then they wouldn't buy a fine pair like these."

"Ah, well, maybe they do make you look a little wealthier, then."

"And the doctor's right. They do break up my long center line," I said, my eyes returning to my nose, something they usually did on those rare accessions when I had the chance to look, really look, into a mirror. "A small blessing, I suppose."

"Clare," Nurse said. She reached out her hand for the mirror. I handed it to her. "There is something I've learned over the years," she said, laying the mirror face down on the table, "something I wish I'd known when I was your age." She looked dreadfully serious, as though she were about to deliver bad news. I turned to face her, to give her my full attention.

"Clare," she said, "you would find it out eventually on your own, but I think it's something you need to know now." She paused, her arms crossed across her nearly nonexistent chest. She stared out the window as though searching among the leaves of the tree outside for words. "All right," she said finally, "doctors go to medical school for at least three years, then do pupilships and other training. Because of all that education, they know a great deal about one particular subject. That is, without a doubt, a great blessing. What is not a blessing is the leap that most of them make from knowing a great deal about something to knowing something about everything, or in the case of surgeons, everything about everything. Doctors are not gods, Clare. Even though some of them would like to think so. They aren't gods. None of the men you'll meet in your life—no matter how wealthy or well educated—none of them are gods."

"I don't think I ever believed they were," I said, but then as I thought about it, I wasn't sure that statement was exactly true.

"That's good," she said. "That's good. That means you're doing better than half the nurses I started school with." She picked up the mirror again, and looking briefly into herself, carried it back to the drawer she'd taken from. She walked stiffly, and her shoulders, those telltale shoulders, were on the climb again. I knew she had more she wanted to say, so I waited.

"He was wrong about your nose, you know," she said quietly. I barely heard her, as she was still looking down into the mirror, which was now lying in the drawer. She turned and said it a bit more loudly. "He was wrong to say the glasses had nothing to mar."

"It's no great matter," I said. "What I mean is that his words were no great matter. Not my nose. My nose is a great matter indeed." I grinned at her. She gazed at me seriously, and I felt the grin evaporate from my face.

"It's so easy for men to pronounce some women beautiful and other women homely," she said. "It's easy for them to say she's too fat. She has a big nose. She looks like a scarecrow in nurses' garb." Her voice quivered slightly and her shoulders crept even higher. She crossed her arms across her chest again. "We make it easy for them to say such things when we simply believe them without questioning their words. Question them, Clare. Even if they are the great and powerful Doctor So-and-So, question them when they tell you something is wrong with the way you look."

"I don't think that eye doctor would be the only one to say it," I replied quietly.

"You are not homely, Clare Keane," Nurse said, her eyes locked on mine.

"'Tis nice of you to say so," I replied. I couldn't hold her gaze. I looked down at the book on the table, ran my finger along the edge of the cover. "Very kind indeed. But I looked in a good many mirrors in my life. I know about my nose, my strong-willed hair, my teeth. It doesn't bother me when people say I'm homely."

"Then you're the only women I've met who isn't bothered," she said. She lowered herself into the desk chair and leaned across the desk toward me. "Don't believe him, Clare. Don't believe any of them. Promise me."

"I won't believe them," I said.

"Do you promise?"

I wasn't sure how not to believe something that appeared obviously to be true. But it seemed so important to Nurse. She reached out and took my hand in hers. So I decided to try, to try not to believe either "the men" she spoke of, or my own eyes. "I promise," I said.

"Good," she said. "Good. Now what do you want to read first? Those glasses look good on you, by the way."

* * *

I was supposed to be in the kitchen working on supper. But Nurse said I needed to try out the new glasses, and that set me to dipping into Nurse's bookshelf. The reading was slow, and when I asked a question about something in one of journals, that got us talking first about her training and then about the miserable six months she spent in a Settlement house on the Lower East side. About the time I started looking for ways to excuse myself and get back to work, the conversation went from there to me, my past and my future. I found myself telling her about the time Mrs. Sullivan stitched Mick and my dreams of being able to do the same for people.

Nurse looked me in the eye. "Is that what you really want?" she asked. "Do you really want to be a nurse?"

There was that question again. What was it that I really wanted from my life?

Perhaps it was all the practice runs I'd had up to that point. Perhaps it was the new world of print that the glasses had just then opened to me. Whatever the reason, that day, when Nurse asked the question, for the first time in my life, I had an answer all wrapped up and ready to deliver.

"I want to be a nurse," I said, clearly, unequivocally. "I want to be a nurse, to deliver babies, to take care of people who are ill. 'Tis what I want more than anything."

Perhaps that's all that the world had been waiting for. It had been waiting for me simply to say it, to speak out into the air my dreams for myself. I had no more than closed my mouth again when Nurse grasped me by the wrist and hauled me to the main office. A couple of quick conversations, a bit of paperwork, and I was reassigned to the infirmary. It was as simple as that. That morning I was a cook's assistant. By late afternoon, I had begun my nurse's training.

The training wasn't official, of course. I hadn't finished primary school let alone graduated from high school. No "reputable" nursing school in the country would take me until I did. But Nurse had thought of that, too. She hauled me from the main office to the principal's office, and enrolled me in the protectory's school. I would study there every morning surrounded by girls a head shorter than me. Then every afternoon, I would go to the infirmary to work, read, and learn. I was on my way to becoming a nurse.

That was, of course, providing that the protectory didn't turn around and send me west the very next day.

* * *

"Where are you supposed to be?" Nurse said, looking up from a couple of pairs of scissors and a handful of probes she was sterilizing in alcohol at the far table. It was midmorning, and I was reading one of her older editions of the *American Journal of Nursing*, an article called "Obstetrical Emergencies." A lot of the words were foreign, but with the new glasses, they were at least shaped like words, not like long bumpy sausages. Despite the slow pace at which I slogged through the article, I was actually understanding bits and pieces of it, and that simple fact made me want to never put the journal down.

"The sisters think I'm out 'getting a bit of air' for morning recess," I said. "But all that the girls in my class are interested in is skipping rope and playing house. I remembered how you said that a sick room should have the same free, pure air that's available outside. So I figured I could get a bit of air in here with you just as well as I could out in the dust of the playground."

"And the playgrounds don't have medical journals," Nurse noted.

"They don't at that," I said with a smile.

Just then the door to the infirmary opened. In came one of the sisters, a highly generic-looking sister with a small boy limping along beside her, tucked protectively under one of her jet-black arms. The boy's face was tear-streaked and blotchy. He looked to be maybe five years old, but with the poor nutrition some of the orphans had before they came to the protectory, size and vigor was no reliable measure of age. One look at his knee left no doubt as to why he was limping. The scrape covering the knee and part of the shin oozed and dripped.

The sister shot a suspicious glance at me, then addressed Nurse in the corner. "Do you have a moment, Miss Lavender?" she said. Nurse's shoulders bristled and rode up along her neck.

"I will as soon as I finish with these instruments," she said. I noticed she hadn't addressed the sister as "Sister." Everyone addressed the sisters as "Sister." I glanced briefly at the face tucked back into the habit. She had noticed too. Nurse used a shiny pair of tongs to pull the probes one by one from the jar, laying them on a cloth-lined tray. I sat at the desk and watched the choppiness of each movement, willing her not to knock something over, willing her shoulders to settle just a bit.

"I could leave the boy with you if you'd like, Nurse," the sister said.

"That's all right, *Sister*," Nurse said, I'm done here. She dropped the lid onto the jar, leaving the remaining scissors still inside. "If you'd be so kind as to lift him up here." Nurse gestured at the examining table as she went to wash her hands. The boy sat atop the table, looked at Nurse, looked at the sister, looked at me, then popped his thumb into his mouth and began sucking furiously. The sister casually reached out and popped the thumb free, laying it gently but firmly in his lap.

"Let's see what we have here." Nurse kicked a rolling chair over to the examining table, sat, put on her glasses, and bent over the knee. Her brow furrowed. Opening the drawer beside the table, she drew out a magnifying glass and again bent over the knee. The glass shook slightly in her hand. Nurse must have noticed the shaking, for drew her elbow tightly against her side, and hunched her shoulders a bit more. That just made the shaking worse.

"He has some tiny bits of stone in there," she said. "They'll have to come out." She drew a bit of gauze out of a glass canister, and opening a big bottle of alcohol, soaked the gauze. The little boy eyed her suspiciously, then rolled over onto his hip to clutch at the sister. The sister gave him a brief hug and settled his bottom firmly onto the examining table again. If Nurse noticed any of this in her preparations, she made no sign. She simply pushed her chair back to the knee, pinned the boy's thigh tightly to the table with one hand, and with the other plopped the bit of gauze atop the wound. The boy let out a shriek that echoed off the high ceiling, off the bare walls, and up and down the institutional corridors. Anyone listening could easily come to the conclusion that the poor lad had been attacked in a particularly merciless fashion.

I rose from my seat, flipping the journal pages-down onto the desk.

"Shh, shh, shh," I said, taking to opposite side of the table from the sister, who stood ramrod straight, her hands gripping the boy by the shoulders, a look of grim resolve on her face. The boy struggled. But with the three-point grip he was in, he wasn't going anywhere.

"Shh," I said. He looked at me briefly, then at Nurse, the sister, me, his eyes imploring. Finding no one to remedy his situation, he took a deep quavering breath and wailed again. I took his hand. "Can you count?" I asked. The boy didn't register what I said immediately. His eyes were on Nurse's hand, which was dabbing bits of dirt from the edges of the wound. He gulped another lungful of air, then let out another wail.

"Look at me, laddie," I said, cupping his chin in my hand. "Look at me. Can you count?" He nodded slightly, his face still contorted with the pain. I took a deep, exaggerated breath and let it out. "How many breaths was that?" I asked. He looked at me as though it was the most ridiculous question he had ever heard, as though he had much more important things to occupy his mind, which I suppose he had. I took another deep breath and let it out noisily. "How many breaths?" I said.

"One," he answered, his voice quivering. He lifted a single finger. "Then another one."

"Good," I said. "Now your turn." I took a deep, slow breath, and motioned for him to do the same. He took a deep, ragged breath, and we both let it out together. "One," I said.

"One," he repeated.

"Now two," I said, and inhaled deeply. He followed my lead, and we let it out slowly. How many?" I said.

"Two," he said.

"Good," I replied, shooting a quick glance at Nurse. She was teasing a bit of stone loose with a tweezers. "And . . . " I took another deep breath, drawing it more slowly this time. The boy followed, then exhaled, then said "three."

"Very good," I said. "How old did you say you were?" I asked. He raised five fingers. "How many is that?" I asked.

"Five," he replied.

"Five," I said. "I think we should do at least five breaths then, don't you?" He nodded. "We're on four," I said. The boy drew a deep slow breath. I nodded and did the same. We exhaled.

"Four," he said, his voice a little steadier. I looked up, the sister was watching me, a faint smile on her face. Nurse shifted a bit in her seat angling her magnifying glass for a better look. She teased back a bit of loose skin and pinched a tiny stone in the tweezers. The boy winced a bit but didn't make a noise. Nurse's hand looked steadier to me.

"What's next," I said.

"Five," the boy replied, watching me for his cue. I inhaled, and he did too. I smiled and nodded. I thought I saw the faintest glimmer of a smile flit across his face.

"One more," Nurse said, looking up as we exhaled. "Just one more stone."

"Six?" I said to the boy. He nodded. We took our breath, and Nurse popped loose the stone, and dabbing at the wound, proclaimed it clean. She wheeled to the cabinet and drew out a bottle of iodine. I looked at it. The boy did too.

"Can you count to seven?" I asked.

* * *

"You were good with him," Nurse commented that afternoon. She was seated at the desk writing something in her log when I came for my afternoon shift. I nodded an acknowledgment and went to the closet in the corner, and pulled out my apron. It was a long apron, so long that it extended far past the hem of my knee-length dress. The bodice buttoned at the shoulders and on the sides. It was a nurse's apron, one of Nurse's old ones. She made me wear it saying that a nurse should never dress for the street while in the infirmary, and she should never dress for the hospital while on the street. She said that when I began nursing school in earnest, I would need to purchase at least two light-colored gingham dresses that I would wear only in the hospital. But for now, she said, the apron would suffice. I buttoned the sides of it, then reached onto the shelf bearing my name, and pulled down a metal chain.

The chain, like the apron, had been Nurse's. It was a grayish gunmetal copy of the one she wore around her neck to hold her glasses while she wasn't using them. Nurse said it was especially important for a nurse to have her glasses handy. If a patient came in with something that needed close attention, it wouldn't do for the nurse on duty to be hunting around for her glasses while the patient suffered. I pulled my glasses case from my skirt pocket, removed the glasses, and threaded the bows into onto the chain.

It had become our rhythm each afternoon. First I put on the apron and the glasses chain. Then I read for a half hour to an hour. Then Nurse showed me a procedure or two. I learned how to make a bed, how to bathe a patient, how to sterilize instruments, how to prepare a tray of instruments for a doctor. I even learned how to hand instruments to a doctor doing surgery, though I doubted our little infirmary had ever seen a surgery. That day I then put the glasses on, pulled one of Nurse's medical journals from the shelf and sat down to finish the article I had begun that morning.

"You were good with him," Nurse said again. It seemed as though she wanted to talk, so I closed the journal, a finger in the obstetrics article I was slogging through.

"Where did you learn that?" she asked. "The counting, I mean. Where did you learn that?"

"On the boat over from Ireland," I replied. "From a woman in the third class who was bringing a baby. She said she counted during hard times because it made her realize she was still alive, still drawing the breaths God gave her. I don't know what made me think of it just then."

"It was a good thought," Nurse said. "Not everyone would have had such a thought."

"'Twas nothing," I said. "Only a bit of comfort, that's all."

"'A bit of comfort' is something many nurses never learn to give," Nurse said, closing her logbook. "For me it was the hardest part of becoming a nurse. I could learn the bookwork with no problems. I could do the procedures. But something about me makes people tense, and that makes me tense, and that makes them tense." She sighed. "A bit of comfort is no small thing," she said. "Nowhere in the world is a bit of comfort a small thing."

I wasn't sure what to say. Apparently Nurse wasn't either. She wiped her pen, capped her inkbottle, all the time with her shoulders creeping up, and her face quivering slightly. She was right. Something about her was making me a bit uneasy.

I glanced down at the journal. "What's 'intrauterine'?" I said. It was the first big word my eyes rested on. I was hoping to learn some of those big words, and had been looking for the right time to ask Nurse. This seemed as good a time as any.

"Intrauterine?" she said.

I nodded and pointed at the word in the journal. "Intrauterine," I said, repronouncing the word with her pronunciation.

"It means inside the uterus, inside the womb," she replied. "Why?"

"I only thought it would be easier to read these articles if I knew more of the words," I said.

"I suppose it would," Nurse replied. "Give me another one."

"hi-po-deer-mick," I said. "H-Y-P-O-D-E-R-M-I-C."

"Hypodermic," Nurse said.

"Hypodermic," I repeated, staring at the word and trying to make the association between the letters and the sound.

"That's the needle you use to give shots," she said.

"They couldn't just call it a needle?" I said.

"I suppose they could," Nurse replied, "but then how would you tell the difference between a sewing needle and a hypodermic needle?"

I nodded in concession.

"Most medical words are Greek or Latin," Nurse said. "Even if there's a perfectly good English word that would do, medical people don't seem to want to use it. Still, once you learn a bit of Greek and Latin, the terms aren't that foreign at all."

"I learned a bit of Irish in school," I said, "enough to say a couple of prayers and to ask to use the privy. But no Latin or Greek."

"No matter," nurse said. She undid the top of the ink bottle again, drew a piece of paper from the drawer and picked up her pen. "Come here," she said. I kicked my wheeled chair over to the desk and bent over the paper.

"So now, this is 'hypodermic,' right?" She drew the word on the page in pointy cursive letters. Even her handwriting was angular, or so it seemed. She drew a line splitting the word into two: "hypo" and "dermic."

"These are the two parts," she said. "'Hypo-' means 'under.' 'Dermic' or 'dermis' means 'skin.' I nodded. She dipped the pen again and wrote "epidermis" on the next line. "What do you see?" she asked.

"There's 'dermis'," I said.

"Do you know what the word means?" she asked.

"Something to do with skin," I said.

"Have you ever heard the word *epidermis* before," she asked.

"I didn't," I answered, beginning to rethink my opinion about its meaning.

"But you know it has something to do with skin," she said.

"I'm not sure," I said.

"Ah, now, don't back down," Nurse replied. "You were right. It does have something to do with skin. 'Dermis' is skin. 'Epi' is 'upon' or 'on top of.' So 'epidermis' is the layer of skin that lies on the very top," she said, striking the skin of her hand with her index finger by way of illustration.

She dipped her pen again and wrote "epiglottis." "Any notion?" she said.

"It's on top of the glottis," I said.

"The glottis is down here,' she said, stroking her throat. "The epiglottis is a small cover that fits over the windpipe when you swallow."

We did "epi-" words, and "intra-" words, and "hypo-" words, and—I have to say it—I fell in love with the tidiness of medical language. It was a little like a well-ordered kitchen, where everything was in its place. You could find the skillet hanging from the hook, the spoon in the drawer, the eggs and butter in the pantry, and when you put them all together on the stove you got fried eggs. The words I was learning were satisfying that way.

"How about this one," she said, "since you seem so interested in the subject. "Obstetrics." She wrote it on the paper.

"It means catching babies, does it not?" I said.

"I wouldn't put it quite so crudely, but yes, that's what it means," she answered. "It has two parts, too." She drew a line between *ob-* and *stetrics*.

She looked at me. I shook my head.

"*Ob-* means in front of or against. So if you were to stand there on the other side of the desk facing me, we'd be "ob." And *stetrics* comes from the Latin word to stand. So an obstetrician is the man who stands opposite a woman while she gives birth.

"Man or woman," I said.

"Well, in this case it's man because an obstetrician is a doctor," Nurse said finally.

"Are there any women doctors?" I asked

"Medical doctors?"

"Well, yes, I suppose," I said. "The kind of doctors who deliver babies."

"There are a few," Nurse replied. "In fact, there's a college in Pennsylvania that trains only women to be doctors."

"They won't let men in at all?"

"Nope. Turnabout is fair play, I say."

"Men don't let women doctors into their colleges in America?" I asked.

"Not into their colleges, or their hospitals, or onto precious medical commissions. At least, they don't want to. If they do, it's because their hand is forced. Because the woman's daddy has money to give to the college. Something of that sort." Nurse replied.

"That wouldn't work for me," I said. "No daddy. No money."

"No matter," Nurse said, "A daddy and money can only take you so far anyway." She began doodling on the sheet of paper with my new words in it. Long fine loops, the kind teachers make students do when they're practicing their cursive. I watched her pen trace the continuous line, fighting to keep it rounded.

"I've met a few woman doctors," Nurse said. "One by the name of Sarah Baker—she's a pediatrician, a children's doctor, here in New York. She was an amazing woman. Fought her way into medical school, fought her way through medical school, became a respected doctor with a good practice. People all over the city knew what a good doctor she was. Eventually, the city of New York recognized her skills and made her Assistant Heath Commissioner for the city. After years of hard work she finally got the recognition she deserved. So do you know what her new city staff did?" I shook my head. "They resigned in protest. Every one of them. To a man. Said they wouldn't work for a woman."

I wasn't sure what to say, so I just sat there and let it sink in.

"Does that make you angry?" Nurse said.

"I'm not sure," I replied. "I don't know many men who would want to take orders from a woman. If a woman is a doctor, she's going to be giving orders, isn't she?"

"They all do seem to," Nurse replied. "Though they mostly order around the nursing staff, and they're all women."

"But if she had them on her staff, Sarah Baker would be giving orders to men, wouldn't she?"

"I suppose," Nurse replied.

That seemed to be the one sticking point. I had no doubt that women could do the job. The strong women I'd grown up around had shown me that women could do pretty much anything they put their mind to. But whether the men around them would accept that strength—that was another story. It would be hard for a woman to do a job if every man on her staff was of the conviction that he knew better than her about every decision she made. Every day she went in to work might mean a battle.

"Do you think you could do that? Give orders to men?" I asked.

"I think for me, trying would be more trouble than it's worth," Nurse said. "You have to pick your fights. Save your energy for the things that matter most to you. If you fight every battle that comes your way, you just end up tired, so tired you might not be able to do the things that really need to be done.

"But if nobody fights this battle—the battle for women to become doctors— all the women who would make good doctors will never have a chance," I said.

"True enough," Nurse said. Her pen ran out of ink, and rather than dip it again just to doodle, she wiped it and placed it in the drawer of her desk.

"So how do you know if the fight is worth it or not?"

"I may be the wrong person to ask about that," Nurse said. "I think some women are cut out to break the mold and do battle, while others are cut out to stay inside the mold and do the best job they can there. Me? I'm no hero. I know that about myself. A month or two into medical school, and they'd have to lock me up in the lunatic asylum. But I am a good nurse."

"Do you think I could be a doctor?" I asked. "Do you think I could fight those battles?"

"Is that what you want?" Nurse replied. "To become a doctor?"

"I don't know," I said.

"Then, no, you couldn't," Nurse said. "If a woman is going to start medical school, she needs to have the conviction that nothing else in this world will ever make her happy, that she has to become a doctor or die trying. If she doesn't have that conviction, she will never survive."

I sat silently, took in what she had said. Now that she had put the feeling into words, I could finally name the desire inside me. That's how I felt about nursing. I didn't think anything else in the world would make me so happy. No other future I could imagine felt quite so right. I was about to open my mouth and say so, when Nurse stood abruptly. She pulled a bottle of disinfectant from the cabinet by the door.

"You get the pan and the broom. I'll teach you how to sweep a hospital floor. Then while you're sweeping, I'll tell you about Elizabeth Blackwell," she said. I stood and fished the broom and pan from the closet. Nurse put a bit of disinfectant in the pan.

"Dip, then sweep, then dip, then sweep," Nurse said. "Work from one wall to the opposite wall, and don't step in the damp places until they dry. The disinfectant kills germs. If you have anyone contagious in the hospital, you have to sweep like this every day." I dipped the broom and began work at the wall on the other side of the beds.

"So then. Elizabeth Blackwell. Do you want to talk about doing battle?" Nurse said. "Elizabeth Blackwell could do battle with the best of them. She was the first woman doctor in America. Strong woman. Strong. When she was in her early twenties, she began studying medicine on her own. She found that she loved it, so much so that she started applying to medical schools. For four years she did that. Studied, applied to colleges, studied some more, all the while being turned down right and left by the schools she applied to." She paused for a moment.

"Help me move this table," she said grasping one side of the examining table. "You need to get behind it with the broom." I grabbed the other side and we slid the head of the table away from the wall.

"Where was I?" she asked.

"Applying to medical school," I said.

"Oh, yes," Nurse replied. "Four years. Finally got accepted at a small school, Geneva College. Do you know why that school let her in?" I looked up from the dust bunnies behind the examining table and shook my head.

"Because they thought it was a joke," Nurse said. "They processed her paperwork, then sat back and waited for the punch line. Turns out the joke was on them. The first day of class, there she stood in all her glory. A woman. And with all the proper admission papers there in her hand. They took her in, but they didn't make it easy. They wouldn't let her watch medical demonstrations because they thought she was too delicate. And then some of the faculty started spreading rumors that she was insane. So do you know what she did? She graduated first in her class. First. She showed them. She became a doctor despite them all. But still they wouldn't let her practice in the hospitals. They wouldn't grant her licenses. She went to Europe for a while, practiced there. She finally ended up working in a small dispensary in the tenement district here in New York. That's where I heard about her. From another woman doctor who had followed in her footsteps."

"And she was the first?" I said.

"In this country, yes," Nurse replied. "There had been a few women doctors in Europe, but in this country, Dr. Blackwell was the first. You have to admire someone like that." I finished sweeping behind the exam table, and grasped the end so we could move it back into place.

"Now that's energy," Nurse said. "She had energy, stamina. Strong woman. And we just hear about the big battles. We don't hear about all the little daily battles, all the little slights and insults and challenges. Those are the things that really wear you down. She's one strong woman; I can tell you that much."

She paused for a moment, the dust rag she had been using on the windowsills still in her hand.

"I'm not that strong," she said finally. "I know that about myself. I could never be an Elizabeth Blackwell. I have to ration my energy, save it for the battles that are important to me."

"Like what?" I said.

Nurse thought for a moment, walked across the floor, dropped the rag into the closet, and closed the door. "When you're finished with the floor, pour the rest of that disinfectant into the trash not down the sink, all right?"

* * *

"Did you ever deliver a baby?" I asked. In the few weeks that I had been working at the infirmary, I'd learned that Nurse was most comfortable talking about medical topics. When she talked anatomy or physiology or nursing training, she relaxed. Her hands stopped shaking, her shoulders slipped down to where normal people kept theirs. People made her nervous. So did loud noises. And nothing made her more nervous than talking about her life outside the infirmary. So I stuck with medical topics like, "did you ever deliver a baby?"

"Not much call for that here," she said. "The girls who come in, well, like that, are usually sent to a home for wayward women first. After they've convalesced, we get them here. The babies, too, sometimes, until they can be placed out."

It was one of those answers that not only didn't answer my original question; it immediately raised a dozen more questions.

"Some of these girls had babies?" I said.

"I would imagine," she replied.

"Some my age?"

"Well, now age doesn't really matter, does it," Nurse replied. "Once you're a woman, you can have a baby. It doesn't matter if you're fourteen or forty."

I thought about that. It was strange how information about sex, even though I already knew it on some level, always seemed new and shocking when I heard it aloud.

"I delivered a baby once," I said. "Abroad, in Ireland. Or at least I helped."

"Did you?" Nurse said.

"I did so," I said.

"I haven't been at a birth since nursing school," she said. "Didn't like it much then."

"Oh, I did," I said. I finished winding the bandage I was rolling. Nurse took it from me.

"Hold out your hand," she said. I held it out. "This is how you bandage a wrist," she said. "You can't just wrap the bandage around the wrist. You have to anchor it to the hand. Always work toward the body, not away." She held the end of the bandage to my palm, then began wrapping.

"Did you really like it?" she said. "Helping at the birth?"

"I did," I said.

"Even with the mess and all the pain the mother went through, you still liked it?"

"It didn't bother me," I said. Nurse looked up from her wrapping and looked me in the eye. "Not much," I said. "Some."

"I passed out the first time," Nurse confessed. "The second time I kept my feet, but I can't say I liked it." She was quiet, wrapped slowly, carefully. When she finished, she tied down the end. "Your turn," she said, picking loose the knot. I unwrapped the bandage, rolled it again, then took the hand Nurse offered.

"There was a woman on the boat from Ireland," I said, starting where she had at the palm. "She went into labor there in her cabin. I was walking the halls and heard her, nearly fought down a doctor for the chance to stay with her. He wouldn't let me. But when I was with her, it was like the pains didn't matter. All that mattered was that I was meant to be there, meant to be helping her."

"And you're fourteen?" Nurse said.

"I am," I said. I crossed the bandage on the palm and made a loop around the wrist.

"Fourteen and looking for opportunities to deliver babies," Nurse said. "You're a strange one, Clare Keane. Has anyone ever told you that?"

"Well, not in so many words," I said, "though I can't say it surprises me any to hear you say so." She chuckled.

"Wait a bit," she said, looking down at the bandage. "Not too tight. You want to support the wrist, but you don't want to cut off circulation to the hand. Loosen it up just a bit."

I unwrapped the last few turns and redid them. "Good," she said. "See how the bandage will move a little when I push it about? That's what you want. Even a bit more if the wrist is still swelling or if you expect the bandage might get wet. And always leave the fingers unbandaged so you check their color. If they go even a little dusky, you need to get the bandage off right away."

I tied the end of the bandage down. "Good," Nurse said. "Now undo it, roll the bandage, and then do it again. Nothing better than practice." I reached in to undo the knot.

Thirty-Five

I hadn't seen much of Annette since I began work in the infirmary. According to Kristie, she'd returned to early morning work in the kitchen because she'd attacked a girl with a knife, cut her apron right off her. I professed shock, but mostly I was relieved to know I wouldn't have to share the lavatory with Annette each morning. It was comforting in more ways than one to picture her at 5:30 A.M. up to her elbows in dishwater, Mrs. Riezler's watchful eye resting heavily upon her.

It was a crisp autumn afternoon when all that changed. I was running an errand for Nurse, delivering some health records to the main office. The grounds were nearly empty as I strolled through the fallen leaves to the administrative building. By the time I'd found the correct administrator and had dropped the papers with his secretary, afternoon recess had released dozens of screaming bodies onto the ball fields and playgrounds. Out the side door of the kitchen drifted several of the older girls. I recognized most of them. Kristie stretched and rolled her shoulders as she walked and talked with a few others. It was a small matter to detour past the kitchen on my way back to the infirmary.

Or at least I thought it would be a small matter. What I didn't factor into the calculation was Annette. She had presumably exited the kitchen through the back door. Just as I approached the kitchen workers, she rounded the corner. She closed the distance between us before I knew what was happening.

"You got me assigned to mornings again, you rat," she shouted. "You squealed to Riezler. Now I have to get up at four in the morning on top of my afternoon shift."

"I did no such thing," I said.

"Liar," she said. She reached out to grab a fistful of my shirtwaist, but I swatted her off. Instead she got my glasses. The chain snapped, then dangled limply from the glasses she clutched tightly in her fist.

"Give them back," I said.

"Come and get them," Annette replied. I looked over at the kitchen crew. They had all backed closer to the kitchen door. So they weren't going to help me. That was fine, so long as none of them were going to back Annette either.

"Give them back," I repeated. "Now." The cool hardness of my voice surprised me.

Annette held them high above her head, like a trophy, and smiled malevolently at me.

"This is the last time I'll say it," I said. "Give them back. Now."

Annette opened her hand, and the glasses fell to the dirt.

Everything from that moment became focused, clear. I could see the glasses fall. I could see the little puff of dust that rose as they hit the ground. I could see Annette shift her weight. I could see her begin to raise the foot closest to the glasses. I knew what she was going to do.

That's when I did it. I took two huge steps in to close the distance, and with all my weight moving forward, I balled my fist, and launched it. It caught her on the point of her chin. Her smile snapped shut. Her head snapped back. And like a sack of flour, she fell in a great heap on the ground.

I picked up my glasses, blew the dust from them, and dropped them and the broken chain in my pocket.

"Did you kill her?" Kristie said, stepping in cautiously to peer down at the pile of Annette on the ground.

"Of course not," I said, "I, I don't think so." I looked down. She was still breathing. "No," I said. "She's only napping."

Kristie chuckled nervously. "A lot of people are a bit grouchy when they wake up from naps," she observed. "And Annette wasn't exactly Miss Sally Sunshine to begin with."

"We'd best get her to the infirmary," I said. Annette was beginning to stir.

"I think it would be best if you left," Kristie said.

"I'm not going anywhere," I said. "Not until I'm ready to leave."

Kristie looked at me, then shook her head. "Don't say I didn't warn you," she said.

Annette groaned, then rolled over a bit and sat up.

"You should probably go to the infirmary," I said. "You passed out."

"You hit me," she said.

"And I'll do it again if I have to," I said. "But for now you should probably have Nurse take a look at you, just to make sure nothing's broken."

Annette hauled herself unsteadily to her feet. "You hit me," she repeated.

I looked her in the eye. I was calm—pumping with energy, but focused, relaxed. "Stop riling me," I said simply. "I'll not stand for it any more."

Annette brushed some dust from her sleeve. Her apron was covered in it. Mrs. Riezler would probably want to know what happened.

"Do you understand me?" I said. "No more."

Annette brushed down the front of her dress with one big sweep of her hand, then turned and strode around back of the kitchen again.

Now I have to say I fully expected cheers, or at least hearty congratulations from the kitchen girls who had watched the entire episode. They had witnessed everything from their place near the side door. Once Annette disappeared, I turned to them. They just looked at me. A couple managed half smiles. Then silently they retreated back inside.

* * *

It didn't take long once the paperwork had been pushed through. But then I suppose that shouldn't have surprised me. One of the things the protectory did was place out children, hundreds and thousands of them. Should it be a shock that they had gotten efficient about it over the years? The news came in on a Friday. We had homes waiting for us in Minnesota and would be leaving as soon as the society could put together a full train car's worth of children.

On Monday we were outfitted. Three of us from my dormitory room were going. After breakfast we reported to Sister Xavier, who handed each of us a small cardboard suitcase. In it we put our second dress, hair ribbons, a change of drawers and stockings, a hairbrush, and whatever personal objects we had come to the orphanage with. In my case that was literally the shirt on my back. In the bottom of the suitcase, I laid the yellow shirtwaist Mrs. Sullivan had made me. It was stained and torn, not something I would wear if I had a dress as nice as the one the protectory had provided me with. But it was all I had of Cork, and I insisted on packing it despite Sister Xavier's pronouncement that it would better serve as a rag.

We made the rounds—to the main administrative building for paperwork, to a storeroom for new coats, then to the cafeteria for a late lunch. Then Sister Xavier took us back to the dormitory where we pushed the suitcases under our beds to wait for morning.

I fervently hoped Tom and Mick were undergoing a similar ritual in their own dormitories. Sister Xavier didn't know if we had all been placed in the same home or even if we would all be going west on the same train.

What she did know was that we had until supper to say our goodbyes. After supper we would be taken to a special confession and Mass for those leaving. After Mass we would be put to bed, and then first thing in the morning, we would be shipped out.

* * *

Kristie was in the kitchen, just where I expected to find her. She was standing side-by-side with Mrs. Riezler, both up to their elbows in bread dough.

"You're leaving," she said.

"I am," I replied. "How did you know?"

"You wouldn't be the first girl sent here to make her goodbyes," Kristie replied. She scraped the dough off her hands and motioned for me to follow. She headed back to the sinks. The smell of fresh bread filled the kitchen. It was a homey smell. I reflected for a moment on the irony of that fact while Kristie washed her hands in the huge institutional sink.

"Where are they sending you?" she said.

"Minnesota, I think," I said. "I don't know much."

"Well, then," Kristie said, and reached out an arm. I walked into it, and gave her a warm hug.

"Good luck," she said.

"And to you," I replied. "God bless."

"I'll need it more than you do," she said, "I'm the one staying here with Annette." She smiled her big smile at me. I'd miss that smile and her wry sense of humor.

"Where is she?" I asked. "Maybe I ought to say goodbye."

"So is it true that the Irish don't feel pain like the rest of us?" Kristie said. "You'd actually walk into her path after what you did to her?"

"I may never see her again—please God that's true. So I thought, well, I'm not sure what I thought. Is she around?"

"Check the pantry," Kristie said. "Last I saw she was peeling potatoes. Maybe she went in there to get more."

"I will," I said. "Thank you for everything, Kristie. For seeing me settled. *Vielen Dank.*"

"*Bitte*," Kristie said and hugged me again. Then she smiled again and returned to her bread dough.

I looked over at the pantry. The door was indeed ajar. I made my way past the lines of girls working and opened it. Sure enough, there was Annette. She was stacking potato sacks. She looked up when I entered. A sour look spread across her face.

Before she could open her mouth, I opened mine. "I'm leaving, Annette. Going west on the train tomorrow. I only wanted to say that I was sorry I had to hit you, and that I don't hold any of what passed between us against you." I was feeling quite noble as I said it, very Christian. Love your enemy. Now that I was leaving, I could do that. I held out my hand for her to shake. It was, after all, how Mick would do it. Establish an understanding with his fists. Then shake the other fellow's hand to seal the new relationship.

Annette looked at my outstretched hand, then tilting her head back slightly and looking down her nose, she said her last words to me: "Good riddance, County Cork." With that she hefted the sack off the stack, muscled it past me in the doorway, and went back to work.

* * *

Nurse didn't appear to be doing anything more than pacing the floor when I arrived at the infirmary. The door was open a crack, and I looked in. Her hands were clasped behind her back, her shoulders rounded. She looked first at the floor, then striding to the window, paused and looked out for a moment, then went back to pacing the floor. She had a worried look on her face.

I gave the door a bit of a shove and entered. Nurse looked up at me. I gave her a weak smile.

"You're late," she said. "I was worried."

"They didn't tell you," I said.

"Who didn't tell me what?"

"The sisters," I said. "They didn't tell you . . . " I paused, trying to find an easy way to say it. There was none. None that I could find on such short notice. Nurse looked into my eyes, then reached behind her for the windowsill and leaned back heavily against it. "I'm leaving," I said. "For Minnesota. The society found a family to take me. I go tomorrow."

"Tomorrow," Nurse echoed.

"Tomorrow," I said. "I'm supposed to be making my goodbyes."

Nurse sighed, then crossed over in front of me to the broom closet and pulled out the broom. She started by the door, stabbing at the floor with small tense strokes. "I supposed you better go make those goodbyes, then," she said, her voice as tight as her grip on the broom.

"I'll keep up with my nursing studies," I said. "And I won't forget what you taught me." She was silent.

"Thank you," I said.

Nurse turned away and began stabbing under one of the beds.

"For everything," I said. "Thank you. I won't forget." I could see Nurse's head nodding slightly.

"Goodbye, Clare," she said, not turning around. I could see the quiver in her shoulders.

"Goodbye, Nurse," I said, opened the door, stepped out, and closed it behind me.

Thirty-Six

Ours was an orphan train. Though we didn't know it at the time, we were part of a phenomenon that resettled hundreds of thousands of children from the cities of the east to the rural areas of the upper Midwest, west and south during the nineteenth and twentieth century. That's the dispassionate, textbook description of the phenomenon. The reality—for all of us—pulsed with all the complexities of family lost and family found, of displacement and sometimes misplacement.

Initially, orphan trains were a little like traveling supermarkets. Not only orphans but also hustlers, street arabs, young prostitutes and thieves were lifted out of the environment that made them, and whisked away by train to a second chance. All along the tracks, families looking for a child, or a farm hand, or a bit of company and help—not that there was much difference between the three in those days—these families would arrive at the station to shop. The orphans would line up in their new clothes, and the shoppers would stroll down the aisles assessing the goods. If they found a child they liked, they would fill out the papers and pay the fees, and they could take their child home with them that evening. It was as simple as that.

Those were the orphan trains of the past. By the time I left the grounds of the Catholic Children's Protectory on my way to my own orphan train on that day in mid September, many states had imposed severe regulations on orphan resettlement. Most of us on my train had been matched to "good Catholic homes" in Minnesota. That match was not always person to family, but the social workers on the train knew that, for example, three families in St. Paul had agreed to take one six-year-old girl each, whereas a family in a rural community wanted two boys in their early adolescence. The social workers would look at the list of requirements and load up the train with the required compliment. The supermarket approach to "placing out" had been scaled back, though not entirely eliminated.

The night before we were to leave on the train, I was told that a family living just outside St. Cloud, Minnesota, was willing to take one boy and one girl between the ages of ten and fifteen. Tom and I were to be that boy and girl. Mick, on the other hand, had not yet received an "assignment."

That's why I was surprised to see him the next morning in his new shirt and trousers, helping one of the brothers load the younger boys into the protectory wagon. His paperboard suitcase was already aboard, sitting at Tom's feet. All night I had braced myself to lose him. But there he was. I came up behind him, laid a hand on his shoulder.

"You're going, too, then," I said.

"So they tell me," he said. The hand he laid on mine was surprisingly gentle, tender. Perhaps he had worried, too.

"Tom and I are going to St. Cloud," I said.

"Mmm," he said, letting go of my hand to scoop up a little girl in a pink dress and swing her onto the wagon. She squealed in delight. Mick gave her one of his buttery best smiles.

"Have they told you where you're going?" I asked.

"West," he said. "Wisconsin or Minnesota probably. That's all I could get out of Brother Andrew yesterday evening." He took me by the elbow and helped me negotiate the step up to the wagon.

"West," I said.

"West," he replied.

The wagon was nearly loaded when Sister Xavier joined us. She whispered something to one of the brothers, who scurried off and returned with a Father to say a blessing over us. We crossed ourselves—Mick on one side of me, Tom on the other. The driver clucked to the horses, and I bid farewell to the Catholic Children's Protectory of New York.

"Do you think they'll let you live in St. Cloud if we explain things to them?" Tom asked Mick. He was seated over the wheel, turned slightly in his seat so he could watch it turn beneath him. Mick, seated on my other side, shook his head.

"I don't think we get a say," I said. "But I would like to know what they have in mind for those who don't have an assignment."

"You could ask the sister," Mick offered. "Maybe she'd tell you more than Brother Andrew told me."

I looked up at Sister Xavier. She was seated in the front of the wagon, her back to the driver. The little girl in the pink dress sat in her lap. Sister Xavier was humming a song, a lively, semi-foreign song. She rocked the little girl in time with the music.

"Trade places with me, Mick," I said, and edged closer to her. I then traded with child after child until I'd made my way far enough forward to speak with Sister Xavier.

"No problem," she said, as we bounced our way through the early-morning streets of New York. "No problem, no problem. Somebody peek him. Somebody always peek him. No problem."

Someone would pick him. It didn't tell me much. And it did nothing to allay my fears. I returned to Mick, took his hand in mine, and resolved not to let go until I absolutely had to.

* * *

The wagon threaded its way through the perpetual chaos of the docks. A ferry waited to take us across the Hudson River to New Jersey and our train. At the foot of the gangplank stood our social worker. She was a tall, pale woman, a head taller than the boat worker manning the mooring lines. She clutched a sheaf of papers tightly to her chest and looked out over the quay, where thirty of us were muscling our bags out of the protectory's supply wagon.

Sister Xavier, her eyes a bit misty, but her energy by no means dimmed, herded us from the wagon to the gangplank. There she rattled off a few words at the social worker. Then without further comment, she spun on her heel, and charged back to the wagon, trailing a couple of young brothers behind her like so much dead weight. As the wagon pulled away from the quay, thirty small heads swiveled to watch it. As it rounded the corner and disappeared from view, each one of those heads snapped back to the social worker. It was she who would have charge of us on our way across the country.

She was a striking woman; the social worker was. Not striking in the sense of beautiful or even handsome, but striking in the sense that her appearance reached out and grabbed you like a slap across the face. She was an impossibly tall woman, impossibly thin, impossibly homely. Now, it wasn't that any one of her features was particularly ugly. I remember a woman back in Cork who had one of the most misshapen noses you would ever hope to run across. It was so bulbous that one would probably never recognize it as a nose had it not been there front-and-center on her face. The social worker wasn't homely in that way. But none of her features seemed to match her other features.

High atop her slender frame lay a face dominated by two large eyes. Beautiful, deep-brown eyes, they were. But the nose that lay between them was far too short, and the mouth that lay beneath that was, well, all wrong. Her two front teeth far outshone her upper lip, which was in turn too big for her lower lip, which was too big for her petite chin. If she were broken up for spare parts, I know a hundred girls who would have loved a dainty chin or button nose like that. In fact, her eyes themselves, her large, soulful eyes, which gave one the impression of a wounded woodland animal, those eyes would be the envy of a Gibson girl except for their unfortunate setting.

The children took her in, eyed her appraisingly from head to toe. She smiled stiffly and announced that her name was Miss Godfrey. Perhaps inevitable that before we had stepped off the ferry, the children christened her Miss Gophery, or simply The Gopher.

* * *

The train tracks began no more than a short skip from where the ferry docked on the New Jersey shore. Line after line, platform after platform, the tracks began at the edge of the country and headed inward. Herded by Miss Godfrey and a handful of porters she'd recruited for the purpose, we walked in a ragged line across the third platform. Waiting for us was our train carriage, the car that would be our home for the next few days.

It was a simple car—rows of wooden seats that folded down at night. Generous windows above them. And above the windows, racks for a couple of dozen identical paperboard suitcases. A privy in the back. A pantry and closet in the front, both bearing conspicuous locks, to which I assumed Miss Godfrey held the key. The seats could hold three children apiece. Mick and Tom and I staked a claim to one on the right side about midway down the car, halfway between the food and the privy. It seemed as likely a place as any.

Through the windows we could see the other passengers boarding the other cars. In days past, an entire train may have been filled with orphans. We, though, were a mere thirty passengers, enough to fill a single car. That car was only one of a long line of passenger cars, all hooked up to an engine and pointed west. As I watched women carrying carpet bags and hat boxes, men lugging suitcases, porters wheeling carts piled high with trunks and parcels, I couldn't help but reflecting upon how odd our own car was. We were all children. We all had very little idea where they were going or what we could expect when we got there. While other travelers were going somewhere, most of us knew little more than what we were leaving behind.

Once we had all settled into seats, Miss Godfrey came by again with her stack of papers, now secured to a tablet of paper by means of a couple of thick red rubber bands. She checked the papers we carried, checked the papers in her fist, laid a hand on a shoulder here and there, smiled. But she didn't say much. Since she didn't talk, neither did we. Most of us only sat, watched out the window, wondered.

* * *

It didn't take long for us to leave the city. The New York skyline was long gone when the sun shining in on my lap shifted overhead. Small towns came and went: Clean white houses on tree-lined streets. Brick churches, each marking its place in the town with a spire. Main streets lined with red-brick shops of two or three storeys. Miss Godfrey brought out sandwiches and milk from the pantry, recruiting some of the older children to help her pass them out. We were licking the red jelly from our fingers when the small towns and gently rolling farmland gave way again to city.

It was nowhere near the city New York was. Trees and open spaces abounded. The tallest buildings were church steeples. Those steeples, the river running through town, the green hills just beyond the outskirts of the city—they weren't foreign. In fact, they triggered in me a great wave of homesickness. In the landscape I could see Ireland: the spires, the Lee, the emerald hills. But Cork was a lifetime ago. The sign on the platform said "Albany."

It still said "Albany" several hours later as I helped Miss Godfrey hand out the bread and mustard sandwiches. She hoped an early supper might help calm the restlessness of some of the younger children. The younger children weren't the only ones who were restless. I was glad for something to do.

Our car had been unhitched from the train we had come with and had been hitched to a new engine and several new cars, not all of them passenger cars from the looks of things. Mick had moved to the back and was talking with a couple of the older boys. Tom had pulled a blank book and pencil from his suitcase and was sketching the wheels of a locomotive on the track opposite. He examined the train carefully. Then with his tongue wedged into the corner of his mouth, he painstakingly copied what he saw. I thought at first that he was drawing the entire train and had just started with the wheel, but when he finished with the complex set of wheels and levers and pistons, he began sketching a coupling in the corner of the page.

"Did you get that book at the orphanage?" I asked. Tom nodded. "'Tis for drawing?"

"And writing," he said.

"A diary?"

"Not really," he replied. He looked up again at the coupling, down again at the drawing, up and down. I watched him. His face was relaxed but utterly focused. Finally he looked up at me.

"You want to see the rest of the book," he said. It wasn't a question.

"I do," I said. "If you want to show me."

He flipped to the first page. It was the drawing of a library shelf. The books were just rectangles, but the shelf brackets had been reproduced in detail. The next was a drawing of a press, a printing press. At least I assumed that's what it would be if the pieces were assembled. Tom had drawn first a lever of some kind, then a roller with arrows showing the path of the paper. The next few pages were more drawings of the press, then came one of a wagon wheel and axle, the eaves of the chapel roof, a bed frame assembly.

"You drew all these," I said.

"I did," he replied.

"They're good," I said. "When did you learn to draw?"

"Well," he said, "it's not so much a matter of drawing as it is of seeing. If you notice things, you can put down what you see." I nodded. I wasn't sure what he meant. He must have known that, so he continued. "I went to the library back at the orphanage, and I asked the librarian if he had any books on engineering, building things. He pulled a few from the shelves for me. All of them had drawings like these. That's when I thought maybe I had better learn to draw. If I want to be an engineer. So I asked one of the brothers for some paper. When I told him what I wanted it for, he said he'd get me some. The next morning he came back with this. These pictures of the press are from the book. I tried to draw it the way the engineer drew. From there I just kind of went to other things."

"When did you find time to draw?" I asked.

"Most places you'd want to draw something there is 'a little bit of air'," he said. "So whenever the brothers told me to go out and get a little bit of air, I'd find both air and something to draw."

I smiled back at him. "I did the same thing only I went to the infirmary," I said.

I watched him draw for a while longer. He had a fair amount of talent; I had to admit that. Plus he had the look on his face that he got when he read, a look of concentration, focus, like he was in another world, a better world maybe.

"Tom," I said, as he held up a sketch of a porter's cart for examination, "how serious are you about wanting to be an engineer?"

"'Tis what I dream of," he said. "More than anything."

"Why?" I asked. "You never met an engineer, did you?"

He shook his head. I watched his face as he thought, tried to formulate an answer. "I want to understand things," he finally said. "I want to build them, make them work right. I want it more than anything."

"I don't know if the people we're going to live with will be able to send you to become an engineer," I said. "Maybe they own a shop. Maybe they're laborers. Maybe they have a farm they want you to work on. You may not be able to become an engineer."

I hated to say it out so baldly, but it was the truth, a truth I had been thinking about almost constantly since we set foot on the train. I could see from Tom's face that he didn't want to hear it. The look was almost one of physical pain. He was a strange boy, Tom was. I don't think I had ever met another boy from the lanes like him—so serious, so focused. I'd never met one who could keep his eyes fixed like Tom did on something so distant and unattainable. It would be a pity if someone like him got stuck as a laborer or dogsbody.

Tom sat beside me, his face tight with thought. He was stroking the ridges of his pencil with his thumb.

"Will you help me?" he asked finally.

"Help you do what?"

"Will you promise to help me become an engineer?" he said. "If the people we go to live with can't afford to send me to school, will you help me?" I wasn't sure what he meant and said so. "By the time I'm old enough for college, you'll be out on your own. And you can get a job near the university, and we can live really closely until I finish my training. And then I'll find work as an engineer, and I'll make it up to you. I promise I will."

The train on the next track began to pull out. For a moment I though we were moving backward. But there was no bump from the slack being taken out of the couplings. It wasn't our turn yet.

"If when you finish secondary school, you still want to go to the university, I'll do my best for you," I said.

"Promise?" Tom said.

"To do my best for you? I promised Mama that last spring. Should I promise you any less now?" Tom nodded. He flipped is little book to a clean page and searched for something else to draw. Finding a signal switch that interested him, he gently leaned back against me, and returned to his drawing.

* * *

The train finally began moving about an hour later. The little towns began to come and go again. But now I began to see something new—smokestacks. Nearly every town seemed to have one or two. The larger towns had dozens. Some oozed white, some grey. The smoke hung in the air, clouding the scenery, giving it a grainy look in the low sunlight. As the sun slipped below the horizon, we stopped in several of these towns, took on passengers for the other cars, let off passengers. I watched the leave-takings, the family reunions from my place perched above the platform, separated from them by just a window, or maybe by more than that.

We were finally pointed west and making good time when Miss Godfrey showed some of the older boys how to fold the seats down to beds. I bedded down in my street clothes, with Tom on one side of me and Mick on the other. My feet hung off the end of the bench and into the aisle, and the wood slats created ridges in whatever flesh rested on them. The makeshift bed was far from comfortable, but I had been up since before first light, and I drifted off quickly.

The train started and stopped, rolled and bumped. The lights of station platforms shone in on us now and then, then dropped away to darkness as we rocked our way through farmland. Miss Godfrey slept sitting up in her seat, facing us. At least I assumed she slept. Every time I looked, her eyes were open, drowsing, but awake, ever scanning the quiet bodies of her charges.

I awoke when the train jolted with a clang. The sign on the platform read "Cleveland." We had been uncoupled from the car in front of us again and were being hooked to the end of a passenger train. I could hear the workers below the window shout to each other as they attached some more cars behind us. The sun was just beginning to peek up over the horizon.

All around me, children stirred, sat, dropped into the aisle to stretch. I looked to the back of the car. The privy had quite a line. I decided to wait. Miss Godfrey stood in the back near the privy door, passing out wet towels for the children to wash the sleep off them. Tom beside me rolled over and curled into a ball, pulling his jacket up over his head.

Mick was nowhere to be seen.

"Tom," I said, bending over his ear. "Tom. Rouse up. Did you see Mick this morning?" Tom groaned from under his jacket. "Tom," I said, "Mick's missing."

"How can he be missing?" Tom said, rolling over and pulling the jacket from his face. "We're on a train." His voice was thick with sleep. His eyes focused on me for a second or two, then closed again.

Tom wasn't going to be any help then. I rose, pulled on my shoes, and worked my way to the back. Perhaps Mick was in the privy. The door opened and a little girl exited, smoothing down her skirts in front. Not the privy then. I made my way forward again, stepping around children stretching and leaning in the aisle. I checked each seat carefully. None of them contained Mick. The panic inside me had risen to near eruption when I heard steps on the front stairs. Mick and another boy entered the car, each bearing a wooden crate of apples.

"Just put them there by the pantry," Miss Godfrey shouted from the back. Some of the children spotted the fruit and were pulled to it.

"Sit down, children, sit down," Miss Godfrey called out. "We'll all have apples for breakfast. At least all of us who behave like good little children will have apples for breakfast." A couple of boys dropped their posteriors summarily into the nearest seat, hands folded and eyes locked on the boxes at the front of the cabin.

Mick threaded his way between their knees back to the seat.

"Where did you go?" I said. "I was worried." I knew full well where he went. He went to get apples. And given Miss Godfrey's response, I could also guess that he went to get them on her instruction. But I had worried, and he had been the cause, so I saw no reason to behave as though nothing at all had happened.

"Washington," Mick said. "I went to Washington. They're famous for their apples. Where do you think I went?" He was grouchier than usual.

"I woke up, and you weren't on the train," I said.

He grunted, and hunched over on himself. He had his left hand tucked into his right armpit, and unless I missed my guess, that was pain on his face.

"Did the apples fight back?" I said, nodding toward the hand.

"No," Mick said curtly.

"Let me see," I said.

"You'll only make a fuss," he said, "or you'll tell the Gopher. 'Tis nothing."

"Let me see," I said, grabbing hold of his arm to pry the hand out from its hiding place.

"Ow," he said. "Get off, Clare."

"I'll get off when you let me see what you're hiding," I said. "Until then, I'll just keep tugging until either your hand breaks off at the wrist or until Miss Godfrey decides to come by and see what all the foostering is about."

Mick looked at me hard, then pulled his hand from under his arm. The thumb was beginning to swell at the bottom joint. It looked to be a fresh injury, but it was already beginning to get a bit purple.

"Can you move it?" I asked, taking the joint lightly between my thumb and forefinger. Mick wagged the thumb a bit and winced. I had no doubt it hurt, but it was moving freely, and without any telltale creaks or pops. "It looks like a sprain," I said. "How did you do it?"

Mick clamped his mouth shut, but looked up at the boy he'd gone to get apples with.

"Were you fighting?" I said.

"No," Mick said. "No, I wasn't fighting. No thanks to Willy, there." He shot a dirty look at the boy guarding the apples. The boy looked to be about fourteen and had a good half a head on Mick. "I caught the dirty ape with his hand in my pocket. I was trying to teach him the difference between my money and his money when this happened."

"What do you mean your money?" I said. "You don't have any money."

"Not much," Mick replied. "But what I have is not his." He said it loudly enough that I'm sure Willy heard. "The man with the apples saw the whole thing, made him give me mine back. But not before the dirty ape broke my thumb."

"I don't think 'tis broken, Mick," I said.

"Well, it sure doesn't work as well as it did an hour ago," Mick replied. "I suppose you're going to tell me I shouldn't get my own back on the bugger."

"I'm going to tell you I don't like the word bugger," I said. "And as for fighting, well, if you have to, you have to. But make sure you have to before you do."

Mick looked at me in shock. "No 'good run is better than a bad stand'?" he said.

"From the looks of him, I'd say he could give you a shirt full of broken bones and not even work up a sweat doing so," I said. "I want you to make sure that it's worth the pain, the pain and the trouble it will cause you with Miss Godfrey. I want you to think of that, Michael Keane, when you're deciding whether to run or stand."

"If I stand," Mick said. "It won't be alone. He'll be the one with a shirt full of sore bones."

I looked up. Miss Godfrey was standing there, looking down at us. "Sore thumb, Mick?" she said.

"Caught it in the apple box, Miss," Mick replied.

"You have to be careful of those apple boxes," Miss Godfrey said. "They can get a boy into more trouble than he knows what to do with."

"Yes, Miss," Mick said.

"Clare," she said, "can you help me get the rest of the children up? I want to have the seats back in place before we pull out of the station."

"That'll do, ma'am," I said. She looked at me curiously. "I will, Miss Godfrey," I said by way of clarification.

"Good," she said, "very good."

I rose and seat-by-seat started shaking children awake. Halfway to the back, Tom squeezed by me on his way back to the privy.

"Look," he said, pointing to the front. Miss Godfrey had Willy trapped in a corner and was giving him a good talking to. Mick sat in our seat, his arms crossed, a look of satisfaction on his face.

* * *

We pulled into Chicago midafternoon. It was a large city, the largest we'd seen since New York. I expected a long wait, but in no time at all we were hooked to a new engine and headed north. By suppertime we were deep into farm country someplace in Wisconsin. At one of many tiny stations, the train stopped. We were fed—bread and mustard again. Then a stocky man with thick jowls and a clerical collar boarded. He and Miss Godfrey whispered a bit at the front of the train. Then Miss Godfrey pulled a fist full of papers from her satchel and began to call names. A tension fell on the carriage. We all sensed that something important was about to happen.

Then it came. Mick's name. I could feel him cringe beside me. The children strode forward one by one. Miss Godfrey smoothed a collar here, buttoned a button there. The children looked at her with anxious eyes. Her answer to all their questions was the same: "Follow Father Baum. He'll take good care of you."

Mick hung back as long as he could. In his good hand, he held my own. His bad hand rested lightly on Tom's knee. When the line in front of Miss Godfrey had dwindled to only a couple of children, he gave my hand a squeeze.

"I'll find you," he said simply, then turned and walked to the front of the car.

"God go with you, Michael Finbarr Joseph Keane," I said to his back. He didn't so much as turn for a goodbye. There was not much more to say.

Tom leaned in against me, and I leaned back. Miss Godfrey straightened Mick's collar, pushed a bit of hair off his face, and with that he was gone.

* * *

It was, perhaps, two or three hours later. The sun had set. We had dropped the seats down into bunks, but Tom and I were still sitting up, watching out the window, waiting. I'm not sure what we were waiting for. Maybe just for some kind of resolution, some sign that Mick was indeed gone.

Through the open window I could hear the sound of crickets. Now and then the telegraph in the stationmaster's office would click to life. I leaned heavily against the side of the car, my cheek against the window. Opposite me, knees to knees, Tom did the same. His face was red with tears that had come and gone. I would imagine mine was, too.

The children all around me were quiet, subdued. Some of the younger ones slept. Most of us, though, simply sat, waited. Miss Godfrey, seated as she was at the front of the car, must have seen it before we did. She stood and descended the stairs to the platform. A sound of wheels on gravel came up behind the station. Then it stopped. I sat up straighter, craned my neck. Miss Godfrey disappeared around the corner. I could hear the sound of quiet voices, but that was all. For long, interminably long minutes, that was all.

Then as we all watched, a small group of children, maybe eight or nine of them—less than half of those who had gone—rounded the corner of the station and stepped up onto the platform. I searched in the dim light of the single lamp for some sight of Mick.

The group walked slowly, herded on one side by Miss Godfrey and on the other by Father Baum. One was a girl; two were clearly too small to be Mick. I thought the tall thin boy might be him, but Mick wasn't that tall, was he? It would have been easier to tell if I could see their faces. But these children walked with their eyes downcast, a shuffle to their step, almost as though someone had deflated them slightly.

As they approached the train, they had to look up to negotiate the high step. I hung my head out the window to look. The tall boy was Mick.

I breathed a sigh of relief. My eyes fogged over with tears. He was still with us. He climbed the stairs, scanned the train, and finding us in the same seat where he had left us, approached and sat down heavily on the edge of the bunk.

"What happened?" I asked, scooting over, swinging my feet down into the aisle, and putting a hand on his shoulder.

"Fish market," he answered, a distinct note of anger in his voice.

"I don't understand," I answered. "You went to a fish market? Here?"

"I went as the fish," Mick said. "We all did. Glassy-eyed. Meat for the eating."

"Mick," I said. "You're making no sense." Tom had scooted in behind me and rested his chin on my shoulder, the shoulder closest to Mick.

I could see the anger and the tears fighting for control of Mick's face. For the moment, he was fighting them both off, but not entirely successfully. I waited.

"They piled us into a wagon, hauled us through the streets to the church," he said. "I could tell something was brewing when we pulled up. The yard was filled with horses and mules and buggies and wagons. And people milling around outside talking. They all stopped when we pulled in. They stopped and gawked."

Mick had found a loose thread hanging off one of his jacket buttons and was twisting it, picking at it. Tom, settled in behind me, was tracing the shoulder seam of my dress with a finger.

"They brought us in, lined us up. The Father came by with a fist full of papers. He asked if I was Michael Keane. I said I was. "Eight," he said. And a woman who was with him, wrote 8 on a piece of paper and pinned it to my jacket. When they finished numbering us all, they let the people file in. One after another. They filed past us, looking us up and down. One man asked to see my teeth. I opened my mouth, and he shook his head and walked on."

He yanked at the button thread. It didn't break, so he raised the fistful of jacket to his mouth and tried to bite it clean.

"Those people wanted to take you home with them?" I asked.

"Clearly not," Mick said. "I'm still here."

"I meant . . . "

"That was the idea," Mick said. "Line up the fish in the bin, let the folks pick the ones they liked best." He spit loose the bit of thread, smoothed the remaining bit down over the button. "The girl beside me started to sing the *Gloria* over and over again. The people would walk past her and smile. Finally one of them pulled her out of the line, and she went to the table where a couple of gentry men in suits sat hunched over the papers." Tom's finger running over my shoulder seam, back and forth, back and forth, was beginning to annoy me a bit. I turned and shook him off. He moved in to sit between the two of us.

"A big fellow came up to me," Mick said. His eyes were glassy, stared at our reflection in the window on the other side of the car. "This fellow felt my arm, lifted my cap, rummaged through my hair looking for nits. Then he said he'd take me. Just like that. The Father came over with his stack of papers and started sorting through them. I looked at him—the fish-man, not the Father—and I knew I couldn't go with him. He had tobacco stains on his face. Not only around his mouth, but down his chin, sticking in the two or three days of growth he had to his beard. He smelled like horse manure, and his hair looked like that was what he used to dress it into place. I looked at all the families picking out a boy on my right and the girl on my left. I looked at all the women, all the nice-looking men in their Sunday suits, and here I was picked by a fat, stinky man in bib overalls and tobacco juice. And I knew I couldn't go with him."

"So did you run?" Tom asked.

"I didn't," Mick answered. "He put out his hand. I think he meant to lay it on my shoulder. But I caught it, and I brought it to my mouth, and I bit him."

"Mick!" I said.

"It was the only thing I could think to do," Mick said. "I didn't bite him hard. In fact, I don't think I broke the skin itself. But he yelped and jumped back, then started swearing a blue streak right there in the church. He kept saying, 'he bit me. The little bastard bit me.' Well, after that there was little danger of anyone picking me. The Father took me aside and gave me a great swat across the mouth. And then he lectured me in the wagon the whole way back here. But I'd do it again."

He sat with his arms crossed tight on his chest. I wasn't sure what to say to him. I wasn't sure there was anything to say in a situation like that. I felt the humiliation creep up the back of my own neck, and I hadn't been the fish myself. Beside me, Tom was stroking the crease in his knickers over and over again. I knew what he was thinking. It was the same thing I was thinking. The same thing Mick was thinking. We were all wondering if that was our future. Would we go home with a coarse, tobacco-stained, smelly lout of a man? Or would we be picked by one of the nice families? There was no answer to that question, not yet. Mick stood and settled his suitcase into the rack above. Then he dropped back onto the bunk, his eyes downcast, and his arms clamped tight across his chest. I returned to my place by the window.

Miss Godfrey was trading papers and saying goodbye to the Father on the platform. The conductor waved her aboard. As she ascended the steps, the train jolted slightly and began to pull out of the station. She strolled down the aisle counting her charges as the station slipped from view. Mick clamped his arms tighter as she passed, his chin on his chest, his eyes on the floor in front of him. She reached out a hand and laid it gently, just for the briefest moment on his shoulder. Mick turned away and stared unseeing at the back of the car. My eyes rested lightly on his cheek. I ached for what he'd been through, but, by all the saints, I was glad just for the sight of him.

* * *

We stopped for what must have been hours at a station whose sign read "Oshkosh." The children asleep on the bunks shifted. Some of them pulled themselves up to look out the windows. Half in and half out of sleep, I felt our car being unhooked and then rehooked again. I'm not sure when we pulled out of the station, but when I awoke, we were passing again through trees, farms, tiny little stations. The towns along the route were small—general stores, machinery dealers, the occasional grain elevator beside the tracks. At one point we saw a team of horses dragging a great log by a chain.

Miss Godfrey and a couple of the boys began to set up the seats for the day. I got up, stretched, and shuffled my way to the back of the car to use the privy. When I came back down the aisle Mick and Tom were seated on the bunk knee-to-knee, forehead to forehead. Their faces were serious. Tom was nodding. I could tell immediately that this was not a mere chat. This was the talk of brothers huddled like co-conspirators over a serious conversation.

I sat down beside them. They fell into silence.

"Did I miss something?" I asked.

Tom shook his head vigorously. The look on his face said I had indeed missed something, something important.

"Mick," I said.

"We were talking about later, after I'm placed out and you and Tom go on to Minnesota," He said. "I was telling Tom he had to take care of you from now on."

"I promised Mick I would," Tom said.

"And don't think I'm not glad of it," I said. "But is that all?"

"Isn't that enough?" Mick replied.

I locked eyes with each of them in turn. Their jaws were clamped shut. I would get no more from them. Not yet.

* * *

Breakfast was barely gone when I felt the train slow beneath us. Beside me, I felt Mick stiffen.

"This could be it," he said.

"It could," I replied. I met his eyes. He held mine for an instant, then looked away. "I think I'm going to go to the privy. Who knows when I'll next get the chance."

"See if you can do something about your hair while you're there. Run some water into your hand and smooth it down. If . . . " I paused, not wanting to say it aloud. "It couldn't hurt," I said finally.

Mick nodded. He looked at me again, a softness in his eyes.

"This might not be the stop," I said. "We might just be taking on passengers."

"Tom," Mick said quietly, "if Miss Godfrey starts calling names again, tell her I'm in the jakes." Tom's eyes looked as though they were about to overflow.

"I will," Tom said. "I'll take care of it." He looked as though he wanted to say more, but Mick quickly turned and strode down the aisle.

The train wheels squealed to a stop. I hung my head out the window and scanned the platform. I'm not sure what I was looking for, a clerical collar maybe, a large wagon waiting just beyond the station house, something that might signal that this was a stop for showing off the remaining unassigned children. A man in a white shirt and black vest, handed a postal sack up to someone in the car ahead of us. The conductor saluted him casually, then waved forward to the engine. The train jerked and began to roll. I pulled my head in, and began breathing again.

Beside me Tom rose.

"Where are you going?" I asked. Tom didn't answer. He simply walked purposefully a couple of seats back to where Willie was sitting. He tapped Willie on the shoulder. Willie looked up from a card game he was playing with his seatmate, another boy of around fifteen. Tom squared his shoulders.

"I am here because of my family's honor," he said. "You insulted my brother. You tried to steal from my family. I'll have an apology, and I'll have it now." He spoke loudly enough that the entire car turned to look.

"Tom," I said, "what do you think you're doing? Sit down." He either didn't hear or ignored me.

"Will you answer, or are you as short on courage as you are on honor?" he said. Willie rose. Tom stepped in and caught him with a solid punch to the gut before he had the chance to fully straighten up. I gasped in shock. I had never seen Tom do anything remotely like that.

I think it took Miss Godfrey a couple of beats to figure out what she was seeing as well, for by the time she rose and made her way through the gathering circle of children, Tom and Willie had disappeared beneath the seats of the train. I worked my way back as well, though it wasn't easy. Most of the children had circled around at the first punch. I could see Willie kneeling on the floor, hunched over, his fists pounding over and over. I couldn't see if the fists were finding their mark—Tom was mostly under the seat—but the sound of dull thuds and Tom's gasps told me that the fight was fast reaching its predictable conclusion. Willie had probably four years and at least thirty pounds on Tom. I picked up a small boy and moved him aside to try to get at them.

"Stop this instant," Miss Godfrey shouted over the cheers of encouragement. "Stop this instant, you ruffians." Willie just kept pounding. "Stop." Miss Godfrey paused for a moment over the melee. Her head and shoulders were visibly shaking. I realized just then that she might not have a notion of what to do. I elbowed between two other children, trying to make my way in to help her.

As it turned out, she needed no help at all. A look of resolve suddenly settled onto her face. She grabbed Willie by the collar. When he didn't stop punching, she shoved him head-first into the seat in front of him. Willie suddenly deflated, all the energy and fight having drained out of him. He looked up at Miss Godfrey, a look of complete shock on his face.

"Stand here," she said, pointing at a spot in the aisle. She spoke with such unquestionable authority that two girls who had been standing close to that spot backed up and made room for Willie to stand precisely where Miss Godfrey had pointed. Willie took his spot immediately. "And you, Thomas Keane," she said. "Pick yourself up off that floor and stand here." Again she jabbed her finger at the aisle. Tom, rising slowly, obviously painfully, took a second or two more, than Willie, but only that.

"The rest of you," Miss Godfrey said, in a quiet, even voice that penetrated the air of the car much more effectively than a shout would have, "the rest of you take your seats, fold your hands on your laps, and set your gaze on the seat back in front of you." The children immediately did as told. The car took on an order and a silence I don't think I'd heard in the forty-eight hours it had been our home.

Tom looked back at me. He was pale, his face blank. Tears were rolling down his cheeks. I could see his shoulders quiver and knew I had to go to him. Rather than taking my seat, I took a step forward. Miss Godfrey turned, stopped me dead in my tracks with her gaze.

"You, too, Clare," she said. "Sit." I thought for a second about disobeying, but only for a second. Something about the incident had transformed Miss Godfrey. She had gone from sheep dog to wolf. Her tiny jaw was set resolutely. Her eyes were calm, intense to the point of iciness. I sat.

We all held our breath, waiting to hear what she was going to say. I think we all expected her to strip the hide off the two of them with her words, maybe even to pull out a paddle and make her point that way. Instead she just said in a quiet, even tone, "follow me."

The two boys, eyes downcast, followed her to the front of the train. Miss Godfrey turned her back to the car, and there, with the two boys partially hidden from our view, proceeded to speak to them. As I watched, the two dissolved beneath her words.

When Tom came back to his seat, his face was red and puffy. I turned his face toward me, looked him over.

"Are you whole?" I asked.

"Most of me," he said.

"What does that mean?" I asked.

Tom's head sagged into his hands. "I can't tell you," he said.

I rubbed his back. "That was an eejit thing to do," I said, "wading in like that with no more concern for your neck than if you had forty of them. 'Tis something I'd expect from Mick, not you."

That's when it dawned on me. Mick must have heard the ruckus from the privy. I looked back to the toilet door. It was ajar. I scanned the car, forward back, forward again. Mick was nowhere to be seen.

"As a matter of fact, the fight *was* Mick's idea," Tom said quietly.

"Where is Mick?" I said.

Tom looked up at me, then out the window. The small town had nearly given way to trees, trees and more trees.

"Tom," I said. "Where is Mick?"

Tom waited, held his breath. As the last house fell by the way, he let the breath out. "He left," he said simply. "He went to find Uncle Ronan. He said he had to, said he couldn't stand another fish market." I looked at Tom in disbelief. I saw there in his eyes the truth of what he was telling me.

"He's gone," I said.

Tom nodded. "He's gone."

* * *

It took me a couple of minutes—a couple of minutes of inner debate, a couple of minutes of raw grief—but eventually I knew what I had to do. I was missing one brother. But I had one brother still sitting right beside me bruised and hurting. I would attend to him. I still had one brother I could keep.

I suppose I might have told Miss Godfrey right away. And maybe she would have stopped the train, hauled us all back to the station, assembled a search party. But by the time they had the chance to fan out into the forest, Mick would be long gone. And if they did find him, what would they do? Lock him up in an industrial school? Line him up at another orphan auction? And faced with those alternatives, wouldn't he just run away again?

Tom sat beside me clutching his ribs, his head bowed, his face pale. I knew how much it killed him entirely to do what he did for his brother. The least I could do was to inventory the damage, care for him the best I knew how.

"Where does it hurt?" I asked.

"You're not going to tell Miss Godfrey?" He said, looking up in surprise.

"When she asks, I'll tell her the truth: that I didn't see Mick since that little station where we took on the postal sack."

"I thought you'd tell her," Tom said.

"He's my brother, too," I said. "Now where does it hurt?"

Tom sighed deeply. I knew it hurt for him in the same place it hurt for me, somewhere deep inside, in that place where worry is spun and anxieties rule. I could feel the sadness creeping up the back of my throat to my eyes. I swallowed it and put on my best nurse's demeanor.

"Where does it hurt?" I asked again.

"Everywhere," he said. "My ribs. My head. My belly. My throat."

"Did he hit you all those places?" I asked. It was a silly question, and I knew it the moment I asked.

"Not my head," Tom said. "I hit that on the seat when I went down." I took his face in my hand, and pulled him closer.

"On the top?" I said.

"Toward the back," Tom replied. If I had looked closer, I wouldn't have had to ask. A small rivulet of blood was trickling down from his hairline into the collar of his dark jacket. I pulled the jacket away from his shirt. The white collar was stained bright red.

"I think you have a nasty cut," I said. "It's bleeding freely." Tom said nothing, only sat. I pulled my glasses from my pocket, put them on my nose, then gently began parting his hair with my fingers, looking for the source of the bleeding. It didn't take long to find it. A small gash it was, maybe an inch and a half long but deep.

"It will probably need to be stitched," I said. "Will I tell Miss Godfrey?"

Tom sat quietly, thinking. "Can you do it?" he asked. "Like Mrs. Sullivan taught you for Mick? Can you do that?"

"I could," I said. "But a doctor would do better."

"If they send me to a doctor, you and I could get separated," he said. "I promised Mick I would stay with you. I gave him my word." He reached out for my hand. His eyes were nothing but fear.

"Fine then, Tommeen," I said. "Fine then."

I looked forward to Miss Godfrey. She was seated in her front seat, but working her way systematically through the children, letting her gaze rest on each one in turn, looking for signs of trouble maybe. Or maybe she was just imposing order again in her mind. She still looked a bit pale.

"I'll need a few things out of my suitcase," I said. "Then I want you to meet me in the privy. And stay out of Willie's reach on the way back."

"You'll not have to tell me twice," Tom said, still hunched over his sore ribs.

I stood and pulled my suitcase from the shelf. Miss Godfrey looked up. I tossed my head back toward the privy. She nodded grimly.

From the suitcase I pulled my old shirtwaist. In the collar was the needle and a bit of white thread from the time I had to mend my apron string. I hadn't meant to steal it. I had stuck it through the collar of my old shirtwaist, meaning to bring it back to the sewing room, and then I had just forgotten. It turned out that omission was a good thing. I wadded it up, and tucked it as inconspicuously as I could under my arm. Then I stood, and without so much as a glance forward, headed to the back.

Tom knocked, then slipped through the door moments later.

"Did she see you?" I asked.

"I don't think so," Tom replied. "She seemed to be intent on examining a little girl who went forward to cry in her lap.

"Good then," I said. "Sit." I shut the lid to the toilet, and Tom sat. I could see him cringe a bit with pain.

"I think you best take off your shirt," I said. "I need to get the blood out of the collar before it dries." Tom unbuttoned his jacket and removed it. The stain on his collar had seeped well down the back of the shirt. He unbuttoned the shirt, removed it, and handed it to me. His eyes went big when he saw the stain.

"Is it that bad?" he said. "The wound. It must be bleeding something terrible."

"'Tis the white of the shirt," I said. "It makes it look like more than it is." I took the collar of the shirt, set it in the sink, and opened the tap. The water flowed slowly from the reservoir. I tested it. It was tepid. I could probably get the worst of the stain out then. I soaked a corner of my old shirtwaist, then with a sudden surge of wistfulness began dabbing at Tom's head. Even a garment as finely made as this one stood little chance against the hard life it had seen in it's two months of existence. None of us stood a chance.

I parted the hair over the wound. It was a clean cut, deep but short. It wouldn't take more than a few stitches.

"All right, Tommeen," I said. "I'll need you to hold the hair back. I don't have a scissors to cut it away, and I don't want it to get into the wound while I'm stitching." Tom nodded. His face was a hard mask of seriousness.

I wet my hand a bit, and slicked down the hair on one side of the cut. "Hold here," I said, taking Tom's hand and planting it atop his head. I smoothed down the remaining hair in the other direction, held it down myself, and dabbed a bit at the cut, wishing for alcohol or iodine, or something to sterilize it. It continued to ooze, and I said a quick prayer that the bleeding was enough to clean the worst of the germs out of it.

"Are you going to do it now?" Tom said, as I rinsed the needle and thread under the tap.

"Are you ready?" I asked.

"I am," Tom said, turning to look at me as much as he could without letting go of his hair.

"Fine, then" I said. "Three stitches, I think. I'll not cut the cotton in between since we don't have a scissors." Tom took a deep breath and nodded slightly. I laid the needle against the edge of the wound to steady it. With the rocking of the train and the poor light of the skylight, this wouldn't have been my first choice in places to stitch up a wound, but it would have to do. I dipped the point of the needle and pushed. It slid through the scalp easily. Tom whimpered, but to his credit, he sat still, his eyes squeezed shut, his face screwed back as though it were trying to scoot back away from the pain.

The stitches were done in less than a minute. I slipped the needle off, and let the last tail of thread dangle. It seemed a better solution than biting it off.

"Now," I said, "let's take a look at the rest of you. What else hurts?"

"Here's the worst," he said, pointing to his ribs on the right side. "I think Willie's left handed. He seemed to make a worse mess of me on this side."

"You're going to have to stop clutching them if you want me to take a look," I said. Reluctantly, he removed his arm. "Where is it the worst?" I said. Tom pointed. Gingerly, I traced the ribs one by one. I was on about the seventh one down when Tom yelped and pulled away.

"That hurts?" I said.

"Don't touch it," he said.

"It could be broken," I said. "If I can feel the break, you need to get to a doctor in the next town."

"And if you can't feel any break?" he asked

"Then you'll probably be fine," I said. "Not that the next few days will be pleasant."

"Check then," he said.

As gently as I could, I traced the rib again. Tom cringed, whimpered a bit, but let me check. The rib seemed fairly smooth. I thought maybe I felt a bit of a bump, but given that I didn't want to push too hard, I couldn't tell. "Take a deep breath, Tom," I said.

Tom drew in a quivering breath, less than a third of a chest's worth before exhaling again.

"It hurts," he said.

"I think it's at least cracked," I said. "Where else did he get you?"

I looked down Tom's throat—he'd taken a glancing blow to the neck. It looked open. I didn't hear any wheezing. His belly wasn't tender so long as I stayed away from the ribs.

"You'll probably live," I said.

"How about the shirt?" he asked.

I drained off the water, and ran a bit more over the collar. The blood seemed to be coming out, at least most of it. It would never have passed one of Mrs. Quillan's inspections, but it wasn't too bad for a lavatory sink and no soap.

"Can you wear just your jacket until this dries?" I asked. Tom nodded, slipped his right arm into the sleeve with a good bit of pain on his face. The left arm didn't look like much fun either. He buttoned the front all the way up, never moving his elbow from his side. I squeezed out the shirt and handed it to him. He stuffed it under the jacket. I took a quick inventory, then opened the door and stepped into the aisle.

Miss Godfrey had her eyes out the window. Most of the children were still sitting quietly, their hands in their laps. We practically tiptoed to our seat. I put Tom on the inside so I could guard his bad ribs, and taking the suitcase from the rack, slipped the old shirtwaist back into it.

We had settled in, and were trying to look interested in the scenery when Miss Godfrey stood, set her stack of papers down on her seat, and without a word strolled back to our seat.

"How serious is the cut?" she asked. I was a bit surprised. I didn't realize she'd noticed.

"It'll do," I said. Miss Godfrey motioned to Tom, who leaned in. She parted his hair gently with her finger tips. "You could have let the doctor do that," she said.

I was silent. I didn't think I could explain, decided not to even try. "It's neat work," she said.

"Thank you," I replied.

"It's the ribs I'm worried about," she said. "I'll cable from the next station, have a doctor waiting for us in St. Paul. It's only about an hour." She looked over at Tom, who had the look of a boy who had just witnessed a magic trick. "Will you hold until then, Thomas?"

"I will, Miss," he said.

"Good," she said.

"I'll need to go with him," I said.

"I suppose you will," she said, "given that you're his only family now."

I looked up in shock. She knew.

"That's the other cable I'll need to send from the next stop," she replied, coolly, as though she were talking about an everyday occurrence, not the disappearance of one of her charges. "Do you know where I should tell them to look for Mick?"

I looked at Tom. Worry was mingling with the pain on his face. He shrugged slightly.

"I don't think I'd know," I said.

"If it were me," she said, "I'd make a beeline for where your uncle was last heard from. Hayward was it?" I nodded. "The sheriff will have every deputy between here and there looking for him," she said. "They'll find him, don't you worry."

"And I'll be able to go with Tom to see the doctor?" I asked.

"I think that would be best," Miss Godfrey said.

"Thank you," I replied.

"No more trouble from the two of you," she said. "Do you understand?"

"We do," I said.

"We do," Tom echoed.

Miss Godfrey laid a hand gently on my shoulder for the barest second, then returned to her seat.

Thirty-Seven

By the time we reached St. Paul, Tom was looking decidedly ragged around the edges. The wagon ride from the train station brought whimpers and tears from him. His voice had gone a bit hoarse, and when I questioned him, he complained of a lump in his throat. His breathing was shallow and obviously painful. As we pulled up in front of a great brick building with "St. Paul Catholic Orphanage" stenciled on the door, Tom was pale enough that the driver asked him if he wanted to be carried in. Tom declined but clung to my elbow as I ushered him through the front door.

The sister at the front desk called us by name. The cable had obviously run ahead of us, and we were escorted immediately into a small sick room with a bed and a chair. Tom lay down gingerly. I pulled the chair over to sit next to him.

"Can you breathe any better lying down?" I asked. Tom's face was thoughtful, but before he could answer, the door opened. A fifty-ish gentry man in a white coat stepped in.

"I'm Dr. Engstrom," he said, closing the door behind him. "This is Thomas?" Tom swung his feet over the edge of the bed and sat slowly, wincing, his face screwed up against the pain. Once upright, he nodded a bit.

"Thomas Keane," he said.

The doctor glanced at me and smiled. "I'm his sister Clare," I said. He acknowledged me with a bit of an incline to his head, but immediately turned his attention to Tom.

"And what would be the trouble, Thomas?"

Tom opened his mouth. "My . . . " His voice came out thin. He coughed gently, then said in a bit louder voice. "My ribs mostly."

"And his throat," I said.

"So I see," Dr. Engstrom replied. He pulled a tongue depressor from the drawer and began his inspection.

While the doctor inspected Tom's throat, I inspected the doctor. Something about the man seemed not quite real. I couldn't quite put my finger on it, but something about him looked almost otherworldly. A man made of butter, he was—pure, yellow-white butter. His face was sculpted into a smooth, yellow ball. His hair was fine and pale, cropped tight and thinning, all the better to see his butter-white scalp beneath. His light beard, which had probably been closely shaved that morning was now in early evening a sandy stubble, neatly camouflaged against the skin of his face. All of it was the pale, yellow-white of freshly churned butter.

He wore the doctor's coat, of course—a brilliant white lab coat, and shiny black shoes, and crisply creased black trousers. And when he reached out to feel Tom's neck and jaw, he did so with fine, long fingers with milky white nails. I caught a whiff of talc on the air.

He switched on a floor light, angled the gooseneck so it shone down Tom's throat, and looked a second time. Then he peered at me through round, wire-rimmed glasses.

"When did he have his tonsils out?" he asked.

"At Ellis Island," I replied. "Just after we landed. Mid August. The thirteenth, I believe. Did they do a good job of it?"

"A good job?" The doctor had switched off the light, plugged his stethoscope into his ears and was listening to Tom's chest. He had a far away look on his face, a look that seemed to compound his somewhat ethereal appearance. "Oh, yes," he said, unplugging the stethoscope. "Not much to removing a tonsil. They did just fine." He smiled a smile at me, one that made him look just like a little boy.

It was then I realized what about him had seemed so unreal. The man had no marks on him, none whatsoever. No scars, no blemishes, no bites, no smudges, nothing. His was pure butter-white skin extending from the rim of his stiff white collar to the top of his evenly cropped head. I don't believe I'd ever seen such a thing before, not since delivering Maura's baby. Back in Cork, we all wore the marks of our life on our faces. We wore the poor nutrition in the form of boils, and blemishes, and terrible teeth. We wore the mark of the tenements on us in the bites from lice and ticks. We wore the streets on us, literally; and the dirt of the lanes worked its way into the small wounds of our lives, creating abscesses that marked us for who we were long after we had left the lanes themselves.

This man had no such marks. I marveled at a life that could be so scar free.

"What is this?" Dr. Engstrom asked. He seemed to be starting his examination at the top and working his way down. He'd worked his way around to the back of Tom and had found the wound I'd stitched up.

"He, um, fell," I said.

"It looks like it was stitched with sewing thread," he said. "Who did it?" I squirmed in my seat. I couldn't quite tell if he was angry or merely curious. He looked up at me.

"I did, sir," I said finally

"You did? How old are you?"

"Fourteen, sir," I said.

"And who taught you to stitch wounds?" He was testing the edges with his fingers, tugging lightly against the stitches.

"A woman back in the lanes," I said. "Back in Ireland. Her name was Mrs. Sarah Sullivan," I added as an afterthought.

"Was she a nurse?" he asked.

"She wasn't," I said. "Just a handywoman. But she raised three boys, and she said stitching wounds was a good skill to have if you have sons or brothers. Especially if they like to fight and you can't afford a doctor."

"*Ja*, I'm sure she's right about that," the doctor said. "I've never seen sutures quite like these before. They're neat. Just the right amount of tension. I'd say your Mrs. Sullivan taught you well, though I can't say I've ever met a fourteen-year-old girl who had the nerves for such a thing. What else did Mrs. Sullivan teach you?"

"I helped her deliver a baby once," I said. "I think maybe I could do it again. And she taught me how to deal used clothing in the market. And she taught me . . . " I paused, remembering our conversation about birth and life and men and how to walk away if it comes to that. "She taught me a power of things about life," I said finally.

"So she taught you basic nursing," he said. "At fourteen."

"She did," I said. "And also a woman back at the protectory in New York. A registered nurse by the name of Lavender. I worked with her for a few weeks. I learned a bit more of the scientific things from herself."

"And what do you propose to do with all that knowledge?" he asked. He'd sat down across from me on a small roll-around stool. Tom continued to sit, bare-chested on the table. It was almost as if the doctor had forgotten about him entirely.

"I would like to be a nurse," I proclaimed without hesitation. "I'll need to finish school first. I never got past my third year. After I finish school here in America, I want to attend nursing school. Buffalo General Hospital maybe, or New Haven. Those are the schools Nurse said were best. It will be a power of work. But I can't think of anything I'd rather do with my life."

"Hmm," he said. Just that, "hmm." Suddenly the proclamation felt slightly less noble, but only slightly. I lifted my chin, looked him in the eye, and smiled. He stood and returned to the table.

After examining Tom's neck and jaw, he worked his way down finally to the ribs. Tom held his breath. The doctor probed gently, then a bit more firmly. Tom cringed.

"I palpated the area on the train," I said. "I thought I felt a bit of swelling, but the bone didn't appear to be offset."

The doctor looked at me, an amused look on his face.

"Only a crack would be my guess," I said, "not a compound fracture."

"Good diagnosis," the doctor said, "just a crack. A green-stick fracture. I want to wrap the area, though, just to give the ribs a bit of support while their healing. It will be painful for him to travel, and I want to keep an eye on him, so we'll keep him here for, say, two weeks. Do you think that's appropriate, doctor?"

I blushed. "I'm sorry," I said.

"Don't be," the doctor replied. "It's a good thing for people to know what they want early in life. It gives them a chance to prepare. My father was a dockman. But I knew by the time I was Thomas' age that I wanted to be a doctor."

He pulled a large roll of bandage from a drawer.

"What do you want to be Thomas?" he asked.

"An engineer, sir," he said.

"Mechanical? Electrical? Civil?" the doctor asked. "Hold this end down will you Clare?" he said, pressing the end of the bandage against the small of Tom's back. I held it, and Dr. Engstrom started winding, round and round Tom's ribs.

"I'm not sure what kind, sir," Tom said. "Maybe bridges."

"Structural engineering then," the doctor said. "Good choice. There's a great call for structural engineers these days." He finished the wrapping and scanned the counters. "Would you hand me those scissors, Clare?" I picked them up, held them as Nurse had taught me, then laid them smartly in Dr. Engstrom's hand. He smiled. "Do you want a job?" he asked. "That was a nicer handoff than my last nurse could do."

I didn't know what to say, so I just smiled. Part of me leaped at the possibility that he was serious. But I doubted it.

"You can put your shirt on now, Thomas," he said. "The ribs could be a lot worse, but you'll still need to stay in bed for a few days. Then you can start getting a little exercise slowly. You'll probably be well enough to travel again in ten days, maybe two weeks."

"What about the lump in his throat?" I asked.

"Globus syndrome," the doctor said.

Syndrome I knew. But *globus* wasn't familiar to me. I teased the word apart. *Glob* plus *us* perhaps. And *glob* meant—what?—"glob" maybe.

"It means he feels like he has a lump in his throat, but it's nothing but the muscles down there bunching up. It's caused by nerves mostly. Or sadness, maybe anxiety. Nothing to worry about."

Sadness, anxiety. I could feel my own throat tightening up just thinking of the last day.

"Thank you," I said.

He removed his stethoscope from his neck and dropped it into his bag along with the scissors and the rest of the bandage. "You said your name is Clare?" he said, fastening the clasp.

"It is, sir," I said.

"Clare and Thomas," he said. "Clare and Thomas." He murmured the names to himself. "Well, then, Clare, I'll be back to check on your brother again tomorrow. When I return, maybe the three of us could chat a bit more," he said. "We could talk about your career in nursing."

"Surely, sir," I said. "I'd like that."

"And I believe I would, too," Dr. Engstrom said.

* * *

The days were crisp and cool, but dry enough that the colored leaves that carpeted the ground crunched and snapped beneath my feet. Tom had been moved to the infirmary, a white, clinical room much like the one I'd spent my time in at the protectory. The sister in charge, however, was as close to the exact opposite of Nurse Lavender as a body could get. She was round and solid, practical and steady. Most of all, she rejected my every offer to help, even when I found myself a broom and asked where I should begin to sweep. She allowed me a few minutes each day with Tom and then shooed me out the door.

I lived in the girl's dormitory, ate in the common dining room, read books in the tiny library. But because I was not a permanent inmate, I wasn't enrolled in classes. I wasn't given chores to do beyond the usual straightening of the dormitory. I wasn't even assigned a number, but rather used a towel and shelf simply labeled "guest." Mostly I walked around the grounds, sat beneath an elm tree that rained its yellow leaves down on me and whatever book I had managed to lay my hand to that day. It was one of the hardest "jobs" I've ever done in my life.

You see, I have never liked idleness. If the body doesn't keep the mind engaged, the mind tends to drift off and look for trouble. Mine drifted to Mick. I pictured him walking alone through the great stands of trees we'd passed through. I pictured him hungry, snatching food where he could, often by stealth and theft. Where would he go? Hayward? St. Croix? If Tom's calculations were to be believed, Wisconsin alone was nearly twice the size of Ireland. How could a boy alone find one man in a state that size?

People like to think of themselves as special, unique, unlike anything that has ever walked the face of the earth. It's easy to understand, of course. Of all the eyes on the face of the earth, it's your eyes that God has chosen for you to see life through. You were the unique gift given to your parents. You are the only one to have lived your life. So, of course, you think of yourself as special.

But thinking of themselves as special leads people to ask some really stupid questions. Questions like, "why me?" Or "how could this happen?"

The simple fact is that very few people on this earth are truly special. Most of us scramble in our own mundane way to make a mark on a world that knows us only as one of thousands of blades of grass, one of millions of tiny twigs being carried downstream by the currents. We aren't special in any kind of great, cosmic sense. So when the eddies of the cosmos pick us up and draw us down, the question is not "how could this happen to me?" but "why shouldn't it happen to me?"

There's something about a great loss—a loss of a parent, a loss of one's livelihood, a loss of one's country—there's something about these great losses that beat the question "how could this happen to me?" right out of you. It takes time, of course. But once you've healed from the initial wounds, once the losses have mellowed down to bone-white scars scratching their lines through the center of you, once you've passed through the loss to the other side, then you know. You know intuitively, instinctively, with a knowledge that lies deeper than your very marrow that bad things can happen. They can happen to you. They can happen to those you love. Destitution, yes. Cancer, sure. Accidents, incidents, murder and mayhem, most definitely. There's nothing special about you to insulate you from these things. Nothing at all.

And that leaves you with a choice. You can cower in the corner, frightened by the big, bad world. Or you can step out, figuring you've seen the worst of it and lived to tell about it, figuring whatever life throws, you will catch whether you want to or not. You can cower, or you can keep busy.

Mick was out in that big, bad world. I had no idea if I would ever see him again. I had no way of knowing what was happening to him. I had no way to tell if he was alive or dead. And there, sitting with my book beneath the orphanage's golden elm, all I could do was catch those terrible facts.

I would have traded my left eye for a broom and house badly in need of cleaning.

* * *

So it was for maybe a week. Life went on like that. Dr. Engstrom came to see Tom every day. Every day he had one of the orphanage employees contact me when he arrived. I'd tuck my book under my arm and make my way to the infirmary. There we'd talked about Tom's progress and about the journey from Ireland. Dr. Engstrom seemed impressed that we had made our way through so much on our own. I told him the truth: that it was little more than necessity that had provided the strength to do so. Nonetheless, he seemed impressed.

He told us about his family, his wife and his son Charlie, who was studying at the university to be an engineer. Each day he brought gadgets for Tom to look at—a stereopticon through which we witnessed the Paris exposition, a dry battery for powering medical instruments, and a Brownie camera, with which he took our picture, Tom there in bed, me propped on the edge of the mattress beside him.

Against all odds, Dr. Engstrom seemed to enjoy our company. In that way, he was vastly different from the gentry men I had met in the past. And we enjoyed his. Within a week, Tom had grown quite fond of him. I could see it all over his face as the two hunched over a photo of the Wabasha Street Bridge Dr. Engstrom had brought in. As for me I found myself looking forward each day to his arrival, and not just because he distracted me from my thoughts. He was a good man, and he genuinely seemed to care about Tom and me. I knew the bit of comfort he offered was temporary, but for that moment it was enough.

* * *

It was on a Thursday, a week and two days from our arrival at the orphanage, that we took off Tom's bandages. We all knew that the time was fast approaching for Tom and me to leave for St. Cloud and our new family. Perhaps that was why when Dr. Engstrom arrived that day, he had no gadget tucked under his arm. On his face was a thoughtful, quiet look, not the boyish grin I'd come to enjoy.

He unwound the bandages into a great pile, then gently prodded the ribs underneath. Tom said the ribs were still tender, but that it didn't hurt nearly so much to breathe. Dr. Engstrom's had him reaching and stretching before he said his first nonmedical word.

"I talked to a friend at the University of Minnesota," he said, "the medical school. He said they are laying plans for a new school of nursing."

"At the university?" I said.

"It's the new trend," Dr. Engstrom replied. "Hospital training was fine back when nursing was no more than changing bedpans and maintaining sick rooms. But in the last ten or twenty years, everything has become more scientific. Electrical devices, sterilization, modern medical advances—a nurse has to know a little about all of them to be useful in a modern hospital."

I was rewinding the bandage Dr. Engstrom had removed from Tom's ribs. Nurse had taught me the correct way and then had insisted I practice until the movement was second nature. Dr. Engstrom watched me for a moment, smiled, then plugged in his stethoscope into his ears, and laid the disk on Tom's chest.

"Good," he said, "it sounds clear. That's always the problem with bed rest and bound ribs. The lungs don't get the chance to work as deeply as they should. It sometimes causes problems."

"Pneumonia?" I said.

"Sometimes," he replied. "Or pleurisy. But I don't see any sign of either of them in Tom." He unplugged his ears. "So what do you think?" he said to me. "Would you like to enter the nursing program at the university? It should be up and running by the time you're old enough."

The question caught me off guard. He was talking as though it were a legitimate possibility. I couldn't see three days into the future, and here he was talking about university.

"Ah, well," I said, "liking something and getting it are two different things, now aren't they?"

"Sure enough," Dr. Engstrom said with a chuckle. "But life has a way of opening doors for those who deserve them opened."

"Mmm," I said, noncommittally. It sounded to me like a rich person's attitude, not one I had seen much of among the laners and orphans of my acquaintance.

"Think about it," Dr. Engstrom said.

"I will," I replied.

He fingered Tom's ribs again, a faraway look on his face, as though he was listening with his fingertips. "Does that hurt?" he asked.

"Only a little," Tom said.

"Good," Dr. Engstrom said. "I think we can leave the bandage off then." He removed his stethoscope from around his neck. "I was an immigrant, too," he said. "Did you know that?" I shook my head. "From Sweden. I was younger than you are. Five."

He put the stethoscope in his bag, then sat and dropped the bag onto his lap. "I didn't speak a word of English. You're lucky that you can at least talk to people."

"Why did you come?" Tom asked.

"Because my family was Catholic," he said.

"Swedish Catholics?" I said. "I don't believe I ever heard such a thing before."

"We're one in a million," he said. "Literally. But there are a few of us. Most of us in America or other countries. My father worked on ships before I was born. He converted halfway across the North Atlantic after a particularly bad storm. He said the ship was all but sunk, and all the people in it mere minutes from the pearly gates. The Catholic sailors started praying to Saint Brendan to save them, and my father, not having a better idea, decided to join them. When Saint Brendan came through for them, my father decided the least he could do was to convert."

He smiled. I smiled back. I hadn't known anyone who had converted before. It was another new idea, and I filed it in the back of my mind to consider later.

"The problem," Dr. Engstrom continued, "was that in Sweden after 1860 you could *be* Catholic if you wanted. But it was tough to *live* as a Catholic. You couldn't get a government job. You couldn't be a teacher. In fact it was very difficult to get any job with a Lutheran employer. Once I was born, and my father settled down on dry land, he was unemployed more than he was employed. He'd work hard, but once his boss found out he was Catholic, he'd be looking for an excuse to fire him. That's why we came to Minnesota. Lots of Swedes. Lots of Catholics. Not many of us who are both, but so long as we're willing to speak German and Latin in church, and so long as we can avoid flashing our rosaries around Swede Hollow, we get along fine."

"Your father wasn't a doctor?" Tom said.

"My father loaded barges down by the river until he died in the war here," Dr. Engstrom said. I must have looked puzzled. "Gettysburg," he said by way of explanation. "The First Minnesota Regiment. During the Civil War. You'll learn about it soon enough. After my father died, my mother and I never had any extra money to throw around. I even spent some time here with the brothers when things got bad enough. So you see when I say 'life has a way of opening doors for those who deserve them opened,' I speak from personal experience."

I held the bandage I'd finished rolling out to him. His eyes were set long, far beyond the wall he was staring at. It took him a moment to see the bandage. He took it from me and sighed.

"Clare, Thomas," he said, "I have something to ask you. Would you consider an invitation to dinner?" I looked at him in surprise. "My wife would like to meet you. I'm afraid I've been talking about the two of you with her, telling her your stories. She would like very much if you'd join us for dinner tomorrow evening. Besides, we have a proposal we'd like to discuss with you." He was packing the last of his instruments back into his black bag, his usual sign that not only the examination but our conversations were over.

"Dinner," I said. I wasn't quite sure what to make of the offer. Not many people had invited me to dinner in my time. Back in Cork there had been wakes, parties for special occasions. But this was no special day that I knew of. On top of that, he was a gentry man, and I was a girl, an orphan girl, a penniless orphan girl at that. Back in Cork the respectable folk didn't invite folks like me to dine with them.

"Tomorrow evening? Around 5:00?" he said. "I'll come and get you, and we can ride the street car." I still wasn't sure what to say, so I just nodded.

"Oh, good," he said. "Mrs. Engstrom will be so pleased. I'd like you to see where we live. You can see if you like it." He snapped shut the bag, and with a grand sweep fed one arm into the sleeve of his huge black coat. "And, Tom make sure you wear your jacket, a sweater, and a scarf around your neck. The evenings are getting chilly, and where we live there can be quite a breeze. I don't want you catching anything before you get all your strength back."

Tom nodded his assent. "Thank you," I added.

"I'll meet you here, shall I? 5:00? To make sure you don't get lost. On the streetcar."

"Thank you," I said again. He smiled, scooped up his bag, and with a nod of his head stepped out the door.

* * *

That evening, Tom got checked out of the infirmary by one of the sisters. I saw him at breakfast the next day, sitting with the boys his age. His color was good, and he looked happy, but I could see the wear of the last week on his face. The brothers led him out with the rest of the boys, and I, following my usual habit, retreated to the library.

I was there picking out the day's book, when a sister strode through the door. "You're Clare Keane?" she said.

"I am," I said. She was holding something in her hand, offering it to me. It was an envelope, bulging, battered about the edges. On the front, the address was simply:

Clare Elizabeth Keane

Thomas Joseph Patrick Keane

The Catholic orphan train

New York to Minnesota

There was no return address, but the postmark said "Hayward Wisc."

"I asked the mailman about it," the sister said. "He said that Wisconsin just sent it to St. Paul, and when it got to the main post office, the men there talked about it, and decided to deliver it to the closest Catholic orphanage in the city. It was a good decision. We keep all the records for the orphans that come in on the trains from back East. I sat down with the records, thinking I would have a terrible time finding you. But there you were on this month's train. I scanned your record, and wouldn't you know you were still here? God must have wanted to you have this letter as soon as possible. I can't imagine it would have found its way so sure without His hand guiding it." She crossed herself with a great deal of solemnity.

I transferred the letter to my left hand and did the same. "Thank you," I said.

"I'll leave you to read it," she replied and closed the door to the library after her.

I sank into one of the chairs, and laid the letter on the great oak table. The handwriting on the front of it was Mick's. My hands shook as I opened it.

Dear Clare and Tom,

I am in Hayward, Wisconsin. It was farther than I thought from the train tracks. A terrible walk entirely, but I am here now. Uncle Ronan is not here but I know where he is. Some men say he worked here this summer but then left. The camp is closing down, and most of the men are going to other camps to find work.

I met a man named Karl Nilsson who knew Uncle Ronan. He says he is in a place called Rainy Lake in Minnesota at the V&RLLC logging camp. He said I could travel with him there next month because he's going to find work there too. We will be taking the logging train, so I don't have to walk. I am very happy for that. The walk wore through my shoes. By the time I got to Hayward I could hardly keep them on my feet. My clothes were powerfully dirty, too. But Nilsson bought me loggers boots and a red wool shirt and heavy wool pants from the wanigan, and now I look just like a timberman.

I have a new job, too. My job is helping Nilsson. He is the camp cook. I chop wood, wash pots, scrub the kitchen, and sometimes he lets me help with the baking. I know what you will say, Clare. I used to think cooking was for

404

women, but best nobody say that around Nilsson. He cooks better than you did, Clare. He's a powerful big man, with forearms the size of my legs. He has a nose like a red apple in the center of his face and a beard like a great, brown bush that grows up almost all the way to his eyes. He calls me Mika, and says that he'll make a cook of me some day.

The food here is good. We get all the donuts we can eat every day, so I'm never hungry. And most days we get pork and flapjacks and beans, and pea soup, and pies Nilsson makes from dry apples or the berries that grow wild in the woods. Every meal we have coffee, not tea. I didn't like it at first, but now I like it fine. Nilsson makes it strong, he says it puts hair on a man's chest. Nilsson says he's going to put some meat on my bones, and I think he has already. I was murderously hungry by the time I found the camp in Hayward, I can tell you that much. But I'm not hungry once since meeting Nilsson. He is mighty good to me.

I hope this letter finds you. Please don't worry. I am well, and happy, and now that I am with the loggers I am well fed. I don't know, but I think maybe God brought me all the way across the ocean so I could meet Nilsson and live here with the loggers. It is a good place for me. I like it very much.

Your devoted brother,

Mika (Mick Keane)

p.s. I miss you.

p.p.s. I'm putting another letter that came here for you. It was addressed care of Uncle Ronan and went first to St. Croix, then here. They were going to send it to Uncle Ronan in Rainy Lake, but I said I would send it to you direct. I didn't open it, but from the return address, it looks like Colum made it to Washington.

The return address said Mr. C. O'Moran, Bellingham, Washington. I looked at the address:

Miss Clare Keane

c/o Mr. Ronan Keane

Lumber Company

St. Croix Falls, Wisconsin, USA

Private. For Miss Keane's eyes only.

It was written in a fair, full hand, the hand of a boy who had still been in school on his fifteenth birthday. I held the envelope in my hands, brought it to my nose, and summoned Colum again to me. I slid a finger inside the flap, and popped it open. Inside was a single sheet of paper.

Dear Clare,

You are that to me, Clare. My dear Clare. We are in Washington. The train tracks that brought us here went on forever, or so it seemed. Seven days, and I am now a half a country from you. My heart tells me I am too far, far and away too far from you.

The trees here in Washington are even bigger than Uncle said, but I am not cutting them, not yet. The very day we arrived in Bellingham, we found it had a high school. It's a lot like my school in Ireland, except here we don't have to pay for me to study. When Da heard that, he said you are going and no mistake. So by day I sit in a desk learning about mathematics and American history and such things. But after school, I will run errands for old Doc Lundquist. That's what everyone calls him, old Doc Lundquist. He was a doctor in Chicago, but he came to Washington to fish in the rivers and to bind up the evils the loggers here do to themselves. I run errands for him and clean his office. He pays me in salmon and helps me with my math homework. And he pays me in coin, 5¢ a day, which I am saving for our house. Doc Lundquist is a smart man, wearing fine suits, and the very Pope in Rome not having a better pocket watch. He says a smart boy like me should stay in school and become a doctor, that a doctor never has worries for money or a roof over his head. He says if I'm going to send for you, I could do better than chopping trees all my life. Well, Clare, would you like to marry a doctor? I think here in America it might just be possible.

Tell me if you get this letter, and if you have an address where I can write you. I miss you dearly, and will write you every Sunday if you tell me where you are.

I am,

Yours forever,

Colum

Mick was safe. Colum still loved me. God had indeed hand delivered that letter into my lap. I believed it then. Now all these years later, I believe it no less.

* * *

The streetcar let us out at the foot of a large hill. The street that led up the hill was wide and lined with pristine sidewalks and huge maple trees that arched across the roadway and dropped their blaze-red leaves on the grey cobblestones. We climbed in silence, and as we did the size of the houses grew. At the bottom, the houses were the size one would expect a small mill owner to live in in Ireland—comfortable, tidy, but not something that shouted wealth. At the top of the hill, perched there for the world to see were the mansions with room for a dozen or more servants, and that only in a back corner. As we continued to climb, I wondered just how far up in the world we were going.

Far enough. Or so it turned out. Dr. Engstrom motioned us onto a sidewalk that led to an imposing house. Upon walls made of great grey stones mortared into a perfect cube, sat a steeply sloped roof with dormers. From the windows I guessed the house had two storeys, four if you counted the attic and cellar. The covered porch that stretched across the front was a good bit larger than our room in Ireland had been.

Dr. Engstrom led us up the neatly painted steps and onto the porch. There he dragged his feet over a bristly mat, carefully brushing every bit of dirt from his shoes. He then opened the door, and stepped in. The floor beneath his feet was oak, a grand oak floor stained and polished until it shone. Seeing it, I made a bit of extra effort with my own shoes on the mat. Tom beside me did the same.

"Never mind that," Dr. Engstrom said. "Never mind, never mind. Just come in." He removed his coat and held his hand out for ours. He hung them on hangers in the front closet.

"Don't you have a maid to do that?" Tom said. I elbowed him hard in the arm.

Dr. Engstrom laughed. "How many maids do you think a man like me should have?" he said.

"Oh, I'd say three or four," Tom said. "Maybe more."

"And a valet, a butler, and gardener?" Dr. Engstrom asked.

Tom shrugged. "Maybe," he said.

Dr. Engstrom laughed again. "I think you overestimate what a doctor in this country makes," he said. "You wouldn't be the first, of course." He wrapped Tom's scarf around the hanger holding his jacket. "No, it's just me and Mrs. Engstrom here, no servants. Mrs. Engstrom takes care of the house. I do the gardening. We had a girl to help with the cleaning and washing, but she quit a few weeks ago, and we haven't been able to replace her." He smiled at me. "Know anyone who's looking for work?" he said.

So that was the "proposal." He wanted to offer me a job. It seemed strange that he would invite me to dinner to do so, but I supposed maybe employers did things differently in America. I made a mental note that I would have to learn those differences and soon if I were to work in service.

"If I were to work in service." How far I had come from those days on the streets of Cork, looking for a position, any position to keep body and soul together. The last month had been filled with fantasy futures, futures in which I was a respected nurse, credentials from prestigious school, delivering babies, comforting the sick. I had adapted oh so quickly to those dreams. But as I stood there with a steady income looking me square in the eye, I understood that the fantasies of the past month or two were one thing. Quite another was a man standing right here before me about to offer me work. I was just about to tell him that I would consider his offer, when I hear a voice from the next room.

"There you are," the woman, presumably Mrs. Engstrom, said. "You're late." Mr. Engstrom popped open his pocket watch and consulted it.

"5:30," he said.

"You said 5:00," Mrs. Engstrom said standing on her tiptoes to give him a quick peck of a kiss.

"I was picking up the children at 5:00," he said. "Half hour to get here. That's 5:30."

"No matter," she said. "These must be the children." She appraised us up and down. "You're Clare," she said to me.

"I am," I said and curtsied in the same way I always had to my employers in Ireland.

"And you would be Thomas." Tom bobbed his head.

"They're charming, Joseph. Just like you said they'd be."

I had never thought of myself as charming before, but so as not to disabuse her of the notion right away, I folded my hands primly in front of me.

"Are you ready for dinner?" she said. "I had hoped we could sit and chat for a while before sitting down at table, but I'm afraid the roast is done. We'll have to do our talking in the dining room." She turned and headed back where she came from. Dr. Engstrom led us out of the entryway and into the living room.

It was a large room trimmed with large dark-stained oak doors and windows. Lots of wood in this house to keep clean. I made a mental note that Mrs. Engstrom was obviously proud of her wood. It all glowed. The floor was covered with a deep red throw rug. And the furniture, if not new, was certainly well-cared-for and very good quality. A beautiful grandfather clock ticked steadily in the corner. The time read 5:33.

The dining room had much the same feel. Deep oak doors, an oak sideboard with beveled glass doors, and a grand oak table in the center of it all. The table was set for four with white linen, china, and crystal. But it wasn't the table that drew me. It was the window. Or maybe I should say windows. Nearly a whole wall of them surrounding a small bay laden with potted flowers. Out the window was a bluff that looked down over the river. The fall colors glowed in the setting sun. The river sparkled. The trees and bushes in the small back yard bid me come stand among them. It was one of the most beautiful sights I had ever seen. I sighed deeply.

"What are you thinking?" Dr. Engstrom said.

"Do we have time to step outside?" I said. It was forward of me, but for some reason I had to get out into the yard. "I want to see the river, the sunset."

"Ida?" Dr. Engstrom called into the kitchen. "How long?"

"Five minutes," Mrs. Engstrom called back.

"Five minutes," Mr. Engstrom said. "We can go out the back. Tom, you stay here. I don't want you out in the chill any more than you have to be, not until those ribs are completely healed." Tom looked disappointed but made no move to follow us.

We walked through the kitchen, a tidy, modern, well-appointed kitchen. It would be a pleasure to work in. A washing machine was hooked to faucets and a drain on the back porch. I might just have time for school in the evenings.

The cool air, the smell of the leaves, the glow of the sunset. The colors seemed more intense, more insistent than anything I had seen for a long time. The river wandered slowly beneath us, the low light glancing off it in shards. I turned to look back at the house. The huge stones stood hard against the painted sky. They looked almost too real, as though they were trying to force themselves into the soft flesh of my mind, trying to tell me something. I took it all in, listened to it, smelled it, looked hard with eyes and heart both. But I couldn't quite understand what it was trying to say.

"Do you think you could live in a place like this?" Dr. Engstrom asked.

"I could," I said. "I don't think I've ever seen a place so beautiful."

"Why do you think I spend so much time in the garden?" Dr. Engstrom said. "I've lived in this city for more than forty-five years, and I still feel the very same way. Right now, though, we'd better be getting inside. Are you ready?" It couldn't have been five minutes already. Or maybe it had been hours. Time didn't seem important. I wasn't ready to go in, but I nodded nonetheless.

Tom was already seated at the table. Mrs. Engstrom, who was putting the last of the serving dishes in front of him, was smiling with obvious fondness for the way Tom looked at food. The dinner looked wonderful, smelled better. Mrs. Engstrom was undoubtedly a good cook, and in Tom that evening she had found someone who would appreciate every bite of her work.

Dr. Engstrom sat at the head of the table. Mrs. Engstrom sat across from him. She placed me so I had a view out the window from where I sat. I had the strong feeling that she would make a good employer, one who realized her servants were not just servants but people.

"We say grace in Swedish," Dr. Engstrom said, folding his hands. "Do you understand any Swedish?"

"*Moder, syster, tack så mycket,*" I said. "That's all."

Dr. Engstrom laughed. "That won't quite cover the whole prayer, but you can pray in your heart in English. And later, if you'd like, I'll teach you the prayer in Swedish."

He bowed his head and half said, half sung the prayer. I understood the Amen, looked up and crossed myself.

They called the meatballs *köttbulle* and the butter *smör*. The potatoes were white and fluffy. And the milk was cold. The sunset deepened into first red, then maroon. I could hear the sounds of the autumn leaves blowing in the soft breeze. Something inside me knew I was meant to be here. I would take the job.

The Engstroms ate quietly. I could feel their eyes on me, could sense the questions they were asking themselves about me, my manners, my ability to fit into their household. Suddenly I didn't want to wait any longer. I wiped my lips on the napkin, took a sip of milk to wash down the last of the rye bread. I looked up at Dr. Engstrom with what I hoped was a casual smile.

"You said you had a proposal for me," I said.

"And have you guessed what it is?" he replied.

"I think I have," I said. "It would have to include Tom, of course. I don't want to be apart from him."

"That's what we had planned," Dr. Engstrom said.

"And you understand that it might be difficult to get a character all the way from Ireland. I'll write, of course. I'm sure I can get someone to send you one, but it may take a little while."

"A character?" Dr. Engstrom said.

"A letter," I said, "something that says I'm a good worker, a moral person."

Dr. Engstrom laughed. "I don't think that will be necessary," he said. "I don't think you could hide the fact that you're a good person and a hard worker even if you wanted to."

"Thank you," I said.

"You're welcome," Dr. Engstrom replied. The room fell silent. I could hear the steady tick of the grandfather clock in the living room interrupted as the chime began to strike six. Tom continued to work on his meal. He looked up at me. I raised my eyebrows in question. He nodded.

"I know I said that it was a nurse I wanted to be," I said, breaking the silence. "But my mother was a servant. I've been a servant since I was eleven. And I am good at it, if you'll forgive me a bit of a boast. If I can get to the place where I can finish my work during the day, I might want to go to school in the evenings. With your permission, of course. And maybe some day I will go to nursing school, but not for a good long while. And in the meantime, I could be very content working for you."

Dr. Engstrom listened quietly to my whole speech, his boyish smile blossoming ever greater as I rambled on. At first I thought it was just because he was pleased that I was taking the job. But the smile grew until he eventually couldn't help himself. His laugh burst forth. He threw back his head and roared with it. I smiled uneasily back at him.

"Gus," Mrs. Engstrom said. "Gustav, is that polite?" But she was stifling a chuckle behind her napkin as well.

"Clare," Dr. Engstrom said, dabbing at the corner of his eyes with his handkerchief. "I think you've misunderstood. I'm not looking for a maid."

"I'm sorry," I said, my mind was scrambling to gather all the clues, to see where I had gone wrong in reading them. "I thought . . . um, I didn't mean to be cheeky. I only thought."

Dr. Engstrom held up his hand, and I stopped short in midapology. "Clare," he said. "I'm not looking for a maid. I'm looking for a daughter. And a son." He looked over at Tom, who for the first time during the meal, stopped eating. He set his fork down and swallowed hard.

"We'd like you to consider becoming part of our family," Mrs. Engstrom said. "We'd like to adopt you."

"Ever since Charlie went away to the university, it's been far too quiet around this house," Dr. Engstrom said. "We always wanted more children, but . . . " He paused.

"But I think God decided not to give us our own because he wanted us to have you instead," Mrs. Engstrom said, finishing his sentence.

"*Ja*," he agreed. "It could be like that. Just like that."

"Yes," Tom said. "I think you're right. I think God brought us to you, too. Don't you Clare?"

I was still stunned. All around me the scenery was shifting. Less than a minute ago, I had been sitting in the house of my employer, my "master," to use the old term. Suddenly I found myself at table with parents. My table. My parents. My new home. My beautiful backyard. My beautiful new life. As all the pieces around me sorted themselves into their new configuration, that is indeed what they looked like.

"We could show you around the house a bit more if you'd like," Mrs. Engstrom said. "Before you answer. We want you to feel comfortable saying yes."

"Clare," Dr. Engstrom said, "do you think it's a coincidence that your whole life has been pointing you toward nursing school and that now, when you're getting ready to find a new family, you should come across one that can send you there? Do you think it's a coincidence that Tom here is so mechanically inclined, just like our Charlie is? Do you think it's a coincidence that you had to stop here in St. Paul, that Tom had to see a doctor, that you two met me just as Mrs. Engstrom and I were talking about adopting? Clare, I think you were sent to us. I think God brought you all the way across the ocean to be our daughter and son. I think we are the future he has prepared for you."

"My future," I said. "Maybe. Yes. I could imagine so."

Susan Lynn Peterson, a former history professor, is the author of four nonfiction books: *Timeline Charts of the Western Church, Starting and Running Your Own Martial Arts School, Legends of the Martial Arts Masters,* and *Western Herbs for Martial Artists and Contact Athletes*. This, her first novel, is the result of several years of research, numerous interviews, and a trip to Cork, Ireland, all aimed at discovering what life was like for her ancestors at the turn of the twentieth century.

www.ingramcontent.com/pod-product-compliance
Lightning Source LLC
Chambersburg PA
CBHW071641260626
47170CB00001B/191